RSK

THEIRS WAS A HERITAGE OF SURVIVAL . . . AND A DESTINY OF BRIGHT PROMISE.

MEIR—Once a man of vast power and wealth, he arrived in Israel a pauper. He would be a rock in a world of shifting sands and, in time, reap a rich reward.

HILLEL—Hard as nails and sharp as a razor, he turned his back on his people, only to come face-to-face with destruction.

LILY—Delicate, dutiful, she risked her father's wrath to cross perilous borders for the sake of the man she loved.

OVADIA—Torn between two worlds, one day he would be forced to make a bitter choice.

SHOSHANA—A dark beauty of dauntless spirit, she defied her family to fight in the Israeli army. She would defy the world to probe the terrifying depths of international intrigue . . . to seize a forbidden love.

FLOWERS OF THE DESERT

Carolyn Haddad

A DELL BOOK

Published by
Dell Publishing Co., Inc.
1 Dag Hammarskjold Plaza
New York, New York 10017

Dell ® TM 681510, Dell Publishing Co., Inc.

ISBN: 0-440-12718-1

Printed in the United States of America

First printing—February 1982

For my children—may your dreams become reality.

FLOWERS
OF
THE
DESERT

PART 1

1

Ovadia was crushed in his sister Lily's arms. Where was his mother? Why had she left him to Lily's care? He felt the darkness surround him in the windowless room. He was afraid.

"Hush!" Lily warned him.

He had been whimpering again. Her mother had ordered her to keep Ovadia close to her and quiet. Quiet. How could she keep him quiet? He was only three. She looked around her and in the dark saw flashes of other faces, other children. Her cousins, her friends, all locked within the large, windowless room in the middle of her father's house in Baghdad. They knew something terrible was happening but not what. The older people wouldn't tell them. They had no time for the children except to lock them away. On this night.

Lily's older brother Hillel sat in the corner with his friends. They knew what was happening, knew what this was all about, but they kept it to themselves, whispering what they would do if it happened to them, when it happened to them. Hillel was fifteen. Why couldn't he take care of Ovadia? She was only eight. It wasn't fair. She wanted to cry, to scream for her mother. Ovadia was fidgeting and clambering all over her. "Stop it, stop it," she cried and struck him.

Ovadia would have wailed, but the sound came first, muffled by the walls of the room, by the walls of their house. It was a storm fast approaching, the sound of men's voices raging in anger and delight. The storm lashed against their street, the street of the Jews. Windows broke, doors were forced open by a thousand blows. The Arabs were in their houses now, making their way down the street to the children in the darkened room. "Please," Lily prayed. "Please. Don't let them get me."

Ovadia heard nothing of his sister's prayer though he sat once again within her arms. He heard only the sound of men calling for help, of women's shrieks cut short, of a hundred cudgels breaking through his infancy, bringing him face to face with what was to be his reality. He was too frightened to call out. He sat still and listened to the crazed sound of a mob calling for Jewish blood. It was a sound that would haunt him throughout his life.

"Mother, mother," the smaller children were calling.

"No one will save us," one of the boys in the corner with Hillel spoke up. "Not mother, or father. Not the British. Not God. We must save ourselves."

The sound of the mob kept them company throughout the night.

"Thank you for being here," Meir Ewan said.

"Your house is as safe as any," Miriam answered. "Maybe safer than most."

"As long as they don't find the children."

"How many are dead, do you think?" Miriam asked. It wasn't a guess. They heard the keening coming from the houses farther up the street. The mob was quieter now as they systematically looted the houses they had broken into.

"Too many," Meir said. "The children . . ." his voice trailed off.

"Do you think they can hear?"

"No," Meir answered. "No. They're probably all sleeping by now. Let's pray they'll be safe."

Light threw itself into the small antechamber where they were sitting. Meir stood as a woman came to him. "How is she, Leah?" he asked.

"It's a bad night to bring forth a child," Leah Haya said, shaking her head.

"It's a good night," Miriam contradicted her. "New life is God's answer to the Arabs. They will never destroy us."

"I leave that sort of talk up to the rabbis," Leah censored her. "All I know is that Salemah is in pain and the baby will not make up its mind what it wants to do. It's the noise. If only she couldn't hear the noise, then maybe she could relax and let it come. But she worries. Will they find her Ovadia? Will they find Lily and Hillel? As if she's the only one who has children in your house."

Miriam gave Meir a look of quiet sympathy. Leah was the wrong person to have here tonight. To her, life itself was a bad omen. But nothing could keep her away from impending tragedy, and for Salemah to have gone into labor on this day of all days was, if not unfortunate, at least inconvenient. "I'll go in and see what has to be done," Miriam said to comfort Meir.

"There's nothing to do but wait," Leah assured her, but Miriam had already entered the bedroom where Salemah lay.

Miriam looked at Salemah contorted in her bedclothes. She took a damp cloth and placed it on the woman's face. The pain subsided. Salemah opened her eyes to see her friend's face. "I will die with this one," she confided.

"No," Miriam said sternly.

"It must be a girl. She is tearing me up inside. She will not come."

"If it is a girl, she will be close to you always."

"Have they gone yet?" Salemah asked.

Miriam was cautious. "Not yet. But soon the British must come and the Arabs will go." Leaving us to bury our dead, she did not add.

"So long?" Salemah said as the pain took her over once more. Miriam felt for the baby. It was down low enough. It should come. Was it facing the wrong way? It shouldn't take this long. Not for Salemah with three living children and several stillborn in her history. They needed a doctor, but no one would fetch him. To step outside on such a night would mean certain death.

Miriam helped Salemah to sit as she felt the spasm once again. "Bear down," she urged softly. Sweating with the effort and the pain, Salemah began to succeed in pushing the child from her womb. "Leah!" Miriam shouted. After the waiting, now everything would happen all too quickly. Leah rushed in and together they made ready for the birth. Miriam watched the crown appear, covered with silken black hair. At the next contraction she held out her hands and the baby slid into them. "A girl," she called out in joy.

"A girl," Leah muttered. "Such a pity. Meir was sure to have wanted another son."

The cord was cut, the baby sponged clean and wrapped in a blanket. The sound of the mob held no terror for the women now. They had shown their strength. They had ensured their survival once again. Miriam held the child out to Salemah. Salemah took the girl and put her to breast. "Shoshana," Salemah said. "It is my daughter Shoshana."

The children were let out of the windowless room the next morning. British army vehicles patrolled the street now. Just in time to pick up the dead. For some children, no parents came. Lily and Ovadia gratefully sought out the face of their father. He waited for them with tea and bread. Hillel had already gone into the streets to survey the damage.

"But where's Mother?" Lily asked, suddenly frightened.

"Come," Meir said with a smile. He took each of them by the hand and led them into their mother's bedroom. They were quite surprised to find her lying in bed instead of working in the kitchen and thought at first that she had been injured last night by the Arabs. But then they noticed what she was holding in her arms.

Lily went up to her mother with a bright smile on her face. She took in the form of this dark, little stranger. "A girl, Shoshana," her mother said softly.

"My sister." Lily responded with growing excitement as her mother passed the baby into her arms.

"Where did that come from?" Ovadia demanded angrily. Salemah and Meir glanced at each other nervously, then laughed. "Did the Arabs leave that?" Ovadia asked.

Salemah tried to explain. "Mother had a big stomach. Now she doesn't have a big stomach anymore."

"You mean you hid her in your stomach when the Arabs came?"

"Something like that," Salemah said nervously to her heretofore youngest. "It's your sister. Shoshana we're calling her."

"I have only one sister. Her name is Lily."

"Well, now you have another one. Isn't that nice?"

It was the wrong question to ask.

"Why is she wearing my amulet?"

Salemah took the child from Lily and fingered the cloth and leather pouch. "All my babies wear this special amulet to protect them from the evil eye. You're a big boy now, so Father's had a new amulet made for you. It's set in gold." She looked at her son and saw his anger and his hurt. "Don't be difficult, Ovadia. I love you as much as ever."

If his mother loved him as much as ever, then why was she clasping that baby when he needed her to hold him. He stalked out of the room.

Meir shook his head at his wife and told her not to worry. He would go after Ovadia and explain it to him. Lily stayed near the bed with her mother. Salemah fell back onto her pillows. "You must help me now," she told her daughter. "I'm tired. Very tired. I must rest until my milk comes in. Take Shoshana and place her in her cradle. Rock her and sing to her. Be my good girl."

Lily took the baby from her mother and carried her to the cradle. Oh, how beautiful to have a child, she thought. This was much better than playing with dolls.

Meir found his youngest son sulking in his room. With all

this grief why must there be still more. "What are you worrying about?" he said to his son. "She's only a girl. It's not as if we had another son. You will still ask the questions at the seder. You will have the afikomen tied to your back. She'll just be there. She'll make life easier for your mother. She'll help clean and cook. You're still a son. Nothing can change that."

Yes, Ovadia thought. His father was right. He was a boy. This Shoshana, whoever she was, was a girl. It would be like another Lily. Someone to take care of and cherish him. He smiled at his father. Now he understood.

"Father! Father!"

Meir rose at the sound of his first son's voice. He went to the railing and looked down upon Hillel in the courtyard.

"Come quickly. They've killed Cousin Ezra. They surrounded him on the street and clubbed him to death. Come. His house is ruined and his family needs us."

Cousin Ezra was dead. Along with several hundred other Jews in this war year of 1941. The Ewans counted themselves lucky that they had not lost more of their own family. They grieved with their neighbors while at the same time they feared a recurrence of the riots if the British could not maintain control of the Iraqi interior.

Still, in spite of political upheaval, there were customs to be observed. Family and friends gathered for shivah, the seven days of mourning, at Meir Ewan's house. For not only had Ezra been killed, but his house had been ransacked, his wife beaten. Until their world was set once again in order, they would be staying with Meir.

"How could he have gone out on such a night?" Jacob asked. Jacob, the family's outcast. He had been the product of Meir's doddering old father's brief marriage to a second wife without quality. It had been brief because Meir's father died almost as soon as Jacob was conceived—the more superstitious felt at the moment of conception. It was Jacob who was rubbed raw by the circumstances. Shunned by the older members of the Ewan clan, neglected by his mother and her new husband, he grew up very much alone and very much used to looking out for himself.

"He was coming home to defend his wife."

"He certainly leaves her defenseless now," Jacob argued. "It would have been better had he stayed where he was."

"What's the matter? Does all this trouble remind you that you're Jewish?" Meir asked. "Or is it only your so-called friends and business associates who are suddenly aware of it?"

"My business—"

"Your business is a whorehouse."

"The Swallow's Nest is not a whorehouse, my brother. It is a bar, plain and simple. Everyone comes there. Everyone who's important. In business and politics. We have music, we have dancers. Men feel free to express themselves, relax from the burdens of the day, talk among friends."

"The Swallow's Nest is a whorehouse," Meir repeated his assertion.

"A bar."

"And upstairs?"

"Well, that's a different story. You didn't ask about that," Jacob objected.

Meir laughed bitterly. "Jacob, you bring dishonor to our family."

"And you bring stupidity." Jacob sat down next to his half-brother to say, "You could move, Meir, move into the new section of Baghdad. My God, you're a building contractor, you could build your own home for next to nothing. You don't have financial worries, you're rich enough. Why do you stay here? Here you will always be subject to the mob. The price of bread goes up. Kill the Jews. That's their answer. Where I live you can have your own house, separated from the neighboring ones, land surrounding it, educated neighbors. It doesn't matter whether you're a Jew or even a Christian. They accept you. You can talk to them on the same level."

"You are deluding yourself."

Jacob looked around to see who had spoken to him. It was a Mr. Aaronsohn. A European, he was a business associate of Nazem Haya, Leah's husband. Aaronsohn had a share in Nazem's import-export firm that crisscrossed the Middle East, Aaronsohn himself being based in Turkey.

"Mr. Aaronsohn, thank you very much for coming to honor my cousin, but you don't know Iraq and you don't know Iraqi Jews," Jacob told him.

"You think you have something new to say," Aaronsohn replied. "You think this exact conversation didn't take place in Germany ten, eight, five, even two years ago. And where are they now?"

"No one knows for sure," Meir said, not wanting to think of the horrible rumors that had come to them via Istanbul.

"I know," Aaronsohn said, thumping his chest. "They are in death camps, rich and poor, educated and ignorant. They are in death camps thinking back to conversations just like this one. What is it now, 1941? In ten years where will you be? This is just the beginning. Like Crystal Night. Mark my words on it."

Meir smiled at him and tried to calm him down. "It can't happen here, Mr. Aaronsohn. We have been living among the Arabs since, well, since Nebuchadnezzar conquered Jerusalem. We know that there will be occasional outbursts like this from time to time. But it's just"—he shrugged his shoulders—"part of being a Jew. We live in peace here. And with the British in Iraq we are secure."

"Oh!" Aaronsohn threw back his head in agony. "The British!" He nearly spat. "Don't you see what's happening? Can't you understand?"

"We understand the situation," Jacob said. "Rashid Ali takes over power in our government. He wants to align Iraq with Hitler's Germany. But the British have stopped him. They've landed planes and plenty of troops. And from what I hear at the Swallow's Nest, my club, Rashid Ali's forces will not get reinforcements from the Germans in time to save themselves."

"So that's what you think, is it?" Aaronsohn asked. "Rashid Ali simply wants to align Iraq with Germany instead of Britian because he thinks Germany will come out the victor."

"What else?" Meir asked. "That's the way of the Arabs."

"Rashid Ali doesn't give a damn about Germany or Britain. He wants an independent Iraq. Independent. With no nation's forces save his own. And if the British leave, who will stop the mob from your street of the Jews? Rashid Ali? The man who incited them?"

"So what is your answer?" Meir asked

"Palestine," Aaronsohn said firmly.

He was greeted with a hoot of laughter from the Jews assembled. "Palestine?" Jacob said. "Israel is a prayer, not an answer."

"The British are in Palestine too, and I hear not as helpful as they are here," Meir said with a smirk.

"You laugh now," Aaronsohn said with Germanic rigidity, "but you will think it over."

"When?" Jacob asked

"When the Arabs ask you to make brick from straw."

There would have been anger then. Iraq was not Egypt. They were not slaves. But the women spared them unpleasantness by choosing that moment to serve tea and cakes. Jacob Ewan used the opportunity of the refreshments to rise and check on the children. However hard he had to be to survive both in his family and his business, he had always had a weakness for children, his own as well as others. He liked Meir's children. Ovadia, who would have hidden behind his mother's skirts if she had not been sitting, and Lily, a beautiful girl much like her mother, Salemah, light in skin with gold running through her dark brown hair. Hillel he was less than pleased with. Hillel was rather priggish. But then so was his father, Meir, at least in his relations with his half brother. So perhaps it was to be expected.

"Salemah," Jacob said in greeting, then pulled up a chair to sit next to his sister-in-law. "So this is the new one."

"Yes," Salemah said. She had the child pressed to her with her face completely covered. She seemed unwilling to show it. Jacob was puzzled. He hadn't heard that the girl was malformed in any way. And he knew that Salemah, always superstitious, had undoubtedly pinned on an amulet to protect the baby from every evil eye, including his own. So what was the problem?

"I've brought her something," Jacob said quietly. "I know this is no time to be giving gifts. But she should be started off right." He took a packet from his suit and unwrapped a necklace with a gold locket. "What is it that you are calling her?"

"Shoshana."

"Shoshana. How pretty. May I see her?" he asked tentatively.

Salemah hesitated, then drew the baby from her breast. Jacob looked down at his niece for the first time. He was delighted. "She's so small, so beautiful. Look at her eyes, Salemah. They will be round and gorgeous some day."

"Thank you for not saying it," Salemah said.

"Saying what?"

"For not noticing how—dark she is."

"Ah." Now he understood. Shoshana was indeed several shades darker than Salemah's other children. And in a woman like Salemah, who had married well exactly because she had light, almost white, skin and was thus desirable on the marriage market, a dark-skinned daughter was not a blessing.

"I don't understand what happened," Salemah confessed. "I don't know whether I ate too much chocolate, or had too many dark thoughts, or whether it was just the frightful time I had having her. The midwife came and gave me some special cream to bathe her with. Perhaps that will help."

"It doesn't matter."

Salemah looked at him. They both knew that was untrue. "She will need a very large dowry for someone to take her as she is," Salemah said seriously.

"Well, perhaps when she grows up, she will look different," Jacob joked. "Anyway, I think she's lovely as she is, and I wish her blessings and happiness. And I wish you

24

would convince your husband to move out of this pesthole before the Arabs riot again and this time take him."

"What are you saying to my wife?" Meir asked Jacob in annoyance.

"Nothing," Jacob answered.

"It's over now," Meir said. "We will bury the dead and make a new beginning. We will live as did our fathers and grandfathers. Nothing has changed."

They ignored Mr. Aaronsohn as he said quietly, almost to himself, "This is only the beginning."

2

Baghdad was a city in which Jews had settled since their Babylonian exile in the sixth century before the common era. It was a city where despite religious prejudices against them and periodic outbursts of violence, they had for the most part prospered. The community had their rich, their poor, but mainly the Jews of Baghdad were small businessmen, skilled craftsmen, professionals, medical personnel, engineers. The Arabs of Iraq admired the Jews even as they envied them. The top officials would send their children to Jewish schools because they knew these schools provided a thorough education. Arabs who could afford it hired Jewish craftsmen because their work was superior. And when they were sick, the Arabs sought out Jewish medical assistance. They lived together, Arab and Jew, not in harmony, not in fellowship, but in a state of coexistence. The Jews relied for their safety on Arab tolerance. It gave life a certain edge. But in 1948 that tolerance was being stretched by forces that neither group could have foreseen a dozen years earlier.

Ten-year-old Ovadia Ewan walked home through the narrow streets of Baghdad toward his own three-story house, which interlocked with the other houses on his street, each facing the outside world with a solid front, yet inside each a different jewel, room upon room surrounding an inner courtyard that opened to the sky. His mind was dissociated from his path, from the sights and smells of this familiar city. Only one locality existed for him now. Israel.

He and his friends could scarcely believe it had happened. Only when the War of Independence started did they understand that it was truly a reality. Israel. They were no longer safe here in Iraq. That's what they were told in the meetings of the Zionist underground, that in 1948 the only place for the Jews of the world was in their own state. Israel. He said the name over and over again. It was his hope, a dream, to settle there. Twice a week he went to the Zionist underground meetings where they studied Hebrew as it was spoken in Ha-Aretz. And sometimes they had speakers who had been smuggled in from the State itself. They spoke of the fields that needed planting, the cities that needed building; they spoke of the opportunity that awaited every Jew who chose to live in this promised land. And the safety, the security. Not scattered and in small groups surrounded by an enemy who had nothing to fear, but together, united, fighting for themselves, defending their land, restoring Zion to its rightful people.

His father Meir Ewan brushed off his dreams. What do we lack here, he asked those who spoke of this foreign biblical land. And in truth Meir and his family lacked nothing. Meir's business thrived. The Arabs sought him out to build for them. Meir could afford to send his sons to the university, could afford to hire maids for his wife and a chauffeur to drive the car he had bought but had never learned to drive himself. There was money to buy gold to adorn his wife and daughters, the finest linen and silver.

Political power, their own state, what did the Jews of Baghdad need of them when they had the money to bribe those who had power to use it for them? This talk of Israel was insane and dangerous.

"Heh, *Yahudi!*"

Why hadn't Ovadia noticed them? He usually kept a sharp eye out for knots of Arab youths, those too young to be conscripted to fight in Palestine, those who felt they had to do battle with the Jews someplace. He didn't know whether to quicken his pace or to keep it steady. He stared straight ahead and walked on.

"Yahudi! Yahudi!"

There were three of them. They were coming for him. They must be about thirteen or fourteen, and he was only ten and pitifully short for his age, as his brother Hillel always managed to mention. He ran for it. He was a good sprinter. But not good enough. He felt hands grab his shirt and circle him around. He didn't see who threw the first punch. Tossing his hands up to protect his face, he dropped his schoolbag. They got him on the nose, then slapped him roughly before one of the shopkeepers called them off. As a parting gesture they opened his satchel, scattered his papers to the wind, and dropped his books in the gutter.

He straightened his clothes as he watched them walk away. Then slowly and with shame he gathered his papers and books together and walked home.

It was hard to miss the blood on his face, but the women managed. His sister Lily and her friend Rebecca just stared at him and said nothing. His mother came out from the kitchen to greet him, presssed her lips together, and fled back inside. Only Shoshana followed him up the stairs to his room. He sat down on the bed and she stared at him.

"Are you coming to the meeting?" she asked.

"Not today I don't think," he said numbly.

"Does it hurt?" He nodded his head. "Did the Arabs do it?"

"Yes."

She put her fist to her mouth and tears welled in her eyes. "When we get to Israel, this will never happen. We will beat them all!" She ended on a note of utter anger. Then she marched out.

Ovadia stayed alone on his bed. He sat there for a long time and then he cried.

* * *

The smell of lamb and green beans in tomato sauce enticed Ovadia downstairs for dinner. Shoshana was busy setting up the table while Lily was inside the kitchen with her mother preparing the food. Hillel was still upstairs studying. He was at the university in Baghdad now and about to take his final exams in civil engineering.

Ovadia could hear his father and Joseph Benjamin washing up out back. They were always out before sunrise on some construction job and never came back without being coated by a layer of dust. Hillel told his father that he should hire workmen to do the running around instead of doing it himself, but Meir insisted he wanted to see that everything was done correctly.

Salemah called the men to the table as she and Lily began putting the dishes out. Joseph came in behind Meir, and Ovadia caught him exchanging a look with Lily. Lily almost smiled, then cast her eyes downward. Shoshana said they were in love, but Shoshana had always been filled with fantasies and romance. "Besides, even if they were in love, they could never do anything about it," he had told her.

"Why?"

"Because Joseph has no money and Father would never let Lily marry him."

Joseph had come to them less than six months ago from Basra. Uncle Jacob had brought him to the house and told Meir the youth needed a place to stay in exchange for work.

"How old are you?" Meir had asked.

"Eighteen," Joseph answered respectfully.

"And why aren't you with your family in Basra."

"I have only a brother in Basra. There was no work," Joseph had explained lamely.

Meir accepted it. No one told him the truth. Nor did he want to know. Joseph had fled from Basra in fear for his life. One of the members of the Zionist cell he belonged to had been picked up by the police. Instead of waiting for him to break, the other members had simply taken off for places unknown. Joseph had made contact with members of a Zionist cell here in Baghdad, but it was not what he had expected. In Basra they had been workers ready to rebuild their homeland after the long exile. Here in Baghdad the Zionist cell was more a debating society, its members university students who found any sort of physical labor beneath them.

The men sat down at the table while Salemah called Hillel. Ovadia took his seat just as Hillel practically tumbled down the stairs into his. Then the women sat down. As the food was being passed, Ovadia kept his eyes averted. He kept them there even after Joseph had asked him what was wrong.

"Ovadia," Joseph said again, "what happened to you?"

Ovadia didn't know whether he could trust his voice. "The Arabs," he started to say.

"This is incredible," Joseph said, putting the rice down. "We are sitting here calmly at the dinner table with your son sitting across from us showing the remnants of a bloody nose and a beating and no one's saying anything."

"I say we should go to Israel," Shoshana piped up.

"Thank you, Shoshi," Joseph replied before continuing. "You are all pretending nothing has happened. How long must this go on?" He raised his voice and pounded on the table.

Meir shook his head at the both of them. "It's all a part of growing up." He shrugged it off. "It's something we all had to go through."

"Why should we have to go through being beaten up on the streets just because we're Jewish? Is that why we have sons, so they can cower in the street until they're beaten up by some Arabs? Is this a way to live?" Joseph asked.

"What do you suggest?" Meir flung back at him. "We are powerless and you know it."

"We are not powerless," he said quietly. "We can fight back. We can get weapons and fight back. I have to go out," he said to no one in particular as the women cleared away the remains of the meal. He left without a word being said to him.

It was a strange night. Ovadia's sleep was filled with

31

dreams, nightmares really. He was afraid. Afraid to go back out on the street. Each time he tumbled from his sleep it was to remember wild, vague figures flying at him. Was it any wonder then when his door creaked open that he sat up with a start and a loud gasp. "Shoshana!" he seethed as he caught her features in the moonlight.

She tiptoed over to his bed and sat cross-legged on it. "Something's happening downstairs," she whispered.

"A burglar? The Arabs?" He got a negative to both. "Then what?"

She took him by the hand and pulled him out of bed. By way of explanation she said, "I saw her light on all night."

Ovadia knew better than to question his sister. He just followed her to the stairwell and gazed downward. It took him a while to sort out the images. But there in what was their dining hall, the table had been moved and the rug rolled back. And the floor itself, a part of it, seemed to be missing. The two culprits were Lily and Joseph.

"Do you think it's treasure they're burying?" Shoshana asked.

Of a sort, Ovadia thought. If handguns were a treasure, and considering the times they certainly might be counted so.

"They're guns." Shoshana had caught on. "Do you realize we'll all be hanged if the Arabs find out about this?" she said excitedly.

Ovadia was troubled. "What would Father say?"

Shoshana looked at him mischievously. "What would Mother say to see Lily and Joseph together without a chaperon?"

Meir Ewan was not as blind as everyone thought him. Like King Belshazzar he could see the handwriting on the wall, but he didn't know what to do about it. It was easy to study history and decide what people should have done, but how to look ahead into the void of the future and see what step he should take. He had thought the tempest would blow past them once Israel was established and the Arab states saw that it could not be dislodged; then he thought life would return to normal. But it had not. There was an unease in his relations with all Arabs now. In 1946 when the Arabs had rioted against the Jews once again, he had been able to call on his friend the police chief to send a guard to his house just in case. Now the police chief no longer knew him.

But to leave. Next year he would be fifty years old. Assuming he could get a good price for his business and his house, how could he start all over again? And, of course, that was just assuming. He had heard of Jews who were "flying to France for a few weeks." Everyone knew they wouldn't be coming back. And their property sold for maybe half of what it was worth. Gold was inflated because Jews like him were snatching up whatever jewelry they could as a solid investment against the day when they might have to flee for their lives.

The door to his office opened. Ewan Construction reflected the sun as Hillel stepped inside. It was rare for his son to visit him at the office. He knew immediately that Hillel's reason for coming would not be good.

"Father." Hillel acknowledged him. "Where's Joseph?"

"He's out working on a new addition. Is he in trouble?"

"Joseph is too stupid to be important to anyone but himself," Hillel answered.

"I had heard."

"There are so many rumors, Father, you can't trust any of them unless you are really in the know."

"I suppose you're right. Well, I for one am glad of your reassurance about Joseph. Sometimes he seems so hotheaded, I'm afraid he'll get us all into trouble."

"The central committee never trusts him with anything that important. What plans are those?" he asked, looking over his father's shoulder.

"Jeremiah Musri's new house."

"You can put them away."

Meir looked up at his son. "Why?"

"He won't be needing them."

"If you have something to say, Hillel, say it."

"You remember the father?"

33

"Joseph Musri, yes."

"He had five sons, and after he died, each son named the next male born Joseph in his honor."

"Yes."

"So the five Musri sons have been known from time to time as Abu Yusef, the father of Joseph."

"Yes."

"Well, one of their second cousins settled in Israel just recently. She gave a letter to a British businessman who was traveling from Israel to Cyprus then on to Iraq. The letter was confiscated by Iraqi authorities. In that letter she says, "Give my greetings to Abu Yusef." The Iraqi authorities contend that this letter indicates collaboration with the enemy. But since they don't know which Abu Yusef the woman was referring to, they've arrested all five sons, confiscated their property, and imprisoned them for six years."

Meir sat back. "When did you hear this?"

"Just now. They were arrested yesterday; sentence was passed this morning. Their families have come to us. We're making sure they're able to leave Baghdad by tonight. Of course they're taking nothing but the clothes on their back, as everything they own now belongs to the state."

"This is incredible," Meir said, shocked. "Why don't the police contact the woman and find out which Abu Yusef she meant?"

"Oh, Father!" Hillel shouted him down. "Look, I've come to you not because you were building a house for Musri but because this should be a sign to you. One day you have everything, the next day nothing. You've got to get your capital out of the country now."

"I've been buying gold with it."

"I've checked your books, Father. You have money just sitting around in your safe."

"It's money I use to operate on."

"And what will you do with it when all your customers are in prison or have fled? Now I've been thinking. Nazem Haya takes money out of the country and invests it in Iran. It's true he takes twenty-percent commission—"

"Twenty-five," Meir corrected him.

34

"Seventy-five percent of something is better than one hundred percent of nothing. Besides, his wife and children are always over at our house. For you he might do it for less. Then when you leave Iraq, and, Father, you must realize that soon it will become a necessity whether you wish it or not, the money will be there waiting for you."

Meir thought it over. "I prefer jewelry."

"I'm telling you, Father, the Musri family was left with nothing. Not jewelry, not so much as a teacup."

"I'll think it over," Meir promised.

"Think quickly. Nazem is going next week. With his own import-export firm he still knows which customs agents to bribe to get the money through. At least we can count on him."

"Maybe," Meir said. But he had less confidence in Nazem Haya than did his son.

The house was full of women. Salemah and Leah were in the kitchen rolling out the dough over and over again, crushing the nuts for the sweet pastry for which their children waited.

Shoshana and Danielle were in the hallway playing with their dolls and dishes, having a tea party for which they needed real tea and real cakes, so they were in and out of the kitchen constantly.

"Isn't Danielle a beauty?" Leah, her mother, asked.

"She certainly is," Salemah agreed. Danielle had been born two years after her Shoshana. She was light and delicate, quiet and obedient, a reproach to her own daughter, who seemed not to know what the word "ladylike" meant. Why Salemah would never know. She set a good example and so did Lily. Already several good families had made inquiries as to how much of a dowry could be expected to follow their older daughter to her marriage bed. Salemah had spoken to her daughter, but Lily had always professed complete disinterest in the idea of marriage to anyone right now. At fifteen that was suspicious. But Salemah had kept a close eye on her daughter. She never snuck out on her own, she never took a particular interest in anyone when they were out visiting, she spent most of her time with her friend Rebecca. If they were not out seeing some weepy romance at the local cinema, they were up in Lily's room giggling together. Well, Salemah supposed that was normal enough. But at fifteen her Lily should be thinking about babies. And a husband, of course.

"He said he loved me," Lily confessed.

"When?" Rebecca asked, eyes wide open.

"Last night when I was in the kitchen washing up. He had to come through to get the truck ready for the next day's work. I was alone in the kitchen and he"—she lowered her voice—"he almost touched me."

"He didn't!" Rebecca shrieked.

"Shh! Do you want to get my mother up here?"

"What do you mean he almost touched you?" Rebecca demanded.

"He stopped when he found me alone in the kitchen. He said, 'The night is warm, isn't it.' I nodded. He said, 'There's a bright moon out tonight.' I looked up at the stars. Then he said very softly, 'I love you.' "

Rebecca giggled hysterically. "What did you do?"

"I ignored him of course. What do you think, silly. So he came close and he said, 'I used to just care about you a lot, but now I think I'm in love with you.' "

"Just thinks he's in love?"

"It's his way of speaking."

"And then he touched you."

"No. I was standing there with my hand sitting in this hot dishwater, and what he was saying was making me so nervous that I started to sweat. It was so embarrassing!" she shrieked. "This one little bead of sweat just trickled from my forehead down to my temple and onto my cheek. He raised his hand as if he was going to wipe it off, then he suddenly just left the kitchen."

Rebecca was disappointed. "What if he had taken it onto his finger and blotted it on his handkerchief and saved his handkerchief forever." They laughed together.

"You know what's awful," Lily said. "People don't sweat in the movies. Not when they're in love, anyway."

"Oh, never mind," Rebecca said. "They don't go to the bathroom either." They fell to the floor in hysterics until Shoshana brought them back to their senses by entering her sister's room without knocking.

"What are you doing here?" Lily snapped.

"Can I get your doll box and bring it downstairs?"

"Yes, yes, get it and go, Shoshi. And don't come back in unless you're invited."

"All right. Sorry," Shoshana huffed as she dragged the doll box to the door and closed it behind her.

The girls had regained control. "Are you going to tell your mother what he said?" Rebecca asked.

"Are you kidding? Do you know what she would do?"

"No."

"She would only tell my father and he would kick Joseph out of the house and I would never see him again."

"Well, then what are you going to do?"

"I don't know. They're trying to marry me off."

"You can't marry Joseph, you know," Rebecca said reasonably. "Your father's rich and he's poor."

"But Joseph says once we get to Israel the difference between my father and him won't matter because it's an egalitarian society."

"What does that mean?"

"I don't know," Lily admitted. They burst out laughing once again.

Shoshana was startled by someone pounding on the door, so startled that she knocked over a teacup. "Mother!" she called to the kitchen. Her mother came out, but not before the pounding resumed.

Salemah nervously twisted the handle and the door slid open. Before her stood three Arabs in their twenties. "Yes?" she asked.

"We're here to collect for the Palestine refugee relief fund," one of the young men stated blandly.

Salemah was terrified. She was alone in the house with only Leah and the girls. "But we gave last week." Her voice quavered.

"Who is it, Mother?" Lily said from the stairs. The Arabs looked up at her. She should have been frightened but she was not. She walked down the stairs and stood next to her mother. "What do you want?" she asked.

"To collect for the Palestinian refugees," one of the Arabs said politely.

"We gave last week."

"The Palestinian refugee problem is a large one. We'll need a lot of money and goods to solve it."

"Do you have any identification from the government authorizing you to collect?" Lily asked.

"I didn't realize we needed any authorization to collect for our poor, suffering brothers. And I'm surprised that a house as rich as this, with so much to lose, would make an issue of helping the less fortunate."

"What do you mean by that?"

"I mean it would be horrible for you if it got out that you were unwilling to support the Palestinians. Some people might consider you Zionist collaborators. The police, for instance."

The police. The one thought Lily connected with the police was the fear that they might find the gun cache beneath the dining room floor and arrest Joseph. "Get them some money, Mother," she said coldly. "I'll wait here."

Shoshana stood at her sister's side. "Oh, what a pretty little girl," one of the Arabs said. Lily put a protective arm around her sister. "That's a beautiful necklace you're wearing," the Arab said.

"My Uncle Jacob gave it to me," Shoshana answered, holding the locket out for him to see. He grabbed it from her and ripped the chain from her neck. "Many little Palestinian girls would like to have a necklace just like this," he explained.

Shoshana was in shock and about to wail when Salemah returned with the money. Lily took it from her mother's hand and thrust it into the Arab's, then closed the door on

38

them. She lifted Shoshana up, took her to her breast, then hugged her into silence. "You foolish, foolish girl," Lily chided angrily. "Don't you ever come to the door again. You run to your room whenever anyone knocks. Do you understand!"

But Shoshana had put her fingers to the back of her neck and drew them away tinged with blood. It startled her into a fit of tears from which only Salemah could help her recover.

"There's no one," Hillel stressed. "They're all against us. No one can protect us. And you see how much good your jewelry did you. Ripped right from her neck."

"Poor thing. They could have raped all the women in the house. There was no one here to defend them," Meir said.

Joseph felt the reproach like a dagger's thrust. Ever since he had come home and found out what had happened, he had been angry and impatient with himself and the movement. What good was it to smuggle a few Jews out when the rest of them remained subject to the tyrannical fits of any Arab. Hillel was worried about their money, why wasn't he worried about their lives?

Pounding at the door again. He would take care of them this time. No matter what the consequences. He rushed to the door before Hillel or Meir could move. He flung it open in a fury.

"Why, Joseph," Jacob Ewan said with a wry smile. "What a dramatic greeting."

Frustrated even in this, Joseph turned and stalked away.

Jacob came into the living room to be greeted by his brother with a kiss on both cheeks.

"So how is your business?" Meir asked politely of his brother.

"Never better," Jacob said with a satisfied smile. "Whatever happens in this world, people will always drink and want women." He laughed out loud at his brother's discomfort.

When tea was served, the children came down to pay their respects. It was only then that Jacob discovered what had happened that afternoon, when Shoshana came to him, her eyes still puffed from her tears. He pulled her up on his lap. "I'll get you another locket," he promised.

"I don't want another locket, I want that one," she insisted.

Jacob smiled at her. "You know, your mother is always insisting that you'll never be feminine enough, but I can see that she is wrong already. Do you know why?"

"No."

"Because you always want what you can't have." She found that less than amusing. "I'll get you another locket," he promised again. "More than that I cannot do." Shoshana slipped from his lap and disappeared.

"I think you've just stopped being her favorite uncle," Meir said with a smile.

"I bet you're happy about that," Jacob replied. "Um?"

"Um. Right now, though, I'd like a little bit of your expertise," Meir said quietly. "Perhaps my study?" He rose and Jacob followed him out.

"Now," Jacob said when they were comfortably settled.

"It's money," Meir said.

"You need some?"

"I would not know how to wash the dirt off your money, Jacob. No, it's mine. Hillel wants me to entrust all my floating capital to Nazem Haya to invest in Tehran for me."

Jacob shrugged. "It's a good idea to get as much out of Baghdad as you can."

"That much I know. But is it a good idea to trust Nazem Haya? Would you trust him? I'm asking you because you trust no one."

"Not true, Meir. I would trust you. However, I ask only one thing: Why is it that Aaronsohn will no longer do business with Nazem Haya?"

"He no longer does business in Iraq. I hear he's spending all his time and money to help resettle European refugees in Israel."

"True, but he broke off with Haya before he broke off with Iraq. He never said anything. But then no one asked him either. No one really cared that much about Nazem Haya except his wife Leah until they needed to get their money out of the country."

"Leah is a frequent guest in our house."

"My sympathies."

"I could put it on the basis of friendship."

"With a healthy profit margin," Jacob reminded him.

"I'm afraid," Meir said. "Everything seems out of control."

"Things will get better," Jacob comforted. He paused. "Or they'll get worse."

Joseph lay in the back room on the main floor. From his window he could see the alleyway leading between the houses. It was convenient. For him to leave, for his comrades to come. He had used it many times at night to slip out to meetings not authorized by Hillel's stodgy Central Zionist Committee. Well, he could afford to be rash. He had no money, no property to worry about. In a way it was a blessing. He was free to pick up and leave whenever the mood struck him. Though less free lately than he had once believed.

It was Lily. When he had heard what had happened to her and Shoshana this afternoon, he could have died. Or murdered. How could she have been so brave and stupid? It wasn't safe for her here anymore. If only he could convince Meir.

But what could he say? I'm worried about your daughter. It would be the same as saying I'm in love with your daughter, and that would be the end of it. Why was it a crime to be born poor? It wasn't his fault that he and his brother had been orphaned and shunted from one aunt to another, whoever had the food to feed them. He was young, he was strong, he was learning a trade. Poor men became rich men all the time, he rehearsed his arguments. But then Meir would point out that becoming rich by marrying a rich man's daughter was a less than honorable way of making it.

The scraping at his door startled him out of his thoughts.

He sat upright and waited. It could have been some animal taking advantage of the darkness. It came again. He slid to the door and asked quietly, "Who is it?"

"It's me."

"Lily?"

"Yes."

"Go back up to your room."

"Either let me in or I'll make a scene."

He rushed over to the chair where he had hung his clothes and slipped them quickly on. Then he opened the door. She skittered inside and he closed the door and locked it. He was about to light the lamp when she reminded him how visible they would be to the windows across the alleyway.

"Why did you come here?" he asked angrily.

"You're not pleased to see me?"

"You know I am. It's just that you're taking too many risks in one day."

"Don't be angry," she pleaded. "I've come to talk to you about what you said the other night."

"What did I say?"

Hurt, she stared accusingly. "You didn't mean it then?"

"Mean what?" He thought back anxiously to what might have passed his lips.

"That you loved me," she stammered.

He looked at her, her nightdress trailing beneath her robe. "You must leave here now," he insisted.

"But why?"

"Because I cannot talk about love with you in my bedroom late at night."

"But I trust you."

"Don't," he said and turned away.

She stared at his back. "I wanted—I wanted to tell you that I feel the same way." He turned. "I love you, Joseph."

"You can't love me," he refused. "Your family wouldn't approve."

She almost giggled. "But that's the way it always happens, doesn't it? Families never approve of young lovers."

"Oh, Lily, this isn't some Arab movie. I'm not Abdul Wahab. This is real life and our world is disintegrating under our feet."

"No, it's not. Not our world, Joseph. That's what I came to tell you. I have a plan."

"You have a plan," he mocked her.

"Yes. If you're serious about loving me, then you want to marry me. Yes or no?"

He shook his head at her. "Lily, think of your family. I have no money."

"I'll have a dowry," she argued back. "Now hush, just listen." She put her hand up to his mouth to quiet him, and he instinctively kissed her palm. She looked at him and was ready to melt into his arms but he backed away. "We can run away and get married. Yes," she insisted before he could reply. "You've gotten other people out over the mountains, you can get us out. We can go to Tehran and get married. Then we can go on to Israel and start a new life, like you're always talking about. What's wrong? Why are you shaking your head?"

"I can't go, Lily. I have commitments here."

"You said you loved me. Isn't that a commitment?"

"There are people here who need me."

"I need you. I don't care about anyone else."

He sat down and took her hand. "Look, I have a better idea. We pledge ourselves to each other secretly." She smiled. He could tell she liked that idea. "Then I arrange for you to go to Tehran and join your relatives. Once you're gone, surely your mother will press your father to leave. Then I'll come and join you. We'll get married and leave for Israel."

She withdrew her hand. "How long before you come?"

"I don't know."

"A year? Two?"

"If the situation keeps deteriorating, we'll all be out of here in two years, or dead."

"You know what I think of your plan?"

"What?"

"It stinks."

"Lily," he protested.

"We both go or neither of us goes."

"You have to go, Lily. You can't keep standing up to the Arabs and not expect some sort of trouble. What if they rape you or something?"

"No one will ever rape me because I'll kill myself first."

"Oh, sure. You can't even quarter a chicken. How do you expect to slit your own throat."

They sat silently together. He could feel her anger. He felt dejected. "Lily." He whispered her name in exasperation. He took her hand and held it between the two of his. It was so soft, so sweet. Who could suppose that the woman under it would be so stubborn. He brought the hand to his lips and kissed it. "Will you marry me?" he asked.

"Yes," she replied immediately.

"Sometime?"

"Sometime," she agreed.

3

"I won't listen," Salemah swore.

"Don't listen," Meir said unkindly. "If you don't listen that means it isn't happening."

"I pray for his soul," Salemah said.

"I don't think I would like to die with thousands of people cheering the hangman on," Lily said.

"I don't think I'd like to die at all," Shoshana added.

They knew from the swelling roar of the crowd that it had happened. Shafeeq Adas was dead, hanged, swinging slowly in the sight of the Arabs who had called for his blood.

"That could have been any of us up there," Meir said softly.

"It will be all of us," Joseph contended.

"Where is Arab justice!" Hillel cried hotly.

"Arab justice? Isn't that too much of a contradiction in terms?" Joseph asked.

Ovadia turned away and stepped out into the courtyard. He couldn't understand why any of this was happening. We're Jews, that's why, his father had explained. It seemed an insufficient answer for all this suffering.

It was the end. The Jews knew it. Even his father knew it. It was time to go.

Meir was worried. Less than six months ago he had entrusted a year's profit to Nazem Haya. The deal was that Nazem should take the money and invest it for him in Tehran. That was the last trip Nazem had made for any of the Jews of Baghdad. They discovered later by discussion among themselves that he had taken the savings of twenty families that last trip of his and simply disappeared. He had left for Tehran and never come back. His wife and her three children were now the object of charity and scorn. And those whose money he had taken out before the final absconding now wondered if their money too had taken wings.

One by one Ovadia's friends were missing from the classroom. He felt naked and anxious as the seats around him became vacant. When in February 1950 the teacher herself left on the same plane his brother Hillel took, he felt the cold of that winter more than usual. He joined Shoshana on the walk home. She was going to an all girls' school and faced the same problem of empty seats and missing teachers. The only one both of them knew would be there tomorrow and the day after was the Arab teacher, assigned to their schools by the government to spy on teachers and students alike.

"She's gone," Shoshana said sadly.

"Who is it this time?" he asked, annoyed. Shoshana's moods always descended on him. He didn't know why she felt he was the only one she could talk to. Perhaps it was their closeness in age.

"Danielle is gone. She came over yesterday to say she was going to leave, but she promised to tell me exactly when it would be. I went over to her house this morning to walk to school with her. There was no answer.

"You know how hard Joseph's been trying to arrange Leah's passage out. She had no papers for her or her children. Nazem must have taken them and sold them."

46

"I don't understand."

"What?"

"Money. For Nazem to cheat everyone in the community for money. What will his boys do when it's time for them to be bar mitzvahed. Who will teach them? Oh, that Nazem Haya. And Father too," she added for good measure.

"Father didn't cheat anyone," Ovadia said angrily.

"No, but he has money. That's his problem. If he didn't have any money, we would be out of here by now. Instead he keeps waiting to get a good price."

"How do you know all this?"

"I listen in the doorway when he's talking to the men. Uncle Jacob too is worried because he says soon they're going to pass a law that all Jews who own property must be Iraqi citizens."

Ovadia considered that. Like most Jews his family had originally come to Iraq from Iran. They had come to see if they could make a living, prosper. If not, they would return to Iran. The Ewans prospered. They had lived in Baghdad for generations but had never given a thought to changing their citizenship. That would mean paperwork, which meant government officials and bribes. So why bother? Now the fact that they were still registered as Iranians might be their salvation. "Father will never do that," Ovadia insisted. "He will never give up our Iranian citizenship. We have our Iranian passports. That's our ticket to safety. Joseph's always saying that."

Jacob Ewan surveyed his kingdom. At four o'clock there weren't many subjects. The tables were neatly arranged, chairs pushed under, counter tops wiped clean. In an hour or so it would be different. There would be circles of men, each with his hand close to his drink. Sheshbesh, cards. Kibitzers. They'd all be there. Gossiping. Useful. The Swallow's Nest was very useful to him. He knew enough about everyone and he knew enough not to talk about it. This, his knowledge, would ensure his safety and that of his family no matter what came to pass. Because he had let it be known from the beginning that if anyone tried anything, he would talk and talk and talk. Only a bullet would silence him. But he didn't think it would ever come to that.

Colonel Hamid had just entered. Poor man, he looked tired. It can be very destructive—this torturing of helpless, innocent people. Jacob took out a bottle of Scotch and poured a shot as the colonel made his way over to the bar.

"Jacob, my friend," the colonel said.

"Sir," Jacob replied, handing him the shot glass. He watched while Hamid sloshed it down, his Adam's apple bobbing appropriately.

"Is Violetta available?"

"Let me check," Jacob said. He reached down and took a receiver off its hook. He spoke a few words into it and put it back down again. "She's occupied at the moment. But she should be free soon. I hope you'll wait. I know she always enjoys your company." He smiled. "You've had a hard day," he said sympathetically.

"Trying to knock some sense into one of yours. Thick-skulled. Very. But we made him see the light."

"What was he, involved in Zionist activities?"

"Forgery."

"Forgery!"

"Papers. A family was caught fleeing with papers saying they were French. Their French was no better than mine."

"Sloppy work."

"Indeed. The father told us whom he bought the papers from to keep his children out of jail. We thought at first it was just monetary gain this forger was after. But it turns out he was also a member of a Zionist cell." Jacob shook his head. "What's wrong with your people, Jacob? We've always had such good relations until recently."

"I don't know," Jacob said. "Propaganda from the Zionist state, probably. It's reached all your young people. They don't seem to realize how well off we've always been in Iraq."

"Always," Hamid confirmed. "Have we ever ill treated any of you?"

48

Jacob thought for a moment. "Well, there was Shafeeq Adas. Hanging him didn't help."

"Oh, him. He was a symbol. Just to keep you Jews in your place."

"Some people saw him as a man more than a symbol, a Jewish man at that."

"Well, it doesn't pay to get too rich, Jacob. Remember that," Hamid said with a smile. "How much for the drink?"

Jacob waved him off. "You are always my guest here, Colonel. You should relax. You have your forger, you have his cell. Soon you will have Violetta. Your day will be complete."

"I only wish. Unfortunately we have to pick up the members of the cell at the dinner hour, so I hope Violetta will be free soon."

"Oh, I'm sure she will be."

"You know there was a funny coincidence with one of the names we were given. Joseph Benjamin. Do you know him?"

Jacob furled his brow. "Yes. Yes, of course. He's a laborer. He helps out my half brother."

Hamid smiled, then laughed. "Just testing you, Jacob."

The phone buzzed. Jacob picked it up, listened, then put it back down. "Violetta's ready," Jacob said. "Enjoy yourself."

"I intend to."

Jacob watched while Colonel Hamid advanced up the stairs. Then he quickly picked up the receiver. "Be generous with the liquor," he said urgently. "Yes, for God's sake, get him drunk."

Jacob looked around the Swallow's Nest. He couldn't leave, but whom could he trust? What if they were waiting for him to leave, waiting outside. As if God answered prayers and created problems at the same time, his elder son stood within the doorway. Jacob watched while Rahamin sought him out and came over to the bar.

"Father, Mother wants to know if you will eat with us

tonight because she wants to know if she should heat the chicken or just make salad."

"Rahamin, come to me and listen closely to what I say. You must go to Uncle Meir's now and tell Joseph Benjamin to leave Baghdad immediately. They know. Leave immediately. They know," he repeated. "You must reach him within the next half hour."

"Yes, Father," Rahamin said. He had never seen his father so serious. He walked quickly out of the restaurant and got back on his bicycle. He didn't really enjoy going to his Uncle Meir's because he always had the feeling no one really approved of his father, not even his mother. But now his father had ordered him to go there and that was his duty. So he pedaled hard and fast.

The Ewan family sat around the table. The blessing had been said over the bread and they began to eat. Lily had wanted to wait for Joseph, but Meir pointed out correctly that Joseph's hours in the house had become quite irregular.

Ovadia went to answer the door when they heard a distinct knocking. He was as surprised to see his cousin Rahamin as Rahamin was surprised to be at his Uncle Meir's house. He held the door open and Rahamin entered. He made his way into the dining room where they were eating.

Salemah rose. "Sit down, Rahamin. Let me give you something to eat."

"I've come to see Joseph Benjamin," the boy said.

"Well, you can sit down and eat while you're waiting," Meir practically ordered.

"You're all sweaty," Salemah pointed out. She got a fresh towel and handed it to him.

"I can't sit down and eat. I must see Joseph immediately," the boy said.

"Why?" Lily asked.

"Father said to give Joseph a message."

"Is Joseph in trouble?"

Rahamin considered how much he should say. "I would think so," he admitted tentatively.

Lily stood, suddenly pale. "Do they know about him?"

"Yes," Rahamin said. She had guessed it. His father could never accuse him of betraying the message.

"Stop screaming, Lily, for God's sake," Meir said angrily as his daughter went into hysterics. "When was this?" Meir asked his nephew.

"Father said I had half an hour to let Joseph know." He checked his watch. "That gives me five more minutes."

The waiting began. The food lay on the table as the family tensed to hear the sound of the front door opening. Shoshana was appointed to keep an eye on the front and to check Joseph's room occasionally in case he slipped in that way. Ovadia was sent off to some friends of Joseph who might know where he was, might be able to warn him.

But he could be anywhere, with anyone. That was the nature of his work.

"I knew he would die before we could get married." Lily wept.

"That is indeed the truth," Meir informed her. "Because you will never marry him. I don't know what you're thinking about."

"She's talking about love, Father," Shoshana said angrily. "Lily's in love with Joseph. They've been in love forever."

"How could you be so stupid?" Meir was stunned. It wasn't enough the police were after a man who lived in his own house, now his daughter was in love with him too.

"There he is!" Shoshana cried. "I see him." She rapped on the window and urged him quickly onward.

Joseph opened the front door with a smile on his face. "What's the matter?" he asked the stunned Ewans.

Rahamin stood before him, his piece well memorized. "Leave immediately. They know."

"They know about you," Lily said urgently, angrily. "Uncle Jacob sent word. They're coming for you."

"For me? Why?" he asked. "And the others? Do they know about the others?"

"Joseph, hurry," Lily pleaded. "We've been waiting forever for you and Rahamin said you only had half an hour."

Rahamin checked his watch. "That was an hour ago," he figured.

It suddenly dawned on Joseph that it was finally happening to him. He ducked off into his room and came back quickly. "The others must be warned. If I—"

He was interrupted by pounding on the door.

Shoshana looked out. "The police," she barely had time to get out before the pounding resumed.

"The roof," Lily said. "The roof." She pushed her lover up the stairs. But before he went, he grabbed her, held her tight, and kissed her.

"Leave my house," Meir said, just loudly enough for Joseph to hear. "And never come back again."

"Exactly my intentions," Joseph said. "See you in Tehran."

Lily watched him until she could see him no longer. Then she pulled Rahamin and Shoshana by the arm. "Get up to your room and stay there. Now!" she ordered, then gave them a shove.

By the time Meir went to the door, the police were through with pounding. They had broken it in.

Joseph saw their cars from the Ewans' roof before he leaped to the next roof and the next after that, leaving the street of the Jews and his immediate troubles behind him.

"Didn't you hear us knocking?" the police asked Meir.

"We heard. But we thought it was some youths playing tricks on us," Meir explained.

We're looking for a man. Joseph Benjamin. Do you know him?"

"Yes," Meir said. "He is my workman. He lives with us."

"Is he here?"

"Oh, not now, no. He is on a trip. Trying to find a buyer for some of my equipment. I expect him back in a few days though. Shall I let him know you've been asking for him?"

The policeman looked at Meir, trying to decide if he was being mocked. "Do you mind if we search the house?"

"Not at all," Meir said. "Feel free."

The police left the front hall and walked through the rooms, searching under and through everything. Lily followed them, Meir followed them, and Salemah followed them in various directions. Lily was with them when they came to Shoshana's room and opened the door. She saw that her sister and Rahamin were playing with blocks.

"Who are they?" the police asked.

Lily thought quickly. If she said this was Rahamin, Jacob Ewan's son, then wouldn't they put two and two together? "This is my sister and brother, Shoshana and Ovadia."

The policeman stared hard at them, then circled them and checked the room. Satisfied, he left.

The police gathered once more in the hallway. "We are not tricked by you," the officer in charge said.

"We're not trying to trick you," Meir protested.

"We will find him, and when he implicates you, it will be your turn."

4

"Let me out!" Lily pounded on the door. She heard people talking downstairs. If only they could hear her, maybe they could convince her father to unlock the door to her room.

Oh, what a fool she had been. The very same evening Joseph had fled, she had announced her intention to follow him as quickly as possible. On her own if necessary. Her father had exploded. Not only had Joseph put the whole house in jeopardy, but she was acting like a whore, chasing after some man who wasn't even worthy to enter her house as a guest. Her father had grabbed her and asked her that all-important question. Why had she answered it honestly? If she had lied and told her father she was no longer a virgin, he would have gladly let her go. She was so stupid! She had done everything wrong. Her father thought there was still hope, so he had locked her in her room.

It had been a week now since Joseph had left and she had seen the downstairs of her own house. She didn't even know if Joseph was safe. They could at least have told her that.

It would have been different if her mother brought her meals. She could get around her mother, make her understand. But it was always her father standing there, and they ended up screaming at each other.

She looked out her window desperately, but it was too high for her to descend safely. She would end up with a broken head, lying in the street. And then Joseph would marry someone else. If only her brother and sister could help her. But she had heard their father forbid them to have anything to do with her. He had caught Shoshana once as Shoshana tried to sneak to Lily's room. Shoshana had gotten a spanking for her effort. One morning Lily had woken up and found a letter pushed under her door. How she had hoped it was news of Joseph. But it wasn't. Just a note saying, "We still love you. Your sister, Shoshi." Stupid girl. Who needed her if she couldn't unlock the door.

The voices downstairs became louder. She pounded on the door with both fists. "Help me! Help me!" she cried. Oh, if they could only hear her. She stopped. She heard several pair of footsteps coming up the stairs. She looked around. She took her hairbrush from her dresser and with both hands batted it against the door. She stopped to call, "Someone help me!" She listened. Someone was definitely coming her way. She batted on the door again. She moved back with excitement when the key entered her lock. The door was being opened and it wasn't even dinnertime. Victory was hers!

Her father was at the door. He moved aside and there behind him was Rebecca. They flew into each other's arms. Her only friend. The door closed on them. Lily pulled apart. "You're not to be locked in here too, are you?"

"No," Rebecca said. Then she put her finger to her lips. They moved over to the bed. "Mother's downstairs," Rebecca said softly. "I'm here to make you give up this foolish idea of marrying Joseph."

"And you call yourself my friend?"

"Shut up and listen. You're really being a silly ass about this. The only thing you've accomplished is to turn your whole family against Joseph and give the neighbors a headache. If you want Joseph, you'll have to use your mind, not your heart."

"Do you have any news of him?" Lily begged.

"Yes. He made it. He's in Tehran. Remember Esperance?"

"Yes, but I never liked her."

"Her family left yesterday, so I gave her news of you to take to Joseph. I also told her to tell him I would help you and we would meet him in Tehran as soon as possible."

"I knew you would help me," Lily said and gave Rebecca a quick hug.

"But you have to repent. After I leave here, you have to dissolve in tears, tell everyone what an awful mistake you made. You have to lull everybody, make them think things are as they were."

"Does your mother know about this?"

"Of course she knows. But she thinks I'm serious when I say Joseph isn't good enough for you. I at least can act."

"Oh, Rebecca, if you were in love the way I am—"

"If I were in love the way you are, I think I could be smart enough to be in Tehran by now."

"I was so afraid the police would catch him."

"They caught two other members of his cell."

"Are they—"

"In prison. Their families go every day, but no one will tell them what's happening. But that's not your concern now. Now you have to sit here and think of all the bad things you can say about Joseph. And also find ways of telling your parents how sorry you are that you've brought them such disgrace."

"I don't think I can."

"Lily, you must. It's the only way. Otherwise the only thing you'll see is this room for the coming months. And I haven't got all that much time to help you."

"Why?"

"We have our tickets. We're leaving in six weeks."

"Time is short then."

"Definitely."

"Okay. I'll do it your way," Lily promised.

The first week after Rebecca left her, she spent lying on her bed crying—at least when her father brought her her meals. By the second week her father had allowed her to kneel, take his hand, kiss it, and beg his pardon for all the disgrace she had brought to them. By the third week she was only under house arrest. So instead of being in her room, she would sit with her mother and listen to Salemah tell her how much she had damaged her chances for a good marriage by this affiliation with Joseph. "I hope some day you'll find it in your heart to forgive me, Mother," she said tearfully. Shoshana always smiled at these moments and Lily felt like kicking her. The little brat would give it all away if she wasn't careful.

Ovadia knew she was faking too. Lily was sure of that. Especially when once at the dinner table she asked her father if he had all the papers ready for their departure.

"Why do you ask that?" Meir said suspiciously.

"Oh," she said in confusion, "I'm mistaken then. I thought the man who came by today was going to buy our house."

"He's interested, yes. But the terms aren't final. When they are, I will get the papers from the proper authorities."

Ovadia came to her later to tell her that even when their father got the papers, they'd all be put on one form so no one could leave separately. Her hopes fell. She would always be under her father's thumb. "But Uncle Jacob has access to unauthorized papers," Ovadia added.

"That's very interesting, Ovadia," she said over her knitting.

"I thought you would find it so," he said with a smirk.

She barely lifted her lashes as she gave him an answering, she hoped, innocuous smile.

The fourth week Rebecca visited her every day. Each day they would go to Lily's room. Each day Rebecca would come down looking a little heavier as she carried out of the Ewans' house clothes and belongings that Lily would need for their short trip to Tehran.

On the fourth day of the fourth week Lily convinced

Shoshana that she should have a sudden acute desire to see the Tigris, running high from the winter rains.

"Must I?" Shoshana said, arranging her tea party.

"You can play with your dolls any day. How often do I ask you to do anything for me?"

"I don't know," Shoshana pondered.

"What if I give you my mama doll. You've always liked her."

Shoshana ran her tongue across her lip. "Your mama doll?"

"Yes."

"The Tigris?"

"Yes."

"All right."

"When Rebecca comes here."

"Okay." She went back to her playing, leaving a spot at the table for the mama doll.

Rebecca came in the afternoon. On cue Shoshana pleaded with her mother to take her to the riverbank so she could see the Tigris flowing high.

"What a silly girl you are," Salemah said to her daughter. "I have the kitchen to clean. I have dinner to make. I can't possibly take you today."

"Do you really want to go, Shoshana?" Lily said kindly.

Well, that sort of puzzled Shoshana. Lily had told her before that she should want to go, now she was asking her and shaking her head yes. That must be the clue. "Yes," Shoshana answered.

"Mother," Lily said demurely. "Couldn't Rebecca and I take Shoshi to the riverbank?"

"Oh, I don't think so, Lily. Your father doesn't want you leaving the house."

"But I feel so sorry for Shoshana. Soon we'll be leaving Iraq and she'll never see the Tigris again. But I understand your point, Mother. I know that you and Father will probably never ever trust me again."

Salemah looked at her daughter, but Lily was busy shucking the peas and seemed not to notice.

"I wouldn't mind a brisk walk near the riverbank," Rebecca said.

"Please, Mother," Shoshana added, swinging into her part.

Salemah stared at her younger, more innocent daughter and smiled. "Well, all right, girls. But not more than two hours or I'll call your father."

"Oh, Mother, you are so sweet. It'll be so good to feel fresh air again," Lily said.

As quickly as possible the three girls were into their coats and out the door.

"Where to?" Rebecca asked.

"My Uncle Jacob's," Lily said with determination.

"We can't go there." Rebecca balked. "My mother would kill me if she heard I was anywhere near the Swallow's Nest."

"It's the only way," Lily insisted. She took Shoshana by the hand and grabbed Rebecca by the elbow as they boarded the bus for her uncle's bistro.

Jacob was at the bar when the three girls arrived. He looked quickly around the club. Arabs only. "Girls," he said as they approached him.

"Uncle Jacob," Lily said sternly. She was a little in awe of him and afraid. It was one thing to see him at home where all the other brothers snubbed him. It was another to face him on his own territory.

"Have you come looking for work?" he asked with a smile.

Rebecca turned pale and would have fled if Lily had not held her firm. "I've come to buy papers for Rebecca and myself," Lily announced.

He stared angrily at her and lowered his voice. "Couldn't you have said it any louder? Perhaps the police around the corner would like to have heard."

She became flustered and worried.

"Come into my office," he ordered. The three of them followed him and sat around his desk. "Now you want papers and passports for you and Rebecca. May I ask why?"

"To join Joseph Benjamin in Tehran."

"Your father's leaving soon. You're going in another two weeks, Rebecca. So why rush it?"

"My father—"

"I know your father doesn't approve of you and Joseph."

"So you can see he'll never let us get together unless I do it on my own. Rebecca will be my chaperon. When my father arrives in Tehran, Joseph and I will be married with his blessing."

"And how will you arrange that?" Jacob asked.

"There are ways," she assured him. He shook his head at her. "Don't you like Joseph?" she asked.

"I like Joseph and I like you. And I think Meir is being very silly. But you're his daughter. Why should I help you defy him?"

She licked her lips and thought. "You don't get along with anyone in the family. This would be a way of getting even."

"That's for children, Lily. I'm too old to get pleasure from causing another man's agony."

She thought again. "When the police came for Joseph, I told them Rahamin was Ovadia so they couldn't trace anything back to you."

He sat forward. "Now there's a reason, Lily. But Rahamin already told me that weeks ago. Why didn't you ask for help then?"

"Because I was locked in my room," she shot back.

He laughed, then considered their case. "All right," he finally said. "For true love's sake and to hurry your father out of Iraq, I'll have papers ready for you and Rebecca by tomorrow morning. You may pick them up from my wife. And if you're caught?"

"I would die first," she promised.

"How will you leave?"

"By train to Basra."

"That's good," he said.

"How much do we owe you?"

"I don't take money from my niece," he told her coldly.

"But the bribes you must pay?"

61

"It's none of your business. Tomorrow morning either of you may stop by my wife's. And what are you going to do with this one?" he asked them about Shoshana. He smiled at her and she returned it.

"Shoshana won't say a word," Lily promised. "Because if she does, I will sneak into her room at night and cut off her tongue."

Shoshana was no longer smiling. Jacob guided the girls out the back way. They would have to walk through the alleyway, bypassing the garbage, but it was safer than leaving through the club.

The next morning after Meir left the house Lily checked to see that her mother was occupied in the kitchen. Indeed, she was plucking a chicken, and that would take her at least an hour.

Lily slipped on her coat and went through Joseph's room, out his window to the alley beyond. She walked slowly down the street, bidding good morning to the neighbors as if it were perfectly ordinary for her to be out on the streets again alone. Then she took the bus to the railway station, where she bought two tickets to Basra. It would be a long trip and arduous, for once the train arrived in Basra, they would have to transfer to the ferry that crossed the Shatt-al-Arab to Abadan and then board another train to Tehran. It would take three days in all but it would be worth it. Because in Tehran there would be Joseph.

Lily waited nervously. Twenty minutes before the train was to leave, Rebecca pulled up in her chauffeur-driven car. She saw Lily, raised an envelope, and smiled. The papers were theirs. Lily came over to join her friend while the chauffeur opened the boot of the car. He removed a suitcase. In exchange Lily gave him one of her gold bracelets. Then he quickly left before he could be recognized. Rebecca and Lily boarded the train, leaving two sets of soon-to-be-enraged parents behind them. But they thought nothing of that. Only of the future. Lily with Joseph, Rebecca with—well, who knows. That was the excitement of it, wasn't it?

* * *

Meir watched from the window of his office as the train slowly pulled itself along the tracks through Baghdad, headed for Basra and the sea. He knew that soon, either by plane or train, he would be on his way out of Iraq too. The time had come.

He was fifty-one. Selling his home and his business, selling most of what he possessed would leave him a ruined man. No matter how hard he bargained, no matter what he threw in, what he was prepared to offer, he could get no more than ten percent of what his holdings were worth. Jewish property was a glut on the market. Everyone was leaving. Everything he had worked for had crumbled. But he had his children to think of. He must salvage their future if not his own.

He would tell his buyers tonight that he would accept their offers. Tomorrow he would start queuing at the various government offices to get his papers in order. Tomorrow Salemah would have to decide what she must take and what she would leave behind. He stood up slowly and walked to the door of his office. It was time to go home.

Ovadia had arrived home a short time before his father left the office. He was instantly alerted to trouble by the sound of his mother and another woman weeping. He looked into the parlor to see his mother with Rebecca's mother, pounding their chest and pulling their hair.

"Lily has disappeared."

He jumped. "Don't sneak up behind me like that again," he warned Shoshana. "And I didn't need you to tell me that. It's obvious from the fact that Rebecca's mother is here."

"Rebecca left her mother a note saying that she and Lily were traveling to Tehran, where Lily would await her parents' blessing for her marriage to Joseph."

"Does Father know?" Ovadia asked.

"No. And I'm not planning to be around when he finds out."

"Keep a lookout by the window. I'll go see if there's anything I can do for Mother."

"I wouldn't bother," Shoshana said. "She keeps beating her heart and asking God why she ever had children."

"Oh."

They sat by the window together, listened to the wails, and waited. For the most part they discussed whether Lily's leaving would improve their chances of immigrating to Israel. "There won't be any pioneering left to do by the time we get there," Shoshana was complaining. Ovadia poked her. The tall figure of their father was coming down the street. They ran up the stairs and for a time pulled each other back and forth in an effort to decide which room to lock themselves into. Shoshana finally won when the downstairs door opened and they were nearer her room than his. "I'm not playing tea party with you," Ovadia warned her. They slammed her door shut and bolted it.

Their day passed like a thunderstorm as the rages of their father flew past them and beyond them then back again. He tried several times to get into their room to ask about Lily but Ovadia claimed the bolt was stuck and they were working on it and would open the door as soon as possible.

Several times they saw him leave the house; then they could relax. But he would be back growing madder than ever. They didn't know what was happening. Was he getting the police after their sister or what?

Someone was knocking on Shoshana's door. They looked at each other. Was it their father? But the rapping was too gentle. "Who is it?" Ovadia asked.

"Mother," came the sweet answer.

Ovadia unlocked the door and threw it open. His mother entered the room with a supper tray.

"How are you, Mother?" Shoshana asked. "Can we help you?"

"Just never have any children of your own. I don't want you to know the pain I'm feeling."

"Where's Father?" Ovadia asked.

"He's gone to see Uncle Jacob. No one else seems to know what's happened to the girls."

Shoshana could barely get down her soup. She could give

her mother the answer she wanted. Maybe she should. But if she did, she could not bear to think of what would happen to her.

Ever since the lunch hour Jacob's stomach had been upset. Lily was an incredibly stupid girl. How had she dared to put it down in writing. He had burned the note as soon as he read it. "Uncle Jacob. Forgot to ask you. Could you tell my father there's a gun cache underneath the dining room table. Thanks for everything. Lily." Now how was he going to tell Meir that without implicating himself in the daughter's disappearance.

Meir would be there soon. He could count on that. All day he had had reports of Meir rushing like a wounded bull through the streets of Baghdad. He would have to be calm, he would have to be courteous, he would have to think fast on his feet, and most importantly, Jacob would have to be ready to duck.

Meir came while Jacob was busy greeting some of his favored British guests. They drank a lot. Meir stood by the bar waiting, his posture menacing. "Where are they?" he growled when Jacob finally made his way over to his brother.

"Keep your voice down. This is a public place. Not your own house," Jacob warned.

"What have you heard?" Meir whispered.

"That they have gone to Tehran to wait for you."

"For me?"

"I'm sure Lily will seek out our relatives in Tehran and stay with them until you arrive."

"And Joseph?"

"Well, he's in Tehran too. Perhaps he will meet her there. I don't know."

"Who gave them the papers, that's what I want to know. Because when I find out, I will slit his throat."

"Well, once he knows that, I'm sure he will take great pains not to be discovered. Look, so Lily went to Tehran. Hillel's already there, as are many members of our family. There's no need to be upset."

"Would they accept a daughter of mine against my wishes?"

"Do you want her to be on her own?"

"She was on her own the minute she stepped out of my house this morning."

"Don't be foolish, Meir. Let her have Joseph. They're going to a new country. Things may be different there."

"Money counts in any country. Money is something that Joseph doesn't have."

"And when you sell everything, how much will you have?" his brother reminded him. "Look, my advice is to forgive and forget."

"And if one of your daughters—"

"I have only sons," Jacob reminded him.

Meir shrugged and turned. "Meir," Jacob called him back. "I'll let you know as soon as I hear they're safe." Meir nodded. "And—" He paused. And he told him about the guns.

At last! Shoshana thought. They were going. She hadn't thought this day would ever come or that the sacrifice she had to make would be so difficult. Her tea set was sold along with all her dolls except the two she held in her arms, and even they didn't feel quite right. The family had been allowed to take only one bag apiece with them, while her father had shipped several trunks with their household goods via air cargo to Tehran.

"Are you holding on to those dolls?"

"Yes, Father." She was annoyed. Last night her mother had taken her dolls away from her and she had slept alone. She didn't like sleeping alone. She wanted something to cuddle. But her mother said the dolls needed an extra special amount of rest too, just like Shoshana, as they were going on a long trip. Whom did she think she was kidding? Shoshana was nine years old after all. She knew that dolls weren't real. They were just friends. She wasn't even grateful to Ovadia for carrying her suitcase, she was so upset.

Meir studied his young daughter as they were waiting

for the taxi to take them to the airport. Salemah had done a good job. No one could see anything different in the dolls. They were the same worn texture as they were yesterday. It was that stupid woman Reba who had caused all this trouble. She melted down all her gold and had the jeweler shape it into an ankle bracelet. As she goes limping up to customs, they take the bracelet from her foot and discover it's solid gold through and through. After that a new rule. No more personal jewelry. And Meir had converted most of the money he had into jewelry. If only Reba had left the week after him instead of the week before.

The dolls. Suitcases could be ripped apart, but would the customs officer take his daughter's dolls? Shoshana would scream bloody murder. So Salemah had taken Shoshana's dolls last night, and together she and Meir had opened up the seams, taken out the stuffing, and embedded the jewelry carefully within the cushioning cotton. Then ever so gently they had restuffed the dolls. It wasn't easy. The jewelry seemed to poke out at every opportunity it got. But finally they were satisfied. The dolls were heavier and fuller, but the seams were along the same lines and the stitches small, delicate, and unobtrusive.

The airport was packed. The lines waiting to pass through customs only increased Meir's anxiety. From the looks of it the officials were confiscating everything. He caught the eye of his wife. She pressed her lips together and said nothing. She put a protective arm around Shoshana to keep the crowd from her.

It was his turn. Meir pushed through first with the luggage and a smile. He hoped it would be one of the last he had to give to an Arab official. He passed over the papers for his wife and two children. His four bags were opened and his goods strewn about. Then they were shoved in and the bags were closed again. The customs official looked up and checked his wife and daughter for jewelry. Salemah averted her eyes but Shoshana stared back at him. The customs official picked up his stamp, quickly smashed it down on their papers, then passed them through.

5

The dolls had disappeared once again. But Shoshana minded less this time. She was too excited to need their comfort. Too much was happening to her, and she plunged breathlessly along with her family into their new state of affairs. So when her mother explained that the dolls were packed away until they settled permanently somewhere, Shoshana chose to accept it.

Their hotel room was beautiful. Tehran was beautiful, everything was beautiful. If confusing. How many relatives did they have? There were so many of them she could barely sort them by appearance and genealogy. She was pleased to see that Ovadia was having the same difficulty. Sometimes they would get together in the corner of their suite and try to decide who belonged to whom and to which side of the family. It was exhausting. And all that kissing and pinching. She felt limp after one of those sessions.

For the most part she couldn't understand what they were saying, though Ovadia assured her the discussion divided itself around two subjects: Lily and immigrating to Israel.

Lily was missing. She and Rebecca had arrived in Tehran and approached their relatives, all of whom refused to accept the girls when it became clear they had left Baghdad against their parents' wishes. The girls had pleaded and been rebuffed. It was not known whether they had had any contact with Joseph. He had disappeared about the same time the girls had.

Hillel was in the process of fawning over some important Israeli visitor to Tehran, so he did not make it to his parents' hotel suite until two days after their arrival. And when he did come, he came like an ill wind. "Do you see what he's done to me?" Hillel asked, holding his face to the light, giving evidence of the fight between him and Meir's erstwhile workman. "How could you, Father?" Hillel demanded. "How could you permit Lily to bring such dishonor on our family?"

"Where is she?" Meir asked.

"Chasing after that good for nothing. He had to hire a gang to take care of me, you know. I had him flat out on the floor so he turns around and pays a gang of six—six—young toughs to beat me up. I had the five of them licked, but then the sixth one jumped me from behind and I never knew what hit me."

"That's awful," Salemah said sympathetically, the only one to believe him. "But where did he get the money to pay them all?"

Hillel gave his mother a deadly look. Shoshana would have smiled, but she sensed that even Ovadia was taking this matter very seriously. "What's the matter?" she asked him quietly.

"I don't like violence," Ovadia replied.

Shoshana couldn't understand. Violence didn't bother her. She was too interested in seeing how everything was going to turn out. What surprised her later was that Joseph chose to arrive only an hour after Hillel, that hour itself filled with acrimony and recrimination between her father and Hillel, each accusing the other of failing in his duty to control Lily. When the knock came at their hotel room

70

door, Hillel changed suddenly. The mean look was gone from his eyes and his face became placid, his smile fixed. Of course the face changed when Ovadia opened the door and Joseph Benjamin walked through.

The first thing Joseph did was to hold up his hand to stop the onslaught, but none came.

"Where's my daughter?" Salemah asked meekly.

Joseph looked at her and said softly, "She is well. She sends her love. Both she and Rebecca are looking forward to rejoining their families."

"What are you doing here?" Hillel challenged.

"I've come to speak to Meir," Joseph answered coldly. He turned to Meir. "I just now heard that you had arrived."

Meir looked at this youth whom he had taken in, who had in turn taken his daughter. The curses of fate. But it was over now. What was done was done and some settlement would have to be reached. Marriage after all was a business. "I want all of you to take a walk," Meir said. "Joseph and I need time to talk."

Meir watched while his family made its way from the hotel suite, watched as Shoshana slid her hand briefly into Joseph's, watched until they closed the door. And then he waited just to be sure no one had forgotten a scarf or a hankie or had some other excuse. He beckoned Joseph. "Sit down," he said.

"It's—"

"Sit down," Meir insisted. "If we're going to talk, I don't want to strain my neck."

Joseph sat down. Now that he was faced with it, he didn't know how to begin.

"Is my daughter still intact?" Meir asked.

"I—"

"I think you know what I mean."

Joseph blushed. "I did not touch her. Not in that way. It was always our desire to have your blessing."

Meir gave an ill-humored laugh. "Do you think this was the way to get it?" he sniffed.

"What other way was there?" Joseph asked. "Lily says—"

"Claims," Meir corrected him.

"Claims then, that she pleaded with you to let her join me in Tehran."

"She is a fool."

"We are in love."

"Love? What do you think your love means to me? What is it worth? You can't take care of her. You are not fit for her. And you knew it!" Meir accused.

"Maybe I am not fit for her in the old ways," Joseph admitted. "But times have changed. I can provide. I will. And we care for each other. What is more important than that?"

"The family. The family is more important. Her family and the one she would marry into. Where is your family by the way?"

"I have a brother."

"Hah!" Meir scoffed.

Joseph sat back. "I'm not perfect. I will admit that. I know I am not what either you or Salemah hoped for. But I will be a good husband to your daughter. Now I have come to you to ask your permission, your blessing for my marriage to your daughter."

"Fine," Meir said with a wave of his hand. "You can have her. After this little escapade of hers, she is without value in any case."

"I think not," Joseph said and pursed his lips.

Well, Meir thought, here comes the bargaining. "You know, Joseph, as well as I do that no one will have Lily now except you. You've compromised her and scandalized our family."

"Yes, but I can make amends by marrying Lily."

"True. And I have given you my permission. What else is there to discuss?"

Joseph lifted his eyes, then lowered them again. "Her dowry," he said finally.

"Ah," Meir said. "So we have not forgotten the old ways after all." He watched with satisfaction while Joseph blushed. Then he said, "I have told you that Lily is no longer worth anything. So what kind of dowry can you expect for something without value?"

"She is not without value to me."

"But that is love," Meir reminded him.

"And I think not for you either," Joseph said.

"What are you trying to say?" Meir asked.

"If I don't marry her," Joseph said softly.

That was all he needed to say. If he didn't marry her, Lily would still be worth nothing. No respectable man would have her. And someone perhaps less than respectable would have her only if she came with a large monetary offering. Therefore Joseph was asking Meir to pay him to take the daughter he had dishonored off Meir's hands. Meir was beaten.

He offered two hundred dinars. Joseph countered it. They both sat staring past each other. The bargaining had begun in earnest.

It took them three hours to hammer out the marriage contract. Joseph received blood and a little bit more from Meir. Meir retaliated by putting into the marriage contract a huge sum of money to be paid by Joseph should he decide to separate from Lily plus an extra clause that if Joseph should ever want a divorce, he would undertake to repay Meir the entire dowry of five hundred dinars plus ten percent interest.

"You'll have no worries," Joseph told him. "I will never separate from Lily."

"Then you'll have no worries," Meir countered.

"And when will the wedding be?"

"That's for the bride and her mother to decide," Meir said. "I'd prefer to have it done here in Tehran and quickly. The longer this takes, the more shame it brings on all of us. But from now on, you are one of our family."

Joseph gratefully took Meir's hand and kissed it. Meir accepted it as his due, though this was a son he would not cherish.

"I will return Lily to you now," Joseph said.

"Her mother will be happy."

* * *

All was forgiven as the rush of wedding activities began. Nothing so excited the women and cleared their heads of scandal as the delight of another sister finding her way into bondage. A few sharp words were spoken, mainly between Salemah and Rebecca and Rebecca's mother; Salemah figured Lily too delicate at this point in her life to be threatened by a harsh tongue. Uncle Ezra had offered his estate north of Tehran for the wedding party, and it was rumored that even the uncle of the Shah had accepted an invitation. It was going to be a grand affair after all.

But Lily would have her way. She wanted no one in attendance except Rebecca as her maid of honor. "Why should I do them the favor? They all turned me out when I needed their help," she said.

Her mother was shocked. "But consider the circumstances," she reminded her daughter.

"Family is family," Lily replied and thus closed the conversation.

She did relent enough to consent to having twenty of her little cousins in the wedding, ten boys and ten girls. She laughed along with the other relatives when the Saturday before the wedding Joseph went up to read from the Torah in the synagogue, followed by the squealing of the male children.

They decided to hold even the wedding itself at her uncle's country estate, and as everyone agreed later, it was the most glorious affair anyone could remember. The ceremony went well. The glass was broken on the first stomp, though no one had doubted Joseph's strength in any case. The groom kissed the bride, then everyone sat down to a lavish wedding feast followed by music and entertainment by two belly dancers imported for the occasion from Lebanon.

"You only live once," Uncle Ezra said. It was he who was paying the expenses. He had never had a daughter of his own, only five sons, considered by everyone a blessing. But he liked weddings and young girls even better.

As the time drew closer for Joseph and Lily to depart,

they constantly avoided each other's eyes. Instead they took delight at greeting relatives and watching what sounded like a hundred young children dash back and forth over the lawns.

"It's time," Salemah said pointedly to her daughter.

Meir would not urge Joseph to it.

There was much tittering and quiet talk as Joseph and Lily prepared to depart. Lily kissed her mother and held her tight. Then she reached for Rebecca, whose attention was wandering slightly to a very presentable second cousin she barely knew she had.

A horse-drawn carriage took them to a cottage on the estate where they would spend their honeymoon. Lily had made Uncle Ezra promise to keep everyone away.

"They will never know where you are," he said. And as they approached the cottage, she could see why. It was hidden from the main estate, nestled in a small valley, surrounded by a clump of trees. She had an uncanny feeling that Uncle Ezra himself perhaps sometimes used this cottage.

The carriage dismissed, Joseph opened the door to find a lamp already lit, a firm bed made up with white coverlets.

"To see the blood," her mother had told her last night. "So that everyone knows you have been chaste."

They didn't look at each other.

"I guess we better undress," she said hesitantly.

Joseph shrugged, enormously embarrassed. He had been with women before, but only what he had paid for. He was afraid to be with Lily.

She had started to take off her wedding dress. Those tiny buttons would take her forever. He wanted to go over and help her, but he was afraid she would be offended. So he stood there and watched as her bodice came open and she slowly dropped the dress off her shoulders and stepped out of it.

His mouth was open. Lily thought she was doing something wrong. She had embarrassed herself already. This couldn't go on every night. She felt sick, faint. A lifetime of this. She wanted to run. She removed her bottom slip.

He was still staring at her. She made a tactical retreat to the bed and slid under the covers, pulling them up to her waist.

She watched while he quickly flew out of his clothes, the fear spreading that he was going to attack her. But when he was down to just his underpants, she couldn't help but laugh.

Joseph thought there was something wrong with his body. "What is it?" he asked breathlessly.

"You look silly in those," she said softly.

"Then I'll take them off," he said with a smile.

Lily was not prepared for what she saw next. She held her lips tightly pressed together. She had helped bathe Leah's children, Ezra and Albert, but neither of them had anything like this.

Joseph moved quickly over to the bed and slid in beside her.

"The light," she said.

"Please. Can we leave it on?"

She sank down and waited for him to touch her.

He didn't know where to begin.

"Will it be like in the movies?" she asked timorously.

"I hope so," he whispered, haltingly laying his hand on her breast.

She felt then that he was just as scared as she was. It made her love him all the more and gave her a feeling of peace and security. She drew him to her. They were man and wife.

Joseph was definite about leaving for Israel as soon as possible. "There's nothing for us here, he says," Lily told her mother as they prepared the meal together.

"Uh," Salemah grunted. She shook her head. "You're too young," she told her daughter. "Why not stay here with us while Joseph finds a place for you. Then you can join him."

"Because I don't want to stay here with you," Lily said ungraciously. "I want to be with my husband. He's quite capable of taking care of me."

"You don't know that yet," Salemah pointed out to her.

"I know it," Lily insisted. "Joseph is a good man and strong. I trust him with my life."

Salemah studied her daughter, then dropped her eyes. "Then," she said hesitantly, "everything so far in your marriage has gone well?"

"You mean—"

"Hush," her mother scolded. "Your sister." They both stared at Shoshana, who stared back with open eyes.

"Everything is going well," Lily confirmed. "I enjoy it."

Salemah looked in shock at her daughter. "It is not to be enjoyed," she told her. "It's something to suffer for the sake of children. Don't enjoy it. Do you want him to think you a whore?"

"He doesn't think that," Lily protested, but wondered.

"It's your duty. That's all. Don't make any more of it."

"You must have felt something sometime," Lily dared to say to her mother.

"I felt it was my responsibility to submit to it."

The meal itself was marred only by the atmosphere created by the presence of Hillel, Joseph, and Lily sitting down at the same table. Still, the conversation centered for the most part on practical matters. Salemah again begged Joseph to let Lily stay with them. Lily spoke for Joseph and said she was traveling with her husband. Ovadia envied them. As much as he enjoyed Tehran, he too wanted to be on his way.

"What will you do when you get there?" Meir asked.

"Try first to find a place to live," Joseph said.

"I've already made inquiries of our relatives there," Meir admitted.

"And?"

"I am puzzled." Meir chose his words carefully while Joseph waited. "I wrote to a cousin of mine—Albert. He lives in Tel Aviv with his family. I wrote to ask him about housing. He wrote back almost immediately and said if I sent him twenty-five hundred Israeli pounds or its equivalent he would reserve a two-room apartment for me in Bnei Brak. That's just outside Tel Aviv."

Joseph did some calculating and then laughed. "Twenty-five hundred Israeli pounds. That's enough to buy a palace in Baghdad. He expects you to pay that for two rooms? What do you say, Hillel?" Joseph asked, forcing himself to address his new brother-in-law.

Hillel stared straight ahead when he answered. "The Jewish Agency has personally given me assurances that each family immigrating to Israel from Iraq will receive an apartment. Everyone will be housed and properly taken care of."

"Then if the Jewish Agency will provide housing like manna, why does Albert stress that I should send him the twenty-five hundred pounds right away before the prices go up?" Meir asked.

"Father," Hillel said calmly, "have you ever considered that Cousin Albert might be a crook?"

"I am certain he is not," Salemah chided her son.

"Well, something fishy is going on," Meir concluded. "Cousin Albert and the Jewish Agency seem to have opposing points of view when it comes to the availability of housing."

"The Jewish Agency represents the state of Israel. It would not lie to its people," Hillel said imperiously.

"Well, we'll soon find out," Joseph said.

"You'll look around for us?" Meir asked.

"Yes, of course. I hope we'll be able to stay together as a family now."

"Be good to Lily," Salemah said. "Remember, she's not very strong."

"I will," Joseph said and smiled.

"She still needs her parents," Salemah warned him.

"She's married," Meir said quickly.

Two weeks later Salemah was preparing another farewell dinner. Her own. She hadn't wanted to do it, much preferring now to leave the last meal up to her relatives. She had enough to do packing her things so soon once again, and she was worried about Lily. Two weeks and no word. But Hillel had explained that two new officials from the Jewish Agency had arrived. "It's important that they know who I am," he explained to his mother.

She understood this. That was the way with business. But she couldn't understand her son. What was he going to be, a Jewish Agency official or an engineer? And if an engineer, then why the dinner party? But it was his last request. Hillel was not traveling with them to Israel; he felt that for the time being the Agency in Tehran would value his services more than an engineering firm in Tel Aviv.

So Salemah prepared the meal with the aid of Shoshana and Ovadia, though their help was more trouble than it was worth. In honor of their guests they made a typical Sabbath meal, even though it wasn't Friday evening. Salemah prepared the kubbah, the chicken with rice, the green beans and beef with tomatoes and fish.

Shoshana was perhaps the family member most excited by the upcoming dinner, for Hillel had told her that the two visiting Israelis were soldiers who had fought in the War of Independence. Even seeing living Israelis was a blessing, but to see actual soldiers brought to Shoshana's mind visions of the Maccabees. For the first time it struck her that she was truly going home to her own country.

What a big disappointment it was then when Hillel escorted his guests into the hotel suite and one of them turned out to be a woman.

Everyone was being very polite, but Shoshana was incensed by Hillel's deception. "I thought you told me these two were soldiers who fought in the War of Independence!" she shouted out.

"Shut up, Shoshana," Hillel said, having little tolerance for any emotions other than his own.

But the Israeli woman laughed. She came over to Shoshana and sat down next to her. "I was a soldier," she told Shoshana. "Women in Israel serve in the army."

"They do?" Shoshana was ecstatic.

"They do?" Salemah echoed in despair.

The man saw it as his responsibility to set Salemah's mind at rest. After all, his first duty was to make sure everyone coming out of Iraq continued on their journey to Israel with a firm resolve. "Married women don't serve in the army," he told her.

Salemah breathed a sigh of relief. Lily was safe. But Shoshana?

The Israeli saw her looking at her younger daughter. "Or religious women," he concluded quickly.

Salemah smiled broadly.

"Good," Shoshana said resolutely. "Because I'm not religious and I'm not going to get married."

Everyone shouted her down and she went off into a corner to sulk until she was called for dinner.

The table was full, overwhelmed not only by the company but by the food upon it. Meir tried to get specific information from the pair of guests, but was given the same placid replies his son gave him that everything would be all right and that he didn't have a thing to worry about.

"Don't bother them now, Father," Hillel said. "Let them eat."

Meir excused himself. "Please," he said, "help yourself."

The two Israelis took Meir at his word. While the Ewan family watched in astonishment, the Israelis grabbed the dishes before them and filled their plates to overflowing before they passed the food on. Then they took up their utensils and began to eat. They didn't stop for anything.

It was the woman who first noticed what effect they were having on the Ewans. She poked the man on his shoulder. He looked up. He had demolished the leg of a chicken and was now breaking open the bone and sucking out the marrow.

"What's the matter?" Meir asked. "Don't they have chicken in Israel?"

"Of course they do," the woman said and smiled. "It's just that—well—we don't have many cooks as good as your wife in Israel."

Salemah beamed at the compliment.

After the Israelis and Hillel had left, the Ewans sat together and discussed the dinner. Everyone assumed the Israelis ate like pigs because they had bad table manners. It was only Meir who guessed at the truth. When asked whàt he thought, he said somberly, "I think they were very, very hungry."

"Hungry?" The word had no meaning for the Ewans.

"They were starving," Meir said. And for the first time his doubts about Israel became real.

6

They were going. Despite any misgivings Meir might have, they were on their way. And his mind was put at ease once they arrived at the airport in Tehran. So unlike the tumultuous exit from Baghdad, here everything was orderly and smoothly organized. Maybe what Hillel had told them about the Jewish Agency was true. Maybe everything would be provided for them. Now Meir could only hope.

When the Ewan family boarded the Constellation, they found that the seats had been ripped out and benches installed in their place, benches without even a headrest. The redecoration was designed to allow as many immigrants as possible to fit into the plane. There were grumbles and mumblings, but for the most part people accepted the situation in which they had no choice.

It was early September when Meir and his family flew into Lod. They made the mistake of assuming that in Israel in September it was winter, so they dressed in their warmest garments. They, like most Iraqis who could afford it, had invested heavily in new clothes for the journey, all tailor-made for them, even though the women of the families were skilled seamstresses who, with their repair work, could make one garment last almost forever. But this was a special day, the most sacred day of their lives, the return to their land, to Israel, and all had dressed appropriately.

The flight to Israel was almost what they expected from their first exposure to flying between Iraq and Iran. When they landed there was a cry of celebration.

What they couldn't understand was why they were not allowed to disembark after the plane had landed in Israel. They peered out the windows; the land looked barren. No one was coming to get them. Could there be some mistake? Had they landed in the wrong country? But no, the attending official had said Israel.

The minutes dragged on. The children became unbearably restless. The heat was oppressive. Outside it was perhaps eighty degrees; inside the plane was well over a hundred.

An hour passed by. Finally from the windows the new immigrants could see a boarding ramp being pushed up to their plane. The door opened and they felt the first rustle of free Israeli air.

A man entered the plane and shouted to them in Arabic, "Don't move. Just stay seated exactly where you are." Then he retreated.

After he left, two men in white coveralls, their faces hidden by gas masks, stepped aboard. The rumble that started in the front of the plane turned to screams as the white clouds of pesticide floated backward, engulfing everyone, soaking through the immigrants' expensive new clothing and into their skins.

There was a silence then as they were left with the settling pesticide. Not only was their clothing ruined, but they, the richest of Iraqi refugees, had been deloused like common beggars.

When they were finally let off the plane, they were surrounded by men in uniform. For Jews in Iraq, like all Jews, uniforms meant oppression. Yet these were their brothers. No longer would they be singled out by the authorities just because they were Jews. The first wave of joy swept through the crowd of immigrants.

Meir expected trouble. Despite the fact that these men in uniform were Jews, authorities were authorities and they thought differently from most men. He was, therefore, pleasantly surprised when a customs official approached him, asked him if he had anything to declare, and when he said no, checked his baggage and sent him on his way.

From the customs area they were sent to board open trucks. Meir climbed on first and had Ovadia hand up their three suitcases. Then Meir helped Salemah and Shoshana onto the truck. Ovadia completed the family by scrambling up last by himself. They settled on one side in the middle of the truck and stared at each other.

"They probably don't have buses in Israel yet," Salemah finally said.

"What's going to happen now?" Shoshana asked.

No one could answer her, so Salemah said, "Oh, you'll see. They'll take us to a nice home, something like our hotel suite in Tehran. Then your father will go out and look for a place to live, nicer than we left in Baghdad."

That answer satisfied everyone except Meir, who, like his daughter, was also wondering what would happen.

He asked other passengers on the truck, but no one knew. Finally a man came to the truck to check them off.

"Where are we going?" Meir asked.

"Sha'ar Ha-Aliyah," the man answered briskly. The gate of immigration. It meant nothing. They would still have to wait and see.

Sha'ar Ha-Aliyah. The gate. The gates to Israel had truly swung open for the Jews of the world, and Meir Ewan's was not the only family to seek its future in this their promised land. The remnants of the massacred Jews of Europe, freed from British internment in Cyprus, freed from other camps throughout that bastion of fallen civilization still waited for their turn to be transported to Israel. But this remnant could not match in numbers alone the Jews from Arab countries who found themselves fleeing from their former homelands when they had a chance, fleeing from their Moslem neighbors, who had come to view Israel as a thorn to be plucked out from under their heel and their own Jews as an annoyance to be trampled under foot. From Yemen, from Tunisia, from Morocco, from Egypt, from Syria, from Iraq alone over one hundred thousand Jews fled to Israel. When the state was declared in May, 1948, six hundred fifty thousand Jews lived in Israel. In the first three years of statehood these six hundred fifty thousand had to absorb one hundred thousand more than their own number. And most of them, like Meir, came through the gate of immigration. Sha'ar Ha-Aliyah.

Sha'ar Ha-Aliyah was, as they later found out, near Haifa. So on the ride from Lod to the camp they saw a good portion of the country, just now in 1950 beginning to build. Many sand dunes, much barrenness, but interspersed in this wasteland were areas of cultivated ground, the kibbutzim that they had heard about from the Zionist underground. However, most Iraqis were like Meir Ewan, small businessmen, great believers in free enterprise. For them the call would be to the established cities, despite all the efforts the government agencies would make to settle them elsewhere in the development towns of the desert, outside the main flow of Israeli life.

As it turned out, Sha'ar Ha-Aliyah was not the hotel suite Salemah had envisioned. This myth was dispelled as soon as they passed through its gates. It was an old abandoned army camp, and Meir knew he would have to be prepared for anything. He tensed like a panther on the attack and nodded at Ovadia. Ovadia knew he also must be ready.

Four open trucks arrived at the same time theirs did. Everyone disembarked and was milling around waiting for someone to bring order out of this chaos. Salemah had grabbed onto Shoshana. They were saying something to Meir but he wasn't listening. He had his ears cocked for the inevitable announcement.

There. The man with the bullhorn. Meir spotted him and gave him his complete attention.

"Everyone! Everybody! Listen, please! Quiet! Everyone is to find an empty cot in the barracks." The man's voice continued to carry past them but Meir paid no attention.

"Quick, Ovadia!" he shouted. He lifted two of the bags, left the other with Salemah, and began sprinting toward the end barracks. He assumed they would have the most places available, as the main thrust of the crowd would be toward the center barracks that stood before them.

Meir whipped his head around once to see Ovadia following him and thought he also caught sight of his daughter Shoshana. He raced down the path of sand and flew into the second to the last barracks. He took no notice of the mass of people already inhabiting the barracks but merely kept his eye out for empty beds.

Three in the center. He spotted them. He threw his suitcase and his coat down on them and looked for another. But Ovadia had gotten there first. Across the way from the three Ovadia had found one and sat on it. Then Shoshana rushed into the barracks and threw herself across the cots her father had already claimed. He laughed at the sight of her small body bridging the cots. It was then that he noticed the other people in the barracks. They were saying something to him, but he couldn't figure out what it was. His first fear was that he had mistakenly taken someone else's cots and would have to start looking all over again.

He stopped. He concentrated. He tried to figure out what these people were saying. "Vuz-vuz," was all he heard. A man across from him kept chattering away. Meir tried to think of the Hebrew word for "empty" but it wasn't there. Then he tried Arabic, Persian. Nothing. Finally he sought out his English. "Okay? Okay?" he asked.

The man across from him smiled. "Okay," the man said. Everything was okay. The strangers came together and clapped each other on the back. "Okay," they repeated over and over to each other.

Meir, assured of his cots, told his children to keep an eye on them while he went back to fetch his wife. He found Salemah waiting anxiously where he had left her.

"It's all right," he told her. "I have the cots." He hoisted the remaining bag and walked in front as he led Salemah to the barracks.

It did not take them long to decide who would get which cot. Ovadia would sleep in the single, Shoshana would be protected in the cot between her parents. With that taken care of, Salemah sat down next to Meir to have a talk. "Did you notice?" she asked quietly. "There are other people in this barracks."

Meir nodded.

"Am I to spend the night among strangers?"

Meir nodded again.

Salemah shook her head.

"What do you suggest?" Meir asked.

"I will not reveal my nakedness to the strangers."

"Good," Meir said.

"You are my husband. It is your duty to provide for me. I will not spend the night here. Not among strangers. They don't even speak our language."

Meir didn't know what to say. His wife was right. She should not be forced to sleep in these barracks with strangers, men and women together. Yet he did not see any houses scattered about. He himself was just thankful they had cots for the night.

Some music was being played over the P.A. system. The man next to Meir said "Okay," to him. Meir turned to stare at him and shook his head in incomprehension. Finally the man held one hand cupped in front of him and with the other dug in and brought to his mouth.

"Ah! Eat," Meir said and mimicked his new friend.

The man nodded and said, "Okay?"

"Okay," Meir repeated.

Meir gathered his family and left the barracks. He discovered a line running around the camp and tried to find the end of it.

It took them an hour to get served. All the time Salemah stared reproachfully at her husband. But what could he do? He no longer controlled his own fate. By the time they got served and went into the dining hall they had little appetite in any case, the noise level in the hall being explosive. Children screaming, mothers yelling for lost children, men shouting back and forth at each other. Meir and his family could hardly understand anything, so different were the languages spoken within the hall.

Nor could his family understand the food they were served. Herring, salad, dark bread, leben, soft cheese. It was nothing like the food they were used to. Only hunger drove them to it. All except for Salemah. She insisted she did not adapt well to change.

The first night, after dinner and the use of the communal toilets, the children sank happily onto the cots and fell immediately asleep. Meir too wanted to sleep, knowing that tomorrow would be even harder than today, for tomorrow he must try to figure out what was going on and what he was supposed to do. But Salemah did not sleep. She did not even lie down. She merely sat at the edge of her cot and stared into his half-open eyes. He wanted to turn away from her, but felt that would be the ultimate betrayal, so he stared back at her for as long as he was able, until his eyes closed.

When he woke the next morning, she was still staring at him. He didn't know, but he suspected that she had slept during the night and had merely awoken early enough to resume her position. He knew what she wanted him to feel and she had succeeded.

Meir didn't understand the camp yet, and that was his first responsibility, to learn what was going on and how to master it.

He ate breakfast on the run that morning, trying to find an Iraqi who had been here longer than he had and who knew what was happening. With perseverance he found one who told him that after breakfast he had to stand in another line, for assignment to a permanent camp.

"Permanent camp?" Meir asked. "I thought we would be assigned housing?"

"That I don't know," the Iraqi answered. "All I know is you stand in another line. They tell you where to go."

They tell you where to go? Meir was in a panic. They?

89

Who were they? He didn't know them. To him they were just another functioning, faceless, feelingless bureaucracy like the one in Baghdad. Unfair. There was a difference. These men didn't take bribes. He found that out from standing in the lines all day, every day, day after day. "What will it take?" he asked those around him. "What will it take to get my assignment to a permanent camp?"

"Where were you born?" one asked him.

"Baghdad," Meir answered.

"Forget it. You don't have what it takes."

What it took was to be born in Poland, or Russia, or Czechoslovakia, in a village somewhere near where the men in the cages who were passing out assignments were born. What it took was to be European and to speak Yiddish, because then you could call out to the men in the cages and like God they would hear your voice in the middle of the multitude and call you forth and send you onward. Arabic was not heard. Arabic was not understood. Day after day the line emptied of white, European faces, day after day more dark ones came to take their place. Dark like Meir, angry, frustrated, uncomprehending. Who would speak to them? Who would speak for them? They waited in line as the days passed and the men in the cages decided their fate.

"Where will you go when you get out of here?" the men asked one another.

Some had places already, relatives waiting to receive them, apartments they had put a deposit on. Meir thought fleetingly of the apartment Albert had written to him about. Should he have? But the question was asked too late.

There were two camps. He had heard that. One near Haifa, the other near Tel Aviv. Tel Aviv was the main city. He had relatives there. That's where he wanted to go.

"Well, you must tell them you want to be sent to the camp near Haifa then," one of the men advised him. Meir turned his back on him. "Look, I know what I'm talking about," the man insisted. "How long have you been here, seven days? Me, two weeks. Two weeks and I've seen things. Believe me, if you tell them you want the one near Tel Aviv, they'll send you to Haifa. You see, whatever you want, they give you the opposite. This is the Israeli way. It never fails. Ask around."

Meir didn't ask around. He didn't want to know. He stood in line. He knew that. And day after day it became less painful. It was an escape from the unspoken reproaches of his wife, Salemah. He did not even leave the line for food. Ovadia brought him that. Ovadia also came to replace him when he had to use the common bathroom. He felt a bond with Ovadia. Ovadia could understand. But the women? They depended on him and all he could do was stand in line.

The tenth day came. He got up, angered and depressed. The sun was hot, the line moved slowly. He no longer bothered to talk to anyone. They might be here tomorrow, they might not. What was the point? He nodded to the few he knew, then stood in line with the rest of them. He got to the head of the line and once more handed over his card.

"Where do you want to go?" the clerk asked him.

Meir was startled. He was so used to hearing, "Nothing for you today."

The clerk looked at him in disgust. "Beit Lidd," he told Meir. "Near Tel Aviv." He stamped Meir's card and sent him on his way.

Meir walked down the line in a state of shock, holding his card stamped Beit Lidd. He mumbled over and over to himself until his voice became louder and he was shouting, "Beit Lidd!" People were applauding him as he moved down the line.

"Beit Lidd," he told Salemah, who waited for him in the barracks. He pretended not to see the tears that ran down her cheeks.

7

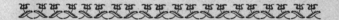

Lily had been waiting for weeks now for her father to arrive. There was so much she had to tell him, but Joseph had forbidden her to write.

"Things will be difficult enough for them anyway," he had told her. "Why add any more burdens on their shoulders."

Perhaps he was right. She didn't know any longer. She didn't even know what had become of her marriage. Ever since they had left Tehran they had not been alone for a minute. First in the barracks at Sha'ar Ha-Aliyah and then this at Beit Lidd. A simple tent that they shared with eight strangers.

She tried not to say anything. It was hard enough on Joseph. She wouldn't make it harder. He was her husband. He needed her support.

Sometimes when she closed her eyes at night, she could see her house in Baghdad, her room, her bed with the clean white sheets and the soft pillows. What would happen to her now? Every night on these straw mattresses hearing the breathing of strangers. Joseph gone all day, desperate to find a place for them to live, some work.

She fought off panic. She was seventeen, she was an adult. She must accept whatever this new life brought her. But oh, she wanted to crawl back into her mother's arms.

The trucks were arriving. Soon her waiting for the day would be over, if her parents weren't among the passengers. She watched closely as the new immigrants disembarked. She couldn't tell. Day after day in this place made every face seem so familiar.

A woman got down from the truck. She seemed to Lily so much like her mother but tired, older, more lined than Lily remembered. A little girl followed. It was Shoshana.

"Mother!" Lily yelled. "Mother! Shoshi! Ovadia! Father! I'm over here."

Her mother looked up and at once that old face turned into the loving, warm one she remembered.

Lily ran past the fence to help. She hugged her family, then told her father he had to stand in line for assignment.

"That sounds familiar," Meir said, no longer expecting anything.

The line moved slowly, but at least it moved. Everyone seemed to get something from the bureaucrat who sat at the desk, protected by two guards.

Meir reached the head of the line. "How many?" the bureaucrat asked him.

He assumed people. "Four," Meir replied.

"D-Twelve." The bureaucrat wrote something, stamped it, and handed the paper to Meir.

Meir veered off to the right, holding the white slip of paper. "D-Twelve. What's this?" he asked his daughter.

"Come, I'll show you," Lily said. She led her bedraggled family deep into the camp to the D section. She continued down until she found the number twelve.

Meir had done well not to expect much. D-Twelve turned out to be a large tent with room enough for eight folding camp beds.

Salemah looked and said softly, "There's been a mistake."

"You have to go over to the supply compound and pick up your mattresses," Lily said quietly. Then continued

94

quickly, "Some, those who came way before, got tents with wooden floors. But this is all that's left now."

"Tents?" Salemah questioned. "Tents like some bedouin. They promised us an apartment. Hillel said the Jewish Agency would have an apartment ready for us." She looked at her daughter. Lily shook her head.

Behind them came another family of four. "Excuse me," the man said. "I think this is our tent."

Meir showed him his slip of paper. He looked down. The man also had D-Twelve written on his.

"They fill up all the cots," Lily explained. "You get to know everyone pretty quickly," she added weakly.

Salemah looked to Meir who looked away.

"Where is the supply compound?" Meir asked quietly.

"Come, I'll show you," Lily said and led her father and Ovadia off to fetch the mattresses.

"Tents," she heard her mother say. "Sleeping on a dirt floor like an animal."

It was confusing for Shoshana. She didn't know what to think. All the tears her mother had shed at Sha'ar Ha-Aliyah, and now they were at Beit Lidd where her father had wanted to go and her mother was still crying. She didn't know what to expect from her parents anymore. Her father, who had once seemed so strong and overpowering, now sat on his cot looking utterly defeated, her mother hurt and mystified. It was not what Shoshana had dreamed about when she dreamed of coming to Israel. She dreamed of a golden dawn, working in the fields, rebuilding the land, dancing and singing as the sun set. Go out and play, her mother had told her. All she could see of Israel was tent upon tent filling up the whole countryside. The miracle was that they had returned. There the miracle stopped.

Ovadia had already found someone to play with. Boys he went to school with in Baghdad. But she had no one and they didn't want her. Boys. They thought they were so tough. But she could run as fast as they could and kick a ball as straight. Oh, well, it didn't matter. She would find her own friends. She walked down one row of tents to the end of the camp and then up another row. The noises—families, babies, children, parents crying. She was glad hers weren't the only ones doing that.

"Shoshana!"

She heard her name being called from inside a tent, but it couldn't have been her name. It must have been another Shoshana.

"Shoshana!" A young girl came out of the tent to face her.

"Danielle? Danielle!" She ran shrieking into the arms of her best friend from Baghdad. "They sold all my dolls and my tea set," she said quickly to assess Danielle of the worst. "But I'm too old for them anyway," she shrugged off the hurt.

"I've missed you."

"You said you were going to say good-bye."

"They came for us in the middle of the night," Danielle explained. "I barely had time to get dressed. It was Joseph's group."

"Joseph married Lily."

"Really?"

Shoshana could see Danielle was shocked. "Yes. They're very happy. I think."

"They're here?"

"Who is that, Danielle?" A woman came to the entrance of the tent and stood there. It was Leah, Danielle's mother. "Why it's little Shoshana," she exclaimed. "Shoshana Ewan. Look, Nazem," Leah called. "Look who's here. Shoshana Ewan."

Shoshana was almost frightened by the appearance of her friend's father. But he looked smaller than she had remembered him, and he had not shaved in days. He just stood there and stared at her.

"Do you have my father's money?" she boldly asked. But she was sorry immediately because she saw she had hurt Danielle. She turned and ran off down between the row of tents.

When she returned to her own tent, she found Joseph

there. She ran to him and he lifted her up and put her on his lap. "Ugh, you're getting heavy," he teased.

"I'm ten," she reminded him. "Do you know—"

"Shoshana, not now," Lily warned. "Father and Joseph are talking."

"But—"

"In a minute, okay, Shoshi," Joseph said kindly. Then he continued his conversation with Meir. "The situation is bad, incredibly bad," Joseph told him. "Tomorrow you come with me, we'll start looking for a place to stay for you. Besides, I think I've found a place to sink my money into."

"But what of the Jewish Agency?" Meir said. "They promised us a place to live."

"You see those tents out there?" Joseph said. "That's what you'll get from the Jewish Agency."

"A place to live," Meir repeated.

"Listen to me!" Joseph said harshly, then added a soft, respectful, "Father," as an afterthought. "There are people who have been living in tents for over a year now, waiting for the Jewish Agency to provide them with apartments. Believe me, there's no hope. You've got to get out and find yourself a place to live now. Every day the prices go up. The inflation is incredible. Nothing will come to us. We must go out and grab it. If you doubt what I'm saying, ask around. You have many relatives here. We've met them all, inside and outside the camp. Get out. Now."

"Is it my turn?" Shoshana asked.

Joseph sighed.

"Yes, your turn," her father said.

"Nazem Haya's here."

"What!" Meir exploded.

"But he doesn't have your money. I asked."

Joseph stared at her and shook his head. "Are you trying out for the diplomatic corp, Shoshi? Look, Meir, don't bother about Nazem. He doesn't have a cent. He lost it all in Egypt. Your money. Everybody's money."

"It's a wonder he hasn't lost his life."

97

"That's been tried," Joseph warned him. "He has a tent with Leah and the three children and three other people. He has bodyguards also, some Moroccan youths that came over on their own."

"But I can still play with Danielle, can't I?" Shoshana asked.

"I would prefer that you have as little to do with the Hayas as possible," her father said.

"How can that be," Salemah spoke up, "when Leah actually helped deliver Shoshana? You might as well give the girl the comfort of her friend since you can give her nothing else."

Shoshana froze. She had never before heard her mother criticize her father. Joseph too was uncomfortable. It was a wife's duty to show her husband respect. He didn't want Lily to get any new ideas. "Tomorrow we'll go out. You can look for a place to stay," he said quickly to his father-in-law.

Unlike Sha'ar Ha-Aliyah, where they had been in quarantine, in Beit Lidd the immigrants were free to leave the camp in search of a place to live and work. Joseph took Meir out with him the very next day. They traveled by several buses, then walked half a mile to where Joseph was thinking of buying property.

"Ramat Gan," Joseph said dreamily. "The garden on the heights."

Meir looked around him. Joseph must have been sunstruck. All Meir saw was emptiness.

They walked along the sparsely populated street until they stood in front of a building.

"It's called a villa," Joseph said proudly.

"Villa! It's a shack!" Meir retorted.

Joseph held up his finger and shook it at him. "Villa," he corrected his father-in-law. "A shack has no indoor plumbing. This does."

He walked up the sand-covered flagstones to the door and knocked upon it. An old woman opened the door.

"Mrs. Finkel," Joseph said in Hebrew and smiled. "This is my father-in-law. He's a builder. He'd like to look at the villa." Joseph had been speaking loudly, his Hebrew elementary but passable.

Mrs. Finkel smiled and politely showed them in. The villa was, in fact, what Meir called it, a shack. It had a basic kitchen with basin and a hot plate. It had a living room, two other rooms that would serve as bedrooms, and a shabby bathroom and toilet.

Meir knocked around, checking on the concrete walls, the floors, the bathroom and kitchen. It was old and gloomy.

"The Finkels are going to Jerusalem to die, that's what they told me," Joseph said. "So they want to sell."

"How much?" Meir asked.

"What do you think of its condition?"

"It's primitive, but sound. Fit for a pig farmer perhaps."

"It has a lovely garden," Joseph said and pointed out the back window.

Meir saw two cactus plants surrounded by sand.

"Nice place to hang up the clothes," Joseph continued. "They're willing to leave some of the furniture."

"How much?" Meir asked again.

"It's the land that's important," Joseph continued. "Land is wealth."

"Joseph, you're sitting on a sand dune. How much do you think a sand dune is worth?"

"Five thousand pounds," Joseph said quickly.

"Five thou—! Are you kidding? Five thousand pounds. First of all you don't have it, second of all you could buy blood with five thousand pounds."

"Let me tell you, Meir, in Israel you can buy practically nothing for five thousand pounds."

"Wait for the Jewish Agency."

"Wait in that tent? Among strangers? I haven't touched my wife since I got here. We need a place to live now."

"So you want a loan!"

"Nothing. Not from you. I'll use the dowry and borrow the rest."

"Borrow? On what? What's your collateral?"

"Lily has her jewelry. I have a strong back. The rest of

the money I'll get as a loan from the Jewish Agency. Low interest rates. And I've already found a job. Working as a plumber at Solel Boneh."

"You're not a plumber!"

"So who knows that but you and me?" Joseph asked. "Besides that, plumbers make better money than workmen. I'll learn."

"I knew you were no good when Lily married you, but I didn't know you were crazy."

"Meir, look at those people in Beit Lidd. Look at those who have remained over a year waiting for the Jewish Agency to give them an apartment. They've got nothing left. No hope, no will, nothing. I've got to take chances or I won't get any place. You will too. You'll see that. You wait a few weeks and you'll see what it's like."

Meir stood by Joseph as he made all the arrangements for purchasing the shack in Ramat Gan. Joseph insisted on this so that Meir would have some idea of how business was conducted in Israel. Then when his turn came, it might be easier for him. Meir welcomed the opportunity to see a solid capitalist transaction take place, even believing as he did that Joseph was making a big mistake. What would Joseph do for money now that he had invested all his ready cash in the villa? How would he succeed as a plumber? Plumber! If he could claim he was a plumber, why not a Rothschild too? And what would Lily say when she arrived at the shack? How would she react to having to make it her home, her first one at that?

Salemah would be sorry to see her go.

Indeed Salemah was already bemoaning the loss. Her daughter's presence kept her intact. She had to put up a brave front for Lily's sake. But when Lily left, what would she do? Shoshana and Ovadia were too young to be the companion Lily had become. They needed her but could give very little comfort in return. Not like her Lily.

"You're off again," Salemah said to her daughter.

"Yes." Lily sighed with relief, not even guessing her mother's need of her. She thought only of her new life. If Joseph had only known how she had hated the time she had to spend in that tent, never daring to breathe or speak or move out from their own limited space. Now her own home, her villa, Joseph had called it.

"It needs a little work," her father had said with more kindness than he usually mustered lately. "The houses in Israel, they're not like Iraqi houses."

Was it a warning? She looked to Joseph. He smiled at her confidently. Anything was better than a tent.

Meir watched them walk away, glad he was not going to be there when his daughter first set eyes on her villa.

Lily in truth had an inkling that something might be wrong when they got off the second bus and started walking up the street. Joseph's steps were light and happy. She swiveled her head to either side, looking for her castle.

When Joseph stopped in front of one of the shacks and walked up the flagstones to the door, she reluctantly followed.

"Ah," Joseph said. "They've left the mezuzah. That means good luck."

Lily was still looking for the garden Joseph had promised her.

He unlocked the door and flung it open for her.

She walked inside and looked around. Silently. "How much did it cost?" she finally asked.

Joseph hesitated before answering. "Have you ever thought of becoming a vegetarian?"

She turned to him. "That much?"

He nodded and shrugged.

"Oh, Joseph," she moaned and pulled him to her as if he were a little boy.

"Please. Wait till I close the door," he objected.

When he did, they realized that for the first time in months they were alone. They hungrily grabbed each other and fought their way into the bedroom, Joseph silently blessing Mrs. Finkel for leaving a cot with a ragged sheet on top of it.

Lily lay underneath Joseph and tried to think of her mother's admonition but couldn't stop herself from responding to the pressure of his body. She screamed and twisted until she finally felt release along with his animal thrusting. She called his name weakly and felt him collapsing onto her breast.

The only thought that dulled her pleasure was that there were no more meal lines to stand on. Now she would have to start cooking for real.

Beit Lidd meant days spent in idleness. No work, no comfort. Empty assurances from officials who left every night and returned to their apartments in the city while the immigrants slept in their tents and dreamed about the future and about the past.

Meir remained in Beit Lidd. He was undecided. He hesitated. His mind moved back and forth between alternatives. He visited Joseph and Lily from time to time and saw the improvements they were making in their villa. He was happy for them. But he couldn't foolishly sink all his money into a place to live like Joseph. He wouldn't at his age take that risk. Yet all that was left to him was the empty promises of the Jewish Agency.

How to get out? *Protectzia,* people told him mysteriously. It was weeks before he got up the courage to ask what *protectzia* was. He discovered it was knowing someone important. Who was important? Someone the clerks knew. Well, he had a son working for the Jewish Agency. That should count for something.

He waited all day to see the man, and when he was finally admitted, he was asked to show his number. He handed his slip of paper to the official, who stamped it and threw it in the basket.

"Nu," the official said.

"My name is Meir Ewan. I have a wife and two children living with me."

"Congratulations."

"I don't want to live in a tent anymore."

"Who does?"

"When I was in Tehran, the Jewish Agency promised me an apartment and a place to work."

"And you'll get it. We always keep our promises."

"When?" Meir asked.

"When? God only knows. A year or two."

"A year or two? But we're living in a tent. There's nothing but dirt under our feet. Why, I had a three-story house in Baghdad."

"You people always say that. Sometimes it's even four-story. Look, we know what conditions were like for you in Iraq. So don't give me the stories about big houses. You're beginning to sound like the Arabs with their orange groves in Jaffa."

"Look, Mister—"

"Don't threaten me, Ewan, because I'll call the guards."

"When I was in Tehran—"

"You're not in Tehran now. You're here."

It was almost on Meir's lips to wish he wasn't. Then he remembered *protectzia*. "My son works for the Jewish Agency in Tehran," Meir said confidentially.

"So what?" the official replied. "We always hire native labor."

Meir sat back totally defeated. "At least," he said, "give me something to do, a job of some sort. I can't sit around this camp all day doing nothing. Man doesn't live by doing nothing."

"Don't give me that," the official said. "There's nothing you Iraqis like better than doing nothing."

Meir, who had worked hard all his life, was seeing the birth of an Israeli truism, that "his" people were lazy, uneducable, barbaric. "Would you tell me something, Mr. Official? Why do you always refer to me as 'you people'? I thought we were one people and that's why we are all here in Israel."

The official said nothing. He didn't have to. He twisted his rubber stamp, the source of all authority in Israel, in his fingers; then he yelled, "Next!"

Hillel came from Tehran at the end of September. When he found out that his parents were living in Beit Lidd, he came out to visit them immediately.

Salemah embraced her son and said, "Hillel, you've come to stay with us."

103

"Live in a tent? Are you crazy?"

Meir squeezed his son by the arm until he saw that he was hurting him. It felt good. "Where is the apartment you promised us in Tehran?" he asked.

"I don't build apartments, Father. I understand you'll have to wait until one is ready. Please let go of me. You act as if this was all my fault."

"You gave me your assurance."

"They gave me their assurances," Hillel shot back. "Look, Father, I know it's frustrating but what can I do? It will only be another year or so." He checked his watch. "I've got to run now. Cousin Albert's having company for dinner so they'll be serving a good meal."

"Albert? You're staying with Albert? Isn't he the one you called a crook in Tehran?"

"Times change, Father. Don't worry. I'm only staying with him till you get your own apartment. Bye, Mother. Give my love to the kids." He retreated from Salemah as she came forward to stand next to her husband.

"But what is going to happen?" she asked Meir.

Meir looked at her but was too angry to say anything. He walked away.

They saw more of Joseph than they saw of Hillel, their own son. As Hillel explained it, he couldn't bear to see his mother suffering, so he had to cut short his visits to her, finally eliminating them altogether. When Joseph came out to visit them, he always brought with him some bit of encouraging news, however small. "Look," Joseph said to Meir, "I've got you this promise of a job."

"Is this anything like the promise of an apartment?" Meir asked.

"It's my boss. I told him you were a building contractor in Baghdad. I told him you were very skilled. Skilled workers they always need. With the job you'll have a salary. So take the money you brought from Iraq and put it into an apartment now." Meir was still undecided. Joseph was exasperated. "Meir, what good is it to sit on your money? Every day it's worth less." Finally he got angry. "All right.

You don't want to buy an apartment. You want to wait here two years in a tent. Fine. At least let Lily and me take Ovadia and Shoshana out of here. Start them in a school."

"The children stay with me. No one says I can't take care of my own children." Meir raised his voice.

"Right. Okay." Joseph stood up. He was becoming equally loud. "When you want that job, when you want a place to stay, let me know. Until then let me tell you that I think you're really a stupid bastard. And if I didn't care about you so much I'd just call you a stubborn old man."

"You have all the answers, don't you, Joseph."

"No. I just have a future. You have nothing but the tents. When will you realize that?"

In the end it was not what Joseph had said to him or what the Jewish Agency had said to him that decided Meir. It was the rain. Beit Lidd was bearable in the summer months because in the summer in Israel there was no rain. But they were well into October now. When the first rain fell, it turned tent D-12 into a field of mud.

"What's to be done for us?" Meir shouted at an official walking through the camp unguarded.

"What do you mean what's to be done?"

"It's raining. Our tent floor is mud."

"So in a few days it'll stop raining and the floor will dry up." The official walked on.

Meir took everything he had with him and left the camp. He would not return until he had found his family a place to live.

He rode into Tel Aviv and sought out Albert at his dry goods store.

"Meir!" Albert said in welcome. "What brings you out on such a wet day?"

"All of Beit Lidd is one big mud puddle," Meir said.

"So what's the surprise?" Albert asked. "It was a mud puddle last winter too."

"I must find a place for my family to live."

Albert looked at Meir in disgust. "Why didn't you send me the twenty-five hundred pounds when I wrote to you?"

"I thought it was too much."

"Are you in for a surprise." Albert called to one of his sons to take over. Then he led Meir out the door of his shop and down the street to Fisher's Contracting. They got into Fisher's car and drove out of Tel Aviv.

"Where are we going?" Meir asked.

"Givatayim," Fisher answered.

"That's near Ramat Gan," Meir said.

"Yes. You know it then?"

"My son-in-law lives in Ramat Gan."

"Beautiful area. Let me tell you, I don't understand why everyone has to live in such a central area as Tel Aviv. Spread out. Give yourself room. That's what I tell my clients."

They stopped on Katznelson Street in Givatayim and got out. Into the apartment building and three flights up, Fisher used his large set of keys to open the door.

He wasn't lying. Meir could see that as he walked through the rooms of the apartment. A large entrance hall-way, large enough to put a dining table, a living room, and two bedrooms. He went to look at the kitchen, checked the faucets, the sink, then the bathroom where he flushed the toilet. He laughed at himself as he watched the water chase itself down the basin. How used he had become to the large holes in the ground Beit Lidd provided. A balcony from the living room, a smaller one outside the kitchen. He could live here comfortably with his wife and three children. That he knew.

"How much?" Meir asked.

"I shouldn't really be doing this, but I'm letting it go for five thousand pounds."

"Five thousand!"

Fisher backed off. "Take it or leave it, my friend. People are begging for apartments around here."

Meir looked around the apartment again. Five thousand would wipe him out. His cash reserves would be nonexistent. Still, Joseph had that job waiting for him. And they couldn't live in the mud forever. No, he had temporized long enough, too long. "I'll take it," he told Fisher.

8

It was raining when Danielle went out that morning. More rain at Beit Lidd was a disaster. She felt the mud suck her down but she plunged along anyway. She and Shoshana were going to the children's tent to see if they could make paper dolls. If there was paper, if there were scissors.

She stood in front of D-Twelve, then stepped inside. Eight faces stared at her. She felt discomforted. Where she expected to find Shoshana, she saw a young woman. And a man. On the other two cots where Shoshana's parents would have been there were two older women.

"They are not here," the man said, the one who had shared the tent with the Ewans ever since the day they arrived at Beit Lidd. "They've gone. Last night. Meir has bought an apartment in Givatayim."

Danielle backed out of tent D-Twelve into the rain. She walked and stumbled down the row of tents, her tears intermingling with the rain upon her face. She was alone. There was always only Shoshana. And now she was gone.

Why wouldn't the other children play with her, the ones she had known in Baghdad? She knew it had something to do with her father. Shoshana said it was because her father had stolen other people's money. Danielle couldn't ask her father about it, but she did ask her mother, and her mother had said something about bad investments. Which wasn't stealing.

She didn't understand why everything was turning out like this. When they had made it safely to Tehran from Iraq, she had been so excited and relieved. That trip had scared her, being bundled in a blanket so she could scarcely breathe. Her two younger brothers were given a sedative so they would sleep during the long truck ride over the mountains into Iran, but she had felt every bump, heard every sound, been terrified each time they were forced to stop. The truck had been so crowded with Jews fleeing Iraq. If they had been caught, they would have been pulled from the truck and shot right there on the mountains and only the scavengers would ever know.

But they had reached Tehran. Once there her mother had heard that Nazem Haya was in an Israeli transit camp awaiting settlement. Before they could unpack, they were on a plane flying into Israel, finding her father at Beit Lidd. "He'll be so pleased to see little Albert. He's never seen little Albert," her mother kept saying. But when they finally found her father, he didn't look pleased to see any of them.

That was nine months ago, and in nine months she had had no friend except Shoshana. The others called her names and they called her father names. Sometimes there were stones, but mainly it was the names, and everyone would turn away when her family walked by.

What would happen to them, Danielle wondered. She stood in the rain and wondered because she did not want to go back into the tent and listen to her mother and father fight.

Joseph held the two letters in his hand as Lily circled around him, promising him a hearty meal in a few minutes. He had his doubts. Lily was a wonderful wife but a lousy cook. Still, he could not fault her. There wasn't that much to cook anyway with the rationing. Two eggs a week per person, a fourth of a pound of meat, a fourth of a pound of chicken, some frozen imported fish, tasteless by any standards. Everything rationed. Wheat, sugar. So he would lose a little weight. He could not work up the excitement that Shoshana and Ovadia had for the new diet. "Look!" Shoshana had said at first, "Cheese from America. And Quackers!" Quaker oats. In the vernacular Quackers. He envied Meir's children their boundless enthusiasm for the new life. They sat in school reading, writing, speaking Hebrew. They also learned how the country was being overrun by vast hordes from the East who brought with them barbaric customs, low intellect, and moral decay. It didn't seem to occur to either Shoshana or Ovadia that these vast, barbaric hordes were themselves.

The first letter was from Tehran. Or rather the envelope was. Inside he found a letter addressed to him, return address Basra. He hurriedly ripped it open.

"Who's it from?" Lily asked.

"Reuben."

"Your brother?"

"Yes." Joseph read quickly. "He thinks he's found a way to get all of his goods out of Basra."

"I'll fix up the other bedroom for them," she finally said. "Now what's the other letter? This is exciting. No one ever sends us anything."

Joseph opened the brown envelope with the staple in the middle. It was a form letter. He sat down to read it and reread the important part: "You are hereby ordered to report to the processing center on December 1, 1950, for tests to determine your aptitude for ZAHAL, the Israel Defense Forces."

"What is it?" Lily stood above him and heaped several half potatoes on his plate.

She mustn't know. Not yet. "A letter from the government welcoming us to Israel."

"Really?"

"Yes."

"Isn't that nice."

109

"Yes, isn't it." He picked up his fork to cut through the potato. The outside was mushy but the inside remained solid as a rock.

Ovadia resented the fact that Shoshana was learning Hebrew faster than he was; he resented the fact that he had to share a bedroom with his sister and Hillel; but most of all he resented the fact that his parents never seemed to smile anymore. Why didn't they at least try to understand. They were pioneers. Pioneers had to suffer to build a new land, sure, but look at all they could achieve. Israel reborn, by them. His father didn't see it that way. His father said things like Some people do more pioneering than others. His mother—the only thing she wanted was to go back to her house in Baghdad.

Respect, yes. He must be respectful to his father, no matter what. And there were times when it was an effort. As when he would read Israel's national poet Bialik, or when he would listen to classical music on the radio. His father would turn the radio to some Arabic station and throw the book across the room. At times like these Ovadia was ashamed, afraid the neighbors would hear Arabic music coming from their apartment.

"Why?" his father seethingly asked him about his reading and his taste in music.

"Because this is what civilized people do," Ovadia answered.

"Read Bialik and eat mashed potatoes?" Meir asked. "Do you know what Bialik says about us? He thinks we're the scum of the Earth. Do you know what all your cultured, civilized people say about us? That we're dirty, shiftless, lazy, naturally inferior. That's what they're saying. Can't you hear them above your Beethoven?"

"Meir, please," Salemah begged.

"They're Israeli," Ovadia exploded with his one envious justification.

"You're Israeli now too. You don't have to be like them to succeed." But that was a lie. He knew it as soon as it passed his lips. He turned away and left the apartment.

God, God, God, what had he done. How could he make it up to his children. The fact that they were born in Baghdad would leave them eternally ostracized in this, their own land.

Lazy, shiftless, no ambition. Where was he to go with his ambition? Oh, he had his job, the job Joseph had found for him. It was a farce. After he had been on the job a week, and that at the lowest pay level of workmen for all his experience, which they dismissed with a wave of the hand, the foreman called him over and asked him to stay after regular hours were over. He was uneasy. He assumed he had been doing something wrong and maybe would be fired.

But no. After work the foreman, at least fifteen years younger than he, had approached him and said, "Meir, why are you working so hard?"

Meir smiled. He didn't understand. "I'm not working hard," he protested.

"Look," the foreman continued, "you don't have to prove anything to anybody. I can see from your work that you're very skilled. Just take it easy."

"I don't understand."

The foreman spelled it out for him. "You're making the other workers look bad, Meir. You're doing twice as much work as they do."

"Maybe they should work harder," Meir suggested.

The foreman smiled politely. "You don't understand our system here, Meir. We're socialists. No one is going to fire us, so we work at our own pace. The job gets done today, tomorrow, the next week, next year. Who cares?"

"But aren't these apartments we're building for the new immigrants coming in?"

"Sure."

"Well, then I'll tell you who cares. They do. They're living in tents in the muck. I'm sure if they had one wish, it would be to get out of there."

"Are you being dense on purpose?" the foreman asked. "Or is it true what they say about you people?"

111

But Meir had worked hard all his life. He couldn't stop because of socialism. So he and the foreman finally came to an agreement. As soon as Meir did his quota of work, he could leave for the day. Why should Meir object? It suited him fine. Because he would pick up what scraps of wood he could and buy others so that he could spend the rest of the day making furniture he didn't have the money to buy.

He was afraid for his children. So afraid. He wanted them to have the best. And he knew they would never get it here.

Joseph was surprised when he came out of the examination room to find Hillel Ewan sitting on the bench, waiting for his turn to be interviewed by the army lieutenant in charge of processing perspective recruits. "You too, eh?" he said with a smile. Hillel barely nodded his recognition. Joseph sat down on the bench across from Hillel and waited. He didn't really know what to say to Hillel. He hadn't seen that much of him. As a civil engineer, Hillel was much in demand. Everything needed building in Israel, and each building plan needed the approval of a civil engineer.

"Joseph Benjamin?"

Oh, God, why was he called first? If Hillel was called first, then at least he'd have an idea of what to expect. He rose, nodded to Hillel, then walked into the office and took a seat across from the army lieutenant.

The lieutenant was shuffling papers in his file. "You're physically fit," the lieutenant said more to the desk than to Joseph.

"Yes," Joseph agreed.

"Mentally alert. Morally fit too, I should imagine."

"I have a wife."

"Morally fit then, for the time being." The lieutenant smiled. "You read and write Hebrew?"

"Yes. From the prayers. But I can read a newspaper and speak well. I pick it up at work."

"Yes. You're a plumber? For how long?"

"Oh." Joseph faked it. "You know."

"No, I don't know. That's why I'm asking."

"Since we came here."

The lieutenant nodded. "Is your wife pregnant?"

"No. I mean it would be a blessing if she was, but so far no sign of it."

"How does she feel about your being in the army?"

"I haven't told her."

"How will she feel, do you think?"

"Oh, she's young. She only has me. I mean her family's here, but we live alone."

"Are you going to apply for an exemption?"

"Oh, no," Joseph protested. "I just don't think she'll be too happy, that's all."

"Have you ever used a gun."

"In Baghdad."

"In what circumstances."

"In the underground. Smuggling people out."

"Did you ever have to fire it?"

"No."

"Are you religious?"

Joseph shrugged. The lieutenant wrote something on a piece of paper and handed it over to Joseph. "Which branch do you think I'll serve in?" Joseph asked.

"You'll probably be in the infantry," he was told.

"How soon?"

The lieutenant shrugged. "I would say very soon."

Hillel watched while Joseph came out of the office. He held up his slip of paper. "Infantry probably," he announced to Hillel. Hillel was glad to see him leave. Of course infantry, the stupid ox. What was Joseph good for except cannon fodder.

He was becoming impatient. He had been here long before Joseph and remained long after Joseph left. Why wasn't his name being called. He had business to attend to and didn't plan to waste the day sitting on some wooden bench waiting for the army.

"Hillel Ewan."

Finally. Now let's get this over with so he could go back to his own life. He took the same chair Joseph and the other call-ups had taken before him. But he sat forward pugnaciously and waited for the lieutenant to dare to speak.

"You're a civil engineer," the lieutenant finally said.

"Yes. And as you can imagine, my time is valuable."

The lieutenant was unmoved. "We have a corps of engineers in the army. Civil engineers, as I'm sure you know, are in great demand."

"I'm too old for the army."

The lieutenant flipped through the file and did some subtraction on a piece of paper close by. "You're twenty-four," he answered. "That's not too old."

"And by the time I get out of the army, how old will I be? Twenty-six, twenty-seven? The years I need to build my career will have passed me by."

The lieutenant looked coldly across his desk. "Mr. Ewan, it is the duty of every citizen of Israel to serve his country. We are in a perpetual state of war for our very survival."

"Don't give me lectures on my duty to Israel. I was the leader of the Zionist underground in Baghdad. When I had to flee for my life to Tehran, I worked with the Jewish Agency encouraging my people to come to Israel, where there were supposed to be apartments and food waiting for them. You reneged on your promise, but still I serve in the government construction firm. Add it up, my years of service in Baghdad, Tehran, and Tel Aviv. And now you want another two years on top of that?"

"Mr. Ewan, there were people who came here right from the concentration camps of Europe, stepped off the ships into uniform, fought and died for this country. They didn't give us a list of how long they spent serving our cause in Auschwitz. You'll be notified when you're to report."

"I'm seeking an exemption."

"That's your right. Now if you'll excuse me, I'm very busy."

* * *

"So you understand." Joseph smiled.

"Of course I understand," Lily said. "Today you went to the processing center. In a few weeks maybe they'll call you up and you'll be a soldier."

"Right."

"And I'll kiss you bravely good-bye."

"That sounds good."

"You promised to protect me and take care of me."

"There's a family allowance. I showed you. You said you knew a few people who wanted you to do some sewing for them. With that and the allowance you should be okay."

"And the widow's allowance?"

He shook his head. "What are you talking about, Lily? I'm not going to die."

"We can leave Israel," she said seriously.

"To go where?"

"Tehran. Listen, Joseph," she said quickly before he cut her off. "I just got a letter from Rebecca. She married that second cousin of hers she met at our wedding. They have a house, a maid, a car, a set of china and silverware, furniture. Do they sound familiar? Do you remember any of them? We can sell this house and fly back to Tehran. We'll be safe there. You can find a job with Uncle Ezra, I'm sure. He liked you."

"Why not go all the way back to Baghdad and find a job with your Uncle Jacob?"

"If you wish."

He turned on her then. "Lily, what was our dream?"

"Whatever it was, it vanished in the dust at Beit Lidd, in the sands of Ramat Gan. There is nothing for us here, Joseph, and if you stay, you won't even have your life left to you."

He studied her carefully to see if she was fully serious. "You never told me before how you felt."

"When was there time? You work all day. At night you complain about my cooking, then wait to fall into bed with me. While you're away, I spent my day trying to keep this villa of yours free from the dirt that blows in from the four

115

corners, trying to keep the plants in our garden alive. I walk up to my mother's, who's a prisoner in her own house and dreams only of returning to Baghdad."

"You are so unhappy?"

"I'm not happy."

He smiled almost to himself. "I worried about this in Tehran. I said to myself, can she take it? You were so strong in Baghdad, Lily, that I marveled at you."

"And now?"

"Oh, my darling," he despaired. He took her gently by the hands. "Do you know that sometimes there comes to a man the opportunity to make an ideal a reality, to see that he can shape history by the work of his hands, the sweat of his brow. You see deprivation, I see opportunity; you see dust, I see grass and flowers; you see death, I see generations of freedom for my sons and yours. For this my life, if I have to give it, is a small price to pay. Israel is a miracle I am privileged to participate in. As God sees fit."

"So everything is perfect."

"Nothing is perfect. Not even you, my sweet. But you will never convince me to leave this imperfect land of ours and become a toiler in someone else's vineyards. I'm going into the army. I will survive. We will have many children." He waited until he was sure she understood. "Now let's skip the part where I complain about your lousy cooking and get right to the part where I fall all over you in bed."

She passively let him take her in his arms and have his way. "If you die," she whispered afterward, "I will name him after you."

"That's a comfort," he muttered into her breasts.

9

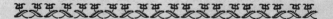

It was Albert's mewing that woke Danielle, his struggling cries almost forcing their way through her sleep. She expected her mother to get up and comfort him, but Albert continued to fret. Danielle rose and went over to him. He was wet again. He would get a spanking for that. Her mother would have to wash out the sheet, and how would it dry in this rain?

January. The rain had started in October and seemed to have never let up. Worst year on record, Danielle had heard some of the officials say. The rain beat down on her tent. It made her feel cold and miserable.

She saw Ezra staring at her. "Albert's wet himself again," she explained. Ezra closed his eyes. He was five and no longer had to worry about such things. He had been out of diapers for a long time.

Danielle looked around. She went over to Ezra's cot and sat down on the edge of it as it sagged inward. He moved to make room for her. "Where are Mother and Father?" she asked.

Ezra sat up and threw the blanket off him. He looked around. His mother's and father's cots were empty. The three Moroccans snored away at the opposite end of the tent.

Danielle looked out the tent flap. She could see the inhabitants of Beit Lidd running through the mud, making their way to the kitchen. Maybe that's where her parents were, but it struck her as strange because usually her mother woke them up and took them with her. She would wait. She got back onto her cot and lay down, but she couldn't relax. She was waiting for the sound of her mother's voice.

Albert was awake now. He wanted to be changed. Danielle scolded him for wetting himself, but she was only his sister and he paid very little attention to her. No sooner was he changed than he was hungry.

"So am I," Ezra added.

She didn't know what to do. If she waited much longer, there would be no food left. But what if she went to the kitchen with her brothers and her mother meanwhile came looking for her. She would get a beating.

"All right, Albert, stop crying," she said irritably. She got out of bed once again and slipped her coat on over her dress. Then she plunged her feet into her muddy shoes. "Let's go," she told her brothers.

Albert wouldn't walk. He wanted to be carried through the mud. He was already built like an ox and she was only eight and slight, but she did her best.

In the kitchen she looked for her mother, even for her father. They were nowhere in sight. Obviously they had gone into Tel Aviv to find a place for them to live. But they could at least have told her.

Danielle picked up their breakfast food and took it back to the tent with her brothers. She fully expected to find her parents there. But the tent was empty except for the three Moroccans, one of whom was awake, lying on his cot and smoking. Soon they would all be awake and playing cards or sheshbesh.

After eating, her brothers began to play and giggle with each other. *"Sheket!"* one of the Moroccans called from his sleep. Everyone knew the Hebrew word for quiet. Danielle felt the safest move for her to make would be to get her brothers out of the tent until her father came back. He at least could control the Moroccans. She told Ezra to get his coat on, helped Albert on with his, and marched them over to the children's tent. She hoped they wouldn't send Albert back because he was too young.

Her parents weren't there for the noon meal. That didn't really mean anything. Because if they had gone into Tel Aviv, they might not make it home till night. At night she put her brothers to bed and sat up waiting. Until she too slipped into sleep.

The next morning she felt herself being nudged awake. It was one of the Moroccans. *"Ayfo aba shelah?"* he asked her.

Where was her father? Well, how did she know? She looked over to her parents' cots, and they were as empty this morning as they had been yesterday morning.

"It's not good," the Moroccan told her.

Yes, she understood that. But whether he meant it wasn't good for her and her brothers or for the Moroccans because they hadn't been paid, she didn't know. She got up and opened the tent flap. It was cloudy. She could go out today and look around Beit Lidd for her parents.

She got the boys up and dressed and took them over to the kitchen for their breakfast. When she got back to the tent, one of the Moroccans had a woman on the cot with him and they were doing things that were perhaps best not seen by little boys. She took her brothers over to the children's tent and promised to be back in time to take them to lunch. They wanted to know where their mother was. Danielle did too. She tried to find her parents first by looking in all the lines people had to wait in at Beit Lidd. When she was unsuccessful there, she forced herself to ask their former neighbors from Baghdad, the same ones who had always done their best to avoid her family at the camp. No, no one had seen her parents, and why was she asking?

Danielle couldn't explain that her parents were missing because they weren't, really. They were just absent. If she said they were missing, then who would take care of her,

119

Ezra, and Albert? That was the question she was afraid to ask, and have answered.

But because Danielle had asked around, her former neighbors now kept a much closer eye on her and her brothers. "Where is your mother?" several women would ask her as she walked by with her two brothers on the way to the kitchen at mealtime.

In the end that's what the official asked her too.

"Where are your parents, little girl? Do you know?"

The official had a translator standing by but she understood him well enough. She sat in a big chair across from his desk and watched him watching her. She was afraid of him because everyone in Beit Lidd said how awful and mean the Jewish Agency officials were.

"I'm not going to eat you," he said.

She had never heard that about him, but she could well believe he might try. He had several gold teeth.

There were some women from her street in Baghdad who told him that Danielle had been taking care of her brothers by herself for a whole week. They had spent months shunning her. Now they had suddenly become interested. The official and the women, no longer paying attention to her, were talking back and forth to each other. They were alone then, the children? Orphans, the women agreed. Victims of immoral caretakers. The women were dismissed and she was left alone with the official and his translator.

The official offered her a piece of chocolate. She knew chocolate was rationed, so he must be going to tell her something very bad, but she took it anyway and ate it before he could change his mind. "We'll try to find your parents for you," he promised. "You know it was a very, very brave thing you did, trying to take care of your brothers the way you did. But a little girl of eight really can't be expected to take care of herself and two little boys, can she?"

"But my parents will be back soon," she assured him.

He smiled. "I hope so," he said. "But in the meantime we have to decide what to do with you."

"Why do you have to do anything?"

"Do you know in Israel there is a program called Aliyat Ha-No'ar? Do you know what that means?"

"*Aliyah*," she answered.

"*Aliyah* for youth. You see, in some countries the parents were never able to leave. And so wanting what was best for their children, they sent the children on ahead to Israel. And sometimes families come to Israel and they are so poor that they can't afford to take care of all their children. Then they come to the Aliyat Ha-No'ar people and say to them, can you help? And do you know what Aliyat Ha-No'ar does?"

"They have the parents fill out forms?" Danielle answered hopefully.

The official laughed. "You've already been in Beit Lidd too long. Aliyat Ha-No'ar takes children like you who need help and places them in kibbutzim throughout the country. Do you know what kibbutzim are?"

"Farms."

"Yes. And there's fresh country air, cows, chickens, horses, fields to plant. Would you and your brothers like to live in a place like that?"

"I think I'd rather wait for my parents."

"When we locate your parents, I will tell them exactly where you are. Okay?"

"I think it would be better if we stayed here because they don't know their way around the country too well."

"I'm going to take you to see Hava now. Hava is in charge of Aliyat Ha-No'ar here, and she can decide where is the best place for you."

"What about my brothers?"

"Your brothers too. You'll stay together as a family." He rose and took her small hand in his. His grip was so firm that she could not run away. And anyway she soon discovered that Ezra and Albert were already with this Hava woman, already being bribed, as she had been, with chocolate.

She sat on the wooden floor in the little office with her

brothers, crying silently to herself. She prayed that some-how someone would save her from these strange events.

"It's time to go now," this Hava said. She had a bright smile on her face, but that didn't disguise the fact that she was taking Danielle away from her last hold on her old life. Even the Moroccans were better than this. Hava lifted Albert and took him down the steps of the cabin out to a waiting pickup truck. Several of the women from Baghdad were there. One of them handed Danielle a bag with her and her brothers' clothes inside. "Poor things," she heard the women mutter.

Hava told them to sit down and hang on. Ezra and Albert cuddled in the truck's corners near the cab. But Danielle knelt and took one long last look around Beit Lidd as the truck pulled through its gates. No sign. No sign anywhere of her mother.

"All right, you bastards! Get up on your feet. Get your boots on. Get your packs on. And your helmets. Get outside for formation on the double or I'll tear up your ass!"

Joseph groaned into his pillow. He had been in the army less than a day and already it was having a deleterious effect on his patriotism. Didn't he just go to bed an hour ago?

"Two hours," someone in the next cot commented.

"Move!"

Joseph threw his clothes on over his underwear, got into his combat boots, and slipped his pack on his shoulders. It wasn't this heavy a few hours ago. He clanked on his steel helmet and hurried through the barracks for formation.

"You there! Line up."

Was it he? He didn't know. He thought he was in line.

"Welcome to the army, boys. We're going to take a midnight stroll that you're all going to enjoy."

The sergeant used hyperbole a lot. As the days wore on, Joseph discovered that more and more. Well, it didn't matter, right? You had so much to do you lost touch with your sense of humor, not to mention reality, in any case. Only one main topic of conversation existed. Whether it was better to do your basic training in the summer months or winter months. Summer was the unanimous vote of this unit, but then they were doing their basic training in the winter. In the mud. Goddamn marching in the mud when everytime you picked up your feet, they were weighted down by an extra five pounds of gook. The obstacle course, wallowing in the mud. The rifle, never clean. Mud again. Some said, okay, but in the summer you get dust. Dust in your goddamn rifle. You get the heat. And the sweat dripping down past your underwear as you do your twenty-mile hikes with a forty-pound pack. And the flies. Don't forget the flies. So it all balanced out. And either summer or winter you were never shaved close enough, your bed was never taut the way it should be.

"Hey, *kooshy*!"

Let him get that guy for hand-to-hand combat. Better yet, bayonet practice. "Don't call me *kooshy*," Joseph snapped at him.

"Sensitive son of a bitch, aren't you?" the redheaded European said. "So what should I call you, '*shahor*'?"

"Just call me Joseph. That's my name."

"I don't know," the redhead said. "Some of you Orientals are so touchy. Look, it doesn't bother me that some of us tan more easily than others. I think you're lucky. You know, you don't need as much camouflage as we redheads do, especially in the mud."

"Hey, Frayman," the sergeant yelled, "you and Benjamin get busy on those goddamn latrines."

"We lucked out today, *kooshy*," the redheaded Moishe Frayman said with a smile.

When they were lying on their cots that night, having one last smoke before lights out, Frayman, two bunks down from Joseph, said to no one in particular, "You know '*kooshy*,' it's just like '*habibi*.' It means 'hey, buddy,' or really 'hey, dark buddy.' It's not meant to be insulting."

Joseph made no reply. He simply fell asleep.

A few days later they were out crawling under some live ammunition fire when Joseph noticed that Frayman had caught himself on some barbed wire. Joseph's first inclination was to crawl past his butt and move on by. But it wouldn't be smart policy. They had had it drilled into them over and over again during basic that they were responsible not just for themselves but for the unit as a whole. Even Frayman.

"Hey, *yekkepotz!*" Joseph yelled from behind. Moishe almost rose to his knees. "Keep down, you asshole." Joseph told him. "You want to be this unit's first fatality?"

"It all depends on how much more of this I have to go through."

"Do you need any help?"

"Only if I want to take my left leg with me."

Joseph crawled over and released Moishe's pants leg from the barbed wire. "Thanks," Frayman said. "*Yekkepotz,* huh. You're really learning, *kooshy.* To be a true Israeli, you have to insult everyone who doesn't share your ethnic origins." But Joseph had already crawled past him. Live ammunition always made him twitchy.

When they were washing up that night, Moishe Frayman came over to Joseph and asked him, "Say, how did you know my family was from Germany?"

"The smell," Joseph replied.

Frayman was puzzled more than insulted. "The smell? But we Germans have the reputation of always being so clean."

"That's what I meant. You smelled like soap."

Frayman smiled and then laughed. After that, they became buddies.

Ovadia rushed out of school as soon as the class was dismissed. Usually he hung around for a while in the classroom with Rosa, his teacher. She would give him written work to improve his Hebrew, guide him on what books he should be reading, encourage him in every way she could to continue with his studies. It was Rosa who had pushed him to take the tests necessary to determine his qualification for a scholarship to high school. She worried about what was going to happen to him after he finished the eighth grade. Would his father be able to pay for his high school education? Probably not. Ovadia hadn't even been bar mitzvahed. His father couldn't afford the party, Ovadia realized. So they would wait till the summer when school was out and he would be bar mitzvahed. Then there would be no need to invite anyone.

"Where are you going in such a hurry?" one of his classmates called out as Ovadia passed him on the sidewalk.

"My brother-in-law is coming home from the army today," Ovadia explained with a smile. He could hardly wait to see Joseph. It had been so long, three months. He wondered what Joseph looked like as a soldier, whether he would recognize him. Maybe Joseph could do something about Lily. Ever since he had left for the army, she had just sort of retired from life. Oh, she did alterations, she took care of the house, she spoke to everyone, but she just wasn't there. Maybe it was Joseph's brother, Reuben, coming so soon after Joseph left for basic training, coming with his wife and two children. Maybe she resented them. That's what his mother thought.

Ovadia passed Lily's house. He stood there for a few moments wondering whether or not he should go up to the door and knock. They would probably like time alone. But still, they could be alone later tonight. And he really wanted to see Joseph in uniform. He walked up to their door and knocked. The door sounded hollow under his hand. He waited. No movement at all from inside. That could mean only one thing. Ovadia raced down Katznelson toward his apartment and bounded up the stairs. He opened the door. As he suspected, Shoshana was already sitting on Joseph's lap. Joseph saw him and rose, sliding Shoshana off. He came to Ovadia, embraced him, and kissed him on both cheeks. "You look marvelous," Joseph boomed. "You've grown at least an inch. Or your hair is getting longer, either one." Ovadia blushed, embarrassed at this attention, but then he forget himself in admiring Joseph's uniform.

"You'll tell me everything." Ovadia wanted him to promise.

"Oh, no, not everything," Joseph said. "I don't want you fleeing the country before you turn eighteen."

Everyone that evening was fascinated by everything Joseph had to say, everyone but Hillel and Lily.

"So when are they going to call you up?" Joseph asked good-naturedly of Hillel.

"I don't know. I have an exemption while I'm working on a *shikkun* in Dimona."

"I thought that *shikkun* was in Beersheba?"

"Well, now there's another one in Dimona."

The evening went on so full of conversation and visitors to welcome Joseph, one of the first of them to be called into the army, that Joseph could almost forget he was sitting next to a silent wife who failed to respond to anything either he or anyone else had to say.

"Did you hear about the Hayas?" one woman said.

"Must we?" Meir asked.

"Abandoned their children."

"What?" Meir said.

"Where did you hear that?" Salemah demanded.

"I didn't have to hear it, I saw it with my own eyes," the woman assured Salemah. "That poor little Danielle dragging around those two brothers of hers, taking care of them a whole week before we all finally got disgusted and called in the authorities."

"Is that Danielle Haya you're talking about?" Shoshana asked, catching some of the drift of the conversation.

"Yes, but don't worry, Shoshi, I'm sure she's being well taken care of," the woman said.

"What do you mean they abandoned their children?" Joseph asked, slightly annoyed.

"Left them. Snuck off one night. We spoke to the official about it a day or so after Danielle had been taken away."

"Taken away where?" Shoshana insisted.

"Just a minute, Shoshi," Joseph said. "They snuck out of Beit Lidd and left their three children alone? For how long?"

"Forever it looks like. That's what I'm trying to tell you."

"Where's Danielle?" Shoshana demanded.

"Quiet!" her father hushed her.

"We asked the official if he had any idea where the Hayas had gone. That was a few days after Danielle was taken." Everyone looked at Shoshana to keep her quiet so the woman could at least finish one thought. "So the official said he had a very good idea where they had gone because there were two exit visas for a Nazem and Leah Haya. They've gone back to Tehran."

"Where did they take the children?" Shoshana asked.

"To some kibbutz. I don't know which one. But wherever it is, I'm sure they're very happy."

But Shoshana wasn't quite so sure. Danielle was never very happy. Shoshana remembered how many tears Danielle had shed at Beit Lidd because no one but Shoshana would play with her. How could she go into a kibbutz and make friends when even Shoshana with her whole family surrounding her had trouble, being so different and all? No, Danielle must be in pain, and Shoshana was not planning to let her suffer alone.

Joseph flopped over on his back. He looked over to Lily who stared up at the ceiling. "You know what I feel I've just made love to? A slightly warm fish. It's a fine welcome back. Thanks. Everyone else from my unit is probably just now leaving the warmth of their families and heading out to see what they can pick up in the fleshpots of Israel. Luckily I have my own woman, who practically ravished me on my return. I could barely fend her off. At least that's what I pictured all during basic training. Certainly not this."

He looked over and saw tears running from her eyes into her hair. He was moved, but only to anger. "It's easy for you to cry, isn't it?" he snapped.

"Just as easy as it is for you to go marching off to war," she replied meanly. "Oh, yes, don't deny it. I saw it all tonight. You just ate it up the way everyone was circling around you, telling you how handsome you looked, how brave. Only you and I know the truth, don't we?"

Joseph propped himself up on his elbows. "What is the truth, Lily? I thought I was handsome and brave."

"Everything is a joke with you. Well, you ran out on me, Joseph."

"Ran out! I was called up to the army. That hardly qualifies as desertion."

"Hillel was called up too, but he always manages to get out of it."

"We've had this discussion before," he said coldly. "I'm not Hillel. If you had wanted to marry someone like Hillel, you could have had your father arrange it in Baghdad."

"Maybe I should have."

Joseph jumped out of bed. She sat up. "Where are you going?"

"Out," he answered.

"To some whore?" she accused.

He almost held his tongue, but, "Better a whore than a bitch, Lily."

She picked up her pillow and ran across the bed. Swinging it at him, she jumped and knocked him to the floor. He raised his hands to protect himself as she formed her fingers into fists and pummeled him on any open spot she could find. Finally she tired of it. "You're not so tough after all, are you?"

"Not so handsome either. I think you've split my lip."

"I didn't," she objected and leaned closer to examine it.

"Kiss it and make it better, Lily."

She licked it and tasted the blood. He grabbed her hair and pushed her lips into his. She couldn't let him, she wouldn't let him make her love him again. But she was sitting on him, and when he pushed his way into her she could no longer resist.

10

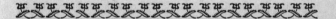

Danielle woke up at Kibbutz Vered before the other children in her house. She had dreamed the same dream again, that her long dress was waiting for her at the edge of her bed. She sat up quickly and glanced down at her toes. Pants and a shirt. Osnat, her *metapelet*, her baby-sitter, teacher, substitute mother, the one who took care of the children, would be there soon to wake everyone up and urge them to get dressed. She would watch carefully out of the corner of her eye to make sure Danielle joined the general frantic effort to get dressed before breakfast was served. That was because of the scenes Danielle had created the first few weeks she had stayed at Kibbutz Vered, when they had wanted to take her long dress away from her. She tried to explain how long dresses were necessary to preserve a girl's modesty. She tried to explain how her mother had taught her never to reveal any part of herself in front of strangers. But they couldn't understand her and she couldn't understand them. They had practically ripped the dress off her when she had arrived and had taken her to the showers where all the boys and girls in her children's house had watched her being scrubbed by Osnat. She was mortified. Boys and girls together in the same children's house. Then she had been given pants to wear when it was cold, shorts when it was warm, shorts that came way up her thigh and showed practically everything.

Danielle cried, of course she cried. They thought it was for her mother. Perhaps it was in part. Osnat and the other *metaplot* were angry at her because she did not fit in. They told her she was being naughty because her actions were upsetting her brothers. She didn't know how that could be true because neither of her brothers was in the same children's house as she was. They were all divided by age, so Albert was with the two and a half to three year olds, Ezra with the four to fives, and she with the eight to nines. They saw each other when they were out on the playground, but other than that they were almost totally separated.

Osnat watched while Danielle got dressed. It annoyed her that after three months in the children's house Danielle still insisted on dressing under her sheet. Osnat was not as ignorant of Danielle's feelings as Danielle thought. There was Sami. He came from Tehran and he understood what Danielle had been telling them when they tried to take away her dress. There had even been a meeting of the *metaplot* with the regional psychologist to discuss her case. His feelings were the same as the *metaplot's*. Old customs and patterns of behavior must be put aside. Everyone had come to Israel to start a new life, and one couldn't start that life if one clung to outmoded patterns of behavior. So while it would be hard for Danielle in the beginning to give up her psychological veil, it would be much easier for her to adjust to her new surroundings later if she looked like everyone else. That's one thing all the children on the kibbutz had to learn. They had to conform to a certain standard of behavior, and neither the time nor the energy of the *metaplot* allowed for any deviation.

There she came from under the sheet like a chicken out of its egg. Fully dressed. "Make your bed, please, Danielle." Even as Osnat said that, she realized Danielle was making her bed. She had tried everything to make Danielle give up her peculiar form of behavior. She had given her extra attention, she had encouraged the children to tease her about her beliefs, she had punished her by not letting her have snacks with the other children. But Danielle seemed to be comforted by her isolation.

Danielle folded her pajamas and placed them under her pillow. Then she came over to her place and sat down for breakfast. She looked around her at the other five children at the table. There was Sami from Tehran. Sometimes they spoke together in their own language when they thought Osnat wouldn't catch them. Hebrew was the only language allowed in the children's house. Except when Osnat's mother came over every now and then to sing Yiddish lullabies to Hilda and Theodore. They were twins who had been at Kibbutz Vered since they were only two years old. They had managed to escape with their father from Germany to Spain and then to Israel. But their father had died during the War of Independence, so they were here. Jonathan was from Poland, Miriam from Greece. Miriam thought she might have an aunt in Israel. They were looking for her. Jonathan had just been found in the port of Haifa, sitting on the dock. No one knew what to make of that. And the only thing he had known was his first name.

Osnat ladled out the oatmeal and the leben. The children passed around the eggs, milk, and salad. Danielle could tell she was gaining weight. That was the nice thing about living on the kibbutz. They had all the food they could possibly eat. Sometimes when Osnat let them, they would go over to the chicken house and very carefully collect eggs for their own breakfast. It was smelly but it was fun to feel the egg so warm in the palm of her hand. Sometimes they took a hike to the cow barn to watch the cows being milked. Once they had seen a cow birthing. It was messy. Danielle much preferred their own little pet, a tabby that they had named Ben-Gurion. She had kittens once, but they were just all of a sudden there when the children woke up in the morning.

"We'll have to get your hair cut when the weather gets warm, Danielle," Osnat threatened.

Danielle fingered her long braids and looked over to

Sami. He gave a very slight shrug. Since it didn't matter what Danielle's opinion on the haircut was anyway, she kept quiet.

Soon they were cleaning the table and wiping it off. In a few minutes they would use it as their school desk for their reading and arithmetic lessons. Danielle looked forward to her lessons. She liked to learn things, especially Hebrew, because then at least Osnat would understand what she said even if she failed to pay attention to her.

Lily knew she was pregnant almost as soon as Joseph's three-day pass was up and she saw him off on his bus down south to his new base.

"In the Negev," he had told her.

"Near Gaza?" she had asked.

"Gaza?" Did he think it funny to pretend that Gaza didn't exist, that the fedayeen weren't coming across the border into Israel nearly every day, attacking public transport, private vehicles, the Israeli army. She saw him turn and wave to her as the bus kicked dust and exhaust into her face, and she knew he was never coming back.

It was a matter of time for both of them now. How long did he have to live? She didn't know. Maybe months. It seemed to her now that this was why they had come to Israel, so he could be killed here in some death of his own choosing rather than on a hangman's gallows in Iraq. Fine. She wouldn't quarrel with God there. Better for Joseph the patriotic death. But she would not have his child and raise it after his death. No, he had chosen his life, she would choose hers. And it did not include having a baby at eighteen and being forced to marry the first man who would take her. Alone she could make it, but not with a child.

She would get an abortion. It was not unheard of in Iraq. Often when women got older and no longer wished the joys of beginning parenthood all over again, they would speak of "accidents" that had deprived them of their intended young. Her mother had tried to have an accident instead of Shoshana. She used an old family recipe that caused her to be violently ill for three days but had no effect on the fetus. When female relatives suggested the name of a few reputable midwives she could go to, she refused. "It's God's will," she had said, since the recipe had failed to work. So Shoshana was born.

In Israel itself one could tell women were not strangers to such acts. How else could the Europeans make sure their families never increased beyond two, especially if their birth control methods failed. She would ask around. Carefully. Some of the women she did alterations for, they might know. They certainly had the money to buy what they wanted, even abortions. She would find a name or two. And when she knew for certain, she would have the baby ripped from her in the same way Arab bullets would rip the life from her husband's body.

Shoshana had lied to her mother. She told Salemah that after school she was going to be over at her new friend's apartment playing. She knew her mother wouldn't suspect anything, and even if she did, what could she do? Salemah would be afraid to leave the house. She would have to wait until her husband got home and by then Shoshana hoped to be home herself.

The bus to downtown Tel Aviv stopped at the corner across from her apartment, so Shoshana stood in a doorway until everyone had boarded the bus before she sprinted up the steps and plopped in her fare. "I want to go to the Jewish Agency, the Sokhnut," she told the bus driver. "Can you tell me where to get off?"

He didn't answer but he did nod, so she could only hope for the best. It was strange being on a bus alone like this. She stood and held onto the rail, but a soldier rose and offered her his seat. She smiled and took it. He reminded her of Joseph.

She was nervous. The bus had been traveling for quite some time, and at the last two stops a lot of people had gotten off. But they were mainly women with net shopping bags. "Ha-Sokhnut," she heard the driver call. She popped up and went to the front of the bus. "Where exactly?" she asked.

"Two blocks up," he told her as he swung open the doors, and she descended.

Two blocks up. She stood on the corner and wondered where up was. She asked directions. Many times. That's one thing she could say about the people of Israel. Even if they didn't know where it was, they gave you directions to it. It was even worse once she found the Jewish Agency building because then she had to find the office that served Aliyat Ha-No'ar. She had never realized, even accounting for all the bureaucracy, that the Sokhnut would be so huge. She was finally sent to the liaison office of the Kibbutz Ha-Me'uhad movement. A woman there told her that the Aliyat Ha-No'ar office was right across the hall. Victory within reach, Shoshana found the office door locked. She returned to the woman in the kibbutz office. "It's locked," Shoshana announced.

"I know it is," the woman said. "I'm in charge and I'm on my tea break."

Shoshana sat down to wait. She stared at the woman until the woman became uncomfortable. "What is it you want?" she asked.

"I want to find my friend. Danielle Haya. She and her two brothers were taken away from Beit Lidd and placed on a kibbutz. Their parents went back to Tehran."

"When was this?"

"Sometime between October and now."

"Sometime between October and now," the woman repeated. "Do you realize how many children we've had between October and now?"

"Yes, but only one of them was my friend."

The woman nodded. "That makes sense to you, I suppose. Okay, you've ruined my tea break. We might as well go see if we can find anything out about your friend. Danielle Haya, was it? How old are you, anyway?"

"I'll be eleven very soon."

The woman smiled. "Where are you from?"

Shoshana already knew the woman meant originally, not Givatayim. "Baghdad," she answered.

"So was your friend, I imagine," the woman muttered as

134

she opened a huge accounting book and began searching. "We do this by month," she explained. "So it would have helped if you had some idea."

"I just learned about it last week."

"Haya, Haya."

"Three of them. Danielle, Ezra, and Albert." She watched while the woman went through October, November, December. "January," the woman claimed victory. "At least that's when we listed her. Kibbutz Vered."

"Kibbutz Vered," Shoshana repeated. "Could you write it down for me?" She watched while the woman carefully printed the Hebrew for her. "And directions?"

"You want a lift there?"

"If possible," Shoshana answered.

"That was a joke. Look, it's a few miles north of Tiberias. You and your family can get a bus at the Central Bus Station for Tiberias. From there they have local buses or you can hitch a ride."

"Do you think she's okay, my friend?"

The woman took Shoshana seriously. "You see, all the children who have been separated from their parents by death or other circumstances are put together in different children's houses from those children whose parents live on the kibbutz. So they all have the same sort of pain in common. Your friend may be happy, she may not be. Some adjust very well, some don't adjust at all. But she is well cared for. She's being given food, clothing, an education, and, I hope, love."

"Thank you," Shoshana offered. She left the office. Now she really had to make plans.

Joseph Benjamin and Moishe Frayman brought up the tail end of a six-man foot patrol that carefully searched the border between Gaza and Israel for any signs of infiltration by bands of fedayeen. They liked it better when they were in the jeeps doing this duty, but there had been stepped-up reports of sniper fire during the night and the commanding officer wanted every square inch of ground examined. So they would walk along their sector of the bor-

135

der checking for signs of suspicious activity. And on their way back they would rake a wide swath of land so anyone crossing the border would leave his footprints clearly visible.

Most of the men in the patrol were smoking, their rifles slung carelessly in their arms. The only alert one was the corporal, who was, respectively, their leader and their main woe.

"Do you realize the only thing standing between the terrorists and the kibbutzim is us?" Moishe asked in wonderment. "Doesn't say very much for the security of Israel, does it."

"Oh, I imagine we'll do okay," Joseph said with a smile.

"You're really gung ho for the army, aren't you? I mean, doesn't it bother you that from our basic training we're the only ones who got Gaza? The others, some are pushing papers in Tel Aviv, others are up in Haifa enjoying the view."

"Others are along the Jordanian border getting shot at."

"The Jordanian border. I don't know. It has an appeal to it. The Dead Sea. Eilat."

"Or Syria. The Hula valley, the mosquitoes."

"Somehow Gaza, it's just all sand."

"Watch your rifle."

"Oh, sorry."

"It has a habit of ending up under my chin when we walk together. Why don't you unsling it and carry it in your arms like the rest of us?"

"Life's kismet, Joseph."

"You sound like my wife."

"You never talk about her much."

"Well, she's a little hard to talk about right now. She keeps assuring me that I'm going to be shot and killed."

"God, she sounds like my mother."

"Anyway, you at least didn't have to end up patrolling the border."

"Oh?"

"You could have been an officer," Joseph reminded him. "They wanted you to be."

"And sign up for another God knows how many years. No, Joseph, my future lies in the land, not the army."

"You're going to become a farmer?"

Moishe gave him a derisive look. "Real estate, you dummy. I'm going to be a builder like dear old Dad, but I'm not going to be working for any government-owned anything. Give me capitalism or give me death."

"Tracks," the corporal shouted. "Spread out."

Moishe unslung his rifle and flicked off the safety. "Goddamn. Trust that bastard to find something."

"Lily?"

"Get lost, Shoshana."

"I need your help."

"I don't have time to help you," Lily snapped.

Shoshana stared resentfully at her sister. What was Lily doing with herself that she didn't have the time. The house was a mess. Lily looked like garbage. She hadn't even combed her hair all day and it was now nearly seven. She couldn't understand her sister. She knew everything had something to do with Joseph, but what? Lily had prevailed. She had married Joseph. Now Joseph was in the army of Israel. What more could Lily want? She would try one more time. "I've found out where Danielle is."

"That's nice," Lily said absently.

"I want you to take a day and come with me up to Tiberias to see her."

"What are you, crazy? Do you realize how far Tiberias is from here? Hours and hours on the bus."

"But it's to see Danielle."

"I wouldn't go across the street to see Danielle, much less to Tiberias."

"I'll go myself then."

"If you even think about it, I'll tell Mother and she'll beat your bottom raw."

"I wouldn't tell you what I'm thinking, so there'll be nothing you can tell Mother," Shoshana said spitefully. "I hate you, Lily."

"Oh, get out of here. Go back and play with your dolls, you stupid little girl."

Shoshana stalked out of her sister's house. She was furious, but what could she do to get even with her sister. She knew. She would write Joseph. Write him in vivid detail exactly the state of his house and the state of his wife. Let Lily try to live with Joseph's knowledge.

Lily sat at the kitchen table, her head in her hands, and cried, hoping the tears would wash away her bitterness, her frustration. But the tears came hard and they did nothing except settle in the dust surrounding her. Why did that drippy Shoshana come over tonight? Her stupid little problem. What did she know about anything? She wasn't three weeks late and nauseous. If only she could convince herself that Joseph would be coming back, that they would be together again, that everything could be as it had been before. That's all she wanted. Over the nights she had needed so much to have Joseph beside her, to talk to him about this thing growing inside her and what it was doing to her. Because Joseph would have known what to do. He always had such clear, simple answers to any problem.

He was never afraid. Not like she was. Terrified of losing. If she could hear his voice and hear him tell her once again that everything would be all right, even if it were a lie, she would believe him.

She sat up and checked the clock on the sink. Eight. It was dark out. But the streets were safe. Her hair, her dress, what a mess she was. But he couldn't see her. She quickly got a scarf from her box and wrapped it around her hair. She slipped a sweater on because it would be chilly. It was a mile to the kiosk and there would be a line waiting for the phone.

Joseph sat on his bunk and played sheshbesh with his neighbor across the way; the board lay on an abandoned orange crate. He played mechanically without thinking. The roll of the dice, the click of the pieces comforted him. He was shaken. Not that he hadn't heard live fire before, but this was the first time it had ever been aimed at him. Moishe had been back and forth to the bathroom all evening. Their eyes met occasionally. They shook their heads and tried to smile. This was it. This was the army. This is what their sergeant had trained them for, why he had threatened to tear up their asses if they didn't perform every maneuver correctly. But were they ready for it? It was a shocker.

"Benjamin!"

Oh, shit. He just hoped it wasn't extra duty tonight. "Yes."

"Telephone."

Telephone! No one got telephone calls. The tent exploded in oohs and ahs. More so because he was the only one who never even got any letters, letter writing not being an Iraqi custom. He jumped from the platform of the tent and raced to the dining hall. "Lily!" he exploded when he heard her voice. "Am I all right? Sure, I'm all right. We saw action today for the first time. Some fedayeen making their way back into Gaza. We got two of them. I mean someone got them, I didn't. One of our boys was hit. Slight wound but he's spending the night in the infirmary. Three of the bastards escaped back into Gaza so we'll have to deal with them next time. God, it was an awful feeling. First time I fired my gun at anyone. I'm glad it wasn't me who got them. Lily?"

She was holding the phone tightly as she slumped against the kiosk wall. "Were you afraid?" she asked.

"Afraid? Well, I practically shit in my pants, but other than that I wasn't afraid at all. So how are you doing? What's happening? How's the family? Lily?"

"Everything's fine," she lied.

"Are you sure?"

"Yes, of course."

"So why did you call?"

"I wanted to hear your voice."

"Oh, Lily, I've missed you so much. I think about you all the time. I—"

"I wanted you to tell me that everything's okay, but you can't, can you."

"Of course everything is okay. What's the—"

"I loved you, Joseph."

"Lily, don't start that again," he said tightly into the phone. "I need you tonight. I need your faith and your love. Lily. Lily? Would you answer me?" He listened while the line hummed. "Lily, are you still there?" They were connected for a few seconds longer and then the line went dead.

Lily put down the receiver. She had the name of a doctor. She would go to him. She would go to him as soon as she had the strength.

Joseph left the dining hall. He couldn't go back to his tent because everyone would ask him whom the call was from and what it had been about. He really didn't know. He just knew that something had come to an end and he could only hope it wasn't his marriage.

Joseph never bothered assembling for mail call; he never got any letters. Sometimes he missed it, when others were sharing their news. But then he thought well, if someone writes, he would only have to write back. He wasn't there when his name was called out, so Moishe Frayman stepped forward and brought Joseph's letter back to the tent.

"For you," Moishe said. He held the letter up to his nose. He studied the letter front and back. "Hey, I know you Orientals are only semi-literate, but can't you do better than write in crayon?"

Joseph grabbed the letter from him. He looked at the back flap. Someone had drawn a very pretty flower over the seal. The return address said S. Ewan. "Shoshana," Joseph guessed.

"Ah. And your wife's name is Lily?"

"This is her little sister."

"Sure."

Joseph warned him off and took the letter to his cot. He unsealed it and ripped out the page. "Dear Joseph, I hate Lily. I've found Danielle. Lily won't go with me to see her. It's only to Tiberias. Lily is a pain. She doesn't keep your house clean. She doesn't comb her hair. She doesn't visit Mother so I am stuck taking Mother everywhere. Is that fair? She doesn't talk to anyone. She doesn't even come over on the Sabbath. How are you? I am fine. Love, Shoshi."

Joseph read and reread the letter. Moishe came over and sat beside him on the cot. "So what does this sexpot have to say?" Joseph handed him the letter. Moishe read it. "How are you? I am fine," he singsonged the ending. They sat silently together. "Look, Joseph, I think your wife might have a problem."

"I know. I don't understand what it is."

"You said she was terrified you might get killed."

"But why? In Iraq she used to stand up to the Arabs by herself and not be afraid."

"So this isn't Iraq. Maybe she figures she has more to lose here if anything happens to you. Look, go to the captain. Demand compassionate leave."

Maybe Moishe was right. Maybe he could get a pass, see Lily, try to make her understand that everything was going to be all right. He walked over to the wooden office and sought out the captain. He didn't like explaining his personal problems to complete strangers, especially to young captains whose wives were always gung ho for their husbands' military careers. He handed over Shoshana's letter. In return he got a two-day pass.

Shoshana carried her school satchel out of the house that morning. Instead of her notebooks, she had packed fruit and cheese and the family's plastic canteen. She had puttered around in the apartment long enough to make sure Ovadia wouldn't be able to wait for her, then she kissed her mother good-bye and swooped down the stairs just in time to catch the bus to Tel Aviv. It took her right to the Central Bus Station, where without any trouble she found the line to Tiberias. It was filled with soldiers, mothers with their children, some old people who traveled there to take the waters, and families who were heading north for a short vacation. Because she was small, she found herself constantly jostled in line. A few times some of the men would try to cut in ahead of her and she would have to make a scene until they backed down. It amazed her and pleased her at the same time. Her mother never would have known how to demand her rightful place. Her mother would never make it as an Israeli.

She saw the bus driver approaching as did everyone else. The pushing started toward the turnstile that would let them on the bus. She knew she would have fruit juice instead of fruit if she didn't keep the satchel over her head. The bus driver unlocked the door. The soldiers, who didn't have to pay, scrambled over the barricades and pushed through the back door of the bus. The civilians went wild trying to give the driver their money so they could get a seat for the long ride into Tiberias.

Shoshana was far enough ahead to get a seat, but the bus was filled and there were still twenty people waiting to get on it. The bus driver moved through the aisle arranging things. Bags went up on top. Children went on mothers' laps. "You there," the bus driver asked Shoshana, "where's your mother?"

"At home," Shoshana shot back.

"You traveling alone?"

"Yes. To visit my friend on Kibbutz Vered," she added.

"Very nice." He wasn't interested. He took her by the hand and put her in the seat behind on the lap of one of the soldiers. There were three of them sitting on seats meant for two small people. They had their guns and they were already sweating in the heated pollution of the bus station.

"I have some fruit. I'll share it with you," Shoshana said quickly as the soldier groaned under her weight.

"Just don't pee in your pants," he said rudely.

"I haven't done that since I was five," she answered sharply.

"It's a long ride, little girl."

She watched while the bus driver made room for everybody. There were a few standing in the aisle and they still had the stop at Petach Tikva. Whoever boarded there would be forced to stand the five hours to Tiberias. Sho-

shana leaned against the window and caught the first breath
of dirty air as the bus pulled out of the station.

His name was Dr. Gelprin. Lily had heard about him
from some of the European women she did alterations for.
He lived in, of all places, Bnei Brak with its fanatical Orthodox community. It didn't matter to her though. The
only thing that mattered was that he existed and that he
could help.

Lily had made an appointment to see him. She was covered by Kupot Holim, the general sick fund, because of
Joseph's job with Solel Boneh, but she knew only too well
she wouldn't get her abortion from Kupot Holim. It wasn't
authorized. It was illegal. She had to search out a private
doctor, the kind rich women or girls in trouble looked for.

His office, like most doctors' offices in Israel, was in his
home. She arrived at the apartment, rang the bell, and
walked in. Another woman was waiting. She had a pretty
maternity frock on and had combed her long blond hair up
into a bun. Lily felt uncomfortable in her housedress and
sandals. She caught the woman glancing at her occasionally. They both knew she didn't belong here.

She had to wait half an hour to see him. She was frightened when he called her into his office. It was filled with
steel and enamel. There was a table with stirrups. If she
had not been so committed to her own course of action,
she would have fled in terror.

"Lily Benjamin?"

"Yes," she replied. He had a nice voice. It was warm.

"How can I help you?" he asked.

"I'm pregnant," she said.

"Um. And you don't belong to Kupot Holim?"

"I do, but I don't want the baby."

"Miss—"

"Please. My husband is in the army. We just came to
Israel from Iraq less than ten months ago. We don't have
any money. I'm working now to get some. It's just not
the right time to have a baby. I can't work and take care of

143

it too. How will I manage? My husband's just finished basic training. There's no one to help. You must understand. I don't want the baby. I want to get rid of it."

The doctor shrugged. "Why do you come to me?"

"I've heard that—"

He cut her off. "You should go to the Kupot Holim doctor. If you're pregnant, you must have a baby. That's the way it goes."

She began to cry. "Please," she said. "I can pay you," she added quickly, bringing forth an object wrapped in a clean white handkerchief from her purse. She unfolded her handkerchief slowly. There, lying in the center, was a gold bracelet with three perfect pearls, a present from her father on her twelfth birthday.

The doctor picked it up and held it between his thumb and forefinger. "It's beautiful," he said. "Where did you get it?"

"It's mine," she answered. "We never sell our jewelry."

"But you're willing to trade it now."

"Yes."

"You're that desperate?"

"Yes," Lily admitted.

"How old are you?"

"Eighteen."

He studied her for a minute. "Wait outside," he told her. "Or if you prefer, you can walk around until five. Then we'll examine you and see what your situation is."

Lily sat in his outer room. She didn't dare to move about on the streets. At five o'clock he came for her, brought her into his examining room, asked her to slip off her panties and lie on the examining table.

She shuddered. She had not expected this. To be seen by a man other than her husband, even if he were a doctor. In Iraq all female problems like this were handled by midwives and women who knew from experience. But she had to go through with it now. She lay on the table and tried not to look when he gently raised her heels into the stirrups, tried not to feel when he poked around in her, hearing him say over and over again, "Relax, relax."

"About two months," he said. "We can do it now. You'll feel cramping and you'll bleed slightly more than your average period."

She froze through the rest of what happened to her, remembering it only in vague flashes. After it was over, she knew the doctor had taken the bracelet and escorted her from the office. After that somehow she had found herself back on the bus to Givatayim.

Joseph had hitched a ride from the Negev to Beersheba, then another from Beersheba to Tel Aviv, where he caught the bus to Givatayim. He arrived home at noon on the day Lily went to see Dr. Gelprin. Shoshana had at least not lied about the state of his villa. It was a mess. Dishes in the sink, the bed unmade, dust sunk deep into the rug. Dirty clothes laying about the bedroom. He didn't know what to make of it. He checked the clock above the sink. Twelve ten. Lily was probably out getting a few things at the market. He tried to decide what to tackle first. He started on the sink. By three he was outside in their backyard. He had the rug hung over the line and was beating it with a wooden paddle.

"Hello," his neighbor called. "How are you doing?"

"Have you seen Lily?" he asked the woman.

"Oh, she left about ten this morning. Headed down toward Givatayim."

"Thanks," Joseph said absently. Well, Lily could be with Salemah, but if Shoshana's letter was totally accurate, she wouldn't be. The only other thing down toward Givatayim was the bus stop across from Meir's apartment. Joseph gave the rug a few extra hard whacks, then lifted it inside and spread it out on the floor. He looked around the villa. The floors should be sponged, but he could do that later tonight after he found Lily.

He left the villa and headed down toward Meir's apartment to see if his missing wife might possibly be there. Salemah was puzzled to see him. Pleased but puzzled. No, she hadn't seen Lily. Hadn't seen her for days since the last time Shoshana had walked her up to see her older daughter.

Ovadia came home. Then Meir. It wasn't a very joyous gathering because the only thing he could think of was Lily's whereabouts. Ovadia went up several times to check the villa but Lily had not returned home.

"Maybe she's with Shoshana," Malemah suggested, noting the absence of her other daughter.

"Shoshana's probably playing with her friends," Ovadia said. "She and Lily haven't been getting along lately."

Joseph thought back to the letter. No, she wouldn't be with Shoshana. He took up his post by the balcony. If she had taken a bus somewhere, this was the stop at which she would get off.

It was over. Lily sat on the bus feeling the pain between her legs and sighed with relief. All gone. Flushed away in the blood that flowed from her. There would be other children at a better time. With Joseph or with someone else if Joseph were killed as she expected. Now she would just try to hold on and forget about what had been inside of her. She looked at the other passengers on the bus. Some stared back at her. She supposed she looked pale. She still felt scared and sick. She watched the street stops pass by. There was her own. She rose and lurched to the front of the bus. The driver stopped and opened the door for her. She felt her legs almost give way under her as she descended the steps. She stood as the bus passed her by. She felt weak, faint. She glanced up to her father's apartment. If she could only make it over there. Her mouth fell when she thought she saw Joseph standing on her father's balcony. All of a sudden she felt something gush from her. She looked and saw blood flowing down her leg before she fainted.

11

⚓⚓⚓⚓⚓⚓⚓⚓⚓⚓⚓⚓⚓⚓⚓⚓

Shoshana arrived in Tiberias at two o'clock in the afternoon. By that time she and the soldiers she had been sitting with had become friends. They had taken turns standing and sitting throughout the long bus ride, shared the food and their water. She had already explained that she was on her way to see a friend at Kibbutz Vered, so when they got off the bus, the soldiers found out for her when the last bus to Tel Aviv left. Four o'clock. That didn't give her much time. And it didn't get back into Tel Aviv until nine. That was late. She was afraid her parents would be worried. But there was no way now to contact them anyway, so she should really put that thought right out of her mind.

"How do I get to Kibbutz Vered?" she asked the soldiers. "Which way is north?"

They took her by the hand and led her to the tramp line where soldiers hitched a ride to their army bases. There was a lot of teasing about her being a young recruit, but she didn't mind. She liked the soldiers. She was going to be one herself someday.

They got a ride sooner than some of the others because of her. Everyone took care of children in Israel. And soon she found herself at the foot of the road leading to Kibbutz Vered, bidding good-bye to the soldiers and sucking in the dust from the departing tender. She started walking up the dirt road. It was so beautiful here that she knew by now Danielle must have come to love it. On one side of her she could see Safad, set in the hills and twinkling in the sunlight, while below her she could see Lake Kinneret. Feeling like a guilty intruder, she jumped when a cow mooed at her. A horse and rider came down the dirt road toward her. The rider looked so much like a cowboy from an American Western. He passed her by while she continued to stare at him. Then he pulled his horse around and came back to her. "Who are you, little girl?"

But she couldn't answer him because the horse's head was so close to her, and every time she moved, the head followed her. The rider saw the problem and dismounted. He pushed the horse slightly away from him. "Who are you?"

"Shoshana Ewan."

"Do we know you here, Shoshana?"

"No."

"Nu?"

"Oh." Shoshana came to her senses. "I'm here to visit Danielle Haya."

"Little Danielle?"

"Do you know her?"

"She came here with her two brothers a couple of months ago. Are you from her family?"

"No, I'm her friend from Tel Aviv. I just heard the awful news about her parents and I've come to tell her that everything will be all right."

He smiled. "Well, that's very nice of you. I'm surprised that your parents let you travel so far alone."

"Oh, they don't know I'm here. Yet."

The cowboy nodded then shook his head. "Well"—he shrugged it off—"first things first. Would you like to see your friend now?"

"Yes, please."

"Would you like to ride the horse back into the kibbutz to her cottage?"

Shoshana's eyes shone. "Could I?"

As an answer, he lifted her up and put her on the saddle. In doing so her dress rode well up past her thighs. She was embarrassed but he seemed not to notice at all. He hoisted himself up, then slowly walked the horse into the kibbutz, pointing out the chicken house, the milking barn, the workshop, the dining hall, the detached cottages where the members lived, and the children's houses.

"I've learned about them in school," Shoshana said. "I think I would miss my parents and brothers."

"We see our children any time we want. It's to let both the father and mother concentrate on our work."

"What do you do?"

"I'm a cowboy."

Shoshana laughed.

"No, really," he said. "When our cows wander away on some of these hills, it's easier to round them up by horse than on foot." He stopped the horse, got off, and lifted Shoshana down after him. She stared across the road. "Banana plants," he told her. "This way to your friend."

Danielle was in the children's house, sitting next to Sami. Even though he was a boy, they had become fast friends. He understood her, not only her language but why she objected to so many of the things Osnat expected of her. They always played together now, Sami and she, sometimes with Ezra if he was out on the playground too. It seemed funny to be running and jumping around, playing cowboys and army instead of with dolls and tea sets as she used to. But Sami would never consent to play with dolls, and she felt it was more important to have his friendship than her dolls.

What made her afraid was that Sami wouldn't be here forever. His parents had sent him away to stay on a kibbutz instead of his sisters, but as soon as they found an apartment and his father work, they were going to send for him. Then she would be alone again.

Sami poked her. She looked up to see Izzy coming toward the cottages with a girl. Another one, she thought sadly, remembering how hard it had been for her to be here at first. When the girl came in and stood at Izzy's side, she looked very familiar and frankly too big to be in this cottage. It didn't take Danielle much longer to realize it was Shoshana Ewan. Fear mingled with her excitement. Was Shoshana to be sent here too? She rose and raced to her friend to embrace her.

Shoshana felt tackled rather than embraced. She did not remember this strange little girl, but she did recognize her voice. "Danielle?"

"Yes! It's me!"

Shoshana pushed her back. Where were her friend's braids? Her hair was shorter than most boys, her body completely uncovered. She was in her underpants and shirt. Shoshana's hand involuntarily rose to her mouth. While she had always wanted to look like an Israeli girl herself, this was perhaps going a bit too far.

Danielle looked down at herself. "We just got up from our nap," she explained weakly. Shoshana fingered her hair. "Cut for the warm weather," Danielle added. She said more but Shoshana didn't hear. She was staring at Danielle and crying.

Sami watched the reunion. On one side there was Danielle and her friend, asking each other a million questions, on the other side were Osnat and Izzy engaged in a furious conversation of their own. Osnat finally broke it off by marching over to Danielle and tapping her friend on the shoulder.

"Little girl," Osnat said, "is it true that you came up to Kibbutz Vered without telling your parents where you were going?"

Shoshana thought it over in the light of the anger in Osnat's eyes. "Basically," she admitted.

"Did it ever occur to you that they might be worried about you?"

"But I'm going to catch the four o'clock bus back."

Osnat checked her watch. "It's five of four now. How do you propose to make it?"

"Five of four!" Shoshana was shaken. Things had definitely gotten out of hand.

Izzy saw her panic and took pity on her. "We can call the police in Tiberias. They can get in touch with the police nearest the girl's home, tell them to contact the girl's parents."

"I just don't think it's a good idea to have a reminder of her past life around here," Osnat said softly, but coldly. "Not when she's just been doing so well."

"There's nothing we can do about it now. We'll get in touch with your parents, Shoshana," the cowboy said. "I don't imagine they're going to be very happy with you."

Shoshana sighed. He was probably right.

"Never mind," Danielle said. "We can still have fun before you go home. Do you want me to show you everything? I can, Osnat, can't I?"

Stuck with the situation, Osnat relented. "Yes, if you're careful not to get in anyone's way."

For Shoshana it was a wonderland. Danielle had freedom, freedom she did not seem to want. Whenever Shoshana praised something, Danielle always had a "yes, but" ready.

"Do you miss your mother?" Shoshana questioned, trying to understand. She could not imagine life without her own mother.

"Not every day anymore. I wish I knew why she left."

"Maybe some day she'll be good enough to come back and tell you," Shoshana said pointedly.

Joseph stood over the pale, inert body of his wife and watched as she stared off into space. He could have easily killed her. How dare she!

It felt like a lifetime, but it was only an evening away that he had seen her fall to the pavement. He didn't even remember running out of the apartment, down three flights of stairs, picking her up and placing her in the taxi passersby had commandeered. He must have because he was with her in the emergency room when the doctor shooed him out. He waited there, soon joined by Meir and Salemah. He had no thought as to what could have caused his wife's collapse. He just remembered being vaguely grateful that something physical was wrong with her. He thought she had been losing her mind.

"Who's the husband?" the doctor asked when he came out from behind the curtain.

Joseph stepped forward. The doctor stared at him in his uniform for a minute, then took him by the arm and led him over to a corner far away from Lily's parents. "Your wife's had a botched abortion. We've cleaned her out. She should be okay with a few days' rest. She'll have to stay in the hospital at least overnight."

"What?" Joseph was stunned.

"Abortion." The doctor repeated the essential fact of the matter.

"But she wasn't even pregnant."

The doctor studied him and shrugged. "It's a classic case. Some fetal material wasn't removed and she started hemorrhaging."

"What fetal material are you talking about?" Joseph asked angrily. "I'm telling you she wasn't pregnant."

"She obviously didn't want you to know."

"You've made a mistake."

"Look, these are the medical facts of the case. That's all I can give you. If you need help, I can try to find you a social worker."

Joseph slumped against the wall.

"She'll be okay. There's no reason why you can't have other children. When she wants one this time. Do you want to see her?"

"No."

"She'll be taken to the ward as soon as she stabilizes. When that happens you'll have to wait for visiting hours. She's right behind that curtain if you change your mind." The doctor almost left. "Are you all right? Is there anything I can do for you?"

"Just tell me who would do such a thing."

"That you'll have to find out from your wife."

When the doctor left, Meir and Salemah walked up to Joseph.

"What is it?" Salemah asked. "What's wrong with my baby?"

Joseph recoiled from her. "The baby is dead," he said harshly. "Dismembered, if I understand it right. However, your daughter, my wife, will be just fine."

"What are you saying?" Meir snapped.

"Lily has had an abortion."

"You're lying."

"Oh, yes, I'm lying. Your own daughter lives right down the street from you and you don't even know she's pregnant. The very least you could have done was look after her while I was in the army."

"She's your wife. You should have looked after her yourself. You shouldn't have gone into the army," Salemah told him.

"Quiet," a nurse called. "There are sick people here."

"Go home," Joseph said softly to his wife's parents. "There's nothing you can do here. It's all been done."

"Can I see her?" Salemah asked.

"Oh, yes, by all means. Help yourself. She's right behind that curtain."

Salemah brushed the curtain aside with a vengeance. Lily looked up, terrified at what she would see in her mother's face, but the face had not changed. It had in it the same love it had shown her every day of her life.

Salemah did not know where to touch her daughter. She patted her cheek awkwardly, she held her hands. "Never mind, never mind, my darling Lily," she lullabied. "They will never know. They can never know. They are just men." She watched in sorrow as Lily let the tears tumble from her eyes. God's curse was to be a woman dependent on a man. "Hold firm, my Lily. You must be strong now and not let everything slip away from you."

"Joseph?"

"Do not listen to what he says to you now. Do not respond. Wait a while. Time will heal the both of you."

"He hates me?"

"Do not provoke him. Be silent and strong."

"Mother."

"I must go now. Your father is waiting." She tried to release her hands but her daughter held on. "You will always be my baby, my beautiful, beautiful Lily," she whispered as Lily relinquished her and she stepped out into the corridor once again.

With Lily's parents gone, Joseph was left alone in the emergency room. He sat on a bench and watched the curtain flutter slightly, knowing that Lily lay beyond it. It took him a long while to suppress his anger enough to go past that curtain. So furious was he that it took him even longer before he could acknowledge that small creature lying on the bed as his wife. And all the time Lily lay staring into the distance, not moving, not reaching out to him.

She couldn't. She was afraid. She could not bear to face him. She could not bear to feel his hurt. If only he had never known. She felt his presence so close to her that it burned. And yet he was like ice and she would not cry.

"If you had enough faith to marry me; if you had enough faith to come to Israel with me, even to Beit Lidd when we had nothing; then why couldn't you have had the faith to have our child?"

The air whispered, the curtain rustled. He was gone.

Ovadia had been left home alone to wait for Shoshana. He didn't know what to do. It was past nine. His parents weren't home. He didn't know what was wrong with Lily. Or where Shoshana was.

Someone pounded on the apartment door. At last, something. He hurried over to answer it. His heart fell when he saw a policeman. "Shoshana!" he gasped.

"Yes," the policeman agreed. "Are your parents home?"

"No. They're at the hospital with my older sister."

The policeman's eyebrows rose and fell.

"Shoshana?" Ovadia asked.

"She's fine. We had a message from the Tiberias police. She's at Kibbutz Vered. She'll take the first bus home to-morrow."

Ovadia felt sick and relieved at the same time. Shoshana was safe, but how was he to tell his parents where she was when they would be so worried about Lily? At the best of times his mother's reaction to Shoshana's going off on her own would be hysteria. And now this. He thanked the po-liceman. He would bury himself in his work. That was the only salvation.

When his parents came home, his mother was crying. That did not surprise him as much as it once would have. She had cried often since they had come to Israel. But now it worried him because of Lily.

"Is Lily—"

"She'll be all right," his father said.

"What happened?"

"She hemorrhaged. She lost a lot of blood."

"Why?"

"She had a miscarriage," Meir decided.

"I didn't even know she was pregnant," Ovadia said, and was instantly sorry as it started another cascade of tears from his mother. He was shocked to see his father take his mother into his arms. They practically never touched. At least not in public. And his father was so gentle with her, a rare occurrence since they had come to Israel where scratching for survival left so many sharp edges. Ovadia sat down at the table and listened while Meir tucked Salemah into their bed.

He pretended to be working when his father came out of the bedroom and took down the bottle of brandy from over the sink. He got down one glass, looked over at Ovadia and asked, "Would you like some?" Ovadia nodded yes more out of companionship than desire. Meir poured Ovadia a glass with the brandy barely covering the bottom. His own glass had a more healthy shot. Meir sat there silently for a few moments taking small, simple sips. Ovadia tried to do likewise, but he hated the taste of brandy. He let it roll against his lips, then put the glass down again.

"Where's your sister?" Meir asked almost mindlessly.

"She's okay," Ovadia assured him.

"She's in bed?"

"Yes," Ovadia said carefully. Well, she must be in bed somewhere.

Meir looked at him suspiciously. Ovadia decided on the truth. "She went to Kibbutz Vered to visit Danielle," he said quickly. "She missed the bus so she'll be coming on the first bus tomorrow. A policeman came and delivered the message."

"And where is Kibbutz Vered?"

"North of Tiberias."

"Tiberias!"

To Ovadia's surprise his father laughed.

"Ovadia, Ovadia, never marry. Or if you must marry, never have daughters."

"Yes, Father," Ovadia agreed. He waited but his father seemed to escape from him. When he did speak, it came silently, sadly.

"There was a time, you know, when I was a young man a few years older than you. I had my whole future before me with no idea what it would be. Your mother asks me that now, what our future will be. I tell her it's all over for us. We have no future. Our lives have been played out. Don't ever look toward the future, Ovadia, because if you knew it, you would not have the will to live it out."

"Yes, Father."

Meir looked to his son. "You don't believe me, do you?"

"It's just that there are so many things I want to do. Like high school. If I get the scholarship. Father. It's so important to me." But his father wasn't listening. He had drifted off somewhere into the night, and the only sign he gave of his presence was the occasional sip of brandy that he took.

Joseph went back to camp and tried his best to separate his military life from his civilian one. The only person he told about Lily's abortion was Moishe.

"Why don't you get a few weeks off?" Moishe asked him.

"I don't want a few weeks off. I don't even know if I ever want to see her again."

"It's not so terrible," Moishe tried to convince him. "I knew several girls in high school who had to do it."

But for Joseph the thought of his unborn child continued to haunt him. And as the days passed he began to wonder also about Lily. During the day when they went on patrol. At night when the others were sleeping. Where was Lily? How was Lily? Soon his anger faded and only his concern remained. He counted the days till his monthly pass as a prisoner counts the bars on his cell door.

Moishe got his pass for the same day Joseph did, which was a lucky break for Joseph as Moishe's father was supervising some work in Dimona and would come by around noon to pick them up and drive them north to Tel Aviv.

"Aside from the ride itself we can be thankful we'll miss a meal," Moishe commented, though he did manage to fill his knapsack with fruits and biscuits for the ride up, lest he starve.

There were ten of Moishe's friends waiting when the government tender pulled into view. Moishe took Joseph by the elbow and told him to get in the cab with him. The other nine sat along the benches in back of the van, but no one complained. It beat hitching a ride, and they would all be in Tel Aviv in plenty of time for the Sabbath meal with their families.

Moishe was squeezed between his father and Joseph. "Papa, this is my friend I've been writing to you about, Joseph Benjamin."

"Hello, sir," Joseph said.

"He's a plumber," Moishe explained. "In real life."

"That's nice," Mr. Frayman said.

"I think he'd be a real asset to our firm."

"Moishe, I'm driving. Don't start that again or I'll have a heart attack."

Moishe blithely turned away and directed his conversation toward Joseph. "When I get out of the army, Papa's going to leave government service and start a private construction firm. He's president for life of course, me, vice-president. He's resisting the idea, but as I say to him, does he want his only son to have a future or does he want his only son to move to Ha-Tikva, marry a Moroccan, and starve to death. He takes it very well, don't you think?"

Joseph barely glanced over at Mr. Frayman, who was turning pink. "That's not right. You should show your father more respect," he whispered.

"Papa, Joseph thinks I should show you more respect."

"He at least knows how to treat his father."

"His father's dead, Papa. Died when he was a little kid." Moishe laughed. Joseph could not understand this war between father and son. He felt uncomfortable. "Seriously, Joseph, think about joining us. You'll do a lot better with us than you would with Solel Boneh. Unless our company folds."

Lily considered that she had been preparing for this day ever since Joseph left her at her parents' almost a month ago. She would try to act normal. She made the supreme effort of cleaning the house from top to bottom the day before Joseph was to arrive. And whenever Shoshana, that little tattletale, came over, she attempted to be sweet to her. She visited her mother every day. She was respectful to her father. She would not let anyone discuss the abortion. That was her affair. And if they dared to mention it, she would get up and walk out. So no one mentioned it anymore. And no one would. Until Joseph came home.

She wasn't sorry. She knew she would have a better chance with him if she fell at his knees and begged his forgiveness. But she couldn't. It would be a lie, and even if he forgave her, he would sense the deception. If he took her back at all, he would have to take her as she was.

At around four she saw him coming. She waited on the sidewalk for him and watched while he drew closer and larger. She had never realized he was such a big man before. She had never felt menaced by him. Would she now? His face was neutral as he came up to her. "Hello, Lily," he said.

She could read nothing into it, neither love nor hate. "Hello," she answered. They walked down their path together and into the house.

"How are you feeling?"

"Fine." She was getting angry. Was this all they would have to say to each other? He could have at least said something about how much better the house looked this time.

"I've missed you."

"Oh?" She wasn't helping any. She watched while he went to the sink, took down a glass, and got a drink of water. "Would you like some cold water? There's a bottle in the icebox."

"No, this is fine."

Wonderful. If it had been warm piss, he would have said the same thing. "Are we through being civilized?" she asked angrily.

"How could you have done it?" he asked furiously, his back still to her.

"I did it. That's all."

"God, I hate you for that, Lily."

"I know you do. I'm not sorry."

He was about to say something else but he stopped himself. "How are you? Are you all right?"

"Yes. I went to the doctor a few days ago. I'm all right."

"The same doctor who did it to you?"

"No, he was private. He costs a lot of money."

"If I were in the habit of beating women, I could beat you to death."

"You didn't have to come home to me."

"You didn't have to be here when I came home."

"Do you want me to leave?"

"If I had wanted you to leave, would I have come home to you?"

"Well, what are you saying?"

He shook his head. "Oh, I don't know," he sighed. He walked into the bedroom, sat down on the bed, and began unlacing his combat boots.

"Your feet smell."

"Thanks."

"Let me wash out your socks for you."

"I need them tomorrow."

"They'll be dry by tomorrow." She took them from him. He lay on the bed and listened to the water running into the metal basin. He closed his eyes.

"You were asleep," she told him.

She lay on the bed, curled within his arms. He looked past her. It was dark out. "What time is it?"

"Eight at least."

"I'm starved."

"We have to go down to my mother's."

"Why?"

"Because I promised Ovadia."

"Ovadia!"

"His teacher's coming over tonight to try to convince Father to let Ovadia accept the scholarship for high school."

"So what's the problem? Your father's always been a hot one for education."

"But other members of the family are coming, and they don't believe Ovadia should go to high school."

"Like who's coming?"

"Like the uncles who believe at fourteen Ovadia should be working and bringing money home instead of being a burden on the family any longer. Like Hillel who believes Ovadia should be apprenticed to an electrician so he can learn a trade."

"But Hillel has a college education."

"Suspicious, isn't it. I think he wants what's left of Father's money to set up his own firm. So he doesn't want Father wasting any on poor Ovadia. There's no one to speak for Ovadia except his teacher. And you, if you'll come."

"This is supposed to be a leave from the army, not a march into battle."

"Ovadia's depending on you."

Joseph sat up. "I can't get those boots on again tonight."

"Put your sandals on. No one will report you."

160

"Do I have your word on that?"

"Come on."

When they arrived at Meir's apartment, everyone was already assembled. Joseph saw with chagrin that he had missed the main meal and that fruit was now being served. Lily sat him down and hurried into the kitchen to prepare him a plate of food from the pots on the stove.

"I'm Joseph Benjamin, brother-in-law." Joseph introduced himself to a graying lady who must be Ovadia's teacher. She was sitting alongside Meir, surrounded by the male relatives, all of whom were shouting at Meir in a language she couldn't understand.

Joseph translated. "They're telling Ovadia's father that with things so tough in Israel financially, why should he deprive himself of another income for the family by sending an able-bodied son to school."

Rosa was flustered. "Could you explain to Mr. Ewan that his son's test scores are at the top of the chart? I'm sure he can get at least a seventy-percent scholarship. I've brought along the test results." She fumbled with a folder.

"Don't bother," Joseph said. "Graphs don't mean anything. It's money that's important."

Rosa sat confused while Joseph translated what she had to say about a seventy-percent scholarship.

One of the uncles responded with carefully correct Hebrew. "Seventy-percent scholarship still leaves Meir with one hundred percent of nothing."

"Yes, but his son will have an education," Rosa said, not understanding the resistance. "What could be more important than that? An education," she screamed above the noise. "At the best high school in Tel Aviv."

"Tichon Hadash, right?" Hillel said.

"Yes."

"But that's an academic high school. What good is it going to do him? No one has the money to send him to college."

"You went to college," Lily said as she handed Joseph his food.

161

"Oh shut up, Lily, those were different times. Education is a luxury now."

Rose understood "luxury." "Education is not a luxury. For Ovadia it's a necessity. Without an education you're condemning him to live a life with which he'll never be satisfied."

"Exactly," Joseph agreed with his mouth full. "How much money can he bring home now? A pitifully small amount. And ten years from now he'll still be bringing in the same amount because he'll still be unskilled labor. You have to invest in the future, Meir. Give Ovadia an education. If he's such a hotshot like she says, he'll be bringing in money by the fistful for your old age."

"We don't have the money now," Hillel said.

"You have the money now," Joseph argued. "Thirty percent Meir can scratch together. And you've got a good job. You're not paying anything to live here. You can help Ovadia. He's your brother."

"I'm saving to start my own company."

Joseph was disgusted. "You owe it to him, Meir. He's your son. You gave Hillel a college degree, you gave Lily a dowry. What is Ovadia asking for? High school for God's sake. It's not the moon."

Ovadia had sat there with his head bowed throughout the whole conversation. If only. If only. If only his father would listen to Rosa and Joseph. All he wanted to do was study and learn. He only felt alive when he had a book in his hands, when he had paper and pencil and a math problem before him. How could this be taken away from him?

Meir watched his son Ovadia suffer. Poor boy, it was his life, that's why he could not share his father's amusement. Meir looked about the room. All the men had gathered to give him advice. Him. Meir Ewan. In Baghdad they had flocked to him. What should we do? they had asked. And now here he was, like them, penniless or nearly so. So now they felt they had the right to come to him to give him advice. Not give Ovadia an education? Who did they think they were even to suggest that his son wouldn't have the best even if it meant that he, Meir, would go without food half the days of the week? "Ovadia."

His father was calling him.

"Yes."

"What do you really want?" Meir asked.

"Tichon Hadash," Ovadia whispered.

Meir shrugged. "Then it's yours." He smiled. Let them beat that.

12

"You are in big trouble," the corporal reported to Joseph.

Surprised, Joseph wondered what the problem could be. Was he being reassigned? "What sort of trouble?"

"I'm only a servant of the mighty. But the captain and two men from military intelligence want to see you in his office."

"Loose talk?" Moishe suggested.

"With whom?" Joseph asked him. God, as if his life weren't complicated enough as it was. He felt his hands perspire as he marched over to the captain's office. He could suspect that the corporal had misread the situation, but as a corporal he had to be extremely sensitive to his commanding officers. And he was. So Joseph was in some sort of trouble. He knocked on the door.

"Come in."

He couldn't believe it. All three were sitting at one long table facing an upright wooden chair that he supposed was meant for him. He saluted.

"Sit down."

He was right. He sat and wondered if he could cross his

legs, but maybe that would be considered disrespectful. Yes, he would sit at attention.

The captain tossed a packet of letters across to him. "Explain these."

Joseph picked them up and examined them. He was surprised. They were letters from Shoshana that he had never received. "They're from my sister-in-law."

"Your sister-in-law?" the captain sneered in disbelief.

"Yes, my sister-in-law. She's an eleven-year-old girl." He was getting angry. He had been waiting for these letters and all the time they had been in some army bureaucrat's hands.

The lieutenant from intelligence spoke up. "Can you explain why they are in French and Arabic. Never Hebrew. Why we can't understand the meaning of them."

Joseph had several quick retorts he could have made, but he didn't want a court-martial. He knew that the army read every letter going into and out of army camps. He pulled open Shoshana's letters and read through them, the French more slowly than the Arabic. They were all phrased obliquely. As far as he could tell, they all had to do with Lily's condition. "What's the problem?" he asked.

"What does this mean?" the lieutenant said. He took the letters from Joseph and read a passage he had previously underlined. " 'I rendezvoused at two o'clock and met the enemy face on. Battle lines were drawn but overcome by triumphant use of mendacity on my part.' All the letters are filled with this pseudo-military garbage. What's this? 'Camouflaged myself as kibbutz member to check out marketplace?' "

Joseph couldn't help but laugh. The officers found it less amusing. "My wife's been having problems since I joined the army. She doesn't want me here. I've been worried about her. So I asked Shoshana to keep an eye on her. I made it out to be sort of a game. You know, like she would be a spy. She obviously took to it very enthusiastically." They didn't believe him. "My God, she's eleven. You can go see for yourself."

"We intend to."

* * *

Joseph rolled back on his cot in hysterics.

"What's the matter?" Moishe asked. He took the letter from his friend's hand and read it. It was written in Hebrew block letters, the way a first grader might do. "Dear Joseph, A dumb, stupid, simian-featured lieutenant from intelligence has ordered me no longer to report on Lily Benjamin, your wife, who lives at 21 Modi'in, Ramat Gan, so the consideration of said subject will remain a mystery to both of us from now on. This order was delivered in the most despicable fashion imaginable, showing not the slightest sign of common decency. Courtesy I don't expect from any lieutenant in intelligence. I am fine. How are you? Love, Shoshana (Shoshi) Ewan, 9 Katznelson, Givatayim."

"What the hell are you laughing for? That's probably going to go into your file."

"Or hers," Joseph said as he wiped the tears from the corner of his eyes.

Their lieutenant blew his whistle and called them all out of their tents for assembly. "We need a squad of volunteers to go out and patrol the area near Kibbutz Goren. They think they've sighted some fedayeen. Corporal Sagan, take Harrel, Pinchas, Frayman, Benjamin, Mizrahi."

"Did we volunteer?" Moishe asked quietly.

"I didn't raise my hand," Joseph answered.

"Get your gear on, boys," the lieutenant ordered.

"Oh, well, we'll miss supper."

"What the hell are you always complaining about the food for, Moishe. You've gained at least twenty pounds."

"It's the starch."

"Let's go," the corporal shouted.

"Gung ho as usual," Moishe said.

"Harrel, you drive; Pinchas, radio. The rest of you pile in," Corporal Sagan ordered as he commandeered a jeep from the motor pool.

They tore out of camp and along the road separating the Gaza border from Kibbutz Goren. The corporal had picked up the binoculars and was studying the land as they drove slowly by it.

"Let's hope nothing appears within ten feet or he'll never see it," Moishe whispered.

"This is it," Mizrahi said.

"Oh, shut up, you dumb ox," Pinchas shouted nervously. "Every time I go out with you, you claim this is it."

"That's all right, Yo-yo," Moishe said. "One of these times you're going to be right."

But it didn't look like this would be the occasion. They had traveled ten miles along the entire border between the kibbutz and Gaza and had spotted no sign of anything. It would be hard with the sun fading in any case. So when they were two miles past the outskirts of the kibbutz's fields, the corporal gave the order to turn around and double-check on the way back to camp.

It was a mine planted under the dirt road that got them. It exploded as soon as the right front wheel rolled over it. The force of the explosion knocked the corporal, Frayman, Benjamin, and Mizrahi out of the jeep. There was no hope for Pinchas at the radio. He was killed either by the explosion or the burst of fire that followed. No one could see Harrel. They assumed he was trapped by the jeep.

"Down!" the corporal shouted. He had heard the first shot before any of them. The fedayeen had been waiting in the sand dunes for them to come back and cross over the mine. Now they had their chance to finish them off.

"Pin them down," the corporal ordered. "Frayman, come help me reach Harrel."

Joseph was emptying his rifle in the direction of the firing. They were out in the open, all of them. Firing continuously at the fedayeen was the only hope for saving themselves.

"He's alive!" the corporal yelled.

Joseph glanced over. Moishe and Corporal Sagan had located Harrel in the wreckage and were trying to get him out, but they couldn't move the jeep. They'd rock it sideways and then it would fall back on Harrel.

Joseph reached down to his belt and grabbed a grenade. It wouldn't get any of the fedayeen. He knew that much.

But it would at least create a momentary screen. He pulled the pin with his teeth, waited, then threw it. Before it landed, he was up on his feet, headed back for the jeep.

"One, two, three!" the corporal shouted. All three of them put their strength against the steel frame and the jeep rolled off Harrel. They fell flat as Mizrahi continued to fire, covering them.

"Let's get them," the corporal ordered.

They began to move then, on their bellies, off the road into the sand, two at a time covered by the other two and then a reversal. The fedayeen retreated under their assault. They stood to run. The Israelis stood to give chase and fire.

"What happened?"

"Who knows." Joseph didn't remember any of it. Not really. There were reinforcements now. Three fedayeen were dead, two captured. Pinchas, what was left of him, was covered by a blanket, Harrel carried away on a stretcher, moaning, calling for his mother. And the medic wanted to know what had happened. Couldn't he see?

"You're hurt."

"What?"

"You're bleeding," the medic pointed out.

Joseph looked down and saw blood running down his leg and swelling out of his boot. He was sick. It reminded him of Lily.

"This was it," Mizrahi said.

"Joseph!" Moishe screamed.

"I don't feel anything."

"That's a bad sign."

"Shut up, Mizrahi," Moishe told him.

"Get into the ambulance," the medic ordered.

"I don't need an ambulance. It's just blood."

"Come on, lean on me," Moishe said. "You're in shock."

All of a sudden, without any reason he could think of, Joseph was crying.

* * *

It was her nightmare come true. Your husband's been wounded. Where they didn't say, how they didn't say. They had just brought her here and dropped her in the corridor. She couldn't stand it. Not the sight of people waiting anxiously like her for some news. An older couple had come by, the woman had been sobbing, the man trying to comfort her. All she wanted was to know what happened.

"Lily?"

"Yes." She looked up to see a redheaded soldier standing near her. "You must be—"

"Moishe Frayman. We were together when it happened."

"How is he? They haven't told me anything."

"He was walking and talking when they took him away in the ambulance. I think he'll be okay." Moishe sat next to her and put his arm around her.

"What happened?"

He shook his head. "We were on patrol. Our jeep ran over a mine. Some fedayeen were waiting for us. One guy got killed."

"I think I saw his parents." She started to cry.

"Yes. No, actually I think that was probably Harrel's parents. His legs were amputated."

"Oh, God," she moaned.

"Yes," Moishe agreed. He was sick about it. God he wasn't cut out for war.

"It seems so selfish but I'm only worried about Joseph."

"Me too, right now." She took his hand. They waited for what seemed like hours but it couldn't have been because it was still dark out when the doctor stood at the head of the hallway and called, "Benjamin."

"Come on, that's us," Moishe said.

The doctor waited for them. "Mrs. Benjamin?"

"Yes."

"I'm his friend," Moishe explained.

"Mrs. Benjamin, I'm sorry to tell you this but your husband received two bullet wounds. One in the thigh, which was basically a flesh wound. The other struck his foot and damaged his tendon. I'm afraid it's going to be a long, hard rehabilitation process for him. But with physical therapy I feel certain in a few years he'll no longer walk with that much of a limp."

"A limp?"

"I'm sorry."

"But how will he fight with a limp?" she asked. "He won't be able to run as fast as the others."

"I'm afraid he's no longer fit for combat, Mrs. Benjamin. I'm sorry."

"No longer fit."

"For combat."

"That's going to break his heart," Moishe said starkly as he squeezed Lily's hand. "Can we see him?"

The doctor hesitated. "For a few moments," he agreed.

All it took was a few moments for Lily to ascertain he was still breathing. That's all she wanted to know now. He wasn't even awake. She leaned over and kissed him and brushed his hair away from his face. After that Moishe took her to the home of a family that offered a spare cot for those who came down to visit their wounded soldiers.

Joseph recovered rapidly. The visits from Lily definitely helped. She seemed once more to be her old self. He supposed it was the news of his loss of a combat-fitness rating. He himself felt terribly guilty about it. Especially when Moishe came by and wondered if they shouldn't have the bullet checked to see if it was Arab or Israeli. He was joking, still Joseph felt he was shirking his duty. He would try very hard to lose the limp sooner than the doctor expected. And then he would apply to rejoin his old unit.

Hillel knew it was time to get out. Joseph's wounds had been a warning to him, especially with the army now breathing hot down his neck, threatening to negate any further delays. Serve in the army? They had to be kidding. Did they really think he would devote another two and a half years of his life to what had become to him a lost cause? To get out in the same penniless state in which he entered, maybe like that stupid ox Joseph with a limp, or dead? For what? So they could sit in their fine apartments, dressed in their fine clothing to attend their Yiddish theater. What did Israel offer him? Nothing. Not now, not in the future. Let them have it and their army service.

Hillel had a slip of paper from a doctor in Tiberias who understood him. "I can't get you out of your army service, but I can get it deferred. Treatment for muscle spasms. Where would you like to go? The United States?"

It had cost Hillel all the money he had to get that medical certificate and the ticket to America and freedom. But could he go without a stake of some sort? He felt not. He hated what he had to do next, but it was in a way his due. Still he did not look forward to it.

His mother was alone in the apartment. Hillel had made sure she would be. He entered with his own key. She was delighted, as she should be, to see him. Hillel was her first-born.

"Hillel?" Salemah called.

He stood in the hallway and looked at her. God, she seemed so small, a small old woman. When did this happen? Who was she? He pitied her. Tears came to his eyes as he hoped they would.

"Hillel?" Salemah came closer, reached up her finger to pluck a tear from his cheek.

He took her hand and let her pull him toward the kitchen table where sat the only chairs they had in the flat. Rough, slightly uneven, made by his father.

"Something has happened."

"Yes, Mother. I must leave you."

"Leave me? But you're never here," she pointed out to him.

This was going to be more difficult than he had expected. He lowered his head and placed a hand over his eyes.

"What is it, Hillel?"

He detected the right note of concern seeping into her question. "Only this, Mother," he answered. "A man can only be abused just so much before he must pick up the cudgel of human rights and fight back. You know how I have suffered since our arrival in Israel. How we have all suffered. And now they want me in their army, probably to die."

"Like Joseph," Salemah said, trying to understand.

"Joseph! Mother, do not compare me to that laborer in the field. Who is he to us? An outcast forced upon us by Lily's delusions. Mother, in my profession I have the opportunity to do such good work if only I have the chance. But what chance is there for me in the army? I'm twenty-five, Mother. I don't want to die."

"Maybe they'll let you be an engineer in the army too."

"Mother, I am not going into the army. I refuse."

"What will happen to you then?" Salemah was becoming agitated.

"I'm leaving Israel for America, Mother. I've spent all the money I could lay my hands on to buy a doctor's certificate saying I need further medical treatment before my army service commences. So they'll let me out of the country. I've already bought my ticket. I'm leaving tomorrow."

"Tomorrow!"

"I wanted to explain it to you, Mother, because you know how close we have always been. I wanted you to know where I was going and why."

"Tomorrow."

"Penniless."

"What?"

"Oh, nothing." He shrugged it off. They sat in silence for a while. Then Hillel said, "Could you, do you think you might pack a sandwich and some fruit for me?"

"But of—"

"You see, I don't have any money left, not even for food."

"No money? But how will you make do in the United States?"

"Oh, I'll get a job."

She sat back relieved.

"After a while I suppose. It seems so unfair."

"What?"

"You know. Father promised me the money to start my own business and then we come here and he doesn't have any money left. Women are lucky. They at least always have their jewels, not empty promises to live with."

"Oh, Hillel, you know your father would help you if he could. He says nothing to me but he has always had a generous heart. If he could provide more—but he can't."

"I know, Mother. I'm only glad that the girls will never know want. They'll receive their share of the family's jewelry. It's I and Ovadia who will have to suffer, as Father will have nothing to leave us. No, I understand. A dowry for a woman is important, what she has to offer her husband. Still it seems funny in a way, doesn't it? Lily and Shoshana will have husbands to provide for them, yet they'll still get your jewelry. I, who want nothing more than to marry and give you your first grandchild, I even at twenty-five have nothing to offer a woman, except hardship and misery."

"Love, Hillel. Marriage thrives on love."

"Love is as empty or as full as one's stomach, Mother. If only"—he laughed—"if only I had something to offer the woman I would love."

They were silent. Salemah thinking, Hillel waiting.

"What will you do if you meet her and marry in America?" his mother asked. "Would you bring her here?"

"I don't know, Mother. America is such a long way away. Of course when we have your first grandchild, I'll come home immediately."

"I would like to give your wife something. To welcome her into the family."

"Your love would be enough, Mother."

Salemah rose slowly and retrieved her jewelry box from inside the kitchen cabinet. She brought it back to the table and sat down with it. She opened it slowly.

Hillel watched while she picked up and discarded each item in the box.

These were Salemah's. Not only her wealth, her dowry, but her history. Bracelets, anklets, rings from her grandmother, her mother, presents for birthdays, marriage, the birth of her children. She had her daughters to think about, but wasn't Hillel right? Didn't he have rights to these too? Not for himself but for his wife. Still what could she part with? She picked up an emerald ring in a gold setting. It made her skin look gray. And here. From Uncle Moshe the butcher whom she never liked, a gold necklace with a locket attached. It had his picture in it. And this bracelet. She had four of these bracelets, perhaps one to each child. Two bands of gold, pearls placed between them. Her grandfather had made these for her wedding day. Then why not for Hillel's wife on her wedding day. Salemah left the bracelet with the ring and the locket. She closed her box and put it away. "You must never sell any of these jewels, Hillel, or melt them down," she counseled.

"Of course not, Mother," he agreed. "And perhaps we shouldn't tell Father."

"Perhaps not," she agreed.

"I will come tonight and tell him I am leaving."

"You will come back though?"

"With your grandchild." He smiled at her, neither of them knowing that this night would be the last time they ever saw each other.

Meir held the letter in his hand. It was from Jacob Ewan. Jacob whom he had seen practically every week of his life, who now seemed so far away, as far away as his life in Baghdad had become. He couldn't think back. He wouldn't. It would be too destructive. He would read Jacob's letter and pretend he couldn't see his house, smell the food, feel the richness of the life he had let escape him. "Dear Meir," the letter began. "May I be not the first, but perhaps the most sincere, to congratulate you on the marriage of your daughter to Joseph Benjamin. I've always liked that boy and I think he will make you a fine son-in-law. As you know, you have always been my favorite brother." Meir wondered at that. What now did Jacob want? "Therefore I am asking your advice. Should I pick up my family, sell my business, and come to Israel? I have been wondering about this as I see practically our entire community preparing itself to be airlifted out of here. Are they right? Am I wrong ? Or is it the other way around? As you know, I am rich here. My business, the Swallow's Nest, continues to do well. I know many high officials and we are very close. Still I wonder if Israel will not continue to be the thorn in the side of our relationships. I have two fine, strong sons who in their time will marry, so I must think also of them, not only of my own well-being. What choice would you advise me to make? What are the conditions in our beloved Zion? Please communicate soon. I am most anxious to hear from you. My love to our entire family and good wishes for the best of health. Your somewhat brother, Jacob."

Meir shook his head at the closing. Jacob, so far away, still had the power to annoy. But Meir saw his duty when it was there. And he did not have to think about this. Jacob had asked for advice. What better advice could Meir give him than to come to Israel? If he wanted to get even with him. No, what could an honest letter document? Lily's abortion, Joseph's brush with death, Hillel cheating his mother out of her own jewelry. That bastard, his own son. Or should he tell Jacob what he himself had become. A common workman with no chance for advancement because he was not born in Russia or Poland, because he did not speak Yiddish. Jacob's letter brought this bitterness back to him, all the hard times. The anger boiled over into the words he placed on the page he would send to Jacob: "Dear brother, I am glad to hear that you and your family are still in good health. My advice is this: Whatever you do, don't come to Israel. I have lost everything, including, you will be happy to note, my control. I am poorer than the beggars of Baghdad. I am a common laborer, trying simply to provide enough food on the table for my family. Do not believe anything that is said to you about Israel. We are treated like dirt here. We are like the sand that blows through our window from the unpaved street below. I understand your wariness in staying in Baghdad. I felt it too.

Get out. Save your family and your money if you can. Go to Lebanon or Europe. But don't come here unless you want to eat the dirt of the desert and like it. We Jews will remain nomads still if this is all Israel can offer us. Excuse my bitterness. It has been a bitter year. With love to our family and wishes for your continued success and good health. Your brother, Meir."

The letter had been sent with a businessman to Cyprus. From Cyprus the businessman mailed it to Baghdad, as there was no mail service between countries at war, Iraq and Israel. Jacob received the letter and sighed with sadness. It did not surprise him that the land of Israel did not live up to its promise. Nothing ever did. What amazed him was that it fell so far short. He could adjust to doing without a little, but not without everything. And yet that's what it would mean if he left Iraq now. Everything would be lost. His money, his power, his position. Choices. A hundred thousand had chosen to flee Iraq. Only twenty-five thousand Jews remained. Sometimes he would walk the streets of the Jews in Baghdad and wonder at their emptiness.

Give me a sign, he prayed to the Lord, but the God of Israel was as usual silent. He would stay a few months. A few years. When things got tough, he would leave Iraq. But for now he was secure. And who was to say that for now was not forever.

He picked out something pretty from the jeweler the next day. It was a gold bracelet with a large ruby. He would find some Britisher he could trust, and when the Englishman left the country, Jacob would have him send the bracelet on to Meir for Shoshana's dowry. Shoshana, that little monkey. He would love to see her again. He would love to see them all. When the time was right.

Peace would come soon. Wars don't go on forever. And then Jacob would see where he would make his next move.

PART 2

13

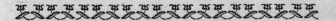

"Be careful."

"Oh, mother, I will be," Shoshana said, annoyed by her mother's concern. It was not as if she was going around the world, only up the street a few blocks to bring her father a bottle of ice-cold juice.

Salemah stood on the balcony and watched her daughter grow smaller on Katznelson street as she disappeared toward Ramat Gan. How the street had changed since they moved there—how long had it been—seven years ago! Gone were the shacks and the sand. In their place stood apartment buildings that almost dwarfed hers, sidewalks, grass. Salemah smiled. She was no longer alone. So many Iraqis had moved into Givatayim and neighboring Ramat Gan that they now had their own synagogue. The grocer was Iraqi, the pharmacist too. She could go walking on the street now and be understood. But most of all it was the right environment for Shoshana, if her daughter only saw fit to take advantage of it.

Salemah couldn't understand why Meir was letting Shoshana get away with murder. Sending her to high school. What good was high school to her when she was only going

181

to get married. Meir had explained to Shoshana the facts of life, how he didn't have any money to give her a real dowry, how the only dowry she had was the beautiful gold bracelet her Uncle Jacob had sent her from Baghdad. "My education will be my dowry," Shoshana had answered. Foolish girl. A man didn't look for an educated wife. He looked for one who could cook and clean and, most importantly, have sons. Then Ovadia, who she thought had more sense, joined in on his sister's side. It was the modern thing to do, educating women. It was the Israeli way. And Meir had fallen for it.

Her silence had shown her displeasure. She had not talked the entire day that Shoshana had gone with her father to sell the bracelet. Then the nerve, Shoshana late at night coming to her and saying, "Mother, I am of value as a person. That's what I will have to offer when and if I get married."

Oh, what a stupid child. Who would accept a woman like that? It was for a man to tell her of her value, not for her to boast of it. It was for a man to recite her worth on the Sabbath eve. Sixteen years old. Shoshana had this year and the next to finish high school. Then what? Her daughter talked about going into the army. Salemah shook her head. She could not believe that child had come from her own womb.

Why couldn't Shoshana be more like Lily? Lily had done what was expected of her. She had gotten married. Of course, not to the man of their choosing. She had had a child. Of course, there was that unfortunate incident when Joseph was in the army. Salemah went back into the apartment and sat down. She really, when she thought of it, did not understand Lily either. But money solves all problems and Lily and Joseph had money now, Salemah noted, looking around at her own still shabby furnishings. Still, would she have risked as much as Lily had for the sake of her husband? Salemah didn't mean physically. Oh, she would lay down her life for Meir. But financially? When Joseph had gotten out of the army and wanted to join that Frayman firm with his friend Moishe, Moishe had been willing to take him on as a plumber. But Joseph wouldn't be satisfied with being a plumber, which he never even was in the first place. No, now he wanted to be a plumbing contractor, and him with a limp. Old Mr. Frayman had told Joseph that Frayman Construction wasn't a charitable organization. If Joseph wanted the subcontracts for the plumbing, he'd have to buy in.

Meir had called Joseph a compulsive gambler. He was right. But Joseph had lured Lily over with all his talk of "our one big chance." They had taken all her jewelry and used it as collateral to secure a loan for him to buy into Frayman Construction. He could have been wrong. He could have lost everything. Instead he was paying back the loan, retrieving Lily's jewelry piece by piece; he had his own truck and five actual plumbers working under him. Joseph had even asked Meir to work with him, but Meir wouldn't. He told her that it would be like taking a handout from his own son-in-law. Joseph still came by occasionally and pleaded his need for Meir's experience. Salemah wished sometimes that Meir would relent. But there was no sign of it. So every day her husband went off at six and sweated in the sun. It was funny how rich Meir had been in Baghdad, how poor, Joseph. And now, not even money for his daughter's dowry.

She had her sons though, Salemah thought resolutely. And sons were a blessing. Ovadia had received an exemption from immediate service in the army so that he could study engineering at the Technion. But that was in Haifa, so she hardly ever saw him except when he could make it home for the weekends. In the summer when he should have been home all the time, he had to serve in the army, first basic training, then this squad-leader course. But he was bright. Everyone said that. To go through high school on a scholarship and then through college on one too. She never was afraid for him. Ovadia always did the right thing. She was sure that even when he fell in love, it would be to the right sort of woman, though there was no sign of that yet. Thank God, he still needed a mother's care.

Salemah often wondered what sort of woman Hi**

married. Diane Shapiro. It was a Jewish name, she knew, but certainly not Iraqi. She worried about Hillel. What sort of food was this Diane cooking for him, how was he living in that strange land America. Hillel had changed his name. Meir had ranted on about that for weeks. She supposed it was the way Hillel had let them know. About six months after he arrived in the United States, Hillel sent a letter telling them to address his mail to Hillel Ewan c/o Hal Evans. Then about a year later he sent them a business card: Hal Evans, Consultant, Mayer, Shapiro, and Rigney, Civil Engineers. Who is this Hal Evans, Meir had written to ask. It's me, Hillel wrote back. No one could pronounce Hillel Ewan and it was too foreign-sounding anyway. Salemah couldn't blame Meir for being enraged. After all, why does a man have sons if not to carry on his name.

She only hoped Hillel was offering this Diane something better than these bitter last years of her own. Diane. Salemah studied the picture of her son and this Diane at their wedding. She was pretty enough. Dark hair and eyes. White-skinned. Ashkenazi. She was the daughter of the Shapiro in Mayer, Shapiro, and Rigney. "That's Hillel for you," Joseph had said at the time. But hadn't Joseph also married the boss's daughter. Though Salemah had to admit with a bitter smile that in all fairness Joseph had not profitted from it.

Hillel had a son now, and the certain expectation of more to come. That's what made Joseph jealous. Salemah could not get enough pictures of this eight-week-old little Brian. Every time Shoshana and Ovadia wrote to Hillel for her, she had them beg Hillel to send more pictures of his son and to ask when, when was he coming. He had promised her that when he had a child, he would come back to her. Eight weeks old. Oh, if she could only hold Brian. Maybe she did not understand the name picked out for him, but she could still give this Diane plenty of advice on how to raise fine children. Or perhaps Salemah better qualify that to fine sons. She was still not entirely certain what was happening with her daughters. Especially Shoshana.

When Shoshana knew she was out of sight of her mother, she crossed the street to walk in the shade. The things she did, suffering in the sun, just because her mother would fret if she did not disappear naturally from view. Oh, it was hot today. The *hamseen*, the hot desert wind from the Negev, was upon them, covering their world in dust and sand. It might be the last one of the season. She could at least hope.

Shoshana reached her father's construction site and looked around for him. She was not too worried about finding him. Several of his coworkers knew who she was and they would let him know she was there. Her eyes stopped to the east of where she was standing. Without knowing it, she smiled. He was perfect. So perfect he reminded her of the statues she had seen in Caesarea. Roman statues. Of gods perhaps. She had touched one, felt the cool ripple of a muscle in marble and wondered. But his muscles were concealed beneath a uniform and his body was leaner than any Roman's. She decided she loved him.

Her father nudged her. She almost dropped the juice bottle. Annoyed, she handed the bottle over and caught him taking a quick glance in the soldier's direction. "Who is he?" she whispered. She watched her father drink from the bottle. He lowered it, gave her a warning look, and took another sip.

The soldier was staring at her. She felt herself blush. She knew she looked pretty, her thick black hair curling around her shoulders, her dark skin made more lustrous by her pink sundress.

The soldier was coming over now. She didn't know where to look so she looked right at him. It was very pleasant.

"Hello, Meir," the soldier said. "Is this beautiful girl your daughter?"

Her father said nothing. Shoshana could see that it bothered him for this youth to call him Meir. But that's the way it was in Israel. Everything was informal and manners were from the bourgeois past.

Getting no help from Meir, the soldier introduced himself. *"Shalom,"* he said. "I'm Danny Ze'ev."

"Shoshana Ewan," she replied shyly.

He stared at her and smiled as if he knew how impressive his appearance was. Shoshana was afraid he wouldn't say anything more. "Do you work here too?" he finally asked.

She laughed. "No. I was just bringing my father something to drink."

"A dutiful daughter. Are you working around here?"

"I don't work," she said. "I go to school."

"High school?"

"Yes."

"Which one?"

"Givatayim."

"That's a new one."

"Yes."

"Academic?"

"Yes."

"I went to the Alliance."

He wanted to impress her. That pleased her but also turned her competitive. He went to the Alliance, a fair enough school, but, "My brother went to Tichon Hadash." And that was the best high school in the country.

"So what made you decide to go to Givatayim?" he asked.

"It was close. And convenient for me." Not to mention, the school's all right if you're only a girl.

"What are you studying?"

"Languages. I want to be in intelligence when I go into the army. Translations. Things like that. You're in the infantry?"

"For a year now. But I'm going to go into the commandos."

"Ooh. That's dangerous."

He shrugged. "Someone's got to do it."

"You have to be in good shape to do that."

"I am," he said. "You too." He smiled. She laughed.

"Shoshana," her father called. She went over to him but

found he wanted nothing more than to get her away from Danny. No luck. She went back to him.

"Say," he said, "I've got to go now. But can I take you out tonight? Maybe go for a show and something to eat."

"Sounds great," she said. She gave him her address.

"Pick you up at seven," he told her before walking off.

She was so flustered she practically forgot to say goodbye to her father.

Meir objected.

"But why, Father?"

"Because I don't like him or his father. I don't like their kind."

"Is he Iraqi?" Salemah asked. They both ignored her.

Shoshana could understand why her father didn't like the Ze'evs. Danny's father was foreman on the job where Meir was working. Meir felt he should have been foreman. True, he should have been a foreman by now, but no way. He had worked himself up from the lowest-grade laborer to the highest-grade laborer and many times had applied to be foreman. There were so many excuses they used to deny him, the latest being that he couldn't write Hebrew, only print it. "So people can read print," he had objected.

"It's easier to read writing," they replied.

"Then why are all the newspapers using print?"

It didn't matter. The only reason he was refused a job as foreman was because he didn't speak Yiddish. He knew it and they knew it and that's all there was to it. But that wouldn't stop him from trying again and again.

It was hard for her father, Shoshana understood. She understood what they had done to him, people like Mr. Ze'ev. But why should the fact that Danny was Mr. Ze'ev's son have anything to do with her seeing him or not.

"He isn't Iraqi, is he?" Salemah asked.

"No, Mother, he isn't," Shoshana said, feeling guilty about her father.

Ovadia came home. He had finished his squad-leader course and now was spending his last few weeks of freedom working as an efficiency expert at the Weizmann Institute. Shoshana always felt safer when Ovadia was home. He at least could understand her needs, he felt them so strongly himself, the need for accommodation, the need for acceptance into a society larger than their own family circle.

"Shoshana's going out with a European tonight." Salemah hit him with it at once.

Ovadia stared at his mother, father, and sister. They were going at it again. He had never seen three people argue so much together since Lily had lived at home. It was obviously a feminine characteristic to cause havoc in the family. "Well, have fun," Ovadia said before he headed off to the shower to get first crack at it. If Shoshana was going out tonight, she would be in the bathroom forever.

Ovadia watched while Shoshana fixed her hair. It was naturally curly and it bounced around her. If he had liked dark women, he would have thought of Shoshana as attractive, maybe even beautiful. But he liked blondes, so her efforts just amused him. Though he could see where a European would like her. Some of them went for the dark, Oriental girls. The contrast pleased them. He supposed Shoshana's date to be one of her high school acquaintances. He didn't see why his father should be upset. No harm could come from that. At least not on the first date. Not from Shoshana.

"How do I look?" Shoshana asked.

Ovadia studied her. Her black hair flowed down to an orange dress Lily had made for her. The dress fit snugly across the bosom and held tight against the waist before it blossomed out over the hips. Their mother found the fit too revealing and the color too flashy. Ovadia supposed that was why Shoshana chose it. "There, right near your forehead, a curl that's slightly out of place."

"Really?" She rushed back to the mirror to check. It was seven. The doorbell rang. "Which one?" she asked desperately.

Ovadia laughed at her. "I was just teasing," he admitted. He got up to answer the door. He was slightly disconcerted to see a soldier rather than a high school student standing before him. No wonder his father had objected.

"Danny Ze'ev," the soldier said, stretching out his hand.

"Ovadia Ewan, Shoshana's brother." They shook hands and Ovadia led Danny into the hallway where Shoshana was waiting. Ovadia didn't like the way Danny was staring at her. Not that he was drooling from the mouth or anything, it was just that lusty glint in his eye.

Meir came out into the hallway. "So you're here," he said to Danny, not too unpleasantly.

"Yes," Danny said. "I found it immediately."

"Won't you come in. My wife would like to meet you."

Danny followed Meir into the living room. "That's called scaring him off," Ovadia whispered hurriedly to Shoshana before she rushed into the living room to protect Danny from her parents. But her mother merely smiled politely when she was introduced and then asked Danny to be seated.

They all sat uncomfortably in the living room while Salemah served fruit and juice. Shoshana was glad to see Danny was polite enough to take some. The conversation was desultory until Danny and Ovadia began discussing the Sinai campaign of last summer. Danny had served with the combat units that had rushed across the desert, rolling over the Egyptians in an effort to reach the Suez Canal and join up with the British and French, of whom the less said the better.

"It must have been awful for you," Shoshana said, perhaps too sympathetically.

"I'm still here," Danny answered with a smile. "That's what counts."

"We were never called up," Ovadia explained, a little bit frustrated. "We had just finished basic training."

"Probably saving you for Jordan if necessary," Danny said.

"Where are you taking my daughter tonight?" Salemah broke in suddenly. It sounded like an accusation.

"To a movie."

189

"We have a movie house, the Nogah, right on the corner. I can see it from the balcony. Then when the movie is over, you can bring Shoshana back here for something to eat."

"Oh," Danny said, a little disconcerted. "I've already bought tickets to a show in Tel Aviv."

"That sounds very nice," Shoshana remarked sternly to cut off any protest. "Perhaps then we should get started."

Their leave-taking was rather hurried as Shoshana practically hustled him out the door before her mother engineered any change in plans.

"That was very interesting," Danny said when they were out on the street corner waiting for the bus.

"Yes. Well, my family likes to make sure I'm going out with the right type of person," she said seriously.

"They've really slipped up this time, haven't they?" He gave her a smile that made her heart flash.

She barely noticed the show. It was American-made with bright colors. Usually she would look upon movies like this as a chance to improve her English. But now she was more concerned with the way Danny held her hand and the way he placed his arm around her shoulder. She felt strange, so excited.

Afterward he took her for a stroll along Dizengoff. She, of course, read about Dizengoff in the papers. Everyone famous in Israel could be found on Dizengoff. The intellectuals, the actors, the politicians, the tourists, the whores. She had never been there before. He stopped at Café Rowal. She had heard of it. They sat down and had coffee. He tried to hold a conversation but she was engaged in her efforts to identify the famous people and failed to pay too close attention. It didn't matter anyway. It was being with him that counted.

They took the bus home, which unfortunately stopped almost in front of her apartment. She looked up as they got off the bus. Her parents were standing on the balcony waiting for her.

"Oh, my," Danny said. He had seen them too.

He took her into the hallway of her apartment building. "You don't have to come up," she told him.

"Of course I do," he said. "But first." He put his arms around her and she felt his hands press into the small of her back and drive her forward. He kissed her full on the lips. She had never known such soft excitement. She felt one hand fall around to her waist and slide up to her breast. She should stop him.

The lights went on in the hallway.

"Your parents," he said.

"That was naughty," she told him.

He smiled. "I'll be thinking about it out in the desert."

"You're going?"

"Tomorrow."

That was it then. "I had a good time," she said as they climbed upward.

"So did I." He smiled confidently before turning her over to her parents who were waiting by the open apartment door.

After they said good night, her mother brought her inside the apartment and looked her over. Shoshana could still feel her nipple erect and pushing against her dress. "What's the matter?" her mother asked. "Does he have a war wound that he can't climb faster?"

Joseph was outside his villa, polishing his fender when Shoshana saw him and waved to him. He waved back. She loved the way he took care of his truck with the words Benjamin and Son printed boldly on the side. Plumbing Contractors. Meir always snorted when he saw that. She supposed it was amusing, Joshua being only two years old. Yet Joseph had big plans for him.

"*Erev tov*, Joseph," she said. "Did you know I was in love?"

He laughed. "Really? With anyone special?"

"I had a date last night." She swung around him.

"I heard all about it. Including those stolen moments in the hall."

She blushed. "You couldn't have heard all about it," she answered smartly, then laughed.

"Shoshana," he scolded.

"So what do you think about it?" she asked.

"One date?"

"I know he's the one for me."

"At sixteen?"

"Lily was seventeen when she married you."

"That was different."

"Why?" He didn't answer. "Oh, Joseph, you're an old man already."

"I was twenty and willing to take Lily on as my wife," he replied seriously. "This guy is in the army and much more likely just to be fooling around."

"Trifling with my affections."

"What?"

"That's the way it's put in books."

"You read too many books."

"Like Lily saw too many movies?" she teased.

He laughed. "Go away. Go in and help your sister. She's making dinner."

"Has she improved any?"

Joseph shook his head sadly.

"Then I guess I'll eat at home tonight," Shoshana said.

Lily had tucked Joshua into bed. Again. Then she came back to her husband in his bed. "Did you like it?" she asked. "It was a new recipe."

He nodded. "It was good, Lily."

"The rice was less burned than usual," she pointed out.

"No one ever said you couldn't learn if you put your mind to it."

She threw herself onto him, laughing. "You're teasing me."

"No," he protested. "It was good."

She settled herself on top of him and let him hold her. "I love you so much, Joseph."

"I love you too."

"Is everything going to work out?"

"It always does."

But it didn't and his lie didn't comfort her.

Yes, Joseph was doing well in business. He and the

Fraymans were thriving in their partnership even if it took a lot of capital, not to mention bribes, to keep it afloat. They weren't rolling in money yet, but the prospects were there for the future. Still none of it would make up for what had happened.

"Do you mind?"

He knew instantly what she was referring to. "No, Lily, I don't mind," tired already of the conversation but knowing she had to go through with it.

When she had gotten pregnant with Joshua, it was such a time of exultation. It was as if they were forgiven the past, the abortion, the distance between them. But when the baby had been born, Lily had hemorrhaged. She had almost died, and afterward the doctor said she would be unable to have any more children. Joseph tried not to be bitter. He had his son Joshua and he had his wife. Still he oftentimes thought it was the doctors who had botched the handling of her case as they so often did. In Iraq the midwives would have saved her and restored her.

Lily felt guilty. If only she hadn't—if only—if only.

"But who knows," Joseph would tell her. "It might have happened with the first one too."

"It's God punishing me," she would say.

"If God were punishing you, he wouldn't have let you have Joshua."

"Oh, yes, as a way of showing me what I am missing. He's vindictive like that."

Joseph would try to hush her, but the same conversation would be repeated at least once a month.

"Be thankful for the child," he would tell her. "And for the love we have for each other."

Danielle Haya worried about her body. She couldn't look in the mirror, not for any length of time. That would be sinful. But she knew her body was changing, pushing out in all the expected areas. They were worried about her at first. Osnat had said she thought girls from Danielle's part of the world developed quickly so they could be married off early—thirteen, fourteen. Danielle didn't bother to tell her most Iraqi girls didn't marry until their twenties. Osnat wouldn't have heard her.

Danielle had just turned fourteen when she got her first period. She should have felt grateful, for by then the girls and the boys had been separated into different houses and she had the benefit of almost everyone else's experience. But she had been uneasy for a whole year, waiting every day for "it" to happen. Then when the miracle did occur, or the "curse" as she remembered her mother calling it, she was given a box of sanitary napkins and the advice that now she could get pregnant. They didn't tell her exactly how she could get pregnant, which was frustrating. But some of the older girls had clever ideas on the matter that sounded rather intriguing and messy at the same time.

Shoshana knew exactly how to get pregnant and how not to get pregnant. "I read it in a book," she had confided to Danielle. Shoshana always sat in the library and read books on the most perilous subjects. Danielle would never have been that brave. If anyone caught her reading something like that, she would be mortified.

Shoshana. Danielle saw her so rarely now. It had been three months since her last visit. It wasn't Shoshana's fault since it all depended on when Joseph would drive up north to see his brother Reuben on the moshav. When he did, he would bring Shoshana to Kibbutz Vered. She would stay overnight and Joseph would pick her up on his way south the next day. Danielle lived for these visits. She could almost taste her old life when Shoshana came to call. It struck her as amusing that Shoshana looked forward to her visits too, because they gave her a taste of a new life. "How lucky you are," Shoshana would say, "to be able to do whatever you want without your parents always breathing down your neck." How thoughtless Shoshana was at times. Or perhaps she honestly didn't realize how much Danielle missed having a family of her own, a real family, one she could love and hate, not one like the kibbutz where she was always expected to be grateful.

She was wrong to feel the way she did about living on

Kibbutz Vered. They had been good to her, and she knew that Ezra and Albert both would never want to live anyplace else. They could take school or leave it, as most of the kibbutzniks did. Their lives were the cattle, the banana plants, the chickens and their eggs. Her life, well, she didn't know what her life was. "Stop being so odd." That's what they told her. That was her life. She was, she had to face it, odd. A misfit, an outcast. A pain in the ass, her gym teacher had told her. Sometimes it amused even her to hold onto a dream of what she had never had, the perfect family. Other times it cut like a knife when the Sabbath meal came and all the families of the kibbutz sat together in the dining hall while the children of Aliyat Ha-No'ar sat alone. She hated her mother then.

Her mother was in Tehran. She and her father had a stall in the *shuk,* the marketplace, selling kitchen utensils. This Danielle had heard from Shoshana who had gotten it from Lily who received this news from her friend Rebecca in Tehran. The Hayas were not doing well, Rebecca reported. Every venture Nazem put his hand to went sour, until now they had the stall that Leah would open and close while Nazem made periodic appearances in between drinks. At least things were normal there, Danielle thought bitterly.

If only Sami were still at Kibbutz Vered. But he had left, was it really four years ago? They had spent two years together. He had taken care of her, protected her, supported her. But then his parents had enough money to bring him home. When he left, he promised to write, he promised to visit. He had done neither, not for four long years. She still waited. But she knew what the truth was. She was alone.

Diane Evans, née Shapiro, was beginning to think she had made a big mistake. The courtship had been exciting, the wedding brilliantly organized, the honeymoon instructive, but for the last three years life seemed to float about her without purpose. She knew what she wanted out of life.

195

She had wanted to get married and have a family. She knew what Hal wanted out of life. He wanted a son. So why couldn't she conceive. She looked over to her coffee table. Where there should have been books by Bernard Malamud, Gerald Green, Philip Roth, Norman Mailer, even John Updike, there stood a towering testament to American publishers' concern with infertility. She had been over and over these books as the doctors had been over and over her. Nothing wrong, they told her. For some women it just took longer than for others. Hal was getting impatient. Every time he made love it was an act of war as he tried to force his seed deep enough into her to do the trick.

She had sounded her mother out very vaguely on her marital distortions. It was always a very troubling experience talking to her mother about anything, because her mother got defensive mighty quickly, as if Diane was blaming her for everything. Well, Diane wouldn't say she wasn't blaming her mother, ever the one to hurry Diane into marriage, any marriage that would look good on paper, specifically *The New York Times*. But now she just wanted to talk to her mother woman to woman, and she supposed her mother wasn't ripe for that yet, for after hours of beating around several bushes, her mother's advice had been succinctly put: Men are peculiar. Children are a blessing many of us could do without. Don't blame infertility on me, I had six. Divorce is out of the question as long as you're a member of this family. What would Grandma Korn say, may she rest in peace.

No, Mother was definitely not ready to communicate on human terms with her daughter.

When Diane thought about it in her calmer moments, she considered that she might be doing Hal an injustice. Maybe his love for children was so intense that the thought of not having one really tore him apart. She saw with tenderness and grief how he fawned over their neighbor's child, little Brian, who was all of ten weeks old. The pictures Hal took of Brian, the pictures Hal made her take of him carrying Brian about in his arms—it was really peculiar.

But if he could love Brian, why did he get hysterical every time she mentioned adoption as a possibility. "I want my own child," he would flare at her.

Well, she was going to an expert now. The expert in Boston. She had her appointment and this should finally settle the issue once and for all. Either the doctor would tell her she was physically incapable of conceiving, or he would confirm Hal's diagnosis that she was simply psychologically disturbed.

14

Jacob Ewan sat in his living room in Baghdad and read the papers.

It was an unsettled time. When was it not in the Middle East? Gamal Abdel Nasser in Egypt spreading his brand of Pan-Arabism to the masses of Arabs in the Fertile Crescent, the Christians and the Moslems fighting in Lebanon. And of course there was always Israel. When Arabs met, they could agree on one thing if nothing else—they would drive the Jews into the sea. That was the purpose Israel served in the Middle East, Jacob thought bitterly, to unite the Arabs where nothing else could.

Iraq was still at war with Israel. Jacob was thus still completely cut off from his family. He had counted on change and change had not come. Now he feared a change of a different sort. There was unrest in Iraq. It came with the transistor radio. Cairo beamed its propaganda broadcasts at the people day and night, urging them to rise up and slay their kings, Faisal II of Iraq, Hussein of Jordan. Would the people listen? They were poor. The oil revenues had brought them nothing. If Jacob were king or merely prime minister, he would see that the poor were well fed, the price of bread and kerosene cheap. But he was not prime minister. Nuri es-Said was and Nuri es-Said had his commitments to the ruling class. Give us time, Nuri es-Said preached to the people. But how much time did Iraq have with Nasser's venomous influence at the back door in Syria.

What stood between Iraq and revolution? The King. Iraq was nearly evenly split between the Sunni and the Shia Moslems, with perhaps a slight majority lying with the Shia. While the Sunni were orthodox and followed the sunna or custom of the Prophet, the Shia cause descended from the early Moslems who rallied to the support of the caliphate of Ali, son-in-law of the Prophet Mohammed. The Shia today still turned to the descendants of Ali, and tenuous as the thread might be, Faisal II was one of these descendants.

Jacob laughed at himself. What a foolish man he was to put his faith in so simple a thing as religion. Religions change. Gods change. Prophets change. And who was to say that Nasser today would not sweep out of Egypt the way the followers of Mohammed swept out of the desert of Arabia over thirteen hundred years ago.

He went into his house. His wife was still in the kitchen cleaning up from dinner. He walked into the kitchen and offered to help her. She refused. "Then why don't you leave it for the maids?" It was a silly question. She would not. Sometimes he wondered what she thought of him. Not that it mattered. He had taken her with little dowry because she had a giggle that pleased him. And he was not, he would have to admit, acceptable to the better families in Baghdad. But he had given her everything that he could, failing respectability, and she had given him two sons. They had come out even. He patted her on the fanny. She twitched him off. By the time she was finished in the kitchen, he was fast asleep in bed.

At five o'clock Jacob woke up with a start.

"What is it?" his wife asked. She put her hand on his forehead. He was sweating.

Jacob looked out the window. It was dawn, but he was

still in his nightmare. The crowd swarmed around him like bees and he was paralyzed. He could hear them still, crying out for Jewish blood.

His wife had gotten up and gone to the open window. She listened, then looked to him. "Not again," she whispered.

Jacob jumped out of bed and called to his sons. "Listen to the radio," he ordered his wife. It had to be another war with Israel. What else would set the Arabs off like this so early in the morning. His sons knew what to do as soon as he called them. They got out the screws and clamps and the large sheets of thick plastic and began affixing them to the windows while Jacob started nailing boards across the front doorway. He was rather proud of himself for thinking of the plastic. That way if neighbors looked out, they would not see plywood over the windows, as if Jacob Ewan expected his home to be stormed. They would see, if they caught anything in the sunlight, clear plastic over the windows, which showed he had nothing to hide or fear. And if they did throw stones, the plastic would protect them until solid wood could be thrown up.

"It's not us this time," his wife came to the front door to tell him.

"What?"

"It's the king. They've killed the king."

So much for the descendants of Ali. But then hadn't Ali himself been struck down with a poisoned sword, murdered right here in Iraq. Yes, Iraq had always loved a good old-fashioned political assassination.

They did not go out of the house for a week. Crown Prince Abdul Ilah's body was given to the crowd. They dragged it through the streets and strung it up naked to the delight of young and old alike. The British embassy was ransacked and burned. Jordanians and Europeans were being taken by truck to an army compound for their own safety. The mob stopped the truck, pulled out the foreigners, and either stabbed them to death or tore them to pieces.

Prime Minister Nuri es-Said, still the fox at seventy,

stayed alive for two days. Then slipping through Baghdad dressed as an old woman, he was spotted by an air force sergeant. He was killed and strung up naked in the city like Abdul Ilah, whom he had served so well. And dead with Nuri es-Said was his entire family. Slaughtered.

No, Jacob Ewan and his family would not leave their house.

They listened though at all hours, to all manner of things. Like Baghdad Radio calling on the people of Jordan to rise up and kill their King Hussein. Like Cairo Radio reporting that King Faisal had died of a heart attack when Crown Prince Abdul Ilah slapped him for urging surrender. They listened and they waited. Even the people of Baghdad could only take so much blood flowing in their streets.

The voice that emerged was that of Brigadier General Abdul Karim Kassem. He spoke of friendship with the Arabs, friendship with the British, a better life for all. Kassem's revolution had taken place on Bastille Day. And now Jacob would wait for the terrors to follow.

Lily watched with delight as Joshua checked the mail. She never ceased to wonder at the sweetness of him. She studied his little legs and arms, his smile, as if each of his component parts was a miracle. And how could she doubt that? She loved her son. Her heart fluttered whenever he was near. Her love for him was so intense that sometimes it worried her. How could she ever bear to let him go? Sometimes she wished for only this reason that she could have other children, so that they could dilute the intensity of her love.

Joshua was crushing the mail. "Keep it neat, Joshua," she scolded. She took the letters from his hand and smoothed them against her thigh. She sorted through them. Most were addressed to Benjamin and Son, Plumbing Contractors. But she smiled with delight when she found one addressed to her from Tehran.

It was Rebecca. How many years had it been since they'd

seen each other. Eight. Since 1950. For a while in the beginning she had not been pleased to hear from Rebecca, because while Rebecca's husband prospered, while Rebecca bore children, Joseph was in the army, she was having an abortion, and they were barely hanging on. But now all was different. She had Joshua. Joseph had his business, and she could write with pride to Rebecca about her life in Israel.

She carefully unfolded the flaps of Rebecca's letter. Joshua, noting his mother's absorption in something other than himself, snuck off to play with the water hose in the backyard. Lily carefully mouthed each word of the letter. She wanted to savor it. First came the news of each of Rebecca's four children, then of her husband. She spread into international matters by touching on the revolution in Iraq and the few Jews who had escaped from that wretched land since then by fleeing into Kurdish-held territory. Rebecca always saved her best news for last. Some juicy bit of gossip about someone they had both known in Baghdad. She would write small and extend it onto the flap, so that sometimes Lily lost the most important words when she opened the letter. But this time she could manage to read it. The name Leah Haya jumped out at her. That didn't surprise her. Rebecca had written often about Leah and Nazem, since they were always embroiled in one scandal or another. This time it wasn't just scandal Rebecca was writing of, it was death. It had happened at the Haya stall in the *shuk*. Nazem was drunk as usual, sharpening knives for those who had time to wait through his clumsiness. One dissatisfied customer claimed a knife wasn't sharp enough to suit his taste. Nazem insisted it was. The argument sailed back and forth from temperate to tempest until Nazem insulted the man's mother. But in the end Nazem proved his point. For the knife that the customer claimed wasn't sharp enough sliced upward through Nazem and into his heart. The funeral—Lily turned the letter sideways—was a grand affair. Everyone came to see Nazem buried in the ground and to see Leah's reaction. All were surprised to find her genuinely sorry

Nazem was dead, as if she enjoyed the beatings he gave her. She made quite a scene at the grave site, claiming that now her children would be practically orphans. Several of the women shouted at Leah for that and tried to strike her with their fists, but the men had held them off and Leah was allowed to flee the cemetery without the appropriate mob following her. And then Leah Haya had simply disappeared. Love, Rebecca.

Lily put the letter down, mystified and annoyed. That was just like Rebecca to end her letter on a high point with Lily waiting for the next installment, which wouldn't come for a couple of months at least. Well, she knew one thing at least: Nazem Haya was dead. She supposed she better go down and break the good news to her mother and father. "Joshua!" she called. She found her son naked in the backyard hosing himself.

Danielle finished listening to Joseph, then put the phone down. Stunned, she stood in the dining hall, not moving. One of the men reading a newspaper came up to her. "What is it, Danielle?"

She looked to him. "My father is dead. He's been murdered."

The man was horrified. "But that's awful." He put his arm around her. Suddenly she felt faint.

"I must tell my brothers," she said, trying to pull herself upright.

"Sit down. You've got to sit down and rest." He led her to a chair but her legs doubled beneath her. He picked her up and carried her to the infirmary. By the time they reached it, she was crying copiously. "My brothers," she kept saying. They gave her some medicine to drink and told her to relax. Her eyes closed in spite of her willing them open. Her father dead, murdered, knifed, her mother vanished. She dreamed about her mother that night, her mother struggling to reach her as she had struggled to leave her mother's womb.

* * *

"It's not me," Diane screamed at her husband. "Physically there is nothing wrong with me. That's what the doctor says. Now you've got to go in to see him."

Hillel felt like hitting her, felt like kicking the crap out of her. But women were not to be touched. At least not in that way. If only she were a man.

He didn't know why his marriage was unraveling, other than the fact that they couldn't have a kid. Diane didn't understand the pressures. She probably thought it was easy to suck up to her old man at work, then come home to face her at night.

All right, he wasn't being fair. Diane was the perfect match for him. If their fathers had arranged it, he couldn't have done any better. As a piece of goods, she was quality. Good-looking, solid, well-formed hips, college-educated, but nothing too deep, English major. A good cook, a good hostess, a good woman. Barren.

If Hillel had been in Iraq, he would have returned her to her parents. But they were in America. Sometimes he thought she had served her purpose, now was the time to move on. He had to scramble for a place in her father's firm when he first came to the United States. It hadn't been easy. Those were days he didn't want to think back on. He wasn't one who derived pleasure from insecurity. In that he was uniquely un-American. No, the days when he struggled both for his livelihood and for Diane were days better left to his nightmares. And now that he had both, he didn't know whether he wanted either. He was taking on a goodly portion of the new work coming into the firm. He thought often of breaking out, starting his own consulting firm. He was good. He was bright. He had always been. But there would be hard years at first if he went out on his own. And he had had enough hard years in Israel. Maybe if Diane's father would make him a partner, maybe then. But fat chance of that without a grandchild to play on.

And what about Diane? Should he trade her in for a new, more fertile model? But how could he possibly explain divorce to his family in Israel? They would want to know why, what was wrong. If he could tell them she was barren, they would understand. But he had already invented a son for himself to cover the humiliation he felt from being married three years without issue. So how could Diane be barren when there was "Brian"?

"Hal, please listen to me," Diane begged.

She had not even worn to bed one of her light, flowing things. It was strictly a cotton pj's night. Well, that was all right, he wasn't in the mood anyway, hadn't been for months, not with all her charts and thermometers. Who ever heard of having a baby with charts and thermometers. He took a good look at her. An accident: That was a possibility. He could divorce Diane, meanwhile write his parents to tell them Diane and Brian had died tragically in a fiery car accident on Route 128. That way he could get rid of Diane and still have the sympathy of his mother, though he wondered how his mother would bear up to losing her only grandchild aside from Lily's, whose child didn't really count anyway because what could Joseph produce in the way of quality.

"Why won't you go to the doctor?" Diane asked tiredly.

"Because I am a man."

"What does that have to do with it? I'm a woman and I went."

"Women go to doctors. It's their sort of thing."

"But, Hal, I'm telling you, the doctor said there was nothing wrong with me. He just wants to check you out."

"Have you ever known me to fail to perform?"

"I'm not discussing your technique, I'm discussing your sperm count."

"If you were a child, Diane, I would wash your mouth out with soap."

"Are you afraid of finding out there is something wrong with you?"

"No one in my family has ever had any trouble having children."

"It's no reflection on you, you know. It's just something that happens in nature."

206

"Are you trying to tell me I'm not man enough for you?"

"It has nothing to do with being a man, Hal. If you have a cold, you're not a man?" She studied him and suddenly thought she understood his fears. "You're all the man I want," she said kindly.

"Don't patronize me."

"I just want to know. I want to know so we can plan the rest of our lives."

Car accident definitely.

"When will you go see the doctor?" she whispered.

"When he finds out what's wrong with you and he wants to let me know what to do about it."

15

"She's back."

"Shoshana!" Lily was annoyed. Her sister had scared the wits out of her. Shoshana stood in the hallway in her dark green poncho dripping rain into a dozen puddles. "Look what you're doing to my floor," Lily moaned.

Shoshana threw off her poncho in one dramatic gesture. "I'll stay in Joshua's room. Don't worry, I've brought a few extra pair of underwear so you won't have to wash out my clothes."

"What is going on? Take your boots off!" Lily yelled at her husband, who had the misfortune to enter the house immediately after Shoshana. "Look at the mud!" Lily went to the veranda and got the sponge while Joseph took off his boots and carefully tried to avoid the puddles Shoshana had created.

"Wreaking havoc again?" he asked his sister-in-law as he kissed her on the cheek.

Shoshana smiled widely, then remembered her purpose. "I'm staying with you for a while, maybe forever until I go into the army."

"Why? Not that we wouldn't be delighted to have you, of course."

"Because—"

"Because she's back," Lily cut in.

"You knew," Shoshana said, surprised. "But how?"

"You told me when you came in."

"Who's back?" Joseph asked.

Shoshana looked to her sister and was pleased to see she had her audience well in hand. "Leah," she said carefully.

"Leah? Leah Haya?" Lily asked, forgetting the mud on the floor. Shoshana nodded triumphantly. "But when?"

"When does the hand of God strike us down? When we least expect it."

"Forget the hand of God for the moment and get to Leah," Joseph advised.

"I left for school this morning. I came home, she was there. She had already moved into my room and taken my bed because it was softer and Mother was sure I would understand. Leah saw me and wept."

"That's understandable," Lily put in.

"Said I reminded her of her dear, dear Danielle, who was in her thoughts every day of her life, not to mention her wonderful Ezra and Albert, how she longed to see them and give them the mother's care she knew they were lacking. I nearly puked."

"I hope you didn't say—"

"Of course I did," she informed her brother-in-law. "I told her I thought her concern came a little late, considering the fact that she had willfully deserted them, despicably leaving them to fend for themselves, parentless, without love, for a full eight years."

"Good for you, Shoshana. And what did she say to that?" Lily asked.

"Nothing. She merely complained about the size of my room, told Mother she was used to better things in Tehran, had Mother apologizing for our apartment," Shoshana finished indignantly.

Lily was disgusted. "She knew Mother was the only one softhearted enough to let her move in with her."

"What does Meir say?" Joseph asked.

"Father wasn't home yet."

"Then don't unpack your bag. I have a feeling your room is going to become suddenly available to you again."

"You'll leave tomorrow, Leah," Meir thundered.

"Meir, Meir." Salemah trailed him around the apartment. "It's a mitzvah to take Leah in," she whispered.

"For one night it's a mitzvah. After that it's sheer stupidity."

"I didn't expect rose petals and trumpets," Leah said, "but to be cast out without pity."

"What can you expect after what Nazem did to everyone and what you did to your own children?"

"Nazem, Nazem. It's always Nazem," she answered him. "Well, Nazem's dead. Leave him in peace."

"No one will ever forget what he did to us, stealing our money."

"What good did it do him? Anyway, you still have your life, don't you?"

"Even an Arab would have had more honor," Meir spat at her. "And you, what you did to your children?"

"They were better off. Think back, Meir. Those were hard times."

"For all of us," Meir agreed. "And many of us were forced to send our children away. But we told them where they were going and why. We didn't just abandon them."

"What could I have done?" Leah cried. "It was either Nazem or the children."

Meir didn't know whether to pity or be disgusted with her stupidity. "Tomorrow, Leah, you leave." He turned to Salemah. "I'll take my supper in my room."

Salemah looked hopelessly after her husband, then turned to Leah and shrugged.

"A fine welcome back," Leah said, greatly offended.

Leah spent a comfortable night despite her troubles. That silly Shoshana's bed was soft and inviting, unlike the straw pallet on the floor she was forced to use in Tehran. Meir's apartment was full of nice things, the bathroom for instance. She didn't have to go outside to use a common privy. And the apartment had hot water, which she might use to take a bath. She could see that it paid Meir well to become a Zionist. Now she would have to hope Zionism would be just as beneficial to her.

No one had told Danielle what was going to happen. Afterward she felt a phone call would have been a pleasing alternative to the shock she was about to receive. But instead she and Ezra and Albert were summoned before a very grave-looking Avi, the *mazkir* or manager of the kibbutz, and told to sit down. It was an office well known to all three of them, not that they had been inside it that often, but it figured prominently in all kibbutz gossip. It was here where the blood was set flowing, where political and moral assassinations took place, where the howls of victory and the rumbles of defeat took on the proportions of a giant screen epic. But today the room was calm, as solemnity swallowed the passions that rose and fell in this room.

Danielle knew immediately that her mother was dead. Why else would all three of them have been summoned here?

"You're to leave us," Avi said.

"No!" Ezra replied. He broke his hand away from Danielle who held onto both his and Albert's.

"Your mother has returned. She has an apartment waiting for you in Tel Aviv. The truck will be here to pick you up in about an hour."

"So we're to be transported like cattle? We came here in a truck, we can leave here in one too!" Ezra shouted in a rage.

"It's not my doing," Avi said, puzzled and hurt. "I would—we all would love to keep you here. But your mother's back and she wants you."

"And when she goes away again and doesn't want us anymore, then what shall we do?"

"You always have a home here."

"Do you mean that?" Ezra asked.

"Would I have said it if I didn't mean it?"

212

"I'm not going to stay with her," Ezra told Danielle once they were out of Avi's office.

"It's not 'her,' it's your mother," Danielle said.

"How can you say that?" he asked in anger. "You're dumb, Danielle, really dumb."

"The kibbutz is our mother and our father," Albert said by rote.

"I hate her."

"You don't know her," Danielle protested. "We have to give her a chance."

"Why? You never liked it here, did you?" Ezra accused.

"I never felt comfortable living here, that's true," Danielle admitted.

"You'll be glad to go back to her."

Danielle thought about it. She didn't know how she would feel seeing her mother again. Curious maybe. But her mother wasn't the reason she looked forward to going to Tel Aviv. "I'll be glad to be myself again," she told Ezra.

"I'm not staying," Ezra threatened.

"You don't have to. Avi said that, didn't he?"

"What does our mother look like anyway?" Albert asked.

Danielle and Ezra looked to each other and smiled. "Last time I saw her, she looked wet," Ezra said, remembering the rain at Beit Lidd.

"It was awful," Danielle said with a shudder. "And the day she left, you had just peed in your pants, as usual."

"I did not!" They laughed at him. "Well, I don't do it anymore," he pointed out correctly.

They dispersed then to their various houses to pack their things. Danielle was alone in her house, as the other girls were in school. She didn't have much to pack, several white blouses and a blue skirt, some workshirts, a pair of jeans, a khaki outfit for youth groups and competitions. She packed them away in a shopping bag she had. She was startled when the door to her house swung open and Osnat rushed toward her. "I just heard," Osnat said breathlessly. "Avi should have told us first, but as usual he acts in his own high-handed manner." Danielle smiled. "I thought I had missed you."

"No," Danielle said. "I think we have around half an hour."

Osnat sat down on Danielle's bed. She was heavy with her third child. "Well, you're getting what you always wanted."

"A chance to return home."

"Things won't be easy, you know. Avi says your mother's on welfare, so you'll probably live in a slum apartment in a bad neighborhood. They're not like we are down there in Tel Aviv. Don't laugh at me, Danielle."

"I'm sure I'll survive it," Danielle said.

"Oh, everyone can survive. We survived the Germans, we survived the Arabs. I know what you're thinking, you've survived Kibbutz Vered." Danielle didn't answer. "We've never gotten along, Danielle, I know that. You've always managed to irritate me. But it's, well, I don't want you to leave Kibbutz Vered with any bad feelings. I know I've hurt you and I probably did everything wrong, but I honestly tried to do what I thought would be best for you. A different *metapelet* would have been better. We discussed this many times in Council. But the other *metaplot* felt that a child's relation to her *metapelet* is much like a child's to her mother. Sometimes it is all love, sometimes there's a mutual antagonism that springs up, like between two strong-willed women. And you certainly had the strongest will I ever ran into."

"Sorry."

"Don't be sorry about it. Better to be strong-willed than to be pushed around."

"I thought it was better to bend than break."

"There you go again," Osnat made her see. "Anyway, what was I saying? I guess it was just—I hope, well, I hope I didn't ruin your life."

Danielle studied Osnat. She too had grown since Danielle had been on the kibbutz. Older, she was married now and had two, almost three, children of her own. Danielle sat down alongside Osnat and slowly, carefully put her arms around her, something she had never done before. Osnat felt soft and slightly puffy and yes, even comforting.

She wanted to tell Osnat that she loved her, but the words wouldn't come because they were untrue. She remembered even now in the glow of parting how many times Osnat had made her life miserable. So instead Danielle said, "No one can ruin my life. I won't let them. Not you, not even my own mother."

"So you think there might be trouble then?" Osnat said.

Danielle stood. "I don't know. I haven't seen her for some years. I don't know what to expect."

"There'll always be a home for you here."

"Yes. That's what Avi said too." But Danielle knew no matter how hard it might be with her mother, she would never come back to the kibbutz, not of her own free will.

Osnat and several others from the kibbutz waited with the Haya children for the truck to come. At the last moment Avi let out Ezra's and Albert's classes so they could wish them farewell. Danielle's classmates were at the regional high school. When the truck came, it was an open pick-up.

"I swear it's the same damn truck," Ezra said.

"It looks a little newer," Danielle told him seriously. They climbed up and gave Albert a helping hand.

"I'll be back," Ezra vowed as the truck pulled away from the kibbutz.

The roar of the engine and the speed of the wind against them made conversation difficult in the back of the truck as it headed toward Hadera, then Tel Aviv. But Danielle felt she had to make an effort with Ezra. She moved over to him and shouted in his ear. "Promise me you'll give it time."

"A week," he answered.

"A week is barely enough to say hello, good-bye. One month."

"A month! That's four weeks."

"A month. Promise me."

He looked at her and nodded. "I'll hate every moment of it though," he swore.

After Herzliya they all moved onto their knees and kept an eye out for Tel Aviv. The sand rolled on almost up to the road and they feared they would never see the city itself. Then it began. More sand, more sea, then the shacks, the villas, the apartment buildings, the city itself. Danielle was excited. She had passed through Tel Aviv several times on class trips and on the way to overnights on the Negev kibbutzim. But to actually live here, to be a part of the city, to be able to call on Shoshana every day of her life. It would be heaven. "Katznelson, Katznelson!" she cried out.

"Katznelson," Albert responded. "One of the leaders of the Labor movement and the founder of *Davar*, the Mapai newspaper."

"No, stupid. Katznelson. It's the street Shoshana lives on."

They turned off Katznelson and drove down almost an entire block before the truck rumbled to a stop. The apartment house they stood in front of was pale green and flaking. The sidewalk in front of it was littered with sunflower seeds and orange peels. Danielle looked up. "We'll have a balcony," she said to the boys, noticing the black railing above them.

An old woman came up the steps from the basement, what Danielle assumed to be the bomb shelter. She looked at the three of them and then to the truck driver.

"Are these the ones?"

"If you're Leah Haya, then these are your children."

Danielle fell back in shock. It couldn't be her mother. Not the mother with long, black hair and perfect teeth, hands so soft and body slender. Not this old woman with gray, tangled hair, two black teeth, slovenly. The driver gave the woman a form to sign and Danielle watched while her mother—it must be—carefully formed each letter of her name.

Ezra got back up on the truck and handed down to each their bags of clothing. Danielle looked to him and felt like telling him to stay on the truck, to go back to the kibbutz. But he remembered his promise and jumped down to join her. The driver wished them well and then sped off.

"I'm your mother," the old woman on the sidewalk said. "Remember me?"

They all shook their heads. She came up to each of them, called them by their name, and embraced them. Danielle had always felt no matter where she was in the world, if her mother came up to her and spoke her name, she would recognize her. Yet she did not know this woman, and she was at this point very uncertain if she wanted to know her.

"Come, we'll go inside," Leah said. The three children followed her down the steps into the basement apartment.

"It's a dungeon," Ezra said.

"And she's our torturer," Albert added with a snicker.

"None of that," Danielle shushed them.

"What's that?" Leah asked, as she turned sharply around. No one answered her. "How do you like it?" The children looked around them. It was one large room with two alcoves, one the bathroom, the other the kitchen.

"Where do we sleep?" Albert asked.

"I have mattresses for the floor. Look, the Sokhnut's given me blankets. That's only till they get in a new supply of cots."

Ezra turned his back on his mother. "A month is too long. We'll have to renegotiate."

"Three weeks."

"Two."

"Done."

"Of course, this is only the beginning," Leah said. "Danielle's fourteen. She can already go to work. And in two years, Ezra, you can leave school. I wish it could be sooner, but the authorities insist I keep you in school until the eighth grade. But more of this later. Who do you think has invited us to dinner? The Ewans!"

Shoshana's presence and Salemah's made life bearable for Danielle. They were her family now, her own mother a mere encumbrance. Danielle had no objection when Ezra and Albert wanted to return to Kibbutz Vered after two weeks. If they had not decided to return, she would have insisted they go.

"But you must come with us," Ezra implored.

"No."

"How can you endure it?"

"I'll manage."

"It's pride."

"No, you're wrong, Ezra," Danielle told him. "Yes, it would be admitting failure if I went back to the kibbutz. In that you're right. There is a certain amount of pride. But here I have Shoshana. And the whole Iraqi community."

"But you also have Mother," Ezra reminded his sister.

"I'll handle her," Danielle said coldly. She held her brothers tight, then watched them board the bus to the central station. She knew they weren't making a mistake. She didn't know whether she was, yet.

It was guerrilla warfare with an adversary less honorable than Osnat, but Danielle soon gained certain tactical advantages. She sought out the welfare official who had dealt with her mother's case. From her Danielle found out that since her family had no means of support, welfare would provide her with a grant to finish her high school education, especially since she had already begun it. She presented her mother with this fact.

"But I don't agree to it," Leah said. "You get out there, work, and make us some money."

"Do you insist upon this, Mother?"

"I do."

"Then I will notify the welfare department that I am returning to the kibbutz. Which means they'll take this apartment from you and you'll be out on the streets again, without even a roof."

Leah made her pay for her triumph in other ways. Leah was always too sick to fix meals, too tired to do the housework. It didn't bother Danielle. She would do the work expected of her, then flee to Shoshana's, where Leah would not go because she feared Meir. Then late at night she would sneak home and sleep, waiting for the morning sun when she could escape her home again.

16

"You won't change your mind?" Ovadia asked as he nervously paced through their apartment.

"Why does it bother you so?" Shoshana asked. "You work with girl soldiers all the time. Am I any less qualified than they are?"

He threw himself down in the chair opposite her. "It's just that I think your attitude is all wrong. You think it's going to be fun, adventurous, exciting. Wrong. You're going to be hot and sticky doing your basic training, and during the rest of your army service you'll be bored, just marking time."

"Did Mother put you up to this?"

"You could be going to a university, starting your career. You're a bright girl, but they won't recognize that. You'll end up as some file clerk with some captain chasing you around his desk, or as a teacher in some godforsaken Arab village, or as a nurse's aide."

"But I know what I want to do."

"Wonderful. Do you think the army cares?"

"They've given you a pretty good job."

"Computers? Only dummies work with computers. The real math is in one's head."

Shoshana couldn't really see how her brother could complain. He had a rather nice job setting up the first computer system the Israeli air force had ever used. He worked in Tel Aviv, he could come home every night, except when he was on night duty. He had never complained except when she talked about going into the army herself. She was sure it was Mother.

Shoshana didn't understand why everyone was upset. She had given them plenty of warning. She had been reasonable enough to agree that if she didn't pass her *bagrut*, her comprehensive high school exams, she would stay home, study, and retake them. But by her total score she was fifth in her class. She thought Danielle would understand but Danielle totally failed her. "You're religious," Danielle had pointed out.

"No."

"But your family is religious. You could easily get an exemption."

"How could I possibly claim to be Israeli if I didn't do my duty to my country?"

"Fifty percent of the girls don't serve."

"Shame on them."

"Fifty percent feel it is their duty to stay home, work to support their family, marry, have children. Why can't you consider marriage instead of the army?"

"I'm not that masochistic." She shrugged Danielle off.

Lily came bursting into the apartment carrying Joshua. "Is she ready?"

"I've been ready since last night," Shoshana answered nervously.

"I hope you know you're breaking Mother's heart."

"Oh, Lily," Ovadia said sharply. "Why can't you two stop it? Every time either of you does something the other doesn't like, you bring up Mother. I think we should stop worrying about Mother and be more concerned about Shoshana's welfare."

"I've never seen Shoshana in a situation where she couldn't take care of herself."

"Exactly," Shoshana said.

"At the expense of everyone else of course. Joseph sends his love and best wishes, by the way."

Salemah came out of the kitchen with a shopping bag full of fruits, vegetables, and cakes. Shoshana gave Ovadia a look. "You can share it with others in your barracks."

"You're going," Salemah said to her daughter.

"Basic training's only six weeks, Mother. Then I'll be back to see you."

Salemah turned away. She didn't understand this one, not at all. What could her daughter possibly want with the army? To leave home for six weeks! No Iraqi woman left home until she went to her husband's. And times could not have changed that much. She didn't think Shoshana had any idea of the disgrace she was bringing to her family.

Ovadia checked his watch. "We have to go," he said. Shoshana stood up quickly. She embraced Lily, gave Joshua a kiss, then came to her mother. Salemah had hoped for a reprieve, but all she saw in her daughter's eyes was the desire to escape. "Nothing can possibly happen to me, Mother," Shoshana whispered as they embraced.

"Remember to hold on to your virginity," Lily said quietly as Shoshana marched to the door.

"I've already held on to it longer than you did," Shoshana shot back.

"I'll see you tonight," Ovadia shouted, as he dragged Shoshana through the door. He took her bag from her and then hurried down the stairs. "Impossible as usual," he told her.

"Not everyone spends his life trying to appease people the way you do."

"Not everyone spends her life starting minor brushfires either," Ovadia admonished.

They stood on the street corner and gave one last wave before they boarded the bus. They took seats and smiled happily at each other. They were free. Shoshana sensed

Ovadia felt it too: As soon as he left the apartment, he was free to be whatever he wanted. So close were their thoughts, she felt he understood her and would support her always.

When they got to the embarkation point, she let Ovadia pick through the crowd of eighteen-year-old girls to find out which bus she should board. It was easier just to stand over to the side and watch everyone milling about. Ovadia pushed his way back through the crowd, grabbed her by the arm, and dragged her to the right line.

"Any words of last advice?" she asked.

"Yes," he said quietly. "Keep your Uzzi clean. They're sticklers about that in the army."

"Right."

"Don't ask any questions."

"What if I don't understand something though?"

"Don't ask any questions," he repeated. "When you ask a question, you ask for trouble. Listen for orders. Don't ask for them to be repeated. Don't volunteer for anything. Keep your eyes downcast on all such occasions. And, Shoshana, there is something I didn't tell you when you were home, in case Mother overheard. There's an expression for new recruits. They're called fresh meat. Can you guess why?"

"Because they are going to pound us into shape?"

"Or feed you to the lions. Shoshana, they are not nice in the army. Yes, sir, or no, sir, should be sufficient for everything. None of your wisecracks."

"Yes, sir." She giggled, only stopping when the bus doors flipped open and the order was given to board.

"Courage," Ovadia said.

"Hold down the home front, Lieutenant." They embraced quickly and she snapped him a salute.

When she got on the bus and it pulled away, Shoshana looked around. She realized that even though everyone was from the Tel Aviv area, she knew not a single girl. She smiled tentatively at the girl sitting next to her, who smiled back, then returned to her copy of *The Magic Mountain* by Thomas Mann. Shoshana only wished she had brought along Ovadia's copy of *Gone with the Wind*. It was obvious from the pockets of noise that many of the girls on the bus knew each other. There was a whole group in front from the Alliance along with a smattering from Ovadia's high school, Tichon Hadash, but from Givatayim only herself.

She felt better once they arrived at the sorting camp near Tel Hashomer, where they would stay for two or three days to be processed into the army. As they disembarked from the bus they were lined up, and those who had been chattering together on the bus ever since Tel Aviv were told to be quiet. It was a new beginning. They were about to become different people. She followed orders. She stood in line. She got her clothes. She stood in line. She got her barracks. Try on the clothes, fix the clothes, the boots were too big, use two pairs of socks. They were heavy, uncomfortable. Tough. They all sounded like elephants as they clomped across the wooden floor in combat boots. Her skirt needed a tuck in the waist. She did that. Then she decided it was too long. She took the hem up a little bit above regulation length. Everyone was doing it. She tried on the skirt again with her oxfords and her white socks. She looked like a grandmother. She put her blouse on over her cotton bra and tucked it into her skirt. She took her hat and went to the common bathroom where mirrors lined the wall. She waited, she jostled for a chance to see herself. Her face came into view. She slipped her hat on and smiled. She was a soldier.

Shoshana was glad when her time at Tel Hashomer was over. She had been in a three-day limbo, meeting other girls but really doing nothing except talking about boys, or if she sat near Miriam Levy, politics. It wasn't what she expected of the army. She hadn't believed the army would be as infected with paperwork as the rest of Israeli life, but she knew from the sorting camp she had been wrong.

When she boarded the second bus, she knew that this time it was the real thing. She even looked like a soldier in her new uniform and heavy backpack. Miriam also had been assigned to her basic training camp. She was glad.

223

Even though she didn't understand most of what Miriam was saying on the trip up. Yes, they were going north to the Galilee. She didn't really know anything about the Galilee except from her visits to Kibbutz Vered. Both Ovadia and Joseph had done their basic in the Negev. She remembered Ovadia saying something like it was harder to dig a foxhole in the Galilee because it wasn't all sand like the Negev. She supposed that would be a part of her training, as she carried a folded shovel in her pack. Once they got to the camp, they were quickly assigned barracks, told to stow their gear and report to the parade ground. Which meant that everyone threw their packs next to their cots and rushed into the common bathroom before hurrying outside once more to line up at attention.

It was funny what happened to them as the weeks passed. Shoshana didn't think there was any one of them in the barracks who hadn't cried hysterically at one time or another. But they were getting tougher and stronger and more cohesive. The spoiled brats from the cities, the North Africans from the Negev, the independent girls from the kibbutzim were all becoming one. They stuck up for each other now, they fought for each other, they shared, they helped each other out.

When the day came and assignments were handed out, many were disappointed. The army did not see fit to send Miriam to an Arab school to teach as she had hoped. They didn't even see fit to send her to a Jewish school. Instead she was to be sent to the air force to become an air traffic controller.

"Well, at least it's not a mechanic," Shoshana tried to cheer her up.

"One of the corporals whispered to me that they considered me too political to be a teacher."

"But conscientious. You have to be conscientious to work in air traffic control. And who knows, you might meet and marry a pilot."

"God, Shoshana, pilots only marry pretty plastic girls with huge smiles and rich fathers. They don't want anyone who can actually think."

"Well, don't rule it out."

"And you?"

"Who will I marry?"

"No, stupid, what did you get?"

Shoshana smiled and unfolded her patch and insignia. "Intelligence!" Miriam shouted, excited for her. It had been Shoshana's dream.

When Shoshana returned home, she found everyone waiting. They had arranged a party for her, and even many of the neighbors dropped by to say hello, how are you doing, congratulations. Shoshana found herself mostly sitting on the couch with Ovadia and Joseph, exchanging army stories. She noticed Danielle looking at her enviously. She hoped this would convince her to join the army when her time came.

Meir could barely face it. It hadn't been so bad when she went off. He had given her his blessing the night before and left early the next morning to miss her departure. But now she was back, in uniform, looking fit and glowing. "Do you think she's changed?" Salemah asked him.

Of course she's changed, Meir felt like saying. You can see it in her, the way she holds herself, the way she laughs and talks. She is no longer a part of us, no meek, submissive Iraqi girl willing to do her parents' and her husband's bidding. She was Israeli now, through and through. The state had claimed her and made her independent. All her parents could do now was hope for the best.

"I'm so starved, Mother, you wouldn't believe it!" Shoshana shouted when Salemah finally served the meal. "The food in the army is awful. And every once in a while they tried to make an Oriental dish, something besides goulash and more goulash, and it tasted like goat turd."

"Shoshana!"

"Well, I'm sorry, Father, but it did. Rice floating in oil and water. Even the canned rations were better." Shoshana sat down and grabbed at the food while her father quickly said the blessing over the bread. By the time he had finished, his daughter's mouth was full.

"The religious girls don't serve," Ovadia reminded his father with a smile.

"Well, I'm glad you're home," Salemah said.

"Where she can keep an eye on you," Lily added with a twinkle.

"I won't be home for long," Shoshana warned her. "Sunday I have to report to my new base."

"But you'll sleep here?" Salemah asked, suddenly worried.

"Yes. And, more importantly, I'll eat here."

Ovadia was in the bathroom when she woke up Sunday morning. She was obviously going to have to fight him for it now that they both had to get ready for work at the same time. When he came out, he was dressed and ready to go. "Good luck," he told her.

She quickly washed and dressed and waved off her mother's offer of breakfast. Not this morning. This morning she was too nervous to eat. Once she was on the road, she had to transfer buses, which made her half an hour late. She was afraid she would be marked AWOL. But at the army gate no one seemed to care. They checked her identification and sent her to the commander's office. That's when her trouble started, because no one knew who she was or why she was supposed to report.

"Well, what do you do?" the commander's assistant asked.

"Translations," Shoshana answered hopefully.

"Oh. That would be Colonel Tal. He's the second building over."

"Right. I should go there?"

"Unless you have something better to do."

Well, no, she didn't.

It was hard to find anyone in the second building willing to take even the slightest interest in her. There were a lot of people in a large open room who seemed to be either buried under huge stacks of paper or rushing back and forth madly across the room.

"*Slicha,* excuse me," she said to one young soldier.

He looked up at her and said in English, "Do you know the Hebrew word for green?"

She was puzzled. "*Yeroq,*" she said.

"Ah. That puts things in a different light." He went back to work.

She was horrified. She had heard the ulpans, where they taught Hebrew intensively, were bad, but they could have at least taught this poor boy the colors.

She moved farther into the hall, trying to find Colonel Tal. She saw a lieutenant staring at her. "Do you—" she started, but he held up his hand and stared past her. She walked on out the large room into a narrow corridor. She traveled down one side of the corridor and then up the other.

"Are you looking for the bathroom?"

The light streamed out from the end office and she couldn't see who was talking to her.

"No," she said rather indignantly. "I'm looking for Colonel Tal, if he exists."

"Ah," he said. "I think I can find him for you. If you'll step this way."

She moved past him and went before him into the office. When he closed the door and moved around her, she saw the *felafels* of a colonel. She was about to salute but he paid no attention to her, looking beneath his seat cushion and under his desk.

"What are you doing?" she asked.

"Looking for Colonel Tal."

"But—but you're Colonel Tal. Your nameplate—"

"Ah, so I am. I knew we would find him if we looked hard enough."

She giggled.

He was immediately taken with her. "What a pretty laugh you have. Are you a virgin?"

She blushed deeply. "Mother was right about the army," she muttered.

He smiled. "Sit down," he said, "and tell me what I can do for you."

"Well, no," she said, taking a seat, "it's what I'm supposed to do for you."

"Oh. Then you're not a virgin."

She cringed backward into her seat. This lieutenant colonel was a madman.

"Name. What's your name?"

"Shoshana—uh, Private Ewan."

"Shoshana. And you can call me David except when I get angry. Then it's Colonel with a salute. Now you were told to report here?"

"No one seems to know where I'm to go. I went over to the commanding officer's and no one had my name down anywhere. I just got out of basic training and told them I did translations so they sent me here."

"And do you do translations?"

"Oh, yes. I'm very good."

"No doubt. What do you translate?"

"Arabic mainly. But I know—"

"Where are you from?"

"Iraq. I also can do French and English." But he had turned his back on her and was fishing through his shelves.

"Classical Arabic?" he threw out at her.

"Yes, and of course Iraqi from radio."

"What else?"

"Egyptian, sort of. I had a girl friend who was Egyptian."

He found what he was looking for and threw it over to her. "Translate," he ordered.

It was the transcript of a speech. She looked it over quickly before starting. "Comrades," she began. "Members of the Ba'athist Brotherhood." She read down the page translating as she went while he listened to her. He stopped her several times to ask questions. "Why did you use 'totalitarian' instead of 'facist'?"

"It seemed to fit," she answered. He said nothing. She went on. The speech was twenty typewritten pages long. By the time she finished, she was mentally exhausted from the strain of simultaneously translating.

When she had completed the speech, he stared at her for a while and said, "Not bad."

"Not bad?" she questioned, rather proud of herself. "What did I do wrong?"

"You don't know the man. You don't know what he's trying to get across. You missed several of his nuances."

He got up and left the office. A minute later he came back with a captain. "Elias," he introduced them, "this is Shoshana Ewan. Elias is in charge of the Iraqi section. Shoshana will come to work for you."

"Can she type?" Elias asked.

"I don't know. Can you type, Shoshana?"

"If I can type, does that mean I can't translate?"

David was puzzled. "You two can decide if she can type or not."

They were dismissed. Elias took her back into the long, noisy hall and set her to work.

17

Jacob Ewan sat in his study, his face ashen. He placed his hand over his heart. It beat irregularly. His son, his Rahamin had just come before him and asked permission to marry. "You are too young," he told him immediately.

"Why, Father? I'm twenty. I'm a man. The girl is from a good family. They will offer a fine dowry."

"Dowry! And what will you do with it? Will you buy your happiness? Will you buy your freedom?"

"Father, please. Calm yourself. You know what the doctor says."

"I will outlive you, Rahamin, mark my words on it."

"Yes, Father."

His son stood bowed before him. His heart broke. "I want you to be happy," he said softly.

"I will be, Father. If I can marry Leila."

No, he would keep calm. "Rahamin, we have discussed your future before. I want you to go abroad to finish your studies."

"That can never be, Father."

"If we are very careful and we wait—"

"Father, we have been waiting two years, ever since the revolution. We will never be free."

"Rahamin!"

"Father, listen to me. They speak about you in certain quarters. You are on their list, Father."

"I have friends."

"Your friends are being taken away in the middle of the night and shot or thrown in prison. Father, you are not a communist and there is no way you can disguise yourself as one."

"His day will come," Jacob hoped.

"Kassem kills those who cross him. He kills those who he thinks even might one day cross him. Be thankful you are a merchant and not political or intellectual or you would be dead already." -

"How dare you speak like that to me?"

"I speak the truth, Father."

"And yet you dare talk of marriage when you expect your father to be dragged off to his death at any minute?"

"I'm only thinking of what you would want, Father. Because if they take you away, and I pray to God it never happens, they will confiscate everything. How will I get a wife then?"

Jacob considered what his son had to say. Rahamin had a point, a valid one, as much as Jacob didn't want to consider it. But if Rahamin married, he would have children. Every man does. And once he had children, he would never have a chance for freedom again. Whole families would not be released from Iraqi captivity. If only his son would receive permission to study overseas, then he would be safe. Maybe more money would do it, though he had already paid out a small fortune in bribes to no effect.

"Leila loves me."

"Why shouldn't she? You're a beautiful child," Jacob said absently. Rahamin came over and kissed his father's hand. "I feel in my heart this is wrong. But your argument does have merit. It would be better to see you settled before anything happens to me. Though if there is to be a wedding, it must be a small one. Nothing to draw attention to ourselves, nothing to stir envy."

"Then I may speak to Leila's father?"

"When the time comes, I will speak to Leila's father," Jacob said sharply. "You are not that skillful a negotiator yet. And besides, I have been thinking about the Kurdish border."

"There is a war going on there."

"More confusion."

"We are watched, Father. We cannot even leave Baghdad."

"If I could smuggle you out one at a time."

"And what would happen to you when they found either Ephraim or myself missing?"

"If you were safe, I wouldn't care."

"Father?"

"Give me time, Rahamin, give me time."

I should have married him, Diane Evans thought as she saw Walter de Gregory approaching her along the hospital corridor. She was not surprised to find him here. From her mother she knew Walter had a residency in pediatrics at Massachusetts General. As a matter of fact, she was amazed she had not run into him sooner. Now she saw him and smiled. He still looked like a teddy bear. Curly, golden hair, slightly flushed face, large, overpowering body. He had wanted to play football but his mother had been afraid he would damage his knees and end up in a wheelchair instead of in medical school. Those were the days. They had gone to high school together and dated occasionally when the urgings of their parents had become too great for Walter. She remembered how uncomfortable he had been on those dates, so uncomfortable it had made her unease seem mere modesty. Then they had gone off to the University of Massachusetts together, passing each other on campus until it became clear that neither had any romantic inclination toward the other. After that they would meet for coffee, in their senior year finally becoming friends. But he had gone on to medical school and she had stayed home waiting to get married. Not that they hadn't heard about each other or seen each other at the temple occasionally on holidays, when their parents would insist they attend, not for religious purposes but to be seen socially.

She blocked his path. He tried to move around her. She blocked his path again, forcing him to look up. How childishly she was acting. "Diane!" She laughed. He was pleased to see her. "What are you doing here?"

"Playing Lady Bountiful." Waiting to get pregnant actually.

"Oh. You're volunteering," he guessed.

"Yes." She was suddenly ashamed. They had gone to college together. He was a doctor, she a volunteer. She blushed.

"Can you come for coffee?" he asked.

"Well, I don't know. I was supposed to stand here and hold up this wall, but I guess I can chance it." She was pleased to see him smile.

It was funny how she missed having friends. She realized that when she sat down and talked to Walter. Marriage had wrenched her away from those she was closest to. It made her more dependent on Hal and Hal's friends, who were really business associates, less dependent on finding those who suited her own needs. She had no one she could really call up and talk to because what she had to say wouldn't be proper, and the people she came into contact with were definitely proper people. They didn't suffer. Or if they did, it was in the privacy of their souls, as even their bedroom was shared. She told Walter everything. How goofy he must find her.

Diane felt better when she went home that day than she had in weeks. She could even make dinner with a smile on her face. That's what it was like talking to Walter. Why couldn't she talk to Hal that way. Probably because they were married. Married couples didn't talk. Hal was in the room in their house set aside as his office when she came home. He barely answered her when she called her greetings. Well, who cared. She had survived another day.

* * *

234

Hillel looked at the letter. "Dearest Parents. And the rest of you: I have the sad duty to inform you that seven days ago my beautiful bride, Diane Shapiro Evans, and my God-given son, Brian, died in a fiery, four-car crash on Route 128. I am bereft and in dire need of your emotional support. I can't tell you how much Diane and Brian meant to me. If only I hadn't bought her that Thunderbird with all the money I've been making, perhaps this would never have happened. Your loving son in America, Hal." They were used to his new name by now.

That was settled. He had written them off. Now he just had to get his nerve up to tell Diane he was divorcing her.

Shoshana would never understand her mother. When Hillel's letter had come, Lily had practically gone into shock. Joseph even had to bring a doctor to their house. And all because Lily thought that what happened to Hillel's child could happen to her Joshua. She would not even let Joseph take Joshua anywhere in the truck after Hillel's letter. Her father had cried and asked why. She had studied the picture of the boy, her nephew, and tried to feel something. She was sorry for Hillel even though she disliked him and found his letter to them revolting. Even at another's death he put himself forward. Ovadia agreed. But what she felt was rather an absense of feeling, that this really wasn't connected to her, this didn't touch her, even as it should since Brian was only her second nephew. But her mother, to whom Brian and Joshua were the sun, said nothing of his death. And while each of them in his own way recovered from the shock of Hillel's letter, her mother stayed the same.

Shoshana asked her father what was happening. Naturally he didn't know. She didn't even think he noticed his wife's unspoken sorrow. She asked Ovadia. He told her not to butt in. Trust Ovadia to avoid trouble. But she couldn't leave it alone. She had to find out what was going on in her mother's mind. She asked of her mother, well, she would admit it, one of her stupider questions. "Do you feel bad about Brian, Mother? And about Diane, of course?"

235

"It's something I can understand," her mother replied.

"The accident?"

"The death." Salemah looked up at her daughter. "Come, I'll show you something." Salemah led Shoshana into her bedroom and took a jewelry box from her bureau drawer. She opened it and lifted the jewel case out. Underneath Shoshana saw several baby pictures. "That's us," she exclaimed.

"Yes," Salemah said. She took out the pictures and spread them on the coverlet. "Who are they?"

Shoshana picked them up and held them like a hand of cards. "This is me." She smiled and laid the picture down. "This is Lily of course. Ovadia. He had the curls. Then Hillel." She held one last picture in her hand. It looked like Brian and yet it didn't. It was too old and old-fashioned.

"Rose," her mother said.

"Rose?"

"She was born when Hillel was two. She died within the year of typhoid."

"But you never talked of her."

"What was there to say? She lived, she died. When it happened, well, that's a different story."

"What does this have to do with Brian?"

"You see, Shoshana, Rose tried to come back to me. I could see her face in Brian's and I was happy to retrieve what I had lost. But God saw fit to take her from me again, and what can I do but accept it. She was meant to be in heaven."

Shoshana was shocked by her mother's fatalism. "And what of Diane?" she shot back angrily.

"That you'll have to ask God about."

"Mother!"

"Shh. We each have to face life in our own way, Shoshana."

"Well, you can't just sit back, let things happen to you and accept them."

Salemah took Rose's picture from her daughter's hand. She studied it, then placed it back in the jewelry box with the others. "We can rush away from it or rush toward it, but the plan of our lives is set down and there is nothing we can do to change it."

"I don't believe you."

"You are young. You still have expectations."

"So should you."

Sad eyes haunted Salemah as she leaned over and kissed her daughter's cheek. "I have work to do," she said. She got up, put the box away, and walked into the kitchen.

Shoshana thankfully went off to work, where everything was basically normal and fatalism was a philosophy, not a way of life. She thought she was doing a good job in the translation bureau. Even though her boss Elias was cold and pedantic, she enjoyed her work. At first she translated mainly stark cut-and-dried official communiqués or radio transcripts or newspaper articles. But sometimes Elias would let her handle something more personal, something with a little bit of flair. Political commentary or, very rarely, personal papers. She enjoyed this most of all because she felt the thrill of throwing herself into someone else's personality. She felt herself merge with the person she was translating and go with him wherever his mind might take her. Even Elias would admire her work on these occasions. "Not bad," he would say.

Seven months after starting work for David Tal in translations, he called her into his office. She really hadn't seen much of him, had tried in many ways to shy away from him. Not that she didn't like him, but she heard he could be somewhat aggressive where women were concerned. It was funny because he wasn't that good-looking and he was always so serious about his work. But he had a good-natured warmth and he was the boss. Many of the girls in translations claimed to have slept with him. They would come in looking fagged out and say simply, "Spent the night with David." While David never seemed to look tired. She wondered. After all he was thirty-six and he had a wife and three children.

She entered his office with some trepidation and stood quietly by his door until he noticed her.

He gazed at her and smiled. "You're beautiful when you're shy," he began.

"I heard you spent last night with Karen," she said impulsively.

"Oooh!" He laughed. "Maybe you're not so shy after all. Anyway I'm sure Karen is nothing compared to you."

She hugged herself protectively. "Why do you always talk like that?"

"It makes women happy," he told her. "But come, sit down, we have work to do." She took a seat, pressed her knees together, and waited. "Elias says you're doing okay. You're being promoted to corporal."

"Thank you."

"That's just an aside. We need someone to go up north for a few weeks. Camp Het near Caesarea. We've brought out two people who worked for us in Iraq, one from Basra, one from the Kurdish highlands. We're having them debriefed, we need someone to handle the translations of the transcripts into Hebrew."

"The Basra one is okay, but I don't know about the Kurdish." Shoshana shook her head. "It's a pretty strange dialect."

"We have someone up there who speaks Kurdish. He'll work on that with you."

"All right."

"You can get away for a few weeks?"

"Of course."

"Avi's going up to Haifa tomorrow. Make arrangements to ride with him. Then report to Captain Gonen."

"Right."

"Good luck."

Shoshana explained why she had to go away to her parents. "I'm rushing toward it," she whispered to her mother. Salemah smiled and nodded.

"How long will you be gone?" her father asked sternly.

"I don't know. A few weeks David said."

"Men and women are together in the camp?"

"Yes, Father, but we sleep separately."

"I should hope so."

"Yes, Father."

"Behave yourself."

"Yes, Father."

It was a relief when Avi picked her up the next morning and they headed north.

That day was incredibly busy for her as after she reached camp, she was taken immediately to Captain Gonen, who placed her in a room with the transcripts and a typewriter. By the end of five hours she was wondering not only why they had to ask so many questions, but why they had to keep asking the same questions over and over again, varying the form very little or not at all.

"Take a break," Captain Gonen came in to tell her finally when she thought she couldn't translate another word. "You can use the time to acquaint yourself with our Kurdish expert."

She bumped into him in the hall. His name was Oren Kohan and he like she had come from Iraq, only not Baghdad but one of the isolated Jewish communities in the north that had a lot of contact with the Kurds.

"He's a real powerhouse, isn't he?" Oren said to her about Captain Gonen. Shoshana made a face. They spent their first half hour together complaining about Gonen's work habits, the next half hour deciding how to go about translating the transcripts.

"I haven't seen you at the translation bureau," she had said to him.

"I haven't been there. I don't know a damn thing about translating. I was just the guy who brought these characters out."

"You went back into Iraq?"

"The mountains. Who knows if it was Iraq or Iran."

"How did you get into that sort of work?" she asked.

"I was in the commandos and then transferred," Oren answered.

It was funny how when Oren said commandos, she had a sudden flash of Danny Ze'ev's face. It amazed her because she hadn't really thought of him for almost a year, so full had her life become with finishing high school, doing

239

basic training, and now working at her job which she loved. "I knew someone who was thinking of going into the commandos once. It was a long time ago."

"Oh, yeah? What was his name?"

She laughed. Danny would be a straw in a haystack to Oren. "It doesn't matter."

They went together to dinner, and when they were in line, Captain Gonen came over to ask them how the work was going. "It's moving right along," Oren told him.

"When can I have it?" Gonen asked.

"A week or so."

Gonen was about to object but just gave them a grim look and walked away.

"We'll be hearing from him," Oren promised her. Then he led her over to a long table that was filled with his friends. She felt strange being the only woman in a group of men, especially these men since they all seemed so rough and boisterous. Anyway she was nervous and that's probably why she jumped when she heard someone call her name.

"Shoshana?" She looked up. "Shoshana Ewan?"

She couldn't believe it. A moment ago she had thought of him and now he appeared? Now when she no longer cared that much. Not like when she was a junior in high school and dreamed about him all the time. She recognized him right away, though he looked older than she had remembered him, more, much more mature. Lines around his eyes and mouth. He rose from the bench where he was sitting and brought his coffee cup over to her, making a place for himself and sitting with his back to the table.

"Danny Ze'ev. Remember me?"

"Of course," she said and smiled.

"How are your parents?" he asked and smiled back. Oh, God, she loved that smile.

She immediately forgot about Oren and the transcripts until Oren interrupted them and told her he would see her tomorrow morning. Five, it had to be, because they started interrogations at six.

"*Nu*," Danny said to her when he had finished his coffee. "Shall we go for a walk?"

He took her down to the sea where they walked along the sand and talked. He was delighted by her. She was still perfectly shy and easily impressed. She wore the blush of ripe, sweet fruit. It made him angry all of a sudden to think that she could keep her innocence while he had been traipsing through the muck of guerrilla warfare, where nothing remained to him except his sanity and his honor. He caught what she was saying, something about working in translations. "So you got your wish?"

"I'm surprised you remembered," she said.

"Oh, I remember everything about that night," he said, pleasing her.

"And you, did you ever become a commando?"

"Oh, yes," he said with bitterness.

"Was it what you wanted?"

"At the time." He studied her. She was puzzled. But of course she wasn't with them two days ago when they had brought back Eli's body, not there when they analyzed their mission, tried to decide what, if anything, had gone wrong. Absent when he tried to keep his voice calm and even while he spoke, because he was in charge of the mission and Eli was his responsibility and now Eli was dead and for God's sake, what had he done wrong? He wanted to scream, to howl his grief like some wild animal, but commanders didn't react to the madness of it all, because commanders accepted casualties as a part of life, even when the casualties were your friends and you had lived with them closely for two years.

"What's wrong?" she asked.

She was so perfect. So dark and perfect that he had to have her. She wouldn't mind. She would understand. He had to have her now.

"We better be getting back," she said.

Oh, yes, she was an animal, that one. She sensed danger and she was ready to sprint. But he had set traps for animals before. Though none with her voice, her darkness.

What was that? She was asking him if he knew Oren. "I worked with him for a year before I went underwater."

"Underwater?"

"Frogman." He puffed out his cheeks and she laughed.

Danny looked for her then on the days following, but she was always closeted with Oren or Gonen or she was alone translating fiercely from morning till late at night. Only on Friday evening did he find her in the mess hall for the Sabbath meal. By then he was desperate for her. "Will you come walking with me again this evening?" he asked her quietly, his request almost whispered into her ear. She smiled. He knew she would.

Shoshana blushed after he left her. The things she had been thinking about ever since she saw him again, the places where she wanted him to put his hands. And now to agree to go for a walk with him? She must be crazy. But not really. Things that she dreamed about didn't happen. People didn't let them happen. She wouldn't let them happen, not outside of marriage.

He hadn't said anything to her when they left camp and headed down toward the sea. He took her hand and almost pulled her along as the waves splashed softly against their feet. "I'm getting wet," she complained. Danny looked back and could no longer see the lights of the camp. He pulled Shoshana to him and forced his lips upon hers. He moved his hand to frame her cheeks and pushed open her lips with his tongue.

She broke away from him. "Don't hurt me," she said. She saw him trying to relax. They moved back from the beach and he pulled her down with him into the sand. She went with him because she wanted to. She felt the pressure of his body on her and did not resist as he pushed his hands inside her blouse to find her breasts.

It was when he moved his hand up her inner thigh that she stopped him. "No," she said sternly.

He mumbled something and pushed on. Rejecting him, she pushed back.

"Goddamn it! What are you waiting for, old age!"

She watched his angry face and felt anger in return. He sighed and apologized almost immediately. "Look," he said, "I'm sorry. I won't hurt you. I have a rubber. Nothing will happen to you."

She shook her head.

"Shoshana," he begged. He took her hand and placed it on him. She could feel his hardness. He quickly undid his pants and placed her hand inside. Then he returned to kissing and fondling her. How she wanted him. She squirmed and moaned with pleasure even through her fears. She had dreamed of this act, dreamed of him on her, and now it was happening and it was still a dream. He pushed his way into her and she felt she had been made for him. She was crazy for him and she let him do what he wanted with her, which was a lot more than she had ever imagined in her silly daydreams. She held on. She held on to him and vowed she would have him forever.

The first thing she thought of when she woke up in her cot the next morning was what would her mother think. It was just something that was not done, ever. Virginity. Nice Iraqi girls didn't lose it. She was just sick with herself and the only time she got up that morning was to vomit.

She tried to pull herself together in time for the Sabbath meal. She washed her hair and washed her body, thoroughly. She sat in the sun for a while, hoping that would purify her. Then she went off to the mess hall, looking straight ahead. She was sure everyone knew about her. She was so ashamed she wished she could just drop dead right there.

Oren came over to her almost immediately upon her sitting down. "Slept through breakfast? What would Captain Gonen say?"

She tried to read something into his words but his face was expressionless.

Danny followed her out of the mess hall. She had not sought him out but she knew he was there. He walked alongside of her, not touching her. Somehow they found an empty piece of ground where they could stand together. There was no place they could go to be alone in the army, except to the beach and she had had enough of that.

"I'm sorry," he said as they stood side by side stupidly in the sun. "I didn't know you were a virgin. I thought—"

"You thought I was Moroccan. You thought I would charge you," she hissed out, angry and embarrassed.

"Shoshana, I didn't know."

"You didn't care."

"Yes, I didn't care either," he admitted. He faced her. "You have a beautiful body," he told her.

She couldn't stand herself. And yet she let him seek her out at night and she willingly went off with him and let him do what he wanted with her. It was wrong, so wrong, but she couldn't stop herself.

Oren caught on. As Shoshana stopped in midsentence and lost track of what she was doing. "Shoshana, he's married." That was all he said. No censure, no nothing.

Oh, God. And yet she continued. She didn't ask him anything. She didn't demand anything.

She was thankful when the job was over. She didn't tell Danny. She just wanted to disappear and she did. Oren kissed her on her forehead good-bye. Then she stepped into the tramp line and waited for a ride down south to Tel Aviv.

It was funny how easy adultery became, Diane thought. They had actually slipped away from the hospital together, rented a hotel room, and wrestled each other into a love embrace on a strange bed. She was mystified. And delighted. "I've never done anything like this before," Walter admitted. Was he talking pleasure or guilt? If it was guilt, he could keep it to himself. She had enough problems of her own without his guilt.

The blame was hers. She had sought him out along the corridors of Mass General pediatrics. She had listened understandingly to the problems he had with his wife and her career. She had sympathized with him. After all, her only aim in life was to be a wife and mother. And of course now to get fucked by Walter de Gregory.

But that came later. First there was the mutual understanding, respect, affection. She told herself. But God, did it feel good. You don't care whom you hurt, she said into her mirror. But whom was she hurting? Well, okay, Walter had his guilt trips, but wasn't that just part of being Jewish? And anyway she needed him. He made her come alive after all those harrowing years of life with Hal, when the only reason they went to bed was to create a child, and when they rose up, they were as barren as when they had lain down.

But with Walter there was joy. There was biting, kicking, screaming. Pleasure. And it even carried over into her life with Hal. That's what surprised her. She even felt a passion for her husband, maybe for the first time. She could come home to him after an hour with Walter and nip him on the neck. Hal would push her away of course, but that was his problem. She would not let him spoil her newfound lustiness.

Sometimes she felt Hal knew about her and Walter. There were moments when she caught him looking at her as if he were about to open his mouth and say something. She would wait anxiously, expectantly, but then he would close his mouth just as suddenly, and she would turn away from him with a smile to make dinner, wash the dishes, pick up the newspapers.

18

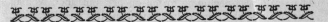

The brit would be held at four the next afternoon. He would hold the child while the mohel circumcised it. It, the child, the boy, Nadav. Nadav. Jacob must get used to the fact that there was a new life on earth, Nadav, his grandchild. Jacob wondered how his son Rahamin and Rahamin's wife, Leila, had decided on him to hold the child, a great honor. Probably they figured it was the last honor he was going to get, as the rumors passed down one street and up the other—Jacob Ewan was to be arrested. Well. So what could he do about it. He would wait until they came for him. That was all.

He was surprised at how calm he felt. He checked his watch. This time tomorrow he might not be alive. Still he took pleasure in dressing in his finest suit and tying his tie just so. Until he looked in the mirror and wondered how a hangman's noose would suit him. He shuddered. But he understood that the noose was for public displays. He would probably be propped up against a wall and shot. That's what he heard had been happening to the others who had just disappeared. No, he didn't mind being dead. It was the dying that bothered him, the moment between life and death, the pain, the parting, the nothingness beyond. But all men died. He would be no exception.

"Are you ready, Jacob?"

His wife looked pretty in the silk print dress he had imported for her from Paris. He would like to see her in the gold jewelry of hers but she refused to wear it. She kept it hidden, even from him. "They will not take it," she vowed. The strain was beginning to tell on her, but good woman that she was, she cried only at night in their bed when she thought him asleep. "It's a great day," he told her.

He wondered what his wife really thought of this day. She wanted the boys free, not married and fathers. He too. And yet every avenue he had tried was blocked by the government, by death, by discovery. So in the end when Rahamin pressed him, he gave in. Maybe somehow, if he were still around, he could gain a release for Ephraim. In a way he was not sorry he had allowed Rahamin to marry. He could think of no greater pleasure on earth than seeing his grandson. He praised God that he had lived so long, he prayed that he might live longer. He laughed. One always clings to what one knows. He had clung too long to Iraq. His wife never said anything, but did she wonder as he did how much better their life would have been had they fled penniless to Israel and seen their grandson born into freedom rather than to stay in Baghdad and celebrate in style his birth into oppression.

The party was held at the house of Leila's father. His wife left him to help in the kitchen as soon as they arrived. He went over to his daughter-in-law and kissed her on the cheek. He took out two presents and placed them into her hands. One was a gold ring with a pearl, the other a smaller ring with jade for the baby Nadav.

"You are very generous, Father," Leila said.

"Oh, well, you have produced a son. If it had been a daughter, it would only have been a ruby." She laughed. "Where is my grandson?"

"Sleeping. In my old room."

"May I see him?"

"Yes. But please don't wake him. I'm—I'm tired, really."

Jacob made his way to the stairway of Leila's house and waved briefly to his son Rahamin, who was engulfed by friends of his from the university. He climbed and guessed that the closed door on the landing would be his grandson's. He opened it carefully and slipped inside before too much light could enter the room. He stood there and waited till his eyes became adjusted, then he studied the small child in the crib with his bottom bunched high up in the air and his pacifier tentatively held between his lips. Nadav was the most beautiful baby Jacob had ever seen, even more glorious than his own two sons. Jacob crossed over to the crib and stood there. He could see the blood vessels run through the thin paper of Nadav's skin. He watched to make sure that the breaths came and were expelled regularly. He wanted so much to pick up and hold the child, but that would have to wait for tomorrow when Nadav would be placed on a pillow on his lap and the mohel would be called upon to practice his art. Poor Nadav, your grandfather would try to ease your pain. The child slept on happily and Jacob slipped out of the room with the same care he had entered.

Coming down the stairs, Jacob noted that everybody had arrived. A party in the Jewish community of Baghdad was not something anyone would avoid, there were so few reasons to celebrate. Unless, of course, Jacob Ewan gave the party. But that was because everyone knew his time was coming. They either wanted to save themselves or him the embarrassment by not being there when it arrived. He circulated, catching sight constantly of Rahamin, who was accepting congratulations for the marvelous feat of producing a son. Leila was ignored except by the women who came to commiserate and ask after her labor, how long the pain, how difficult the birth.

It wasn't that anyone was particularly avoiding Jacob. There were nods and pleasantries. But it was different from even months ago when deals would have been discussed, financing arranged. They knew, everybody knew. He was marked.

When Jacob saw that everyone had had enough time to eat, drink, and gossip, he signaled to his man. The oud and *dumbak* players from his club, the Swallow's Nest, gathered their instruments and started with an uncertain beat, then moved quickly on to a rhythm the crowd knew well. A circle was made before the players, and when the rhythm was slow and sensuous enough, the belly dancers appeared, first one and then the other, taking turns, competing with each other for the tips that would come their way. The crowd whooped with joy. Jacob was delighted.

His wife came to stand next to him. "From the Swallow's Nest?" she asked.

"Yes. Lebanese. Good, aren't they?"

"The blond especially." She looked at him. She knew he had a weakness for blonds, but she could see nothing on his face. She might suggest. She would never ask.

Jacob smiled at her and touched her cheek. The blond was not the breeder of his sons.

"Why are you standing by the door?"

"To make sure no one gets out without giving Leila a gift."

"I have been your wife too long, Jacob. I don't deserve that sort of answer."

"I—this is just the sort of thing they would do. To come now. If they do, I can see them. I will leave before they come into the house."

"I won't let them take you."

"You will tell everyone I was taken ill. You will ask Ephraim to escort you home. Nothing must spoil this party for our grandson." He turned to her. Her hair was more gray than brown. When had that happened. "They may not come."

"They may not come tonight," she added. She waited beside him. "I want to hold you, Jacob."

"That would be unseemly," he told her. "Now go back and join the party."

As she took her first step, he pinched her on the rear. She jumped. She turned in anger but laughed when she saw him smile. She rejoined the party. A few minutes later she looked over to the door. He was gone.

When Jacob had seen the first jeep turn into the street, he had slipped out the front door and quickly walked toward it. He wanted the disturbance to be as far away from the party as possible. Behind the jeep was a command car. He stood on the sidewalk looking at them as they passed. He thought for sure they would recognize him, but they continued to drive slowly along. He had the strange feeling of seeing his destiny pass him by. He could have kept walking, but the jeep and the command car stopped in front of Leila's father's house. He rushed back there. "Excuse me," he said to the captain who had gotten out of the command car, "are you by any chance looking for me?"

The captain just stared at him. Jacob wouldn't say that Arabs were slow on the uptake but— "Are you Jacob Ewan?"

"Yes, I am. Shall we go?"

The captain looked longingly at the front door of the house. So that was his purpose then. Not only to arrest Jacob but to break up the party and put the fear of God, not to mention Mohammed and Brigadier General Abdul Karim Kassem, into the Jews attending the party. No, Jacob wouldn't allow that. He slid quickly into the command car and tapped on the driver's shoulder. "*Ya'allah*," he told him. "If you get me to the prison inside of ten minutes, I'll give you my watch." He held it out for the driver to see. It was Swiss-made, gold-plated. The driver gunned the motor and the captain slid back inside the car. The loss of the watch didn't bother Jacob in the least. They would take everything from him once he got to the prison in any case. At least this way he would know where it was going. He smiled at the captain in reassurance. The captain looked uncomfortably back at him.

* * *

She had confided in David. He had noticed something was wrong, something had been ever since she returned from Caesarea. As she spoke, she felt relief flood through her, despite her shame. Her affair with Danny was a burden she no longer wanted to carry alone. "I don't know why I did it," she confessed. "It was so wrong."

He shrugged. "Right and wrong. Wait twenty years. They won't have the same meaning."

"I'll never get married now. No one will have me."

"What are you talking about?"

"You don't know what it's like for Iraqis. I mean, if a woman's not a virgin. My husband would return me to my father."

"I can just see the sign now: Used goods. Going cheap."

"It's not funny, David." She was hurt but felt like giggling at the same time.

He put his arm around her. "You put too high a price on your virginity, my dear. Besides, you can always fake it. An ooh in the right place, a few winces."

"So what'll I do for blood?"

"Slit your wrists. He'll be so panicked he won't worry about where it's coming from." She sort of laughed. "Look," he continued, "chances are you won't marry an Iraqi anyway. I don't know why you would want to. They treat their wives abominably and still get what they want on the side."

That settled it for David. He lived in a world where passions and appetites were understood and were governed only by qualities of good sense or the lack of it. She wished she could belong to that world, but her own heritage still weighed heavily upon her. But she was functioning. She kissed her mother every morning. She came home early on Friday to help clean the house for the Sabbath. She even went out on innocuous little dates with friends of Ovadia's or acquaintances of her cousins. She smiled and she talked and she listened. And she was bored. Some of them were nice enough, sweet even, others were braggarts and simpletons; she found the two often went together. But none of them came up to her and overpowered her the way Danny had, none of them could melt her by just being there staring at her with those beautiful eyes of his. No one was like Danny. No one ever would be. She wanted Danny. She wanted his excitement. She would have no other.

And yet she knew she was crazy. She would never even see Danny again. He was married. And if she did see him, she would turn around and walk the other way because it was wrong to want him. And he had used her while she didn't know how to use back.

The only thing special to Shoshana now was her work. She loved it. It had restored her innocence and given her peace. Whenever her thoughts turned to Danny, she would pick up her headphones and begin her simultaneous translations from Iraqi radio news broadcasts.

On Hanukah she was promoted to sergeant. Ovadia was very happy for her when he heard the news. "Don't worry," she told him on one of his weekend visits from Haifa, where he was getting his M.S., "I won't ever make lieutenant."

"Of course you will," he told her.

Her mother and father didn't understand any of this. They were just waiting for the day she would get out of the army and get married, start to have children, what she should have been doing all along.

Military intelligence had a Hanukah party for all its units and their families at its base outside Tel Aviv. It wasn't as impressive as the tank corps or the paratroopers. Intelligence had nothing to demonstrate except its wit, which was sometimes questionable. The children would be bored. The colonel in charge was trying to arrange for helicopter rides but the air force wasn't being cooperative. They talked about a cutback in fuel consumption. So there would be juice and doughnuts and latkes and everyone would go home with indigestion. It would be a regular party.

Shoshana went with a group of friends from the Iraqi division. It seemed strange that all the translators from the different languages stuck together, but that's how it worked out. Except for the British, who made it a point to cast their pearls before the natives. Nobody could understand why.

When they got to the camp, they headed immediately for the food, knowing that would be the first to go. They weren't mistaken. Already the depletion was great. They grabbed armloads, sat in a circle, and ate themselves sick. When they finished, they got up to join the rest of the party. The object was for the girl soldiers to meet the boy soldiers with the officers and wives standing off to one side, talking about their children and each other.

Shoshana had a good time flirting. She wasn't as obvious as a lot of the girls, but her dark good looks brought her many blond suitors. "But how could I possibly date a private?" she asked one of them.

As she was walking around the camp looking for her friends, she bumped into David. She smiled at him. Even though he had comforted her, she had been embarrassed when they first met after she had confessed to him. But he had treated her normally and she soon forgot. He was with a woman now, bosomy, kind, aging face. "Shoshana," he said, "I'd like you to meet my wife, Hava. Shoshana is one of our best new translators," he told his wife.

"It's a pleasure to meet you, Mrs. Tal. I've heard so much about you."

"All good I hope," the woman said good-naturedly.

"Of course."

They walked past her. David whipped around and gave her a look but Shoshana hid her smile by turning away.

"Shoshana!" someone called her. She seemed to be utterly in the family section now. She looked and saw someone waving. It was Oren Kohan. She waved back and went over to join him.

"Shoshana, *shalom*." He leaned over and kissed her on both cheeks. "I'd like you to meet my wife, Nurit."

"It's a pleasure," Shoshana said, then to Oren, "I didn't think you were in the army anymore."

"I'm not. But we had to show off our news to everyone."

"Oh," Shoshana said, glancing down at the baby in Nurit's arms. "How old?"

"Six weeks."

"How precious. May I hold him?"

"Of course." Nurit passed the baby over to Shoshana and then shook out her arms. The baby craddled comfortably in Shoshana's arms while she instinctively rocked and cooed at the child.

"*Hag sameah*," someone said to her left. She glanced up. "Ours?" he added by just moving his lips.

Oren took the baby from Shoshana while Nurit greeted Danny Ze'ev, and Shoshana for a second caught Oren's eye.

"This is my wife Ronit," Danny said.

Shoshana was sure she mumbled something appropriate while staring at Ronit, blond, freckles, already wide, spreading hips with thick ankles. She did remember distinctly saying, "Excuse me, I have to go find my friends before they leave without me." She turned and left quickly. Later she thought she had been too abrupt, too noticeably so. But she tried not to consider it. Why did these things play constantly over and over in her mind?

Danny caught up with her.

"What do you want?" she asked him coldly.

"I wanted to say good-bye to you. I missed that chance in Caesarea."

"I heard your wife was coming up and I didn't want to be in the way."

"Bullshit."

"Why did you come up to me just then? You could have easily avoided me," she said angrily.

"Why should I want to avoid you?"

"Adultery?"

"That wasn't adultery," he said to her. "That was love."

"Bullshit." She said it for the first time in her life.

He looked straight ahead and smiled. Then he laughed. She veered off from him but he followed after her.

"Stop trailing after me."

He laughed again. Where was she leading him? Away from the party? Into the evening? She tried to turn back. He blocked her.

"Out of my way," she said, anger mixed with fear.

He took her face in his hands and kissed her. She broke away. "Stop it!"

"Why?" he asked angrily.

"Because you're married."

"Do you think that's my fault?" he shot back.

"Oh, I'm sorry," she said sweetly. "Did you get her pregnant?"

He moved on her. She ran. He ran after her and tackled her. He picked her up and started walking off with her. "Don't scream," he told her. "It would only embarrass both of us."

She didn't. She stared up at him and past him at the darkness. It was comfortable being carried like this, the way she had carried Nurit's baby, but where was he taking her? He was climbing clumsily on something and she felt rough metal push against her skin. She soon found herself perched next to a tank turret. He was opening the lid.

"Are you mad?" she asked him.

"It's an old one, just for show."

"There isn't enough room," she protested.

"Just keep your knees bent," he joked. He had the lid open and was lowering her inside. When her feet touched the floor and she looked around, she was surprised at how much room there was inside a tank. Danny came down, closed the lid and crouched next to her. It wasn't a matter of running away now. The situation was too intriguing.

"It's dirty," she complained.

"You can sit on me," he told her, drawing her close and unbuttoning her blouse. "You've been promoted," he noticed.

"Does that make me more exciting?" she asked.

He smiled. "I'm not status conscious," he said, lifting her shirt off her arms and dragging her down. She realized when he touched her between her legs how much she had missed it.

Shoshana was different after her second run-in with Danny Ze'ev. She knew she had changed but she didn't care. There was nothing she could do about it, there was nothing that she wanted except to be with him. There were moments when she suffered total despair, moments when she was in her parents' apartment at night, wearing her gown, brushing her hair, when they were in the next room sleeping, sharing a bed, so safe, the way she should be. But she hardened herself. She told herself no, it was not to be, not for her. She knew it was self-destructive, she knew it was wrong, she knew it was stupid. But she did it anyway. She would hurt later. And suffer. She had read enough books to know that. But now she would get what she wanted. And she wanted Danny.

"You're nuts," David would say.

"How do you know?"

"I know."

She was a fallen woman. The thought that had once frightened her now amused her. But it also strangely enough improved her work. She threw herself into it. Her emotional needs, warped as they were, were fulfilled. So while the other girls panicked as their army service was drawing to a close without a husband in sight yet, she did not. She concentrated on her work.

"What a dynamo," Elias said to her once, threatened by her precision.

She was always discreet with Danny. That was why she was surprised that David knew. She wondered sometimes if Danny was bragging.

"How could I brag?" he asked her. "If my father knew, if Ronit's father knew, do you know what would happen to me?"

According to Danny, his marriage had been a business merger. He and Ronit had known each other as children. Her father was a contractor, his father a foreman and moving up politically. What could be more convenient than a marriage. Danny couldn't see any objection at the time. He knew he would end up marrying someone like Ronit.

"Even after meeting me you agreed to marry her?" she asked, joking and yet not.

"And what would have been my parents' reaction if I wanted to marry you?" he retorted.

"You mean I'm good enough to fuck but not to marry."

"Where are you picking up these vulgarisms?"

"From you," she answered.

"Can you see me approaching my father and telling him I want to marry Shoshana Ewan. That *schwartza*, he would have said. 'Where does she come from? She can't even offer you money.' "

"Very flattering," Shoshana said coldly.

"And what would your parents have said?" he asked defensively.

Marriage with Danny? They would have been horrified. Her father hated Danny's father as it was, and her mother would never accept Danny as a son-in-law. She disliked the Europeans even as she feared them. They were destroying her and her way of life. She did not understand them, she did not want to be near them.

Shoshana asked herself why she was such a fool! She could examine it rationally over a cup of coffee at work. She could see that she was being used and being hurt and next time he called she would say no. But at night when she slid into bed, she felt him slide in next to her, felt his hands along her body, tossed in shame and wanted him. She went out of her way to fix a time and a place to see him.

It was a Friday evening when she called him. Her father was at the synagogue, her mother over at Lily's where they would all meet later for the Sabbath meal. She had the apartment alone. For an hour maybe. Danny was only too willing to come up and join her.

They never wasted any time when they got together. Time was too precious and she delighted in every little thing he did. He was never quick with her, only when he had come back from some mission, and she had learned to understand and yield to his needs on those occasions as he

258

had learned what pleased her in her various moods. Now they were on the Persian carpet that used to be in her room in Baghdad. They were fondling each other, Shoshana's skirt was up, her blouse open, Danny's legs between hers. It was Danny who heard the click in the hallway, but before he could do anything about it, the front door opened.

"Mother!" Shoshana screeched. Salemah stood there, shocked.

Danny rose quickly and pulled Shoshana up with him. He didn't know what to do. He looked back and forth between mother and daughter.

"Go, Danny," Shoshana said quietly. "Go now."

"Are you sure?"

"Go."

He walked past Salemah and left.

Salemah was galvanized as the door closed. In a fury she rushed at her daughter and began beating her with her fists, screaming at her. "Whore! Tramp! Slut!"

Shoshana did not brush her off. She took it all, knowing she deserved every blow. She fell to the ground crying hysterically.

"Those Ashkenazim, those Ashkenazim!" her mother screamed. "They've taken our livelihood, they've taken our bread, they've taken our dignity, and now they've taken our daughters. God curse them. God curse them on the face of the earth!"

"Mother," Shoshana mumbled, grabbing hold of her mother's knees. "Forgive me, please forgive me."

Salemah placed her hand absently on Shoshana's head her rage depleted. "You will be the death of me, Shoshana," she said weakly. "The death."

"Don't tell Father. Please," Shoshana begged.

After eight years of marriage Diana Evans was pregnant. The father of the child was not her husband. She couldn't swear to it of course. She had after all laid herself open, as it were, to Hal's approaches. And even though he approached her only once a week, he had managed the other six days to be heartily appreciative of her company, cuddling, warm, responsive, like the Hal of her courting days.

She sensed at times he was insincere. He often had that look upon his face as if he were about to say something dreadful. She had long ago lost the fear that he had found out about her affair. No, she thought, he was probably having one of his own and was being so nice to her to make up for it.

When she had gotten pregnant, she had discovered the meaning of love, the only meaning love could have, that of a mother for her child. And when her child moved for the first time against her belly, the earth moved as it had not with any man. This was hers, to love, nourish, and protect. She prayed for a daughter.

She did not tell Walter she was pregnant. What would have been the point? She and Walter were friends and lovers in that order. They clung to each other for comfort, the sex being a mere reaffirmation of their warmth. So how could she tell Walter she was pregnant and he was the father, or worse yet she didn't know who the father was? Were it a passionate relationship in which they couldn't wait to get into a corner with each other, she might have been tempted. But she didn't even feel the slightest bit jealous when she saw Walter and his wife, Mary, featured at some political fund raiser. She always cut the picture out of the newspaper and gave it to him and he reciprocated when she and Hal made the temple bulletin at one of the fund raisers for Israel. "Your wife is beautiful," she would tell Walter. "She keeps herself well," he would reply noncommittally. And his daughter? Could she tear Walter away from the daughter she knew he loved? No, the best solution, the only solution was what she had done the other day. She had said good-bye.

"Is it something I said?" he had asked.

She laughed. "It's time," she had told him. "Circumstances beyond my control, beyond ours."

"No."

"You'll always be my friend and lover."

They had both tried to be gracious, but it had been uncomfortable dressing together for the last time, and the parting kiss had been bitter. She would tell Hal that night. He would be pleased, even though he had given up hope of their ever having a child.

Hal had met a rich widow. She had brought in an architect's plans to have them independently evaluated. He knew she was his kind of woman when he took her out for lunch and they ended up in bed.

She would do. He had been waiting to find someone like her to replace Diane for several years now. Someone certifiably fertile. The widow had two young children. He was seeing her tomorrow to look over her present home. It would give him a better chance to check out the quality of her goods, both personal and otherwise. He would get a credit rating done on her, and depending on the outcome of that, he would get to work. It was about time he set up his own firm in any case.

"I'm home, dear," Diane called.

Home. That brought up the question of community property. He would need a good lawyer. He knew several from B'nai B'rith who had the same view of women he held. There was no reason why Diane should get much. She was strong and healthy with no encumbrances such as children to hold her back from earning her own living. He would be glad to stop busting his balls keeping her in the style of living to which her father had accustomed her.

She came into his study. He stood up to greet her. She put her arms around his waist and they kissed. "I have a surprise for you," she told him.

I have a surprise for you too, he thought. "New dress?"

"You're not very imaginative." Diane took his hand and placed it over her stomach. He hoped she didn't want sex. It wasn't their night. "New life."

He pushed her away. "What?"

She smiled at him. "It's what you've always wanted, Hal. I'm four months pregnant."

19

Other people used the time prison afforded them to write books cataloguing their philosophy of life. Jacob Ewan used the time to improve his game of sheshbesh. He felt he was a better man for it, certainly a richer man; and since he was in prison for the crime of capitalism, he knew he could not compound his guilt any further by side bets on his own ability.

He had thought when he had been carted away to prison after the birth of his grandson to have some unexpected truth about himself revealed. But in point of fact the only truth that kept coming home to him was one he already knew: He should have left Iraq when he had the chance. He thought at least in the interrogation cell he would find one ideologically pure, if tyrannical, force against which to pit his wits. But pureness obviously isolated itself in the Defense Ministry with General Kassem while the jailers were interested in baksheesh. So as soon as his wife found out which prison he had been taken to, his living conditions improved immeasurably as the money began funneling from her hands into the jailers'. He even convinced them not to confiscate his property because if they did, he would have no more money left to pay them with and the property they confiscated would go to the anonymous government instead of into their very own pockets.

While he was in prison in Baghdad, he was allowed to see his wife once a week. He had not been formally charged with anything. There was no word of a trial. She had paid her way in to see many officials and they claimed never to have heard of him.

"What will happen to you?" his wife asked.

It was a puzzling question. If there was no charge against him, he should by rights be released. But if he demanded his release, wouldn't they find something to charge him with? National politics was not a game he played. And yet here he was involved in it. Kassem's national policy was like a flashlight swinging around in the dark. The jails were full of political prisoners, those like himself who were no immediate threat to Kassem or his government, thus he took no interest in them. The ones he was interested in died quickly. So perhaps Jacob better not pique interest. He told his wife to stop making inquiries. He would rot quietly in jail until something told him the time for getting out had come.

After six months in a Baghdad prison, Jacob was ordered to gather his belongings. His initial response was that he was about to be taken out and shot. But then why would they march him off with his razor, books, and change of clothing.

"Sorry to see you go, Mr. Ewan," one of the guards said to Jacob as he helped him into the van. Indeed he should be, Jacob thought, I've made him rich.

When all the prisoners were seated, the doors to the truck were closed and padlocked. The truck took off but the prisoners remained silent. Most like Jacob had been in prison for months. Their curiosity had dissipated as the days dragged on. Even now as they might be going to their deaths, each sat thinking his own thoughts about the future.

However it was not the ominous pockmarked wall they saw next, but the Rashid military base. They were unloaded off the trucks, unshackled, and led away to a barracks. There each was given a cot and a carton for his personal belongings. Then they were left on their own.

"We're free," one of the men said.

Well, not quite. Jacob had not the temerity to open the barracks door first. He left that to another man. But when the man stepped out of the door and no shots were fired, they all pushed their way into the open air. Freedom in their case wasn't the absence of guards but the ability to stand out under the open sky.

"Jacob! Jacob Ewan!"

Jacob turned to see who had called his name. He was amazed to recognize a former minister in the government who frequented the Swallow's Nest. He walked over to the man.

"You've just arrived," the minister said.

"Yes. But—"

The minister waved him off. "Oh, you'll find all the upper crust of Baghdad here."

"But why you?"

"Pro-Western sympathies," the minister called out heartily. He introduced Jacob to his friends, many of whom Jacob already knew from the club. They formed an easy alliance based on their recent misfortune.

And so Jacob became part of the never-ending sheshbesh tournament. He did better at that than toss the rock, another camp favorite. Toss the rock was really a young man's game. Like the other new men he had his interview with an officer from internal security, one Musa al Haykal. Al Haykal arranged for him to write and receive letters from his wife. He also tried to reassure him. "Don't be afraid," he told Jacob. "Capitalism isn't so much of a crime that you would be shot for it. Unless there is an extreme shift in government policy of course. And even those of you who are most near to being condemned to death, I like to tell this story to. You will remember Colonel Abdul Salam Aref, he who with our great leader Kassem overthrew the villainous corrupt government of our late king and his uncle? Well, he was also here, here in Rashid under sentence of death. And do you know what Kassem did?"

"He pardoned Aref."

"There. You see."

"But Kassem always said Aref was like a son to him. How many of us does he consider his sons?"

"All of Iraq are his sons," Al Haykal said strongly.

Yet there were those who were taken away and did not return, not even for burial.

They all lived on rumor. Perhaps that was part of being a political prisoner, the only criminals in camp being the guards who grew rich on bribes. For the rest it was ideology, plots, and counterplots. Who was Kassem after now? Who would be up against the wall tomorrow? Jacob lived on, eighteen months in jail already. The year 1963 came while he was at Rashid, the month of January chilled him till he thought he would never be warm again. Then February where he could only look forward to March and a warm spring.

Ramadan arrived. He fasted with the Moslems from sunup to sundown. No need to make it perfectly clear how different he was from them. They slept and gossiped their days away. The war with the Kurds on the Iraqi border was going badly. Israel had a hand in supplying the Kurds, that was certain. He said nothing. Nothing would provoke him. He knew how to survive.

One cold Friday morning in the middle of February, they were sitting around listening to the transistor. All of a sudden the station went dead. They looked up at each other while the owner of the radio twisted the dial to make sure nothing had happened to the radio itself. No, Beirut was coming in strong. There was only one reason the radio went dead in Iraq. Something had happened with the government.

Jacob got up with the rest of them. The safest place to be was in the barracks. Preferably on the floor underneath your cot. The courtyard emptied as everyone sought his own safety.

At nine thirty that morning the radio station came back on the air. The cult of personality was over, they declared. General Kassem and his aides were found guilty of crimes against the Iraqi people and were executed as befitted their guilt.

"What will happen to us?" one of the prisoners called out.

The answer would be given when they discovered who had led the revolt against Kassem, who had him killed. They discovered in short order that it was their former prisonmate Abdul Salam Aref, he who had led the revolt against the king with Kassem, he whom Kassem had first sentenced to death for treason and then pardoned. Aref was now in charge of Iraq.

As to what would happen to the prisoners in the Rashid army base, it seemed they had been forgotten. Their greatest fear was that Kassem's man, who was still in charge, would order them mowed down, machine-gunned to death. But they waited, both sides now, the jailers and the jailed, and neither side knew the new definition of their relationship.

On the third day after the coup, the tanks of Aref broke down the barriers of Rashid and liberated them.

Jacob Ewan felt tired as he made his way slowly down the streets of Baghdad to his house. There was a curfew and he was not supposed to be out on the streets, yet he shuffled like an old man toward his house. They stopped him. Of course. The paramilitary men in green armbands signifying they were members of Aref's new order.

Curfew, they told him, rifles pointed at his heart.

He held out his papers. They took them and waited till they found someone who could read.

"But you are a Jew," their lieutenant said.

Jacob nodded his head.

"You've just been released from Rashid. But everyone important was at Rashid. What were you imprisoned for?"

"Capitalism," Jacob said softly.

The lieutenant nodded sympathetically. He handed the papers back to Jacob. "An enemy of Kassem's is a friend of ours," he assured Jacob. Then he ordered his men to escort Jacob to his house.

His wife was in shock when she saw him. "I thought you were dead, I thought they had killed you," she almost wailed. "You're old," she noted suddenly.

His lips curved slightly upward. He had not been old a week ago. A week ago there had been a certain order to his life. But with the revolution that order had been swept away. He was Kassem's enemy so he was Aref's friend. He knew neither of them. He had been sitting so close to death until the tanks came to Rashid, and now he was free, a hero of sorts for enduring.

"They have lists," his wife was saying.

"The little green men?"

"The ones with green armbands, yes. They have lists of communists and communist sympathizers. They're rounding them up and executing them. They showed the revolution on television, the bodies anyway. Someone held Kassem up by the hair so we could see that he was truly dead."

Jacob let his wife help him to his chair. She had preserved it with a white cloth so that no one could sit on it aside from himself. Now she whipped the cloth away. Who dared to say that Iraq was not advancing into the modern age? Only five years ago when the king, his uncle, and Nuri es-Said had been killed, the people had to rush into the streets to see their dismembered bodies. Now they could sit comfortably at home and watch it on television.

Jacob knew only one thing. He had to get out.

Meir Ewan followed the revolution in Iraq closely in the newspapers. He read and savored the analyses. Then he shrugged them away. Why did anyone try to take a rational approach to Iraqi affairs? Why didn't they understand, as he did, that Iraq under whatever government thrived on blood sacrifice? He threw the papers aside. He felt safe, comfortable, even as the rain beat down on his balcony. He was free, his children were free. Thank God he had left.

"Eh, Salemah?" he called. "Thank God we left when we did."

But she made no response. He didn't understand her lately. She was folded with sorrow and he could not see the reason. Their son Hillel in America had remarried and had another boy. He did not really understand Hillel's letter. It was all very confusing. Hillel had written that he had married Diane's younger sister and had had a son by her. Steven this time. Hillel's new wife looked remarkably like his old one, but then they were sisters. That news should have cheered Salemah, and she did brighten for a moment or two when she got a letter from Hillel with a picture of his new son. But she remained unbearably sad, as if she were in mourning.

"I said it's good that we left." He had gotten up and walked over to her. She was mending his shirt collar.

"Where?" As if she had been paying no attention.

"It's good that we left Iraq. There's death there."

"I wonder how your brother is."

Meir shook his head. He couldn't bear to think of him. What could he do for Jacob now. "It's good that we left," he said softly. He went over to the radio and turned it on. Perhaps there was some more recent news.

He watched absently when his daughter came into the apartment. It was eight o'clock. He didn't like Shoshana working so late, but she said she had to. It was part of her job. She barely said hello to him before she went over to her mother. They were talking quietly together. There was a secret between them that he would dearly love to know, but they would never let him in on it. He turned back to his radio and twisted the dials.

She had lived too long. She looked over to her husband, Meir, by the radio. She wished she were a man. Men feel nothing. Everything happens to them. Nothing happens within them. She did not tell her husband about Shoshana. How could she? How could she betray her own daughter? She wanted no harm to come to Shoshana and yet the greatest harm had already been done.

Why had this happened? Why? Why? It tore at her heart. How had she failed Shoshana? Hadn't she told her often enough what happens to girls like—like her daughter. Danielle knew. That surprised her because Danielle had kept the secret so well. She and Danielle had gotten together with Shoshana and had tried to force her to promise to give up this boy, the married man. But Shoshana wouldn't. "If I promised you that, it would be a promise I would break so what's the point?"

"Can't you see it's wrong?" she had begged of her daughter.

"Of course it's wrong. I know it's wrong. But there it is."

How had it happened!

And if there would be a baby? "We take precautions," Shoshana had said briskly.

Precautions? What should her daughter know of precautions? Her beautiful baby daughter. Everyone said yes. everyone always said Shoshana would get into trouble. She always knew her own mind, she always went her own way. So why should this surprise Salemah? Neither tears nor anger would move her Shoshana.

She wanted to tell Lily, have Lily talk to Shoshana. But Lily would use her knowledge as a knife, and then the shame would descend on the whole family instead of just mother and daughter. If they were in Baghdad, they would go to this boy's parents and put a stop to this immediately. There were ways in Baghdad to handle such things. But here his parents wouldn't even let them through the door, here she could not even speak their language, here they used her daughter like a whore and Shoshana called it love.

She was tired. So tired. She hadn't the will to fight anymore, not even the will to complain. She just wanted to lie down and rest, sleep. Thank God for Danielle. She came over after work to see how she was. Always. She could mother Danielle. Danielle was so sweet, so beautiful, so obedient. She could not understand why Leah abused her so.

Salemah got up to go to bed. Meir didn't notice. She walked past her daughter's bedroom. Shoshana was reading a book instead of doing something useful like mending her clothes. She looked up. "How's your stomach tonight, Mother? Is it any better?" Salemah didn't answer. "We'll go to the doctor tomorrow and check on the tests. I'll come home early from work."

Salemah nodded. It was one less day that she could spend with that man.

Ovadia was back at the Technion getting his M.S. in engineering. He was out of the army, even though they had offered to make him a captain if he stayed or break him down to a sergeant in the reserves if he decided to leave. Sergeant wasn't too bad, he had to concede. So he wouldn't wear his officer's cap again, but it was better than spending the next twenty years working on computers. Besides, he had a dream, one of nebulous safety and fulfillment. He wanted to go to the United States, he wanted to study there, get his Ph.D. there, see what it was like. Not to make money like Hillel, to buy his wife a Thunderbird so she could wreck herself on the highway, just to, well, experience something different. He didn't even know why he wanted to go, maybe because he felt slightly claustrophobic in Israel. He knew what was open to him, and suddenly at twenty-four it just wasn't enough. He wanted opportunities. America was the land of opportunities. He wanted America.

He told Shoshana of course. He always told Shoshana everything. She listened and smiled, encouraged him; but through it all, he found her distracted, incredibly so every weekend he saw her. He finally thought he had discovered why when he came down late in February to find Shoshana very upset.

"She says she's in pain," Shoshana told her brother.

"Mother?"

"Yes."

It didn't surprise Ovadia. His mother was always in pain, had been since they left Iraq and came to Israel. Some of it was real, some of it was emotional, most of it was depression. The real had been a cyst removed from her lung, but that was almost ten years ago. They had grown used to their mother's complaining, they would laugh it off. Lily would always go with her to Kupot Holim where the doctors could find nothing, so they sent her home with pills for her nerves, for her high blood pressure. But now Shoshana was worried. Why?

"I caused it," she said.

"Caused what?"

"The pain."

Ovadia sighed. He didn't know how to react. Hadn't they all caused their mother pain, Lily, Shoshana, Hillel, even her Ovadia, the good one.

"She said I'd be the death of her," Shoshana said as she cried into her handkerchief.

"She says that to everyone," Ovadia pointed out.

"She had a reason," Shoshana said. Ovadia waited. "I've been seeing someone."

"Oh?" He thought that an appropriate response.

"Mother doesn't—he's not to Mother's tastes."

"Oh." Ovadia mulled it over. "Is he Moroccan or European?"

"European."

"Don't be stupid," he told her quickly. "You know what those Europeans are like. You must know by now. You've been in the army long enough."

"I thought some of your best friends were Europeans."

"All my friends are Europeans," Ovadia said. And it was true. He lived in a different world from that of his father and mother, Lily and Joseph. He had traveled by his brains into the hierarchy of Israeli life. First a scholarship to high school, then Atudah Academait in the army allowing him to get his B.S. before he served, now he would be receiving his M.S. All on scholarship. All by passing test after test, being better than anyone else because that was the only way he could get what he wanted from Israeli society. And wherever he went in Israel there were only Europeans—no Orientals. In the army too it was rare for his people to make Atudah Academait, rare for them to become officers. Cooks, that's the kind of job they were trained for, cooks learning how to prepare schnitzel, boiled chicken, and mashed potatoes, Ashkenazi fare because the Ashkenazim controlled everything in Israel, even his stomach.

"Do you remember Shimshon?" Ovadia asked his sister.

"The corporal from Egypt?"

"Yes."

"Vaguely."

"Well, he was like you, dating an Ashkenazi. He wanted to marry her, she wanted to marry him."

"Are they happy?"

"Her parents didn't allow it. He wasn't good enough for her. None of us are good enough for them. None of us. We'll always be outsiders here."

"How can you say that after serving in the army?"

"I deny it. I deny it to myself all the time. I tell myself I'm just like them, but I'm not. I don't walk with their assurance, I don't act with their self-confidence. I'm always running to catch up with them even when I'm far ahead."

"That's just you," she told him.

"Remember when we were kids, when we first came here?" He smiled.

"How could I forget?"

"Remember how we used to love to eat 'Israeli' foods. You especially."

"You too," she reminded him.

"But you, how you used to force Mother to make you mashed potatoes instead of rice so we'd be like everybody else in the apartment house."

"Remember sometimes she'd serve them cold? Yech!"

"That's what this boy is Shoshana. Mashed potatoes."

"Ovadia."

"You want what everyone else has. You can't have it, Shoshana. You'll have to settle for rice."

She laughed. "I'm not settling for anything."

"Has he asked you to marry him?"

"No."

Ovadia didn't say anything.

"It's not like that," Shoshana said. "You don't, you couldn't understand."

"I remember once in high school rumor had it that Ziona was going out with a Yemenite."

"So?"

"She got pregnant."

"What happened?"

"She married Gil, her boyfriend from high school. But when the baby came out, it was brown."

She laughed, he joined her.

Their mother got worse. Lily was over at the house all the time. "I don't know what to do for her," she complained to anyone who would listen. "I'm afraid. When she's sleeping, Joshua makes noise and wakes her up."

It was always her now. Never Mother this or Mother that, but always Salemah was addressed as 'her,' as if she no longer had a rational part in her own existence. The sisters discussed and bickered. Danielle came over to do what she could. They took Salemah to doctor after doctor. Nothing.

"Is it me, Mother?" Shoshana asked once. "Is that it? Am I causing you the pain?"

"In the heart. Not in the stomach."

Even Meir didn't know what to do. His life, all their lives had depended and revolved around Salemah. Now she was fading and they walked around dumb and distracted, each fearing to face the truth. Salemah was dying.

Shoshana went to work one day, but instead of sitting down at her usual desk, she went to David's office. David was in conference. "I'll wait outside the door," she told him.

"Why don't you get some work done," Elias suggested.

"I can't," she replied.

When the meeting broke up, Shoshana went into David's office and closed the door on everyone.

"What do you want, a court-martial?" David asked her jokingly.

"Who cares," she said. "I only have a few more months anyway."

"I've been meaning to speak to you about that."

"It can wait," she told him. He was taken aback. "It's my mother, David. She's sick."

He changed immediately. "Oh, I'm sorry. Do you want some time off?"

"I don't know what to do. She keeps going to Kupot Holim with pain in her stomach, they keep sending her home again. She's really suffering. I can't stand it any longer."

"What can I do?" he asked sympathetically.

"Give me a name of a reliable doctor."

He thought about it. "Stomach pains?"

"Yes."

He pointed to a chair, then picked up the phone and called his wife. The conversation was about Rahel, a friend of theirs, and it was involved and medical. "Yes, but who—" He couldn't get a word in. He looked at Shoshana and raised his eyes upward. "Who, darling, was her doctor? Dr. Nogel? Private? At the clinic when? Thursdays. Right. Thanks, my sweet. I'll be home in time for dinner." He shrugged. He pushed down the button and dialed another number. He had to go through several people to get what he wanted, each time introducing himself as Colonel Tal. "I should have been a general," he whispered once to Shoshana. Finally he succeeded and hung up the phone. "Thursday at eleven."

Dr. Nogel was cold and forbidding but at least he seemed competent. He took Salemah's complaint seriously.

"There's a swelling in the stomach area," he said. "Has she had this condition before?"

"Well, she's always been swollen. From childbirth," Shoshana answered. Both ignored the patient on the table.

"How many?"

"Four live births, no, five," she corrected herself. "There miscarriages."

He nodded. "And the cyst?"

"Nineteen fifty-four."

275

"Benign?"

"Yes."

"Well." He left the patient, telling her to get dressed, while guiding Shoshana out the door. "Your mother might have an abdominal cyst this time," he told her. "There's no way of knowing except to operate."

"Operate?"

"Yes." The doctor looked questioningly at her.

"Is it safe?" Shoshana asked.

"Safer than not knowing," Dr. Nogel said. "Don't worry. She'll have the best. I always send my patients to Hadassah in Jerusalem."

Shoshana nodded, trying to take it all in.

"She should be admitted as soon as possible. Sunday I would say."

"Sunday," Shoshana repeated dumbly.

"Can that be arranged?"

"Of course," she said.

"All right. I'll send her chart down and tell them to expect her."

Ovadia was called home from Haifa. The family decided that he and Shoshana should stay with their mother in Jerusalem until she was operated on. "They'll find nothing," Lily assured her brother.

"I hope they find something," Shoshana said. "I hope they can stop the pain."

"They will, Shoshana," Joseph assured her quietly. Shoshana crumpled into Joseph's arms.

"Why can't they operate on her here in Tel Aviv?" Lily said. "Then we could all be with her."

"Because she needs the best," Shoshana said, "and the best is in Jerusalem."

"But Father—"

Meir, another person outside the theater of their existence. They were to be humored now, Meir and Salemah, to be coaxed and scolded. Their strength had ebbed, their power dissipated. Decisions were being made for them and they no longer seemed to care.

"Father, you'll come down with us to Jerusalem to see her settled, all right?" Shoshana asked.

"We'll take a taxi," Ovadia said. "It'll be more comfortable for Mother."

"Taxi? We could use Joseph's pick-up," Lily suggested.

"A pick-up to take Mother to the hospital!" Shoshana screamed.

"A pick-up is more like an ambulance than a taxi is," Lily screamed back.

"Oh, girls," Joseph moaned.

"You think I don't care as much about Mother as you do?" Lily accused.

"Stop it!" Joseph shouted. He looked around at his in-laws. They stared at him. He realized they were not used to hearing him scream. Even Joshua was hanging onto Lily's skirt. He lowered his voice. "The pick-up doesn't have the same suspension as an ambulance. Lily didn't know that or she wouldn't have suggested we use it. A taxi would be best. I think we can all agree on that. Now, Lily, why don't you go into the kitchen and make us all tea."

"I'll make the tea," Salemah said. "This is still my house." She rose, then fell back into her chair.

"Mother, no one wants tea," Shoshana wept. "No one."

But Salemah got up anyway and they sat silently together listening to her move about the kitchen.

"I should stay," Meir said when they reached the hospital in Jerusalem.

But Ovadia had checked with admitting. "They don't know when they're going to operate," he told his father. "We'll watch over her."

"This is not the time to stop working," his father said.

"I know, Father. Mother wouldn't want you to. She knows how bothered you are by hospitals."

"But she needs me."

"We'll be here, Father," Shoshana told him. "And Jerusalem is only a short bus ride away. We'll call immediately."

"I should get back to work. This is no time to lose my job."

Ovadia and Shoshana looked at each other. Shoshana put her arm around her father and walked him to the local bus stop.

They waited. The surgery was Wednesday morning. They talked about their life in Israel, they went to see the sights of Jerusalem, they visited their mother, called their father. The waiting made them feel as if they were suspended in time. But their mother was more comfortable in the hospital. They gave her something for the pain.

The doctor called them into his office after the operation.

"What is it?" Shoshana asked after they were seated and no one was saying anything. "Was it a cyst?"

The doctor paused as if he didn't know what to say. He plunged in. "It's cancer."

"Cancer," Ovadia repeated numbly.

"It's spread too far," the doctor continued. "There's just absolutely no way of cutting it out."

"What does that mean?" Shoshana asked anxiously.

The doctor thought he had explained it. "She has stomach cancer," he said.

"But what does that mean?" Shoshana asked more insistently.

"She's dying," the doctor answered.

Shoshana burst into tears and Ovadia could see the doctor flinch at this display of emotion.

It became necessary for them to get all the details. Somehow they had to know everything about something they didn't want to face. How long? He didn't know. Months, maybe, maybe a year, maybe longer. The cancer was eating away at her. When it did it's job, she'd be dead. "What a terrific way to end your life," Shoshana said bitterly.

Ovadia went home to tell Father and Lily. Lily could not stop weeping. Meir and Joseph and Ovadia sat around the table staring at the grain in the wood. "What shall we tell her?" Meir said.

"Nothing," Joseph answered. "Tell her nothing. She wouldn't want to know. It would only scare her."

"Let her go on like this till she dies," Ovadia said, whether questioning or censoring he didn't know.

"We must contact Hillel," Lily said. "Mother would want to see him again. And see his child."

"Yes," Meir said. "I will write to him immediately."

20

Hillel was suspicious when he opened the air letter from Israel and saw the Rashi script of his father's hand. It worried him. He assumed his father would be asking for money and he didn't know how to respond. He was in shock when he discovered that the letter was not for money but instead demanded something of himself. The request was more difficult than he expected.

"What is it, Hal?"

He looked up at Diane. She sat in the glow of the television watching him and folding the diapers.

"Nothing." His mother was dying. Cancer, the letter said. Now his father wanted him to come to her, bring his wife and son. Come to say good-bye. He could say good-bye by telephone. Bye-bye, Mama, the way Diane was trying to teach little Stevie. Jesus.

How could his father expect him to go back to Israel? Didn't he know the minute Hillel stepped off the plane, he'd be arrested for evading his army duty. Another thing he hadn't told Diane. She thought he was a paratrooper.

And to bring Diane and Steven? How was Diane supposed to understand that she had died years ago in a traffic accident?

All right. Let's say he chanced going back to Israel to see his mother—Diane was out—would his wife let him take Steven along, without her? Not a chance. Especially when she heard he was going to Israel, where she had begged him to take her ever since they were married. These American Jews. The richer they became, the less satisfied they were with Miami Beach.

No! He would write his father. He would make it clear to him that the closest he could reasonably get to Givatayim was Cyprus. It was a short plane ride. His mother could meet him there. He would send the fare for both his father and mother. And there would even be time to go to the beach, get out in the sun a little.

Joseph put on his glasses and read the letter Hillel had sent his father. Where it had infuriated Meir, it simply made Joseph sad.

"I will kill him," Meir fumed.

"No, you won't," Joseph said and put his arm around his father-in-law. They were in Joseph's office. Meir had brought the letter to him as soon as he got off work and picked it up at his apartment. He was too angry to stay at home and let Salemah see that something was wrong, especially since she would recognize Hillel's handwriting.

"What can we do? She asks for him. Sometimes I think she knows."

Joseph walked slowly over to the coffee pot and poured himself a cup. He shrugged. "We can go to Cyprus and force him to come back with us."

"Do you think we can?"

"It's worth a try." Joseph looked at the letter again and set the dates in his mind. "You have money for the tickets. You and Ovadia can fly over and try to make him understand that this is the last chance he will have to see his mother. The doctor is sure she cannot travel?"

"Yes. She wanted to go to Jerusalem to King David's tomb, but the doctor said it would be too much for her."

"You and Ovadia go. Even Hillel can't refuse such a plea."

But when Ovadia read Hillel's letter, he would not accompany his father. "I don't go to beg him to do what is right." And he would not budge, which was much unlike Ovadia, who tried his best to accommodate everyone.

But it was a strange time for all of them. They were in limbo. Everyone knew everything except Salemah. They told her that the cyst had been removed and she would be given pills to take to make her more comfortable after the operation. She didn't question them even when the pain continued. After all, they had spoken to the doctor and he should know.

Shoshana was being separated from the army. David brought her into his office for a talk. "You know I'm leaving too," he told her.

"No, I didn't know," she said.

"Yes. There's nothing more I can do here. Haim's retiring over at security."

"Oh."

"I'm taking his place."

"That's good. That should be challenging," she said numbly.

"What are you going to do?"

"Stay home. Take care of my mother."

"I mean for a living," he specified.

"I can't think about it now, David. I can't think about anything."

"I'm offering you a job with me. It's open when you want it."

She was suddenly interested. "Same sort of work?" she asked.

"The same. Maybe more intriguing. I haven't gotten into it myself yet."

"You mean it?"

"Well, of course I mean it," he said, slightly annoyed.

"You're not just sorry for me."

"When I'm sorry for people, I pat them on the head. You're good at your work. Sometimes inspired. I want you with me. I should warn you though. There is one drawback. While I'll be moving into Haim's spot, Yossi Leskov will be taking over Amos's. He'll be our boss. You know how I can usually get along with anyone."

Shoshana smiled. He didn't have to explain further. They both knew about Yossi Leskov from military intelligence. He was a schemer, not an analyst, not a scholar. But maybe that was what was needed, someone like Yossi with his underhanded methods of collecting information. Of course she had never considered a career before. She didn't know why. Her major aim all these years had been the army, and she had never thought past that. But now, the thought of a career, she liked it.

"Are you still seeing Danny?"

"Danny?" She came back to the present. "Danny, yes. Why? Is that a security violation."

David smiled.

"My mother caught us once, you know." Why did she blurt that out? "She said I'd be the death of her."

"You're not," David told her sternly.

She bit her lip. "I try to be rational." She was silent. "David? Am I an awful person?"

He stared at her. "You're a woman," he said, as if that explained everything. "Would you give me your hand?" he asked.

She held it out. He took her hand in his and kissed her palm. David was warm. David was always warm for her.

Despite David's assurances, Shoshana still felt guilty, still felt responsible for her mother's illness. It surprised her to find that Lily, of all people, did too. They had grown closer these past months, watching over their mother as she moved slowly through her days. "Do you remember how angry she was when I wanted to marry Joseph?" Lily asked tearfully. "It probably started then."

Shoshana thought Lily insane. "How can you say that?"

"Or when I had the abortion. She's the only one who stood by me, helped me fight it out."

"She's happy for you, Lily. She knows you love Joseph, and Joshua has been her life ever since you had him."

"Still—"

They all saw in the disease eating its way through their mother's body the reflection of their own sins and their own mortality. And they each tried to make their peace without saying good-bye.

Ovadia didn't know what to do. He had received his acceptance from Princeton University for September 1963 to study toward his Ph.D. and had been awarded a fellowship that would make it possible financially. He wanted to go to Princeton more than anything, but what about his mother?

"You have to go," Shoshana told him. "You can't give this up. This is your chance."

"But how can I leave her."

"What is it, it's May. You don't have to go until August. You can wait and see how she's doing. But don't turn down that offer."

"How can I tell her?"

"She'll be happy for you," Shoshana assured him. "And if you don't go, she'll know there's something wrong. Besides, as soon as it looks like it's . . . near, I'll call you. You can fly back. Don't worry."

"Like Hillel?"

"Don't compare yourself to Hillel! Don't ever."

When the time came to go to Cyprus, Meir persuaded Joseph to come with him. Joseph had wanted Meir to take Shoshana or even Lily, but both girls had convinced Meir that they should stay with their mother. So Joseph was pressed into service because he spoke English and maybe he could say something to Hillel that would bring him home.

When Salemah heard they were going to Cyprus to meet with her firstborn, she grew wild with excitement. She made Lily stay the day with her so they could bake all the foods she knew Hillel must have missed since his exodus from Israel. When she had boxed the food and handed it to Meir before he left, she said, "Tell him I miss him and would like to see him too. If it's possible."

Meir smiled. "I'll get him here," he promised his wife.

When Joseph and Meir got off the plane in Nicosia, Hillel was waiting for them with a limousine he had hired. He was not pleased to see Joseph, but he gave his father a warm embrace. And Meir, despite his anger, was moved to tears by the sight of his son after so many years.

"Come," Hillel said. "I have the best hotel suite in Nicosia reserved for us."

"I don't need a hotel suite," Meir told him, getting down to business immediately. "Your mother needs to see you now. We can go to your hotel, check out, and be on the next flight back to Tel Aviv."

"I'll do anything I can for her," Hillel said dutifully.

"Then go to Tel Aviv to see her. She's been asking for you. She's dying."

"I cannot go to Tel Aviv because of the army, Father," Hillel said calmly. "You know what the Israelis will do to me."

"Ovadia says no. Ovadia says if you come in on a U.S. passport, they won't pay any attention to you."

"What does Ovadia know!" Hillel exploded. "Does he know about the lists they keep? It's a police state. Why should I take the risk?"

"She gave you life."

"If she knew what would happen to me, do you think she would want me to come? Now I'm willing to provide for her," he said more calmly.

"Provide what? A gravestone?"

"Father, don't get excited. A man your age must control himself."

"I hope some day your children turn away from you," Meir said quietly. They rode the rest of the way in silence.

When they got to the hotel, Meir said, "At least let your wife and child see her."

"My wife doesn't even know her and my child is too small to travel without its mother. Steven is still being breast-fed." A lie.

"Hillel, you must come and see your mother." Joseph spoke for the first time.

Hillel ignored him. "Tonight we'll go out for a big dinner and then we'll visit several nightclubs. How about that, Father? You probably haven't been to a nightclub since the Swallow's Nest. Does anyone ever hear from Uncle Jacob? I thought about him during the latest coup. That man, with his money he could have come to America. You must come to the United States someday, Father. You'd love it. Everything is wrapped in cellophane. It's so clean."

"Ovadia is probably going to the United States in September to study," Joseph said softly. "I'm sure he'll be glad to have you show him around."

"Ovadia? Coming to the States? But not near Boston?"

"What do you have to hide, Hillel?" Joseph asked with a slight smile.

Hillel turned from him. "So, Father, what'll it be? Your choice of nightclubs."

Meir looked at his son. "Do you understand what I'm telling you, Hillel. Maybe it's the shock of it. Your mother has asked to see you. This is your last chance."

"I understand, Father," Hillel said severely. "Don't you think after losing Diane and my Brian that I understand death?" He let a tear slip from his eye. He was pleased to see his father reach out to him. "But would my seeing her save her life? Would it in the final analysis make one hour's difference? She would live or die on the second set aside for her by the Almighty. I have a new wife and a new son. And I will not be thrown into some Israeli prison for years while they rot alone in America."

"Wrap them in cellophane," Joseph suggested. "It will keep them fresh."

"Bring her here, Father," Hillel begged. He reached into his pocket and took out some traveler's checks. "Here, here is the money. Another ticket for you. Bring a nurse with you, if you must."

"She can't travel," Meir stressed. "She can barely make it up and down a flight of stairs. She is in pain. She asks for you."

Hillel shook his head. "Mother would never put herself, her own desires before my welfare."

"No," Joseph said coldly. "She never would."

In the end the only compromise Hillel would make was

to arrange to call his mother and speak to her over the phone. He could have done that from New York. Nevertheless Salemah was inordinately grateful to hear from Hillel. And after Hillel spoke to her, he demanded to speak to Lily, Shoshana, and Ovadia. Lily and Shoshana spoke briefly to him. Ovadia would not come to the phone.

"Ovadia," Salemah pleaded.

But Hillel's desertion of his mother was more than Ovadia could take. He walked away, he ran from the post office where they had received this call and he would not return.

Salemah had noted her husband's depression ever since he returned from Cyprus. "Why?" she asked him as they sat alone one night in their apartment.

He understood. "I promised to bring you Hillel. I failed."

"I spoke to him on the telephone. It was enough."

Meir studied his wife. She was sorting and mending sheets. Last night she had gone through the napkins. "What are you doing all that work for?"

She continued as if she had not heard him. He didn't ask again. "Meir." She caught his attention. "I have something to tell you. I don't want you to get upset."

"I won't."

"You know you have a temper. When you were younger and you got mad, whooh! We all had to keep out of your way."

"But not now."

"Now you're older. We all get old, Meir. Meir. I'm dying." He looked up at her as if someone had torn a knife across his heart. "Shh," she told him. "Just listen. I didn't think at first it was possible because of what the doctor had told Shoshana and Ovadia. But I feel it now. It's coming."

"No."

"Meir, you never listened to me. Maybe I always talked too much, so you could never sort out the important from the unimportant. But now, be quiet and listen. I've made a list. I'm going through everything we have and making sure it's in good condition."

"But why?"

"Do you think I want someone going through my things and saying what a sloppy housekeeper I was?" she asked angrily as she rethreaded her needle. "But this is nothing. There are more important things I'm leaving behind than the linens. That's those four children of ours. And, Meir, you must never tell them I'm dying because it would upset them. They must not know. You will promise."

"Yes. I promise."

"Now I think that Lily and Joseph are happy. Hillel?" She shrugged. "What can we say about him? He has been a stranger to us for so long. But he always knew how to take care of himself."

"True." Meir nodded bitterly.

"Ovadia tells me he's received money from America to study. He must go. Because he's always wanted to study. Sometimes I think he doesn't want anything else. " She shook her head. "He mustn't stay here on my account. You'll see to that?"

"Yes," Meir promised.

"Shoshana." She stopped herself after speaking her daughter's name, fearing her voice would break.

"You'll want me to see she makes a good match."

"No," Salemah said sharply. "Shoshana will not marry. She has said that often to me. She has her reasons."

"What reasons?"

"Woman's reasons." She knew that would stop Meir. He would not press into matters that were too murky for the masculine mind. Above all things she must protect Shoshana since her daughter was not capable of protecting herself. "You must not press her into marriage," she continued. "She has a fine future in front of her. She has a—a career." Salemah said the word carefully. Meir waved that off. "A career is very important to a girl like Shoshana. She should have been a boy." It would have solved everything, Salemah thought bitterly. She would never say even to herself that Shoshana should never have been born. "So what do you think?"

"I don't agree with you about Shoshana."

"But I am her mother. And it is my dying wish." She teased him with a smile.

Meir got up and went over to the couch where his wife sat. He put his arm awkwardly around her. "And what of me?" he said. "Since you're ordering everyone's life."

"You will remarry."

"No," he protested.

"Meir, you don't know how to cook, you don't know how to clean, you don't know how to do the wash. Since you are no longer rich enough to hire a maid, you'll remarry."

Meir sat with his arm around his wife thinking back to the day he first saw her, his marriage day when the veil had been raised and that face had stared up at him. And now they were old and she was dying.

"I am at peace, Meir," she said, guessing his thoughts. "I have been content to be your wife."

"Despite everything?"

"Because of everything."

It happened on one of the first days of August, 1963. It was a quiet day, hot. Meir had left for work. Ovadia had to go down to the American consulate to check on his visa. Shoshana was still in her room. She came out, dressed for work. "Do you want me to do the dishes before I go?" she called out.

"No, leave them," Salemah said. "It will give me something to do."

"It's no trouble for me."

"For me either," her mother said, defending, still, her position in the family.

Shoshana laughed and came over to kiss her mother good-bye. "I love you, Mother," she said. Her mother grunted as Shoshana brushed her cheek with her lips. Then she was gone.

Salemah felt a breeze drifting through the window as she lay on her bed. Shoshana, her baby, what would become of her? She would have to speak to Lily about it. All the children growing up and going their ways. Thank God for the grandchildren. She rose from the bed to get at the dishes,

lked over to him. "How to get to Princeton?" he asked
nidly.

"You want your bags carried?" the porter asked.
Ovadia didn't understand. He began sweating more pro-

then sank back again. It was hard getting up that morning. Leave the dishes for an hour. She would just take a little nap, then do them before Meir came home for his lunch. Yes, she needed to rest.

When Meir came home for lunch that day, he found Salemah asleep on the bed. He could not wake her. He had expected this for some time. The doctor said she would slip into a coma first, then die. He straightened the covers around her.

He checked the apartment and found the breakfast dishes in the sink. He filled the tub with hot water and washed them quickly, dried them, and put them away. Now everything was the way she would have wanted it. Now he could go get the family and bring them to her.

21

What impressed Ovadia right off about the United States was its efficiency. He had flown to New York at the very last minute. The thirty-day mourning period for his mother was over at sunset. He took the next flight out. He was used to dealing with Israeli authorities—papers, rubber stamps, and argumentative hostility with every step. What a pleasure then was passport control in New York, where not only did the official smile at him as he stamped Ovadia's passport, but he also said, "Welcome to our country." And he seemed to mean it.

In a way coming to America was like coming to Israel. It was September and hot in New York. But Ovadia was wearing two suit jackets and his winter topcoat as he had no room for them in the two cardboard cases he was carrying. Now what to do after he had gotten through passport control and customs. He had to get to Princeton that night. Registration was the next morning. He spent some time looking around, trying to sort out the English. It panicked him for a minute. How could he possibly learn to speak and comprehend this language? He must have been crazy to come here. He saw a black man in a uniform and fusely. "Princeton?" he asked again.

"Bags?"

"No, Princeton."

"You want to get to Princeton?" the porter asked.

Ovadia smiled.

The porter smiled. "You're losing me a fee, man." Ovadia didn't understand. "Come 'ere."

Ovadia followed him to the entranceway. He stepped on a mat and the door shot open. He was startled. He stepped back. The porter laughed.

"You see that bus there?" the porter asked. Ovadia nodded. "You take that bus, you hear, to West Side Terminal. West Side," he repeated. "You get out of West Side Terminal and cross the street to Port Authority. You got that? Port Authority. From there you ask information for the bus to Princeton. Right?"

"West Side Terminal, cross street, Port Authority," Ovadia repeated, grimly determined.

"Right. Okay, up you go now," the porter said, heaving his bags into the waiting belly of the bus. Ovadia was shaken. "Don't worry," the porter said. "They'll be there when you get off the bus. Good luck now." He waved. Ovadia waved back.

Somehow he made it. By some miracle he arrived at Port Authority just in time to catch the last bus out for Princeton. He said to the bus driver, "Please, you tell me when Princeton University?"

The bus driver looked at him and shook his head, but an hour and a half later the bus driver was calling, "Palmer Square!" He turned around. "That's you, buddy."

Ovadia shot up and stumbled forward, trying to pass his two suitcases down the aisle. He had barely dropped off the bus before the bus driver closed the doors and motored off.

The security guard quickly found him. Ovadia was short

294

and dark and certainly looked suspicious. And at eleven thirty at night what was he doing standing in front of Old Nassau.

"I'm graduate student," Ovadia announced. "Where do I go?"

The security guard laughed, helped Ovadia into his car, and drove him over to the graduate college. "What have you got in those suitcases?" the guard asked.

"Stamps," Ovadia said.

"Stamps?" That stopped all conversation.

As soon as Ovadia arrived at the graduate college, he was given the key to his room and directions on how to get there. He couldn't believe it when he opened the door and closed it again. A room of his own. After his apartment in Tel Aviv, the tents in the army, rented rooms shared with others at the Technion, now this. But he couldn't really savor it yet. It was twelve New York time, six A.M. in Tel Aviv. Now all he wanted was sleep.

When he looked out the window the next morning, it was green. Green all over with paved paths cautiously cutting across the grass. Not a grain of sand in sight. He laughed with pleasure. And breakfast. Americans ate more for breakfast than most people in Israel ate for the day. The stores. Registration left him exhausted but not too exhausted to walk through the stores. Everything, even objects for which there was no use, was for sale. The United States was a wonderland, a paradise, and with a sudden quickening of his heart, Ovadia knew he would never want to leave here.

He made friends quickly, mainly among other engineering graduate students. They saw each other over and over again as they took the same courses, they ate together, they went out to the movies together, to mixers, to the bars. Ovadia had to develop a taste for beer. It wasn't hard. People seemed to enjoy his company, perhaps because he provided them with so much amusement as he continuously mispronounced words. English annoyed him. Why couldn't they spell words the way they were pronounced. How could "Wednesday" be "Wensday."

He wrote many letters home to his family in these early days, especially since he knew how lonely his father would be and how hard it was on Shoshana caring for him and holding a job at the same time. Shoshana always wrote back saying that Father wanted to know if he had contacted Hillel. He avoided the subject in each letter he wrote. He had no intention of seeking Hillel out, not after the way his brother had neglected their mother. So instead he filled his letters with every facet of American life, what they ate, what they wore, what movies they saw, what was on television. There was no television in Israel. Jordan had it, other Arab countries had it, but not Israel. So the rich Israelis bought their television sets with one hundred percent or more sales tax added to customs, and they turned their antennas toward the Arab states surrounding them. But for Ovadia television in America was a first. Everything was a first.

Then Kennedy was assassinated. The country sagged, dragged down into the morass by age and loss, despair and sorrow. The United States jigsawed into the young and the old, the white and the black, the rich and the poor, the loudmouths and the silent majority.

Ovadia returned to his work. He could not sort through what was happening to America, but he could understand mathematics. That was one of the beauties of his studies. Equations meant something, numbers could be figured out, could be made to prove something. Words were mere camouflage and most of the time meant nothing at all.

David Tal, his stomach contracted in anger and frustration, left the staff meeting to walk back to his own department. Why did he let Yossi Leskov, his boss, do this to him. It might not lead to an early grave but surely there was an ulcer working itself up inside of him. They had just gone over the budget. Research was being cut while more money was funneled into operations. David needed that money for computers and programmers to store what his department translated. But Yossi couldn't see it. He was satisfied with the metal files that littered every corner of

David's domain. One day, David thought. Yossi will want something quick and it won't be there. Then research would get its computers. Until then it was antacid pills.

He caught sight of Shoshana. She at least still respected his opinions. He walked over to her and caught her reading an air letter from America. "How's your brother?" he guessed.

"David!" Shoshana smiled brightly up at him. "I'll assume you mean Ovadia, not Hillel."

"Right."

"He's fine." Shoshana mulled it over. "A little of the exuberance has gone out of his letters since Kennedy's assassination."

"I can see why."

"It's so incredible. One can see this happening in Baghdad but not in the United States?"

David sighed. "Well, it just goes to prove there are nuts everywhere."

"Assassination is government policy in Iraq," she reminded him sternly. "One would hope this is not the case in America."

"Don't worry. No one's going to assassinate Lyndon Baines Johnson."

"How do you know that?"

"Because the people who hate him are for gun control." She laughed. "David, you are too cynical."

"Not cyncial. Just getting old. I keep telling you that. How's the work going?"

She was busy transcribing messages from the new government in Iraq.

"I don't know. Intriguing. Depressing."

"You're getting sick of the Ba'aths already? I wouldn't. I have a feeling they're going to be around for a long time."

"It's just that I don't understand the Ba'aths."

"So introduce me to someone who does."

"They call themselves the Arab Socialist Renaissance party, yet there's no renaissance in Iraq. From all the reports we've had, there's only confusion. And socialism seems to mean when a gang of thugs takes what it wants from those who have more than they do. So I don't really see where any policy is being instituted."

"I'm glad you're a translator and not a political analyst," David told her.

"In other words I should just keep translating and not try to figure it out. After all, Iraq was my country, David. You can't expect me to feel nothing. I have relatives there still."

"Just don't slant your work to fit any preconception you might have."

"Is that why you came by, to reprimand me?"

"My God, Shoshana, just because I'm your boss and you're my willing slave."

She smiled. "I'm not your willing slave."

"Whose willing slave are you then?"

"Oh. That's why you came by. David, my personal life is my own."

"But to meet him on company time? I tried to find you yesterday at three and you were missing."

She grinned, thinking back to yesterday afternoon.

"Shoshana," David said sternly, "work comes first."

"Well, I did try to find you yesterday around eleven to tell you I'd be leaving a bit early but you were out. On personal business, your secretary managed to let slip."

"I had to exchange some dollars on the black market. As you can see, I put my spare time to good use. I wish you'd do the same." He got up to go. "A word to the wise." He found her smirking. "It's a hopeless situation," he reminded her.

"I'm used to that. After all, I deal with Iraqi politics all day."

Shoshana didn't leave work early that day. She didn't have to. She and Danny planned to meet later that night after she had fixed her father's meal and straightened up the apartment.

She hated to go back to the apartment. Her father had become so depressed since her mother died. Nothing was right with him now. He went to work and then he came home and moped. He didn't seem to want to do anything except sit on the balcony and stare at the activity on Katznelson street. Well, with the winter days that would soon cease. Then what would he do? She hated to think about it. He had gotten so crabby. And religious. All of a sudden after sixty-four years he was Orthodox. He never considered the strain it put on her. No one ever thought of the strain living with her father put on her except her. And Danny, now that he was back from England. Lily lived right up the street but she never seemed to manage to get down to their father's to do any of the cooking or the cleaning. Lily considered it a big deal that she had her father and Shoshana over for the Sabbath eve meal, never thinking that Shoshana had to prepare food for him every night. And listen to his mumbling. He never spoke clearly. He mumbled. And she was expected to catch what he was saying because when she didn't, he just flared at her as if she were a total simpleton who would never get anything right.

She wished she were Ovadia or even Hillel. She wished she were far away in America. She wished she were anywhere but in Givatayim living alone with her father.

"I'm home," she called out as she unlatched their front door. There he was, the balcony closed to conserve heat, sitting by the window, staring out. "I'm home, Father," she said more gently. He paid no attention to her. She threw her coat and purse down on her bed and went into the kitchen. She tried not to think. In a few hours she would be with Danny and that would make everything all right.

Danny waited in his friend's room for Shoshana to appear. He checked his watch. Half an hour late already. But Shoshana was worth the wait. She was worth everything.

He hoped she wore her hair down tonight. He liked it down around her face and shoulders. He would ask her to undress in front of him, watch while she pulled her sweater over her head, which sent her hair tumbling up and down again. Beautiful. She was beautiful and exciting. She came to him so openly and desired him so. All he wanted to do was protect her and keep her. Save her. He laughed. Or was it savor her.

He supposed it was only physical, nothing more. He should hope it was nothing more. He was always comparing Shoshana to his wife, Ronit. Ronit, who had the audacity to have a daughter instead of the son he expected. Adee, his daughter, was cute enough. He enjoyed holding her and cooing to her when he was alone with her, which was hardly ever. Ronit and he were both only children so the grandparents were over at their flat all the time. And Ronit had gained, God, enough weight to produce an elephant. She could barely make it into her old house dresses, and she never found time to put on make-up or do more than brush through her cropped hair. Shoshana came to him perfect, smelling of flowers, not soured milk. But then Shoshana hadn't had his child. Thank God.

When the knock on the door came, he opened it to find Shoshana looking flustered. "I'm late," she announced.

"I've waited."

"My father is driving me crazy."

"You said that yesterday."

"At least you listened. Sometimes I think the only reason you see me is to—"

"That too." He pulled her into his arms.

"Hold me. Just for a minute."

He held her but he could not stop his hands from working down along her back. "Why are you so desperate for me?" she asked him suddenly.

"Because I love you." That was the easy answer. The truth was he didn't know. He did know that the only time he felt really alive was when he was underwater with his men or when he was under the covers with Shoshana. Someday he would figure it all out. Someday he would stop feeling and start thinking. Now he would just concentrate on the intensity of Shoshana's moans and answer them with some utterings of his own.

She was sweating. He wiped the beads from her upper lip. "It's winter," she said, amazed.

"It's always summer when I'm in bed with you."

"Are you going away again?"

"Yes—to Bermuda."

"But why Bermuda? And why now? You just got back from three months in England. How much training do you need just to splash around in the water?" She somehow didn't get the same thrill underwater he did. They had tried it once together, scuba diving off Eilat, but she was so afraid water would get into her mouth and choke her that she barely noticed the fish and the coral he was busy pointing out to her.

"At least you look great in a bikini," he had said to her afterward to make her feel better. But it only made her remember how she had to keep pulling at the bottom half of her suit so she wouldn't be exposed.

"It's not just splashing around in the water. It's learning how to attack, how to plant devices that'll cripple the enemy's navy, how to conduct raids from the sea."

"Variations on a theme."

"Exactly."

"Danny, has it ever occurred to you that no one in Israel knows or cares about the navy?"

"They will. Someday. Until then I'm content to be your unsung hero."

"If you leave me alone much longer, you'll be unremembered."

"You have your work."

"And my father."

There were drawbacks to Shoshana. She made demands. But the good thing about her was that he never remembered the demands when he was separated from her.

At twenty years of age Danielle understood money. It was a commodity, something one traded. Not bartered. That was different. Bartering, that was trading your effort for someone else's effort. Money wasn't an effort. Money was there like a second skin. It felt good and rough between one's fingers, against one's body. There was money in the bank, some of it real, some of it fabricated on paper.

She was separated from the real money by a glass partition. She dealt with the fabrication. "That's all right," one of her friends in accounting told her. "Real money is worth less every day. We can create a paradise on paper."

She wasn't so envious of the tellers. Paper money, yes. She liked that sensation. But coins bothered her. They clinked and they splattered. They were heavy, flashy. Coins were vulgar. Not everyone found them so. Some of the tellers spent lunch hours going through their cash drawers. They collected. Especially those who dealt with the overseas trade.

Overseas accounts would be her specialty. She had spent eighteen months moving around the accounting department, learning the business. "Because you're bright," her boss told her. "Not like some of the girls who come here, put in their hours and leave. You actually want to know." She certainly did. And now that she was working with Mr. Frankel, she hoped to delve deeper into the mysteries of banking. Mr. Frankel was a good teacher. She supposed for that she must have been an apt student to have given him such encouragement. He explained the intricacies of theoretically—always theoretically—avoiding Israel's tax laws; how one hid one's money in foreign bank accounts; how one could double one's savings by illegally sending them overseas to friends or relatives and then bringing the money back on the wings of a rising inflation; how the most valuable people to know in the Israeli financial world were those who traveled abroad frequently or at regular intervals. Pilots, stewards, army officers training overseas in the United States or Great Britain. What was the proper cut to give them of money you wanted secreted in foreign bank accounts. She found it fascinating.

Shoshana found it less so. When Danielle would turn to talk of money with Shoshana, her friend would only talk of Danny. Danielle had met Danny. She thought it was about time. After all, Shoshana was her best friend and Shoshana had been seeing Danny for over three years now. Three years. She couldn't believe it had been that long. The only people who did not know of Shoshana's relationship with Danny were Shoshana's family and, she hoped, Danny's wife. She warned Shoshana that she was headed for disaster, but Shoshana no longer seemed to care. Anyhow when Danielle learned that Danny, having just returned from England, was about to set off again for Bermuda, she decided it was an appropriate time to be introduced. They got together for coffee after the workday finished. She found Danny outwardly friendly but rather reserved.

Still Danny was amenable to meeting her again, "on a business matter," as she phrased it. He did not even find it odd when she requested that he open an account in her name in Bermuda, nor did he question her when she passed him an envelope with five one-hundred-dollar bills American. She supposed his commando training had readied him for life's little surprises.

Danielle felt safer after dispatching him with the money. It had become heavy on her hands. What, she asked herself often, would happen if her mother found it? Five hundred dollars and over a year's work would have simply disappeared into her mother's pocket, and she knew that neither she nor Leah would ever bring the subject up. Not that Leah didn't know her daughter was trading on the black market. Everyone on the block knew that. After all she did work in a bank only two blocks from Lilienblum Street, the center of the black money market. She had to know by now whom to trade with and how to transact business. And she looked so innocent. Who would suspect her? The neighbors trusted her. That's how she made her first commissions. A check from a retailer here, an embarrassing excess of profits from the corner store elsewhere. She was only too glad to help out. For a percentage that she denied to her mother she took. Not that Leah totally believed her. Danielle sometimes upon returning home would find her things in disarray. But Danielle knew if there was one place her mother would not look, it was in the old rags used to do the cleaning, and that's where she kept the money. Until she found Danny.

Her first move from neighborhood to high finance came from Joseph Benjamin, Shoshana's brother-in-law. He had let her handle a few piddling amounts before he broached the subject of his overabundance of riches. She, of course, assured him immediately that she understood the hazardous cash flow in the construction business. On the one hand he had to keep enough money in reserve to buy information—she wouldn't call it passing out bribes—on where the government was planning to build and what bid they would accept, on the other hand there were the overwhelming profits to be made from selling the *shikunim* once they were built to the right sort of people, those who could pay extra under the table. And, of course, what if one were suddenly audited by some uniquely diligent tax official? How could one explain that one's profits were perhaps triple what one's books stated them to be? Indeed she would be glad to help Joseph find some anonymous resting place for his money in a New York bank.

"Danielle, how can I ever thank you?"

She told him her commission. He laughed. "It doesn't matter," he shrugged it off. "I was doing business with someone else before, but him I couldn't trust."

"You can trust me, Joseph," she assured him, the ghost of her treacherous father Nazem Haya suddenly rising between them.

"I know I can." He chased the ghost away.

And he could. They all could. She would redeem the family name, restore their honor. And at the same time make money. For her dowry, for Ezra, for Albert. But not for her mother.

22

Ovadia read the latest epistle from his father via Shoshana. They were on him again. Why hadn't he gone to see Hillel? Even Joseph in a short burst of written affection had chided him for not making the trip to Boston, Joseph saying that he understood how Ovadia felt about Hillel's treatment of Salemah, but all that should be buried in the past by now. Ovadia wondered at Joseph's choice of words.

Ovadia's excuse to his family had always been that he was too busy with his studies. In actual fact he had spoken several awkward times with Hillel over the phone, conversations dutifully recorded in his letters home. But never in any of his short, abrupt conversations with his brother had Hillel invited him to Boston to meet his family. Ovadia didn't think it strange of his brother. First Hillel was thoughtless, second Hillel most assuredly knew how Ovadia felt about him. Cowardly, insensitive, well the list could go on and on. Not that Ovadia found himself so perfect, but at least he felt the burden of his responsibilities. Except to his brother, as the letters from home never failed to point out.

Well, okay. It was spring vacation. He had a week. More than enough time to finish the work he wanted to do. So he would take three days off, Greyhound up to Boston, map his way to Brookline, and find his brother. He thought of calling first, but he couldn't face it. So he would be Israeli. He would come uninvited.

Diane was sure Steven was advanced for his age. She had compared notes in the neighborhood. What month had the others sat up, started drinking from a cup, grabbed the rail of their playpens to pull themselves upright? When had they walked and talked? Steven was definitely brighter than the others. Not that she would brag. Too much. After all, as her mother had said, by the time they were twenty-one who cared when they had walked or talked. The important thing was whether they were in or out of jail. Diane supposed so. Still, right now she was perusing a book on potty training. She didn't want to make any mistakes. She had to be a perfect mother.

She looked at Steven. He was eating and drooling his animal crackers. That was all right. Mess was a stage to go through. Sometimes looking around her house, she felt that she had never left it. She tried occasionally to decide whom Steven looked like. Walter knew. She had assumed the parental grapevine had been busy because he had called before the birth to ask, "Is it mine?"

"No," she had answered. "It's mine." Steven was her personal possession, her wealth.

Her mother had been hysterical when Diane had chosen Dr. Palberg as her pediatrician. "What's wrong with Walter de Gregory? He'd probably give you a discount on the shots?" But she couldn't face Walter again, not with their child between them.

It wasn't too bad living with Hal. It struck her finally that she would never have a happy marriage. Steven had not brought them together. Evidently the tie that bound them was very loose indeed. She realized that she never honestly had understood her husband, probably never would understand him. She supposed there were worse things in life than not being committed to one's spouse.

Though she wanted to be happy, she expected she would hang on like everybody else.

Sometimes she wondered if she was glad or sad that Hal had so little time for her. She could ridicule him behind his back. The organization man. He ran for president of anything—his country club, his engineering society, the local UJA appeal. He had to feel important. He wanted fame more than fortune now that he had succeeded in becoming a partner—in her father's firm. It was probably her fault that he craved so much attention from others, as she was no longer capable of giving him at home that which he needed. Still she barely saw him that much anymore. With his meetings and his business trips he was hardly ever at home. Like now in the middle of Passover he had taken off for Chicago. It didn't really bother her. At least with him gone she could have bread and crackers in the house. He had been insisting ever since Steven was born that she become more Orthodox in her religious practices. She had asked if he wanted her to act like a hypocrite, and Hal had replied that there were worse things to be.

If she were to be honest with herself, Diane would admit she was lonely. She had joined a new sorority when she had Steven, that of motherhood. While it sufficed during the day, it did not make up for the sweetness she had felt with Walter. But that was over. Until she wanted a second child, she thought humorlessly to herself.

Five o'clock. It was time to think about getting supper. With Hal gone it was easy. She could have hot dogs or hamburgers or frozen food. She would lead Steven to the refrigerator and let him take his choice. Though she knew what it would be. Cottage cheese. How he could possibly choose cottage cheese when she only selected it on diet days was beyond her. She rose from her chair and headed for the kitchen. The buzz brought her to a halt.

"Door, Mommy," Steven said. That kid was so damned bright.

The first thing Diane thought when she opened the door was "pygmy." Okay, he was a little bit taller, but he was dark and his face was certainly more African than American, though she didn't think he was a Negro. It was hard to tell exactly what he was.

The second thing that struck her was that he was paying very little attention to her but had his eyes, crossed as they seemed to be behind his thick lenses, fixed on her child. "This must be Steven," he said, stepping into her house. Her son responded with a giggle. The strange little man took a giant panda from a shopping bag and thrust it into Steven's waiting, crumb-encrusted palms.

"Excuse me," Diane said. "Do I know you?"

The man turned to face her. He held out his hand. "I'm Ovadia Ewan," he offered. "I know I'm not expected; but I found myself with a few free days during spring break, and I decided to come up and visit you."

Diane realized she was dealing with a crazy. "Was there any particular reason you decided to visit me out of all the people in the Boston metropolitan area?"

Ovadia looked startled. He went back to the door and checked the number. "This is the Evans' house, isn't it? This is Steven, isn't he?"

"Yes."

"Well, I'm Hillel's brother. He must have mentioned me."

"Hillel?" Diane suddenly threw her hands up to her mouth. "Oh, Hal. You're Hal's brother?"

"Yes." Ovadia smiled. "How stupid of me. Yes. Hal Evans. Hillel Ewan. One and the same. I haven't changed my name. Ovadia Ewan."

"U-in," Diane tried.

"Everyone in America says it that way," Ovadia complained. "It's short *e*—E-wan, rhymes with 'don.' Almost."

"Ewan. Ovadia Ewan."

"Right."

"Hal's brother."

"Yes. His only brother. The one at Princeton."

"Have you just come to this country?"

"Last September."

"Last September?"

"Hal must have—"

"No, he didn't."

"Ah." Ovadia mulled that over. "Well then I'm really a shock to you."

"Hal's not here. He's in Chicago."

"Oh."

"I guess he didn't expect you."

"No."

Diane laughed. "This is really stupid. I'm just flabbergasted or dumbfounded or something."

"I usually don't take people by surprise."

"Look, I was just about to make something to eat. Have you eaten?"

"I've been traveling all day. I had an egg salad sandwich with me but it spoiled."

"I have—oh, the hell with it. Let's go out to eat." She let Ovadia follow her around the house while she got Steven ready. "You don't keep kosher, do you?"

"Not in America," Ovadia answered. "It's too much trouble."

"You want to try a lobster?"

Ovadia grimaced.

"All right, we'll start on shrimp. Out of the shells."

But when they got to the seafood house, Ovadia ordered plain fish, broiled, while Steven and Diane had fried shrimp. "I know it's not elegant but I love them," Diane admitted. "Now I have to hear all about your family," she rushed on. "Hal is so secretive, he hardly tells me anything. Imagine your being in this country since September and I never even heard of you. You must think I'm terrible for not inviting you up for the holidays."

"Actually I'm not here to talk about me. My family is dying to know more about you. They've been after me to visit you ever since I got here. We were all very upset to hear about Diane and Brian."

Diane stopped chewing. "Diane and Brian?" she repeated.

Ovadia stared at her. He floundered. "I'm sorry, I realize the subject must be very painful for you. I'll understand if you don't want to mention it."

"Mention what?"

"Diane and Brian. Hillel's first family. The one killed on the expressway."

"Hillel—Hal had a first family? You mean not only does he have a brother he didn't bother to tell me about but I'm his second wife?"

"But you're Diane's sister, Shelia."

"Shelia is my sister. She lives in Colorado. I'm Diane."

"You're Diane! And Brian?"

"Brian? Brian who?"

Ovadia fiddled with his wallet in his pants pocket. He flipped it open and showed to Diane a picture of a blond, smiling little boy. "That's Brian all right," Diane said. "I can show you Brian. He's my next-door neighbor's child."

Ovadia slumped, Diane sat back. Neither of them took another bite.

They went home. They talked for hours, forever, before Ovadia left. She couldn't believe the well of deceit in which she was drowning. Fairy tales about her and her make-believe son, Hal's treatment of his mother, his lying about—his lying about everything.

After Ovadia left, she went to her bedroom and tried to sleep. It was impossible. She turned on her light. Three o'clock. Things look worse at three o'clock than they do at seven in the morning. But seven came and she saw no resolution except one. Flight. She could not stay within a thousand miles of Hal Evans. She would not take that chance.

She checked their joint checking and savings account. The banks opened at eight thirty. She would be there. She would take the cash box Hal kept hidden in the office safe. She'd put in a call to her stockbroker at nine, tell him to sell all the stock in her name that Hal had purchased for income tax purposes and have the money sent to her sister in Colorado. She had until four to get out. That was when Hal's plane arrived from Chicago. She left a note: "Dear Hillel: I know all about you. I know how you killed me and Brian off. I know how you lied about your military service in Israel. I know you deserted your mother.

"I am leaving with Steven. I will establish residency elsewhere and get a divorce. If you try to stop me, interfere with me in any way, try to make contact either physically or through the mail, I will tell the world about you. That includes my father and his business partners, the rabbi, the Federal Bureau of Investigation, and the Israeli embassy. I'm not joking. Diane."

Ovadia found himself the next day on the bus back to Princeton. Two whole days in buses traveling to Boston and back. And all for what? Well, he got a chance to see Steven and Diane. And he sure had a lot to write home about. But he couldn't shake the feeling that somehow he had put his foot in it.

Jacob Ewan spent the second night of Passover at his club, the Swallow's Nest. His eyes circled the darkness and sought out the knots of men. He didn't like it. They weren't drinking, they weren't dealing cards, they weren't playing sheshbesh, they weren't looking for women. They were talking. Talk meant conspiracy. That's all he needed. He didn't mind the Swallow's Nest being a den of iniquity, but a den of conspirators, well, that was infinitely more dangerous.

He sighed. He had been out of jail for over a year but he still felt confined. Even more so now that his son Rahamin had had a second child, a girl this time, Melina. Thank God his second son Ephraim was busy studying and seemed to have no time for women except the little tart upstairs, the blond one with the lisp. She was acceptable for his son. She didn't threaten him with a need for respectability.

Jacob had given up. It was simply that. There was no order in his life. There was no rationale for his daily existence. He no longer tried to leave Baghdad with his family. He no longer had any hopes. How could he with Iraqi politics overwhelmed by the fratricide of the Ba'athist Brotherhood.

The Ba'aths, the Arab Socialist Renaissance party, had taken over Iraq when Kassem was killed. It had seemed at first that they only co-opted Abdul Salam Aref's services to deal with Kassem. Though they did throw Aref the sop of the presidency while the real power lay in the premiership, which they gave to their own man, Hassan al-Bakr. It seemed for a time that the Ba'aths had nothing to worry about, especially since one month after they seized power in Iraq, the Ba'aths also came to the force in the Syrian government.

However, the Ba'aths of Iraq held absolute power for only ten months. Then when the radical Ba'aths moved on the moderate wing of the party, Aref stepped in. November 18, 1963, the new revolution. The next revolution. Their Ba'ath National Guard, a band of thugs who terrorized anyone with the semblance of prosperity, Jacob included, had been roughly disbanded after several days' fighting. Colonel Aref was given a promotion to Field Marshal Aref, the real power was shifted from the premiership to the presidency, which Aref continued to hold. And to ensure he held it, Aref put his older brother, Rahman, in charge of his security forces.

Jacob would wait. He hoped Aref could solidify his position. He longed for the days of an absolute ruler when right and wrong were clearly defined, instead of Iraq as it was now, coup after coup, the only universal being uncertainty.

Jacob looked up. The British were here. He like the British. They very much resembled Jews. They seemed to survive everything. This particular group had been coming to his place at least twice a week. They were a mix. Businessmen, newspaper reporters, embassy officials. He thought at first they might want some of his women. But British wives seemed quite adept at supplying the needs of their men, husbands and otherwise. He smiled broadly as they claimed a table and waved him over. He knew it was dangerous to be overly friendly with foreigners in a country as xenophobic as Iraq, but his case was too far gone to warrant a remedy, so he made it a point to go all out for his British guests.

"Gentlemen?"

"Only half of us, I'm afraid," one of them said, as they

gave their orders. Jacob snapped his fingers and one of his waiters went for the drinks, while Jacob exchanged with the Englishmen the rare bits of gossip he knew they would enjoy. The several knots of Arabs broke up. They didn't trust a foreign presence. They rose and snuck off into the night. Jacob watched with pleasure as his club filled with more normal activity. The furtive whispering ceased, Arabs who only wished to drink, smoke, and watch the dancers came into the Swallow's Nest. The night hours lingered until even he longed to return to his bed, after he counted and locked up the cash. He noted with amusement one of the Englishmen bringing him the empty bottles. This man always did so even after Jacob had assured him that he had boys hired for exactly that purpose. Jacob moved behind the counter to meet the Englishman with the bottles. He put his hands around the cold glass, but the Englishman held on until he caught Jacob's eye. "I should wish you *hag sameah*, should I not?" the Englishman asked.

Jacob was startled. His features froze. *Hag sameah* was a Hebrew phrase for happy holiday. Was this Englishman a Jew? "Thank you very much," Jacob said cautiously.

"I bring you greetings from your brother Meir. He wishes you well."

Jacob hugged the bottles as the Englishman turned and walked away. In a few minutes they were all gone, through the door and out into the night.

Jacob stayed to supervise the washing up. The Englishman was perhaps not an Englishman at all. The Englishman—could he be an Israeli? For the first time in years Jacob dared to hope.

Shoshana looked radiant. Her sister said so, Joseph, her father. The only one who did not comment on it was Danielle. But then Danielle knew the reason why. Danny had returned from Bermuda. Not only that, but he had assured her that he had completed his training and the navy wasn't planning to send him away again, soon. Relief.

They were sitting comfortably in Lily's new apartment. Joseph had finally sold his plot of land, and in return not only had he gotten the money, some under the table in American dollars so both he and the buyer could declare less on their income tax, but he had also demanded and gotten a three-bedroom, two-bathroom apartment in the newer section of Ramat Gan. Italian tile in the kitchen, rugs on the floor, new furniture from Denmark. Lily loved it. "It's so much easier to keep clean," she sighed. Joshua missed being able to play outside at a single step, he missed his friends at his old school. But he was learning to play in the stairwell with his new friends and the schools were the same everywhere. He wasn't interested.

The conversation centered around Ovadia's latest letter, which was being passed from hand to hand. It wasn't the bombshell of a month ago. Thank God. Lily now said that Shoshana should never have read that letter to their father, but what exactly was Shoshana to do. Meir had gotten home first, picked up the mail, and was waiting with Ovadia's letter in hand when she returned. Had she any idea of what Ovadia had to say, she might not have plunged into the letter with such abandon, but she thought it the usual university report. The words had shocked her as much as they had shocked Meir. But her reaction was not as swift as her father's. Meir had immediately grabbed her by the arm and urged her on to the post office where he had her place an international call to Boston. Hillel was at home. Shoshana listened while her father raved on about the worst thing Hillel had done, poisoning his mother's last hours with regret that she had never seen her grandchild, not to mention the grief he had caused the entire family over the death of a fictitious Brian. When he was through—he gave Hillel no chance to reply—Meir flung the phone at Shoshana.

"Who told Father?" Hillel finally sputtered.

"We received a letter from Ovadia. He said he went up to visit you, but you weren't there, so he had a talk with your wife."

"I have no wife."

"Oh? Well, whoever the woman was then."

"I have no wife. Ovadia has taken my wife from me."

But it was over, in the past. Now they sat quietly, comfortably, a family grouping. Lily was bringing out the cake while Danielle finished clearing the table. Shoshana looked to Joseph and smiled. It was nice being able to relax and let someone else do the work. When the cake and tea were served, Lily sat down and said, "Joseph has an announcement to make." She was beaming. Shoshana thought, hoped for a moment Lily might have by some miracle become pregnant. "It's about you, Shoshana," Lily continued to speak as Joseph just started to open his mouth. "It's for your birthday."

"My birthday?" Shoshana smiled. She was surprised. It wasn't their custom to celebrate birthdays, except for very young children. Nor anniversaries, nor Hanukah with the giving of gifts, as she had seen some Westerners in the translation bureau do. She hadn't gotten a birthday gift since she had come to Israel. The only thing her family tried constantly to provide was something new to wear for Passover and Rosh Hashanah.

"It took a while to arrange. That's why the gift was late," Danielle explained.

They all waited. "So come on, Joseph. Speak up," Lily urged him, none too gently.

Joseph took an envelope out of his pocket and handed it to Shoshana.

"Thank you," she said. She slipped her fingernail under the flap and the envelope unsealed. She took out a bankbook. From America, New York. She opened it up, turned it sideways, saw her name and Ovadia's and the amount of her savings.

"For your dowry," Joseph explained with a smile.

Shoshana let the bankbook drop to the table. "I told you I wasn't going to get married," she said evenly to all of them.

"We know," Lily answered with a smile. "But that's because you were ashamed to start looking for a husband without the dowry behind you to make the arrangement a serious one. Now you have your dowry. See, we understood you all along."

"No, you didn't understand me at all." Shoshana pushed herself away from the table and stood up. "That you could be involved in this," she said angrily to Danielle, who glanced away too hurt to meet her gaze.

Shoshana walked from the table and got her coat. "Where are you going?" Meir asked.

"I'm going out. Over to a friend's. I told you that before." She threw on her coat and went out the door.

Joseph followed her but had to run to catch up with her, so fast was she moving. He grabbed her by the arm and pulled her around. "Shoshana, what is it?" he demanded.

"I told you before I didn't want a dowry. I told you I wasn't going to get married. I don't want you interfering in my personal life. And don't insult me again with your money." She pulled away from him and walked off.

It took her twenty minutes to reach Oren Kohan's flat. By that time she had cooled off considerably. She liked visiting Oren and Nurit. Lately when Oren was away, Nurit and she would take in a movie together or go shopping if Nurit's mother could take care of her three children. Tonight both Oren and Nurit were at home having a small get-together with friends. Oren had called the office to tell her Danny was included. She couldn't pass it up. She didn't know whether Danny's wife, Ronit, would be there or not. She hoped in a way Ronit was there, as she wanted to see what Danny would do. But when she got to the party, she found Danny alone, joking with Oren.

"Talk about windswept," Oren said as she came up to them, rubbing her arms for warmth.

"Don't tease her," Danny said. "I can tell she's upset about something. See those little crinkles on the bottom lid of her eyes. That's a sure sign." He put his arm around her and held her close. Obviously Ronit was at home.

They whispered together for a while until she felt calm.

It took Oren awhile to isolate her. "I'm going back," he told her. "Anything I should know that I don't know already?"

"I've gotten several transcripts on those mock trials the new regime is holding. You know, tried in two minutes, executed in one. But most of them were from Kassem's time."

"Any reports on the Kurds? Come across any infiltration that I might not have been briefed on?"

"Is that where you're going? Back to the Kurds?"

"Answer me first."

"Nothing really, Oren. Everything is still so unstable in Iraq, I don't know if they could have time to infiltrate anyone into the Kurdish organizations, anyone new that is. There are several coup attempts in the planning stages from what we know. But that's nothing new. An Egyptian report was intercepted, some Egyptian colonel attached to the Iraqi army. He said that the army was loyal enough to Aref, but the guns weren't only in Aref's hands so Nasser should move slowly on his commitments. What will you do with the Kurds? Fight alongside them?"

"Yes. Try to take enough high-ranking Iraqi prisoners so we can find out the state of their army. Keep in touch with Nurit. She enjoys your company."

Diane Evans drove through Sante Fe, New Mexico, three times before she decided this was the city she wanted. The evenings thrilled her. The silence of the desert, the beauty of the skies. And then there was the relatively low cost of living. What money she had, she had to make last. But would she find work? She was assured by the woman who rented her a two-bedroom apartment that she had come to Santa Fe at just the right time. For in the summer Santa Fe's population tripled with tourism. She still had a month or so to pick and choose what would suit her.

Diane found her situation grimly amusing. All she had ever wanted was to be a wife and mother. Now she found herself pushed to the fore of woman's liberation by the lack of a reliable husband. Finding a job she didn't mind as much as trying to arrange day care for her child, her precious Steven whom she loved and desired to nurture. But she would have to leave that to Mrs. Zwicky. Mrs. Zwicky who had a house with a fenced yard, who had a jungle gym, a swing, some records, blocks, cots, blankets, diapers, and five other children. Mrs. Zwicky would feed and potty train Steven while Diane was off working, being a part of the real world, a world she didn't want, a clerk in a store. It wasn't the amount of time, it was the quality, other mothers said. But how could quality matter when for eight hours she would not see Steven smile, laugh, or cry, for ten hours he would be sleeping. And for the hours left she would be cooking, cleaning, watching television, and trying to find her little boy again.

But work, yes, she must think of herself as a professional woman now. If one could call a clerk in a store professional. She was hired because she put on her make-up well. She could thank Jordan Marsh's cosmetic clinic for that one. It made her look classy. It made her look like the kind of person who could ask outrageous prices for the handcrafted goods displayed at Chez Laurie's and get away with it. The owner hoped. She would check out Diane's sales figures as the season got underway.

It was lunchtime. Andrew Harris sat in the Swallow's Nest and watched Jacob Ewan work his customers. Jacob was good at it. Inoffensive, unobtrusive, a natural. Yossi Leskov had been right about Jacob Ewan, had summed him up perfectly when he had briefed Harris in Tel Aviv. Though Harris didn't feel Yossi was right about sending him here to Baghdad, Iraq, of all places. The caliphate, Scheherazade's *Thousand and One Nights,* all gone with the centuries. Nothing remained. Except the Arabs. Iraq wasn't a front-line state. Sure, it was important to know what was going on here, but that information could be just as easily gathered from the newspapers, the radio, government reports, from those Israelis already in the mountains with the Kurds. Iraq was too weak to be hazardous to Israel. He suspected his bosses were bartering the information they got from him with the United States. The United States would be more interested in Iraq with its oil and potential Russian connections than Israel would be. His services could be put to better use in England or France. But Yossi had built

Harris's cover as an ex-patriot Britisher in Canada, then Argentina, and on into Baghdad, where he spent his time selling office machinery to businessmen who fucked up the equipment the day after it was delivered. He should open his own repair business. At least that way he could have some money on the side. Not that there was any place he'd want to spend it here. Besides, he wasn't to bring notice to himself. Just leave it at friendly Andrew Harris, lips frozen into a slight, innocuous smile.

Jacob Ewan came over to him and Harris offered him a seat. Jacob nodded and sat down.

"Have you done it?" Harris asked, looking as if he were talking about the weather.

"Yes. My sons and I installed them early this morning."

"Both the tapes and the cameras?"

"I have said yes."

"And you can control them."

"When anyone important comes to see one of my girls, I can record his session."

Harris studied him. "I'm surprised you didn't think of that before."

"Why? I always knew who was in which room."

"True. But with the film you could blackmail them. Gain your freedom."

"Mr. Harris, you have a very naive view of what such a film can accomplish. If I had even attempted to blackmail anyone in such a way, I would no longer have been here for you to contact. Do you realize how easy it is to round up a band of thugs to attack a Jewish home? Not only do they get the pleasure of murdering a Jew, but they also can take the opportunity to pillage a wealthy household. If I had attempted blackmail, I would have been dead within twenty-four hours and the Swallow's Nest firebombed no doubt. Now selling someone information detrimental to his enemy is something one can do for political profit if one is very careful. I do try to be."

"I hope you wouldn't even consider selling information about me."

319

Jacob searched the Englishman's face. "How could I do that, Mr. Harris, when you have promised to free my sons, my family. When, Mr. Harris?"

Harris slipped Jacob an envelope. "In it you'll find a photocopy of your Swiss accounts. One for you and each of your sons. You'll notice that not only have I deposited what I promised you, but I've also managed to transfer the money you gave me here from Baghdad to Zurich."

"Very nice. Money is always important. What's more important is to move my family from here to Zurich."

"I've told you, if you like, we can try to get Ephraim out now. He's alone, a student. It shouldn't be too difficult to move him. But that might make it more difficult for the rest of you to leave. However if we wait awhile, we might be able to move you all."

"How long?"

Harris shrugged. He tried to recall the gesture instantly by squaring his shoulders to the chair. His shrug was still much too Middle Eastern. "I'm being honest with you. I don't know."

Jacob sat back. "I'll think it over."

"In the meantime we're interested in this Sadah al-Bakr. You know him?"

"Of course. He's a colonel. He was in charge of the forces that routed the Ba'ath National Guard."

"Pro-Western, we understand."

"Pro-Aref."

"Let us know whom he meets with, what he does, what he wants."

"Yes. And . . ."

"Yes?"

"If you could, Mr. Harris, I would like to know how my relatives in Israel are doing, what they're doing? Can you understand?"

"I'll do my best," Harris assured him.

23

In the summer of 1966 life was not difficult for Ovadia to understand. It had no mystifying force. It was simply plain hard work. He was coming to the end of his student days at Princeton. Regretfully. He had already accepted a job as assistant professor at the University of Illinois in Urbana for the fall term. They expected his thesis to be completed and approved by then. So did his advisor. Only Ovadia had his doubts. His mind wasn't on his work. He spent time improving his swimming strokes at the quarry, he sampled new ice cream combinations at Buxton's, he bought a Ping-Pong paddle at the sports shop. All the time he should have been at his thesis, revising, reworking. Engineering didn't excite his thoughts as much as women did. But the days were going by, his affairs had fallen flat, and he was still alone. At twenty-eight it was a definite fact—he needed a wife. He contemplated making a fast trip home to Giva-tayim. It wouldn't take long for a marriage to be arranged for him. That's the way the Indian students did it. But did he really want an Iraqi wife? She would cook for him, keep his house clean, raise his children. But what would they talk about? Iraqi women had no other world than their families. He did not want to spend the rest of his life talking about the price of eggs with the woman he supposedly would love. Yet American women, while more exciting than the Iraqi variety, were also more uncertain. He thought back sadly to his affair of a year ago. He and she had rendezvoused several times in the back seat of his '56 Ford, both proclaiming undying love, then she had simply stopped returning his calls. If an Iraqi woman had found herself so compromised, she would have been on her hands and knees begging him to marry her. And of course he would have because he was a man of honor.

It was Tuesday night, the night the folk dance society met on the Princeton commons. He tried never to miss a gathering. He had met several girls through folk dancing. He sighed remembering one of them. She used to be a regular when he asked her out for a date. After one evening with him, she never returned. He didn't feel they had had that bad a time together, and he was really sorry he had ruined folk dancing for her.

He slipped on his blue Bermudas and tucked in his white shirt. He looked at himself in the mirror. He always hoped the mirror would tell him something different, but it never did. So at least he didn't have to look at himself when he was out on the commons.

The music drew Roberta Davidson as she walked across the campus. Princeton comforted her. As soon as she stepped within the confines of the campus, she felt at peace. And if she wanted not to feel at peace, she only had to sprint across Nassau street to where the Italians and blacks, the townies intermingled with the Ivy League. It was a good place to work, she supposed, because Princeton reminded her of Tarrytown where she had grown up, but in Princeton she was alone.

Roberta had recently left her job as a gym teacher. She had found a job in physical therapy. When it went well, she felt instant gratification. But there were the cases of those who chose not to improve even though they had the ability to move forward. She was not a patient woman.

Roberta liked physical therapy for another reason. There was always a need for a therapist. She could find a job wherever she wanted to. Especially with the Vietnam War heating up, she thought grimly. So she had come to Princeton.

Roberta followed the music to the graduate commons. The area was crowded. She had to walk along the stone wall and push through a knot of men before she discovered what was happening. There were people out on the grass dancing. The music was coming from a record player attached to a loudspeaker. "What's this?" she asked no one in particular.

"Folk dancing," came a reply.

Folk dancing. She remembered teaching folk dancing at school. It always brought a "yuck" response, and she had to admit she wasn't too good at it herself. She had trouble remembering the steps in order and which was her right foot, which her left. She walked along the wall and picked out an empty spot near a big oak tree to lean against. As she stood watching, she heard the announcer call out the next dance. Then she saw this midget eyeing her. Well, he wasn't a midget exactly. But he was short, about her height, and he was dark. He was wearing baggy blue Bermudas and had very hairy legs. He walked by her once and was standing by the tree. He was staring straight at her, she was looking away, praying to God that he wouldn't ask her to dance. He started in her direction, really not looking at her until the last moment when he stood two feet away and asked her to dance.

"Well, I really don't know how—"

"Oh, it's a simple one," he said, brushing off her objection. "I'll teach you."

The preparation had started. He dragged her into the circle and the Dubeleska Polka began. They exchanged a few pleasantries and Roberta even thought she was getting some of the steps right. What the stranger had failed to tell her was that this was a change-partners dance. He stamped and clapped and circled on to the next. She found herself alone, so she scurried back to the wall, leaving another dancer halfway round the circle without a partner. God, the humiliation.

"Hi."

"Hi."

He had come up to her after the dance was over. "What happened?"

"I had no partner." She tried to be sweet about it.

"You should have just stood in the circle till someone came over to you."

She didn't know what to say. "Are you from India?" she asked. He was that dark.

"No," he answered. He had a slight accent that she couldn't place. "Israel. My name is Ovadia Ewan."

"Oh," she exclaimed. "Israel. I remember when I was a checker at a grocery store, I met someone from Israel. He had left the country."

"It's tough. You can call me Ovadia."

"Ovadia," she repeated.

"Um—uh, do you have a name?"

"Yes," she replied.

"Oh." The next dance was called. "This is a good one," he told her. "It's a line dance. Anyone can do it." He took her hand and dragged her across the grass.

"Well, perhaps not anyone," he conceded a few minutes later after they had dropped out.

"I hate making a fool of myself," she said tersely.

"Have you been in Princeton long?"

"Roberta."

Roberta? Was that a new month? "Sorry?"

"My name is Roberta Davidson."

"Oh." Ovadia had to pause to figure out where the conversation was going.

"My grandfather's name was Robert," she told him, apropos of nothing. "He didn't approve of my mother's marriage so she named me after him."

"Well," Ovadia said kindly, "that must have been a wise decision."

"Are you studying here?"

he couldn't—drive that is. They edged out of the town and got on the road leading to Washington's Crossing. "It's a back road," he told her. "More scenic."

"Uh, couldn't you speed it up a little."

"We're going fifteen," he said. "That's about the right speed for this sort of pavement."

She wondered why he couldn't notice the long line of cars behind him with lights flashing and horns blaring. "Don't you think we better speed up before the people behind us get angry?"

"I'm not going to do anything foolhardy just because there are people following me, Roberta. I'm driving defensively and safely," he informed her as he swerved out over the center line just as a car was passing them.

"What was he saying?" Ovadia asked as the other driver gave him the finger. Roberta sank farther down in her seat.

It became even less funny when they arrived at the park to find it closed and had no choice but to circle around and start back.

"Well, you can see what the trees look like," he said, waving one arm while hopelessly trying to steer with the other.

"Please let me out," she moaned.

"What?"

"Please stop the car and let me out. You're going to kill me and I'm too young to die."

"What's the matter?" he asked as a car shrieked by him, horn blasting.

"You are without a doubt the worst driver I have ever ridden with. Now will you stop the car please and let me out so I can walk home?"

"You're joking."

She tried to laugh. "Hasn't anyone ever told you what a bad driver you are?"

"Only my friends. But they were just kidding me."

"No, they weren't," she assured him, gripping her seat as they entered a traffic circle.

"Now let me see," he said.

"I'm getting dizzy!"

"I'm just trying to figure which exit I should take," he explained as he drove continuously around the traffic circle.

She was emotionally exhausted when they got back to her house. "Thanks for the unique evening," she told him as they stood in the doorway. She opened the door and slipped inside.

Two minutes later with her earrings off and her stockings removed she heard a knock at the door. She went to open it up and there were the books she had forgotten in the car.

"Oh, thanks," she said. "I'd forgotten these in my rush to hit terra firma. See you at folk dancing on Tuesday." She shut the door in his face.

"See you," he said weakly.

There was something about him, Roberta thought, as she pondered away her hours between Friday night and Tuesday. Despite all his faults—and after one date she could name them more easily than his merits—she found herself attracted to him. There was in him a quality so weird that if he didn't turn you off, he turned you on.

She met him for folk dancing, she met him every day after that for two weeks. She didn't understand his dreams, she didn't understand his fantasies, she didn't understand anything about him. She must have been in love. The third week of their acquaintance they decided to drive up to her parents in Tarrytown and announce their impending marriage.

Roberta had forewarned her parents, giving them all the information she thought necessary. As they drove up to the house Roberta noticed her father in his rose garden. Everyone in her family had a small garden plot lying somewhere around their Tudor-style home. Whether it was flower or vegetable, hers always seemed to fade before the summer was quite over. She beeped her horn. Her father came slowly out to the driveway. His manners were impeccable. He held his hand out to Ovadia, repeated Ovadia's name so he was sure he pronounced it correctly, and bid him welcome. Her mother had come out to join them. Her face was set in a certain rigor that Roberta remembered from past occasions, but this time the lines were a little deeper. So this was the man her daughter wanted to marry. "Won't you come in?" Her mother forced the words through tight teeth.

They sat around the living room, the beige carpet unmarked beneath them. Coffee rolled out on a cart laden with their silver service. "So you're going to Princeton?" said as if her mother meant, so this is who they're letting in now. "And where are you from?"

"Israel."

"Israel? My. What religion do they practice in Israel?"

"You can practice any religion you like in Israel. It's a free country. Like America."

"But what religion exactly, Ovadia, do you practice?"

"I'm a Jew."

Roberta wanted to jump up and down in her seat and clap her hands. To her mother's credit the smile remained fixed on her face as she rose and said, "Excuse us, Ovadia, Roberta and I have luncheon to make in the kitchen."

Roberta rose, gave Ovadia a bright smile, and trailed after her mother.

"How could you!" Her mother turned on her as soon as the antiqued kitchen door swung shut on them, sealing them off from the rest of the house.

"How could I what?"

"A Jew, for Christ's sake."

"Mother, in this day and age religion doesn't really matter."

Her mother flashed her a look of steel. Religion did matter to at least one person in the kitchen. Her mother, born a Baptist, had parlayed her husband's station as a rising corporate executive into membership in the Episcopalian church when they first moved to Tarrytown. She lived in fear of anyone discovering her true dogmatic origins.

"What about your children? What will they be?"

"Ovadia seems to want them to be Jews. It doesn't matter to me."

"Jewish grandchildren?" Her mother leaned heavily against the kitchen sink.

"Mother, what does it matter? He's a good person, he has a good job, we'll have a good life together."

Her mother shook her head. "You don't know anything about this boy."

"Of course I do. What do you want to know? Ask me."

"What about his family?"

"They're in Israel. Except for his brother who's in Boston, but he never sees him."

"Israel. Do you even know where Israel is?"

"I looked it up on a map after I met him."

"Have they always lived in Israel?"

"No."

"Ah. The Wandering Jew. Do I dare ask where they came from originally?"

"Baghdad."

"Baghdad," her mother repeated slowly, hopelessly. "Roberta, no one is from Baghdad. Except Alladin, or was it Ali Baba."

"I'll get my storybook out and look it up."

"You know this marriage cannot take place, don't you?"

"No, I don't, Mother. If you don't want to share in it, fine. But I will marry Ovadia the first week in September. That gives you around six weeks to get used to the idea."

"And if it doesn't work out?"

Roberta shrugged. "I'll get a divorce."

"That's some way to start a marriage."

Roberta sighed. "Mother, I'm old enough to know what I want. It'll work out."

The day passed in quiet turmoil. Ovadia might have sensed something was wrong, but he never quite caught on to what it was. He thought his only faux pas came when he told Mr. Davidson that he found American football boring. He went to bed and listened to the noises of this strange house, which would have served for at least three families in Israel. It was good to be in the United States.

* * *

The wedding was small, as very few people could fit into the rabbi's study. The vows were repeated in Hebrew. Her mother later confessed she felt better about that since she couldn't really understand what was going on. Once Roberta and Ovadia were married, the wedding party rushed from the rabbi's study to a large restaurant reception her parents had arranged in honor of the ceremony. It was hard to tell it was a wedding reception. Even the cake looked more like a birthday cake. But Roberta didn't mind. She spent three hours being positively gracious. "You're so like your mother," one woman even had the nerve to say. And then it was over. She and Ovadia got into her Ford Falcon and drove away.

"How did it go, do you think?" Ovadia asked uncertainly. He had been upset that no one had thought to bring a glass to the wedding, so he had had to break a flashbulb for good luck.

"I think it went the way all weddings go. No one will be speaking to each other for the next couple of months. Luckily since we'll be in Urbana, that will cut down on our long-distance phone bills."

"Do you think they still minded?"

"It's just that the rabbi looked so Jewish." She laughed when he took her seriously.

Well could she laugh. She had faced her parents with the fact, fought it out with them. He still had to break the news to his father, that he had married a Christian. Sometimes he thought of fudging it. Instead of calling her Roberta Davidson, he could change it slightly to Roberta Ben-David. But no, if he did lie about her, she would some day find out. Hadn't Diane, Hillel's ex-wife, found out. And he never wanted Roberta to think he was ashamed of the fact that he had married a Christian. He wasn't ashamed at all. He was simply scared. What would his father say?

24

Shoshana couldn't believe that Ovadia would do this to her again. Another letter, another automatic translation, another explosion from her father. She thought in a way this was worse than the revelation about Hillel. Hillel was expected to be sneaky. But Ovadia? Her father's world exploded. How could Ovadia marry a Christian. The last Christians they had spoken to were from Baghdad and that was sixteen years ago. Her father ranted on against his son, against the United States that allowed such things to happen, against Roberta whoever she was.

Meir took a pad of paper and a pen, threw them at his daughter. "You will write to Ovadia. Tell him I want the marriage dissolved immediately."

"No, I won't, Father. I will write to Ovadia and send him our best wishes."

"Not mine."

"Then mine alone."

"I want him to put an end to it."

"They're married, Father," Shoshana said patiently.

"Not binding."

"By a rabbi."

"American."

"Certified in Israel. Ovadia wrote you."

"But she's a Christian!"

"So she's a Christian. Father, the world is not made up of only Jews."

"My world is," he told her furiously.

"And look what happened to Hillel. He married a Jewish girl—"

"Don't say anything about your brother. Pick up that pen. I will tell you what to write." Shoshana remained seated with her hands folded. "Did you hear me!" Meir demanded.

She stood and walked stiffly out of the apartment, ignoring her father's orders to get back inside.

She went to Lily's. With every step she took, her anger grew. Why should she have to put up with that cantankerous old man when everyone else was living a normal, healthy life. By the time she reached Lily's, she was furious. She pushed the button and her anger grew as no one responded.

"Who is it?" Joshua finally asked through the intercom.

"Your aunt," she spat out. Joshua buzzed her in. She couldn't believe Lily had left him there alone. The elevator was out of order. Perpetually. She climbed four flights of stairs, her face getting red from the effort and her anger. Joshua held the apartment door open for her. "Where's your mother?" she asked.

"In the bedroom with Father."

Naturally. There was nothing like wedded bliss. She imagined. She went up the hallway and pounded on her sister's bedroom door. "Lily, come out of there," she raged. She turned and saw Joshua staring open mouthed at her.

"They didn't want to be disturbed," he explained awkwardly.

"Right. I'm the only one in the world who deserves to be disturbed," she screamed at her nephew.

Joseph opened the door and slipped out. He had on his undershirt and a pair of pants. He was barefoot. "What a pleasant surprise," he said grimly to her.

She stared at him until her mouth broke and she began to laugh. He might have smiled vaguely. "This better be important," he told her.

"Is Lily coming out? I have a few words I would like to address to her."

Her sister opened the bedroom door. She wore an old house dress and her hair was down. It was longer than her own and Shoshana was surprised to notice a few gray strands in it. "I have a few words to address to you too. If you ever come into my apartment and bang on my bedroom door again—"

"How dare you," Shoshana attacked. "I have to spend my whole life in an apartment with our father. I never have any privacy at all. Furthermore I have to deal with his outbursts all the time. You see him once or twice a week and you're oh, so sweet and loving. He always comes away from you telling me what a good daughter Lily is, implying that I am not."

"Well, perhaps you should be sweeter to him."

"Well, perhaps you should have him at your place for a month. Then we'll see how sweet and loving you find each other."

"What brought this on?" Joseph asked.

"Ovadia is married." Lily and Joseph were too stunned to respond. "To a Christian," Shoshana finished.

Lily walked slowly up the hall, then turned. "Father will say kaddish for him," she whispered.

"That's a brilliant thought," Shoshana said nastily. "Why don't you run right over there and suggest it to him?"

"Where's the letter Ovadia sent?" Joseph asked.

Shoshana took it out of her pocket and handed it to him. She watched him read it. When he finished, he shrugged his shoulders and handed the letter to Lily. "He was such a sweet little boy," Lily remarked to no one in particular.

Disgusted, Shoshana walked out of the apartment.

She went back to work. Her office was the only place she could really be alone. And even there sounds could be heard coming from beyond the door. They had finally gotten the money to convert to computer use in a big way.

Everything was being stored for future retrieval on these tiny little bits. All day long they received mini-lectures on computer use and misuse. They all had their own codes for access to the system. There was a whole new batch of intelligence personnel, some shunted over from the army. Instead of the quiet scholarship their department was used to, the humming and the clicking of the computer could now be heard. She liked computers. They were a marvel. But she was afraid of them too. What if she made a mistake. What if she blew the whole system. Twenty years of intelligence erased by a thwarted fuse. But no, they had a backup system. And backups for the backup.

Still she was glad she was out of straight translations now. She would hate to be the person who decided what was of value in the daily Iraqi newspapers. God forbid he should miss a small item about someone unimportant who would become the central figure in the next coup. But was her own work in misinformation of such great value? She sometimes had the feeling they were creating more monsters than they were taming. It wasn't even Iraq Israel was worried about. It was Egypt. So anything Israel could do to thwart Egypt and Nasser's grand design was undertaken. Though since the death of Field Marshal Aref in a helicopter crash five months ago, the danger of Iraq and Egypt uniting had lessened considerably. So, aided by military and political analysts, her work went on.

Sometimes she thought she should try her hand at Israeli politics. It had been in enough of a mess ever since 1963 when Ben-Gurion was forced to retire, to hand over the leadership of his Mapai party and thus the government to Levi Eshkol. The squabbling continued unabated though, for if it wasn't the Lavon affair—determining responsibility for the security mishap in Egypt of the early fifties when Western installations had been vandalized on Israeli intelligence orders in an attempt to turn the West against Egypt— then it was the struggle for leadership within Mapai between the old pioneers like Eshkol and the young guard—Shimon Peres, Moshe Dayan, all protégés of Ben-Gurion. Eshkol, rather than see political power fall into the hands of the younger members of his own party whose socialist zeal he mistrusted, turned to Ahdut Ha-Avodah of Yigal Allon and Israel Galili. Eshkol also called Lavon's followers back into party power, thus offending Ben-Gurion, whose protégés had scapegoated Lavon for the Egyptian security mishap. Ben-Gurion broke with his old friend Levi Eshkol; he ended his lifelong membership in Mapai and founded a new party with his young supporters, Rafi, the Workers' List of Israel. There was so much mudslinging and acrimony in the 1965 election that its wasted energy could have powered Israel for a year. She hadn't voted for Rafi, nor had she voted for Mapai. Neither of those parties spoke for her. She often wondered whom they did speak for in the country except the power elite and other politicians. She had voted for Gahal, but since Gahal combined both the Liberal and the Herut lists, her vote for Gahal was also a vote for Menahem Begin. When the dust had settled and the final ballot box stuffed, the Mapai alignment had kept its majority. She wondered sometimes if there wasn't some woman sitting over in Baghdad who had the same trouble figuring out Israeli politics as she had with the Iraqi coups.

David knocked on her door and opened it. "I saw that you had signed back in. What's the problem?"

"No problem. I just didn't have any place to go."

"What does that mean?"

"I have no place to sleep tonight."

"Is this the invitation I've been waiting for?"

"No."

David closed the door and sat down. "Shoshana, do you know that Rumanian? The one who's been hanging around here, working on the computer system?"

"Georgi, sure."

"He's interested in you. He keeps asking if you're seeing anyone, if he should ask you for a date. So far everyone's been very tactful. No one's mentioned the frog. Hasn't he been stationed in Eilat for the last few months? You must be lonely."

"He's coming home next week for a month."

"A month. Wow. Georgi is a good type. He's solid. While at the same time resourceful. I understand he's even a gourmet cook."

"Do you know why?" she asked him.

"No."

"Because his mother is blind and he's the only one left at home to do the cooking. His apartment, by the way, is in his mother's name and anyone he marries will have to live there with his mother and take care of them both."

David whistled. "You should be in operations. Well, look, his mother might do very well with your father. In which case your father can go live with his mother and you and Georgi can have the apartment you're living in now."

"Good night, David."

"Will you go out with him?"

"If he asks me, I might make myself available this Friday."

David stood up, leaned over, and kissed her on the cheek. "You're sweet. The poor simple soul doesn't know what he's letting himself in for. *Leila tov.*"

"Bye-bye." She waved him out.

Which didn't solve the problem of tonight. She took out a piece of paper and picked up her pen. "Dear Ovadia, We were all so pleased and happy to hear about your marriage. It came as a shock, as you can imagine. I wish you had given us some advance warning. But now that you are married, we look forward to hearing more about Roberta. She sounds very nice, just the right sort of wife for you, lively and intelligent. Please send us a picture. When do you think you will come here so we can meet her? I feel very proud of you. Now I can not only tell my friends that my son is a professor but a married professor at that. Mazel tov. Your loving father." Shoshana left a space for her father to sign. "That goes double for me," she added underneath, signed in her own name.

She folded the letter carefully, put it in an envelope, and stuck it in her purse. As she was leaving her office, the phone rang. She picked it up. It was Georgi. Their date for

Friday night was on. David was an incurable romantic. Or an incurable meddler.

She signed out of the building and took the bus home. Her father was sitting by the radio drinking tea. "All right," she said to him, "I give up. I've written your letter." He paid no attention to her. She drew up a chair and took the letter out of her purse. She began to read. " 'Dear Ovadia, That a son of mine should take such a step without at least conferring with his father has shocked and dismayed me. Especially since that son is you, my Ovadia. What madness has entered your blood in America? My advice is to cleanse yourself of all impurities. Let me hear from you soon on this matter.' And here, Father, I've left a place for you to sign."

Meir took the letter from her hand and looked it over. "And what does it say after I sign my name?"

"That's a short note from me. It says as his sister I would like to know more about what's going on. See, there's my name. Shoshana." She pointed out the letters to him.

She held out her pen. He took it, squinted at her, then signed the letter. Shoshana did not dare sigh. She took the letter, refolded it, and sealed it in its envelope.

Danny was glad to be back in Tel Aviv. He had had enough of Eilat, for a while anyway. Not that he expected hardship pay for doing his duty, but it would have been nice to have a little extra money to be able to eat in the restaurants overpriced for Israelis but suitable for the tourist trade. He was sick of the steakeyas, the sprawling cafés, the ice cream stands, the junk shops, the whores of Eilat. It was good to get home to his family. Ronit was a decent cook. His apartment was comfortable, just the place to relax in, even with Adee's mess. He had to admit he was fonder than he had expected of his daughter. She had those cute puffy cheeks and blond shaggy hair that was still too short and uneven to cut. His mother told him Adee looked just like he had when he was a baby. Maybe that's why he was so fond of her. *"Aba,"* he kept saying to Adee over and over again, hoping she would call for him. Sometimes she obliged him, but more often she called *ema* for her mother. He should come home more often and stay longer.

They were waiting for him to decide what to do, his family and the navy. It was his choice now, whether to stay in Eilat or to ask for a posting in the Mediterranean. He felt the Mediterranean suited him better. Eilat made him feel claustrophobic. Its gulf stretched narrowly from the southern tip of Israel, disjoining the Egyptian Sinai peninsula from Jordan and Saudi Arabia. One could stand in Eilat and wave to the Jordanians if one so desired, as Aqaba, their sister city to Eilat, lay only a short way off, divided by a desert border. Sometimes small boats from one port or the other wandered by misfortune into the enemy's port. It was hard, impossible not to touch each other's navigational waters when sailing in the Gulf of Aqaba. He wasn't big on deserts—the Negev bored him, but he longed to set foot on Sinai if the interior matched the beauty of its coast.

Shoshana had not visited him while he was in Eilat. She claimed she couldn't get away. He accused her of not loving him anymore. She protested violently that she did. It was all so silly, so childish. He didn't know why they had argued like that and over the phone, which he knew was being monitored.

Still she seemed excited when he called to tell her he was returning to Tel Aviv. They arranged to meet and he was there right on time after swearing to Ronit that he was going out to visit an old friend. Shoshana was two minutes late. He was wild for her, but she shuddered under his touch. "What's the matter?" he asked anxiously. She unbuttoned her blouse from her belly up to her throat and timidly took it off. There were three scab lines running across her left chest. "What in God's name happened?"

She smiled tiredly. "David fixed me up with a Rumanian."

Danny gave a short laugh. "When was this?"

"Friday."

"I mean—"

"After he took me to a nightclub in Jaffa. He said I owed it to him."

Danny wasn't laughing anymore. "What's his name?"

"It doesn't matter. I fought him off."

"I'll call David and find out from him."

"Don't. I can take care of myself."

"Sure." He held out his arms to her. She came carefully into them. He was soon assured that everything remained the same between them. There was the same sweetness, the same sadness, the same intensity, the same sense of loss when they parted.

Shoshana came to work the next day to find David hanging around her office door. "I'm sorry about Friday," he told her.

Danny wasn't kidding, the jerk. "That's all right," she said, embarrassed.

"Georgi would have been here to apologize himself, but he's over at Kupot Holim having some stitches put in."

Shoshana burst into laughter. Oh, Danny, oh, how she loved him.

Diane felt safe in Sante Fe. Though the process of building a new life for herself was more difficult than she had expected. She was lonely at first. She knew no one, and somehow it was not enough to work eight hours, then come home and take care of Steven and call that a life. There were things she would do if she were the old Diane. She would join the temple, join Hadassah, maybe the League of Women Voters, something middle class, respectable. But those organizations, those women had no room for her. They met while she worked. They were at home with their families while she was alone in her apartment with Steven. She felt sorry for herself. She had never been so totally on her own.

Slowly as the months passed, she began to establish tentative contacts, mainly with the artists who sold their work to the store. They would come by to ask about sales, to deliver more of their handicrafts. But during the summer everyone was taken up with the tourist trade. There was no time to relax and enjoy something as simple as friendship. After Labor Day the season slackened. Slowly Diane reached out to some of the women artists she had met. Would they like to go for lunch on Saturday, excuse me, but I have this child I have to bring along. She found a few she liked. Some even shared her predicament, being separated or going through the divorce process, some had children too. It was a comfort to know she was not disgracefully alone.

She didn't think of men. Not yet. She couldn't until she was completely severed from Hal, until she no longer had to mention him as part of her life. She was considering legally changing her name and Steven's back to Shapiro. The only surprise in her life came from Walter. Somehow, well, how else but through the mothers, he had found out about her and Hal. He had also discovered that the only one who knew her whereabouts was her sister, Shelia. Shelia was being very loyal under torturous circumstances. She had not told their parents where Diane had fled. Shelia became the conduit for the messages of anguish and wrath that tided back and forth from Sante Fe to Boston. One of those messages was from Walter. He wanted to offer his aid and comfort. She sent a letter back to him, saying in essence she could take care of herself. The next letter he sent had a check for one hundred dollars. She sent it back to him; she didn't need it. He returned it. If she didn't need it, she should use it to start a bank account for their child. He didn't say Steven. He said "their child." It frightened her. Mostly because she did not have the will or desire to argue his point. She endorsed the check and started the savings account. Every month after that a check secreted in a sheet of white paper arrived in the mail. She sometimes wondered how he was declaring this on his income tax, but her mother had written her that Dr. de Gregory had set up in private practice, so she was sure he had a good tax accountant.

Of Hal she heard much but answered little. He was going around Boston with a broken heart. People were fawning all over him in an absolute shared sorrow. He dined out on his tragedy. Good riddance. Good riddance, you bastard. She was safe. She was alone.

25

Ronit Ze'ev had stood it long enough. She left Adee with her mother-in-law. Now she was rummaging through her closet for something to wear. Something impressive.

How could Danny think she didn't know about his "old friend"? He didn't even try to hide it anymore. They all had affairs, all the men when they were away for months at a time. One expected something quick, something meaningless. The women too were not immune to these opportunities. Except for her. But then she had to spend so much time taking care of Adee and forcing herself to stay out of the kitchen to get her weight down.

Danny wasn't being fair. He had been seeing this same woman off and on for years. All Ronit's friends in the unit had told her about this Shoshana Ewan. She looked Yemenite though some said she was Iraqi. What could you expect from a woman like that? She probably even had Danny supporting her.

Ronit would have let things go on as they had. God knows she didn't want Danny to be mad at her. But this latest was too great an insult. He had beaten up another man to protect his whore's honor.

Enough was enough.

She would wear the brown dress. It was cut to make her look thin. Now she would have to look for the sweater and the perfume Danny had brought her from Bermuda. That Shoshana Ewan had to see whom she was dealing with.

Shoshana was in her office trying to clear up a few items of work that someone had thoughtfully left for her. Marked urgent, of course. Everything in David's department was urgent. Including David. It seemed almost as soon as she had returned to her office, he came down to find out what she was doing there. She could think of several replies but he was faster. "Did Oren give you the tapes?"

"No."

"Didn't you understand why you were sent to military intelligence?"

"No, David, I didn't." She said it very calmly. She was proud of herself.

"Oren has over fifty tapes from Iraqi soldiers that you're to translate. I listened to a few of them. Pretty interesting. However there's a slight problem. The soldiers are speaking all sorts of dialects. Sometimes Oren had to use an internal translator, someone who could translate the soldiers' dialects into one that Oren could understand. So we'd appreciate having both versions. Just in case there's something missing. Do you think you can work overtime on supervising this? It's pretty important."

Shoshana rose.

"Where are you going?"

"Out for lunch."

"Lunch?" David checked his watch. "Shoshana, it's quitting time, not lunchtime."

"I haven't had lunch yet."

"Oh."

"I'll be back after I eat." She grabbed her sweater and slipped it on as she walked down the corridor. She looked through the closed windows. The sweater would probably not be enough. Winter was upon them. It depressed her as it always did. Still the cool air would wake her. She walked into it and braced herself for its onslaught. She took absolutely no notice of the woman who was watching her and following her down the street. The woman caught up with her and grabbed her arm. Shoshana turned. "Shoshana Ewan?" the woman asked.

"Yes?" Shoshana said. She had no idea who this blond, plump, freckled woman was, even though the woman was waiting for recognition.

"I'm Ronit Ze'ev," she finally said.

"Oh, yes," Shoshana said with a slight smile. "How are you?"

Ronit pressed her lips together and did not answer. "Perhaps we could find some place to talk."

"Coffee?"

"Fine."

Shoshana led her down a side street and into a café frequented at lunch hour by people at work. Now it was practically empty. They ordered and Shoshana waited. It was not, after all, her game.

"I've come to ask you to stop seeing my husband," Ronit said.

Shoshana didn't know what to reply. She had no intention of not seeing Danny.

"Did you hear me?"

"First of all, lower your voice," Shoshana said.

"Don't try to pretend that you're civilized," Ronit shot back.

Shoshana waited for a minute. "I realize you're upset," she said calmly and softly, "but do let's try to get through this with a modicum of manners. Now, have you spoken to Danny?"

"I wouldn't take up his time with this."

"Then why are you bothering me?"

"Because you have some sort of hold over him."

"I believe it's called love."

"He doesn't love you."

"Why don't you ask him? Are you afraid of his answer?"

"You can never have him, you know. He may degrade

himself by sleeping with you, but he would never marry you. He would never humiliate himself by being seen with someone like you."

"Then how did you find out about us?"

"Friends in the unit. They saw you together."

"Danny hanging his head in humiliation, no doubt."

"You can't have him."

"Neither can you," Shoshana pointed out.

"Once the newness wears off, he'll drop you like the slut you are."

"We've been together for six years. You've been married for eight, I believe."

Ronit began crying. Shoshana immediately felt not only shame for herself, but sympathy for this woman. "Look, I'm sorry," she said quickly. "But I loved Danny before you did."

"I've loved Danny since I was twelve," Ronit slobbered.

Shoshana conceded her a point. "I just—I don't know what to do," she admitted.

"Stop seeing him." It was very plain to Ronit.

"Talk to Danny," Shoshana said to her. "If he wants to end it, I won't fight for him."

"I can't."

"He's your husband."

"I can ruin you," Ronit threatened.

"Danny's already done that," Shoshana said. She patted Ronit's hand, then left. She would return to the office without lunch. Perhaps it was better to work on an empty stomach.

Over the next few weeks she barely had time for Danny. So busy was she with the translations that when he called, she couldn't make it and when she called, he couldn't make it. At that point she thought Ronit had gotten to him and he had agreed to end it. But then he called to let her know he was going north near Rosh Hanikra for two weeks, so if she wanted to see him, it was now or never. Things were the same between them, the familiar warmth still existed. He did not bring up Ronit. Neither did she. It was, after all, his business with his wife. Later she was to concede that this was a blunder on her part. If she had brought up her meeting with Ronit, Danny would surely have taken some action and in this case some action would have been better than nothing. But Shoshana was to discover to her sorrow that Ronit's tactical skills were more finely honed than her own. For Ronit struck as soon as Danny had departed from the scene.

Meir was forced to invite Ze'ev in. He didn't do it from desire. He knew the distaste was evident on his face as it was on Ze'ev's. But what was he to do when the man was standing on his doorstep and asking if he might step inside for a moment.

Ze'ev looked disdainfully around Meir's apartment, then settled himself gingerly on the edge of Meir's sofa. Meir offered him neither coffee nor tea.

"What is it you want?" Meir asked icily.

"It's about your daughter."

"I have several."

"Shoshana." Ze'ev looked at him for the first time. Meir hated to hear the sound of his child's name on that man's tongue. He waited for Ze'ev to continue. "I understand from my daughter-in-law that your daughter—Shoshana—is my son's mistress."

Meir forced his hands to his side. "What are you saying?" he growled.

"Look, I don't like you any more than you like me," Ze'ev stressed. "And I don't like coming here to discuss this with you either. But someone had to do it. Your daughter has been sleeping with my son for years now. She's ruining my son's marriage. My son has a wife and child and your daughter has been trying to take him away from them at every opportunity. So far she's failed. But I don't want to see it go on any longer."

They both looked up when the door opened. Shoshana came into the apartment and was shocked to find the two men together. She recognized Danny's father from seeing him at her father's construction site, and she knew instantly this was not a social call. She saw Danny's father rise, look knowingly at Meir, then walk past her out the door. Shoshana went to her father. "What did he have to say?"

"What do you think he had to say?" Meir said coldly.

"I don't know."

"What he said about you and his son, is it true?" Meir asked. He waited for an answer.

"Yes," she admitted.

Somehow it did not matter to Meir that his daughter had so defiled herself. What mattered was that she had defiled herself with the Ze'evs. The Ze'evs who kept him still a slave in his own land, living on a worker's pension, struggling to buy a chicken for the Sabbath. The Ze'evs who robbed people like him blind then asked out loud how Israel could survive the primitive onslaught of the Eastern immigrant. For Shoshana to go to his son and let his son use her, destroy her the way the father had him. How could she be so stupid. Meir did not know what he was doing, but he held Shoshana by the hair, slapped and kicked her till she broke away, wrested the door open, and escaped. "Shoshana! Shoshana!" he cried out for her, but she was gone and he could only sink to his knees and cry for his lost child.

"Shoshana!"

"Please help me."

"Oh, my God, Shoshana!" Nurit stood helpless at the door. Shoshana pushed herself in, then held her hands over her face when Nurit's children came to see what the matter was.

Nurit rushed them into their room and closed the door. Then she took Shoshana into her bedroom, helped her to lie down, and covered her with a blanket. "We have to get a doctor."

"No."

Nurit rushed about bringing warm wet towels to Shoshana. Then she hurried into the living room and called Oren.

Shoshana must have blacked out because the next thing

she felt was someone examining her bruised body. It was Oren. "Who?" he asked her.

She mumbled something and tried to sink back into unconsciousness.

"Shoshana!" he called, stressing his desire for her cooperation by applying cold towels to her face.

"My father," she got out.

"He found out about Danny?"

"His father," she mumbled.

"Danny's father told your father?"

"Yes."

"Great."

Shoshana wasn't worried. Oren was Iraqi. He understood the situation. It wasn't uncommon in their part of the world for girls who dishonored their families in such a way to have their throats slit by their fathers or brothers to restore the family name.

"Nothing broken," Oren said to his wife. "Best to let her sleep." Then he reconsidered. "Shoshana, where's that schmuck Danny?"

"No. You musn't tell him!"

"Fuck that! Where is he?"

"Oren, please," Nurit begged.

"No! This has gone on long enough," he said harshly. "Never mind. I'm going to find out for myself."

Shoshana fell into a troubled sleep. She had bad dreams and woke up crying. Always the same, her mother reaching out to her from the grave.

She didn't want to wake up. Not ever again. But she felt someone's face buried in her neck and she heard Danny saying, "Don't worry, my darling, I'm going to kill your father."

Danny always knew the right thing to say, she thought weakly. She had to get up to stop him. But she couldn't. She was too weary.

She heard shouting from another room. She heard Danny's voice and Oren's. She thought she heard David's. She couldn't decipher what they were saying, but she heard David distinctly say over and over again, "Goddamn toad."

Shoshana lapsed away again. When she awoke, she got up to use the toilet. Nurit heard her and came to help her to the bathroom. When she washed her hands, she got the first look at her face. It was darker than before. In spots. She started to cry. Again. Nurit helped her back into bed and brought her tea and soup.

"Did Danny kill my—"

"No." Nurit laughed. "You don't think Oren would let Danny do anything so stupid, do you? No, he went to see his own father. That's all I know so far. He'll be here shortly."

And he was. He came to the door and looked at her. "You're a mess," he said. "We're in a mess." He came over and sat down next to her.

"You don't have to be."

"Oh, shut up," he brushed her off. "I've got compassionate leave for a few days. We've got to get moving."

"I don't know what you mean," she said sullenly.

"I've had it out with my father, her father, and Ronit. What is worse I had it out with Ronit's mother. Boy, you should've been there for that."

"I'm glad I wasn't."

"The words that woman knows."

"I'm sorry, Danny."

"Sorry? Why the hell didn't you tell me Ronit had been to see you? We might have been able to stop all this shit before it got started."

"I thought Ronit would speak to you when the time was right. I suggested she—"

"You don't know Ronit."

"No."

"Sneaky little bitch, wasn't she."

"Did she kick you out?"

"If only."

"So?"

"So the way it looks now, I move out, we get an apartment, I try to get a divorce. She's going to fight me on that. She'll use the *ketubbah* against me. It'll have to be arbitrated."

Shoshana didn't know what to say. She couldn't face this all of a sudden. "But do you want to move out?"

"It's either move out or give you up. Those were the choices everybody gave me," he explained.

"You could give me up," she suggested weakly.

"I've thought about it," he admitted.

"And?" He didn't say anything. "You don't have to feel guilty," she assured him. "I have some friends I can move in with till I get a place of my own."

"You're going to make me say it, aren't you?"

"Say what?"

"That I love you more than I love Ronit. More than I love my family. Are you satisfied?"

"I didn't ask."

"I didn't ask either," he said angrily. "It just happened. I—I need you. Don't make me say more than that."

"Danny." Ronit stood at the door of their bedroom watching him pack. "Don't think you're doing an honorable thing because you're not." He didn't answer her. "I'm your wife. I have your child. You never really considered me, Danny. You've never looked at me and asked what I wanted. I . . ." She faltered. "Oh, there's been too much screaming here already. Maybe—maybe I should have let it go on. I've always loved you, Danny. Even when we were kids. Do you remember the time you jumped off the third-floor balcony onto Mrs. Herzog's awning to prove that canvas could break a fall?"

"It was stupid."

"I thought it was the bravest thing I had ever seen. Still is. That I've seen."

"What does this have to do with anything, Ronit?"

"We've lived our lives together, you and I. I know you, I know how you grew up and what you want. I understand that you have to go away and do these crazy things and I'm always here waiting for you to come back. And you always have come back, Danny, you have to admit that. I've been here with our child in our apartment, keeping our lives together. For you. Look, I understand I can't fill all your

needs. So I settle for the ones that matter most to me.
Being your wife. Having your child. You can't have that
with that woman."

"Shoshana is quite capable of being a wife and mother."

"Not yours," she said too harshly.

"Ronit," he warned.

"I will not give you a divorce, Danny. You better face
that right now. You'll be living in sin with Shoshana. Any
child you have will be a bastard. Your friends won't treat
her as they treat me. You won't be welcomed anywhere.
Neither your family nor her family will have anything to
do with you or her. You won't see Adee."

"Threats."

"Do you think you're doing her any good by moving in
with her? You can't give her anything, Danny. Not money,
because I'm going to go to the navy and make sure the
rightful part of your salary comes to me. Not respectability.
Of course that obviously means nothing to her in any case."

"You've made these points before. At a higher decibel, I
will admit."

"Maybe if I had been beaten up by my father, maybe
then you could care about me."

Danny closed his bag and left his apartment. But he was
not to escape. His mother was waiting for him in her car at
the bottom of the apartment steps. He shook his head in
tired disgust. She leaned across the front seat and opened
the door for him. He wanted to walk past but she was his
mother. He got in the car and closed the door. She said
nothing. She stepped on the gas and pulled out of his street.
When she turned onto Derech Haifa, she pulled off the
highway onto the sand. He was afraid he would have to
push her out. "Pick up the envelope on the front seat," she
ordered.

He did.

"Open it."

He took several folded and stapled papers from the envelope. Straightening them, he read through them and discovered it was a contract to an apartment in Shoshana's
name. "That's very generous of you, Mother."

"If you say you must have this woman, then you must have her."

"What's the catch?"

"If you've had both Ronit and Shoshana for six years, I don't see any reason for you not to continue with the situation."

"Mother—"

"Look, I know you. You feel guilty because of what happened to this girl. Well, now she'll have her own apartment. Her father can't touch her. You can see each other whenever you like."

"It won't work, Mother. Ronit—"

"Ronit won't say anything. She's too afraid of losing you."

"But Shoshana will."

"What can she say? She can't expect you to give up your family and your child for her."

"I've already told her I will."

"In the heat of the moment. No one will hold you to it."

"She will."

"You will tell her that she should move into this apartment, that you'll join her there permanently when you sort things out with Ronit."

"In other words deceive them both."

"Danny, you're my child. I can't keep quiet when you toss away a wife and a child of your own. I beg you as your mother, give this woman her apartment, visit her, have a child by her. I don't care. But don't separate from Ronit and Adee. Promise me, Danny."

"Mother—"

She grabbed his hand. Hers was so small in his, yet he could not resist it. Ashamed, he looked down and mumbled, "I'll speak to Shoshana about it. I'll see what she has to say."

His mother sighed in relief. He sat there silently while the tears rolled down her cheeks. When she finally started the car, the wheels spun. He had judged the situation correctly. He would have to get out and push.

Shoshana waited expectantly for Danny. She knew she

could count on him, that he would take care of her. If he hadn't been there for her, she would have been a total loss, she would have floundered, she would have sunk, she would have drowned. Danny was her life preserver.

She tried to make herself look presentable, but it had been too short a time. Her bruises remained.

Nurit opened the door for Danny when he rang and Shoshana stepped out contritely to meet him. She found herself embarrassed. "I've circled some apartments that might be possibilities," she said timidly.

"That's all right," he told her. "I already have an apartment."

She waited for an explanation, but he gave her none; so she got her coat, thanked Nurit, and they left together. Even in the car Danny didn't enlighten her. "Where is it?" she asked.

"Bat Yam."

"Bat Yam? That's a pretty long way for me to travel to work. How many rooms?"

He didn't answer her. When they got to Bat Yam, he stopped the car at several intersections to ask people for directions. After finally finding the apartment house he was looking for, he got out of the car and waited for Shoshana. Then he let her follow him into the apartment house up one flight of stairs to the second floor. The key was in the envelope. He opened the door. It wasn't a bad apartment. The kitchen was nicely tiled. It had one bedroom, a hallway, a balcony that overlooked a small park.

"It's pleasant," Shoshana said. "When did you find it?"

"An hour ago."

"How much does it cost?"

"Nothing." Danny put the key back in the envelope and handed the envelope over to her. "It's yours."

Shoshana removed the papers from the envelope and studied them. "Very generous," she said. "So do you want to explain?"

He made an attempt. "I can't move in with you right now."

She cut him off sharply. "Where does this apartment come from?"

He tried honesty. "My parents." She dropped the papers to the floor. "Shoshana," he pleaded.

"What do you mean you can't move in with me right now?"

"It's just—I think it might be better if we gave things time to cool down."

"And meanwhile you'll come and visit me here when you like."

"You're making it sound—"

"That's what it is. You want me to be your mistress, your whore, your slut. What are you thinking, Danny, that that's what I am already? You told me you loved me!"

"I do love you. But I can't."

"Can't what? Can't give up everything for me? But I have no choice, Danny. I have nothing left. Except you."

"It's my mother. She made me promise not to leave Ronit. Not yet."

"My mother tried to make me promise not to see you again. I refused."

"If you had heard her."

"I saw you when my mother was dying and we were doing part of the killing."

"I'm sorry." He would not even look at her.

That was it. She turned away from him and willed herself to step toward the door.

"Keep the apartment," he said.

"No."

"Be sensible."

"Drop dead." She was through the door and galloping down the stairs.

He followed after her. "Look, let me take you someplace at least."

"You've already taken me to the sun and back, Danny. You can't do more than that."

"What are you going to do?" he asked her urgently.

She shrugged. "Who knows. Maybe I should try to find someone who'll make a higher bid."

She walked quickly down the sidewalk. He caught up with her. "Don't say that."

She turned roughly to face him. "Don't talk to me, don't touch me, don't come near me. Ever again." She walked away. He did not follow.

She found the bus line that would take her down into Tel Aviv to her work. She would have forgotten about her peculiar looks if the stares of her fellow passengers hadn't reminded her. Even at security in her own building the air was pregnant. Everyone had heard. Naturally. This was the sort of affair one relished if it happened to someone else. She took her card and headed for David's office. She knocked primly. He was in conference, but when he saw her, he finished his instructions quickly and showed everybody out. They were alone together across the desk. "Not out apartment hunting?"

"Do I look okay to you, David, poised, well under control?"

"Yes," he said carefully.

"You probably expected me to be hysterical, suicidal, on the verge of insanity."

"Finding the right apartment can be trying."

"I'm not going to cry."

"Good."

"Or break."

He waited.

"Danny's dropped me." She watched while David nodded and shrugged. "Please don't say I told you so."

He said nothing. He got out a clean sheet of white paper and drew lines vertical and horizontal. "Well. Let's analyze the situation." He put her name at the top of the page. "You have a job. So what you basically need is a place to live." Which wasn't easy to find in Israel, where apartments were not for rent. Everyone bought apartments the way people in America bought houses, except that the apartments in Israel cost more than the houses in the United States. "You can't go back to your father's?"

"No."

"Georgi and his blind mother I imagine are still out."

358

She smiled. "Danny gave me an apartment. From his parents to him to me, so he could see me when he wanted to and still keep his marriage together."

David studied her. "Sweet." He gave it another thought. "You know, Shoshana—"

"No."

"It would solve all your problems."

"So would suicide."

David drew a few more lines. "Money."

"None to speak of."

"Can you get money?"

"I can't ask."

"Give me a list of people. I'll ask."

Joseph Benjamin sat in his office after the working day was finished. He had agreed to meet with David Tal, Shoshana's boss, but conditions being what they were with Lily and the family, he couldn't possibly ask David to his house. The office would serve. He had heard enough about the situation in the past few days to last him a lifetime. The trouble was, he still didn't know what to think. There were two sides to the situation, the male side and Shoshana's side. Mistresses come with a certain economic level, like cars and apartments, and now the television set he had just bought Lily. Moishe Frayman, his partner, had a mistress. He put her on his payroll as a secretary and set her up in an apartment. Joseph didn't have a mistress because he had Lily and she was enough for him.

When David Tal made his appearance, Joseph tried to greet him with a semblance of politeness, even though he had his suspicions that David had known about Shoshana and this Danny Ze'ev long before her family had found out.

"It's about Shoshana of course," David said after taking the proffered cup of coffee.

"Yes. Of course. How is she?"

"Not well. You know she was to move in with Danny?"

"No."

"Well, that fell through. She's staying at my house till I

359

can find her a place to live. For that she needs money, which she doesn't have. I've come to you first. You seem to be the most prosperous of her relatives and friends. A simple yes or no will suffice. Will you help her?"

"What did you mean it fell through?"

"What?"

"Moving in with her soldier friend."

"Well." David shrugged. "Complications set in."

"What sort of complications?"

"Does it matter?"

"To me."

"He offered her an apartment. He wanted to keep her on the side. She expected something more substantial."

Joseph laughed out loud. "What a fool she is then."

"Yes, well—"

"You tell her from me, that she's a fool."

"Sure. That's bound to make her feel better. Uh, can you help her or not? If not, I would appreciate your letting me know so I can cross your name off her list and—"

"Her list? She expected me to help her?"

"Well, as you say, she's a fool."

Joseph felt himself getting angry. "What does she want?"

"She needs a place to stay."

"She had a place to stay. At her father's."

"All right. More specifically what she needs is money to buy her own apartment. Can you help her or not?"

It was as if Joseph's mind had split down the middle. Half of him said let Shoshana suffer the fate she deserved. Let her go to the social welfare agencies and see what they had to offer her. If they could find an apartment for Leah, they could find one for Shoshana. But the other half, he couldn't deny her. Because she was his wife's sister, because he remembered her in Baghdad, and in the camps, and in the army, because maybe her world was no longer the same as his. "I'll think about it."

"I have no time for you to think about it," David insisted.

"I'll give you an answer by tomorrow night. Surely you can stand to have her around that long."

Moishe Frayman knocked on the door of the Tal household. This was the first time since the army that the "old man," as he called his partner, Joseph Benjamin, had so deeply involved him in his personal affairs. They had discussed it, this Shoshana business. For Moishe it was no big thing. He knew it was an unhappy affair, but it wasn't the tragedy Joseph thought it was. So this Shoshana would go on, find someone else. Maybe it would turn out better the second time. For him the big tragedy was letting go of the apartment. He, big-hearted lunk that he knew he was, was settling the apartment on Shoshana Ewan for cost, which was Joseph's and his agreed-upon price. He could have sold the apartment for double what Joseph was paying him. But friendship was friendship, and he had done his deals with various relatives of his own before this, so he shouldn't complain. He wouldn't complain.

"Shoshana Ewan, please," Moishe said when the door was finally opened.

The high school girl who had answered the door called into the kitchen and a very striking young woman made her appearance through the doorway. Striking, if you discounted the yellowing bruises. "Yes," she said.

Moishe couldn't decide whether he was more impressed by her long, curling hair or by the fullness of her breasts. "You're Shoshana Ewan?"

"Yes." David had come out of the living room to stand by her.

"I'm Moishe Frayman, Joseph's partner. I have something for you." He fumbled with the folder in his inside pocket. "It's papers to an apartment. No entrance hall but two bedrooms and a balcony. It wasn't moving because of the entrance and the mosquitoes. It's in a North Tel Aviv *shikkun*, a few blocks from the Yarkon. These are your papers. You'll have to sign the contract."

David took the papers from Moishe's hands and studied them. He nodded. "What are the financial arrangements?"

"Joseph's taking care of them."

"But you're asking Shoshana to sign a contract where the price has been left blank."

"When it's tax time, we'll fill in a price," Moishe said, annoyed. He had expected gratitude, not a lawyer.

"Give me the papers and I'll sign," Shoshana said. "Joseph wouldn't hurt me."

"Oh, yes, like Danny wouldn't," David muttered under his breath.

She grabbed the papers from him and signed her name quickly. Then she handed one copy back to Moishe. In return he gave her two keys.

Before dawn Danny Ze'ev rose from alongside his wife. He put the contract to Shoshana's apartment into an envelope and addressed it to her at work. Then he took his bag, went into his daughter's room and gave her a kiss. After that he left for Eilat.

26

Danielle saw Shoshana waiting at the corner, looking around for her. She called her friend's name. Shoshana glanced her way and waved. She carefully crossed the street and joined Danielle. They decided on a milk bar for lunch. It was April and they'd soon have to shed their bulky sweaters for something thinner. They wanted to be ready.

"You look happy today," Danielle said. She was always amazed at her friend's resilience. After such a tragedy she would have committed suicide rather than face the rest of her life.

"I am happy," Shoshana said. She leaned forward conspiratorily. "We've just shot down six Syrian MiGs. It should be on the next news report. We've picked up Syrian transmissions. They're already claiming it was our planes they shot down. That should teach those bastards a lesson."

Danielle shivered. "What's the matter?" Shoshana asked.

"Every time I hear a report from the Syrian border, which let's face it is about every day, I'm afraid. Ezra's there, you know."

"I know." Shoshana took her friend's hand.

"He says there's no place else he wanted to be, that that's his land, that's where he farms, that's what he wants to defend. And you know Joseph's brother, Reuben? The moshav's fields were set on fire last week. His children have to sleep in air raid shelters underground like foxes in their dens. Why do the Syrians do things like that?"

"Because they control the Heights, it's as simple as that. I was up there once on an outing with a group from army intelligence. All the Syrians have to do is spit and it lands on our fields."

"I wouldn't mind the spit, it's the bombs that bother me."

"And Albert?"

"He called me at work last week," Danielle said. "I don't think they ever taught him how to write. He's on the Jordanian border across from Jenin. He enjoys looking for the fedayeen infiltrators every night. He thinks it's exciting."

Shoshana laughed. "He's so young."

"He's nineteen," Danielle said. "He's old enough to die."

"Don't say it," Shoshana hushed her. "You'll bring the evil eye down on him."

"I don't understand why we must fight, fight, fight."

"Would you rather be in Baghdad?"

Danielle sighed. "I just want peace. I'm tired of sacrifice. And I haven't even made any." She laughed and Shoshana joined her.

"How's the family?" Shoshana leaned forward to ask.

"Oh. I was afraid you would ask. Lily says she never wants to speak to you or hear from you again."

"But she hasn't ever since my father kicked me out."

"Now she's more definite about it. Your father has re-married and she blames you."

Shoshana let her mouth hang open. "When did this happen?"

"We don't know exactly. You see, last Friday night he showed up at Lily's apartment with this woman and he said, 'This is Rahel, my new wife.' I wouldn't say Lily became hysterical immediately, but she called Joseph into the kitchen, slid the door shut, and screamed at him for over half an hour. Meanwhile I was in the living room trying to strike up an interesting conversation with Rahel. She also made an effort, though it was rather difficult as we missed at least every third word what with the racket coming from the kitchen."

"Poor Danielle. Why do you put up with us?"

Danielle shrugged. "Because I have no family of my own. Not with me anyway."

Shoshana would not mention Leah, Danielle never did. "So what is this Rahel like?"

"She seems a nice enough woman. Her daughter's family lived with her and her daughter kept having babies, so even though it was Rahel's apartment, there was no room for her. When Meir came along, she probably saw it as a golden opportunity to move once again into a place of her own. And Lily naturally thinks your father betrayed your mother and that you betrayed all of them, especially since if you had remained at home, your father wouldn't have gone looking for a wife." Danielle paused. "Any message for Lily this week?"

Shoshana thought it over and smiled slyly. "It's remarkable, isn't it. We're all so full of surprises. Hillel and his lies, Ovadia and his Christian wife, me and that schmuck bastard. And now Father. We must have inherited it from him. But tell Lily that it all started with her running off to marry Joseph. And see what she says to that."

"Thanks but I think I'll leave that message undelivered."

Shoshana had to get back to work. There would be reports coming in from all over the Arab world on the downing of the Syrian MiGs. There was no peace, not even a semblance of peace on the borders in the spring of 1967. From Syria, from Jordan came not only the irregular forces of Ahmed Shukairy's Palestinian Liberation Army, but also attacks carried out with the assistance of regular Syrian and Jordanian forces, plus Egyptian encouragement for the fedayeen from Gaza. It was depressing keeping up with these reports, and she wondered at Israel's threats to teach them a lesson. What lesson could Israel teach? She had hit them at Es Samu in Jordan, blown up their houses, beaten back the regular Jordanian forces. What good did such retaliation do when it did not stop the infiltration. But she was not in military intelligence, though sometimes she felt she was. Except today when David wanted a retranslation of the mutual defense pact between Iraq and Egypt. Anyone could have handled it, as it was in the traditional classical Arabic. But David said they had obtained a Photostat with individual notations from the Iraqi foreign minister, so they wanted to know what he was thinking. Some times she wished nothing would ever be written down again.

The buses had all but stopped by the time she reached her apartment. If she noticed the dark figure in the hallway, she was too tired to care, until he stepped out and called her name.

"Joseph! My God, don't do that again. You startled me." She shook her head. "What are you doing here?"

"Waiting to talk to you."

She gave him a puzzled smile and opened the apartment door. She didn't have any idea why Joseph would want to talk to her now, when he had made it plain earlier that he wanted nothing to do with her. After Moishe Frayman had given her the contract to the apartment, she had called Joseph at work many times to ask how he wanted her to pay him back. He was never in. She had left messages. He never called back. And so all of a sudden he shows up? Well, perhaps now he needed the money. But he should have come to her during working hours.

After she flicked on the light, she watched him look around the apartment. "You should get someone in to plaster that crack," he told her as he stared at the ceiling.

"Sometime I will," she assured him. "What did you want, Joseph?" She tried to put some warmth in her voice. After all, Joseph had saved her when there were very few to step forward to do the honors. However, she had heard from neither him nor Lily since the fight with her father. She was tired of being their outcast. If they didn't care, neither would she. If he wanted his money, she had some of it, thanks to Danny of all people. When she had gotten that contract on the apartment in Bat Yam that he had sent her, she had wanted to tear it up and flush it down the toilet. It was Danielle who convinced her to rent the apartment, it was Danielle who took care of renting it, collecting the fees. If she stuck by Danielle's advice, she would surely be wealthy. "No, I don't have much furniture," she said as Joseph paced through the rooms. "You'll notice though there is a bed in the bedroom."

Joseph blushed. "I'm not here to fight with you," he protested.

"Then why are you here?"

"To tell you that your father remarried."

She didn't know whether to act surprised or to inform him that Danielle had already told her. "Oh?"

"A woman named Rahel. She has three children of her own. They're all grown and have families."

"Well. I hope they'll be very happy."

"Lily's—upset."

Here it came. "Lily's always upset. What is it, does she blame me?" Shoshana asked.

Joseph closed his eyes in pain. "How did it happen?"

"Would you like some tea?"

"I don't like what's happening to the family. I don't like it that we're all torn apart after what we've come through together. Was he that boy? That's what your father said, the one you met while you were in high school."

"Yes." What did it matter. "I met him later in the army. I didn't know he was married until after I started sleeping with him. By then it didn't matter. Well, it mattered, but I managed to suffocate my misgivings."

"You loved him?"

"Of course. What other reason should I give for doing something so catastrophic?"

"It was his fault. He should have cared more for you."

"What matters to us doesn't matter to him."

"I loved your sister for years, but I never ever would have defiled her. What he did to you was wrong." Joseph had decided. "Do you ever hear from him?"

"No. Nothing." Well, not exactly true. She had heard

about him the same way she heard about her family, through mutual friends. He seemed to be surviving well in Eilat, even if he suddenly took life a little bit more seriously. Yes, and she was feeling great, she told his friends. Happy as a lark. Work going well, life in order. The best thing that ever could have happened to her, him walking out on her and letting her fall flat on her fanny. She needed the exercise of picking herself up again.

"Tell Lily I'd like to see her," Shoshana suggested softly.

Joseph shook his head. "She won't. Your father has forbidden it."

She stiffened. "Tell Lily our father forbade her from seeing you. Yet I was the one who lied to our mother so she could escape to Tehran with Rebecca."

"I'll tell her," Joseph promised. He turned from her and left her alone in the apartment with her sorrow.

PART 3

27

Of all the holidays in Israel, Yom Ha-Atzma'ut, Independence Day, was Shoshana's favorite. Even with the solemn Day of Remembrance, Yom Ha-Zikaron, preceding it, when the sacrifice of the fallen was noted, she always felt like celebrating. Because for her there was so much to celebrate, her own private exodus from the captivity of Babylon to freedom in this, her land, and she would not forget it. Even when her freedom was mingled with sorrow. There were others who took a more cynical view of the freedom Israel offered them. But they could not remember as Shoshana did, the constriction of Jewish life outside Ha-Aretz, her Zion.

This Independence Day she was spending with Oren and Nurit. The night before she had gone down with friends to the Iriyah, where they had eaten candy apples, been hit on the head and fanny with plastic hammers, and danced the hora. Now it was a private party with friends and their families. She sat with the women and talked about the rise in the price of clothing and how much the customs on an imported television set was. Now that Israel had its own television broadcasting authority, there was a rush, despite

371

the expense, to buy a set. Since Israel was a bilingual state, the broadcast authority divided its programming into Hebrew and Arabic. And since the Iraqi Jews would control the Arabic broadcasts as they did the Arabic radio service, Shoshana would have stood a good chance of getting a job with them. Several other Iraqis had already left the resources and translations bureaus of the security service for television, but she chose to stay, mainly because David was offering her a promotion as soon as her boss retired. All that was hush-hush for the time being because if her boss knew a woman would be replacing him, he would never retire.

It was so noisy at the party that at first no one heard the phone ring. Nurit's little boy finally grabbed it and called to his Uncle Matti, who was a lieutenant colonel in the tank corp. Matti took the call, listened, hung up. No one paid much attention to him. He grabbed his wife, they stepped out of the circle and spoke a few quick words in the hall before he thanked Nurit and Oren and disappeared.

The phone rang again. This time everyone heard it. It was for Gil in military intelligence. He held the phone for barely five seconds. He kissed his wife and his two sons. "See you," he said to the rest of the party. He was gone.

The men looked at each other. Oren turned on the radio. He switched from Gal Aleph to Gal Bet to Galei Zahal. There was music, there were interviews. But there were no telltale phrases like white dragon, Jacob's delight, Sami's sewing circle. There was no general mobilization. Oren turned off the radio and shrugged. The party resumed, although quieter than before.

The phone rang. No one wanted to answer it. Oren finally picked it up. He listened for about a minute, then put the phone down and walked into his bedroom. Nurit quickly followed. Everyone fell silent. A few minutes later Nurit called her three children in to say good-bye to their father. Oren came out of the bedroom with a small traveling case. He smiled and said, "Once more into the breach." Shoshana guessed Kurdistan.

That sort of killed the party. The men took turns waiting to call in to see if they were needed, when they might be needed, what they should do. Shoshana waited until they were through, then she called the office. The operator told her that her name had been checked, so could Shoshana tell her where she would be for the rest of the day and night. If she wasn't called, she should report to the office at six thirty the next morning for a briefing. It might be a good idea to bring a small cosmetic case and a change of clothing.

"All right, everybody, let's settle down." David looked harried already and the morning had barely started. Someone whispered that he had been working all night. "Quiet, please, in the back!" He waited. "Now," he announced, "we have a slight problem."

"That must mean war's going to break out any minute," one of Shoshana's friends whispered.

"Quiet. Please," he begged. "The Egyptian forces have started to mobilize. We have reports of tanks rumbling through the streets of Cairo. We hear that Egyptian army units are moving into the Sinai and up toward our borders. We hear that the Soviet government has passed on false intelligence reports to both Egypt and Syria, informing them that our forces have massed along the Syrian border, that we are poised for an attack on Syria. Syria seems to be invoking its mutual defense pact with the UAR. Nasser seems to be responding with this partial mobilization.

"However, there are several reasons why we should not be too worried about these developments yet. First of all, we are not massed along the Syrian border, a fact of which we are assuring the Russians, the Syrians, and the Egyptians. Second, between us and the Egyptians stands the United Nations Emergency Force, which has been there ever since 1957. Last, you all know that Egypt is involved in a disastrous war in Yemen. It has poured its troops and equipment into that war. So we feel that right now Egypt is not ready for a total confrontation with us. Right now we're here to collect as much raw data as we can. Let's let the analysts analyze this time. What's not important to you might be important to them."

Someone had made a dart board of U Thant's picture and placed the words "war criminal" underneath. Shoshana couldn't blame them. U Thant, if anyone, must be given credit for stoking the fires of this latest round of madness. He had withdrawn the United Nations Emergency Forces stationed between Israel's and Egypt's troops. Nasser asks. It is given. Don't bother with the fact that it meant certain death, a bloodletting that would drench the sands of the Middle East. What does it matter? Nations will play their little games. Nations survive. Only the people die.

What surprised everyone was that the United Nations acted so swiftly. It usually took weeks of fumbling for it to make the smallest of movements, but U Thant had really cut through the red tape on this one. And it had set the Arab world ablaze. No longer could Syria scoff at Nasser's pretentions to leadership, claim that Egypt was hiding behind the skirts of the UN force. Nasser had proven Egypt's determination, and his cries for the destruction of Israel rung out from North Africa across the Arab East.

Still there were some in Israel who said, even as the mobilization of Zahal and the Arab forces continued, that Nasser's words amounted to nothing but hot air.

Words do not kill and the Arabs' words were always mightier than their deeds. Then on May 22, Nasser blockaded the Strait of Tiran, an international waterway. No Israeli flagships would be allowed through.

"Isn't Danny down there?" one of Shoshana's coworkers tactlessly asked her.

The patrol boat churned through the waters of the Gulf of Aqaba. "What does this mean, *'causus belli'*?" one of Danny's men asked him.

"It means 'act of war,'" Danny translated.

"Act of war? Act of war is when someone shoots a gun at you or fires a missile."

Danny laughed. "This act of war means it's a provocation to war. Egypt has closed the Strait of Tiran. We have an international guarantee that they're to be open to us. If they are kept closed, we will be, as Nasser says, 'strangled.' We need the strait open. It's our southern shipping route, our oil lifeline."

"So let's open the strait."

"Yes, let's," Danny agreed.

And yet there were no orders to open the Strait of Tiran. They waited for the prime minister, Levi Eshkol, and their foreign minister, Abba Eban, to arrange for an international flotilla to honor its previous commitment and break the Egyptian blockade. But it seemed as if every ship in the Western fleet was occupied elsewhere. The international commitment given to Israel in 1957 wasn't worth shit and everyone in Israel knew it, except the government. So the Israeli navy would wait while the days passed and Nasser's blockade became the new reality. If this status quo continued much longer, Nasser wouldn't even have to fight. He would have gained his victory without losing a man.

"Guess what, everybody? Cairo radio's favorite, the Hashimite whore, the dwarf of Amman, our own little Hussi has flown to Cairo. At this moment while we are sitting here drinking tea, King Hussein is meeting with Nasser and our special friend Ahmed Shukairy, who's spent the last few years trying to overthrow him, to arrange for a joint military command. My prediction, fellow citizens, Hussein will be flying back to Amman with his own Egyptian general to take charge of Jordan's Arab Legion."

"Dalia, take a couple hours off and get some sleep," David advised. "You're obviously hysterical."

"What's hysterical about that?" David was asked. "The noose is complete. Syria, Egypt, and now Jordan. And how many troops from every other Arab country have been airlifted to the front line. Ask Shoshana about Iraq."

Shoshana sighed. She had already made her report. What was it, May 30 and Iraq had airlifted one army unit into the Sinai to fight alongside the Egyptians at Sharm el Sheikh. Now more of its army had moved in between the Syrians and the Jordanians along Israel's northern borders. It was the same with every Arab nation. They wanted to be in on the kill. Ahmed Shukairy, head of the Palestinian Liberation Army, spoke for them all when he said, "We will wipe Israel off the face of the map and no Jew will remain alive." Those Israelis who owned television sets could see for themselves as in every Arab capital the masses demonstrated. Death to Israel. Death to the Jews.

Shoshana was tired, she was worried. The government of Israel vacillated and floundered. It expected international action to save it and no action was forthcoming. The Arabs saw Israel as weak, as easy pickings, and they would attack her sooner or later. So the Israeli people waited for the Arabs to decide their fate because the Eshkol government was still searching for a compromise in a situation in which one couldn't compromise. And the general frustration was building inside Israel, as they realized the longer they delayed, the more the Arabs mobilized, the more deaths there would be in what had to come.

It was her night to go home. They took turns, though some would not leave even though after two weeks the crisis had sapped them of most of their energy. But she wanted to rest tonight, to be away, to think. She hadn't been quite right since she had heard that the Egyptians had mined the Strait of Tiran. She tried to label it a national problem, but she realized that the mining of the strait was Danny's problem, and she didn't want to think of him solving it.

It was only by happenstance that when she was leaving the office, she saw the green Volkswagen with its headlights painted blackout blue pull away from the curb. The driver was an analyst for European affairs. "Need a ride?" he asked. "Ramat Gan?"

If he hadn't asked, she would never have thought of visiting her sister, but suddenly she couldn't stand to be alone any longer. So she piled in. The streets were empty. The buses were gone, the trucks were gone, the men were gone.

The latest figure she saw was eighty percent mobilization. Their Volkswagen was the only car they spotted from Tel Aviv to Ramat Gan.

It seemed strange for Shoshana to be going up the familiar steps to Lily's apartment. She had not paused to think of what her sister's reaction might be. And she did not pause now. She simply rang the bell. Lily answered almost immediately. When she saw Shoshana, she fell on her and embraced her. Shoshana let the tears fall from her eyes as they hugged and comforted each other. "Joseph?" Shoshana finally asked when they parted.

"He's in the Negev. That's all I know. He told me to write him, so I do every day. He's been gone for a week. His unit, you know. He collected them in his truck and drove them south. I wish to God he had never bought that truck."

"He'll be all right." Shoshana said that meaningless phrase.

"I hope so. I think maybe he will be because they've converted the truck into an ambulance now and so maybe the Egyptians won't bomb him. Do you think?"

Shoshana said nothing. She walked into the apartment to find the television on.

"Jordan," Lily explained as the Arabic came wafting to them through the speaker. "They showed Baghdad earlier. You should have seen it. It's like that riot of 'forty-one or 'forty-eight. Pick a year. Baghdadis don't change. But you must know all about it. It's your work after all."

Shoshana sat numbly on the sofa. She didn't care to discuss her work, or Iraq. She came to be at home, with her family. But Lily kept asking questions. Shoshana tried to sort through what had been in the papers and what was in the intelligence reports. She certainly couldn't tell Lily that the Kurds had started a major push against the Iraqi army. Thus the greater portion of Iraqi forces would be pinned down dealing with this internal problem.

"Where's Joshua?" Shoshana asked.

Lily put her finger to her lip. "Sleeping," she said quietly. "He's so tired. His class spent most of the day filling sandbags, and after he was through with that, he went down to the post office to help deliver mail. From the way he acts, you would think his bar mitzvah was this year instead of next year."

"You should be proud of him, Lily."

"Oh, I'm proud of all of them. And scared." She put her arm around her younger sister. "I've been teaching."

Shoshana smiled. "No."

"Yes. Arabic of all things. The regular teacher was called up."

"And Danielle?"

"Oh, Danielle. She's in paradise. She says she's never seen the bank so busy. It seems everyone in the world supports us except the Arabs and the governments. The people are with us. It feels better to know we are not so alone as it would seem when watching television." She trailed off. "Father and Rahel are baking bread to send to the front," she said suddenly.

"Are they? Doesn't it spoil?"

"I don't know. They bake bread in the morning, then in the afternoon they go to the first aid station and roll bandages." She paused. "How are you, Shoshana? You look tired."

Shoshana leaned back. "I am tired. It's the waiting more than anything. And the uncertainty. All these facts are swimming around in my head and I don't know what they'll add up to."

"Is—should I ask about him?"

"He's in the Gulf of Aqaba on a patrol boat. Waiting like the rest of us."

"Do you hear from him?"

"No."

Roberta was hysterical. She had never learned so quickly to care so much about a country that hadn't really mattered to her a year ago. She thought it was the meeting of the Israeli Student Organization that had done it. The same people who couldn't even decide what juice to buy now came together in a single mind. Decisions were made at the snap of a finger. What had been splintered now coalesced into a single unit. But what touched her more than anything was that she was discussed. She was pregnant. If Ovadia were called up, a family was delegated to take her in and care for her. She had not heard from her own family, but these strangers were ready to provide for her when their own country was threatened with destruction.

But what could happen, what would happen, she asked Ovadia over and over again. And would he go.

"I'll go if they call me," he said. "I'm not in a fighting unit. I'm in the scientific reserves."

"What the hell does that mean?"

"That's the point, isn't it?" he answered angrily. "When computers fight wars, I'll be in great demand." Talk about frayed nerves. Ovadia got in touch with a friend of his at the Weizmann Institute who was in the same unit. No, they hadn't been called up yet. As a matter of fact the scientists and the old men were the only males still walking the streets of Israel.

Most of the Israelis in Urbana who were married stayed with their families to finish their semester studies. The single ones began to slip away. They had gotten tickets aboard El Al. They were going home to fight.

Diane Evans felt strange. It happened in the store, it happened on the streets of Sante Fe. People would come up to her, they would ask her if she was a Jew. When she answered yes, they would say to her, "We're with you. We're with you all the way."

This was heaven for Hal Evans, née Hillel Ewan. He was in demand. He never knew he had it in him, but when his brethren in the UJA called and asked him to speak on the need for Jews to support Israel financially in its hour of need, he was ready, and he did it so well he was considered a financial evangelist. He discussed his glorious days as a Zionist youth in Baghdad, his outstanding service as a paratrooper in the Israeli army, the tragic back injury he received on his last jump that had caused him to come to this great land of America for medical treatment, and now the commitment he felt to support not only Israel but Jews everywhere. "For never forget," he would tell his audiences in conclusion, "that if Israel falls, we fall with it."

For the first time in his life Jacob Ewan had guns in his home. The cries in the streets were not just against Israel, they were against himself and his sons. And this time if it came to it, he would not go alone. All his money, all his guile had not stopped him from being spat on in the streets as a dirty Jew. Well, he had learned in the last few days no longer to walk in the streets. His neighbors didn't know him; faces stared through him as he passed down his street. He felt the growing within him of a siege mentality. He had one of his Arab workers from the Swallow's Nest bring him food, supplies, and he ordered his son Rahamin and his family into his house and then his son Ephraim. Ephraim was being more difficult. He told his father that he was a Jew, not a Zionist, so the Arabs would not hurt him. Where had Jacob gone wrong with him? Ephraim was a fool.

Rahamin didn't want to see the guns. "If they come into the house and find them, they will kill us," he argued.

"Once they are in the house, they will kill us anyway," Jacob retorted. "Why should we die alone?"

And they were alone. With the building of tension, with the masses gathered in the square every day to demand the death of Israel and Western imperialism, the Englishmen, the Americans, the Europeans had fled. Including Mr. Harris. Without a word, without the outstretching of a hand, Mr. Harris had simply vanished.

Alone, the Jews of Baghdad waited for what must come.

The sounds of jubilation reached through her closed office door, forcing Shoshana out to ask what the celebration was about.

"Moshe Dayan has joined the government as defense minister."

Shoshana threw up her hands. "Finally!" she said.

It had just been too much. Eshkol's government sat around making pronouncements and waited for the world to act. With every muted statement from the Israeli government, the Arabs became more angrily demanding. Dayan, Shoshana thought. Now there was someone the Arabs could understand.

It was the first of June. From all over Israel the people girded themselves for battle. For that was what appointing Dayan as defense minister meant. War would come soon. The UN would take no action. The United States backed off from sending an international fleet through the strait, and President Johnson now proposed a peace mission for his vice-president throughout the Middle East. But more serious rumors were being heard in Tel Aviv, that the United States and Russia were getting together to discuss a solution to the crisis that would allow for foreign flagships, but no Israeli flagships, to pass through the Strait of Tiran to Eilat. If the superpowers agreed, they might try to impose their will on the smaller states of the Middle East. Israel was worried. The time for action had come. Nor could the Israeli economy stand this continued mobilization of its work force.

Danny Ze'ev had been called back to Eilat. He was studying the charts as his commander explained to him what he wanted done. "Can you and your men do it?"

"We can do it," Danny said. "You want us to blockade the blockade, we'll blockade the blockade."

"You've got the timing?"

"Tonight, stage one, tomorrow, stage two. Count on it."

"You know, Danny, if you encounter too much resistance, I have word from general command that they're going to send paratroopers down to take Sharm al-Sheikh."

"Yes. Well, it seems to me that Sharm should be our field of operation."

The commander smiled. "Seems to me it should be too." They laughed and shook hands on it.

Danny left naval headquarters and hit the streets of Eilat. Across the way he could see the beginning of lights in
Aqaba. Tonight or tomorrow, June 4 or June 5, it would
begin. He could already feel the adrenaline pumping
through his body, could already sense the cold serenity of
his wet suit, his goggles, the warmth of the water as he
splashed backward into it. He loved it, he wanted it, he was
scared, he was insane.

He thought of her as he passed the post office with its
rows of phones hanging on the outside wall. He wanted to
call her, tell her he was going, that it was about to happen
and he was thinking about her. But she had told him never
to come near her, never to talk to her again, forever. Forever. Fuck it, this was forever. He might be dead before
morning. He picked up the phone and aggressively dialed
her number. It rang and was picked up. "Shoshana Ewan,
please," he said sharply. Naturally she couldn't be at her
desk to answer her own phone.

"Shoshana is in operations."

"Would you get her out of operations?"

"No, I couldn't. We're on wartime footing, you know."

"No. I had no idea." *Bitch.*

"Can I take a message for her?"

"Yes. Tell her I love her and if she doesn't like it, tough
shit."

The girl on the other end sighed. "What name shall I
give?" she asked nastily.

"If she has to ask the name, then the message won't matter." Danny hung up the phone. He'd have to hope his
mission tonight went better than that phone call.

Joseph Benjamin sat under the stars of the Negev and
froze his ass off. Two people from his unit were missing.
One was in Great Britain as a fund raiser, the other was in
Hadassah Hospital being treated for ulcers, though just
being in Jerusalem under siege as it was would give him
ulcers. Better the desert, he thought, as he sat shivering.
Moishe Frayman walked casually over to him, his Uzzi

hanging from his shoulder. "I'd forgotten how cold the desert can be," Joseph said.

"I hear it's even worse in the Sinai," Moishe replied, sitting down next to him. "You know, Joseph, you don't have to be here. With your injury—"

"It's my truck—the army says I have the right to drive it into battle."

"You men okay?" their lieutenant walked by to ask. "Want some coffee?" He poured some into their cups. He must have been twenty-five at the most.

Moishe shook his head in wonderment. "Little pisser," he said.

"Don't knock youth, Moishe. They're the ones who buy our apartments."

"That's what I'm getting at, Joseph. What if we're both blown away at the same time? What's going to happen to the business?"

"Look, we're going into Sinai, not Gaza. We'll be okay. We always have been."

"Sure," Moishe said heavily. "Still and all, I can't wait until I hit forty-five. Enough of war already."

Joseph laughed. "You'll make a great civil guard."

"Damn right I will. Nothing is safer than patrolling the streets of Herzliya."

The meeting in operations had broken up and Shoshana had her marching orders, so she rushed back to her office to get her things. It was off to military intelligence again, but this time she was glad. At least she would be in the thick of things. She frowned when she saw the message on her desk. "I love you. If you don't like it, tough shit'?" she read aloud.

The department secretary came over. "Some guy called around an hour ago. Didn't leave his name."

"Danny. Where can I reach him?"

"He didn't leave a number either."

Shoshana panicked when she saw David and the major approaching her. "Danny called. I have to get back to him."

David took the message from her and read it. "Hearts and flowers as usual." The major looked at his watch.

"I don't know where he is," Shoshana explained.

"Shoshana, go with the nice major. Danny will be fine."

"How do you know?" she asked David.

"Because the navy is superfluous. If he were with the army or air force, I might be worried about him. Now scat. The time has come."

Danny and his men had been dropped off south of Dahab in the Gulf of Aqaba. They moved swiftly and silently through the waters of the gulf on the black rafts especially constructed for the commando units until their point man had triangulated their position. The Strait of Tiran was open to them. The Egyptian guns lay to their right, the island narrowing the channel to their left. He ordered his men to get ready. He would leave Dov and Yossi on board to guard their retreat. One by one he signaled his men over the side until only he was left to join them. He pushed himself off the raft and sank noiselessly into the sea. They were waiting for him. They had their orders. They fanned out in a vee with him in the lead. He felt no fear in the water. He had drilled for operations like this over and over again. What he did was second nature to him, even, on this mission, tedious. When they finally surfaced one by one, it felt as if they had been below forever. He looked at his men. They all agreed with him. Nothing. They tipped themselves back into the raft and returned to their mother ship.

The report was radioed to Tel Aviv that night. Contrary to Egyptian claims, the Strait of Tiran was not mined. But Danny and his men would not rest. They had to prepare for their next night's work, which might be more deadly.

Roberta Ewan would remember the time forever. It was 6:56 on the morning of June 5, 1967. The phone rang. She picked it up. She knew the voice instantly. It was an Israeli friend. "It's begun," was all he had to say. Why did she thank him.

She called to Ovadia. They ran into the living room and turned on the *Today* show. It took them a while to understand the gist of what was being said, but when they did, it seemed to be believed that the Israeli air force in the first hours of battle had almost totally knocked out the opposing Arab air forces of Egypt, Syria, Jordan, even Iraq, which had dared send one of its planes to strafe Netanya. The map was up on the screen and they watched as S. L. A. Marshall pointed out what had reportedly happened to the Arab air forces. "If the reports are true," General Marshall said, "then Israel has won the war."

"But the reports, are they true?" Roberta asked desperately. There had been such a torrent of words coming from the Middle East of late that who knew what to believe.

Ovadia stared at the screen and said finally, "It's Israel's policy never to lie to her people in times of crisis." He turned to her, smiled, grabbed her, and embraced her. They sat there in front of the television set watching the terrible miracle take place.

There was no miracle for Joseph as the push into the Sinai began. He was separated from his friend Moishe Frayman as he started his truck and picked up the medics assigned to him. He would rush after the war, he and his young friends, but there would be no glory. Joseph wouldn't see the triumph of battle because his head would be down and his hands would be bloodied as he helped lift the bodies of the fallen to bring them as swiftly as possible back to the aid stations for medical attention, if it were not already too late.

"When you go to Nablus city, when you go/ When you go to Nablus city, when you go/ Then Mohammed very easy—"

"Shut up, Haya!"

Albert clamped his mouth shut. His lieutenant didn't like his singing, he wouldn't sing. Orders were orders, yes, sir. And he wanted orders. He was so damned tired of waiting for orders that even his own singing didn't inspire him.

And when they came, they were beauts. Move through Jenin, move down toward Nablus, prepare yourself to take the Damia Bridge. Yes, sir, very well, sir. The fact that the Damia Bridge was on the Jordan river and they'd have to take the entire West Bank of the Jordan to get to it didn't disturb him one bit. Though he could see the lieutenant was slightly flustered. Well, such is the burden of command.

Oh, but he was going to get them. Where were they now, these Arabs who had threatened to push them into the sea. Let them come, let them try. Albert Haya, formerly of Baghdad, future member of Kibbutz Vered, best Arabic speaking soldier in his unit, was waiting for them. Waiting for them, hell, he was coming to get them. He would push them back to Baghdad, visit his old house for a few hours, then make a return flight to Israel. Another Operation Magic Carpet, this time all his own.

So he wouldn't be the first into the West Bank. No, the planes had come over this morning like birds swooping down to their nests. Then the tank corp had gone in, one on one with the Arab Legion. Now the half tracks. That was he. Later the reserves would come in to mop up and hold. They all had their orders. It was on to the Jordan.

Shoshana sat with the headphones pressed against her ears. She didn't even notice anymore the pain their pressure was causing. Someone tapped on her shoulder. It was the major. He had a lieutenant as a replacement for her. She was surprised. That was why she had been seconded to military intelligence, to free the men for combat positions.

"You haven't slept in thirty-six hours," the major reminded her. "Get some rest. We have some broadcasts we'd like you to do later."

Thirty-six hours. She couldn't believe it. She went into the hallway and looked to the window. Those weren't blackout curtains. It was night. The first day of the war was ending. "A present for you," the major said. He shook out a slightly wet piece of paper and handed it to her.

She stared at it. It was all smoke and craters. "What is it?" she asked.

"*Habbaniya*. With love and kisses."

She smiled. The Iraqi air force base lay in ruins. She found the conference room with the cots set up for quick naps. It would have surprised her how soon she fell asleep if she had been awake to notice.

Danny checked his equipment and his men. Night was falling on the first day of the war and he was about to execute the second half of the venture that had begun the night before. So far the Gulf of Aqaba and the Straits of Tiran were a naval field of operations. The army had not pushed down the Sinai coast to Sharm al-Sheikh as it had in 1956. It was left to the navy to handle the Egyptian forces there while the army cut through the northern Sinai passes, thus loping off any Egyptian support for the garrison of Arab troops stationed at Sharm. Unless, of course, the Egyptians resupplied through the Gulf of Suez, which was his mission, to make sure they did not.

It was familiar territory for them this night as their craft skimmed almost noiselessly through the Straits. They had explored every inch of this last night. They knew nothing under the water would get them, and in the darkness, unless the Egyptians used flares, they were safe.

Dov was sitting nervously, almost wringing his hands. Danny wasn't used to seeing his friend so aggravated at the thought of battle. "What's the matter?" Danny asked.

"I'm afraid we'll get the wrong island."

Danny laughed. Islands lay like stepping stones between Egypt and the Sinai peninsula. One of them was particularly advantageous for spotting ships traveling from the Red Sea up the Gulf of Suez to the canal. It was used by Egypt as just that, an observation post. Danny and his men would take it, set up their launchers, and blast away at any Egyptian boat sent in to resupply Sharm. Danny had no fear of Egyptian retaliation from the mainland. He had been briefed before he left. The Egyptian air force was destroyed, including Hurghada, the base right across from the islands. The Egyptian navy was busy in the Mediterranean and along the canal. If Danny and his men wanted the island, it would be theirs, once they took the garrison.

The motors were cut as soon as the island came into view. Momentum propelled the boat farther toward land until it rocked to a halt almost in position. Danny gave his men the thumbs-up sign and led them as one by one they slipped into the water with their weapons and swam away. When they came up on the beach, he waited until all were accounted for. Then he signaled them to divide into two squads. He led his squad across the high rocky terrain until they were behind and to the left of the observation post. It was sitting there just as intelligence had said it would be. The back side of the post was totally blind. He checked his watch and waited. He had allowed himself five minutes too much time and his men were restless, psyched up for battle but knowing they had to wait. He consoled himself with the fact that it would give them time to catch their breath.

At his signal they began their descent to the post. He knew that the other squad would be coming in on the beach from the right side. They could hear Egyptian voices floating up to them. Then one particular voice crying a warning before the shooting started. The Egyptians made the mistake of rushing out of the observation post instead of into it, where they could have held Danny and his men off for a time and radioed for help. As it was, they were easy targets, caught in a cross fire, and after seeing his men dropping, the Egyptian commander gave the order to surrender.

It was a mopping-up operation after that. The Egyptians lost five dead, seven wounded, a heavy toll for a post staffed with only twenty soldiers. Danny's men broke into their details. One trained as a medic treated the Egyptian wounded while another had their countrymen remove the dead. Three were in charge of the prisoners. One went to the radio with his Egyptian counterpart to assure Egyptian central command if necessary that the observation post was secure and also to set up a communications link with Israeli command. The rest of his men readied their missile launchers and signaled their craft to come to port. The island was taken. The only thing Danny and his men regretted was that they could not raise the flag. Their presence on the island was to be kept a surprise.

It was as if the water could wash away the blood. Joseph Benjamin jumped into the Suez Canal and let its wetness sweep over him. God, it had been a long sixty hours. He had seen, well, he had seen too much. He had been at Abu Agheila if only to take care of the wounded. Had he been an infantry soldier, perhaps he would have felt the exhilaration of battle, but as it was, he felt more like a woman who had cleansed and shrouded her only son. Still the victory was sweet and in time he might be jubilant. He climbed out of the canal and sat in the sun. Where had all these cameras come from? Israeli soldiers were probably the only ones who carried both a rifle and a camera into war.

He got up and started walking back to the medic's tent. He heard sort of a rumble through the troops and he wondered what was happening. "Jerusalem," one of the soldiers shouted, throwing up his helmet. "Jerusalem is ours. All of it!"

Joseph felt himself shiver, then he smiled. Naturally, he thought. This is the age of miracles.

"Danny," one of his men pleaded.

"Our orders are to stay here," Danny scolded him. "The war's not over yet."

His men were pissed off with him. Good-natured about it but still pissed. They didn't understand why they had to stay on the island when Sharm al-Sheikh had been taken and the strait was opened once again. All they could get was secondhand reports on it, and they wanted to see it firsthand. Especially since the navy had retaken Sharm, had landed to find the enemy missing, had raised the Israeli flag, had sat and waited cockily while the paratroopers who had dropped at Ras Nusrani hiked down to meet them. It hadn't fazed the paratroopers of course. They just continued around the southern tip of the Sinai and moved up the eastern coast to a-Tur and the Abu Rudeis oil fields.

"When are we going to see it all!" his men wanted to know.

Danny's heart was with them but his orders were to remain on the island.

Ezra Haya was near hysteria. It was June 9. There were ceasefires on the Egyptian and Jordanian fronts and Syria still retained the Heights. Where was the justice in any of this? Syria had practically started the war with its incessant bombardment of Israeli settlements, its call on Nasser for his military assistance, and now it should get off scot-free?

Ezra's only relief during the day was the note he had received from his smart-ass brother. "Dear Ezra, I'm at the Damia Bridge on the Jordan River. Inspirational scenery. Wish you were here. Keep helmet in place." And this written on an Arab Legion training manual. Thank God Albert was safe.

What made Ezra think that all was not lost was when he saw the bulldozers. And his lieutenant was called away for a briefing. Tanks were brought to the fore also. Old, bulky Sherman tanks, but tanks nonetheless.

His lieutenant came back and called Ezra and the other sergeants to him. "Okay, we move," was all he said.

"Where?" Ezra asked.

"Straight up Tel Azaziat."

No one said anything. If those were the orders, they would be followed. The soldiers would go up the hill straight into the face of the Syrian guns.

The assault started at high noon. The bulldozers moved in first to clean the large boulders out of the path of the tanks that followed. The Syrians must have thought them crazy. This wasn't tank terrain. And yet there were the Israeli tanks inching their way up the hill. The entrenched

Syrian tanks simply blasted many a bulldozer and a Sherman tank to a halt. And then it was the Israeli infantry's turn. It was the infantry who would finally have to take out the Syrian guns one by one. Ezra watched as the signal was given. The lieutenant followed their captain, as Ezra followed his lieutenant, as his men followed him straight into the killing power of the Syrian guns. He dared to look up, to see several times where he was going. He could almost feel the heat of the bullets pouring down on him. When they were within a hundred feet of the ridge, their lieutenant fell. Ezra looked around for the captain and saw his body below him. He pulled a grenade and arced it toward the Syrian entrenchment. "Come on," he called to his men, "follow me!"

He could not pinpoint later what had happened after his lieutenant had gone down. He remembered almost tumbling into the trenches upon the surprised Syrians, and he had the distinct impression that he was nearly alone. In a place too confined to fire, he used his rifle butt to whip all those Syrians surrounding him, and when someone grabbed his rifle away from him, he pulled out his bayonet and plunged onward. He must have seemed like a man possessed, but if he had not cleared a way for himself, he would have soon been trampled beneath the feet of his enemy.

And then he suddenly no longer had the feeling he was alone as he heard other voices, Israeli voices, joining him in the trenches as they cut down the Syrians.

When he came out of the trenches, Ezra knew the blood upon him was his own. Yet there he was at the top of Tel Azaziat staring down with a mixture of exhilaration and horror. They had made it, but the cost lay beneath him. He turned from his fallen comrades and vomited.

Shoshana felt like a vulture as she studied the lists of dead and wounded, always looking for names she hoped would not appear. Joseph was safe. Lily had heard from him. Even though the streets of Tel Aviv were filling with men who had been demobilized, Joseph continued to work on as a medic, but there was little to fear now. Shoshana had heard from Danielle that Albert was also okay. Danny must be safe. His name was on no list. Over and over again she had checked. And she found many familiar names, those wounded, those dead. Amidst the enormous triumph came the stories of horror. Mothers who thought their sons were studying in America only to find they had come home to join their unit and died in the street fighting for Jerusalem. Wives who assumed their husbands were still in the Sinai with the troops when they had actually joined the Golani units and been killed in the Syrian assault. The cost was too high but everyone agreed with a sad determination that it must be paid.

When the reports from the Syrian front came in, Shoshana saw the name of Ezra Haya, wounded. Before she let Danielle know, as she promised she would, she called the northern military command to find out what she could. Ezra was in serious but stable condition in a hospital in Safed. In the taking of Tel Azaziat he was a hero, the commander assured Shoshana. But they all were, Shoshana thought, as she put down the phone. They all had to be.

"Where are you going?" Albert asked the woman with the child clutched in her arms and the bundles piled on top of her head. "We won't hurt you. Come on back." The woman paid no attention to him. She walked across the river into Jordan. "What's wrong with these people?" Albert asked no one in particular.

"They're afraid," one of the soldiers answered.

"Let them leave," another replied. "Who needs them in our land."

Albert was a little slow to catch the quick transition. He couldn't understand it. He knew from listening to the radio that Israel was exhorting all Arab residents of the West Bank to stay where they were, but still they came and crossed over into Jordan, where they had no hope of a decent future. He tried to talk to them in Arabic, to explain to them how much better it would be for them to stay. Especially the women with children because they reminded him of what it must have been like for his mother to travel alone with no hope. Sometimes the Arabs said they would be back if it looked like the Jews weren't being too destructive, but they couldn't take that chance just yet. Others just didn't want any part of living under Israeli occupation. What could he do except watch them leave. Until he got notice from his lieutenant that his brother had been wounded and would he like a day off to go see him.

Danielle reached the Safed hospital half an hour before Albert did to find Ezra patched and resting in a general ward. She was surprised to see him so bruised, as she had expected a gunshot wound or something equally anonymous. But he explained to her that he had been involved in hand-to-hand combat. The ward was filled with women volunteers giving what comfort they could. "Just keep the woman with the oranges away from me," Ezra muttered.

"Was it terrible?" Danielle whispered.

"Terrible, yes," Ezra answered and the tears welled up in his eyes. "So many dead. But it was worth it to be free of them."

She held her brother as best she could. She remembered him as the little boy she had mothered in Beit Lidd, and now here he was a soldier, bigger and stronger than she would ever grow, seeing things that she would never want to see. How could she protect him now?

And then Albert showed up. "I knew it. I said if I leave my brother alone, he's going to do something stupid like get wounded. And you didn't disappoint me."

Ezra almost laughed. Danielle watched while her brothers grasped each other's hands. How strong they were. She was overwhelmed by them. They sat around and talked of the Syrians and the Arab Legion and even the UN until Albert asked about that dear to all of them, Kibbutz Vered.

Kibbutz Vered was free now. Free from the guns, free from the infiltrators. But a price had been paid. Aside from the wounded, they had lost two men and one of them was the husband of Osnat, Danielle's *metapelet*. "I must go to her," Danielle said.

After leaving their brother, she and Albert hitched a ride

to the kibbutz. They were both welcomed with shouts of joy, especially Albert, and even in Osnat's household there were smiles of greeting. Danielle moved slowly to Osnat, put her arms around her and expressed her sorrow. Osnat thanked her. "He fell at Tel Faqr. That's the hill next to the one your brother was fighting on."

"They say it was murderous," Danielle commented softly.

"Too many," Osnat agreed. "I console myself by thinking how happy Arik would be if he knew that we are free of them, those Syrians, and by his efforts. How happy I should be that he died for something he believed in and not in some senseless auto accident. And yet, he's dead, you know, and it hurts. It hurts terribly." Osnat started to cry and there were clucks of sympathy and tea and hugs. She would recover. She would tell her children about their father and they would know what his sacrifice had meant when they could walk in their fields, look up into the hills, and not be afraid.

Danny sat atop Mount Sinai and surveyed the desert. It was perhaps more beautiful than he had expected. He wished he was a psalmist so he could put his thoughts to rhyme and music, but it must all be there in the Bible someplace, what he was feeling, for his people had said and felt the same things since time immemorial. There must be something said about the grandeur of this desert, which could so touch and humble, so overwhelm those who sat among its peaks. Danny felt overwhelmed with gratitude. His usual arrogance had been replaced by a religiosity he did not know he possessed. They could not have done this alone. He sensed that as he sat on Mount Sinai and let the wind whip across him.

"Time to descend," someone called. The sun was about to fall. It did not tarry in the desert. And when he went down, his thoughts would descend too. The problem lay before him. His leave. He was the last of his men to get leave, the last to ask for it. Because he did not know if he had the guts to go where he wanted to go. It was easy to fight a war. It was not so easy to love. He just didn't know the right tactics. He was always blundering into some ambush and retreating. Yet he knew whom he had wanted to share it with, this victory, whom he wanted to crush in his arms and say, "Hey, I'm alive." Would he do it? Finally. That was the question he could probably not answer until he found himself in Tel Aviv.

28

In Baghdad Jacob Ewan was afraid. He had not seen his sons in months. Sixty-three days to be exact. It gave him time to think about what kind of father he should have been, what he should have taught his sons as they grew. Not honor, not respectability, not pride, not love. All those were useless to them now, for there was only one thing a Jew in Baghdad needed and that was the will to survive. This he had taught neither Rahamin nor Ephraim. Somewhere in the prison they were as solitary as he, if they were not already dead. God curse the Arabs.

He laughed. God had cursed the Arabs. He and his sons had remained free long enough to hear of Israel's great victory. And then the army had come for them, into their house before dawn broke, scurrying like pack rats through the rooms, confiscating what was in reach, using their rifle butts to find what was hidden. Oh how he wished then that he had remained in the old section of Baghdad, where his sons might have climbed up the stairs and escaped to the roofs of their neighbors. But here he was with his own villa and no place to run. He was not even allowed to bring the women and children together. They each had to stay put in their separate rooms while the army searched. He could merely wince at the sounds coming from the next bedroom, the voice of Leila, Rahamin's wife, as she tried to protect Nadav and Melina from the sight of those animals.

In the end they had found a shortwave radio. Used to transmit messages to Israel, the officer charged. Spying. That meant automatic hanging. Jacob said nothing. A book on the Kabala. Ephraim's. Used to encode secret messages to be transmitted on the shortwave radio. The radio couldn't send anything but that was overlooked. Money. British pounds. How could they fit that in? Jacob's lips curved slightly. He was sure they would fit that not into their reports but into their pockets. Twelve silver dessert plates engraved with the Star of David. Jacob chanced a quick look at his wife. It had been illegal for over twenty years to have the Star of David emblazoned on anything. How many jewelers had earned their keep enclosing the star in other forms and yet his wife kept these plates?

"They were a gift from my grandmother on our wedding," she explained weakly. Where had she hidden them all these years? It didn't matter now. They were dropped into the sack with the radio and the book.

He was allowed to get dressed finally. In front of his wife and the army. She lowered her head in shame. He grasped her hand on his way out and squeezed it tight. Then he left between two soldiers. There was a police van waiting outside his house. He was familiar with negotiating the step up. He remembered it from the last time he was arrested. He waited there calmly and could just glimpse through the open door several of his neighbors peering out cautiously from behind their windows. His sons were brought out one by one. Rahamin quiet with anger, then Ephraim struggling, tossed into the van, a welt already rising on his cheek. Ephraim fell into his arms and wept. "This is what I have raised you for," Jacob said guiltily, silently cursing himself for his own stupidity. He felt the futility of it all as he realized that freedom for him lay only in death.

And yet there was hope. As the days passed and he was

not hanged, the fear eased even as the pain of that fear remained. His cell was bearable. His blanket was infested but that was to be expected. The cell stank, but no hygenic measures were taken so he would save his complaints. He counted his days not by the rising and the setting of the sun. There was no sun in his cell. There was only a gray settled darkness enlivened once a day by the bringing of food. Always the same. A bowl of rice and water. He distrusted the water as he found his constant diarrhea turning into dysentery. But drink he must to survive. Over the weeks no one spoke to him and he called out to no one. No words said to a simple guard would affect his fate.

On the sixty-fourth day the door to his cell swung open. He averted his face as the dim hall light struck him. "*Ya'allah,*" the guard said to him. Jacob felt like a drunken man as he struggled to his feet. He tried to move forward but he stumbled back. Disgusted, the guard came into the cell, grabbed him by the arm, and pulled him outward. Jacob almost threw them both off balance before another guard grabbed his other arm and he was led securely down a hallway he vaguely remembered and propelled up two flights of stairs. He knew from the way his legs did not recover that he was not young anymore.

It was another hallway now. Then a door was kicked open and he was dragged inside and placed on a chair. He tried to keep himself from flopping around on it, but found he had very little physical control over his own body. A light was flicked on and his eyes seemed to burst backward inside his head. How could simple light cause such unbearable pain? He snapped his head downward and tried to shield his eyes with his hands. A guard grabbed him by the hair and swiveled his face toward the light. Just when Jacob thought he could stand it no longer, the light was switched off. He stared vacantly as the circles before his eyes began slowly to dance their disappearance. Then he looked up and tried to focus.

"It has been a long time, my friend. Several years. And how sorry I am once again to find you in similar circumstances."

Jacob tried to discern who the speaker was, but a white handkerchief was held over the lower half of the speaker's face so that Jacob could not recognize him. "My sons?" Jacob asked.

"You don't know me, do you?"

"The handkerchief," Jacob explained weakly.

"Excuse me," the speaker said, letting the handkerchief fall. "The stench is enormous. When was the last time you bathed?"

"When was the last day I was home?" Jacob replied. Jacob studied the man's face carefully.

"The Rashid prison camp," the man offered helpfully.

"Yes. Musa al Haykal. You're the one who told me not to give up hope."

"And I bring you the same message today," Musa said smoothly. "But really, I don't think we can talk until you've been scrubbed down. Having been in the army most of my life, I am not by nature a delicate man, but the smell is truly horrendously offensive."

He snapped his fingers, and the next thing Jacob knew, he was being bruised by a jet stream of cold water. "Soap," Jacob called out. A bar was thrown to him and he lathered his body as the cold water played against it. When the water was shut off, he was freezing. He knew he was alive. It was a good feeling. Even the rough prison garment he was given felt good and clean against his skin.

"Ah. Much better," Musa al Haykal said as Jacob was brought back before him. "I have coffee waiting for you. And some fresh bread. Your wife has brought you and your sons a fine meal every day. I must say, the guards are going to miss it. If you are released."

"If?"

"The charges against you are strong."

"You and I both know that my life is in the hands of the state. The charges have no validity. Their only meaning is what the state decides to make of them."

"You deny you are an Israeli spy?"

"Of course I deny it. How crazy do you think I am? To

spy for Israel? It would be insane. If they have spies in Iraq, and to be sensible, one must assume they have, they would not ask a Jew."

"Perhaps," Musa said thoughtfully.

"People know me here in Baghdad. You may ask any of them what they think of me."

Musa continued to study him. "It's not the people who know you I'm interested in. It's the people you know."

"Whom do I know?" Jacob protested.

"Everyone," Musa pointed out to him. "The Swallow's Nest. Everyone comes there. Everyone."

"Is that what is upsetting you? The Swallow's Nest? I'll close it. I'll sell it. What do you want? Whatever you want is yours."

"A partnership."

"A share in the profits?"

Musa smiled. "No, Jacob. Not a share in the profits. I want the information you glean. I want the tapes you make. The profits, they're all yours." Al Haykal watched while whatever color was in Jacob's face fell from it. "Yes. I've been over there. I've checked out the rooms. They're wired, Jacob. Did you know that?"

"Some of my—"

"Please don't insult me with your explanations. What you did before was your business. What you do from now on is mine. Mine. And no one else's. If you love your sons."

"My sons?"

"Yes. They're still alive. For the time being. They'll remain alive. As long as we're partners." Musa reached across the desk with his right hand extended. Jacob quickly grabbed it firmly in his. The bargain was sealed. The Ewans would live. For a while longer.

Danielle Haya sat at her desk and thought about last night's birthday dinner Shoshana and Danny had made for her. Was she really twenty-six? And if she was, what did she have to show for it?

Shoshana had Danny, for two years now. One day shortly after the war Shoshana had come home from work and there he had been, waiting for her. Now they lived together. For Shoshana it was as simple as that. Danielle only wished love would be simple for her.

Men. She in truth did not understand them, was, she would have admitted, somewhat afraid of them. Her mother spoke about men, about the dirty things they liked to do, especially with a little encouragement. "Most men aren't as good or as decent as my Nazem, rest his soul, was."

Danielle hardly remembered her father. He came back to her sometimes as a brooding presence. She could not really understand what her mother saw to admire in him, unless it was his absence. And her mother had been alone all these years. She did not seem to need a man the way Shoshana needed this Danny, or even Lily her Joseph, which was a respectable union, even though her mother whispered that Lily took too much pleasure in Joseph's company. What was marriage then if not pleasurable. "A duty," her mother had responded.

Danielle feared she would never have the opportunity to find out. She had met men at the bank. But if their timidity served them well at work, it did not enhance them outside of it. She had met distant relatives at family gatherings. It was whispered to her that she could do worse. But she had in her small moments of rebellion hoped that she could do better.

She wanted to fall in love. She wanted to be delirious and silly, to do all the stupid things women in love did. If she could allow herself. Everyone fell in love. Shoshana was happy even when she was unhappy. Ovadia. He had been so quiet and shy. Now he was married with one son and another on the way. Even he must have known the right words to say, the right way to say them. No one had said those words to her. Perhaps no one ever would. That thought left her sad, empty, and frightened.

But life went on, even bleak, dismal lives like her own. She worked at the bank, she came home. Every evening at seven fifteen she was at the kitchen sink making dinner, because every day it seemed, just before she got home, her mother would develop a terrible headache that would confine her to her bed until dinner was ready. Danielle objected, but not too strongly. She liked these few minutes of solitude when she allowed her mind to roam. Later when she went to bed, she would be tired and would fall quickly to sleep, only to wake up with the alarm. But now she stared out the kitchen window, which was just about level with the small backyard, and thought her own special thoughts.

Today her thoughts were a little less quiet than usual. The Margolises two flights above her were having two new armchairs delivered. The truck had backed in till it was right next to the entrance of the building, which meant it was almost opposite her nose. She watched while the driver hopped out of the truck and unlatched the back, grabbing one of the chairs. She studied his body from the anonymity of her kitchen. He was wearing a red plaid shirt and black trousers. She could see his thigh muscles pressing against the material of his trousers. She felt a slight stirring between her legs. She tried to still it. It happened all too frequently lately and sometimes she was tempted to touch herself to calm her nerves. The man disappeared. Soon he came back to fight with the second chair. When the delivery was completed, he climbed back into his truck. Danielle felt safe once more. The engine started and she expected to see the truck pull away. Instead she heard a slight spinning sound which grew louder, and then she caught a spray of sand from the churning wheels. The truck was stuck in the backyard. The driver tried a quicker acceleration, which did nothing for him but shot a sandstorm into her kitchen, all over her, all over the food. She was furious. In a moment of sheer hysterical anger which she rarely gave way to, she rushed outside and began beating on the truck door with a wooden spoon.

"Hey, lady!"

"Don't you give me lady. Look what you've done to my kitchen, look what you've done to me, you—you—

bastard!" she screamed at him, shocked a moment later by her intolerable use of that awful word.

The driver of the truck watched her expression turn from anger to horror and began laughing at her.

"Oh!" she shrieked and rushed back into her apartment, slamming the shutters to the kitchen. She didn't know what to do, where to begin to clean up.

She heard a rapping at the shutters. She ignored it. But it came again. She violently threw the shutters open. He was there by her window, smiling in at her. "*Shalom*," he said, his teeth flashing.

"*Shalom*," she said coldly. "Look what you've done."

"If you'll help me get my truck loose, I'll take you out to dinner."

It was too crazy. And she didn't believe she was doing it. But she actually let him lift her through her own kitchen window. What was she thinking of? She only hoped her mother's headache got worse so she wouldn't come out to the kitchen to see what was happening.

"Now here's what you do," he was saying after he seated her in the cab of his pickup. "You press very gently on the gas when I say go. Let up on the clutch. Slowly with your left foot. Or you'll stall."

"Where will you be?"

"In the back, pushing."

"But I don't know how to drive."

"Would you rather push?" he asked. She watched him circle around behind. "Ready!" he shouted.

She did what he told her but the truck stalled.

"Too fast on the clutch," he shouted. Well, how was she supposed to know? "Hold it," he called. She watched while he circled out to the sidewalk and asked some men returning home from work to help him with his truck. Now Danielle was really scared, but the driver came around to her, opened the truck door. He would push against the door, operating the clutch with his hand. All she had to do was press down on the gas pedal.

He forgot to tell her about the brake. With the men pushing and the driver working the clutch, the truck shot forward, leaving them in the sand and her headed straight for the other apartment building. In horror she covered her eyes with her hands and drew her legs up toward her body. The truck lurched to a stop.

"You are incredibly stupid," the driver hurried over to tell her. "Do you realize you could have ruined my truck!" She was too petrified to react. He stood on the running board and pushed her over. Then he got into the driver's seat, restarted the engine, and slowly put the truck into gear. It moved. He waved his thanks to the men who had pushed him and turned the steering wheel, maneuvering slowly out over the curb onto the street.

"Where are you taking me?" she asked nervously.

"Out to dinner. Like I promised."

"I thought I was incredibly stupid?"

"Yeah, well, you're a woman." He shrugged it off.

Dinner? She wouldn't be able to eat. But her appetite revived slightly when she thought what her mother's reaction would be to the mess in the kitchen. At least this time Leah would know what a real headache felt like.

Danielle was uncomfortable in the cab of the truck. The driver spoke not a word, only glanced at her a few times with a smirk. She rearranged her legs under her dress and sat primly with her hands folded in her lap. He almost guffawed. He was truly beginning to annoy her. "Perhaps you'd just better drop me off someplace," she suggested.

"I will. Right after I turn this corner." They had traveled south toward Jaffa and were on the outskirts of the Ha-Tikva section of Tel Aviv when he pulled up onto the sidewalk and parked. He got out of the cab and waited for her to dismount. She felt awkward. It was like jumping off a mountain. He secured her by the elbow when she landed and took her back around to the main street, led her into a small steakeya. He had such effrontery that he didn't even ask her what she wanted. Instead he ordered houmus and eggplant salad, kebabs, pita, and orange drink. *"B'te'avon,"* he said to her as she viciously ripped off a piece of pita and dug into the houmus. The food was good, she had to admit it. It was raw and spicy. He bought her another orange drink when she finished her first and watched her eat. "Don't you ever say anything?" she asked him.

"I buy the food. It's your place to be entertaining," he teased. She looked away from him. "What's your name then?" he asked her.

"Danielle," she thrust back.

"Danielle." His smile changed to something softer, sweeter. "I was in love with a girl named Danielle once."

"Really?" She was unimpressed.

"When I was a boy. She was a weird little girl. All arms and legs and eyes. Like a half-grown chicken."

"How flattering. What happened to her? Did she get wise to you?"

He sighed. "I don't know what happened to her. We were parted by circumstances. And I never saw her again."

Danielle mellowed. "You mean by the immigration?"

"Oh, no, we were already here. You see, my parents had to put me in a kibbutz when we first came to Israel. They had no money, no place to live. And this Danielle, her parents had simply abandoned her and fled back to Persia and —what's wrong?"

Danielle felt really faint for the first time in her life. She could sense the blood fall from her face as the room swirled. The driver grabbed the cold drink bottle and rolled it against her forehead. It shocked her into an almost speedy recovery. "What's your name?" she whispered.

"Are you all right?" He was panicked.

"Your name?" she repeated.

"Sami."

"Sami from Kibbutz Vered?" She saw the look of shock and recognition pass across his face. "I'm your Danielle and you deserted me. You stinking bastard!" What could she do to him? She took all the plates sitting on the table and one by one dropped them on him as he watched in horror and the angry owner of the café screamed at them. Then she rose, walked, ran out of the steakeya. Sami. God, it was Sami. He had come back to her.

* * *

Shoshana sat on the couch, her eyes passing from the television set back to Danny's shirt collar, and to the television set again. Danny was engrossed in the paper. She let the shirt fall to her lap as she pushed her new glasses up to the bridge of her nose again. Danny had noticed. He smiled. "You look good in them," he told her.

"They're only for reading," she reminded him.

The doorbell rang. "Your friends, I'm sure," she said. "And would you please kick them out before twelve?"

Danny rose and went to the door. When he opened it, he saw a disheveled Danielle Haya. He called Shoshana, grabbed Danielle by the waist, and quickly force marched her to the couch.

"Danielle!" Shoshana was horrified. "What is it? What's happened? Tea," she ordered Danny, but he stood there. "Your mother? The family? Lily? My father?"

Danielle just stared emptily back at her friend.

"She's been raped," Danny guessed.

That brought Danielle around. "No, I have not!" she protested.

"Then what happened?" he demanded.

"Sami." She uttered that single word.

"Sami attacked you?"

"Do I look like I've been attacked?"

"Yes," he told her.

Danielle looked down at herself. There were food stains on her dress. She patted her hair. It had come loose from its bun. She rose from the couch and hurried into Shoshana's bathroom. Shoshana gave Danny a disgusted look and rushed into the kitchen to make tea.

With a good cup of hot tea in her, Danielle was soon able to communicate. She told Shoshana and Danny exactly what had happened to her that evening. "Do you think I offended him by dumping all those dishes on him?" she asked finally. Danny laughed wildly. "But don't you see, Danny, how he deserted me when I really needed him?"

"I understand perfectly," Shoshana agreed.

"That was years ago when he was a little boy. The fact that he said he loved you and he remembered you still should make up for the desertion." Danny tried to put things in perspective.

"But he promised to write. He promised to visit. I never saw him again. I was alone. Always."

Danny didn't know what to say. He shrugged.

"So you think he'll never want to see me again?"

"Well, you've obviously made your second lasting impression," Danny joked. No one found it amusing.

"Did he have his name on the side of the truck or anything?" Shoshana asked.

Danielle shook her head. "I don't remember."

"But he knows where you live," Danny pointed out.

Danielle sighed. "Much good that will do me." She rose. "I better go now."

"I'll drive you," Danny offered.

"No."

"Yes," he insisted.

Actually Danielle was glad for Danny's offer. She didn't want anyone to see her in the state she was in, not even her mother, though she feared that would be impossible. Leah by now was certainly waiting by the kitchen and wondering.

Danny dropped her off and she fleetingly thanked him. She watched him leave, then slowly made her way around the apartment building to her basement entrance.

"Danielle?"

She looked up. It was Sami. Her first instinct was to run.

He approached her with a smile on his face. "Danielle? Is it really you? Danielle Haya? With the two brothers? Ezra? Albert? Danielle. You're not so funny looking anymore." When he was almost upon her, he reached his arms out for her and pulled her to him, kissing her full on the lips. She could not pull away. Her mouth instinctively opened and his tongue was inside her. She felt his hips pressing against her as one of his hands slid down to her backside while the other pressed the small of her back into his chest. She felt faint again and dizzy. But this time she didn't want to throw anything at him. She just wanted him to carry her away.

"M-m-m."

He broke away. "What?"

"You mustn't."

He took her face in his hands and drew his fingers through her hair, releasing the pins. Slowly, carefully, he kissed her forehead, her cheeks, her eyes, her nose. When he came to her mouth, it was already open to him. For the first time her arms came to life and awkwardly encircled him. He slid his hand around to her breast. She did not stop him as he played with her nipple beneath the material, pulling it and rubbing it between his fingers. She felt a sweet sickness flaming across her body. She fell back. He caught her. "You mustn't," she insisted.

"I've been looking for you all my life."

"Well, I've been right here in Givatayim," she retorted angrily.

He laughed. He took her hand and held it in both of his. "We're going to be married. You know that, don't you?"

She studied him. He was still so dark and beautiful, and brave and daring, smiling, happy, assured. Wonderful, loving. Her Sami. "Yes," she said. "I know that. We will be married."

Sami's family overwhelmed Danielle. She couldn't remember ever feeling so much love before in her life, and they all said the same thing to her: "So you're Danielle." His mother went on and on about all the girls they had introduced Sami to. "He would always say," his mother told her, " 'She all right, but she's not Danielle.' None of us really believed you existed, but here you are at last."

Why, if she had been so awkward and weird as a child, had he been so impressed by her that he wanted to wait for her? Or someone like her. "Because I knew what it felt like to care for someone as a child, and I wanted to know that feeling again," he explained to her.

Sometimes she was so afraid that his love for her would evaporate. After all, he hadn't seen her in seventeen years.

But his love never faltered, remained steadfast, not that he gave it much time to be tested. He wanted to be married immediately. But there were other considerations, financial and familial, to consider. Financially, he assured her, he was doing okay. His truck was almost paid for, he had a string of clients for whom he made deliveries. And where would they live, she asked him. He would borrow against his truck, against his livelihood, against his life to buy them an apartment. Meanwhile they would share a room in his father's apartment.

As much as she liked—loved—Sami's mother, his sisters, his brother, even his father the shoemaker, she could not see sharing a room with his brother, with his whole family in their tiny apartment in Jaffa. "So what do you propose, a bomb shelter?" Sami asked her.

At that she surprised him with her financial nest egg. "You robbed a bank!" he declared.

"When one works in a bank, one doesn't have to rob it," she explained.

He was justifiably speechless. She watched his face and could see him alternating between pride in her, awe, and resistance, as if it were not manly to accept her monetary offering. "It's my dowry," she convinced him. "I believe in the old ways." Which he should have known after struggling with her every night to touch more than her lips and her breasts. Still soon it wouldn't matter. They would have their apartment. They would be together forever.

She was so happy during those weeks she and Sami hunted for an apartment. They spent their Shabbats driving up to Kibbutz Vered to visit her brothers and, of course, Osnat. Danielle felt she really had a family now. Osnat acted like both the mother of the bride and the mother of the groom. It was she who suggested it would only be appropiate for them to marry on Kibbutz Vered and they both took instantly to the idea.

"You don't have any bad feelings left toward the kibbutz, do you?" Sami asked her quietly.

"Not since the kibbutz gave me you," she assured him.

Besides, she was calculating how much she would save on the reception, since Osnat promised them the kibbutz would provide. Poor Sami. Thoughts like that never seemed to strike him. She would have to keep a close eye on his business for him.

So it was settled. The date and place of the wedding was set, her dress was chosen and being altered, the contract on their apartment was ready to be signed, their basic furniture had been selected and was ready to be delivered by Sami himself, if need be. What was left except to kiss her old world good-bye.

Leah was left.

Leah had bided her time, waiting to make her move. She hadn't butted in when they had sat on her sofa and made their plans together. They hardly gave her a thought as she crouched quietly and listened. But when she was sure that everything was set, she asked them one night when Sami brought her daughter home when she would be able to see the apartment.

"Don't worry," Sami told her with a smile. "We'll invite you over as soon as we're settled in." Leah got on his nerves. He didn't know whether it was what Danielle had to say about her that influenced him, or the fact that she always sat in a corner like a dark, looming presence when they got together, or the fact that she had abandoned his poor Danielle so long ago, but he got itchy when he spent too much time near her. He was allergic, he told his own mother. She insisted it was just because Leah would be his mother-in-law, that was why he automatically didn't like her.

"I just wanted to know what the apartment looked like so I would know what I needed to bring to my room and what I could leave here and sell with this apartment."

Danielle froze. She had never expected this from her mother. Even though she had had her suspicions ever since she had met Sami and declared her intentions. Her mother had made no protestations, even seemed to encourage the match.

411

"Oh, you're moving to a room?" Sami said carefully. "Well, that will probably be better for you. Danielle tells me how difficult it is for you to keep this place clean no matter how hard you try. A room will be just about right for you."

Leah had to decide whether to press the matter or let it drop. But nothing would be gained by letting it drop. "When will I be able to see it?" she insisted.

"See what, Mrs. Haya?"

"My room in your new apartment."

"Mother, there is—"

Sami stilled her. It would be better coming from him, not from her own daughter. "Mrs. Haya, there is no room for you in our new apartment. There's no room for anybody but Danielle and me and when we have him, our child."

"I'm sure Danielle feels differently."

"Whether Danielle feels differently or not doesn't matter to me." He could not let Danielle take any of the responsibility for this rejection. "She will be my wife. I will make the decisions."

"Danielle?" her mother snapped.

"I'm sure, if you'll remember your own marriage," Sami continued calmly, "that's the way it was."

Leah waited for Danielle to say something, but her daughter, pale and frightened as she was, held her tongue. Danielle only wished Sami wouldn't have to leave her alone with her mother; but Leah, noting her daughter's silence, kicked him out almost immediately.

Lily was nervously removing the skin from the breast of the chicken. She didn't know why the breast always gave her so much trouble. The leg skin came off easily, the neck also. The breast skin was the largest. She liked to keep it whole so she could stuff it with rice and meat for Joseph, especially tonight, when he would be returning from his reserve duty, but for some reason it always broke or tore.

"Would you like me to help you?" Shoshana asked.

412

"No!" Lily snapped.

Even Danielle was shocked by Lily's vehemence. She had come to Lily's apartment to get away from her mother, and all she had done was step into some other family's mess. In a way it was a comfort. She was tired of the crying and screaming that went on in her basement, her mother claiming that she had taken Danielle in when Danielle had no other place to go. It wasn't true; Danielle knew it wasn't true. But the lies her mother told were so often repeated, she was beginning to believe them. She felt such guilt it was like a stone pressing against her heart. And Leah was always in the kitchen now making the food when Danielle came home. She even washed the floors. Maybe Danielle did owe her something, but not the rest of her life.

Sami held firm. Well could he. He didn't have to live with Leah. He didn't even have to see her, as Leah refused him entrance to her house. If only Danielle could spend this last week before her wedding someplace else. Perferably on the moon.

"If you—"

"Shoshi, if it's one thing I don't need, it's advice on how to cook from you."

Danielle was suddenly grateful she didn't have a sister as well as a mother.

"What is the matter with you?" Shoshana asked Lily.

"I don't like it."

"You don't like what?"

"I don't like Joshua going over to your apartment and spending time with Danny."

Shoshana was surprised. "What harm is it doing Joshua? We don't have any children of our own and Danny loves the boy."

"Oh, Shoshi!" Lily was shocked. "How can you even talk about children when you're not even married? He hasn't gotten his divorce yet. What excuse has he given you this week?"

Shoshana flushed. Anger, shame, sadness intermingled. "He's trying," she objected gently.

"Even you can't believe that any longer," Lily said. "Besides, every time Joshua goes over there, he comes back with talk of how he's going to be a commando like Danny."

"What's wrong with that?"

"I'm not going to let him be a commando. I'm not going to let him be in any fighting unit. He's my only son. Those are the rules. If you have only one son, they can't force him into combat."

"I don't think anyone would force Joshua to fight. He would realize it was his duty."

"It's his duty to stay alive. It's his duty to get married and have children. Those are the laws of God. I've had enough of war, enough of Joseph's driving his truck all over those sand dunes. Every day there's a new death in the papers. There are mine fields down there. That's what Joseph says. He says as soon as our boys leave an area, the Egyptians come across the canal and plant mines. This is aside from barraging our boys with artillery day and night. I thought your beloved Danny was supposed to take care of this sort of thing with his dashing commando raids?"

"Danny dashes to the Egyptians side of the canal, for which he risks his life every day. It's the army's job to clear the mine fields."

"And Joseph's job to pick up the bodies where the mines are. Well, I don't want Joshua to be one of those bodies. He's all I have. So just keep Danny away from him."

"You don't have to worry. Danny and his unit are permanently stationed along the canal now."

"Does that mean he won't be coming to my wedding?" Danielle asked.

Shoshana tried to read into that question Danielle's wishes. "He was planning to ask for the day off. But if you'd prefer that he didn't come, I'm sure he'd be more than happy to stay along the Suez protecting the construction workers who go down into the Sinai and bring back wheelbarrows full of government money."

Lily dropped the chicken and turned on her sister. "Are you accusing Joseph of fleecing the government?"

"I'm not accusing Joseph of anything. I'm merely saying

that the road to the Sinai and back is paved with gold for those who receive, by whatever means, government contracts."

"Do you realize how many tractor drivers are being killed making the Sinai safe for the army?"

"Joseph and Moishe Frayman are not tractor drivers, Lily."

"By developing the Sinai, Joseph and Mr. Frayman-to-you are doing what they think of as their patriotic duty. They could easily sit in their offices here in Tel Aviv and build high rises in Ra'anana and Ramat Aviv for the new immigrants."

"They're doing that too, Lily. So don't criticize Danny. He's not getting rich off the war."

"I'll tell Joseph what you have to say," Lily threatened.

"Do. I'd love to hear his reaction, but since I haven't been invited to stay—"

"I've invited Father to welcome Joseph home from the reserves," Lily explained.

"Of course."

Shoshana stormed out of Lily's apartment, barely saying good-bye to her sister or Danielle. It had been awful of her to attack Joseph, she knew. Not that everything she had to say wasn't true. It was. But why should Joseph be blamed for grabbing at what was available? She wouldn't have said anything if Lily hadn't criticized Danny. Danny had been under so much pressure lately. He came home every other weekend, but his mind never really left the canal. It was like a sieve, he had told her. It wasn't the same as the English Channel, which had for so long protected Britain from European invaders. The Suez Canal could be crossed, and was crossed, daily by hostile forces. Egyptian commando units slipped over to the Israeli side and mined it. Their artillery was in easy range of Israeli fortifications. Danny's commandos in retaliation crossed over to attack Egyptian installations. The air force was called out, the paratroopers. "It's not a war," he told Shoshana in disgust, "it's just a perpetual bloodbath. They're picking us off one by one, and we don't have Egypt's problem of overpopulation to fall back on."

"So what can we do?" she had asked him.

He shook his head. "You would think after such a victory there would be some peace. But we're not going to live to see it, Shoshana. Not in our lifetime."

She was worried about him. She was worried about them. He was so tired. She tried not to add to his burdens, but she couldn't stop him from sensing the undercurrent of anger she felt every time she thought of his divorce not coming through, and she thought of it every time she saw him.

Why was Ronit being so stubborn? She had lost him. She must be able to see that. Though who knew. Maybe something went on between them when he went to pick up Adee. He claimed not. But could she believe him? He talked about Adee all the time. When he wasn't talking about the canal. He loved his daughter. Maybe if she could have a part of that. But he had promised Ronit that he would never bring Adee into Shoshana's presence. So every other Saturday he spent with his daughter. She got to see him on Friday and Saturday nights when they would make love, or he would use her, as she sometimes thought of it. He was always so tired! If she brought up the divorce, he didn't want to talk about it. What was left to her. Four nights a month and a few phone calls? She was twenty-eight. She wanted at least the security of marriage. She wanted children. "What do you want me to do?" he kept asking her. Something. Anything. She just didn't know anymore.

Luckily she always had her work. David said he didn't object to Danny anymore because now he was only a phantom in her life. So she could work overtime any time David called her. He had all but promised her that when the head of the Iraqi section retired, the job was hers. She had whispered the news to Danny. He had just grunted and fallen over on his stomach to sleep.

Well, even if her own life was in a shambles, it was some consolation that Israel was in better shape. It wasn't only

Joseph and Moishe Frayman who were becoming rich. It seemed as if the whole country shared in a rainbow of prosperity after the war. New immigrants from the West brought money and a desire for material goods happily emulated by even the most frugal of Israelis. Tourism rose drastically, as not only Jews but Christians came to see Greater Israel. All the holy places were in one country now. There was no difficulty with passports and visas as there had been when Jordan controlled East Jerusalem, Bethlehem, and Hebron. The building boom was sustained by Arab workers who poured into Israel proper from Gaza, from the West Bank. No one stopped to ask any questions. Never had Israel seemed so open, so free from threats. The deaths of Israeli soldiers on the borders were a horrible thing. But the borders now were so distant that they didn't seem to have the same impact as a death occuring only a ten-minute bus ride away. And above all there was still that overwhelming exuberance that they had done it, they had won, they were victorious, alive. They had survived. It gave one a feeling of great confidence, though Shoshana herself would have felt more confident if she were like Danielle and in a week she, and not Danielle, was going to be married.

Danielle had solved all her problems. Or they had been resolved for her. She had left Tel Aviv four days before her wedding. As soon as she had picked up her wedding dress after its final alteration, she had boarded a bus to the kibbutz. She had told Sami it was safer that way. She had to leave Givatayim if she wanted to start her marriage sane. Her mother was making threatening sounds about not coming to her wedding, and she almost didn't know what to do, especially when Leah started whispering things like, "God curse you the way you have cursed me." It wasn't good. Lily had given her an amulet to ward off all misfortunes but Leah had noticed it immediately. "Nothing will protect you from a mother's vengeance," Leah had said. Danielle had to leave.

It was funny how in her desperation she would still turn

to the Ewans for comfort. She was overwhelmed by their kindness, not only the daughters, who had been her friends for so many years now, but Meir Ewan himself asked her to call on him before her wedding day. She came to his apartment when she knew Rahel would be out and made both herself and Meir tea, listening while he reminisced. Some of the stories she had heard before. Stories of Baghdad, of their families, how Leah had helped during the birth of his youngest child. He did not mention Shoshana by name. Other stories were dark and menacing. Stories of betrayal, fear, and greed. Stories about her father and her mother. "You have fulfilled the commandments," Meir firmly told her. "You have honored your father by restoring the name of Haya to respect, you and your brothers. And you particularly have honored your mother by supporting her when she should have been supporting you. What more can God ask for? Now there is a new commandment. You are to marry. You will honor your husband above all men. And women," he added pointedly.

"Lily has been speaking to you."

"As usual." She watched while he reached his hand into his breast pocket and drew forth a handkerchief. He unfolded it and inside she saw a gold bracelet studded with rubies. "For your wedding, Danielle."

"But this was your wife's. It should go either to Lily or—or your other daughter."

He sat forward and slipped it onto her wrist. "Salemah loved you like a daughter."

"I couldn't."

"You must. We all want you to have it."

She wore the bracelet now. It would look good against her skin, against the whiteness of her wedding dress. She looked out the window of Osnat's kibbutz apartment. "Is Sami here yet?" she asked anxiously.

"Relax," Osnat said to her. "The wedding's not for two hours."

"But he should be here to get ready."

"What does he have to do? Just stand there and repeat the vows."

Danielle couldn't imagine how Osnat could be so calm. Just two hours now and she'd be a married woman. She was scared to death, she couldn't wait. There would be the ceremony itself, then the food and the dancing. Then afterward. Oh, she was going to be sick. She had asked Shoshana about it. Her friend, if anyone, should know about matters of sexual intimacy. Would it hurt, should she scream, would she like it? "I already want to," she admitted, disturbed with herself.

Shoshana laughed. "Well, I should hope so. You're going to marry him after all."

"What if he doesn't like my body?"

"What's not to like?"

"I think he's had some experience in these matters."

"Good."

Good? How could it be good? He would think she was a fumbling idiot.

"Just tell him to be gentle," Shoshana suggested with a smile.

Where was Shoshana? She was supposed to help. Two hours to her wedding and no one was here yet. It was obvious. No one was coming.

Danny stood around waiting for the wedding to begin. Shoshana had insisted they get there at least an hour before the wedding so that she could help Danielle prepare. "Her hair, her dress, everything has to be perfect." Shoshana had really been galvanized by the forthcoming event. He was simply uncomfortable. Not only because he knew Lily and Joseph would be there, but because he guessed what Shoshana must be thinking. This should be she. She should be getting married. She hadn't said anything on the long drive up, practically hadn't said anything at all. But he didn't have to be a mind reader. He knew Shoshana. Had to know her after all these years. He would give anything he had to make her happy. But all she wanted was his name and his child. It was an impossible situation. How could three people cause each other so much pain? If only Ronit would let him go. Sometimes in his darkest fantasies he would think about hiring someone to kill Ronit. He never thought about killing her himself. She had been his wife. She was the mother of his child. But someone else with a knife appealed to him. Especially when every time he went to pick up Adee, Ronit asked in her sinister fashion, "Are you happy, Danny?"

Now Shoshana he had thoughts of killing with his bare hands. There were days when she was impossible. He would come home on leave and she would start on him immediately. Why haven't you gotten that divorce, when are we going to get married, I'm getting old, I want a child. From one room to another around the apartment, he couldn't escape her. And then when she had exhausted both of them, she would break down and say, "You're sorry, aren't you. You're sorry that you ever met me." And he would explain to her as gently as possible that he wasn't sorry, that she was like a toothache he had gotten used to.

But she was right about one thing. The situation was becoming more impossible with every passing month. Something was going to break, but he'd be damned if it was going to be him. He had plans, he had ideas. He would work something out. The navy was always applauding him on his tactics. He'd have to work on some for his own life. And soon.

Danny was glad to see more people arriving for the wedding. They had come in groups by *sherut*, cars, tenders, whatever was available. It was a long drive from Tel Aviv. Danny spoke to the few he knew and was introduced to Danielle's brothers. He was amazed. They weren't at all like her, had absolutely none of her shyness. Shoshana rushed out and attacked him. "Has Sami arrived yet?"

"No."

"She's afraid he's not coming."

"He has a mother, a father, three sisters, and a brother to make sure he gets here. Don't worry about it." She looked at him as if he was at fault before she rushed back in to Danielle.

Danny's stomach froze when he saw Joseph Benjamin's tender pull into the kibbutz. He moved back and tried to lose himself in the crowd as he watched Joseph get out and help Lily and Joshua out of the back. From the other side of the cab two women of very similar ages stepped down. He was going to assume that one of them must be Danielle's mother. But who was the other one? He watched while Joseph waited to help someone else down from the tender. Him he recognized immediately. It was Meir Ewan, Shoshana's father. He felt the same tension he felt before battle. Shoshana couldn't have known. She would have mentioned it.

His attention was diverted from the Ewans by the dashing up of another truck. Thank God it was Sami. He watched with a smile as Albert went up to ask Sami what had taken him so long while Ezra rushed to give Danielle the news.

Sami went around shaking hands with those he knew. "How do you feel?" Danny asked him.

"I'm going to drop dead," Sami confessed. "My mother and sisters have been crying the whole trip up here. My father's been giving me advice, my brother's been snickering. Give me my tank in the Sinai anytime."

The rabbi called Sami over to sign the marriage contract just as Danielle, with Shoshana and Osnat at her side, came out of the apartment. Sami smiled happily at Danielle as she nervously studied him. "She's worth every penny," Sami declared.

While the crowd laughed, Danny slipped forward and Shoshana took her place next to him. "You should give him some words of advice before he signs," she suggested slyly.

"Don't look now, but your father and his new wife came with Joseph," he replied.

She tightened as he slipped his arm around her waist. "Stay with me," she exacted.

"Always," he promised.

Sami signed the contract and the rabbi began trying to organize the wedding. Everyone pushed forward so they would be able to see. Ezra and Albert, Joseph and Sami's brother grabbed the four poles of the huppah and held it high over the heads of Danielle and Sami as they quietly, solemnly, nervously repeated their marriage vows. The crowd was silent then as a glass wrapped in a white handkerchief was laid down. Sami hesitated, then picked up his foot and smashed it down. "Mazel tov!" the crowd shouted as one. The bride and groom kissed. Then Danielle turned in one direction, Sami in the other, and they were caught in a thousand embraces.

As the hours passed by, Danny was pleased to see that the wedding dinner and dancing weren't going to be as bad as either Shoshana or he had feared. They kept as far away from her family as possible, joining the general crowd only when Sami and Danielle were raised on chairs to be swept together and apart again. But as the dancing drew longer into the night, Shoshana became more and more convinced that she should say something to Meir. "He is my father, after all. I don't hate him for what happened. It still hurts, but I can't really blame him." It was almost a question she was asking him.

"Wait till Danielle and Sami leave," Danny suggested. He didn't want anything to mar their wedding. Especially since Danielle was now in the process of saying her final farewells. She came up to Shoshana and embraced her tightly, then she surprised even herself as she threw her arms around Danny too and whispered to both of them, "Wish me luck."

They laughed and watched her run off with Sami to his truck. "Were we ever that innocent?" Danny asked her.

"I was," she retorted.

Meir Ewan had kept his eye on Shoshana the entire evening. He watched as she talked and laughed, mingled with the other guests. He noticed how Ze'ev stayed with her, protected her, engulfed her. Meir had caught Ze'ev's eye several times during the evening as he steered Shoshana away from her family. But what should he expect from that boy. Why should Ze'ev let Shoshana share any part of her family's life. Maybe she would leave him.

But no, she couldn't. She was lost to them. She had made her choice and she was living with it, no matter what it had cost all of them. The blame was hers. The shame was Meir's. But at least he had expected her maybe to have the decency to come up to her own father and beg his forgiveness.

"Ready?" Shoshana asked Danny nervously. "What are you doing?"

"Getting the car keys ready so we can make a dash for it."

"Such confidence." She took Danny by the hand and slowly snaked him through the crowd toward her father. Her father had stared at her at first, then turned away as he sensed her coming toward him, until now she stood alongside of him while he pretended not to notice.

"Father," she spoke softly to him. She waited. And waited. When he turned toward her, there were tears in his eyes. "Oh, Father," she cried. She threw her arms around him and sobbed into his chest.

Danny stood back and watched while Meir's arms slowly enfolded his daughter. Thank God, he thought. At last that's over.

29

It was five of nine in the morning. Diane was in the back of Chez Laurie's checking the stock book while the new salesgirl lay in wait for any early customer who might happen to drop by. Laurie was in the great Southwest somewhere searching for Indian artifacts. The Indian phenomenon had become very big among Easterners, and Laurie always tried to provide her customers with the unnecessary extravagances of life. Even her Anglo artists were directed toward Indian motifs. And now Diane was checking for blankets that the tourists could get much cheaper from the roadside stands. Though she had to admit Laurie had an eye for quality. The buzzer sounding in the stockroom startled her. The first customer of the day, she automatically smiled even though she was out of sight. Diane hated the tourist season, hated it especially today as she fingered the letter from her mother in her pocket. She should be thankful that it wasn't all about Hal, whom her mother wrote of even though their divorce was final. No, this time it was about Walter de Gregory. He had gotten a divorce. As her mother put it, "I knew exactly what to say to Walter's mother after my heartbreak with you." She wrote of ru-

mors that Walter's wife wanted her freedom while Walter
wanted a nurse at the hospital. Diane had cried. Walter
was her last, her best fantasy. She should have been allowed to keep him. But time and love tumble on. As she
had no doubt from studying her face in the mirror. Oh,
Walter, Walter, it could have been great.

By twelve thirty they had had between forty and fifty
patrons. The new salesgirl had been instructed to trail behind the younger ones, making sure nothing was broken or
swiped, while Diane took care of the older, more respectable variety. The influx of the hippies and the backpackers
into Sante Fe in recent years was something to behold.
Though Diane imagined that by now they had made their
way into every corner of American life. But why did they
ask her where they could buy or find peyote? Did she look
the type? And why were they frequenting a high-priced
tourist joint like Chez Laurie's? She would expect most of
these youngsters to prefer dealing with the Indian crafts
workers who set up in front of the museum.

"Perhaps a larger size," Diane suggested to a woman
who was trying to slip a silver ring onto her finger.

"I've always worn a size six ring," the woman complained. It was obviously Diane's fault that her finger was
fatter. But Diane sympathized, knowing that shocking feeling. She had always worn a size nine skirt, but now she was
expanding toward an eleven. Still if the woman got that
ring caught on her finger, Diane would have to use a hack-
saw.

"Excuse me, miss?"

Diane looked up. A man alone. He looked like the type
to be buying a birthday present for his wife. "Yes?"

He smiled. "Diane?"

She stared, then threw one hand to her forehead. "Walter?"

"Yes." He was delighted with his surprise.

"My God! What are you doing here?"

"Well, if you really want to know, I have one week's
vacation in which to woo you and wed you before returning
to my practice."

426

"Excuse me. Miss?" The woman with the ring was begging for her attention.

"I left in the middle of pre-school examinations. I'm probably losing half of my practice just standing here talking to you."

"You have a lot of nerve, you know that?" Diane said to him.

"Miss!" The finger lady was really beginning to bug her.

"I might be remarried, I might have a man. I might not want to marry you."

Walter's face dropped. "Are any of those things true?"

"No," she conceded. "But they might have been."

"I had to see you, to find out before I chanced meeting Steven."

"Diane," the new salesgirl called out even after she had been warned to call her Ms. Shapiro in front of the customers. "She can't get the ring back over her knuckle."

Diane knew this was going to happen. She looked down at the woman's now puffy finger. The knuckle of her ring finger was red and swollen.

"Stand back everyone and give her air," Walter said. "I'm a doctor."

They laughed about it that evening after Steven had been tucked finally into bed, despite his excitement brought on by their exhilaration. "You have to develop a sense of humor over small catastrophes. I've learned that dealing with kids," he pontificated. He fell silent. "Steven's terrific by the way."

"He takes after his father," she told him softly.

"And his mother. We made a good pair."

"That was years ago. Seven years ago. We were both married."

"And now we both aren't."

"There has been, as they say, much water under the bridge."

"In Sante Fe?"

"Even here life goes on." She plowed her furrow.

"For you?"

427

"What do you want me to say, Walter? I've thought of you, of course."

"At least once a month. I always see your signature on the back of the check. I give it a little kiss before I stick it with the others."

"Why are you being so flippant?"

"I don't know. Maybe I'm afraid."

"You just got your divorce."

"You know?"

"My mother."

"Thank God for our mothers."

"Why don't you wait a few years. Divorce isn't a pretty thing to go through. It takes time to recover. You shouldn't jump into something else right away."

"You're right."

She was disappointed.

"Diane, you know damn well that my marriage wasn't so hot when we were together. It didn't improve after you and I split. My wife was swept away from me on the tides of liberation. We had what was called an open marriage. It didn't work. Not for either of us. It was so loose and open that we found we had no ties that bound us together except our daughter, whom we both love. I couldn't live that way. We ended it. The divorce was a legal document. But the end came a long time before the courts stamped finis on our marriage. Though we do have what is known in the trade as a friendly divorce. We refrain from hitting each other and calling each other names in front of our daughter."

Diane smiled. "And the nurse?"

Walter rolled his eyes. "Oh, my God. Your mother obviously writes thorough reports. All right. Before the nurse there was a doctor; before the doctor, a professional chef. Her I liked. She catered a friend's bar mitzvah. And you?" He watched while Diane blushed. "You see? What does it matter? I'm not asking you to be a number of a harem. I'm asking you to be my wife."

"And if we marry, will you have mistresses?"

"No." He moved to convince her. "I've tried it. It doesn't work. Not for me. Not for the way I see my marriage to you."

Diane shrugged. "I have my life here."

He considered what she was trying to say. "Are you so attached to Chez Laurie's?"

"No," she admitted.

"Look, we can give it a shot. If it doesn't work out, we can always get a divorce."

"Oh, Walter."

"I love you. Sitting with you now, it's as if we were in college together, or high school, or grade school. It's as if we've always been together."

"You hated me in grade school and high school."

"I didn't hate you. Our mothers—"

Diane laughed. "What are they going to say?"

Walter smiled. He leaned over to kiss her. She bit his lips. "I have to check on Steven," she whispered.

Her son was asleep. She tiptoed from his room and closed his door. Then she led Walter into her bedroom. He shut the door and locked it. She smiled. "It's been a long time."

He moved on her like an elephant charging. There was no escape. He pushed his hands over her body, while she raised her hips against him. "You're hard," she told him.

"You better believe it. I've been hard all night waiting for this."

She practically tore his pants from his legs in her eagerness to get at him. "Rape," he called feebly as she guided him quickly in. Her hips became frantic in an effort to urge him as deep as possible. She began screaming even before she started to come and come as he moved harshly inside her until she was drifting someplace near heaven.

If one can live long enough, one can see anything. The Arefs were gone. Baghdad was free of them and their cronies, all done in by their own corruption. Over a year ago now. The 1968 coup, as opposed to the '58 or any other year since then you might like to mention. The Ba'aths were definitely in control, though which Ba'aths was always a matter of reading the entrails. The coup itself had not been all that bloody. Rahman Aref had been overtaken in his palace at three o'clock one July morning and put on an airliner for London. Paid off, some said. A military-revolutionary council took his place, the power falling to Ahmed Hassan al-Bakr. What Aref was for, al-Bakr was against. Which meant ties to Nasser of Egypt were loosened, and in another turnabout, the communists of Iraq were released from jail. Which made life impossible for those Iraqis who were friendly toward the West. These pro-Westerners began to disappear from the streets, from their homes, businesses, never to be seen again. Another endless Iraqi purge in the making.

Jacob had hoped Musa al Haykal would have been swept away in this repeating revolution, but he feared that al Haykal like himself was a survivor. Al Haykal had been with Kassem, he had been against Kassem; he had been with the Arefs, and he had been against them. And now? Al Haykal knew how to serve whoever was in power as he, Jacob, must learn how to serve at Haykal.

Still there were advantages to be gained from working for al Haykal. For the past two years he had been blessed by a lack of government interference in all his affairs. He and his sons had prospered. Rahamin had had another daughter, Ahouvah, while Ephraim had been allowed to finish his studies in pharmacology and get his license. Al Haykal had even found an Arab who would front for Ephraim, claim ownership of the drugstore Jacob had bought for his son. Al Haykal had been most accommodating, a real gentleman in his dealings, which was more than Jacob could say about Mr. Harris.

Andrew Harris had returned to Baghdad after the Six Day War but during the time Jacob and his sons remained locked up in prison. Jacob had been out of prison only a month before Harris had the nerve to reenter the Swallow's Nest, to try to renew his former relationship with Jacob.

"Where were you?" Jacob asked him.

"You're safe."

"Do you always run for cover the minute trouble starts? Perhaps you better go back home and take a few more lessons from your army."

But Harris didn't leave. He persistently stayed until he got what he wanted from Jacob. He was pleased, more than pleased with Jacob's relations with Musa al Haykal. He saw endless possibilities in using such a relationship, and Jacob was only too willing to comply for guarantees this time of his sons' safety. Harris put up no more arguments. The stakes were too high. It wasn't just gossip he was getting from the Swallow's Nest, it was a major pipeline into Iraqi internal affairs. Harris would do whatever he could for Jacob. Gladly.

But it was too late. Rahamin and Ephraim were not children any longer. They had their own ideas about the way they wanted to live; and since their father's connection with al Haykal, life in Baghdad had become very sweet indeed. "You are crazy," he told them. "Do you think that whatever he gives to us cannot just as easily be taken away?" But they would not listen to him. "I said this too," he pleaded with them. "When all the Jews left Iraq, I said why should I leave? Look at what I would be leaving, my business, my home, my money. But I discovered over the years that none of these things mattered. What mattered to me was you, your freedom, your survival."

"We are surviving very well, Father," Rahamin told him.

"But think of your children."

"I am. I'm thirty years old. How can I drop everything here and start life over in a new country? You ask the impossible, Father." He put his arm around Jacob. "You will protect us," he assured his father. "You always have."

And then disaster struck. Ephraim chose to fall in love. It was time, he explained to his father. He had his business, he had his own home. He needed a wife and children to fill it. "But you can get a wife and children in England," Jacob told him.

"And leave you and Mother and Rahamin behind?"

Jacob shook his head. Ephraim was never the smart one. Jacob knew the girl. Tina. Beautiful, fine family, good dowry, but what was the point? No, this time he would insist. Ephraim would go. If necessary Tina could be sent after him. He spoke to Harris about it. He was firm, he was insistent. Harris came through with an escape route. On paper it looked good. Ephraim would take a holiday in the mountains. Instead of returning to Baghdad, he would wander in the hills and be set upon by bandits. Remnants of his clothing would be found along with his identity card. By that time Ephraim would have been liberated into friendly Kurdish hands and transported to Iran. "How can we count on the Kurds? How much will we have to pay them?"

"I'll take care of that," Harris promised. "We have men working with the Kurds."

"Perhaps Ephraim should be given false papers in case that plan falls through."

"And if he's found with the papers, how long do you think it will take for him to talk? He'll lead to you, you'll lead to me. No thanks."

"That would happen in any case."

Harris smiled like death. "You are my lifeline and I am yours," he reminded Jacob.

Ephraim wouldn't go. Jacob laid the plan before him and he kicked like a mule. Jacob had to use all his paternal authority to enforce his will upon his younger son. When Ephraim finally reluctantly agreed, he said, "I must tell Tina."

"Are you a complete idiot?" Jacob asked him. "I know Tina. The minute you tell her, she'll start blubbering all over the place. The flood of her tears will lead a trail to our door. You are to tell no one. Not your mother, not your brother, certainly not Tina. I will tell them all when you are safe."

Jacob thought it would never happen. His son was not being very good about it. And his wife couldn't understand why Ephraim should shed tears upon leaving her for a vacation in the mountains. She was suspicious. Jacob comforted her, quieted her. She knew her husband. She knew when not to ask any questions.

The days of Ephraim's vacation seemed to be interminable for Jacob. And yet there was nothing to worry about until the fifth day, a day he spent working hard in the Swallow's Nest and lying sleepless at night. He longed to call Harris, to find out what was going on. But he feared that Harris would know no more than he did.

Day six. Day seven. Ephraim had not returned. But on the other hand, there was no word from Harris on his son's safety. Jacob didn't know what to think or what to tell his family.

The problem was solved for him. On his way home that night he saw a car he recognized as al Haykal's and an army auto parked outside his house. He walked in past the guard to find al Haykal in his living room having tea with his wife and his son Ephraim. Ephraim stood suddenly upon seeing Jacob and shouted, "Father, I didn't—"

Al Haykal cut him off. Jacob studied his son. His face was bruised and his hand was bandaged. Jacob ordered his wife and son out of the room.

Al Haykal tsked as Jacob sat down across from him. "I'm disappointed, Jacob, naturally," Al Haykal began. "I thought there was a bond of trust between us. And yet you tried to smuggle your son out of our mutual homeland. You can imagine how shocked I was. Here I had sent my men along quietly to accompany Ephraim. I said to myself— and my men—I can't let my old friend Jacob Ewan send his son off to the mountains without some protection. The mountains can prove very dangerous. Disreputable people live in the mountains, people who are not friendly to our central government. How pleased I was when my men were actually able to prevent Ephraim's abduction. It was unfortunate that we only took one of those bandits and that one died very quickly, before we could examine his statement. You can imagine my disappointment. Why, Jacob?" he asked sharply.

"You must know," Jacob said to him. "The life of a Jew in Iraq is not an easy one."

"You have my sympathies, but Ephraim told me it was your idea that he should leave, that all he wanted to do was stay and marry this Tina. Let me make a suggestion. Give Ephraim your permission. This marriage sounds like a very safe idea. Much safer than trying to cross me. I still need you, Jacob. You're lucky. Maybe you won't be so lucky if I ever find out how you got in touch with the Kurds." Al Haykal rose to go. "Thank your wife for the tea, Jacob. And remember, friendship can be a very fragile thing."

Hal Evans, née Hillel Ewan, was in shock. Diane Shapiro had returned to Boston. Why? He had kept his part of the bargain. He had not sought her out in any way. And yet here she was in the world's greatest provincial city instead of in that out-west watering hole she had been confined to for the last half dozen years.

No announcement in the papers heralded her return. But he knew it the moment she alighted from the flurry of phone calls he began receiving. Women. Let no one claim they were not the more vindictive of the species.

Diane was returning and marrying Dr. Walter de Gregory. Well, what had it to do with him? His place was secure. He had become a major speaker for Jewish causes in Boston, respected by everyone, invited to both mayor's and governor's conclaves, asked to the dinner parties of the powerful. Anything that Diane said about him now would simply be considered sour grapes.

He let it pass. The wedding came and went, it flickered into eternity along with a *Boston Globe* account featuring a picture of the bride and groom flanked by their mothers. It didn't matter to him, it didn't touch him. He wouldn't have given it another thought, except—except everyone else was thinking about it for him. Everyone suddenly seemed to have his best interests at heart. During the Sabbath meal, over Oneg Shabbat, now that his son was so close again, when was he going to demand visiting rights? How could he explain to these viciously well-meaning people that a son was something to possess? A man must have a son as he must have guts, strength—to be American about it, balls. Therefore, how could Steven be his son any more than Diane was his wife? Were they in his house? Were they under his thumb? What angered him was not the absence of visiting rights, but the loss of a family that should have been his to control. He had expected by this time to be a patriarch of his own tribe.

So he avoided the issue until Diane took an action that was a calculated public slap in the face, an act which, as a man with balls, he could no longer ignore. Walter de Gregory was going to legally adopt his son. Steven Evans was to become Steven de Gregory. Hal Evans's name was to be left to crumble in the dust, his flesh and his blood not to be called on to say kaddish for him, to carry on his seed. Steven was to have a new father and Hal Evans, with his death, was to be wiped from the face of the earth. It was not to be tolerated.

Hal Evans was pleased to see Diane again, pleased because her complexion was sallow and her eyes encircled. He had done this to her with the custody suit, and from the look she gave him, she knew that it was he who still held the power in their relationship. Her new husband was being calm about this, probably didn't want the boy in any case. Hal would have to give his lawyer a bonus for this. Here they were coming meekly to his lawyer's office, accepting Styrofoam cups of coffee while he glowed and gloated. Even their lawyer smiled at him. He must realize he was dealing with one smart cookie.

They were settled now. Diane didn't want the coffee, she didn't even want to be in the same room with that bastard. He looked so smug all she wanted to do was rake her nails across his eyes. Walter put his hand over hers. He must have known.

"Well," Hal's lawyer said, "I guess we better get started."

"Yes," the de Gregory's lawyer agreed. "Mr. Evans, we'd like to settle this whole matter out of court."

"Fine with me," Hal said. "All they have to do is give up custody of my son."

Walter had to hold Diane back.

"Will you tell us why you consider him to be your son?" their lawyer asked.

"I fathered him."

"Leaving that aside for the moment, did you since your marital separation support Steven in any way? Physically, emotionally, monetarily?"

"He was always in my thoughts."

"That's touching but—"

"My wife is a vindictive woman. She threatened to tell the most vicious kinds of lies about me if I made contact with her or my son."

"We won't go into these so-called lies right now. Suffice it to say that they would all come out in the hearing." The lawyer went on but Diane was pleased to see that Hal was shaken by his little aside. "Dr. de Gregory, did you in any way support the child under discussion since Diane's separation from her first husband?"

"Yes. As soon as I found out how to reach her, I sent Diane a check in the mail each month. A hundred dollars."

"What was it for, Dr. de Gregory?"

"Child support."

"Do you still have the letter in which Walter tells you he is sending the money specifically for the child, Diane?"

"Yes."

"Wait a second," Hal said. "It's not as if Diane didn't have money from me. Before she fled Boston, she stole all my money."

"I didn't steal anything," Diane protested. "That money was either in our joint account or under my name alone."

"But it was my money. What did you do to earn it?"

"I lived with you."

"Please," Hal's lawyer tried to calm them.

"In any case," their lawyer replied, "she certainly didn't have enough money to support the child for six years. You made no objection to the divorce?"

"None," Hal admitted. "I wouldn't hold someone to me who didn't want to be there."

"Have you tried to see your son since Walter and Diane have returned to Boston?"

"I was awaiting the outcome of this case."

"That may attest to your good manners but certainly not to your concern for your son," their lawyer snapped.

"Now wait a minute," Hal's lawyer protested.

"Sorry," he conceded. "Now, Walter, would you mind telling us why you felt compelled to send Diane a check every month for Steven's support?"

"Steven is my child."

"Not yet he isn't," Hal pointed out.

"Steven is my child," Walter told him directly. "We have the blood tests to prove it. I've also seen your sperm count. from the tests you were forced to take. You couldn't have possibly fathered Steven. Not Steven, not any other child. You're functionally sterile."

Diane watched Hal's face. She stood. "When we find out what date the hearing is going to be, I'm going to let everyone know so the court will be well packed with your friends cheering you on."

Hal decided not to pursue custody. Steven had been contaminated with another man's seed. Not that Hal believed he was actually infertile. But what if he was? He had spent all those years insisting that women use something to protect themselves from his vigorous masculinity. He couldn't let anyone find out about this. Not ever. So he'd let that slut keep the child. It didn't matter to him anymore anyway. He didn't need her, he didn't need the child. He had all he needed in his breast pocket. An engraved personal invitation from Golda Meir. As an outstanding fund raiser for the United Jewish Appeal, he was invited to meet with her—with Golda!—in Jerusalem. He could go back to Israel now and his family would see how important he had become. He didn't need to fear the army or anyone. He had his American passport, and he had his invitation from Golda Meir.

30

Shoshana swished several dresses before her. "Which do you think looks better on me?" she asked her sister.

"Why do you care?" Lily responded.

Shoshana lay the dresses on the bed. "What's wrong?"

Lily wouldn't say. She got up and paced around Shoshana's bedroom, picking up things, putting them down. "Your dresser top's a mess."

"Clean it up if you like." Shoshana hadn't seen Lily distressed like this in a long time. It could be trouble with Joseph, though Shoshana doubted it. Joseph always gave in. Or if he didn't give in, he'd just listen to Lily and let her temper tantrum ride itself out. Shoshana didn't think she could stand a man like that. She was used to Danny's fighting back. Then it didn't seem so ridiculous when the storm was over and they had both made idiots of themselves. It was easier to laugh it away.

"I wish he hadn't come," Lily said.

"Lily," Shoshana placated.

"I hate him!"

Shoshana slumped down on her bed. So she would be like Joseph. She would let Lily get it out of her system.

Naturally it had been a shock to find out after so many years Hillel was coming home. They had had sporadic letters, newspaper clippings showing him with Peres, with Allon, with Eban, Dayan, Sapir. "Prominent Boston Fund Raiser," he was always called. They hadn't thought much about it. Prominent fund raisers littered the pages of *The Jerusalem Post*. They had very little to do with life in Israel itself. They gave money, which was an easy thing for them to do. Israel, the poor relative, accepted the funds with thanks and resentment. Not that the fund raisers ever felt the resentment. When they came to Israel for their conferences, they stayed at the best hotels and were ferried back and forth across the land in air-conditioned buses. They never met real Israelis nor saw how real Israelis lived. For them Jerusalem or Tel Aviv was just Chicago or New York with a different climate and language. So Hillel had become one of these strange, foreign Jews. What did it matter?

"How come he's invited to meet with Golda Meir and my Joseph's not?" Lily asked bitterly.

"Oh, Lily, why in God's name would Joseph want to meet with Golda Meir of all people? She doesn't even speak our language. She couldn't care less about us. All she's interested in is conniving with her Labor party cohorts. For them the country can go to the dogs as long as they're in power."

"Hillel told Father he got a personal invitation."

"Personal invitation? They run those off by the hundreds in the printing office. If Joseph wants one, I can get him one easy." Shoshana smiled at her sister. "You're being ridiculous about this, Lily. Try to keep your sense of humor." Lily huffed. "He gets his jollies by attempting to convince people he's important. Why should it bother you? We all know he's a schmuck."

Lily didn't see Hillel in the same light as her sister. He had always tried to control them, to ruin everybody's life. He would try to do it still. It galled her, that was all. Her Joseph had stayed in Israel, built up a business from nothing, served in the army, been permanently crippled with that limp, still insisted on doing his reserve duty and fighting in the war. What did he get? Nobody even knew he was alive. But when someone like Hillel, who fled to America to escape the army and the hardships and from there raised money for the UJA but offered nothing of himself came, he was welcomed back to Israel on a red carpet. And to announce his second coming, he put ads in all the papers, Hebrew and English: "Hal Evans (Hillel Ewan) will be in Israel September 9–15 and may be reached at 54 Katznelson Street, Givatayim."

"Wear your navy dress," Lily told Shoshana after her sister had brought out a yellow flowered one. "You'll want to look respectable."

Shoshana tossed the yellow one back on the bed and picked up the navy. She threw off her robe and slipped the dress on over her head. Lily was right of course. She must look demure. This would be the first time she had been in her father's apartment since she had been thrown out so many years ago. Lily had said many of the relatives would stop by to see Hillel, and they of course all knew about her. It made the situation very threatening. At best she would be snubbed. At worst, well, God only knew. She had called Danny to discuss it with him. "Stop trying to be a heroine. Don't go." That was his advice. But she felt for her father's sake she had to go. She had not seen him often since Danielle's wedding. But sometimes when Father was going to Lily's and Lily knew Danny would be away, she would invite her sister. Slowly lines had been cast out to each other, and she and her father exchanged a few thoughts, innocuous as they were. The weather, inflation, television. And now he had told Lily that he would like to see Shoshana there when Hillel came for Shabbat. So she would go, for her father's sake.

Joshua thought he looked spiffy in his Gadna uniform. His khakis were clean and pressed, thanks to his mother's invaluable service. He didn't know why she didn't like to see him in khaki, especially since in three years he would be wearing the uniform of the Israel Defense Forces.

441

He stopped before 54 Katznelson and looked up to see the light in his grandfather's apartment. The light and the people. It was crowded with relatives he barely knew. And he would have to be polite. His mother would insist on that. "Be Iraqi," she would say on these occasions. He was curious about his Uncle Hillel. His mother and father had been holding unusually frenetic conversations ever since they had heard he was coming. When Joshua had asked about him, his mother would say, "He's your uncle, that's all." So Joshua had to rely on half-remembered stories from his early years. Well this visit didn't really upset him. How long was Hillel staying? Only a week. He couldn't be that bad.

Joshua started up the steps and was surprised to meet his Aunt Shoshana rushing down. They kissed. "My, don't you look handsome," Shoshana said, but he noticed a tightness in her voice.

"Am I that late?" he asked over her departure.

"No. Your parents are waiting for you." She saw him hesitate. "I just felt claustrophobic, that's all," she explained before she raced off.

Joshua shrugged his shoulders sadly as his aunt disappeared. At fifteen he thought he understood love. He certainly had a pressing desire for Ilanit. Still he didn't think he would ever let himself fall in love the way Aunt Shoshana had with Danny Ze'ev. What was the point of all that pain. Someday, maybe when he married, he would understand it.

Exhausted, Shoshana returned to her apartment. It had gone about as she had expected. The relatives had conspired to ignore her, especially after she approached Hillel to kiss him, and he had rebuffed her by saying, "What are you doing in our father's apartment? From what I have heard about you, you have no business among us." No one had exactly leaped to her defense. Not her father, not Lily. She had stayed an hour to show she couldn't be forced out, then had quietly left.

She was surprised to see the light on in her apartment

when she unlocked the door, more surprised to find Danny coming out of the kitchen. "What are you doing here?" she asked with delight.

"I had a few days coming. I thought you might need me," he explained.

She came to him and threw her arms around his neck. "Oh, I do, Danny. I really do."

"That bad."

"Horrible."

"I know of some quick relief."

"Oh, Danny, as much as I love you, I'm not in the mood for sex."

He stood back, offended. "I was going to suggest stopping by Haggai's for cake and coffee."

She laughed. "Sorry."

"But now I'm offended to think you didn't want me."

"I do want you." She brightened. "Now."

"Now? But you just said—"

She didn't want to go to Haggai's. But how was she to tell Danny? He had been Haggai's friend since high school. And because Haggai was a member of military intelligence, Shoshana had to work with him. Still he made her uncomfortable, more so lately, ever since his wife had been having an affair with her boss at the ministry of housing. Haggai knew there was someone. His wife knew he knew. But they never said anything about it to each other. It might have been better if they had, even if their recriminations had torn their marriage completely asunder. As it was, now Haggai felt he had to prove something to his wife, maybe his masculinity, and he tried to do it with Shoshana. She couldn't have been more displeased. She neither wanted nor encouraged Haggai's attentions. Yet he never missed an opportunity to foist them on her. Had she told Danny, he might have laughed it off as harmless flirting on Haggai's part, or he might have taken it seriously, spoken to, fought with Haggai. Which she didn't want. So she kept silent. If she had been married to Danny—but she wasn't.

She didn't know why Haggai and his wife insisted on

entertaining together anyway. Everyone knew about them. What kind of act were they trying to put on?

"We have to go there," Danny said. "He's my friend and he especially asked us to come."

"I know he's your friend," she stressed. "But he makes me uncomfortable."

"What do you mean he makes you uncomfortable?"

"I mean the situation makes me uncomfortable." She skirted the issue.

Danny shrugged. "Haggai has always stood by me, Shoshana. He doesn't refuse to have me in his apartment because I'm no longer living with Ronit, with whom both Haggai and I went to high school. You have to support your friends at times like these."

"Right," she agreed. "We'll go to Haggai's."

"Only after you take off that awful navy dress," he ordered. "It makes you look like you're in mourning."

Shoshana's spirits did pick up as she slipped on the yellow floral dress she had intended to wear in the first place. It was so good to have Danny home unexpectedly. It took moments like this to make her realize how much she depended on him emotionally. Her life was such a void without him. Though she couldn't say cake at Haggai's was that much better than meeting with the relatives at her father's. Aside from fending off Haggai's offensive comments, she was teased by all. Haggai, Oren, Dov, even Danny. They wanted to know if she was the sister of THE Hillel Ewan who had plastered his name all over their newspapers for the last week.

"I really think he's insane," Shoshana said, deciding that her brother wasn't worth defending. "You should have seen him preening. He talks about his personal invitation to meet with Golda Meir. He intimates that if he could but tell us, there are conspiratorial deals between him and Golda, secret services she desires him to render. I mean, I think he's gone off the deep end."

"Who knows." Oren shrugged.

"Oh, Oren, he's a draft dodger. What could she possibly want from him? And this personal invitation, he showed it around. It's the usual governmental 'Golda Meir, Prime Minister of Israel, cordially invites Mr. High and Mighty . . .'"

"Sealed with a kiss?" Danny asked.

"So why does he think he's being specially anointed?" Oren asked. "Any Jew with enough money can get a special invitation to meet with any Israeli prime minister, unless the Jew's Israeli himself."

"Who knows? What's with you?" she asked, noting Oren's crazy smile.

"I don't know," Oren said. "I just had sort of an inspiration. Maybe Hillel will be called on by Golda Meir to serve." Danny started to laugh.

"I don't want to hear any of this!" Shoshana said. She covered her ears, but it didn't work very well.

As Hillel Ewan was leaving his Cousin Ephraim's apartment, he didn't notice the white Fiat, its army license plates carefully covered with mud, trailing along after him. He had more important things to think of. Cousin Ephraim had a daughter. Sarah, her name was. She was eighteen, a quiet, religious girl. Ephraim was looking for a husband for her. He had heard Hillel was divorced. Would he be interested in taking a look at the girl? Interested, yes. Hillel felt he needed a wife, someone to stand at his side for others to see how he was admired. And this girl, she had said nothing in his presence. Most impressive. She was probably overwhelmed by him. The difference in their ages—should that bother him? She eighteen, he forty-three? But wouldn't a young, tender child like that need a man of his experience? He would think about it, Hillel had told Cousin Ephraim. Think about it very seriously. It was a big step to marry a woman he barely knew and take her to America.

Women made him nervous now, though he would admit that to no one. After Diane and what she had done to him, how could he trust another woman ever again? Even this innocent-seeming Sarah. Had not Lily and Shoshana been innocent at one time? And yet now look at them. Lily barely speaking to him, belittling all his achievements, and

Shoshana turning into a whore. It was embarrassing to have her around. Where were the women of biblical virtue?

Golda Meir. Now there was a woman he could admire. And even though there had been a hundred of them in the dining room in Jerusalem, he knew from the way she looked at him when she spoke about Zionistic zeal that she had been thoroughly briefed on his earlier career in Baghdad and had been overcome by her own approval. Then afterward when he had pushed his way forward to tell her, "I got your invitation and of course came immediately," the look of mystery she gave him made him realize it wouldn't be safe to talk further on the subject in front of all these other clowns, who had no real idea of what sacrifice and triumph meant. No, just he and Golda held tight in a bond formed by the common knowledge of his own superiority. Well, if he was called on, he would serve. That was the way it was with a man like him. He didn't even mind when he was nudged aside by her security guards. They had a place in the scheme of things, even if it was only as muscle backed by a latent mentality.

"Slow the goddamned car down!" Oren snapped.

Danny instantly obeyed. Hillel was walking down Bialik Street. They'd have to wait until he passed Hadar before they dared take him.

"Okay," Oren said as they reached the residential section. "Pull a few feet ahead of him and continue crawling."

Danny did as he was told. He paid attention to his driving. He let Oren jump out of the car and make the grab. Before he knew it, Hillel was in the car between Haggai and Oren and Danny was being given orders to step on the gas. They took off down Katznelson and roared toward the Nahal Ayalon bridge and Derech Haifa.

"I'm sorry we had to do it this way," Oren spoke to Hillel in a perfect Iraqi dialect to calm any incipient panic. "You know why you're here, don't you?"

"Is it—"

"Golda," Haggai answered before Hillel could finish.

"I thought so," Hillel said. It really had not surprised him too much when a car had rolled up quickly beside him and the pedestrian footsteps behind him had hastened, arriving just in time to push him quickly into the backseat. "You may tell her that I am ready."

"It's tricky," Oren explained. "You can't be seen anymore with her in public."

"Will I get a medal?"

"All of Israel will know of your deed eventually," Haggai promised him.

"That's all I ask," Hillel said.

Oren took a key out of his pocket and pressed it into Hillel's palm. "It's the key to her Ramat Aviv apartment," he explained. "It's safer if you don't knock. She's expecting you. We'll drop you off three houses down. You'll have to make it the rest of the way on foot."

"I understand the need for security," Hillel told him curtly.

Danny pulled to a quiet stop on a street just off Derech Haifa in Ramat Aviv. Oren wished Hillel luck, then let him crawl over his legs to make it out the open car door. Oren held the car door shut while ordering Danny to make a U and return the way he came.

"Are you sure Golda's in Jerusalem tonight?" Haggai asked.

"I don't slip up," Oren informed him. He liked Haggai well enough, but anyone stuck in military intelligence was bound not to be too bright.

"What now?" Danny asked.

"Now home to bed, my friends, and let events take their course," Oren suggested.

"Do you realize we could be court-martialed and you could be fired for this?" Haggai asked.

Oren gave Haggai a look. "Don't forget to kick the mud off your license plates," he told Danny, as Danny dropped him off at his apartment.

* * *

Shoshana lay sound asleep within Danny's arms. He had to get up at five tomorrow morning and head back to base, so they had both gone to sleep early. She was surprised to be awoken by the phone, more surprised when she knew Danny was awake but he wasn't picking the phone up. She reached over him to grab it and felt her breasts drag along his hairy chest. He smiled. "Hello."

"Shoshana? It's Lily."

"Lily?" She sat up. "What's the matter?"

"It's Hillel. He's been arrested. He was caught trying to break into Golda Meir's apartment."

Shoshana looked quickly to Danny. He was trying to feign sleep but there was a curious smile on his lips.

"Shoshana!" Lily exploded.

"That's shocking," Shoshana said, she hoped expressively.

"What are we going to do?" Lily asked.

"I can't think of anything right now," Shoshana admitted. "But I'll ask Danny and see if he has any ideas. I'll call you back in the morning." She put down the phone and lay her body on top of Danny's. "That was naughty, Danny," she whispered.

"I hope you're going to punish me," he said.

She licked his lips. "What do you think you deserve?" she asked him.

But his hands were already removing her gown.

31

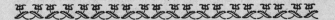

Danielle had her account book before her and was working with both her red and black pens. It had been a struggle. Sami at first had not wanted her to take charge of his business accounts. He had felt as the man he should be in charge of the money. And yet he didn't have any system.

She didn't mind. She was happy. More than happy, she was content. She had never known such a feeling of peace. At first she couldn't understand it. She would wake up wondering why she felt so good. Then there would be a haunting anxiety that this couldn't go on. Yet it did, and she understood the reason for it. Sami was constant. He was her constant. He was her life.

It had been a year. Could one be happy for a year? There had been bad moments. She had occasions when she exploded at him for something, and he would pay no attention to her. Her anger seemed not to reach him, and she hated not being taken seriously. She would tackle him, sit on him, force him to listen to her pour out her wrath, and he just smiled heavenly upward. Her mother's visits hadn't helped of course. It had been nice the first few months when Leah refused to visit them. But all of a sudden she had taken Danielle up on some vague invitation, and now she made it a practice to drop in at least twice a week, more after they had splurged and bought a television set. Sami called Leah "the log," since she sat immobile as long as the set was on, except for moving her lips as she tried to follow the subtitles. It was frustrating for Leah, as she could barely make out the Hebrew letters and form them into words. So frustrating that she would watch the Arabic programming and the Hebrew news, but leave as soon as the American programs came on. They were never sorry to see her go.

Her brother Ezra had gotten married six months after she had. His wife was from Argentina. She had been at an absorption center in the Galilee when her ulpan class had taken a tour of Kibbutz Vered. It must have been love at first sight because her Hebrew was practically nonexistent. Paula was her name. She was the only member of her family in Israel, so the wedding must have been very lonely for her. As soon as they had gotten married and had a short honeymoon in Tiberias, Ezra had resettled in Kibbutz El Al along the Syrian border. Danielle worried about this, especially since Paula was already pregnant.

Danielle was jealous of her. She longed to have Sami's child. And yet they waited. It made good sense to wait, they told each other. They needed a nest egg, money to fall back on in case of hard times, because when Danielle had their child, she wanted to stop working. She wanted to stay home with their baby, nurse him, care for him, love him. And Sami wanted that too. So they both worked harder now, waiting for the day when they would have a child.

Hillel studied his new wife across the living room from him. She was knitting, knitting and watching television. Her needles clicked as her eyes darted from her hands up to the set, then back down again. She was a real find, this Sarah of his. She wanted nothing more than to stay at home and please him. Of course there were drawbacks to bringing a girl like Sarah from a primitive country like Israel to the more advanced society of the United States. She seemed unwilling to go out on her own. She didn't want to learn how to drive a car, so he had to do all the shopping and fetching himself. She didn't even seem to understand how to go about cooking American food. He had brought home a chicken wrapped in plastic. She had placed the whole thing in the electric oven. Only the smell had alerted him to something wrong. He tried to explain to her that the chicken had to be taken from the plastic, then washed and put in a baking dish. He thought he had gotten through to her, but the next day she did the same thing with some steak he had bought. He asked her how she could have forgotten to remove the steak from the plastic. Her excuse was that it was steak this time, not chicken. Sarah was certainly a delightful and endearing child, but perhaps a bit slow. She was repeatedly ruining the fresh store-bought food, so he compromised by buying only frozen food and removing the outer cardboard box before he put it in the freezer. That way dinner was always a surprise.

One thing he could not fault her on was her feminine fecundity, for she had become pregnant it seemed from the very first that he had slept with her. He was angry at himself then for letting Diane bamboozle him out of custody of Steven. He should have known. What with Walter de Gregory being a doctor himself, he probably had an easy time bribing the technicians to alter the test results of one Hal Evans. Sterile, heh? Well he had shown them with Sarah. He was just sort of sad that their lovemaking had to cease with the advent of her morning sickness, but he tried to understand her discomfort. He had once guided her delicate hand to his penis and shown her how to pump it to give him some relief. When she at last understood what he wanted, she had quickly withdrawn her hand, scolding him for asking her to do something contrary to the halakah, their common orthodox faith. True, his seed should not be spilled upon the ground. Even into a handkerchief, she assured him, it was against their laws. She was Orthodox, she was pure. She made no demands on him except one. She wanted him to put her green card, her permanent residence permission from the United States immigration authorities, into her hand instead of the ṣafe-deposit box. She asked for it night and day. She would not be happy, she told him, until she got it. But he explained to her that she didn't need it as he would let her go nowhere without him. This did not please her. She wanted it in her wallet like every other immigrant. Perhaps then— Perhaps then, he suggested, when her morning sickness was over, she would allow him to— But before he got to finish the thought, never mind the deed, she would rush away to the bathroom.

Sarah had been the one good thing to come out of that trip to Israel. It had been a disaster ever since the Shin Bet had picked him up trying to "break into" Golda's apartment. "Call her," he had screamed at them as they handcuffed him and dragged him away. "Ring the doorbell, she's right inside waiting for me." It was only later when he had returned to the States and had time to think about it that he understood. It was the Mossad. They were testing him. They were checking to see if he could avoid their own forces and enter Golda's house without being caught. If he had passed that test, he would have been ready for a regular assignment. But he had failed, failed miserably. His interrogators hadn't believed a word he said. The three men in the car they dismissed when he couldn't even give them the color and make of the car. But it had been so fast. Golda had wished to see him. His interrogators claimed they had contacted Golda Meir. She had never even heard of him. He had shown them his personal invitation to dine with her. Personal invitation, they questioned. There were over five hundred people at that dinner. But his picture shaking Golda's hand? They showed him her eyes. She was looking past him. Obviously her eye focus had been distorted by the camera's flash, but they chose not to understand that. The questions they asked him. Over and over again. And then to be humiliated by Shoshana, the way she had sauntered into the interrogation room and said, "Hello, boys," to his tormentors. She had assured them that he was completely harmless, that he just suffered from delusions of grandeur. They had been doubtful, but after a conference with Shoshana and their superiors, they had escorted him to the airport and helped him board the first plane out. It had been embarrassing being force marched up the aisle of a 747 and having the onboard security guard told in a loud voice to keep an eye on him. But he thought he had quieted the other passengers' minds if not his own by explaining he was prone to heart seizures and Golda Meir herself had wanted him to have special care on the trip home.

He was glad to see that his family didn't believe any of this garbage that was being spouted against him. Sarah was the proof of that. Cousin Ephraim would never have sent Sarah over to him if he had believed Hillel to be less than honorable. He could always expect his father and his family to honor him. Now if he could only somehow assure Mossad that he was worthy of their trust.

Shoshana checked the papers on her desk, put the ones she would need into a file, the others back into her cabinet, which she then locked. Her watch said five of seven. Just enough time to make it to the conference room. The halls would be quiet now, almost everyone gone. She liked working at night. The dark soothed her. Work also postponed the loneliness she would feel if she got home too early. She left her office and locked her door. Passing by David's office, she knocked on the door and swiftly opened it. "Do you have the maps?" she asked him.

"You need them now?"

"I'm meeting Haggai. He wants to go over Iraqi military placement along their Syrian-Jordanian triangle. I thought it would help if I had the specific emplacements."

"Do you have the character profiles of their high command?"

"Yes."

"So go over them first. I'll send the maps down in half an hour."

"Okay. Conference Room B." She started to close the door. "David, you know what? We're getting old."

"Speak for yourself, dearie."

Smiling, she made her way down to the conference room. Haggai was already waiting for her. She leaned over and kissed him on the cheek. "Um, you smell good," he told her. "I hope that's for me." She sighed. Haggai never grew up. She often wondered what he was trying to prove by his overt sexual comments. No one paid any attention to him anymore. He had just gotten to be a nuisance.

She sat down at the table and started removing her papers from her file and placing them strategically on the tabletop. Meanwhile Haggai had moved around, brushed her hair aside, and kissed the nape of her neck. Bored, she sighed and pushed him away. "Stop it," she told him. "We have work to do." Maybe it was Tzahal. She didn't know what turned professional military men into such crass sexual bores. They all felt they had to come on with this macho image. Whom were they trying to impress? Not their wives, certainly not their mistresses. Danny was sometimes the most insecure man she knew. Maybe the new recruits liked their officers rough and ready. She didn't know, she couldn't remember.

"Do you want to check the new profiles?" she asked.

Haggai shrugged. "What's the point? We already know what the Iraqis are capable of."

"How can you already know when we've just gotten new data in?" she replied. "Several Russian transports were seen landing in the interior last week. We know exactly what was delivered."

He sighed. "You can give the Arabs all the military equipment in the world. It's just so much junk if it's not used right."

She didn't say anything. It wasn't her place to. This had been going on for several years now. Military intelligence had taken over. Everything the other services collected was fed to military intelligence for analysis. It bothered her. These were not cautious men. What made them good battlefield commanders made them lousy analysts. The military had targets and objectives and the officers were used to overcoming any obstacle thrown in their way. It was good military science but a perversion of intelligence, where sometimes the objective was not to accomplish anything but to know, to understand. She knew men and women who spent their lives checking out little insignificant items, trying to fit them into the jigsaw of Arab intentions. There was no objective but to comprehend and be prepared.

Haggai drew a chair close to Shoshana and sat down, rifling through a few of the documents. "You're killing me with that perfume," he told her, after giving up the pretense of concentrating.

"Haggai, I'm not wearing any perfume."

"Oh." He leaned over and kissed her on the lips. She smelled liquor on his breath.

"Stop it," she told him coldly.

"Why?"

"You're being childish and you're acting like an idiot."

"Did I tell you I'm still not getting along with my wife?"

"Everyone knows."

"Oh. Yeah. Everyone knows everything in Israel. I forgot. Do you know whom she's sleeping with?"

Shoshana lowered her eyes, feeling his pain. "Haggai, you will regret this in the morning."

He put his arm around her and tried to kiss her cheek. She pushed him away. "I've always had this thing for you, Shoshana. Ever since we went swimming together off Eilat. Remember? You were wearing that pink bathing suit. I could see your nipples through the material. They were hard."

"I see. You're going to be impossible tonight. I was with Danny. Danny's your friend." She hated it when men drank. They seemed to think being drunk relieved them of all responsibility.

"Danny wouldn't mind about us. He's very generous. And you must be some terrific piece if he'd keep you around for so many years."

She slapped him across the face and rose to go, but he grabbed hold of her arm and pulled her down so she was sitting on his lap. He held her tight, she could barely move. She was angry but also for the first time afraid. "What are you trying to prove? I'm not your wife. Go take it out on her."

"You're not anyone's wife," he reminded her. He took her head and forced it toward his lips.

She pushed and flailed out against him. He pushed back and they fell from the chair onto the floor. She hit her head and moaned. Haggai clamped his hand across her mouth and pinioned her. "It's not going to hurt you," he told her through rough gasps of breath, "and it's going to make me feel so much better." He watched as she shook her head and her eyes grew wild in fright, tears gathering at their corners. It made him feel good. The bitch. "It's nothing you haven't done before," he pointed out as he fumbled with the buttons of his pants. He was already hard, he hadn't been so hard in months. He put his hands inside her pants and drew them down past her knees as he watched her eyes shriek. "You're not going to say anything to Danny or anyone," he told her as he settled himself on top of her. "Because I'm going to tell everyone you asked for it. And who's going to believe you didn't?"

It was nine o'clock when David finished clearing his desk and locking everything up. He came out of his office to find the night clerk typing away at her desk. "I'm going home now," he told her.

"Uh, David, what do you want me to do with these?" She held out the maps he had given her over an hour ago.

"You were to take them down to Conference Room B."

"I tried but the door was locked and no one answered my knocking. I think there was someone in there though."

David gave her a puzzled look. The door shouldn't have been locked. And Shoshana wouldn't have finished the briefing without this map. He took the map from the clerk and walked down the west corridor to Conference Room B. He knocked on the door and waited. When he tried the knob, it turned. The door opened. The room was dark. They must have left. Except the room didn't feel empty to him. He turned on the lights and noticed the chairs scattered about the room. Their disorder annoyed him. He went into the room, lay the maps on the table, and began straightening the chairs. He almost missed her because she was huddled in a corner; but there was Shoshana, and it became very obvious why the door had been locked and the chairs knocked about. He closed the door and secured it. Then he walked over to Shoshana. She seemed not to notice him. He crouched down next to her and helped her arrange her clothes. Other than that he was afraid to touch her. "Do you want to go to the police?" he asked her. She made absolutely no response except to pull away from him. "Do you want me to handle it?" She nodded her head yes.

Somehow he got her out of the building and into his car. He drove her home, fumbled through her purse for her keys, and settled her in her bedroom. "Do you want me to stay with you?" he asked. "Shall I call a doctor? Lily? Danielle? Anyone?" But she had turned away from him and was curled like a little ball on top of her bed. He covered her with her comforter, turned out the lights, and left her. When he got home, his wife, Hava, asked what was the matter with him, he looked sick. He couldn't tell her. He wouldn't tell anyone. Why spread the shame.

But he could not sleep that night, could not stop thinking about it. He blamed Danny. He tried to assess his own feelings for Shoshana. Maybe they were in the way of his judgment. She had appealed to him ever since he first met her. She had struck him as wonderfully innocent, a pure pleasure, even during the continuing Danny fiasco. To him Danny was the villain, Shoshana merely love-crazed. David wanted to protect her. As a father might? Well, not really. She stirred him in a very special way. But she was unaware of it, unaware of everything except Danny. And, thank God, her work.

"It's three thirty and you're still awake," Hava informed him. "Can I help?"

Ignoring her, he rose from the bed and called the chief of military intelligence, demanding a meeting in an hour's time at the Kiriyah.

* * *

457

David had left word to be called as soon as Shoshana showed up for work. When it was ten and she hadn't appeared, he knew he shouldn't wait any longer. Especially when she didn't answer her phone. He tended to panic during personal crises. He hated facing the unpleasant. Her apartment building in the middle of the morning was very quiet. Both wives and husbands worked while their children were off in school or *gan*. Though he did hear a baby cry behind one of the doors as he rushed up the two flights of stairs to Shoshana's apartment. He knocked on the door rather forcefully. There was no responding sound from within. He hoped he wasn't going to have to attempt to break the door down. It looked particularly solid, and he was sure it would remain long after he dislocated his shoulder. He knocked again.

"Who is it?"

Thank God. Shoshana. "It's me. David."

"Go away."

He could hear her voice clearly. She must be leaning up against the door. "Are you all right?" It wasn't too profound, but . . .

"No."

At least she was being honest. "What can I do?" he asked.

"Nothing." She hesitated. "What do you want to do, kiss it and make it better?" she said with quiet hysteria.

"Let's not be obscene." They stood with the door between them; he was desperately trying to think of something reassuring to say. He would attempt an appeal to her sense of responsibility. "There's work waiting for you at the office. If you'll let me in, I'll explain what it is." Nothing. "Should I call your sister or—"

"Don't call anyone!"

"Okay, don't get excited. I just thought—what are you planning to do?" He waited. "Nothing foolish I hope. Shoshana?" He could sense her waiting on the other side of the door. If only he could find the magic words to say. "That's a violation of the commandments, you know."

"You're not religious."

"I am in matters of life and death. Please let me in, Shoshana. I know if we talk, you'll feel better."

"No. Please go away, David. I need time."

"Will you wait for me then?"

"Wait for you?"

"Yes. Wait for me. I'll be back at four to check on you. After all our years together, you should be able to wait six hours for me. Promise?" He held his breath.

"Promise," she answered softly. He put his hand up against the door, then retreated.

Between now and four he would have to figure out a way to get into that apartment. He knew someone who had the key, both literally and figuratively. With dismay, David supposed that had to be his next step. He negotiated the side streets with care but was glad when he hit the highway. He needed the speed and the open road in order to think. An hour north of Tel Aviv he turned east off the main highway and made his way to Camp Het. Despite his government identification and his high security clearance, he was left waiting at the gate while someone went off in search of Colonel Ze'ev.

Danny hurried from the mess hall when he heard that David Tal was waiting at the gate for him. David did not seek him out of friendship. He would only come if Shoshana was in trouble. David had spotted him and was coming forward to meet him, pushing past the guard whom Danny waved off. "What is it?" Danny asked.

"We need somewhere quiet to talk," David said calmly. "Private also."

Danny looked around. David was asking a lot. He beckoned him. They went down to the sand and got into a rubber raft, which Danny pushed off and paddled away from the beach. Once off, he started the motor and they moved farther away from the shore.

"I gather you know I get seasick," David told him.

Danny laughed. "It figures. Why are you here?"

David kept his eye on Danny rather than the rocking raft. It helped. "First, let's have an agreement that you'll listen to what I say without interrupting because there are some things I'm going to say that will be very upsetting, and if you start screaming and jumping about, I'll never finish what I have to say, and we'll probably end up in the water. In which case I'll have to count on you to rescue me and bring me to shore, and I don't want to have to be grateful to you for the rest of my life. Agreed then, your silence?"

Danny considered it, his dislike for David entirely too evident. "We'll see."

"Danny—"

"Okay. Agreed."

"It's not very pleasant. But please hear me out." He took a deep breath before he began. "Shoshana was raped last night. I wish I could say she's okay, but she's not." David watched while the vessel in Danny's temple throbbed, but true to his military discipline, he said not a word. "She was raped by a friend of yours. It's not going to help to beat him up like you beat up the Rumanian. Besides I've already taken care of him. What was done to Shoshana was done. And there's nothing we can do to take it away." He paused. "I blame you. I don't like you, Danny. I never have. Maybe it's my fault. Maybe it's because I've never tried to understand you. But you've used Shoshana. Right from the beginning. You took away her virginity, wasn't it right here in this camp, and you didn't give a damn about her. You were already married, your wife wasn't available, so you used Shoshana. Do you know how she felt afterward? I do. Because she came to me with it. She felt like dirt. She had almost recovered when she met you at the Hanukah party. After that nothing could stop you. You had absolutely no sense of decency where she was concerned. I heard it all, Danny. She wouldn't talk to you about it because she was afraid of losing you, the poor stupid bitch. Her mother was dying. That proved no obstacle. You poisoned relations between Shoshana and her family. I was even grateful that she broke off with you when your offer to set her up in an apartment wasn't accepted. I thought, now finally Shoshana will have a life of her own to live. But there you were, a hero back from the war, and she couldn't resist you. What have you ever given her, Danny? A good time in bed? That's about it as far as I can figure. For that she's sacrificed her respectability, her place in society, her chance for marriage, for children, for real happiness. Why do you think it was she who was raped, Danny? Because of you. If she were your wife, no one would have touched her. But everyone knows that she's your whore. It pains me. I would rather cut my tongue out than call her a whore. But that's what she's become, thanks to you. Okay, I'm through. I just had to get that off my chest once and for all."

"I love Shoshana," Danny said intensely.

"Oh God, give it up," David answered angrily. "What kind of love is it that ruins another person's life?"

"Are you saying if I love her, let her go?"

"I said everything I had to say."

"I could kill you."

"Big deal," David derided him. "You better go see her. I don't know what to say to her. I don't have the words. Now please take the raft into shore before I puke."

David waited while Danny informed the base commander he was leaving for Tel Aviv. The ride down together was unpleasant. They held only one conversation: "Why don't you admit it?" Danny asked. "You're in love with Shoshana too. You're just angry because she chose me."

David thought that one over. "If I were in love with Shoshana," he said carefully, "I'd be too much of a gentleman to admit it. Even to myself."

Danny quietly unlocked the door to their apartment and let himself in. He found Shoshana sitting in their bedroom. He had startled her. She looked up at him and turned away without saying a word. He came to her and attempted to put his hand on her shoulder but she shrugged him off. "Don't touch me," she pleaded.

He tried several times to start a conversation with her, but she wouldn't answer. He wanted to find out who, but she wouldn't say. He wanted to comfort her, but he could give none. He pulled up a chair, and they sat five feet away from each other. They didn't talk, they didn't touch.

The hours passed. The light in their room changed to dusk, to darkness and still they didn't move. "It's funny, isn't it?" she finally said. "Other women get married, have children, I get raped." He helped her to wash then and change, to get ready for bed. He held the covers open while she slid between them. He tucked her in and watched while she curled up protectively. Then he resumed his place on the chair and sat quietly while she fell asleep. He stayed there the whole night. It was his death watch. When morning came, he helped her up, helped her dress; he fed her breakfast and took her to work. There he left her.

Jonathan Ben-Gal, chief of naval operations, was available when Danny Ze'ev wanted to see him. He rose and shook hands with his top commando. "My God, Danny, where have you been. I thought we were going to have to declare you AWOL." But his smile was not matched by an answering one from Danny. "Sit down," he said, his mood changing. "What can I do for you?"

"I want to resign. Effective immediately," Danny said.

"You want to resign? What are you, crazy?"

"Jonathan, I've been serving with the navy for sixteen years. I think you owe it to me to let me resign when I want to."

"I can't believe this. One day I have you training all our new little webbed feet up in Caesarea, next day you're down here in Tel Aviv asking to resign. I knew you weren't too thrilled with being an instructor, but this isn't the way to go about changing your assignment."

"It had nothing to do with that."

"So what does it have to do with?"

"Personal reasons."

Jonathan sighed. Everyone knew about Danny's perpetual permanent triangle, but why the explosion now? "Can you tell me about it?" he asked sympathetically.

Danny stumbled, thinking of a way to put it. "I love Shoshana," he began. "She's everything to me. But— It's not working out. I can't give her what she wants most. I think I'm destroying her."

"So you want to resign from the navy? This is the answer?"

"I want to leave the country."

Jonathan sat back.

"If I go, if I stay away from her," Danny explained, "she'll find someone else."

"And that'll make you happy?" Danny didn't answer. "Danny, you're giving up your career."

"So what? In another ten years I'll be asked to retire."

"What will you do?"

"I thought maybe you could arrange it so I can have my leave time to study abroad."

Jonathan shrugged. It could of course be arranged. It was part of their benefits to enable officers to have their university studies supported. "Do you really want to be a student?"

Danny laughed. "No. But I need time to organize my life."

Jonathan thought about it. He hated to lose Danny. He was a good officer—bright, dedicated, committed to his men, a natural leader. He should be able to find something for him that would suit both Danny's purposes and the navy's. "Look, can you hang around for a few hours? Give me time to make some arrangements?"

"Yes. But, Jonathan, I mean it. I want out today."

Jonathan calmed him. "I understand. Today it is."

Four hours later Jonathan came back and walked Danny down to the cafeteria. They went through the line, then found a relatively private place to sit. "How would you like to be a naval attaché?" Jonathan asked. Danny laughed at him. "No, I'm serious," Jonathan said. "I've talked to the defense minister; I've talked to the chief of staff. Reuben's about finished his tour of duty in London. He's not going to like this because he wanted to extend his stay, but we'll send him to France or Nigeria or someplace. Our foreign ministry has sent out feelers to the British. They're agreeable to having you on such short notice because you've trained there so they have a file on you. They know we're not trying to pull a fast one. So what do you say?"

"Naval attaché? I don't know anything about diplomacy."

"Yes. That's going to be a problem. But you do know about the navy. What can you lose? Go to England. Spend a month with Reuben learning the ropes. If you don't think you can handle it, Reuben will be glad to stay on. And the month away will at least have served your purpose."

Danny nodded his head. "Thanks, Jonathan."

"You can pick up your assignment and papers tomorrow."

"Tomorrow?"

"Danny, you can't expect the impossible. Stay on base tonight."

Yes, Danny thought, it would give him a chance to say good-bye.

When Shoshana arrived from work that night, he had just about finished packing. The things he wouldn't be taking with him he put in boxes and hoped maybe she would make some arrangement to call his parents to store them. There wasn't really much he was leaving behind. Mainly corals and shells, photograph albums, navy mementos. Very few things meant so much to him that he would save them. So when Shoshana came home, his bags were by the door and he was waiting for her.

"What's this?" she asked.

"I've been given a new posting," he told her quite truthfully. He could see that she was still numbed by what had happened. She looked sick and tired. Maybe he shouldn't leave her now. But if not now, when?

"Where are you going?"

"London."

"Perhaps I can—"

"Shoshana." She looked up and he knew she knew what he was going to say before he said it. "We've got to end it."

"No."

"It's not good anymore."

She started to cry. "Danny, the rape was not my fault."

He rushed to her and crushed her in his arms. "Don't

ever say it was, don't ever think it was," he told her harshly.

"Then why?" she begged him.

"Because," he was desperate for words, "I can't marry you, I can't give you a child, I can't even protect you. Not even that."

"But I don't want any of those things. I just want you."

He held her face between his hands. "You want to be married. You want a child. Let our love die, Shoshana. You can have what you want with someone else."

"Never."

He blocked her lips with his palm. "You must. You must stop loving me." But she wouldn't. "I'm not going to love you from this moment on," he threatened.

She smiled at him. "Danny, you're a fool. You can't kill love."

"I'm not going to kill it. I'm going to let it die." He wanted to hold her, to kiss her, to take her to bed and feel her body moving against his. He dropped his hands from her, picked up his bags, and left the apartment. He hoped he had said enough, he hoped she would no longer cling to him as he still clung to her. She had told him he couldn't kill love. Maybe she was wrong. Maybe he could. Maybe one move on his part would end it, would free her if not him. He stood by a pay phone on the way to his base. He dialed his number. "Ronit?" he said when his wife answered. "I'm leaving tomorrow for London. I'm going to be the naval attaché there. If you and Adee want to come along, contact Jonathan and he'll make the arrangements." He hung up the phone. Shoshana would hear about this. It would be the one unforgivable act, letting Ronit return to him. She would hate him for it. He felt sick, he felt dead. It was over.

32

Sarah Evans paced around her husband's bedroom nervously. Shaul lay naked on Hillel's bed, his curly head propped up on the pillow, his now flaccid penis resting quietly between his legs. "Stop it," he told her. "You'll lose your balance and fall on your stomach."

"A hell of a lot you care about my stomach or the baby inside of it," she attacked.

"I'm here, aren't I?"

She came back to the bed and stood over him. His body was young and lean. When he held her, when he made love to her, he was strong and forceful. She let her hand drop down to his chest. Her fingers twined their way through his hair. He pulled her down, she fell awkwardly onto him. "We're together," he told her.

She straightened herself. "But not the way we planned."

"So?"

"Do you know how much I sweated getting my hands on that green card? Every day I begged him, I bargained for it with my body. Just so you and I could be together."

"We are together. That's what I'm telling you."

"And after your tourist visa expires, where will we be?"

Shaul sighed. Sarah was becoming a real nag. "Look, how do you think I got into this country in the first place? Do you think with my criminal record, they're just going to hand me a visa? I bought it, you silly girl. Now do you think the woman I bought it from is going to give a call to Washington, saying, hey, look out for Shaul Darom? Or do you think the Israeli police are going to contact the police here and say, you got a real bad one on your hands? Drop it, Sarah. In six months everyone's going to forget I ever existed."

"But you need papers."

"Papers can be bought. Everything can be bought. And your cousin has the money to buy it with. What the hell do you want to rush out onto the streets for? We got everything we need right here. Including each other."

"I can't stand it, Shaul. I can't stand for him to touch me."

"Baby, have I ever asked you to sell yourself for me? No. That's not my game. Even now when it would be so easy for you to go along with him. I mean how long can it take with an old guy like that? A few minutes? I don't ask you to do it. I know how you feel. I respect that."

"I don't want our child to have his name."

"How can the kid have his name. We're married."

"Not by a rabbi.".

"Look, when I said those words to you, when I said, *'harei at mekudeshet li'* in front of Dado and Topaz, that's legal. I said it and I meant it, Sarah. You're my wife. For now, forever. And as such I intend to provide for you. So can you think of any better way to live than this? We don't have to lift a finger. That stupid schmuck you married provides everything." He laughed but didn't see her crack a smile. "We can't afford to live elsewhere the way we live here," he told her sternly. "When I get myself established, we'll see what we can do."

"If you'd just get a job, we could—"

"A job? What the hell are you talking about? Work my ass off all day. For what? Peanuts? I'm talking about big money, Sarah."

"What are you going to do, join the army here and sell off their equipment like you did in Israel?"

He laughed. "They didn't catch me for a year."

"And then you were court-martialed and put in a military prison."

"They say it beats the regular lockups." His face turned grim. "Anyway, Sarah, we all have a price to pay for what we do. Even our love costs us," he said, patting her stomach.

"I hope I never find the price too high," she threatened him.

They heard a car drive up. Sarah moved to the bedroom window and looked out over the driveway. "It's him," she said. She looked over her shoulder. Shaul lay in bed as naked as before. "Hurry up and get dressed," she ordered. "He may be dumb but he's not blind." She left the bedroom and had reached the foot of the stairs when Hal Evans opened the door. She tried to greet him with a smile. It never came out just right. He barely nodded at her as he pushed past her on the way up the stairs. "Where are you going?" she asked.

"To pack," Hal announced.

Sarah swore under her breath. What would they do now. She had closed the door of the bedroom but Shaul was still inside.

Hal turned the handle of his bedroom door and pushed it open. He was surprised to find Shaul in his pants and T-shirt straightening out the sheets. "What are you doing here?" he asked.

Shaul looked calmly up at him, his face registering surprise. "Making the bed," he said, as if it was the most natural thing in the world to be doing. "You know how it is with Sarah now. She could have the baby any day. She doesn't feel well when she bends over the bed."

"She doesn't seem to feel well most of the time," Hal snapped. He was getting sick of her moods. He had taken a wife so that he could enjoy her. But Sarah refused to let him within five feet of her. At least her disposition had improved since their cousin Shaul had shown up. That was a surprise and a half in itself. Shaul had just arrived one day claiming to be the son of Cousin Ephraim's younger sister's second marriage. He would only stay for a few days until he got settled. But it had been two months now. Not that Hal had much reason to complain. Besides helping put Sarah in a better mood than he had managed, this Shaul knew enough English to do the shopping. He knew how to cook, he cleaned the house, which was more than Sarah had ever attempted. And he stayed with Sarah when Hal had to travel. That was good. Sarah had always been afraid to be left alone in this big house with no one to look after her.

"I have to leave for a few days," Hal said.

"Oh, not again," Shaul sympathized. "That's some sort of job being a professional fund raiser. I hope at least it pays well."

"Well enough," Hal told him. "Of course the pay is nothing compared to the feeling of satisfaction I get from raising money for Jews everywhere."

"I'm sure a lot more Jews would be grateful if they got the money raised for them directly instead of having to beg for it from the Jewish Agency," Shaul commented.

"Don't I remember," Hal said bitterly. "But that's all in the past. Now they respect me for what I am."

"They respect you because you're an American Jew now and not a Baghdadi anymore," Shaul said with a smile as he fluffed up the pillow he had half an hour before placed under Sarah's ass.

"What you say might be true," Hal admitted. "Is that what you're trying to become? An American Jew?"

"I wouldn't mind it."

"You should get a job then."

"Oh, I intend to. As soon as Sarah has the baby. I don't want to leave her alone with you traveling all the time."

"Why? She has a telephone. She can call the hospital."

"She's afraid to be left alone. She can't speak English so well. How long are you going to be gone this trip?"

"Two weeks."

"I hate to bring it up, but we're going to need money to

live on." Shaul watched while Hal handed him a hundred dollars. "I hope it's enough."

"It should be."

"Maybe you should leave Sarah some money. You know, open an account in the bank in case there are any emergencies."

"I did that with my first wife. She cleaned me out when she left. I don't make the same mistake twice. Now if you'll excuse me, I've got to pack."

Shaul practically backed out of the room bowing. This was going to be tougher than he thought. He had wanted to stay out of the drug trade because he had heard the Mafia was strong in Boston, but if he didn't come up with another idea quick, he might have to get in touch with his Israeli connections in Canada and see what could be arranged.

Andrew Harris was having a devil of a time putting the recorder in place. It would have been much easier to use a transmitter but not much safer. He supposed he should opt for safety. He didn't want to end up before a firing squad or hanging from some rope. Still, he wasn't as apprehensive about this eventuality as he used to be. The politicians of Iraq were all too busy killing each other off to be worried about the likes of him. No sooner had he spotted a source than that source found himself up against some wall. The number of prominent disappearances was becoming as common as it was terrifying. There must be some way to end a political career without murder. But not in Iraq. He had accomplished some things in his too long a stay here though. He had a string of agents now. Some Christian women, a few Kurds in the capital, three Sunni officers in the army. It was costing him money, but he was sending back useful information to Tel Aviv. Training manuals in Arabic for all the Russian weapons that had been pouring into Iraq since the rapprochement with the communists under the Ba'aths. A constant update on military deployment. He had a network within the governmental bureaucracy of people who could get things done for a price. Jacob Ewan.

Poor Jacob. Harris thought now Jacob helped him with

471

no thought toward getting his family out, but merely as an act of final vindictiveness against al Haykal. Harris couldn't blame him. After the fiasco of Ephraim's attempted escape, al Haykal had kept the Ewan family on a short rope. They were watched constantly, never allowed to travel outside Baghdad's city limits without a special pass signed personally by al Haykal, and even then he provided a personal escort. "I'm waiting for the day when he is brought low," Jacob would mutter. Sure, like some day the messiah will come, Harris thought. Al Haykal was a fox and he played a treacherous game. Close friendship with al Haykal was the kiss of death for many a politician. Once al Haykal knew all, he betrayed all. And yet the politicians continued to dance around him like miller moths. Why? Harris thought it was that secret, inviting, quiet smile al Haykal kept upon his face, a smile that betrayed nothing, but offered everything. And al Haykal was a power in internal security. If one side could own him, he could offer them much. So they bid for his favors and his influence and he burned them up.

Harris wasn't the only one who could spot a survivor. Which explained Harris's presence underneath Jacob's desk. Colonel Gasbakian, the senior Soviet advisor for political affairs, had also singled al Haykal out. The colonel and al Haykal had met casually at the Swallow's Nest several times over the past six months. So Jacob had reported. Then one night al Haykal had asked Jacob to leave the back entrance to his office open after the rest of the Swallow's Nest was closed and Jacob himself had left for home. Harris cursed himself, for Jacob had not been able to reach him in time. Instead he had left one of his swallows sitting quietly on the stairs, waiting, watching. She had seen the Russian come out of Jacob's office and search for a bottle of liquor. As he closed the door to the office, the swallow had caught sight of al Haykal. What Harris would have given to have heard what was said. But he figured if they had used it once, they would use it again. And this time he would hear what was said. If al Haykal was selling out to the Russians, he wanted to know how, why, and what for.

Some pictures of the two of them together wouldn't hurt either. Al Haykal wasn't the only one who was skilled at blackmail.

Jacob watched Harris work. "Are you through yet?" he asked nervously.

There was no answer from under the desk. Harris shouldn't be here. What if al Haykal should walk in now. He never bothered to knock. He figured he owned the Swallow's Nest. Which he did. Along with Jacob's soul and the lives of his family, which had increased by three since Ephraim had not only married Tina but managed to father two children in short order. "For God's sake, when are you going to finish!"

Harris slid himself out from under the desk and smiled. "It's working."

"Bravo. Now would you get the hell out of here."

"You need a vacation."

"Thanks. What do you suggest? London or Paris? Or perhaps Baghdad?"

"I'll be back," Harris promised.

"I don't doubt that."

"When I figure out how to install a camera."

Harris smiled a farewell while Jacob suppressed a groan. He left the Swallow's Nest and walked toward the Street of Ba'athist Solidarity. Jacob would cooperate despite any misgivings. The pictures of al Haykal and his Russian counterpart would start flowing into Yossi Leskov's hands in Tel Aviv. Tel Aviv. God, if only he were there. But he was here in Baghdad and the more successful he became, the longer he would be forced to stay, the more Yossi would demand of him, until somebody somewhere would overstep an invisible line and all would be lost.

33

Roberta was packing away her life. There wasn't much to it. Two children, four suitcases full of clothes. They were leaving Urbana. It had been six years since they had come here, six years in the deadness of the Midwest, and now they were getting out. But only for a year, for Ovadia's sabbatical from the university. It was a sabbatical they both needed, a time of rest not only from work, but they would also leave behind the pain of living in America. Never had Roberta seen such a time, nor could she imagine such anger and agony trampling across the land as it had in 1972. The Vietnam War and White House politics crazed the people of America and caused them to feed upon themselves in an orgy of destruction. She couldn't understand any of it. The Vietnam era was not her America of the fifties—small-town picnics and parades, fall-out shelter drills. Vietnam was wrong and all *her* American presidents, such as Washington, Jefferson, Lincoln, Eisenhower saw the difference between right and wrong and then chose the right. But Richard Nixon was in the White House now and the values of the United States were being undercut by both the right and the left, by those in power and those seeking it.

The revolution—not evolution, certainly—came to Illinois more slowly than it had to the rest of the country, but it came with the inevitability of the five o'clock news. The mood on campus was electric. Cambodia and Kent State turned on the switch. But she saw only the horror of it as she had crossed Green Street and observed the campus blockaded by the National Guard. She couldn't believe that this was happening in the United States of America. She wouldn't believe it. One night she had been free to wander the campus because a baby-sitter waited with her children while she was on her way to pick up Ovadia from a conference. The National Guard was placed along Wright Street in an effort to hold a horde of students in. In from what? This was their town. But the trashing had come nights before and the merchants wanted no more of it.

The students were gathered facing the militia. It was a strange confrontation of youth against youth. The guardsmen were holding their rifles nervously. The students were milling before them good-naturedly. Roberta was surprised to see as much wonder on the students' faces as she felt inside her. A boy was standing next to her. "Look over there," he said. "Beyond the line. Artillery pieces. See that soldier?" he said. "That's a bazooka." A bazooka?

How does one use a bazooka against a crowd of students? Was this government-sponsored theater of the absurd? Her world had gone mad and she was glad she was leaving.

But Israel? She had to wonder. She was worried. It was a strange country with a foreign tongue; and even though she had visited once with Ovadia and met his family, it was not the same as living there. Would she be able to work, she wanted to know. Ovadia had asked her why she would want to work when she could stay home and take care of the children. He had asked her that same question when Zachary was six months old and she had decided that staring at him eight hours a day just wasn't what life was supposed to be about. Ovadia was horrified when she had hired a baby-sitter and had gone back to the hospital to work. "How can you possibly not enjoy staying home with your baby?" he had asked her, mystified. "Because Zack doesn't say anything. He just lies there and gurgles." She had offered Ovadia the obvious alternative. He could stay home and take care of Zachary himself. He looked at her as if she were mad. Of course it didn't stop her from having another child, Deborah, eighteen months later. She liked having children. It was just caring for them afterward that didn't really set her on fire.

She pressed Ovadia: Was he going to be very religious in Israel? He answered that one didn't have to be religious in Israel because one didn't have to struggle to remain a Jew there. A cheap shot at her certainly since they struggled all the time in Urbana. This was after she had practically fainted despite her medical experience when Zachary was subjected to his brit. It was the most primitive act she had ever seen. Then Ovadia had offered money to the synagogue for the pidyon, to protect himself from the necessity of offering his firstborn son for the priesthood. Really, if he thought she was going to let Zachary go anywhere near a synagogue or a church, he was sadly mistaken. On that she had held firm. She must protect her babies from all religious maniacs.

She spent the last days in Urbana cleaning the house and packing away their goods. They had shipped some boxes on ahead of them with their basic American necessities. She remembered a call she had gotten from a security official at Kennedy airport asking her if it were true they were only shipping household goods. "It's true," she told him.

"Look, you don't have to lie to me. I'm security."

"I'm not lying!"

"Are you sure?"

Still, when they arrived in Israel, she found that her three hundred feet of Reynold's aluminum foil had been carefully unrolled foot by foot. But she had to admit, she was terribly impressed that they had rerolled it so neatly.

The trip to Israel on September 4, 1972 had been a little more harried, a little more tense an atmosphere than they expected, but they were so exhausted after four flights with two small children—Ovadia's cheaper way—that they never thought to wonder why. When they landed and were checked through customs at Lod airport, Joseph Benjamin met them. He looked grim. "Did they announce the news on your flight?" he asked.

"No. What news?" Ovadia responded.

"Eleven of our athletes were murdered at Munich."

Roberta could not fathom this act of terrorism. Nor could she understand the decision in the interests of sportsmanship for the Olympic games to continue. But then this was Munich, this was Germany; and even though the deed was done by Palestinian terrorists, the blood of eleven more Jews killed on German soil wouldn't matter all that much. Welcome to the reality of Israel.

Roberta followed Shoshana madly in and out of the lunchtime crowd in downtown Tel Aviv. Shoshana kept throwing questions back at her. She tried to answer them but gave up, figuring Shoshana couldn't hear her even though she turned back several times to guess at what Roberta might have been saying. They hurried into a small steakeya; Shoshana pushed Roberta down at an empty table and went to order at the counter. It looked like the Chicago commodities exchange. Roberta was glad she had someone to do the pushing and shoving for her. Whenever she had gone out alone, she always came home empty-handed. She was still not used to shouting for attention, therefore no one noticed her.

Shoshana brought back two bottles of Tempo. "Is this it?" Roberta asked.

"We have to wait for our pitas. I hope you like hot sauce and pickles."

"No. Not really."

"Oh. Sorry. Well, anyway," Shoshana smiled. "How's it going? I haven't seen you in a week. You should really come to Father's on Friday night. Ovadia keeps saying something like you want to be alone. What could you possi-

478

bly find to do alone? Your children are so adorable, Roberta, I just love them. Already they're speaking a little bit of Hebrew. How is your ulpan going? Do you really like the cottage I rented for you? I figured it had a washing machine and a refrigerator, what else would an American need."

"A stove. Shoshana, I—" Roberta had thought she almost had Shoshana's attention but her sister-in-law popped up and hustled to the counter. This was going to be more difficult than she imagined. But she had to try to appeal to Shoshana for help. Shoshana after all should understand. She was always working. She should understand that Roberta also had a need for work, something outside the home. Now all she had was her ulpan, her Hebrew-language class, which she would admit she did enjoy. She and Ovadia's "cottage" was in Ramat Aviv near Beit Brodetsky, an absorption center where new immigrants were given a flat and a place to eat and to learn Hebrew until they found jobs and apartments of their own. She had made friends among the new immigrants, one of them especially, Margaret, a nurse from South Africa, who was becoming as fed up with being a "new immigrant" as Roberta was with being a housewife. Margaret at least knew more Hebrew. She had been a Zionist in South Africa. But she agreed with Roberta that their ulpan had turned into a very destructive gripe session and that really it would be better to go out and live life, learn Hebrew that way instead of merely studying it.

So Roberta would appeal to Shoshana. If she ever came back to the table. She hadn't noticed Shoshana being called or anything. But here she was back with two pitas and a spoon for Roberta to dig out the hot sauce.

"Now," Shoshana said, waiting.

Roberta hesitated before she spoke. She didn't know what else was going to pop up, but it seemed as if Shoshana was really ready to listen. "I'm bored," she announced.

"Bored? With two children and a husband?"

"Incredible as that may seem to you, my children are

in *gan* till one. Ovadia is always over at the university. Except for my ulpan, I'm left alone in the house—cottage. I don't know the language, what should I do all morning?"

"But you can make dinner for your family, do the clothes, sew, read. That's what Lily does. You can visit Lily," Shoshana suggested brilliantly.

"I didn't come to Israel to be a housewife. I need a job."

Shoshana looked nonplussed. "How does Ovadia feel about this?"

"Who cares?"

Shoshana drew in her breath. Who cares what a husband thinks? Poor Ovadia. Was this the way wives were in America? "You don't speak Hebrew. What sort of job do you think you can get?"

"I'm a physical therapist. I brought my license and my degrees. How different can medicine be from one country to another?"

Those were the days of her innocence as Roberta thought back on them later. Appalling innocence. Shoshana couldn't guarantee her a job, but she did arrange an interview for her with Tuvia, the head of administration at Tel Hashomer Hospital in Ramat Gan. Tuvia was willing to give her a chance, even though they had a lot of Russian medical personnel immigrating to Israel at that time whom they were testing out at the hospital. But she could have a part-time job to coincide with her childern's *gan* hours. She was so grateful she didn't even think to assess the salary, but as Ovadia explained it to her later, she made enough each month to cover one meal out in a restaurant.

It didn't matter though. She was just happy to be doing something, happy and terrified. She found herself in the same position Zacky and Deborah were in. With Hebrew she would have to sink or swim. Not so with the Russian immigrants. They at least spoke Yiddish, as did most of the hospital administration. Luckily for her, most Israeli doctors also spoke English. Still, after working in the hospital for a month, she was suffering from severe culture shock. Preventive medicine did not exist in Israel. They immunized their children against very few diseases, letting mumps and measles fall where they might. More offensive, they did not immunize their children against German measles unless the child hadn't gotten them by the time he reached twelve. Meanwhile there were pregnant women constantly being exposed to the risks of deformity in their newborn babies because of this. Pap tests were unheard of for women. The only time a Pap test was given was to confirm uterine cancer, after it had already developed. Antibiotics were not given in large enough dosages to knock out the infection, but were dribbled into the patient until he built up a resistance and they did no good whatsoever. Patients in the hospital were treated like animals. There was a dire shortage of nurses, so those patients who complained or acted up in any way were never attended to. The Russians who were flooding the hospitals had no concept of Western medicine. They had no familiarity with Western drugs, which they dispensed indiscriminately to unsuspecting patients. The only competence seemed to be found in the pathology department, where they took a certain glee in proving that a patient had lived a long life despite, not because of, Israeli medical care. And these poor, dedicated pathologists practically had to be body snatchers to evade Orthodox Jewish strictures. They even worked in laboratories with secret exits in case of rabbinical guerrilla attacks. Roberta felt at times as if she was working in a madhouse.

It wasn't as if the medical establishment didn't know better, it did. But incompetence was built into the entire Israeli system, and not only in medicine, so it was accepted. Doctors were not even bothered that whenever they went on strike for higher wages, the death rate in Israel fell. For them it was a sign that they had been overtreating rather than maltreating.

On the other hand she could see the problem the patients caused as they constantly demanded medical attention. Most workers in Israel belonged to Kupat Holim, which was the Histadrut sick fund. Kupat Holim was a medical clinic, much like an emergency room in United States hospitals where people queued for hours to be seen by a doctor. Most did not need medical attention. But those who did, and even those who didn't, got so frustrated that patients physically attacking the Kupat Holim medical personnel were not uncommon and were generally applauded by the people of Israel. One could only be dehumanized so far by the bureaucracy without striking back, and the breaking point in Israel could be reached every day.

She and Ovadia belonged to Kupat Holim Maccabee, which was an independent sick fund where the doctors had their own offices. They had a good family doctor, a Dr. Deutch, whom she really appreciated the one time she did fall ill and he made an immediate house call. But their pediatrician, who could have answered several of their questions by telephone and spared herself and them a lot of time, insisted on seeing them and each child in person. She got paid by the number of patients she saw, not by the answers she gave on the telephone.

Roberta found herself not alone in facing up to the deficiencies of medicine in Israel. The hospital staff broke into three main camps. There were the Anglo-Saxons, the Israelis, and the Russians. The Anglo-Saxons were those like her who had come from the more civilized countries of the West—Great Britain, South Africa, Australia, Canada, the United States. They had a sense of responsibility toward their patients and toward their profession. There were many Israeli doctors who felt the same way. The Russians were sloppy, careless, ignorant. There were also many Israelis who worked on the Russian model.

Roberta only mingled with the Anglo-Saxons and the Israelis like her. It was too distressing to be around the others. She was fortunate in that almost as soon as she came to Tel Hashomer, Margaret also accepted a job there as a nurse, so they could exchange gossip and outrages whenever they found the time. Their friendship was solidified when Roberta overheard a telephone call between Margaret and her husband. Margaret's daughter had just been taken to a doctor in Tel Aviv who told her husband their child had angina. Margaret was both puzzled and panicked until Roberta, old pro that she had become with two children of her own, stepped in to explain that angina in Israel was not some sort of heart disease but a bad sore throat. The doctors called it angina when there were white specks in the throat that only they could see. They charged more for angina than they did for a sore throat. "I should have guessed," Margaret said, relieved and angry.

But as close as Roberta and Margaret became after working together, Roberta soon discovered that when they left work, they lived in different societies, which affected their attitude toward the patients they dealt with. Margaret was strictly Anglo-Saxon in outlook. For her a stiff upper lip was as necessary as a good cup of tea. She found both lacking at Tel Hashomer. Her patients were not always Europeans who had been trained by their culture to hold their grief and agony within them. There were many Oriental Jews in the hospital whose philosophy seemed to be if one were in pain, everyone should be aware of it. While Europeans would be embarrassed to show their emotions, the Orientals were embarrassed for those who couldn't express them. Margaret found this trait repulsive and barbaric. She found most Oriental traits to be antipathetic to her.

But Margaret's new prejudices against the Orientals were common. Israelis had grown up disparaging Eastern mores, manners, customs, even intelligence. Thus the "second Israel" of the Oriental immigrants came into being. By the time the Orientals started flooding into Israel in the early 1950's, the Ashkenazim had already a tight control on the government, the Histadrut (the labor union), and most importantly the money that poured into Israel from the Diaspora. It created a lock-out for the Orientals from the start. And, too, the Ashkenazim controlled the state-run media. The state decided what was heard on these stations. The only time Eastern culture was mentioned was to point out its barbarism. So people like the Ewans saw their culture debased, derided, neglected, forgotten. The Oriental Jews were forced to rebuild their lives in Israel from the cornerstone up.

Roberta wondered what favor her friends thought they

were doing her by assuring her that Ovadia was different from "the others." The truth of the matter was that Ovadia wasn't all that different. A little brighter perhaps, a little more determined to push his way to the top, which she pointed out he had found only in another country, not in Israel where the opportunities for his advancement were not opened to him. The truth of the matter was that there were thousands of Ovadias lost because of the way those in power perceived the Orientals. She saw it in the way her own son Zacky was treated. The product of two relatively intelligent college-educated human beings, a child who at four started reading *Time* magazine, his Israeli teacher told them that if Zack worked hard, he might be a good mechanic. Well, Roberta certainly hoped Zack became a good mechanic. It was a very useful talent to have. But she also saw something more for him, some adventurous, creative future not open to him as an Iraqi in Israel.

Still, for a year she and her children could survive anything. She hoped. She was speaking Hebrew now, limited but functional. She had learned to change her money on the black market, she had learned to write checks to herself so they could be passed from payee to payee and no one would have to declare them on his income tax. Most importantly she had learned not to be a shy, sensitive, shrinking, tear-filled American. This was the hardest lesson of all because she had been brought up to feel that good manners were probably the most important key to a civilized society. This maxim had to be dropped by the wayside if she were to survive in Israel. She learned to push, to shove, she learned to toss insults in Hebrew and Arabic; she learned how to get what she wanted in a society where only the loudest voices were heard, though she would admit she occasionally suffered from battle fatigue.

Danielle Nissan and Joseph Benjamin were going over his books, trying to hide money. It was a challenge. Frayman Construction Company had been doing a booming business ever since the immigrant explosion. Joseph had

had to hire many new workers. He had also started a country-wide repair service with his own fleet of trucks. "To fall back on in case the boom goes bust," he explained. Sometimes Joshua joined the meetings between Joseph and Danielle of his own accord, other times his father insisted he attend. He was a senior in high school now. After the army he would have to take an active part in running the business. Joseph was going to turn the repair side over to him. "I don't know anything about plumbing," Joshua had protested. "Neither did I," Joseph reminded him. He was worried about his son. He wanted him to pass his *bagrut,* his comprehensive high school exam, but all Joshua was interested in was Gadna and thoughts of the army. Joshua's best friend had been selected for pilot training and Joshua was just a little bit jealous. He wanted to be in the tank corps now, like Sami, or maybe artillery. He didn't know, Joseph didn't have the heart to tell him yet that Lily wasn't going to let him join any combat unit. Joshua was their only son and as such Lily could insist he be assigned away from the front. And she would insist. Too many young men had died along the Suez Canal from Egyptian sniper fire and bombardments. She wouldn't let her son be one of them.

Danielle paused over a column of figures, then started from the top again. "We don't have to do this tonight," Joseph said.

"No. It's all right," Danielle insisted.

"I hope you're not paying any attention to your mother."

"I don't want to talk about it, Joseph."

"Lily—well, look what she did and she still has Joshua."

Danielle glanced up at him and smiled. It must have cost him a lot to mention that. "The doctor says it happens a lot with the first pregnancy," she said, more to reassure herself than him.

"Of course it does. In a month or two you can try again."

"Six months. The doctor says."

"Six months then. It's not so long. You're young."

Danielle had been crushed. Four months into her pregnancy, everything going beautifully, she had never been so happy; then one night she had woken up with cramps and it was all over. Sami had to take her to the hospital to stop the bleeding. Why had it happened?

True, the doctor said many women naturally abort during their first pregnancy. But her mother had whispered that she had cursed her, that Danielle would never have any children because of the disrespect shown to Leah. Sami had been furious when Danielle, in tears, told him what Leah had said. He was ready to kill. But Lily had calmed them and told them of the amulet her mother, Salemah, had worn when she was pregnant. Lily had it still and would lend it to Danielle until, when, if Shoshana ever needed it. Danielle wore it now. She didn't believe in it of course. But what harm could it do?

Ovadia had to think about going to the store to pick up the fresh bread and milk. But he awaited the sounding of an alarm to rouse the rest of his family. It was funny how easily his family had fallen into the routine of living in Israel. He went to get food while they dressed, all ate breakfast, went to school, to work. The cottage Shoshana had rented for them was pleasant. Roberta barely complained, only about the mice that inhabited it. He smiled. What would his wife have done if she had been his mother, if she had come from a house with servants in Baghdad to a tent in Beit Lidd? Roberta wouldn't survive it. But then had his mother? Roberta, Roberta, he despaired of his marriage with her. Roberta had always been so outspoken that at first he thought he would never have to say anything. But she made demands on him. She never asked for his love. She assumed that. Too bad, because love would have been an easy thing for him to give. But she wanted more. She wanted him to leave Urbana, perhaps to stay in Ramat Aviv. Why should he leave America?

He could live here. He knew that. He had lived in Israel before. He could go back to that sort of life. He had been offered a job at the Weizmann Institute. "Take it now," he had been told. "We can't guarantee it later with all these Russians coming in." But he had talked to Roberta about it and she had refused the Weizmann Institute. "It's very nice there," she had said, "but it's just like America. I mean if we're going to live in Israel, let's live in Israel. If America, America, not an imitation."

Why couldn't she appreciate how easy life was in the United States? In less than ten years he had a wife, two children, a house, and a professorship. Not bad for someone who had landed in New York with two suitcases and his brain. Where else but in America could life be so good, so free. So secure! To come back to Israel where every day was a struggle for economic survival, what was the purpose? What did she get out of life here that she couldn't just as readily get out of life in Urbana? She never had the answer. When she found it, maybe he would be forced to listen to her.

The water nozzle outside their bedroom window flushed on.

"Oh, my God!" Roberta shot out of bed and opened the shutters. "Would you please stop using our water," she said distinctly in English to the Arab right outside.

Ovadia drew back. The Arab protested. "I don't care," Roberta countered. "You've been using our water for the past month. We have to pay for it." The Arab said something else. "Not again," Roberta finished off, closing the shutters on him.

"What did you do that for?" Ovadia asked.

"Well, my God, they've been remodeling that cottage down the street for months now. They use our water to mix the cement, for everything. I don't mind if they just get a drink here but this guy comes and takes a bath here six thirty promptly every morning."

"But he's an Arab!"

"So what?"

"So what do you think he's going to do?"

"So what do you think he's going to do?" she retorted. "Throw a grenade in here?" She relented when she saw that that was exactly what Ovadia thought the Arab would do. Then she laughed. "Don't worry," she said. "Mommy will protect you."

He turned from her. "I'll go get the rolls," he said.

"Some milk too," she added.

He dressed quickly and left their cottage. He looked to the right toward the Arabs but they paid no attention to him. He set off for Isaac's two blocks away.

She couldn't protect him. She didn't know, but he knew. He remembered. In Baghdad, 1941, in their house, he was three years old. He hadn't heard or understood all the whispering but he knew something was wrong. And when the night came, all the children on the street had been gathered into his father's house and locked in a windowless closet on the top floor, told to keep quiet no matter what. He remembered his sister Lily holding tightly onto him as they heard the roar of the Arab mob descending on their street, breaking into their homes, plundering and killing. The screams, the wails of the women. He had been so afraid one of them had been his mother. It went on all night. There was no one to stop the Arabs. They were just Jews after all and legitimate targets. The next morning the children were let out and sent home to mourn the dead. Yes, he was afraid of the Arabs. Because he knew them and he knew how easily they could turn and kill. But Roberta understood none of that. Roberta understood nothing. She was American.

Roberta reached Tel Hashomer five minutes late. The buses had backed up and gotten snarled in traffic. Some of her patients had already arrived for their appointments. Others came early, hoping they could be fit in. And these were just the outpatients. She smiled vaguely at all of them. They wouldn't be offended. They knew her Hebrew was still weak. She checked the schedule of hospital patients assigned to her. Four new amputees, one breast cancer, three nerve disorders, assorted elbow and leg ailments. She checked the causes. Illness, yes that existed even in Israeli hospitals. Along with terrorist bombings, war zone injuries, car accidents. She breathed deeply and called out the first name. She was ready to begin her morning of small victories and terrible defeats.

What touched her most over her months of working in the hospital were the soldiers from the front lines. They were like puppies looking up to her, hoping for her assurance that everything would be right. It wouldn't be. Once a leg or arm is gone, it's gone. And yet these boys hung on with the same tenacity that allows a lone tree to survive on a sheer cliff. The soldiers were like the tree of Israel. Their roots in the land were deep. They and their country would survive.

Michael came to fetch her for lunch. He was an orthopedic surgeon with whom she had worked often over the long months. At first he had been cold and abrupt with her, arrogant. Typically Israeli, always seeking self-protection by cloaking himself in a rotten personality. But over the months of working together they had become buddies, until now there was practically nothing they could not say to each other. When Michael didn't come to get her, she sometimes worked straight through her shift, not wanting to disappoint those who had made the long trek out to Tel Hashomer. But today he was there with his Giveret Ewan, may-I-see-you-for-consultation look.

They went to the *miznon* and bought sandwiches and soda. This winter day was nice so they walked out on the grounds looking for a sunny place to eat, usually someone's car hood, anything to get away from the stench of the hospital.

"Today?" Michael asked.

"Today I nearly killed a patient."

"Only one?"

She laughed. "Oh, it was so awful. It was this guy, he was driving a *sherut* up from Jerusalem, tried to pass a truck, ran head-on into a Fiat. The family in the Fiat, all dead. Five of them. The two *sherut* passengers sitting next to the driver—kaput, plus two in the backseat courtesy of the truck. That's nine deaths in one accident. And the sherut driver can't see that he's to blame. Why do they give these crazy people licenses?"

"Or why don't they take the license away?" Michael asked. "It's funny, isn't it. If there had been nine people killed in some military action, there would have been national mourning and an investigation; but on the road in Israel it's just considered an everyday occurrence."

"I can't listen to this man's blathering. I can't treat him. And yet I know I must."

"Duty first," Michael said, drifting away.

She looked at him and realized she loved Michael. Not in the way she loved Ovadia. Nothing so sensual. But Michael was her soulmate. He could share himself where Ovadia couldn't. She had never had a male soulmate before. There had been girl friends who would know exactly what she was feeling, but this was the first time it had happened with a man. He was Israeli, she supposed that was why. Israeli men were different. They seemed honestly to like women, to feel comfortable with them. There was no constant sexual friction in their conversation. They accepted women as equal partners in a dialogue. "An agorah for your thoughts," she said quietly.

He shrugged. "I was just remembering. During the war all the dead and wounded came to us. Jew, Arab, it didn't matter. I was working on an Egyptian sergeant when they brought back the body of my brother. There was no time to grieve, no time to mourn. I stopped in mid-suture and looked down at this Egyptian and thought, but for you my brother would be in Tel Aviv selling insurance. I wanted to kill him. I wanted to take the scissors and plunge them into this Egyptian's heart."

"So what did you do?"

"He had some of the neatest sutures I did during the war. I was so overwhelmed with guilt for those primitive feelings of mine that I took an extra long time trying not to hurt him, to patch him up perfectly. He was very grateful. He kissed my hand. He had expected us to be monsters. And I was."

"But you weren't."

"I am so sick of being a Jew. I am tired of balancing the

ethics of my life between war and peace, love and hate, life and death. I despair of ever deciding what is right or wrong on the West Bank, Gaza, the Golan. I want to be an Arab. I want to lose myself in a frenzy of emotionalism. I want the release of fury in their ritualistic bloodletting. I am tired of Moses and his law. I don't want always to have to do the right thing. Can you understand?" he asked quietly.

"I'm not Jewish."

He laughed. "That's right. I keep forgetting."

"Sometimes I do too. It's very hard to live in Israel and not consider oneself Jewish. My son, Zack, if he were in America, he would want to be a policeman, a fireman. Do you know what he wants to be here?"

"A fighter pilot."

"How did you know?"

"They all do."

Shoshana was sometimes shocked when she caught sight of more than her hair or her eyes in the mirror. It seemed many times as if she were not Shoshana at all but someone different, deader. She asked David once if he had noticed any difference in her. He had told her she looked happy, serene. "Are you sure I don't look deceased?" she asked him, and he had laughed at first, thinking she had been joking. But when he found that she was not, he had busied her with extra work and introduced her to that new immigrant from Russia who had sold him his samovar. She had seen this immigrant several times, but she dropped him.

How could Danny go back to Ronit? This was the one item that nagged at her. At first when she had heard it, if Danny had been there, she would have taken a knife and sliced open his belly. Ronit, that pig! She must be in her glory. And Danny couldn't be satisfied with her sexually. Which meant he probably had taken another mistress in London. Sometimes she tried to get her hands on the raw reports that came in from Great Britain, but usually they caught on to her. Iraq and Great Britain were just not that

491

close in the files. Still it seemed he hadn't even given a thought to her since he left. He never sent regards, not even a postcard of Buckingham Palace. He had told her to let their love die. It had not. It had certainly soured when she found out about Ronit's joining him. But die? She supposed it would never really be dead until another love took its place. She had tried to find that love. She had searched for it among second cousins, friends, friends of friends, new immigrants. Nothing. She had some good times. She had some laughs, some cries. But nothing, nothing like Danny. "Choose one," Lily would beg her. "Love will grow in time." But how could Shoshana be sure? And if she wasn't sure, why should she take a chance?

34

Hillel parked his car on a side street and made his way quietly up the winding sidewalk toward his house. His suspicions had been aroused when after Gil had reached eight months of age, Sarah still refused him marital relations because she was breast-feeding and didn't want to sour her milk. How long could a woman, even one like Sarah, go without sex and not look as strung out as she felt. And this cousin of hers, this Shaul Darom, had made himself completely at home in Hillel's house despite the repeated hints Hillel dropped that he should go. What did Shaul find so interesting around Hillel's house if it wasn't his cousin, Hillel's wife. Sarah.

Sarah lay naked in the master bedroom of her split-level house as Shaul poured over her body. She had just finished feeding Gil, and now her boy was asleep; but her breasts still tingled with the sensation of his sucking. She wondered, was it right to feel this way after nursing? She would ask her mother, no, her sister if she ever returned to Israel. Her sister had written her. Be careful, she had said. Her husband, that Hal Evans, has written to their father making inquiries about "cousin" Shaul Darom. So far their father had written nothing in return, not wanting to shame the family any further than her early pregnancy had. But she and Shaul must have a care.

"Shaul," she moaned. How could she have a care when he was between her legs, eating away at her while she arched against him and called his name. She never could resist him. Not from the first. Not from when he put his hands on her and told her what he wanted. She knew even then who he was, how cruel he could be, but never to her. "In me, Shaul, in me," she begged. He moved his dripping body up along hers as she lifted her hips and threw her legs around him to hasten his entry. She waited for the first thrust, gloried when it came and he ground against her. Her little shrieks gathered as he plowed her, each shriek becoming slightly louder as he worked his way to the top.

"Shaul!" she exploded. It was not with her usual intonation. He lifted his head to find her eyes wide with fright. He glanced over to the doorway. Hillel was standing there in shock, watching them. Maybe he didn't do it this way. "Were you invited?" Shaul asked him.

He regretted that later. It was a trigger. Hillel sprang at them, and Shaul had to leave poor Sarah lying there while he moved fast and brought Hillel down with one quick punch to the stomach.

Sarah looked at him as if he were a madman. "What are we going to do?" she screamed.

He gave her a look that shut her up. Then he gently kicked Hillel in the ribs as he lay on the rug. "Hey, killer," he said, "are you going to stay down there all day?"

Hillel stared up at the two naked people sitting on his bed. "Get out of my house," he ordered them. Shaul Darom just gazed down at him and smiled. With effort Hillel grabbed onto the edge of the bed and rose. "I mean it," he said when he was upright. "I want you both out of here. You slut," he whispered hoarsely to Sarah.

Shaul rose again as Sarah begged him not to do anything. He grabbed Hillel by the nose and pulled him out of the bedroom. "I don't want you saying that sort of thing to Sarah," he warned Hillel. "She's a very sensitive girl. And no talk about getting out of this house either. I don't want to break up this happy family unit."

"What are you talking about?" Hillel said. "You think I don't know that Gil's not my child?"

Shaul smiled at him. "I think you didn't know till half an hour ago."

"I can prove Gil's not my child. So why should I have the two of you around?"

The smile never left Shaul's face as he said, "Come here, I want to show you something." Hillel followed him down the stairs and into the basement. He only hoped that none of the neighbors was peeking through the curtains, as Shaul remained completely naked. Once in the basement Shaul moved through several storage cases till he found what he was looking for. He took out a box and opened it up. He held up strands of pearls and ribbons of gold. "Nice, aren't they?" he asked.

Hillel was mystified.

"Stolen property," Shaul explained. "You see, you kept telling me to get a job. You were an older man giving me advice, and I respected you for that. Especially since you kept us on such a tight household budget."

"I will tell the police," Hillel threatened.

"You could try," Shaul concluded. "You're such an outstanding citizen that you might recover from the bad publicity. Then again while they're investigating, something might happen to you. Car accident. Mugging?"

"They'd catch you."

"Me? You've got to be crazy. I wouldn't have to do it. I'm not alone in this. So if I thought our operation was threatened, I'd just pick up the phone and make a call. Any time, any hour, any day. But I'm not—I'm not a killer at heart. My basic philosophy is live and let live. I thought that was yours too. I thought you understood. That's why I was ever so surprised when you did something so perverted as standing in the doorway watching us. There are porno films for that sort of thing. Or if you have the money, hire a couple of people. Now I think you'll discover that I'm very easy to get along with. We both are, Sarah and I. You'll find your clothes washed, your meals made. Perhaps the bedroom arrangements will have to be switched now that the charade is over. But these are all arrangements we can work out together. As friends. Understand?"

"You're not even Iraqi, are you?" Hillel asked.

"Iraqi, Algerian, what does it matter? We're all Jews. That's what counts." He smiled. "You understand that, don't you?"

Hillel didn't answer. He turned around and walked up the basement stairs. He had more important things to think about. The benefit taking place in Miami Beach for one. After the fund raising was over, he'd contemplate attending to his own slum clearance.

Joshua Benjamin waited while the sergeant looked over his papers. "You can drive a truck?" the sergeant said.

"Yes. Safely," Joshua pointed out and was pleased to note the sergeant's smile.

"So you want to be in an armored division?"

"Something like that, yes."

The sergeant shrugged. "I see you're an only son."

"Yes."

"Do your parents have any idea you want to go into a combat unit?"

"Sure."

"So there's no problem there?"

"No, of course not."

"Because sometimes boys come in and feel it's their duty to serve in a combat unit while their parents feel it's their duty to stay alive and produce grandchildren."

"I've been in Gadna all through high school. My best friend's going through pilot training. I don't want to make Tzahal my career, but I don't want to shirk my responsibility."

"There's lots of things you can do behind the front lines. There's enough glory for everyone."

"I don't want to be a *jobnik*. Sorry."

The sergeant laughed and handed him a mimeographed sheet of paper. "Your parents have to sign this. It's a permission slip for you to be in a combat unit."

"Isn't that rather childish."

"Also rather necessary."

Joshua took the slip and rose. "Any idea when I'll be called?"

The sergeant shook his head. "None. But you'll be working with your father until you're called up, right? So we'll find you. Don't worry." He shook Joshua's hand and told him to send in the next boy on the way out.

Joshua left the center and boarded a bus for home. He studied the permission slip, read it carefully. He knew damn well his parents weren't going to sign it, especially his mother who became teary-eyed every time she thought of him in uniform. She could really be embarrassing sometimes. Well, it didn't matter. He had friends. One signature was as good as another.

Roberta and Ovadia walked slowly along Rehov Einstein in Ramat Aviv, accompanying their daughter's *gan*. All their friends had told them the Independence Day celebration was an event not to be missed; so when the *gannenet* had asked for parents to volunteer, she and Ovadia had agreed, as had Margaret, her South African friend, who had to retire from the hospital with her expanding pregnancy. Everyone who came to Israel seemed to get pregnant. It was like an industrial quota that had to be filled. Now the children from all over Ramat Aviv were pouring into the local military camp for the celebration. Roberta wondered how many mothers like her had to rush out to buy white shirts and blue shorts for their children. Probably only the new immigrants, as everyone else seemed to have them already from previous festive occasions.

Roberta was proud of her children. There was such a difference between them now in May from last September when they had first come. Now no one ever mistook them for Americans. She was the only one of her family who didn't speak perfect Hebrew. Last September everything they did seemed to be unsettled. Now all was perfectly natural, even confronting the aggravating bureaucracy. And even as she longed for her home, her stove, her dishwasher, her television, her possessions in Urbana, she didn't know how she was going to return to that staid, uneventful existence. Life in Israel was not what anyone would call comfortable, but at least one felt life had meaning. Each person in Israel mattered for good or ill. This was not the case in the United States.

Ovadia poked her. There was Zack with his *gan* just three classes away from Deborah's. She went over to say hello to her son, but at five he was already a tough guy with his *haverim*, and mommies were excluded.

Now all the classes were drawn up into circles with their teachers while the lead teacher stood on a platform and directed the singing. It was a massive if disharmonious display of young talent. Then the soldiers from the camp came around and gave each child a flag to wave while *"Ha-Degel Sheli"* and *"Kol ha-Aretz Degalim"* were sung. Finally the grand moment came when the head of the army camp, a colonel, rose to speak to the youngsters, none of them older than six. Roberta didn't pay attention to most of the remarks, as Hebrew still had a tendency to slide over her, but the last one before the singing of *"Ha-Tikva"* caught her attention. The colonel said, "Now I want all of you to be good little boys and girls so that when you grow up you can be good soldiers." The children applauded, quieting only with the playing of the national anthem.

Roberta was startled. She watched as her future air traffic controller and her future fighter pilot streamed out of the camp with their classes. "Ovadia—"

"Don't say it," he warned her. "Not here." He had made it through a whole year in Israel without being called for the reserves. He didn't want to make himself the center of attention in an army camp.

"Good boys and girls so they can be good soldiers?"

"Well, what do you want them to do, spring it on them when they're eighteen?"

"I don't like this attitude. It's not right for young children to grow up expecting to fight for their country."

"Write a letter to the chief of staff."

She wouldn't write a letter to the chief of staff. She had already written enough letters of complaint. People in high places, if they compared notes, might think there was a crackpot named Roberta Ewan let loose with a pen in Israel. Still, it bothered her. What did she want for her children? They were so young she barely gave it a thought. But she had a feeling the Israeli army was not it.

Joshua was in his room combing his hair when his mother came in, as usual without knocking. She watched him for a while, then asked, "Are you going out?"

"Yes, Mom." He picked up some money on his desk and put it in his pocket along with his comb.

"Where?"

"Ilanit is having a small Independence Day party."

"How small?" she asked accusingly.

"A few classmates, that's all," he said, annoyed.

"Has your father spoken to you about certain things?"

He blushed. "Mother," he pleaded. He pushed past her and went out into the hallway. "Good-bye, Father," he called.

"Have a good time," Joseph told him absentmindedly.

Lily watched her son go. Then she walked over to where Joseph was reading the newspaper. "Do you think you should have encouraged him?"

"What?" He wasn't paying any attention to her.

She raised her voice. "He's going over to that Ilanit's again and you told him to have a good time."

Joseph looked up at her and finally understood. He laughed and pulled her down into his lap. "I worry about him, Joseph," Lily said sternly. "He's over at her place every chance he gets. Her parents are going to think he doesn't have a home of his own. And what if they're doing things?" She did not specify.

Joseph sighed. "Joshua's a good boy. He's seeing a lot of

Ilanit because she's smart and they study together for their *bagrut*."

"You've really been taken in, haven't you? Have you seen her with that long blond hair of hers all braided on top of her head? I don't think they do much studying. And she's not even Iraqi."

"In a few months they'll both be in the army and then it will be all over between them," Joseph said. He fingered her hair. "Old woman." He kissed her. "Wouldn't you like blond grandchildren?"

She smiled at him. Their son eighteen. They had lived a lifetime together and yet it seemed so short. It had been a good forever. "Do you know from our bedroom window we can probably see the fireworks at the Iriyah?"

"Um." He smiled at her as she reached inside his shirt. "It sounds promising."

Roberta was rushing through the wards trying to find Lieutenant Magen. She had spent hours with him trying to convince him physical rehabilitation was worth the effort. One day he would come, the next day he wouldn't. And his injuries weren't even that serious. If they had been due to enemy action, she was sure Lieutenant Magen would have acted heroically to overcome his disability, but this was a military car crash in Ashdod. Nothing glorious, just your typical Israeli maniacal driving. For people who supposedly held life so dear, they all had a definite tendency toward highway suicide.

Frustrated, she tore off down the corridor and found her way blocked by a delegation of military personnel come to cheer up the troops. She could tell by the width of the bars who was the commanding officer, so she placed herself in front of him, demanding attention. Orders would probably be her only way to reach Lieutenant Magen. "Are you from the air force?" she rudely interrupted his goodwill spiel to one of the soldiers.

"Navy," the commander answered, slightly surprised at being addressed by one of the staff members. She quickly explained about Lieutenant Magen. The commander promised he would try to find him and have a talk with him. Orders were out. They didn't do things that way in Israel. She hated humanistic armies.

But she was pleased to see that Lieutenant Magen meekly showed up for his therapy, even if he arrived just as she was about to take her break. Duty first, she continued working with him. She was almost through with his session when the naval officer showed up and gave Lieutenant Magen a few more words of encouragement. She thanked him profusely. 'Next time I'll know what the navy uniform looks like," she promised.

"There's not many of us," he admitted. "My name is Johnathan Ben-Gal."

She nodded, recognizing his name from the newspaper. "You're in charge of the navy."

"Yes."

She hesitated, fearing she should keep her mouth shut. But, "I knew of someone in the navy once. Danny Ze'ev?"

"Yes, Danny! He's in London now. How do you know Danny?"

She leaned against her parallel bars. "Well, I don't know him exactly but he used to be—um—how would one put this? He used to live with my sister-in-law." She saw this Jonathan was very puzzled. "Shoshana Ewan."

"Shoshana! You can't possibly be Shoshana's sister-in-law."

"You know her then?"

"Of course."

"I married her brother. He got his degree in America. We met there."

He shook his head. "Shoshana. How is she?"

Roberta shrugged. "Whatever happened between them? Do you know? I hear rumors from the rest of the family, but they basically want to forget about it."

"I just saw him last week," Jonathan confessed.

"And?"

"He asked about her."

"So? How confusing. They both still care for each other, but she's here and he's in London. What happened?"

Jonathan shrugged. "I can't figure it myself. He's obviously unhappy in London with his wife. He talked about Shoshana for half an hour, saying over and over again how he had done the right thing for both of them. It was very strange. One day two years ago he walked into my office and claimed he had to leave Israel because he was destroying her."

"So now neither of them is happy."

"It must be true love."

Joseph put the phone down and stopped his son from leaving the apartment.

"But I have to go over to Ilanit's house to study," Joshua protested.

"Not tonight. You can call her and tell her you can't come."

"Oh, come on!" he moaned.

"Call her!"

Lily came out of the kitchen. She stared at her husband. Joseph never raised his voice. Not at their son.

Joseph ordered Lily back into the kitchen.

"How dare you?" Joseph said once Lily had gone.

"Dare I what, Father? I didn't do anything," he said quickly.

"The army just called."

"Oh." Joshua thought he was beginning to understand.

"They were checking on the signatures."

"I can explain that."

Joseph's response was to slap Joshua hard across the face. He watched while tears gathered at the corners of his son's eyes. Why, how had he done that? He grabbed Joshua and held him tight, kissing the bruised cheek. He held him in his arms and rocked him even though they were the same height. "You can't go," he told him.

Joshua pulled away from his father. He was horrified at what had just happened because he never believed his father could be so upset with him. But that did not change his mind about the army. "I must."

"You can't. We won't let you."

"Father, do you think I want everyone to laugh at me? There's little Joshua. He can't play with guns because his mommy and daddy don't want him hurt."

Joseph stared at his son in astonishment. "You don't play with guns in the army," he told him. "Is that what you think? Go with Roberta one day to the hospital. Let her show you what a gun can do. Go to Kiryat Shaul. See how neat the graves are. See how many. That's what comes from playing with guns, Joshua."

"You're always talking about duty."

"You have a duty to serve in the army. And you'll fulfill it. But you don't have a duty to fight. You are our only son. What would we do the rest of our lives without you?"

"Nothing's going to happen to me."

"Nothing's ever going to happen to anyone. But it does. Now forget this nonsense."

"I cannot forget it, Father. I am a man."

"If you were a man, you would have come to me with this paper and asked me to sign it," Joseph flashed. "Now go into your room and study."

Joshua turned in anger from his father and marched to his room. Who did his father think he was, ordering him around like that. He wouldn't take it. He didn't have to anymore. One more month and he'd be free of them. He would be in the army, he would marry Ilanit, make his own living, start a business of his own. What right did his father have to tell him where to study, when to eat, how much to spend? He was sick of it. He took out his knapsack and threw some clothes in it. And his books. He still had to pass that damned *bagrut*. He slipped the knapsack on and walked out of his bedroom. His mother and father were conspiring near the kitchen. He tried to quietly make it to the front door.

"Where are you going?" Joseph asked him sharply. Joshua shrugged. "Get back to your room."

"I'm not going back to my room. I'm not going to stay here anymore. Then you won't have any say over what I do. I'm sick and tired of being the focus of your life. It's not my fault Mother couldn't have any more children. I won't bear the burden for it."

His father was moving on him. But he had the tactical advantage. Joshua was already at the door and his father's limp would slow him down considerably. He rushed out of their front door and raced down the stairs before his father made it to the first landing. Finally. He would be free.

"Thanks a lot," Shoshana said when Joshua finally explained what had happened. She was less sympathetic than he had expected. "Why did you choose me? Wasn't there someone else you could have bugged?"

"I knew you would understand. After all, Danny was an only child."

"Danny is long gone. Lily is my sister. You are her baby, the center of her life. No, I don't understand, Joshua. I served in the army. I didn't go into combat. Ovadia, why don't you talk to him? He was a *jobnik*. There was nothing shameful in it."

"But he was bright. He had a purpose. They had a place for him."

"They'll find a place for you too."

"Yeah. Filing papers."

"It's not a question of being either in Tel Aviv or on the Golan," Shoshana explained. "If you're not in a combat unit, you can be with the support units. At the front."

"Like what support unit?"

"Like ordnance."

"Oh, yeah. How exciting."

"Maybe not exciting, but what they do is vital. And you're a good mechanic. They'd probably be pleased to have you if you expressed a preference. Do you realize how quickly they can turn a tank around and make it serviceable again after it's been hit by enemy fire? They're very important if you don't have all the tanks in the world, which we don't."

He wasn't convinced. "And what will Ilanit think of me when she finds out my parents won't let me go into combat and I didn't do anything about it?"

"First of all, there's nothing you will be able to do about it. I can guarantee you that. I know your mother. Nothing will make her give her permission for you to have combat status. Second, if that's what you think makes a man, rushing off into combat with your rifle blazing, then I feel sorry both for you and for Ilanit."

"Why? Wasn't that a turn-on with Danny?" he asked hostilely.

She was annoyed. Little boys were all the same, and all men were little boys. "Turn-on? I take it you're addressing me in the sexual vernacular? No. It wasn't. Every time I knew Danny was away fighting, my stomach was tight." She made a fist. "I was like that the whole time until I knew he was safe again. I hated him for it, Joshua, hated him because he enjoyed it. He didn't think about the fear or the danger, but I was left here at home waiting and praying, hoping and hanging on. You have the wrong idea of what women want in a man. Not a hero, not a martyr. Someone who's strong, responsible, someone who cares, someone who knows how to love. Someone who's there for you when you need him. We want the same thing in a man as you would want in a woman."

Joshua actually hung his head. "You think I'm wrong then?"

"I think you have to compromise. It'll hurt you; it'll make you angry. But you'll be more of a man for accepting this decision of your parents than you would be for marching off into combat."

"I don't believe it."

"Not now. But when you have your own son, you'll understand." She stood up. "I'm going to call Lily. She'll never forgive me when she learns you rushed over here to me. But I'm going to be brave about it. I'll tell her you'll stay the night and be home tomorrow."

"Will you help me with my Arabic then?"

Surprised, she looked at him. "Do you need it?"

"I'm not so great with the grammar."

Shoshana shook her head. Only one generation removed and their heritage had come to this. Would it all be forgotten in his son's time?

Hesitation marked every step Roberta had taken to Shoshana's apartment. It was none of her business, she told herself. Besides, how well did she know Shoshana? She was Ovadia's sister, that was all. It was not as if they were intimates. She tried to remove herself from too close an involvement in Ovadia's family. They were always scrapping with each other about something, so why was she sticking her nose in concerning Shoshana and Danny. She was a fool, that was why.

She came bearing gifts, a bottle of wine and some cake. Shoshana had just washed her hair and was definitely surprised to see her. "What's this?" she asked.

"I thought we'd get drunk together," Roberta explained. "It's an old American custom." Shoshana left the door open. "Ovadia's not coming. It's just me," Roberta informed her.

Shoshana closed the door and continued toweling down her hair. She was surprised to see her sister-in-law, especially in the middle of the week and alone at that. They saw each other on Shabbat mainly with the kids and the rest of the family. During the week they were both too busy and too tired after their work was over. But now here Roberta was.

"Bourbon would have been quicker," Roberta explained as she brought two glasses from the kitchen and filled them with wine. "But I had the feeling you were much too Israeli to take to bourbon."

"Is there madness in your method?" Shoshana said, as she took a sip from her glass and sat down on the couch.

"I don't know," Roberta said, still standing. "If we ever got drunk enough, there might be." She paced the floor. "You see, I don't understand you. I don't understand Ovadia, right, so how could I understand you?"

"What's to understand about Ovadia?"

"Do you know he talks in his sleep? Some language I don't even recognize. Not Hebrew, not Arabic. Do you know he's afraid of things? I'm not afraid of anything, Shoshana. I don't think it's bravery. I think it's probably ignorance, but there it is." Shoshana smiled. "You agree with me?"

"You're an American." To Shoshana that was the explanation.

"I met Jonathan Ben-Gal a week ago."

Shoshana said nothing. Now she knew why Roberta had brought the wine. Her sister-in-law wanted to pry. But she had closed that part of her life off, and she didn't want to open it again, not for Roberta. It wasn't dead as Danny had wished. It was just sealed tight, condemned.

"If you don't want to hear this, I won't go on."

"I don't want to hear this."

Roberta nodded, smiled. "You're right of course. Ben-Gal indicated that Danny was rather miserable. And since you seem to be too, I thought—but it's none of my business. I'm sorry I've intruded. Keep the wine. It's definitely too sweet for me." She left.

Roberta felt guilty. Why couldn't she have kept her mouth shut? Why open old wounds? She was glad Shoshana had more sense than she had. She should never have brought Danny up. But the conversation with Ben-Gal kept preying on her mind. If Shoshana knew, maybe everything would be all right again. But Shoshana saw what she hadn't. Everything wouldn't be all right again. It would just be the same. And why get into that?

The phone rang. At first she thought it was the neighbor's because they got a lot of late phone calls, but the ringing didn't stop. Ovadia refused to wake up, so she slipped out of bed into her clogs and made her way to the living room. She picked it up. "Hello?"

"Roberta, it's me."

"Shoshana?"

"Yes. What did you mean when you said Danny was miserable?"

507

35

Shoshana would go to London. That was all there was to
it. Jonathan had said he was miserable. How miserable?
Stupid Roberta, she didn't even bother trying to find out.
How did Danny look? Were the lines any deeper around
his eyes? Had he stopped eating? Or had he gotten fat?
Roberta hadn't found out anything!

No, it was up to her. She didn't have any pride. She
would crawl on her hands and knees to him. Hands and
knees? On her belly if need be. She couldn't wait.

"Ta-dum!"

David looked up from his desk and sniffed. He had gotten his early summer cold, which he could barely distin-
guish from his spring cold. And here was Shoshana a veri-
table flower garden of smiles standing before him like a
goddess. This was indeed a change from the grim gray lady
of the past months. "What's with you?"

"I've come to collect my vacation."

"Didn't you just have it?"

"When?" she asked angrily.

"The seder."

"Oh, very funny, David. I'm serious this time. I want it now." She was leaning over his desk. He looked into her eyes; she bent over and kissed him full on the lips. He was startled.

"Where do you plan to go?"

"Guess?" She caught him looking at his watch. "London." His face dropped. "David," she warned him

"Shoshana," he echoed.

"He's miserable."

"Wonderful. He should be."

"David, I love him."

David studied her. Her face was flushed, her eyes were bright. She was obviously a feverish romantic. "Sit down," he told her. "Let's talk about this. I'd like to understand the workings of a sick mind. You know as well as I do if you do get back together with Danny, nothing's going to change. His wife won't let him go, especially now that she's seen he will come back to her."

"Something's going to change."

"What?"

"I'm going to have a baby."

"Goddamn, Shoshana, whose is it?"

She laughed. "It will be Danny's. All those months ever since he left me, I said to myself, I slept with him all those years and now I'm empty. I won't be empty again, David. I'm going to have his child."

"Why?" David asked insistently. "Why him?"

She shook her head slowly and smiled. "I don't know." She placed her hand on his. "Love him for my sake."

"Let me get you a courier slot to London. It'll at least pay the travel expenses. We won't count the emotional costs."

"I don't want him to know I'm coming. I want it to be a surprise."

"I'll put your name down as Madam X on the ticket."

"You're wonderful, David."

"No, I'm not. I'm jealous," he said softly, but she was already out the door.

* * *

Shoshana was afraid. It was so silly because she knew the English language as perfectly as any foreign-speaking person could, and yet here she was in London on foreign soil and her mind froze. How did Ovadia do it? How did he talk, think, make love in English? And Danny? She took a bus in from Heathrow. At Travel they told her that would be the cheapest. One of the girls had a friend Shoshana could have stayed with, but that would not have suited her purpose, so she made a reservation at a small, inexpensive hotel near Russell Square. She had to go to the embassy first to sign over her briefcase. She was so excited she didn't even mind the security check. Any minute now she might see Danny and then—well, she at least expected lightning and thunder. But when she finally completed all the bureaucratic signings and countersignings and asked if it might be possible to see the naval attaché, she was told he was out for the day, in Cornwall. Her face fell so abruptly that the receptionist took pity on her. "Colonel Ze'ev usually stops at the Golden Coach for a pint after work."

"A whole pint?" Shoshana asked. The boy had obviously become an alcoholic without her. But she got directions and found out when after work might be. Then she checked into her hotel and tried to get some rest. She wanted to look young and beautiful, but she would settle for classy and attractive. She closed her eyes, letting her thoughts swirl between Danny and the wonderful shopping at Mark's and Spenser's. Of all the sights in London everyone told her that was the one not to be missed. She fell into a short, fitful sleep.

When she woke, she bathed and perfumed herself. She slipped into a new dress from Maskit, touted for that very special occasion, and hoped this evening would live up to it. Though of course he wouldn't be able to see her dress, as she had to wear her raincoat on top of it. England's summer was about like Israel's winter.

This time when she stepped into the streets of London, she felt more at ease with her surroundings but less at ease with herself. What if she saw Danny and he didn't want her? Worse yet, what if she didn't see Danny at all?

She had to know one way or the other. Tonight.

The Golden Coach, when she reached it, was unimpressive. It was a bar filled with wooden tables, hazy blue smoke, and lots of people just off from work. She made her way inside and sat down on one of the empty chairs at a long table. A barmaid came over to her almost immediately, even before she could ascertain who was in the pub, and asked her what she wanted. For the first time Shoshana realized she hadn't eaten since she left the plane. "Do you have sandwiches?" Shoshana asked.

The barmaid spewed off a list of which Shoshana recognized only cheese, which she gratefully grasped at.

"And a pint?" the barmaid asked.

"Fine," Shoshana said timidly.

With the barmaid gone Shoshana was able to concentrate on studying the patrons of the Golden Coach. Most of them wore suits. They were grouped together in friendly conversations, so it took her longer than she expected to realize her disappointment. Danny was not among them. Should she go? Should she wait?

She was interrupted by the barmaid again, bringing her sandwich and pint. It took her an embarrassingly long time to figure out how much to pay and tip. The barmaid gave her a patient, tired little smile and Shoshana felt ridiculous. Well, she would drink whatever this was, eat her sandwich, then go. She could see him tomorrow at the embassy. But could she bear to spend that night alone in her hotel room? She watched the door of the pub as it opened and closed a thousand times. Until he came.

She did not understand why she didn't recognize him immediately. She was in a way surprised to notice how old he looked upon seeing him after this absence. She supposed because she always thought of him the way she first saw him. And yet in a way he still had that youthful strength that had first attracted her at the building site too many years ago.

She studied him happily. He seemed rather vague. He had come in with two friends of his, and he sometimes listened to what they were saying, sometimes talked to several women at the bar who seemed to know them. But he wasn't attached. None of the women were with him. She hoped.

He first noticed her when she was taking a bite of her sandwich. How gauche. But what should she do, leave it with tooth marks or bite the piece off? She bit it off and chewed as gracefully as she could, but it didn't matter because his eyes passed right over her. So much for two souls seeking one another out.

But his eyes returned to her just as she was taking a sip of this pint, which turned out to be ghastly. She put the mug down and tried to wipe her lips delicately. He was staring at her suspiciously now. Perhaps his sight was deteriorating. Or maybe she looked as old to him as he did to her. She allowed herself a smile. He recognized that smile.

He came over slowly and sat down. "Shoshana?"

"Danny?"

"Is that you?"

She reached over and took his hands to show him she was no ghost. It was electric. "I came to tell you that I love you," she happily declared.

He held onto her hands as if they were a life preserver. "I thought we decided that we couldn't."

"You decided that we shouldn't. You idiot."

"It was a good decision, Shoshana."

She looked away from him.

"What is it?" he asked anxiously.

She smiled at him. It was a friendly smile. Not a loving one. "Jonathan told Roberta, my sister-in-law, you were miserable. I misjudged the situation. I thought you were miserable without me." With a sigh she unsteadily rose and left him.

She was weak. It was as if she was walking on a pillow, she seemed to have trouble getting her feet to move from one piece of pavement to another. She was glad it was cold outside. She felt like collapsing but the cold would keep her going. Someone's arm wrapped around her, supporting her.

It took her a while to realize it was Danny. But then who else would it have been? They stopped. She looked into his eyes and saw pain. "I don't want to hurt you anymore."

"You left me once. You thought it best. Should I leave you now in hopes of avoiding some future sorrow we can't even guess at? I can't be that brave, Danny. I don't want to spend another moment without you."

His arms covered her and she felt her body close against his. His lips came to hers. They tasted of salt and beer and passion. They were incredibly soft, smooth, inviting. He broke off. "We can't," he told her.

"What . . ." She failed.

"Not here in the street. They don't do it that way in England."

"I have a room."

She led him there. Every step she took she felt her body become more alive. He unlocked the door for her. She stepped inside and waited for him. He came to her and slowly began to undress her. Whatever she remembered about their lovemaking, there was a difference in this union. They touched each other as if they were blind. Every curve, every wrinkle, every smile, every tear was new. Danny leaned over her and made her climax without him, watching each thrust of her body, each contortion of her face, as she desperately called for him. "I've dreamed of this," he told her as he at last joined her and she could feel him searching within her. "I've dreamed of that agony since the day I left you. I've tried to remember whether you came in pain or joy."

"Regret," she told him. "Only regretting that it couldn't go on forever. But now it can. Now we know that it has to." She urged him on, rocking her body against his, feeling him carrying on his terrible work within, and let the sun streak to her.

Afterward there wasn't enough time to say everything, but they tried. She had forgotten amidst the turmoil and the lovemaking how much fun they actually had together, how much laughter they shared, even at their bleakest moments. Like now—what was Ronit going to say? "Not again," Shoshana suggested. Danny thought of more insightful comments like, "You schmuck." And then Jonathan Ben-Gal, how quickly could he get Danny transferred back to Israel. It was such a mess. But they had time, her two-week vacation to straighten it out, in their own minds at least. They decided to spend the vacation in Britain and on the continent. It was a good time. The best. They felt like children sneaking away on a forbidden holiday. They toured London, Scotland, Paris, the south of France. It gave them time to realize that nothing had changed. Nothing ever would. She confessed to him about wanting a child no matter what. He had kissed her and redoubled his effort. And then it was over. They left each other in Paris. He flew back to London, she to Tel Aviv.

Ronit sat in the living room of their London apartment and listened to what Danny had to say. She was grim, more because she had been expecting this than from the words he was mouthing.

Danny awkwardly tried to explain.

"Why can't you love me, Danny?"

Danny paused to consider whether she really wanted an answer. He knew he had made her suffer. She wasn't young anymore. What had been pleasantly plump in her youth had turned to flab. She never exercised. Her face bordered on middle age. But she had been good to him since they came to London. She had not reproached him with Shoshana or anything else. Of course she had gotten what she wanted. Him. And London. It had been embarrassing for her among their circle before he called her, and now she was the envy of all her friends in Israel. She loved being an embassy wife and all it entailed in that closed society.

He didn't hate Ronit the way he had when they were feuding over the divorce. But he didn't love her either. "We were too young," he said weakly. "I didn't know what I wanted. I just fell into things. Like our marriage. I know now what I want."

"And it's not me."

"If we had met ten years later, I could have been decent to you. I would have been understanding."

"Not so immature?"

"Yes."

"But if we had met ten years later, you would have been married to Shoshana. Would she be the one you deceived and humiliated?"

Danny sucked in his breath. "I'm sorry," he said too kindly.

"Does she know about your other women?" Ronit waited. "Does she? No, of course not. You didn't tell her, did you?"

"Shoshana's no fool. She knows I wouldn't go two years without—"

"Someone other than your wife? And her? Has she gone without?"

"I didn't ask her. I never will."

"You can have it, Danny."

"What?"

"The divorce. You're not worth fighting over. I don't think I should give you that satisfaction anymore."

He dared to breathe again. "Thank you, Ronit."

"Two conditions. I expect you to continue to support Adee and me."

"Agreed."

"And I don't want you to get the divorce until your term of service here is over. I don't need everyone laughing at me in London. When we get back to Tel Aviv, it will be bad enough."

"That's okay with me." He rose. "Shall we wait to tell Adee?"

"Yes. No sense in ruining what's left for her." She watched him put on his coat and walk to the door of their apartment. It was obvious he couldn't wait to leave. "Danny!" He looked up at her. "I hate you."

"I'm sorry," he said meekly before he left. His eyes hadn't even flickered. Her hatred meant nothing to him, her love equally nothing. She had lost him.

* * *

Roberta was counting hand luggage and children, trying to hang on to everything among the swarm of relatives that had come to see her and Ovadia off at Lod airport. It was the beginning of September, 1973, and they were leaving Israel. She had not really wanted to go but was confused as to whether she wanted to stay or not. If she could have lingered in limbo in Israel, she would have been happy. If she didn't have to accept Israel's daily problems as indelibly her own. The inflation, the discomfort, death on the highway, litter, bureaucracy, all the little petty harassments that could drive one crazy if one had no choice except to live with them. Michael had told her to join them, stay at the hospital with him and work her ass off. She might have had Ovadia been willing, which he wasn't, except one thing about Israel really bothered her. The total corruption that pervaded the society in all dealings—writing checks, claiming car allowances, dealing with banks and/or the black market, trying to get by by lying and deception. She was not a law-and-order type person, but it bothered her that laws meant nothing in Israel. They weren't even made to be broken, they were made to be flouted. Traffic laws. No one cared. Tickets were torn up under the noses of policemen who did nothing. Criminals were treated as *boychiks* who had a bad day, they had gotten caught. Government corruption, cheating on one's taxes, padding one's salary, these were the accepted norms. And yet everyone claimed their personal integrity was intact. Well, she wasn't quite so sure that the line between personal and public morality could be so finely drawn. Her conclusion after a year in Israel was that nothing worked except its army. When Michael had told her she had reached that conclusion only because she had never been on an army base, she was really worried. Yet life in Israel could be pleasant, was pleasant, fulfilling, good friends, happy and sad times shared. A real community. Unlike the United States. Unlike Urbana. "We'll come back," Ovadia promised her when she bemoaned the thought of reentering the American mainstream. But her anxieties were not stayed. "What's your problem?" he finally snapped. "You're not even Jewish." She laughed. The poor man. She might not have converted according to the halakah, but one year in Israel had certainly warped her WASP identity.

Lily was crying. "Joshua wished so much that he could come and see you off," she said. But Joshua was just about to finish his basic training, and then he would be sent immediately to an ordnance unit for lessons on repairing tanks. He was happy. A little moody at times for not being in a combat unit like many of his friends, but he could see how fixing tanks might be worthwhile, though how he would ever use it in civilian life, he didn't know. "He'll be safe," was all Lily could think of.

"Keep making money," Roberta told Joseph in a final embrace.

Shoshana was there, glowing. She was pregnant. She had confided to Ovadia and Roberta two days before they were to leave Israel, as long as they swore not to tell anyone else. "Well, I'm glad to see Danny wasn't too exhausted by his transcontinental flights," Roberta commented. But Ovadia took the situation more seriously. It was one thing to take a lover, even that was unacceptable. But to have a child out of wedlock? Shoshana hushed him. Danny had finally straightened everything out with the navy. He would be returning to his regular duties after Yom Kippur. As soon as he and Ronit set foot in Israel, they would get a divorce. It would be a matter of days. Ronit had already agreed to it. So a baby coming a month or two early wouldn't matter to anyone. "Finally things are working for you," Roberta said.

"Yes. Thanks to you," Shoshana had whispered. It had been their secret, the part Roberta had played getting Danny and Shoshana back together. Somehow neither felt the family would applaud her efforts.

They talked aimlessly now as they waited for the flight to be called. Ovadia stood patiently listening to his father claim he hadn't fled Iraq to have both of his sons wind up in America, where he never would have a chance to see his grandchildren growing up. "Good point," Roberta whispered in her husband's ear. Ovadia grimaced and was saved by the flight announcement. "We'll be back," he promised his family.

Roberta counted hand luggage and children again, as she stepped onto the escalator on their way to flight departures. She chanced a look back once, but the only salt that formed was from the tears running down her cheeks.

36

Andrew Harris was worried. He had been worried for a long time, six months at least, but now his anxieties were growing. All his agents came in with the same report. Iraqi army and air force units were involved in intensive exercises. He studied the newspapers, he listened to gossip, he read confidential government reports. He could find no internal reason for the beefing up of combat units. The Kurds, they will be with us always. Syria? Iran? Where?

He held the newspaper before him. September 14, 1973. The only thing they all agreed on was that yesterday fourteen planes had been downed off the coast of Latakia in Syria. A dogfight between the Zionist aggressors and the courageous Syrian air force. Some papers split the losses evenly; some had all planes being Israeli; others ten Israeli, four Syrian. He couldn't stand the suspense. He had asked Tel Aviv. Thirteen to one. One Israeli plane lost, its pilot rescued at sea. So what did this mean? He had sent word to Yossi in Tel Aviv about the agreement between the Iraqi and the Egyptian government. Iraq would provide units to fight alongside its Syrian brothers in case of war with Israel. Was this to be it? Was this what they were preparing for? If this was the case, there must be some coordination between Iraqi and Syrian policymakers. He would have to seek this evidence out, send it back to Tel Aviv, make sure Israel was prepared for every eventuality. He went through a mental list of those who could be most helpful to him. He finished his coffee rather too quickly, dropped some coins on the plate, and rose to go. He didn't like it. Something was happening and he hadn't quite figured out what it was.

Shoshana went through the motions of working. Along with the rest of the country she looked forward to Rosh Hashanah, the start of the new year and the days that followed that would culminate in Yom Kippur. But this year she would not fast. Pregnant women were exempted from fasting. She smiled. In less than two weeks Danny would be home. He would be hers.

"What are you doing?"

She looked up and was surprised to see Oren. He had been flying around the Mideast like a maniac the past several weeks, so she could understand why he looked so strung out, but was that any reason to snap at her. "I'm working."

"With that dreamy look on your face?"

She smiled lazily. "How are you?"

"I'll tell you how I am, I'm sick." He came into her office, closed the door tight, and sat down. "Have you been hearing anything?"

"About the buildup, you mean? Of course. Hasn't everyone?" Both the Syrian and Egyptian forces along the borders were conducting war games within sight of Israeli units.

"Have you seen the aerials?"

"Not to study them," she admitted.

"There's going to be war, Shoshana."

She scoffed at him. "That's what we thought in May."

"Not May. Now. Gabby came back from Europe with a set of battle orders from the Egyptian high command. Brigade by brigade. Yossi studied them and took them over to military intelligence."

She didn't know what to say. "So what's happening?"

He laughed harshly. "Nothing."

"Nothing?"

"No mobilization. Nothing. They're thinking about calling a state of alert. They don't believe Yossi. They don't believe our reports from Egypt, Syria, Morocco, Iraq. They say only they have the complete picture, only they can make the final evaluation."

"They" was military intelligence. "Maybe they're right," Shoshana said tentatively.

"And if they're wrong?" Oren asked. "Don't you think they might reevaluate what we've been giving them? And even if they don't trust us or our sources, shouldn't their own aerial reconnaissance be worth a thousand words?"

"War?" Surely he was being an alarmist. "After we beat them so badly last time?"

"This is 'seventy-three, Shoshana, not 'sixty-seven." He rose. "I'm off."

"Where?"

"Can't say. How's Danny." He caught the full flower of her smile. "Safe in London, heh? Keep him there."

Oren left. Others left and came back again. All with pieces, but for which puzzle? She was worried; David was uneasy, on edge. No one said anything. But it was always there, that uncompleted sentence. "Do you think there will be—" Danny was safe. That was her consolation. He was in London.

When Danny got to his office in the embassy, he sat down at his desk and took a pen from the top drawer. With a great deal of pleasure, he crossed off another day. October 1. In less than a week now he would be with Shoshana. In less than two weeks they would be married. At last. It had been hell living with Ronit these past months. It had been a mistake. Lying in bed with her at night, knowing she was hating him. Once, just once he had tried to touch her, hold her, comfort her. She had pushed him away. What had he done to her? To them? He wished he could hate her. It was easier when he had hated her. But Ronit wouldn't be hated, wouldn't be loved, wouldn't be pitied. It was a cold war, a one-sided truce being declared only in the presence of their daughter, Adee.

Danny absently picked up the latest intelligence briefing from the Israeli navy. He read through it quickly, then re-read it, picking it apart phrase by phrase. Due to the redeployment of the Egyptian and Syrian navies over the past month, navy intelligence had concluded that war was imminent. Danny was surprised. There had been talk of course of the buildup, but everyone pooh-poohed it. Yet here was Jonathan Ben-Gal declaring a state of emergency for the navy. Danny picked up the phone and dialed home, his real home, naval headquarters. "Jonathan, do you need me?" he asked.

"It wouldn't hurt."

Danny was on the first plane back to Tel Aviv. With his kit bag in hand, he passed briskly through customs and reported immediately to naval headquarters, where he was welcomed like a long-lost son. They had just the spot for him. And even though general headquarters had insisted they lower their state of alert, the navy would not be caught napping. Jonathan was already giving orders for the deployment of his fleet against the Syrians and the Egyptians.

Shoshana had come home for a bite to eat and a few hours' rest. She was more tired than she had been before and sometimes she felt like a balloon, even though she knew her pregnancy didn't show as yet. Still, she must be careful. She remembered how heart-breaking Danielle's miscarriage had been, and she didn't want it happening to her.

The shower was running in her bathroom. It didn't startle her, it didn't frighten her. She knew when she heard about the state of emergency in the navy that Danny would come home. She went into the bathroom and surprised him as he was grabbing blindly for his towel. She handed it to him and watched while he quickly wiped his face free of water. He still had a beautiful body. She studied it with fascination while the remnants of the shower water coarsed slowly through his hair, winding its way down between his toes and into the drain.

"Lusting after me?"

"Go back to London."

He didn't take her seriously. Instead he waited for her while she slowly undressed. "How is he?" Danny asked, as he placed a hand on her belly.

"Go back to London?"

He lay her down on the bed and began kissing her. He was so gentle that she was afraid he would not take her. But it was just his way of making it last. Then she knew that he would be reporting for duty and she would not see him until it was all over. "I don't want to hurt you," he whispered. As if pain mattered. Not pain, not pleasure, only this, the way they moved together, the way they locked onto each other and did not surface for a very long time.

"Where?" she asked him.

"The Gulf of Suez."

"Why?"

"Because I know it like the back of my hand."

"Maybe it won't be war."

"Don't worry. We'll win."

"At what cost? It's not a soccer game."

He propped himself up on his elbow and gazed down at her. "I know that. I know the costs as well as you. They're my men."

"You're all I have, Danny. Remember that."

He smiled. "I'm invincible." He slipped down and kissed her stomach. "Milk," he told her. "Plenty of it. We must secure his future."

If only milk alone would do the trick.

He slept beside her that night, peaceful and content. At four in the morning a car came to pick him up. He promised to call. She waved good-bye from their balcony. A week, two weeks. She would force him to retire when this was over. He could become a businessman or a tour boat operator or something. They had their child to think of now. Enough was enough.

"What are you saying to us?" Ezra Haya asked the captain from the IDF. The men of El Al looked on as the women and children stood off to the side.

"I'm saying we want you to evacuate," the captain insisted.

"Evacuate a settlement? Israel doesn't evacuate settlements."

"Look!" The captain was losing his patience. It had been the same in all of the Golan settlements. These *halutzim* took a lot of convincing. Of course they'd have to be nuts choosing to live under the Syrian guns on the Golan anyway. "There is a large concentration of Syrian forces right across from you. Tanks. Thousands of them. And what if they start to roll?"

"There have always been tanks positioned across from us."

"Not in these concentrations. Your land might become a battlefield. We would feel much better if you withdrew, so we wouldn't have to worry about protecting civilian settlements as such. Believe me, we're going to have enough on our hands just dealing with the Syrians."

"If there is going to be a war," Ezra asked, "why haven't we been mobilized?"

"I'm not the chief of staff," the captain answered.

Ezra looked around him. The men of the kibbutz conferred and agreed that they were going nowhere. But the women and children? Perhaps it would be better to evacuate them. Move them to a kibbutz in the interior. Then in a few days when this war scare blew over, they could come back.

At four thirty on the morning of October 6, Yom Kippur, the Day of Atonement, Danny checked in with Shoshana. He had called every day for the past five days whenever he had the chance. One day he hadn't called till nearly midnight and she had been frantic. He had explained that he didn't want to wake her by calling early in the morning. After five minutes' worth of her complete, senseless rage, he figured out that she would rather be woken then left waiting and worried. They never said much, but that wasn't important. It was just hearing each other's voices, knowing each was still there. After Danny piped himself off, Shoshana tried to fall back to sleep, but ten minutes later the phone rang again. It was David. "It's today," he announced. "Call your section in."

Her first instinct was to call Danny back. But then he would already be prepared. He had expected this. So she telephoned her secretary and her assistant. They in their turn would notify two more who would notify two more until the whole Iraqi section was alerted. She went into the kitchen, poured a glass of milk for herself, and sipped it between dressing and putting on her make-up.

By midmorning as the rest of the country was in the synagogue praying, she reported to David's office for tea and consultation. She had in her hand a list of probable Iraqi units to be sent to the Syrian front and the personality profiles of their commanders. David flipped through her work and threw it aside. She was afraid. For him, of him, she did not know. "Can I help?" she asked softly.

David glanced at her. The sun was behind her and she looked so soft. He smiled briefly, remembering the visit to his house from Danny over a month ago when he had been in Israel to make arrangements for his return and, of course, to see Shoshana. He had come to David angry and exultant. "Your advice," he had told him, "was about the shittiest piece of advice I ever had the stupidity to take. So let me warn you, don't interfere with me and Shoshana again. My wife is giving me a divorce, Shoshana and I are to be married. I'm sure she'll want to invite you. Don't come."

"My concern was for Shoshana, not you," he had told Danny. "Just don't hurt her again."

"I didn't tell her it was you who kept us apart for two years."

"I won't be around to pick up the pieces for you again, Danny."

"Take my advice and don't be around at all."

"Why are you smiling?" Shoshana asked.

"The world has gone mad," David said grimly. "They have just started mobilizing now. This war is supposed to start at sunset—"

"Sunset? What a stupid time to start a war. There must be something wrong."

"And the government has decided. No preemptive strikes. We are going to sit back and let them attack us to prove to the world we didn't start this war."

Danielle had been to the synagogue early in the morning with Sami, but she had decided to slip away after an hour or two. She always got a headache when she fasted, so if she was going to make it through the day, she had better lie down. She entered her apartment and smelled the chicken simmering comfortably along on the Sabbath hot plate. It would be very tender and tasty, and if she didn't go to her bedroom now, she might be tempted to go into the kitchen for a nibble. She lay down on her bed and closed her eyes. The streets were so quiet on Yom Kippur. No cars, no buses, nothing moved except people walking back and forth to the synagogue. She must have drifted off because she awoke to hear shouts in the streets. Who dared break this peace? She rose and hurried to her balcony. She couldn't have slept an entire day, and yet there were men rushing back and forth below her and buses rolling through the roadways. It was unbelievable. She caught sight of Sami running from the direction of the synagogue. If she had not held the door open for him, he would have burst right through it. "What's the matter?" she asked him. "What's happened?"

"It's the goddamned Arabs," he shouted at her as he strode into their bedroom to grab his beret and identification.

"What do you mean?" she asked anxiously as she rushed in after him.

"The Arabs, those barbarians are going to attack us."

"But they can't attack us," Danielle said. "It's Yom Kippur."

He laughed at her. "Do you think they have any respect for our holy days, for God even? You lived among them long enough to know the only thing they respect is power and blood."

"When are you going?" she asked.

"Now" he said. "What does it look like?"

Now! Sami was leaving her now? For war? Her mouth hung open. How could there be a war when no one had heard about it? In '67 they had had days, weeks to prepare. But now?

"Wait." She hurried into the kitchen and grabbed some fruit, apples, oranges, all she had, washed them well, and slipped them into a plastic bag. He was watching her now and smiling. She looked up quickly, then took the cake she had made and some cookies and placed them into another bag. She put them all together in her net shopping bag and handed them to him.

"I don't think there's that much room in the tank," he kidded.

"You share them with your friends," she told him. "It's good to have something refreshing." They stared at each other. "You have to go now?" she asked.

"Now," he said.

"Where will you be? So I can think of you."

He shrugged. "The Sinai probably. That's where our crew has always been."

They came together and she felt his roughness against her skin. "I'll be back," he called to her at the door. "That's a promise. Keep the chicken on the stove for me."

She waved, but he was gone.

They were waiting for him. Joseph's call-up code was announced at the synagogue, and by the time he returned home, they were waiting by his van.

"Let's go," the lieutenant ordered. "We've got to pick up the men."

"Where to?"

"North."

He looked up at his apartment. Lily was on the balcony waving frantically to him. "Joseph," she called hysterically, "find Joshua. Bring him home."

"Come on, *habibi*," the lieutenant hurried him. "We've got to pick them up."

"Joseph," Lily shrieked, "bring me my son!"

The sergeant with the lieutenant stared upward sympathetically. "He needs time with his wife," he said.

"We all need time with our wives," the lieutenant answered. "Including the reserves isolated on the Heights."

Joseph had his duty. He tore himself away from his wife's pleading, got into the van with the two soldiers, and drove off.

Lily cursed Joseph. And his trucks. He was forty-three for God's sake. Time to give up war. Time to let the younger men fight. Except among the younger men was her son. He was safe. She felt guilty. But he was safe in the Galilee learning how to be a mechanic. Joseph would find him and bring him home to her. He knew that Joshua was her life.

It was two o'clock in the afternoon. She hadn't noticed when the air-raid sirens had begun to screech. They were lost among her wails, among the wails of all the wives and mothers of Israel.

Ezra Haya later looked upon it as an incredible joke, how he and a handful of kibbutz members were going to save El Al from the Syrian army. The tanks crushed El Al as they ground up the entire Golan. The army evacuated them, but not before they had a chance to see the entire Galilee laid open to the Syrian assault. He hadn't had time to grab his dog tags and his beret. Nor had anyone bothered to come to El Al to issue mobilization orders. But he reported to his unit of the Golani Brigade and they were definitely glad to see him. The war was not going well. Already members of their brigade had been lost or captured as the Syrians overran the Israeli position on Mount

Hermon. They didn't know if they could hold the Syrians back. "But we have to, don't we?" Ezra said to his new lieutenant. "We have no choice."

His lieutenant's eyes shifted nervously. He was green. Just out of the officers' corps. He was afraid. "There are reports that some of our infantry are running away from the Syrians."

Ezra looked around at his platoon. Half he knew from reserve duty, from '67. They could count on each other. They wouldn't fail each other. The rest were young kids doing their regular service. This was the first battle for them, and he knew they couldn't help but think about how they would react. He would speak to the reservists. He was their sergeant. He had led them up Tel Azaziat and they had survived. He would create a buddy system. One reservist, one regular. They would make it through. Or die trying. "Don't worry," Ezra told his new lieutenant. "None of us is going to be running away."

Joshua Benjamin was in the mess hall drinking coffee when his instructor approached him. "Benjamin!" he called. Joshua rose and walked outside with him. "We're in trouble," his instructor began. "The war is not going well on the Golan. Our men are barely holding on. The reserves are coming up, but slowly. Meanwhile we're one tank against five, one tank against ten, sometimes one tank against twenty. And the Iraqis and Jordanians are on their way with more tanks. We don't have enough unless we repair them, turn them around, and send them back into battle. For that we need men."

"I'll do what I can."

"We need men at the front, Joshua. We need men on the spot who, when the tank is knocked out, can go in and put it right. I'd like you to go with me because I've watched you these past few weeks and you're good. You have a knack for guessing what's wrong. But you're an only son."

"I volunteer."

His instructor patted him on the cheek. "We're taking that half-track up. Report to it in ten minutes."

* * *

"I mean they're like the Chinese," Dov was saying to Danny aboard their missile boat. "They can just keep coming and coming and coming. They're overpopulated, we're underpopulated."

"Shut up, Dov," Danny said quietly.

"Doesn't it bother you even a little bit?"

"Our field of operations is the Gulf of Suez not the Suez Canal." He said it evenly, calmly. But Dov's remark festered in him. "Of course it bothers me!" he burst out with immediate regret.

Dov smiled and clapped him on the back. It released the tension, but it did nothing to alleviate the horror of what was happening to the north of them. The Egyptians had not only successfully crossed the canal, but they were successfully beating back Israel's immediate counterattack. At night from the gulf they could see the firepower directed against their own forces. During the day they could spot Israeli Phantoms falling from the sky, victims of the SAM missile umbrella that sheltered Egyptian troops from Israeli air power. But he was right when he told Dov it wasn't their problem. Their problem was keeping Egyptian troops from being ferried across the Gulf of Suez to the southern Sinai. And so far between the commandos and the missile boats, they had been totally successful. Though they could not stop the helicopters that crossed above them. Sometimes he felt like a prisoner on the boat, felt he wasn't doing his share to stop the Egyptians, to put an end to their war machine, to bring Israel its victory.

"Do you think they'll try to ferry any more over?" Dov asked.

"They might try. But they won't succeed if they don't have the boats to do it with."

"Nu?"

"I think we might take a little trip into the Gardakah harbor tonight. See what's afloat that shouldn't be."

Lily was afraid to leave her apartment. Joshua had called her once, almost as soon as the war began. He had wanted to find out about his father, and she had told her son that Joseph had some men to deliver, then he would come to Joshua's camp and bring him home. "Oh, Mother, you're crazy," he had said to her over the phone. To his own mother. But she had rights, rights to keep her son alive, which would be best accomplished by bringing him here to Tel Aviv.

Why hadn't he called again? Or why hadn't she heard from Joseph? What were they doing that they couldn't give a thought to her feelings? Was she just supposed to sit at home and wait? Like Danielle? Danielle always assured her that everything would be okay. But how did she know?

Lily decided to call her son's base. It would be a tangle getting through, but she could wait no longer. She dialed the number and soon found the phone being passed from one hand to another, but not to Joshua's. He was unavailable, she was told. So she asked for a friend of his who had done basic with him. Shmuel would certainly know where her son was.

Shmuel did. He told her Joshua had been sent forward to help repair tanks on the Heights. Shmuel asked her to call his mother, tell her that he was quite safe. The conversation ended. Somehow. And somehow she managed to dial Shmuel's number and speak to his mother. And then? What happened? She didn't know. She was on her bed crying. Her men were gone, she was alone. And she was terrified.

Shoshana was working in her office, solidly and carefully, trying not to think of what was happening beyond the tape that lay in front of her. She among all her family knew the price and the extent of the initial Arab successes. But what was essential now was to concentrate on doing her part to turn the tide in Israel's favor, as it must be turned. Yet she found this concentration coming hard. How had it happened? When everyone knew it was coming, why weren't they prepared to strike first? What madness had overtaken Israel?

Danny was safe. She would have heard if he was not. It

was the nights that she feared most. Because she knew Danny operated then. She knew the commandos would slip into the Egyptian harbors and destroy what they could. The navy was having an active war. All along the coasts of Syria and Egypt they patrolled with their missile boats, taking on all comers.

Oren was back. He was in uniform now and hurrying up to the Golan Heights. "The Iraqi brigades are moving up to the front," he told her. "Tanks. They are all coming with tanks."

She had never known so many tanks existed in the world. "How are things going?" she asked.

"We're just about holding them. We're organizing for a counterattack." He shook his head. "*Aze balagan,* Shoshana. We have tanks without ammunition, we have ammunition without tanks. We have breakdowns all along the line. It looks like some of the matériel hasn't been checked in years. We don't have enough night equipment. The boys up there are not only fighting and dying, they're freezing their asses off. We don't even have warm-enough clothing to issue the reserves. Someone's going to pay. Someone's got to."

She reached her hand out to him. "Have a care."

"When you get my tapes, edit out the anguish."

Oren was gone. The halls were quiet, solemn. Occasionally she would hear David's flashes of anger booming out from his office like thunder. But that was it. It would have been better if there were more citizens in Israel, she thought, better if they all didn't have brothers, lovers, fathers, husbands at the front. But they all did. And they all waited. To hear. Anything.

Her phone rang. She picked it up instantly and was only vaguely listening to the voice on the other end. Whoever was speaking was going on a mile a minute. "Wait a second," Shoshana cut in briskly. "Who is this? Ilanit? Ilanit who? Oh, Joshua's girl friend." Shoshana listened while Ilanit explained her problem. It seemed Ilanit had come to visit Lily after volunteering at the hospital since she hadn't been called up yet. Lily had answered the door but seemed not to be "in touch with reality," as Ilanit put it. But then who was, who would want to be at such a time. Ilanit continued. She had finally gotten out of Lily what was wrong. Joshua had been sent to the front to help repair tanks that had been knocked out of action. Lily was afraid Joshua would be killed. "So what should I do?" Ilanit asked. Shoshana shrugged. Hold her hand, put your arm around her—what else could she come up with? "She said to call you. You know people who could get Joshua sent back to base. Should I take her to the hospital?"

"No," Shoshana said quickly. "They have enough to do. How bad is she?"

"Bad. She doesn't seem to hear most of the time. I have to keep repeating things."

"Look, Ilanit, take her to my father's. I'll call Danielle. They'll all have to take care of each other now."

"Okay. Shoshana, will Joshua be all right?"

Shoshana thought back to what Oren had told her. "Of course," she said automatically. She had no time to figure the odds.

Joshua was paired with someone old enough to be his father. They had been working all day, all night, stopping only long enough to pee. At first Joshua had not counted the human cost. He had been too afraid of the shelling. He had been afraid. They actually had moved into crippled tanks within range of Syrian firepower to repair them. He was scared. He watched Evan, his partner, work calmly and efficiently. Evan said nothing about Joshua's shaking hands until the shaking stopped. "First time is always a shocker," Evan told him. "You'll be all right." And Joshua guessed he would be. The shelling had stopped bothering him as much. He didn't flinch when the boom came close. But maybe his body was out of flinches. Maybe he was just too tired. As soon as they finished with one tank, a fresh crew came to claim it. But it was the men who had been fighting since the Syrian assault began that broke his heart.

They had stood nearly alone defending Israel for forty-eight hours. Their faces were black with soot, their eyes streaked with red. Many had been wounded and yet they fought on. Many had been killed.

They waited by a tank now for an evacuation team to take away the bodies so they could go in to see what was wrong. He looked at the faces of the dead and saw that some were little older than himself, while some were old enough to have a wife, children. Evan poked him. They climbed in. The floor was covered with blood. Joshua started crying. "We lubricate with oil, not tears," Evan rebuked him quietly. "Tomorrow, the next day will be better. We'll start sweeping them back. You'll see. The Syrians will run for it. Then you and I will walk through the battlefield, hop into their tanks, start the ignition, and drive them home. There's always an end to it, kid. You'll see."

Sami Nissan looked out from his turret and swore his head off. He had never been in such a goddamned frustrating fuck-up in all his life. Defend the Bar-Lev fortifications; no, don't defend the fortfications. Outflank them to the north. No, pull south. Hold the Egyptians at the canal. No, pull back and give yourself more maneuverability. He was near tears with anger. All he wanted was one goddamn direct order. The only thing that could be said in their favor was that they wouldn't starve to death. Everyone in his crew had brought enough care packages to open a supermarket. He gave the thumbs-up sign to the tanks on either side of him. Night would fall shortly and they would be exposed once more to the ferocious fireworks of the Egyptian artillery barrage.

His radio man patched him in to Yair, his brigade commander. "Sami, orders have been given for the fortifications along the Bar-Lev line to be evacuated. When it's dark, they are going to try to make it out. Amnon's going in to pick them up in your sector. You still have three tanks?"

"Right."

"Send one of them down to sector ten to outflank the

Egyptians in the south. You and the others go up north. Draw them away from Amnon."

"Right." Sami looked to the commanders of his other tanks. They had heard. "Yossi," he called to his right, "take yours to the south. You'll be passing by Shaul's platoon. Ask for some support."

"What flank is he talking about?" Yossi called back. "There's no goddamn flank. There's just one Egyptian army from here to the Mediterranean."

"There's got to be a flank somewhere," Sami shouted. He muttered under his breath, "That's what they say in all the manuals."

"Ammunition?" Yossi called.

Ammunition. There was plenty of ammunition at Refidim. Too bad they couldn't get it up to the front. "Make it last," he shouted. He tapped on his tank and his driver took off for the north to find the Egyptian flank, barring that, the entire Egyptian army.

Albert Haya showed up at his mobilization point in the Negev. This was after they didn't call him on Saturday or Sunday. Two days of the war gone by and he was sitting on his moshav tending his flowers. "I'm here," he announced to anyone who would listen.

"What are you, infantry?" a lieutenant asked him.

"Right."

"We don't need you. We've got to get the tank crews and the artillery down there fast."

"Don't you think they might need our help?"

"Who knows. I have a list. I follow the list."

"Well, there must be something I can do. Hey, what's happening down there anyway?"

The lieutenant looked up at him and said very quietly, "Your guess is as good as the general command's."

Sami found he had gone too far north. They had encountered five Egyptian tanks fanning out for their night positions and had taken them out. But there would be more to take their place. Each night the Egyptian tanks moved forward and Egyptian infantry formed their lines of support. Each day they had to be beaten back. It was bothersome at night. It was hard to keep track of your position. There were so few Israeli tanks in the area that one false move by him and he would be swallowed by the Egyptians and never find his way back to the Israeli lines. He was not engaged now. He was waiting for word from Amnon before he moved forward. But somewhere to the south of him he could see a firefight beginning. He watched for half an hour, waiting for word.

"Sami!" It was Yair. "Move south toward the Canal. Give Tuvia support."

"Right." So that must have been Tuvia where the fire was coming from. Forget Amnon now. He gave the signal and his driver and Lior's tank behind him moved south through the dunes while he kept an eye out, ready to give the order to fire. He saw a half-track coming at him and gave the coordinates but not the order to fire. It was theirs. It was swarming with the wounded being evacuated behind Israeli lines. They were traveling south in the path the half-track had come from when two Egyptian tanks came at them from the north. They took them without much trouble and were traversing the next dune when a company of Egyptian infantry rose and began firing at them. God, he hated these dunes. He ducked and started firing with his mounted machine gun as he gave the order to drive right through them. "Lior's been hit," his driver reported.

"Shit." Lior was his second tank commander. "Lior?"

"Yes." Lior's voice came through the earphones.

"How bad?"

"Can't move."

"Can you fire?"

"Yes."

"Back up," Sami told his driver. "Make a line with Lior."

"Go, Sami," Lior said.

"Go where? There are Egyptians everywhere. Who's to say the ones at the canal are any more worth fighting than these?" It wasn't Zahal's policy to desert its wounded. And

538

it sure as hell wasn't Sami's policy to desert Lior. If he could get Lior's crew onto his tank, they could move again. But they were pinned down by the damned infantry. They were like ants. God, the ignominy of it all. One of his tanks being taken by an infantry unit. "Lior, hang on. I'm going to try to squash these bastards." He gave his driver the order and they dashed forward spitting sand and firing. Damn, if he had had his own infantry for support, he wouldn't have had to worry about such annoyances.

"Sami, to the south," Lior called.

The infantry had pulled back, but a line of tanks was coming up on Sami and they weren't Israeli. Even as he swung his turret for the first shot, Sami gave his driver orders to move into a new line with Lior.

Fantastic! He loved his crew. So accurate, so clean, so perfect. So much Russian scrap to be collected after the war.

"Sami, to the north."

Goddamn! Where did all these tanks come from? He swung to the north.

"Sami, I'm out."

"Out what, Lior?" Sami asked as his tank continued to fire.

"Out of shells."

"All right," Sami said very calmly. "Evacuate. Come to mama."

Sami stood in his turret and with his machine gun covered Lior's men as they made it to his tank. He helped them onto the tracks and told his driver to reverse and get them the hell out of there.

"Sami, behind you," Lior called.

Sami looked around and couldn't believe it. Five Egyptian tanks had come around his rear. To what did he owe this honor? He was surrounded. His only line of escape lay toward the ten Egyptian tanks they had previously knocked out, and that was toward the Egyptian concentration. "Yair, support," he radioed.

"Can you hold out a few hours?"

"No." He waited.

"No support, Sami."

"Keep firing," Sami told his crew. Think, think, think. The greatest good. "Lior, take the men and try to make it back to our line on foot."

"I'm not leaving you, Sami."

"Goddamn it, that's a direct order! Evacuate," he told his crew.

They hesitated until he started pulling them out by the sleeve. If they were going to make it, they'd have to do it fast. But of course they wouldn't all make it. No, not all of them. Maybe not any. But it was better than letting them sit in this tank and be blown to pieces. He slipped into the driver's seat and threw himself firing at the tanks behind him. He didn't bother to say the *"Shema' Yisrael."* It had all been in God's hands from the beginning.

"Where is he?"

"Danny," Dov calmed him.

"Where the fuck is he?" Danny counted his men again. Avi was missing and they were floating like sitting ducks in the Egyptian harbor of Gardakah. The seconds were like hours. Their work was through; they had to get out. Even the Egyptian navy wouldn't be afraid of the bogeyman forever.

"I'll go down," Dov volunteered.

"You stay here," Danny ordered. "I'll find him." Danny pulled his mask over his face, bit on his air tube, and slipped underneath the water. Haste makes waste, he told himself as he slipped by the anti-personnel devices that littered the underwater depths. He checked where they had been before. He checked the Egyptian flotilla. No Avi. He backed away now as he counted the seconds off to himself. He saw a light flashing over by the fishing boats. If that was Avi, he'd have him court-martialed. Fishing boats he wasn't that worried about. He swam quickly over to where he had spotted the light seconds before. There was Avi entangled in the fine, strong threads of a fishing net, his hand unable to reach his knife. Even as Danny all too slowly cut him loose, he had to admire the fisherman's ingenuity. What a fish they would have caught.

Avi was panicked. He was thrashing. He really did look like a fish in a net. Danny cut the final strand and signaled Avi to follow him. He started off through the water. Sixth sense made him turn back. Avi had frozen. He went back to get him. He placed Avi's hands on his leg and signaled for him to hold on. Carefully, cautiously, Danny swam through the thicket of anti-personnel devices back to his own craft. Avi saw and recognized the hull, but instead of waiting to be maneuvered, he made a rush for the surface. Stunned, Danny tried to grab him when he saw what he was swimming into, but it was too late.

The explosion filled Dov's ears. He watched in horror as Avi's body shot through the surface of the water and landed smack on top again. "Pull him in," he ordered. His men obeyed and nervously awaited the order to depart. But it didn't come. Instead Dov searched the waters around him until he spotted Danny's body ballooning slowly to the surface. He pulled his best friend aboard the craft and gave the order to leave. Danny was bleeding from his ears, his nose, his mouth. Dov rocked him in his arms and watched him die.

David Tal had just dismissed his staff from morning conference. There was none of the usual banter, just clues thrown back and forth about what to look for. It was depressing. Not the war, his staff. They all looked five, ten years older. The war? Well they were no longer being pushed back. They were holding. In some areas there were counterattacks. Israel would not be overrun, though one would never guess it from the casualty figures.

There was a knock on his door, which had been left open for emergency consultations. He looked up and saw a navy major framed in his doorway. He expected another demand for assistance from his already short staff. "What is it?" David asked brusquely.

"They told me to come to you," the major said.

"Wonderful. So you're here."

"I've come about Colonel Ze'ev."

David's heart stopped.

"They told me you would be the best person to approach about this."

"Is he dead?"

"Yes," the major said softly.

Oh God, he would never forgive the bastard. To die on Shoshana like this. It was so typical of Danny, so god-damned typical. David felt tears well in his eyes and desperately tried to beat them back. "Well, what did you come to me for?" he asked harshly.

"I understand that Shoshana Ewan works for you."

"So?"

"So I thought it would be helpful if you—"

"No," David said abruptly. "You have a team for exactly this purpose. You don't need me. You won't use me for this."

"We've sent the team to his wife and his parents. You'll have to admit that his is an unusual case. That's why we thought—"

"Well, you thought wrong."

"It's best to have someone she knows to lean on."

"Not me."

"Look . . ." The major didn't know what to say. "She shouldn't be alone," he ended lamely.

Shoshana. How could he? He didn't want to have this responsibility. He didn't want to see what this death would do to her. But he didn't want to leave her alone. David got up and led the major down the hall to Shoshana's office.

Shoshana knew what was coming as soon as she saw the navy uniform trailing in behind David.

"May we come in?" David asked.

"No," she said.

They came in anyway and closed the door, tight.

"Is he injured badly?" she asked hopefully.

David took the extra chair in her room and pulled it around next to hers. "He's dead, Shoshana."

A wave of exhaustion hit her and tears began to fall

quietly from her eyes. David put out his hand and she grabbed it with both of hers and held on tight. "How did it happen?" she asked.

The major stepped forward. "Colonel Ze'ev's men—"

"You may call him Danny," she interrupted sharply. "Everybody did."

The major's voice softened. "Danny's men were attacking an Egyptian naval installation. When they returned to their craft, one of the men was missing. Danny went to look for him. As far as we can figure out, when the other man was surfacing, he touched off an anti-personnel device."

"Danny died in the water then?" Shoshana had to know.

"On the craft," the major said. "But he never regained consciousness after he was pulled from the water."

"I see. And the other boy was dead too."

"Yes. I'm afraid so."

Shoshana thought it over. "Someone must tell Danny's parents."

"We've already done so."

"Yes. Of course you would. And his wife?"

"Someone in the embassy . . ."

"Yes."

"He's to be buried tomorrow at the military cemetery. Nine thirty."

"Not today?"

"His wife and child have to fly in from London."

She nodded as if she were understanding all of this. "I'll be there."

"There will be someone to direct you."

"Thank you for coming."

The major thankfully withdrew. But Shoshana still held on to David.

"You'll want to go home," David said softly to her.

"Yes," she agreed.

"I'll have a car brought around."

"Thank you."

"Would you like me to call your sister? Anybody?"

"No. Everyone has her own worries. In any case I'd like to be alone."

"Shoshana—"

"David, I'm going to ask you a favor and I know it'll be very hard for you, but please, I need you now."

"What is it, Shoshana?"

"I want you to come with me tomorrow to Danny's funeral. Please. I'll be alone. And I don't think I can stand it alone."

"I'll pick you up at nine," David promised her.

While Shoshana was being driven back to her apartment, the army found Danielle at Meir Ewan's apartment, where everyone was trying to decide what to do with Lily who, when she wasn't laughing or crying hysterically, sat staring vacantly into space.

"We're looking for Danielle Nissan," the captain said when Rahel answered the door. Rahel escorted them in to where Danielle was standing.

"Danielle Nissan?" the captain said.

"Yes."

"I'm sorry to report that your husband Sami is missing in action."

Danielle laughed in his face. "What do you mean missing in action? Sami's so big no one could miss him."

The captain glanced at the solider who accompanied him. He tried to explain himself. "Sami's tank in the Sinai, there are fears that it's been overtaken by the enemy. We haven't been able to raise him for over twelve hours now."

"Well, keep trying," Danielle told him.

"We will," the captain assured her. "But we fear the worst."

"The worst? What worst?"

"The last time your husband was seen, he was charging a formation of Egyptian tanks."

"So?" Danielle said. "Sami and his crew are quite efficient when it comes to dealing with Egyptian tanks. You don't know them. They'll come back okay."

"Sami was alone," the captain said. "He ordered his

crew and that of another tank to evacuate and make it back to Israeli lines on foot. It was very heroic of him, an act of complete self-sacrifice."

"You mean he was alone against the Egyptians?"

"I'm afraid so," the captain said.

"They've taken Sami!" Leah wailed. "God's called him."

"Oh, Mother, shut up!" Danielle shouted. She turned to the captain. "No matter what, Sami will survive. I know. He promised to come home to me. I'll be going back to my apartment now to wait for him."

"Someone should go with her," the captain said quietly to the assembled family members, but no one made a move.

Danielle left swiftly. She had had enough of crazy people for one day. She just wanted to get back to the quiet of her own apartment and wait for her husband. He would be back. She had kept the chicken for him. In the freezer. They would eat it and laugh over this day together.

The funeral was for the two of them, Danny and Avi, the other commando. Shoshana's fears of being alone were unfounded. David had brought along Hava, his wife, and once they arrived at the burial site, Nurit, Oren's wife, came over to join her while Jonathan Ben-Gal and several others Danny had served with expressed their sympathy, their regret. The words didn't really seem to matter anyway, as she felt she was only half-conscious; events and people floated above her while she was somehow in touch with Danny, whose body had been shrouded and whose presence she felt alongside of her also staring into the hole where his body would be lowered.

In her semi-conscious state she did not give much thought to Danny's family, but they were there in strength. Ronit and beautiful little Adee to whom Shoshana tried to smile. But she looked away. Almost ten now she had Danny's coloring, but it was obvious she ate in her mother's kitchen. Ronit wore black but remained tearless. Shoshana let her eyes linger on Danny's father, who held in his arms Danny's mother, who was quietly sobbing. His father's eyes met hers and she found nothing in them but hatred, even now when it no longer mattered. She stared back. Let him break away; she would not yield, not after all these years.

She wasn't aware that she had cried out. But she must have. She felt physical pain as the first handful of dirt fell upon the body in the open grave. "Shameful," she heard them muttering from Danny's side. David held on to her and held her up as one by one the mourners grabbed a handful of soil and settled it upon the body. When it was her turn, she could not, so David pressed some into her hand then opened it above the grave.

His father said kaddish for Danny Ze'ev, the grave was filled in, the military salute was given, the flag folded and handed to Ronit. Shoshana started crying again. "It's not fair," she whispered.

"Shh," David hushed her.

The mourners broke away. For most of them it was back to duty as the war still raged on. Jonathan Ben-Gal came over, pressed something into her hand, and closed her fist over it. She knew what it was. It was Danny's military disc and insignia. She thankfully slipped them into her purse. It was something at least. "Dov says to tell you that they are going to clear out Gardakah so there is not one Egyptian naval vessel left in port," Jonathan told her. She smiled. Gardakah. Where the hell was Gardakah that Danny had to die there?

David was leading her back to the car. He would not allow her to look back. They passed several other funerals on their way. Empty, she felt so empty.

Her path crossed Ronit's at the parking lot. She and her daughter were in a group waiting for their car. Shoshana mindlessly reached out to brush Adee's hair, but the child moved away. "You will never have him now," Ronit told her very coldly, very calmly.

David opened the car door for her and practically pushed her in. "Enough scenes," he muttered. Hava slipped in the backseat and David quickly pulled out of the lot.

When they moved into traffic, Shoshana said, "The flag should have been mine. Danny was mine. Everyone knows that."

"Everyone knows that," David echoed. "So it's only right that his wife gets the flag. She has the daughter."

"I have a child too," Shoshana claimed.

"Where?" he asked. Funerals did nothing to improve his mood, especially this one.

"David, please," his wife begged tearfully. She was worried about her own sons and hoped she would not have to go through anything like this for them.

"The child is in me," Shoshana said. "Danny's child. And it will be a son."

Albert Haya waited at Refidim in the middle of the Sinai. His whole unit was there. Men whom he had fought alongside of on the West Bank six—was it only six years ago? And new men, conscripts doing their regular service. They sat on their asses and waited for the order to move out. They swatted flies, they told each other about new wives, new kids. The war raged on in front of them and they had nothing to do with it. He called his wife Segal every day. He lined up and waited his turn. That's how he found out about Sami being missing. Danielle had called Segal to ask her to ask Albert to look for Sami when he had a moment to spare. "What hope?" Segal asked.

Albert couldn't reassure her. The east bank of the canal was a killing ground for both sides. He would ask around, he promised. Maybe some of the wounded had news of him. And Ezra? He had reported to the Golani Brigade. Since then Paula hadn't heard from him. Albert's time was up. He put the phone down and walked off.

Ezra, his brother. Well. So no one had heard from him. It wasn't unusual in this war. Too many times soldiers being evacuated from the front had carried messages for their buddies. By the time they delivered these to the families their buddies were already dead. Ezra would be okay. He wasn't crazy. Maybe a little bit too solid, but he would survive. He had to. Albert didn't want to think of life without an older brother.

Shoshana needed her family. Not that Hava hadn't been kind to her but what could Hava say. No, now Shoshana needed someone to mourn with. She needed her sister. She would return to her father's house.

"But how will you get there?" Hava protested. "There're no buses."

"I'll hitch a ride," Shoshana assured her. "Thank you for taking me in today. Tell David I'll be back at work as soon as possible."

"You're suffering from shock."

"Yes," Shoshana agreed. Yet Danny in death was still near to her. What she could not contemplate now were the months, the years ahead with out him.

It was six o' clock when she reached Givatayim and slowly, tiredly climbed up the steps to her father's. She smiled briefly, remembering the time Danny had caught her on the stairwell, had kissed her and embraced her. He was such a naughty boy, always.

She didn't have a key. She rang and Rahel let her in with no comment. She saw Lily sitting quietly by the window. She did not even turn her head at Shoshana's entrance. Shoshana took a chair, much as David had taken one the day before, and placed it opposite her sister. She took Lily's motionless hand in hers and said to her quietly, "Lily, Danny's dead."

Lily's eyes became alive. She looked at her sister with horror and compassion, then together they began screaming and wailing, their mourning of the dead.

Lily held her like a mother, she cried with her, she comforted her. "We will go back to my apartment," she told Shoshana. "You will rest there. We will talk." Shoshana agreed numbly. When they left, their father was sitting in his chair, crying silently, and reciting the prayer for the dead.

* * *

Joseph Benjamin found out about his son being at the front when he evacuated several of the wounded to what should have been Joshua's base in the Galilee, only to find his son missing. He was shocked, he feared for him. But there was no time to be angry or upset with his son. His van had been turned into a makeshift ambulance, and he made dozens of trips a day ferrying the wounded from the battle line to the medical unit where help, he hoped, awaited them. He studied carefully those he carried, looked perversely for the face he had seen every day for the last eighteen years. They were all so young. He was the "old man" to them. The old man with the taxi, they would say, here he comes. As the troops moved farther into Syrian territory, he moved up too, asking about his son and his unit. None had heard or some thought they had but weren't sure. They were more interested in coffee, chewing gum, warm clothes. He brought what he could. He scavenged what he could find for them.

A freak accident brought them together. An ordnance crew was bringing back a Russian prize intact. Disoriented from lack of sleep, one member of the crew fell off the tank and was almost crushed by a passing half-track. Joseph was directed to the scene.

"This is heaven. A little peace," the crew member was mumbling as he stared at the winter sky.

He would be all right. Joseph could see that. Not like some of the earlier ones he had carried. Joseph was bent over, carefully moving the crew member to a stretcher, when someone came up to him and roughly pushed him over, literally pounced on him and dragged him down in the mud. The soliders watching pulled them apart. Joseph was startled and wondered what he had done to offend. He didn't even recognize this grimy oaf.

Joshua stared at him, waiting. "It's me, Father," he finally had to say impatiently.

An involuntary moan escaped from Joseph's lips as he grabbed his son and held him in a long-lasting embrace. Before the war if he had done this to Joshua in front of his friends, his son would have broken away embarrassed. Now Joshua held on to him too and couldn't let go. There were tears in both their eyes when they moved apart.

"Mama?" Joshua asked.

Joseph examined him. "You're a mess," he said. "I don't know. I haven't seen her since the war started. Are you okay?"

Joshua shrugged. He couldn't speak.

"Of course he's okay." Evan came up and clapped Joshua on the shoulder. "We couldn't have made it without him." He introduced himself to Joseph, as did the whole group of them, giving Joseph messages to give to their families in case he got south before they did.

Joshua returned to his father's embrace and whispered in his ear, "You were right, Father. About war. I never want to have to see any of this ever again." Joseph squeezed him tight. If only. If only he could make that happen for his son.

"I'm lying here bleeding to death," the crew member reminded them. They gathered around and lifted him gently into the van. It was time for Joseph to go. "Keep your head down and your helmet on," Joseph told his son. "There's a lot of head wounds going around."

"Worse than the flu," one of the boys said.

"I'll be careful, Father," Joshua promised him.

Joseph wanted to say more but what was there to say. He looked closely at his son, got into the van, and drove away. Joshua was alive so far. That was a good sign.

Danielle waited with her in-laws for word of Sami. Days passed. They called for news. There was none to give them. He was still missing in action; the army had tacked on, "presumed dead."

Danielle had vivid dreams of Sami, lost in the Sinai, being hunted down by the Egyptians, but always evading them to fulfill his promise to her. He was coming home to her, she knew that. Right now he was hiding in some sand dune eating the fruit and cake she had packed for him. She was worried about that because all the boys coming back from the Sinai complained about the heat and flies. She didn't want the flies to get on the food she had prepared for him and she hoped Sami was taking precautions against them.

Sami's mother and sisters gave up before she did. But they hadn't heard Sami's last words. They didn't know him the way she did.

The Israeli army broke through the Egyptian lines and crossed the Canal. She followed every step of their military exploits, including the strangulation of the Egyptian Third Army, because she knew that Sami's life depended on their success. She had heard about Danny. She was sorry for him and for Shoshana. And she was gratified to hear that Lily had nothing to worry about after all. Both Joseph and Joshua were safe. But her concerns were all fixed on Sami.

Albert had called. He had told her he had met someone named Lior, who was in the tank next to Sami's just before they evacuated. Lior said that Sami had sacrificed himself to save the others. Lior had told him that he had looked back and Sami's tank had definitely been hit. He didn't think Sami could have survived. "I know that he did," she told her brother. What did Albert know? He was such a baby. And anyway Lior had not seen Sami dead.

She thought now that maybe Sami had not really had enough food to survive, so perhaps he had no choice other than to turn himself over to the Egyptians as their prisoner. But now he would be returned. After all, if the Egyptians wanted their Third Army back, they would have to return Sami. Though her dreams were less vivid, and she no longer really was sure where Sami was. If only she knew where. Instead of waiting each day for word of him.

Ezra Haya was so tired. Yet it was left to him to relay the orders to his men. Their lieutenant had been killed while crossing the Purple Line to hold the Syrian territory taken by the Israeli tanks. The brigade commander had remembered Ezra. "Tel Azaziat," he had said, and threw his arm around Ezra. "Well, another hill to climb, eh?"

Yes, another hill. If Mount Hermon could be considered

a hill. The Syrians had taken the Israeli positions on Mount Hermon at the beginning of the war. They had killed—too many. And Ezra feared for the captured, those who had fallen into barbaric Syrian hands. Now Israel had to take Mount Hermon back. For defense, for observation, Mount Hermon was necessary, Ezra told his men. Israel needs it, we'll get it back for her. He was firm, he was forceful.

He was tired. His men were so tired. The war should have been over for them. October 20 and Israel had retaken the entire Golan, had beaten back and broken the Syrians, the Moroccans, the Iraqis, the Jordanians. The road to Damascus was wide open to them. But politics intervened there. They would not take the capital of Syria. So why couldn't they go home now to their wives and children, to rebuild.

The attack on Mount Hermon would be two-pronged. The paratroopers would be landed on the heights above the clouds to overtake the Syrian position on Mount Hermon, and the Golani Brigade would move up from the base to retake the Israeli positions.

The paratroopers achieved their goal with relatively little cost in human lives, but when Ezra led his men up the base of the Golan behind several Israeli tanks, he found a different story. In the darkness of the night the Syrian commandos seemed to be behind every rock, in every pit of the hillside. And the Syrian commandos had night-vision, telescopic lenses which the Israelis did not. "Scramble, scramble!" Ezra told his men. But wherever they moved, they found themselves in the Syrian sights and one by one they were being picked off.

Ezra knew they couldn't lie there. They had to move forward to show the Syrians there was nothing they could do to stop this army. And yet his men saw their dead and wounded being dragged down the slope they still had to climb.

Orders were passed back for Ezra's platoon to move up and replace those that had fallen. He said to his men, "The sooner we do this, the sooner we all go home." It was more effective than just giving the simple order to advance.

They rose and others followed. One by one the Syrian commandos were flushed out. Mount Hermon was retaken.

That was, yes, Ezra wasn't quite sure. But that was October 22 in the morning. That evening the Syrians accepted the cease-fire. But it wouldn't matter for fifty-one members of his brigade. Because they had died taking Mount Hermon.

Danielle was beginning to get worried. The war was over. The prisoner exchange between Egypt and Israel was about to take place. Sami's name was not on the prisoner list. But that could have been a mistake. She went out to the airport anyway. She waited but he did not materialize.

Shoshana and Lily hung around her all the time. She could not understand that. They told her she had tried to kill Leah when her mother came to her apartment. How ridiculous. Her own mother. But when she saw what she thought was her own mother, it was Sami's mother who came to her every day. She assured her mother-in-law, "There will be news soon. We'll hear from Sami very soon now." And yet the waiting continued. Day after day.

It did not feel to Roberta as if the war was over because the pain never left her.

In Urbana Roberta was home on Yom Kippur fixing the night's meal. Ovadia had taken their two children to the Hillel organization for the Orthodox services, having never gotten used to what the American Jews thought of as Judaism. She always stayed home. Since she had never observed Yom Kippur as a child, it meant nothing to her. Ovadia returned around noon, earlier than she had expected him.

"Hi," she had called. "Were the kids good?"

He looked sick, weak. "There's a war going on," he said. "The Arabs have attacked us."

At first she thought he was joking. The Arabs attacking Israel? Not with Israel's highly touted intelligence, not with the Israeli army and its state of preparedness. And not on Yom Kippur. They turned on the radio and waited. And waited and waited, in horror, as day in and day out the Israelis failed to repeat the victory of 1967, as Israeli pilots were shot from the sky by Russian missiles, as Israeli tank crews were destroyed and the war stalemated.

The newspapers in Urbana headlined University of Illinois football. The war in the Middle East that held the fate of their family and friends drew a couple of paragraphs. They stuck together with the rest of the Israelis in Urbana, all calling each other with any news, letting each other know if they were able to get through by telephone and what was happening when they did. The miracle was that those inside Israel itself, parents and friends, were trying to keep up the spirits of those isolated in the States.

There were no smiles, there was no comfort as day turned into day and still the state of Israel was threatened. Too much was at stake now, too many of those close to them were doing the fighting, and the war was going too disastrously.

And then she heard Danny had died. Shoshana called to tell them. Shoshana was strong. "I haven't miscarried," she promised Roberta. "And I won't. It's what I live for now." Danielle's husband was missing. Along the canal. Presumed dead.

Roberta listened to the radio out of a sense of masochistic duty. There was nothing to do but endure. "Can't you do something?" she had asked Ovadia over and over again.

"What can I do?" he retorted. "They have my number. If they need me, I'll go. I'm not even assigned to a unit anymore. I haven't held a gun since squad leader course."

She knew he was right but there must be something. And yet what? None of the Israelis in Urbana had been called up, even one who was a captain in the infantry. It wasn't a matter of fighting and dying. It was a matter of stopping the onslaught. She found things inside of her had changed. She could no longer read about Israel, listen to the records they had brought home, no longer listen to Arabic music especially, even though she had grown fond of it during her stay in Israel. What bothered her most was the isolation. She had talked to her mother about the war over the phone. "Well, I feel sorry for Ovadia," her mother had said. "But it shouldn't bother you. It's none of your concern." It was none of America's concern. No one cared, certainly not in Urbana. Roberta found some bitter irony in the fact that the Israelis had always struck her as being more than slightly paranoid. There was always the feeling in Israel that the whole world was against them, that they stood alone. During the Yom Kippur War this paranoia was proved accurate. "What do we need Israel for," one American had so aptly put it. "They can only sell us oranges."

As the details of the war were revealed, it became perfectly obvious that the Israeli government was less than ready for this war. Its use of intelligence had failed, the preparedness had failed, the leadership itself had failed. Analysts now were claiming it was a great Israeli victory that they could come back within three days of such a disastrous initial position to take the offensive and bring Egypt and Syria to their knees. And yet what sort of victory was it that left over two thousand men—fathers, sons, husbands—dead.

She had no answers. Only her anger and her pain. As the months passed, she gave the only response to the war that she knew how to give. She got pregnant. *Am Yisrael Hai.* The people of Israel lived. Within her.

PART 4

37

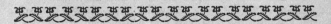

It had all seemed so easy. Al Haykal would fall. Jacob had been approached by a band of al Haykal's enemies. It was to happen at the Swallow's Nest. Al Haykal invited to the club for dinner, after the second course the minister for foreign affairs would show up with his own armed guard and arrest al Haykal for treason. Treason. What surer way would lead to al Haykal's downfall? How easily internal sabotage could be made responsible for the disastrous showing of the Iraqi troops against the Zionist entity.

The day came. Al Haykal did not. Neither did the foreign minister. It didn't take a clairvoyant to guess what had happened. Jacob left the club by the rear door, circled through the sewer of alleys until he was safely away from the danger zone.

He turned to Andrew Harris. Whom else could he turn to? Those who he thought were safe had by now probably disappeared into the eternal fire of Iraqi politics. He told Harris everything. The response: You fool!

Yes. He was a fool. Finally and forever.

"Look, I can get you out," Harris told him. "If we move quickly."

"Me? What does it matter to me? I'm fifty-seven years old. I have high blood pressure. A few hours, a few days under al Haykal's thumb and I'll probably have a heart attack. It's my sons. My sons!"

Andrew Harris slowly shook his head.

"You must."

"No way." Harris saw Jacob's heart turn. "As much as I would want to, it's impossible. You must know that."

"I'm afraid for them. He will kill me. He will confiscate all my property. The least that will happen to my sons is poverty. The most?" He raised his hands in answer to his own question.

"There is nothing—"

"After all these years?"

"Let me get you out. From there you can work for your sons' release."

Jacob rose slowly and left Andrew Harris alone. After he had gone, Harris realized he should have killed Jacob. Because Jacob would talk, Jacob would try to deal. Jacob Ewan had spent his life doing deals, and Harris knew he would be part of any deal Jacob attempted. Why? Why had Ewan been so stupid as to try to trap al Haykal? He would have to leave. In a way he wasn't sorry. Iraq was never his sort of country. And after the war all he wanted to do was go home, see his wife and children, help bury the dead. He set up his radio for one more transmission to Tel Aviv to tell them he was coming out. Then he went to his bathroom, carefully slit open a tube of shaving cream, and took out a new identity neatly wrapped in plastic. He looked out the window of his apartment. No increase in traffic, no unfamiliar cars. He checked his front door. Hall unoccupied. He slipped out and strode down the stairs, exiting through the servants' entrance. From there he made his way to a certain stamp collector, the first step on his escape route home. The stamp collector had a phone. Harris made three calls. The recipients would finish the work. His network would be closed down, waiting reactivation. And in two days he would be home in Tel Aviv.

* * *

When Jacob left Harris's, he had tried to return to his own house but had been picked up when he was a block away. He caught sight of the lamp shining through his window before he was hustled into a car and taken to the city prison. He was put in a cell. No one bothered him. No one talked to him. No one fed him or beat him. He fell asleep.

The next morning he woke with the dawn. Something had startled him, and yet still confused from sleep, he could not figure what it was. The sound came again. Sort of like a loud clap. From outside. Jacob stood on his bed and tried to see out his small, narrow window. The sound came again. He reached for the bars, dug his toes into the cement block, and pulled himself on an eye level with the window. One glimpse, then he broke his grip and fell back onto the cot. Better he should not have seen. The conspirators, including the foreign minister, were being hanged one by one. The foreign minister! That surprised him. The man was from a prominent family. One that had money, power, connections. A family who would not forget. Al Haykal feared no one if he would hang the foreign minister.

It was curious, knowing that his death was coming so soon and still he felt hungry. But there was no food. No water. Nothing.

Al Haykal came at noon. "Did you see this morning?" he asked Jacob.

"Yes." Jacob nodded solemnly.

"Tomorrow it will be you. You have been such a disappointment, Jacob. You were a man I thought too cautious to involve himself in such foolishness."

"I hoped finally you would get what you deserved. There is a hell waiting for you someplace, Musa."

Al Haykal stared at him, amazed. "I never knew you hated me so. I thought I had always treated you fairly."

"I've wanted only one thing in life. Freedom for my sons. And that you did not allow me. With you gone, there might have been a way."

"And now? What have you gained for them?"

561

"Perhaps their freedom still."

Al Haykal laughed.

"A bargain?"

Still smiling, al Haykal asked Jacob what kind of bargain he could possibly make when he had less than twenty-four hours to live.

"I was accused once of working for the Israelis. Do you remember? Yes, you do. I see. I told you it would be ridiculous of them to recruit a Jew. And you believed me. I lied to you, Musa."

Al Haykal frowned. "You're lying now."

"No." Jacob waited until he was sure al Haykal was taking him seriously. "A deal. The freedom of my sons for the top Israeli agent in Baghdad. Oh, yes, I can see what you are thinking. You can beat it out of me. Perhaps. But I am counting on my love for my sons and my age to cheat you out of this one victory, Musa. So if you want my information before you hang me, we strike a bargain."

"And why do you not bargain for your own life? That worries me."

"Why would I want to live longer? I have seen enough to sicken me for a thousand years to come. It no longer matters to me, not to survive under any conditions. I will opt for the serenity of death. And you? Will you opt for this great victory? The capture of an Israeli spy?"

Al Haykal gauged his man. "Okay," he said.

"Your word," Jacob demanded. "You are treacherous but a man of your word. Quite a contradiction to live with, isn't it?"

Al Haykal walked over to Jacob and held out his hand. Jacob took it. "I give you my word. Your sons will be free."

"Now. Before I speak to you."

"Now."

Jacob ate then. Food and water were brought to him almost as soon as al Haykal disappeared. Would it be tomorrow or the next day that he would cease to eat? It did not seem to matter. He took pleasure in every swallow. Al Haykal returned to him that evening. "They are on their way to freedom," he told Jacob. "There is no way I can call them back."

"Your word?"

"My word."

Jacob immediately reciprocated by telling al Haykal everything he knew about Andrew Harris, which when it got to the telling was very little. He knew Harris, he knew what he did, he knew where he could be found. He swore that was all he knew. Only Harris. No one else. It seemed enough for al Haykal.

Empty. Al Haykal pushed around the stack of books, the piles of newspapers. He checked the refrigerator. Nothing had as yet turned rancid in Andrew Harris's apartment. One might think he had just stepped out for supper at some local café. And yet why did al Haykal have the feeling that he would never see this Mr. Harris again? The tube of shaving cream, split so meticulously then tossed in the basket?

Perhaps it was better this way. This Andrew Harris, what did he know? They had both used Jacob Ewan. It was as bad as sharing the same woman, only this time it was he al Haykal who was the cuckold. It worried him a great deal. Harris's disappearance or his death were imperative in such circumstances. His intense interrogation by someone other than al Haykal might prove very embarrassing. Not all the acquaintances one makes should see the light of day.

Jacob had prepared himself for death even as he lay awake on his last night. He had tried to balance in his own mind the deals of his life. He came out wanting. He had fasted over Yom Kippur, he had prayed. He had wiped the slate clean for another year. Then he had betrayed Andrew Harris. He would be condemned by God and man. He said the prayers that he knew by heart over and over in his mind to ward off his weakness. He dreamed of his youth, his wife, his children, his grandchildren. He said good-bye.

When they came to get him shortly before dawn, he was ready. He made no protests even as he was spat on and pushed around. One final act, one final passage and he would be free. He walked by himself out into the courtyard. Numbness had overtaken him. He noted al Haykal waiting for him alongside the wooden structure with three nooses. Three?

"We did not want you to die alone," al Haykal said with a smile.

Some more poor conspirators, Jacob thought. Until al Haykal signaled and the door on the opposite side of the courtyard opened.

Two men stumbled out, moving slowly with their guard toward the gallows. Jacob averted his eyes. At such a time a man should be alone. Yet as they approached and stood next to him, Jacob raised his head. He gasped and fell backward. He was staring into the faces of Rahamin and Ephraim. His sons.

"You wanted freedom for your sons," al Haykal said. "This is the only freedom the state of Iraq provides for its Jews."

Jacob fell to his knees, ripped open his shirt, and pressed the dirt of Iraq to his chest. No matter how hard he was kicked and beaten he would not choose which son was to be hanged first.

38

"Well if you are pregnant, and it looks like that's certainly the case, then you must put in your claims now," Oren was telling her as Shoshana sat with Oren and David in the office cafeteria.

"I don't need anything," she said.

"You may not need anything now, but when the baby comes, you will need help. And if it's Danny's—"

"If it's Danny's!" she objected.

"I mean—look, we know it's Danny's, so you and the child are entitled to survivors' benefits."

"Why should I haggle with them?" Shoshana asked. "Look what the rabbis did to us all those years when Danny was trying to get a divorce."

"With the government it's different," David said. "You are his *yedu'ah batzibur*. You have a case. It's common knowledge that Danny's been living with you off and on since 1966. That's longer than he lived with his wife. So his daughter might get benefits, but you and your child also deserve a fair share."

"Oh, I don't know."

"Just sign the papers. We'll expedite them."

"I feel like a vulture."

"That's what the funds are for," Oren said.

Shoshana looked at the papers in front of her. It was true, she would need help with the baby, and this would mean a free education for him and other benefits, but to have to go through this sort of thing again. Still she signed. Oren promised to get the affidavits she needed and submit them for her. She didn't know what she would have done without Oren and David over these past months. It had been hell.

Work had helped. She had gone back almost immediately and stayed long, hard hours. She had tried not to overdo it because she knew that the most important thing now was not to miscarry, to have the baby she and Danny had planned on. Still at night when she was forced back to her apartment at David's insistence, she could not sleep for hours on end as the events of her life with Danny passed like a kaleidoscope on the ceiling above her head. At first it was a constant ache. Then some days she thought she was managing only to be plunged into deeper stages of despair. Why had it happened? She still could not believe it. And yet she felt she was lucky in that she had no regrets. There were no last words unspoken between them. There was no anger, no resentment. The child had given them peace. She knew how fortunate she was when a week ago to this day the army had notified Danielle that Sami's body had been located and identified, was being returned to Israeli hands for burial. It had been a horrendous experience. She had thought that Danielle surely had just been keeping up a good front, that she really couldn't have believed Sami was alive after being declared missing, presumed dead, for three months. But Danielle had bargained with her heart that Sami still might be alive. It was awful. When Sami was buried, Danielle seemed to shed some vital part of her being.

"We never said good-bye because he would be back," Danielle told her. "Sometimes I expect him still. If only I had had a child. If I had had a son. He died without a son. His life has ended entirely," she said sadly.

"We will remember him," Shoshana promised. And when she lit a candle for Danny on Friday evenings, she lit one also for Sami.

She was close now to Danielle, as close as she could be, though she sensed perhaps unfairly that her advancing pregnancy was disturbing Danielle. She was glad to see how Sami's family took Danielle in as relations between Danielle and her own mother cooled.

It was Leah's fault really. No sooner had Sami been buried than she had suggested in her sly little fashion that now would be the time to move into Danielle's apartment. She didn't even add to be close to her daughter in this time of need.

Danielle had turned on Leah and screamed that it was her mother's doing that Sami was dead, that Leah had wished and prayed for it from the day Danielle was married, had put a curse on Sami and taken him from Danielle. Now she could not bear to be near her mother, even to see her face. So Danielle turned once more to the Ewans.

Shoshana's relations with her family improved. They had to. She had no place else to turn, and with the baby coming, she would need help. Her father had invited her to move back into his apartment but she wouldn't. Instead she turned more to her sister and Joseph for help, and they were always there when she needed them, despite their own worries for Joshua, who had sent her a very moving letter upon learning of the death of Danny. She treasured that letter all the more, knowing it was probably one of the few Joshua had ever written in his life. Lily always complained about not hearing from him.

Of Danny's family she saw thankfully nothing. She did not even show up at the thirty-day memorial service but waited until it was long over to pay her private respects at the grave. Her bouquet of flowers was small compared to those left from the morning, but she placed them on the grave, took a rock and stood it on the stone, then said the prayers. She was interrupted by thoughts of Danny pouring through her mind, asking her things like had she drunk her

milk. It made her laugh almost, and she broke off her
prayers to assure him that she had and he could rest in
peace.

She didn't know how long she had been standing there or
how long she had been crying, but when she turned to go,
she was startled to find Danny's father standing behind her
a short way off. He shouldn't have been there. This was
her time. She stared coldly at him, wiped the tears from
her eyes, and walked off, sensing his eyes following her,
wishing her dead. But she would not die. She would live to
see Danny's son grow and prosper, she would live to see
Danny's grandchildren be born to bless his name. That
would be her revenge. Danny's son. Her son. And no one
could take him away from her.

Ilanit was afraid. She had not seen Joshua Benjamin in
over two months, and she feared he would not want to see
her now. Something had come between them. At first she
thought it was only the deaths. She knew how close he had
been to Danny especially. And to have the war take Danny
and Sami and oh, so many others, some of them friends
they had just graduated with, it was incomprehensible.

Joshua didn't talk to her the way he had before. He
didn't phone her or write her as he promised. Her mother
said Forget him. Don't go chasing after boys, it never
works, was her mother's advice. And yet she loved Joshua,
had loved him ever since they were fifteen. They had
made all sorts of pacts and vows together. And now this,
this absence.

Most of the girls who had finished basic training with
her were going home to their parents. She was going to
Joshua. If he would have her.

She didn't arrive at his base until four thirty in the afternoon, by which time she assumed he would be off-duty. He
was. He was also quite surprised to see her when he met
her at the gate. She had expected him to throw his arms
around her and kiss her. Instead he just stared at her as if
he didn't know what to do with her.

"It's me, Ilanit," she announced.

He smiled, something like his old self. "I know who you are," he assured her. He got a pass to go outside his base, slung a loaded Uzi over his shoulder, and they set off toward one of the Galilean hills surrounding Safed. The ground squished under them from the recent rain, but the day was pleasant for all that. They could almost look forward to the ending of another winter.

"You look silly with those shoes and socks," he told her.

"It's regulation. I just finished basic training."

"I thought it would be about now. Congratulations." He took her hand and pulled her off the well-beaten track.

"Where are we going?" she asked.

"There are some rocks up ahead. About half a kilometer. Nice for a picnic. Or a chat."

She let him guide her over a path that only he could see. She wanted to complain about the branches slapping against her bare legs, but she didn't think it soldierly so she kept quiet. Finally he located her on a stone slab that overlooked Safed.

"It's beautiful," she said, taking in the glistening city.

"When the sun falls, Safed turns all sorts of colors. If I were an artist, I would paint it." He sat next to her and felt her tenseness. "Why are you here?" he asked without looking at her.

"Because I love you." She answered so simply that he looked at her to see if it was true. It was. "You haven't written or called or anything," she chided him. "Don't you care for me anymore?"

He leaned over, took her in his arms, and carefully found her lips. Then he kissed her not urgently but finally, forcefully, with endurance. "I do love you, Ilanit," he answered her.

"Then why . . ." She didn't know how to say it. "Is it the war?" she asked as she watched him try to contain himself.

"I can't tell you," he said almost angrily.

"Why?"

569

"You must never know."

"But why? Did you do something during the war you're not proud of? Did you run away?"

He smiled. "No. I didn't run away. That would be simple. Concrete. Something to deal with. It's nothing that I did. It's what I saw that's made the change."

"What did you see? You can tell me surely."

"I can't tell you, Ilanit. I never want you to have any idea of what it was like."

"What are you doing, trying to protect me?"

"Protect you?" He considered it. "Yes," he guessed. "If I were your father, I wouldn't have let you join the army. I would have seen you married off and pregnant instead."

"I'm not such a coward, Joshua. You can share these things with me." But when he looked at her, she knew he would not. "You're not protecting me, you know, you're isolating me." She had gotten mad. It made him withdraw. They sat on the rock and watched the sun going down on the city of Safed. Joshua was so silent, so still that he scared her. She wanted desperately to reach him, desperately for him to reach out to her. But how? "You can if you want to," she finally told him.

He looked up at her, mystified. "Can what?"

"Sleep with me."

"Sleep with you?"

"Make love to me," she spelled it out for him.

He laughed in her face. "You mean fuck you?"

"Don't be disgusting," she snapped angrily. Flushed, she turned away from him.

"Look, I don't want to sleep with you, make love to you, fuck you now," he said softly. "It wouldn't be right. Not for you, nor for me. My God, think of all the times you impressed upon me the necessity of waiting for marriage."

"I've offered you my body," she flared. "The least you can do is be gracious enough to accept. I'm not damaged goods. You'd be the first."

"Why do you want to sleep with me all of a sudden?" he retorted.

"Because I'm afraid of what's happened to you," she answered automatically.

"That's a great reason."

"Because I love you."

"It's getting better."

"Because you've been avoiding me since the war and I don't know what I've done wrong, I don't know why you've stopped loving me. We used to be so close. We used to talk about everything. And now one of us has stopped talking."

"But I can't say it to you because I don't want you to know—"

She watched as in midsentence Joshua stopped talking. His lips began to tremble and tears flooded out of his eyes. She called his name in anguish and held him tight against her breast. Who had dared hurt her Joshua so, she would murder him. "It was awful," he admitted. "Oh, God, Ilanit, when I saw the bodies—minutes before they had been living, breathing, dreaming, and then nothing." She watched him smile distantly. "I knew then my mother had been right. If I had a child, I could not sacrifice him."

Ilanit took his hand. "But he would want to sacrifice himself."

"Oh, yeah?" he shot back cynically. "Okay. Maybe you're right. And let's face it, I'm how old, nineteen? There'll be other wars for me, for the both of us. But don't expect me to march off nobly. I'll do it to survive because Israel's survival and my survival are one and the same."

They sat silently together. Before they knew it, it was night. "You don't want to sleep with me now," Joshua told her, exhausted.

"Now more than ever," she promised him.

"Not yet," he held back.

"You pick the time and place. I'll be there."

They kissed and petted as they had in high school. "Besides, when I get back to base, the guys are going to ask me how much I got."

"How gross."

"If I looked too happy, they would know."

"That's all right. We talk about it in our barracks too,"

she informed him. He was so shocked that she had to laugh.

Frustrated but happy, they made their way back to the main gate of Joshua's camp, where he snared her a ride into Tel Aviv. "Next time," he whispered to her, "I promise not to cry."

"It's okay whatever you do," she told him. "But next time I promise you I won't try to seduce you." She left him in an acute state of disappointment.

The pains started April fifth. It was a beautiful day and she cursed herself for having to work in an office. She had often wondered how she would recognize when the baby was ready, whether the pains were real or false. But everyone assured her she would know when the time came. They were right. She called Lily who told her she would meet her at the hospital and to hurry there.

Her doctor had told her she had to go to the hospital immediately. She was old, thirty-two, and this was her first birth, there might be complications.

She stopped in to tell David. "I'm going to have my baby now."

He looked up at her quickly. He was still pissed off at her because she insisted on quitting work. "You can have maternity leave," he had told her.

"I want more than maternity leave, I only want to work part time."

"Well, fine. I'll arrange it."

"I know you only too well, David. You say part time but you'll want me full time. I've got to be with my baby."

She had found part-time work at Tel Aviv University, translating for scholars who had no faculty for languages. It would be easy. There would be no pressure. David was unhappy.

"Are you taking a bus?" he called out to her.

"I thought I'd walk," she said.

"Walk?" He swore. "Are you crazy."

"It's such a nice day."

"You want to have the baby on the sidewalk?"

"It takes longer than that," she reminded him, and with three kids of his own, he should certainly have known that.

"Who's walking with you?" he asked.

"I'm walking alone."

He grumbled, got up, and accompanied her to the hospital. She was grateful for his presence because sometimes the pains would immobilize her. But she did walk and she made it to the hospital in plenty of time. Once there Lily took over from David. That was a mistake. While David had been calm, supportive, Lily rushed around hysterically, demanding to know of Shoshana if she was all right.

"She's all right, she's all right." David stared her down. "She's just having a baby. It's not as if this is unexpected."

Shoshana was afraid he would never forgive her for complicating his life, but he looked at her softly and said, "Let me know what it is and good luck."

"What an unbearable man," Lily whispered. "How could you have worked with him all those years?"

Shoshana just smiled. She would not start an argument with Lily now. She needed her sister to hold her hand when the pains came. As each crescendoed, she repeated strongly to herself, "For Danny." But her resolve was not so fanatic that she did not sigh with gratitude when she was carted away to the delivery room. There the pain was more intense but at least she knew it was almost at an end.

"I can see the head," the doctor told her. "One more push."

She pushed. It seemed like an eternity. Then she heard something gurgling below her. It was her child.

"It's a boy," the doctor announced.

Smiling and crying, she curled upward and saw a red little creature being sponged off. To her the baby looked just like Danny.

Lily rushed homeward after being assured that Shoshana was resting quietly, happily. She promised to return early tomorrow with an overnight case and plenty of magazines. Meanwhile Shoshana should be thinking, when she had a spare moment, of what exactly she wanted Lily to buy for her. What kind of crib, how many diapers, T-shirts, what kind of playthings? And of course the brit. What would she call the child? There was so much to do, no time to waste. Joseph would have to help her buy everything Shoshana needed. Baby carriage! How could she forget that? Shoshana must have a baby carriage so she could roll the boy to the milk bar, sit at the tables out in the open, have tea with cake and chat with the rest of the young mothers. Joseph would have to move everything into Shoshana's apartment. It would be such hard work. If only Sami—but Sami was dead. And Joshua with all those strong young muscles of his was in the army, never home. Her father couldn't help. One of Joseph's workers would have to assist him. That was all.

She wondered at the way Americans did these things. Roberta—yes, Ovadia would have to be notified—said Americans bought everything before the baby was born, prepared a whole room to bring the baby home to, with crib, changing table, toys. That seemed awfully risky to Lily. It was never done in Israel. One might shop around, make lists of what one wanted and where it should be bought, maybe even put it on order; but to buy anything before the baby came, no. That was considered bad luck. Because what if, God forbid, something happened and there was no baby to bring home with you? Then how could one live with such a reminder as a nursery? But of course Americans were always so optimistic. Even Roberta, five months along in her pregnancy as she was, sounded cheerful in her letters to Shoshana.

Lily huffed and puffed her way up the stairs of her high-rise apartment house. The elevators were out of order and the elevator repairmen on strike. Everything would appear to be normal in Israel again, until she got to her apartment. She unlocked the door to find Joseph and Danielle sitting quietly together. If she had not come, she guessed they would sit this way forever, statues frozen in fear and despair. "Break out a bottle of wine," Lily told them cheerfully. "Shoshana's had her baby. A boy!"

They rose and smiled tightly at her. Life goes on, she

wanted to shout to them, but they were stuck in time, stuck in October 1973. The toast was perfunctory and when the glasses were set down, Danielle pleaded a headache and gathered her things to go.

"Would you like to come shopping with me for Shoshana's things?" Lily asked.

"No."

"Visit Shoshana and the baby tomorrow?"

"No." Danielle said it quietly, resolutely.

"That was cruel of you, Lily," Joseph chided after Danielle had left.

"And what should I have done?"

"You know how she feels, how she must feel, Shoshana having a baby and all."

"Oh, yes, I understand perfectly. It's not enough that Shoshana's lost Danny, now she should lose the baby. That way no one could resent her for having a little bit of happiness. And we, you and I, we shouldn't be living in this luxury apartment. We should be living in a slum, sharing a bathroom with twenty families. More than that, wouldn't it have been great for our image if Joshua had been permanently crippled in the war, better yet, killed?"

"Lily!"

"I'm sick of your guilt, Joseph." He moved toward her to enfold her. "Don't touch me! Don't come near me. I'm going to call Father. Then I'm going to call Ovadia. After that I'm going to prepare a list of things Shoshana needs. And if necessary, we will buy them with our money. I'm not ashamed of the way you made it."

She huffed and Joseph turned away from her. He wouldn't bother her for the rest of the evening. Instead he would sit around and mope. He acted as if the Agranat Commission, which had just submitted its report on the failure of both the government and the military in the Yom Kippur War, had personally laid all the blame on his shoulders. "It's all our faults," Joseph had said to her when the report came in, absolving neatly as it did the government ministers from primary responsibility. "God has turned his back on Israel."

She had asked him to enumerate his crimes, and for the first time Joseph told her exactly how he ran his business. How he and Frayman participated in bribing government officials to get the information they needed to buy profitable property to build profitable flats. How they had managed consistently to undervalue their worth. "But nobody pays their taxes and everybody bribes government officials," she confronted him. "It's just good business."

"But it's not the way it's supposed to be," Joseph stressed.

"Yes, but it's the way it is. In Iraq—"

"This isn't Iraq, Lily. This is Israel. And we came here with a dream. A dream I've corrupted."

"How?" She struggled to understand. "We came here with nothing. We had nothing. Don't you remember? I do. I remember standing in line for eggs, rice, milk, bread, chicken, what they called meat. I remember when no sooner had I swept that god-awful cottage in Ramat Gan than it would be buried in the sand with one gust of wind. I remember how you could barely walk a straight line at the end of the day you worked so hard. For our dream. So we could live well, have a family, be free. You've corrupted nothing, Joseph. The system corrupts. Systems always do. Look at where you and Moishe Frayman have been. Where there were sand dunes now there are villas, where there were shacks now there are apartment buildings, schools, gardens. How can this be wrong? We came to build a country. And we've done it."

"But how have we done it?"

"What does it matter?" she asked him angrily. "It exists." Reflection, she believed, was not good for the soul. That was why it was demanded on only one day of the year, Yom Kippur. But now since the war Yom Kippur had a new, more deadly meaning in Israel. Not only one's soul but one's country had to be torn apart and examined. And if one found nothing good, what then? Women understood instinctively what was important in life. Where would they sleep, what would they eat, how many months gone was she, was the child healthy. In the end these realities were all that mattered.

39

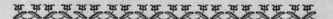

Hal Evans slumped back in his armchair and let the *Globe*, Boston's survey of mankind, slip from his fingers and stretch itself out on the rug. Times change, he recited significantly to himself. Gone Golda, going Nixon, and age pattered ever after him with the running of Gil's four-year-old feet. The nations of the earth had created a new phenomenon of the throw-away leader. Richard M. Nixon, a man Hal felt an immediate kinship with, was being thrown out on a technicality, supposedly perverting the American system.

Hal had wept bitter tears when Golda Meir had resigned last April in the aftermath of the Yom Kippur War. He felt as if his one remaining foothold in Israel had been cut loose. Now he would have to start all over from scratch with the new prime minister, Yitzhak Rabin, one of the reasons he would be traveling to Israel early this July, to solidify relations with the new regime. And to carry out a certain more nefarious deed that had been in the planning several months now, ever since Sarah's second pregnancy had begun to make itself obvious.

How dare they deal him such a humiliating blow. But

they felt secure. Oh, those fools. Just because Sarah had become a fixture at his side at some of Boston's better dinner parties, just because every one of his acquaintances assumed he had a happy marriage, they thought they could pull off this sordid second pregnancy. Well he had a very unpleasant surprise in store for them once they set down in Israel. Oh, yes, Shaul was coming with them, with Hal and his devoted wife, Sarah. Shaul Darom thought it safe to travel to Israel now that Sarah had her United States citizenship and he his green card. However Shaul got it and for how much Hal had to wonder. Well, Shaul could kiss the United States good-bye once he stepped on that El Al flight for Tel Aviv. He could kiss it all good-bye.

Sarah Evans was amazed and mystified by her legal husband's actions upon their arrival in Israel. She had pestered him before the trip: What was he planning to say to her father? Where were they going to stay? At her father's place? At his father's place? He said nothing except, "You'll see."

She was afraid. She didn't want to go back to Israel because she knew he was planning something. She warned Shaul but Shaul laughed her off. "There's nothing he can do to us," Shaul protested. Return her to her father, she suggested. Claim she had been sent to him under false pretenses. Her father would not deny knowing she was pregnant when he proposed Hal Evans marry her. Her father had that much honor at least. It doesn't matter, Shaul insisted. He had no use for Hal anymore except for appearance's sake. He had taken all his ill-gotten gains and invested them in a restaurant in Brookline called Daromah's, hired an Israeli family to run it for him, and watched it flourish. "Laundering the money," he explained to her proudly, "like the Republicans." She wished to God Shaul had let her divorce Hal before the second pregnancy began to blossom but Shaul refused. He said it wasn't the right time emotionally what with Hal being so depressed over Golda Meir's resignation. She suspected Shaul's attitude might be slightly more callous. It was easier to let Hal support the children than to take the responsibility for his own kids himself. Shaul was shocked and appeased her with a diamond bracelet. She couldn't help wondering who had worn it the week before.

So she had not expected Hal's—or Hillel as he called himself in Israel—surprise. Upon their arrival they were greeted by members of her family, including her father and mother, her sister, brother-in-law, nieces, nephews. It had been a long time and all had wanted a glimpse of Gil, who was her son no matter who the father was. Sarah surprised herself by shedding a copious amount of tears as she was held in her mother's embrace. She had not realized the tension she lived under until she was cosseted by her family. How glad she was to be among them again. Even her father seemed genuinely glad to see her despite the near catastrophe of Gil's precarious conception. Of course, he might not have been so happy had he realized that Shaul had accompanied them to Israel. But Shaul, ever sensitive to her needs, had made himself scarce.

It was Hillel who stopped her brother-in-law from picking up her and Gil's things and placing them in the taxi they had waiting. "I've already rented a car," he informed them grandly. "From America. A Dodge Dart." Her family was impressed. But of course that was why Hillel had rented the American car, to be impressive. It was his greatest need. Even though she did not sleep with him anymore, she lived with him closely enough to know that. Quickly Sarah offered her mother and father a ride back to Ramat Gan. They could certainly fit into the car, and she did not want to be alone with Hillel any more than was necessary. "But we're not going to Ramat Gan," he contradicted her. "Though I'll be glad to give a ride to anyone who wants it."

"We're not going to stay with my parents?"

"You deserve the best, Sarah," he said to her. "Therefore I've prepared a little surprise for you."

The surprise was a luxury apartment in the Bavli section of North Tel Aviv. Five rooms filled with Danish furniture. The door to the apartment was protected by a mezuzah and a plaque announcing the new owner of the flat.

Hal Evans—Fund Raiser. Her family was overwhelmed, but when they left her, wishing her all the best, she was scared. "What's the meaning of all this?" she asked accusingly.

"No meaning at all," Hillel told her calmly. "I thought since we are a bi-national family, it would only be appropriate for us to own homes in both countries. You're not pleased?"

"What are you trying to pull?"

"Why, Sarah," he said, feigning shock. "What am I trying to pull? You fly over to Boston to marry me, already pregnant; you import your boyfriend, who usurps my place in my own bed; you pretend you're a dutiful wife; you even manage to prove my virility by getting pregnant a second time; and then you ask me what I'm trying to pull? What do you think I'm trying to pull?" He looked at her mockingly but left her alone to unpack Gil's things and put the tired child to sleep. He did not even try to share the bed with her. She was definitely disturbed.

"He's up to something," Sarah told her boyfriend, as she paced around the plush white Danish couch.

Shaul studied Sarah. There was something in her that did not react well to stress. In the month they had been in Israel, her eyes had receded, her skin had almost turned yellow. He worried about her, especially since she vowed she was not going back to Boston, would never return to the States to live in the same house with the mad Hillel again. When Shaul asked her why, she said, "He gives me the creeps." So he could understand that, he could sympathize with her; but what was he supposed to do, return to the United States and live with Hal Evans alone? "Ever since he's found out about the second pregnancy, he's been acting strange."

"So who wanted to get pregnant again?" Shaul asked her sharply. "Who said Gil needs a brother?"

"Or sister."

"God, Sarah!" She had angered him but she didn't care anymore. "Anyway, what has he done to you? He gives you the creeps? Why? You said everything has been going all right, that he's gone most of the day conducting his deals and at night you go either to his family or your family. So what's the matter? Does he treat you badly in front of the families?"

"No. He acts kind, considerate, as if everything is all right between us."

"So?"

"But it isn't!"

"So maybe he doesn't want anyone to know. Has that ever occurred to you? You know how he feels about looking good in front of other people."

She slumped against the arm of the couch. "It's easy for you to rationalize all of this. You haven't been around him. You haven't seen him. It's like he's waiting for something to happen."

Shaul took her in his arms and held her tight. "It'll be okay," he comforted her. Women were a problem universally shared by all men. He had discovered that on his travels around the country this past month, looking up his old friends. Five years and they were all married. Every single one of them. Married, with children, still living in slums most of them, living by theft, extortion, drugs. And no matter how many jobs his friends pulled, they couldn't keep up with Israel's inflation rate. That's what Sarah didn't realize, how good they had it. It was simple for a woman. She got married, she had a man to take care of her. She got pregnant, she had a man to take care of her and the child. That was her dream. But what about a man's dream? Nothing could come of it because he was out breaking his balls, trying to keep his wife and children in food and clothing. It made him sick. It made him angry. All his friends, whether they were criminals or straight, it was the same damn story. They envied his streets of gold in America, no matter how he paved them, and he feared returning to their sort of life. No matter how hard he worked or what he did, he would end up with nothing.

Sometimes his mind told him to drop Sarah, especially when she got like this, just to pick up and leave her. But his heart told him he needed her because he loved her. Stupid. Stupid, stupid, stupid. Her and Gil and the new one. It had been a month since he had seen Sarah. He pushed her into the bedroom, locked the door. He took her violently and quickly. She didn't complain. She didn't mind. She wanted him as much as he wanted her. That was the hell of it. That was their lifetime mistake.

"So it's all set then?" he asked her, looking at the ceiling, inexplicably depressed.

"Yes."

"How?"

"A short trip to show Gil Israel. That's what I told my parents."

"Does Hillel know you're coming with me?"

"Yes."

Shaul had arranged it. Another bit of his madness. His father dead, his mother had moved south to Dimona to live with his sister. He wanted to show off Sarah and Gil to his family. Another man's wife, supposedly another man's child. But his mother would understand. She knew what life was. And she had appreciated him more ever since Shaul had sent her money every month from America. Finally his mother could buy something decent for herself. If his sister didn't confiscate the check as soon as it came. He made a note to check on that. "You'll love my mother," he promised Sarah. She smiled at him and leaned over to kiss him. He was such a little boy, she thought, even when she was frightened of him.

Frightened of everything lately. As when the doorbell rang and she jumped while Shaul lay there calmly. "My family," she guessed. "Shaul!" She pushed him. He got up and dressed while she slipped on a summer house dress that neatly covered her expanding belly. She was straightening the covers of the bed just as the doorbell rang again. She hurried to get it, noting with dismay that Gil had woken up from his nap half an hour early. She had expected her mother or her sister, maybe a cousin or two, but it was the police. "Shaul," she called instinctively.

Shaul came out into the hallway, stared grimly at the

uniform, then up to the face and smiled. "Captain Mizrahi," he said, "what a pleasure. Captain? You've been promoted since I left." He laughed. Gil, dressed in his underwear and carrying his blanket, pranced over to Shaul, who lifted him and held him happily in his arms. "You'll be wanting to see the great Hal Evans, I presume," Shaul guessed.

"Oh, no," the captain said. "It was you I came to see, Darom."

"Well, please sit down then," Shaul said with a smirk. "Sarah, make some coffee for the captain, will you?"

"Tea, if you don't mind," Mizrahi countered.

Sarah busied herself in the kitchen, trying to make as little noise as possible so she could hear what they were saying in the living room. She prepared the tray, brought it out, and set it before the captain. Then she poured tea for both Mizrahi and Shaul, catching up on their conversation, which was, remarkably, what had happened since they last saw each other five years before when Mizrahi had tried to prove Shaul guilty of arson in the burning of a boutique.

She sat down very close to Shaul. Gil transferred from one parent to another as they waited for Captain Mizrahi to come to the point of his visit. "We see you've been traveling around Israel quite a bit."

"Shaul's visiting friends," Sarah said, quickly rising to her man's defense.

Captain Mizrahi smiled conspiratorialy at Shaul. "We know that," he assured Sarah. "We know whom he's been seeing and most of what's been said. Some of it has not been too smart," he warned Shaul.

"People ask me for my advice, I try to give it," Shaul explained.

"We prefer you in America," Mizrahi said. "It's quieter, safer on the streets of Tel Aviv when you're not around. But you start giving us any trouble here, you start making any trans-Atlantic deals, and we'll be in touch with our American counterparts. Don't think you're free of us over there, Darom. We have men everywhere."

"Always with their hand out?"

"He didn't mean that," Sarah interposed.

"We know about Canada; we know how you got the money to start that very successful and, I hear, very good restaurant. As far as I am concerned, you're a legitimate businessman now. Don't go making any trouble for yourself by associating with people who aren't in your league."

"I'm sure he won't," Sarah filled in for her silent partner. "All Shaul has ever wanted was a chance to make a go of something. And as you said, the restaurant is a success. Believe me, he'll take your advice. We have another child on the way," she finished lamely.

Now it was Mizrahi's turn to smirk. "Mazel tov," he congratulated Shaul. As he rose to go, Sarah caught a menacing glance from Shaul. But their fight would have to be postponed because as Captain Mizrahi opened the door to leave, he found the way blocked by Hal Evans returning home.

There were hasty introductions, allowing Hillel time enough to ask if anything was wrong. "Just seeing an old friend of mine," Mizrahi explained.

"Cousin Shaul's not in any trouble, is he?" Hillel asked all too innocently.

"Trouble? No," the captain told him. "Not yet."

Hillel sighed meaningfully. He put his arm around Shaul's shoulder while Shaul shifted awkwardly. "I know that Cousin Shaul has had his problems with you people. But I want to assure you that ever since I've taken him under my wing, he has trod the straight and narrow. If it's one thing I'm proud of in my life, it's the turnaround I've been able to make in my cousin's life."

"Well, sure," Mizrahi said uncertainly. After he said his good-byes and left, Shaul pushed Hillel away and asked "What the hell was that all about?"

Hal merely smiled at him and walked away. "Don't leave me," Sarah begged. Shaul studied Hillel's back uncertainly. "Tomorrow I'll pick you up," he told her. "Only one more night." He gave Gil a kiss, then he was gone.

* * *

Hillel Ewan lay quietly in bed waiting for his moment to strike. When he first came to Israel, he had had several alternative ideas aside from the one he started out with in Boston. But they had fallen by the wayside. Returning her to her parents? But they already knew their daughter was a whore. Discovering Shaul in bed with Sarah and killing them both? Pleading temporary insanity? But would he have been set free completely and immediately? So he had stuck to his main course, a plan he had gone over and over again in his mind ever since he had decided to come back to Israel for a visit. He had been nice to Sarah, oh, so pleasant, she didn't know what was happening. His relatives, her relatives, all had seen what a contented marriage he had. There would be no questions, no suspicions, especially when they saw him in mourning. It was perfect really. He knew Shaul wouldn't leave Sarah alone forever. And now Shaul was taking her and Gil down to Dimona. Hillel had even suggested they use his Dodge Dart and the stupid fools had agreed. It had to be a Dodge Dart—even though he anguished over its rental price—because it was an American car in the diagram, the one on how to wire the ignition so the car would explode in flames the minute the key was turned. He didn't want to chance it with a European model. Besides, Avis must have insurance to cover the car, so would it pursue him for its month's rental after the Dart went up in flames? Especially since he would be the bereaved father and widower?

Two o'clock. They would surely be asleep by now. Everyone in Israel must be asleep by now. Hillel reached under his bed and found his flashlight. He carefully snuck to his briefcase, unlocked and unzipped its most secure compartment. He reached in and took out the handbills. He had printed them himself at one of the amusement arcades in Boston's combat zone. It was a Palestinian manifesto demanding the evacuation of occupied territory and the release of all political prisoners in Israeli jails. These would be found carefully scattered near the car to leave no confusion in the minds of the police as to who was responsible for this dastardly deed. He carefully reached his hand into the briefcase for the most important item: the explosive. He wished he could have brought the diagram on how to wire the car with him, but that he had memorized. And he was after all an engineer. A civil engineer who had visited a construction site of an old friend and found out exactly which explosive to use. People with a little bit of knowledge were ever so helpful.

Hillel slipped his pants on over his pajamas and stuck his feet into his slippers. He opened the door to his room and moved like a cat to the front hallway where he let himself out of the apartment. He plunged downstairs and found his car parked on the street where he had left it. Carefully unlatching the hood, he set to work.

The trouble of it was that both wires were gray and dirty, not at all the same colors they were in the diagram. But even that didn't bother him. It just meant it wouldn't be the five-minute operation he had envisaged when he had meticulously assembled the same device on his Continental in his own garage. No, and here the wires were twisting one way and then seemed to lap back. What was he to make of it? He put down the explosive at his feet and leaned over into the car to separate and straighten the wires he needed. Good. Now he was ready to make his move. He bent over to reach for the explosive, brought it up to attach it. He checked the wires carefully once again. Then he checked the markings on the wire he would be inserting. Electrical charges all worked in the same fashion. He was sure. Almost. It was like replacing a light switch. All that could happen would be nothing. Sure. Theoretically. But his hands were sweating as he carefully encircled the loose frayed wire of the car's ignition around the explosive's terminals. By the time the last coil was in place, his hands were soaking and sweat dripped down his temples into the car itself. He nestled the explosive gently into place and then stood straight with relief. Done. Victory. He took out his handkerchief, wiped his face and hands, then sighed happily. He could feel his heartbeat become normal again as without thinking, he reached up for the hood of the car and slammed it into place. Do not jar! was his last thought as the explosive did its deadly work six hours too soon.

None of the Ewans could comprehend it. Last evening Hillel was alive, this morning he was dead. Why? Shoshana wondered if she was in a state of shock. She must be because she tried to come to terms with how Hillel had died, but she never quite made it. There were deaths that modern man could understand and expect: Warfare, car accidents, heart attacks, cancer. But terrorism, the taking of a single life for inexplicable reasons, was more than she could fathom. That's when living or dying depended on madness alone.

Now they had to decide how they would mourn Hillel, he whom they hardly knew. She had just left her father's apartment. No matter what the crisis, her first duty was to her three-month-old son, Ehud, and he needed to eat, to sleep. She could not breast-feed in front of all the visitors. Lily, Joseph, her father, even Rahel had been sitting around the apartment stunned, not really responding to the expressions of condolence. Sarah, Hillel's pregnant wife, had come by with Gil to discuss the funeral arrangements for the next morning, to decide where the shivah would be held. She looked more frightened than mournful. The poor girl. Shoshana understood only too well how she must feel now, suddenly having to fend for herself with no man to take care of her. Relatives, acquaintances, the police—Meir Ewan's apartment had been a madhouse.

She got off the bus with Ehud, her little Udie, and carried him against her shoulder to her own apartment. He was wide awake now, whimpering, ready to eat. She felt her breasts bursting with milk as she sat down in the rocking chair given to her by her former coworkers and unbuttoned her blouse. She moved her nipple to the baby's mouth and he latched on immediately, his small hand anxiously patting the softness of her breast. She leaned back then, closed her eyes, and let her son nurse. She thought of Danny. How many months? Ten. Ten months without him.

Sometimes she thought she could not bear it. So many deaths.

When Ehud was finished nursing, she burped him and put him down in his crib for his nap. She would rest too, sleep. It had been a long day, and tonight she would have to return to her father's. She had just about tucked herself in when the doorbell rang. It annoyed her because she knew it had to be about Hillel, and she would have been more pleased if the mourners had waited to find her at her father's. Getting up, she slipped on her dress and went to the door. She was surprised to find Oren, a police officer, and a civilian waiting in the hallway. "Oren?"

"Hi." He came forward to kiss her and asked to come in. She stood back while all three men shuffled inside her apartment. "Shoshana Ewan, this is Captain Oded Mizrahi from the police and Ben Yairi from internal security. I don't think you've met."

"No." She held out her hand to them. "Shall I make some tea?"

Oren sighed. "No, I think not. I think maybe we better sit down. Maybe you better too. We have some difficult things to discuss."

All sociability left Shoshana's face. "About what?" she asked apprehensively.

"About your brother, Hillel Ewan," Yairi from Shin Bet took over. "Did you know him well?"

Shoshana considered it. "He left Israel almost as soon as we got here. I was only ten. He was already grown. Most of what I knew about him I heard from listening to others talk. Lily, Joseph Benjamin, my brother-in-law. He would know as much about Hillel as anyone in Israel."

"But when he came back in sixty-seven," Yairi wanted to know, "what did you think of him?"

"He's dead," Shoshana reminded him.

"Shoshana," Oren urged, "please. This is necessary."

She took a deep breath. "I never liked Hillel. I don't think any of us really did. Except my mother, of course. He was the sort of man who had to hold all the power in his hand. To do this, he lied, he manipulated, he hurt. His

588

one goal in life was to be important, to be somebody, to be recognized. For anything. I don't think he was all there. He had dreams of grandeur that had no root in reality."

"Do you think he would go so far in his dreams of glory that he would link up with the Palestinian terrorists?"

Absolutely not!" She was shocked that Yairi had even suggested such a thing.

"He hated Israel."

"When he left, yes. I don't think Israel was important to him one way or another after a while. But because of his connection to it as a fund raiser, he could meet important people. That's what mattered to him. How could you possibly suggest he was connected with the Palestinians? What sort of slander is that?"

"The handbills found next to his body were printed in America."

"You're suggesting he blew himself up?"

"It's happened before. Over and over again with inexperienced terrorists."

"Well, if he was going to blow something up, why would he choose his own car?"

"You said it yourself. He wanted to be important. What could make him more noticeable than to be a subject of a Palestinian attack."

"I can't believe you."

"What do you know of Sarah?" Captain Mizrahi suddenly broke in.

"His wife? She's a distant relative. A cousin of some sort. I vaguely know her. She seems young, vulnerable."

"Did they have a happy marriage?"

"Oh, how do I know," she said, exasperated. "How could one be happy married to Hillel? Oh, God, I didn't mean that."

"Do you know a Shaul Darom?"

"Shaul Darom? No. Who's he?" Mizrahi did not answer her, but smiled instead. They rose as if to go. "Wait a second," Shoshana demanded. "What's going on?"

All the men looked to each other questioningly. "Can

you keep a secret?" Oren asked finally. "I mean now that you're out of the government."

"Are secrets kept in the government? Don't provoke me."

He smiled. "I know. That can be very dangerous. There are two theories about how your brother died. Shin Bet thinks either he had some tenuous connection with the terrorists and he was setting the explosion to insinuate himself into our power structure, or he was doing it on his own to attract attention. Like when he tried to break into Golda Meir's apartment."

"But—"

Oren rushed on quickly before she could speak. "On the other hand, Mizrahi here and the police believe your brother was trying to murder his wife, her child, and her boyfriend."

"What!"

Mizrahi took up the explanation. "Your brother's wife, Sarah, before she left for the States to marry Hillel Ewan, was keeping company with Shaul Darom, a minor but bothersome criminal on the local scene. We suspect she was already pregnant with Darom's child when she married Hillel. Yesterday she as much as admitted to me that the second child was also Shaul's. Shaul was taking Sarah and Gil down to Dimona today to meet his mother. Shaul said Hillel had offered him the rented Dodge Dart, almost demanded that he take it. I think that if your brother had done it right, the minute Darom turned the key in the ignition, he, Sarah, and little Gil would have been blown to bits."

Shoshana turned in shock to Oren. "We'll probably never know," Oren told her. "In any case he's dead, so that's the end of it."

"Unless he was connected to the Palestinians," Yairi interjected.

"What are you going to do about it? I mean what are you going to say to the newspapers and everything? I don't think my father should have to suffer this scandal," Shoshana protested.

"We're just planning to say that the police are still investigating this mysterious death, something like that," Mizrahi said. "Tomorrow he'll be buried. The newspapers will forget him a few days after that."

"The government is planning to send the minister of transportation," Oren said. "No one too high up, but someone high enough to show respect for an ardent fund raiser."

"The minister of transportation. How fitting," Shoshana said glumly.

Oren reached out to her and held her in his arms. Then he took a few minutes off from official duties to have a look at Udie, after which they departed, leaving her mind swirling and her body weak.

"He would have been pleased," Lily said. They had all come back to Meir Ewan's apartment after the funeral. The sisters had brought cakes and sweets. Rahel provided the tea and coffee as the mourners passed in and out of the apartment expressing their regret. "The minister of transportation giving the eulogy; that's something, isn't it?"

"Yes," Shoshana told her sister. "It's something." She glanced around the room and saw Sarah sitting on a straight-back chair, the same look of apprehension and fear on her face as before. Shoshana didn't know how she should feel toward her sister-in-law. Hatred, fury, pity? Who was this Shaul Darom anyway? She guessed he wouldn't dare show up now. But could he be far away? Sarah caught her looking at her. Shoshana gave her a smile of encouragement; Sarah tentatively smiled back. Live and let live. What other way was there?

"You're angry at me, aren't you?"

Shoshana looked at Lily strangely. "Why should I be angry at you?"

"Because I'm being such a hypocrite."

Shoshana hushed her. Then she whispered, "We're all being hypocrites. Just because you hate someone doesn't mean you wish him dead. So go through the motions of mourning. That's what the shivah is for. When it's over, we can rise up happy."

"Father's not happy that Ovadia didn't come."

"I talked to Ovadia on the phone. He said he never saw Hillel when he was alive, what good would it do to come to the funeral, especially since Roberta would be stuck at home with two children and the birth less than a month away."

Lily nodded her head sagely. Ovadia was no hypocrite.

But the rest of the family seemed to be as they listened and nodded their way through seven days of mourning, while relatives and acquaintances came by to tell them what a great man Hillel Ewan, or occasionally Hal Evans, had been. Shoshana didn't mind it except when it upset Udie's schedule. She saw many of her friends from work who came over to her father's to express their regret to her. They gossiped and even had a quiet laugh or two together. David stopped by. Twice. Both times he sat next to her trying to convince her to come back to work. She adamantly refused even as he went into detail after detail of how the Iraqi section was falling to pieces without her. "Have some respect for the dead," she warned him. So he sat there silently next to her, sipping his tea.

Shaul walked up the street and looked at the spot where nine days ago Hillel Ewan had blown himself and a Dodge Dart to oblivion in this quiet, residential section of Tel Aviv. There should be some plaque, some mark bearing the legend, "Here lie pieces of one of the biggest shits to ever walk the earth." Blow up Gil? The bastard. Oh, yeah, Shaul believed Captain Mizrahi when the policeman told him the bomb had been meant for him and Sarah. After that act Hillel had put on, what else could it mean? Well, they were rid of him. For good. Now his only problem was Sarah, getting her to go back to Boston to collect her inheritance. She refused, said he could handle it for her. She would give him her power of attorney. But her father had put his foot in and stopped that. Her father wanted the power of attorney for himself. Poor Sarah, the sooner he married her, the better. And the sooner would take place when they arrived in Boston, got a license and the blood tests. Sarah wouldn't fight it. She would want a name, his name for their second child. And he would see that they stayed in America for a year or so operating his restaurant. Then they could sell the house in Brookline, come back to Tel Aviv, and use the money to open a second restaurant in Dizengoff. "Daromah's: Boston—Tel Aviv." She would like that. Yes, Shaul saw a good life for himself. Sarah, two kids, two restaurants, two passports, and all of Hillel Ewan's earthly possessions.

40

Shoshana wondered if everyone dreaded the coming of October, 1974 as much as she did. She did not want to reevaluate; she did not want to remember; she did not want to study her regrets. She tried to think ahead, to concentrate on the growth of her son and her work at the university. If she had to remember how much she had lost, how could she ever go on? Danny is dead, she told herself on that awful anniversary. Yet even as she did so, she looked in the mirror and her face was pale, her eyes sunken, her hair had lost its luster. If Danny was dead, she must also be dead because she could not live without him.

It was a duty one paid to the dead, to remember them on that day. A duty. She did not think it a burden to visit her mother's grave. There was a fullness in her mother's life for all the pain she had suffered toward the end. Shoshana felt her mother was at peace. But Danny, he, they all were so young, those who had fallen. What might have been lay buried in the ground, so cold, so silent.

Oren had called and asked her if she wanted a ride to the scheduled memorial service. She told him no, she could not face all those people again, not Ronit, not Danny's father. She would go later when everyone else had cleared out. She wanted to be alone with Danny because there were a lot of things she had to discuss with him. That had just slipped out. Oren must have thought her crazy. But he didn't comment on it.

"Well, do you want a ride later?" he had asked.

"No. I'll take a bus."

"Don't be a martyr. I'll pick you up at three."

She had accepted gratefully because she was bringing Ehud along and by bus it would have been complicated.

Oren, who had already been to the grave in the morning, told her he would wait in the parking lot for her.

When she got to the grave, she was unpleasantly shocked to find Danny's father still there. She froze in hatred and took the last few steps cautiously. His father waited for her, staring not so much at her as at her child.

Angered, she said, "You had your chance to be with your son this morning. Now it's my turn. Clear out."

He didn't move. "I've been waiting for you all day," he said coldly. "I understand that you have Danny's son." She pressed the squirming child more closely to her. "We want to adopt him," the man continued. "We'll pay you for your effort."

"You filth," she hissed. "Get out of here. You couldn't take Danny away from me, you won't take our son. That your eyes are even gazing at him makes me sick. If Danny could rise from his grave, he would strike you down."

He stared at her still. She held the child's face from him. "Think about it," he said. "The child is illegitimate. You were never married to my son. If you give up the child, you can start a new life for yourself. If you keep the child, all your men will ask where it came from."

"I can promise you this: You will never see this child, you will never hold this child. He will never be a part of your life. You cut off your son, you cut off your heirs. You may think about that for the rest of your days. And all your money and your influence can't bring Danny back to you or bring you his son. Now get out of here. Go back to your comfortable sewer. Let the dead rest in peace."

Slowly, without another word, he left her. She was tight and tense all over. She could not think about Danny, just what they were still trying to do to both of them.

Someone came up beside her. She turned quickly, expecting to see Danny's father again. It was Oren.

"I saw—"

"Yes," she said.

"What did he want?"

"Hah! What do you think?"

"Not Ehud," Oren said in disbelief.

"Yes."

"What chutzpah."

"Over Danny's grave! I can't think of anything now."

"Shall I say the prayers?" Oren asked.

"Yes," Shoshana said weakly.

Oren began the memorial and Shoshana swayed slightly in time to his rhythm. "That was beautiful," she said when he finished.

"They are our prayers, not theirs," Oren said, good Iraqi that he was. Shoshana laughed. "Shall we each tell a story about Danny?" Oren said. "As a way of remembering."

"Yes, okay," she agreed.

"Well, okay. Once when Danny and I were stationed in Caesarea, this girl—"

"Don't continue," Shoshana said happily. "It was one of the most miserable moments in my life."

"How do you know you were the girl I was going to talk about?"

Shoshana laughed. "Oh, you're right," she said. "With Danny one never knew."

"He was never unfaithful to you, Shoshana."

"Oh, Oren."

Oren shrugged. "He loved you. That's what I meant. He never grew up knowing how to do what was right. Maybe the Ze'evs of this world don't teach their children right from wrong. But he tried to find his way to you in everything he did. In the end he succeeded so the rest doesn't matter. Don't cry for God's sake," he said, annoyed.

She tried to push away the tears. "Do you think that's all that's needed to remain faithful to someone, to be in love forever?"

"Love is like a ghost. It just floats around somewhere waiting to haunt us. Don't build a stone memorial to Danny in your heart. It would sicken him. He wasn't much on sentimentality. He would expect you to remember the happy times and go on with your life. And of course never let Ehud forget who his father was." He smiled at her. "So anyway that's my story of the daring commando and the beautiful young maiden. Like all Iraqi stories it has a melancholy ending. Now its your turn."

She thought. "I have to come up with one uncensored. Okay. Do you want to know why the baby's named Ehud?"

"I have wondered," Oren conceded.

"Well, you know that Danny was an only child. When he was growing up, he used to say, he got very lonely. So he had a make-believe friend and he called him Ehud. He said if, I mean when—he never expected otherwise—he had a son, he wanted him to be named Ehud because some of his happiest moments were with this make-believe friend."

Oren studied the child sitting on her lap. "He looks like Danny, you know?"

"He smiles like him too. Come on, Udie. Smile for your Uncle Oren."

"No, no, no," Oren said as he got up. "You're just like Nurit. All the time I have to sit for hours waiting for our brats to smile. Believe me, it's not worth it."

"Well, no wonder with that attitude you don't get a smile," she said indignantly.

He helped her up. "You'll be okay," he said.

"I know."

And she was okay. She thought she would not live through the memorial for Danny, but she had, and some of the sadness slipped away. Oren was right. She would remember the happy times. There were so many of them. And she would go on. With Ehud, with her family, with Danielle. Her life could be, was full. It was just a matter of reaching out for those around her. She could have so much if she was willing. Even her relationship with her father had been restored. Now with the university starting up again, she had asked Lily if her sister could care for Ehud during the mornings while she worked. Instead her father had volunteered to come over three mornings a week to save her from carrying everything to Lily's. Lily was upset and Shoshana slightly worried at first. After all, what did her father know about taking care of babies. Yet Udie was dry, well fed, and happy when she returned from work. And her father was delighted with his new-gained insights into motherhood.

So her life was full. And yet there was that singular absence. No one loved her as Danny had. She was afraid no one ever would, afraid for the first time in her life of being alone forever. She did not think she could live without being in love with someone.

Joshua Benjamin was jackknifed over a jeep trying to choke his wrench around the right bolt when someone came behind him and tickled his ribs. He shot up and turned furiously on his attacker.

"Ilanit!"

She laughed, her white teeth shining, her blond hair glinting beneath the sun. "Were you going to use that wrench for something?" she asked mischievously.

He noticed that he still held the tool clenched in his fist. Turning, he placed it on the jeep's fender. "What are you doing here? Are you on leave?"

"No. My general had to see your general, and he very nicely offered to let me accompany him. After I told him about you, of course."

"Oh, sure," he noted with a sardonic smile. "I can imagine what goes on between you and your general. Corporal Burg," he added pointedly.

She dusted off her new stripe. "I happen to be a very efficient typist."

"Uh huh. And being as beautiful as Batsheva doesn't hurt."

"Can you get some time off?" she asked hopefully.

Joshua looked around the area. "Uh, lieutenant," he called. "I've got to take this jeep out on a test run. I can't quite figure out what's wrong with it."

The lieutenant looked from Joshua to the blond, then waved them on their way. "Hop in," Joshua told her as he slammed down the hood, swung himself into the driver's seat, and started the motor.

They were off. Joshua drove her north from the Kinneret into the Golan, the land lying lush and green on both sides of the road as the curves took them up and down the hills until the jeep struggled valiantly to the top of a crest. Joshua cut the motor and they stared out into the countryside.

"It's beautiful," Ilanit said.

"Quiet. That's what I like about it."

They looked at each other. Without saying a word, they left the jeep and walked slowly down the hill together. Joshua turned and took her into his arms. "I'm not afraid," she promised him. "I am," he admitted.

And yet he didn't seem to be. His hands were so firm, his body so strong; she knew whatever happened, he would be there for her, protecting her, supporting her, loving her. "Oh, Joshua!" She called out his name, looked up into the sky, and knew this was what she wanted for her eternity.

Meir Ewan had finished changing his grandchild Ehud and was now dressing him in his knit leggings and sweater. It disturbed him sometimes to see the way Shoshana carried the boy about with so little on him. A baby should be bundled, kept warm and secure. If Salemah were here, she would show Shoshana how to do all these things, but Salemah was long dead and Rahel, his second wife, had time only for her own grandchildren. He was glad he could come over these days to take care of Udie the way he was meant to be taken care of. He supposed he had Shoshana's work to thank for that. Though why she would work when she had a child he would never understand. Well, he had to face it. He would probably never understand anything about his younger daughter. She was so foreign to him even as he loved her. But he would no longer chide her or criticize her. He had no more time to spend in anger or separation because he had no more time for regrets. He was old. His generation was dying out. Who knew when his time might come. So why start a fight he couldn't finish?

"Come on, Udie," he said to the struggling child. "Time to go on our walk." And he would be walking soon. Ten months old and he crawled faster than Meir's eyes could see. He pulled himself up on his crib and playpen, bounced around like a monkey. He dribbled from his mouth and splashed out syllables. "*Saba*," Meir said to him as he picked Ehud up and carried him to the door. "Can you call your grandfather *saba*? *Sa-ba*."

"Ba-ba," the boy bubbled.

Meir laughed happily. "Good, good. Almost. *Saba* will be the first word from your mouth." Meir placed Ehud in his stroller and unchained it from the downstairs railing before pushing it out onto the sidewalk. He stopped for a minute to wrap his scarf tighter around his neck. The sun still shone in December, but the winds were cold. He buttoned his jacket and pushed the child toward the park. He had many friends at the park now. If he hadn't been married a second time, there would have been plenty of action for him along the benches, as the grandmothers were out in style, all looking after their grandchildren while their daughters worked. And Rahel wondered why he was gaining weight. Well, what could he do when all the women offered him fruit and cookies? Refuse? He called out a happy greeting to all he knew, then he parked the stroller and took Udie out. He held the child up by his two hands and let Udie struggle to put one foot in front of the other. Udie almost pedaled with excitement. The sandpile lay within sight and he could hardly wait to get at it, to nuzzle into it and throw the sand up into the air to come down on

601

his clothes, his hair, on other children. Udie was already the terror of the playground, like his father must have been, Meir thought sadly.

"He's a fine boy," a voice next to him said. Meir looked up and saw Danny's father. His heart turned cold. Shoshana had told him briefly of Ze'ev's efforts to claim the child, told him to be careful, not to let any stranger pick him up, walk away with him. As if he needed to be told. "That he is," Meir said sternly. "A very fine boy, my grandson."

"Mine too. My son was his father."

"How can you be sure of that? You've always been so prompt to brand my daughter a whore."

"I'm ready to let bygones be bygones."

"It's too late."

"You're not being fair to the child. I can offer him so much more than the Ewans can."

"Hah! The way I read it in the newspapers, you may not be around to fulfill any promises. You and the father of Danny's wife seem to be in some sort of trouble. Taking bribes or giving? I forget which."

"Everyone who has any wealth is being persecuted. You should be glad you're poor."

"A man who has sons and grandsons is never lacking," Meir told him coldly.

Ze'ev backed off. "Your son-in-law, how's he feeling right about now? I understand Frayman Construction Company might be at the center of one of the juicier government scandals."

"Joseph will be okay," Meir assured him. "We Iraqis have a knack for survival."

"Ba-ba," Ehud cried from the center of a sandstorm.

"If you'll excuse me," Meir said, "my grandson is calling me." He rose, his limbs stiff, and sunk down into the sand next to Udie. It was time to make tunnels so he could stick his arm through and wiggle his fingers at Ehud like magic, then hear the child peal with laughter. He looked at Ehud, studied his face, even as Ze'ev behind him must be doing.

He had several teeth now, his skin was lighter then the Ewans' but darker than the Ze-evs'. His hair was brown like Danny's but curly like Shoshana's. And his tongue was calling for ba-ba; he belonged to them. Ze'ev had it all. Money, a large apartment, a big car, while Meir had only his small apartment and a small pension. But Ze'ev had lost his son and through his cruelty had lost his grandson. So who was the winner? Meir knew the answer to that when Ehud reached out and played pat a cake on Meir's rough-shaven cheeks.

41

Sergeant Joshua Benjamin returned to his family for Hanukah, 1975 from his base in the Galilee. He was in charge of training new ordnance recruits now. His commander wanted him to stay on in the regular army, go for officer's training, make it his profession, but Joshua declined. His father and Benjamin and Son needed him more than the army. Though his father never said anything, Joshua followed the stories in the papers as faithfully as anyone. It seemed as if after the Yom Kippur War there was a witch-hunt in the country that would not stop until the highest in the land were tumbled. And his father was caught up in it along with Moishe Frayman and all the others. Questions asked, books poured over. He had spoken to his father about it on an earlier leave. "All I can do now is confess to nothing," Joseph had said, "because to confess to anything is to admit to everything. So I have pitted Danielle Nissan's brain against the best tax accountants in Israel. So far she's coming out on top."

"And Frayman?"

"Moishe," Joseph pondered. He became moody again

and Joshua was sorry he had asked. "Moishe, I see him every day. Every day he looks at me and asks if I expect him to commit suicide like the dentist or the doctor or the party official. I tell him no, but he wonders and is happy his father didn't live to see this."

"Will it be okay?"

"When they have bigger fish to fry, they'll leave us alone," Joseph assured him.

His father looked happier this time. Perhaps it was Hanukah, perhaps it was seeing him again after all these months. His mother had made doughnuts filled with jelly, light fluffy things, so much better than the army's, which gave all but the heartiest stomach cramps.

Aunt Shoshana was there that night with her son. Joshua couldn't believe how much Ehud had grown and all the new words he was learning. He wasn't even two yet. He held him on his lap and kept him there till Udie was calling him Joshua instead of just Shua which always sounded like a sneeze to him. "He's wonderful, Aunt."

"I know," Shoshana replied.

Joshua set Ehud down and soon both of his little cousin's hands were filled with cookies. "Well, I came home to tell you something."

Lily tensed and came to stand by Joseph, resting her hand on his shoulder. She was only afraid her son was going to tell them he would stay in the army.

Joshua was pleased to see he had everyone's attention. "Ilanit and I are going to be married." Joshua was so busy happily accepting congratulations from his father and Shoshana that he didn't notice his mother's rage.

"What do you mean you and Ilanit are going to get married? How dare you?" she snapped at her son.

Joseph turned to look at his wife and saw her inflamed. "What's the matter with you, Lily?" he asked her quietly.

"Have you forgotten our ways?" Lily asked her son angrily. "You don't announce you're getting married. You speak to your father about it. Your father will then speak to her father, and they'll see if they can come to some agreement. Then they'll inform you whether you're getting married or not."

The family stared at her in a certain fascinated kind of horror until Shoshana burst out laughing. "Lily's absolutely right," she told her shocked and hurt nephew. "Let me tell you about the old ways. The old way is to demand to marry someone your father doesn't approve of. Then your father locks you in your room while your beloved flees from Baghdad to Tehran to wait for you, just ahead of the police who are searching for him because of his Zionist activities. Pretty soon your father unlocks your door because you've pretended to forget your beloved. You and your girl friend conspire to flee Iraq with the help of a disreputable uncle. You enlist the aid of your poor gullible little sister, forcing her to lie to her own mother. Then you scurry to Tehran with your girl friend, where in the company of your intended you wait for the arrival of your father. You know your father will be forced to let you marry the man you love now because you have dishonored yourself and no other man will have you."

Even Joseph was laughing at Lily by the time Shoshana finished. "Well, at least I got married," Lily flung back at her sister.

"Don't be such a hypocrite," Shoshana retorted. "You've always been afraid of losing Joshua. Now you think because he's going to be married, you'll never see him again. Tell him you're happy for him and you'll be glad to have Ilanit for a daughter-in-law."

"I certainly will be," Joseph assured his son.

Lily saw they were all aligned against her, even Joseph, whom she would speak to later. "I will be glad to take Ilanit under consideration as a candidate for daughter-in-law," she conceded.

"Well, consider it fast, Mother, because I've invited her and her family over for the Shabbat dinner tomorrow night."

"Oh, Joshua, you couldn't have!"

* * *

Lily worked furiously in her kitchen, her fury coming either from anger or despair at ever being ready in time. Joshua's list of dos and don'ts were still coursing through her mind. Do boil the potatoes, boil the chicken. Don't make rice or anything spicy. Thank God Joseph had vetoed that. "They're coming to our house, they'll have our food," Joseph had set his son straight. "Besides, they probably haven't eaten well since they last went to an Oriental restaurant." Lily had called on both Shoshana and Danielle to make their best dishes and bring them over by four in the afternoon. If she had had three days, she would have made pacha, stuffed lamb stomach, but as it was, she made barakas while Shoshana brought over stuffed vegetables in tomato sauce along with her lemon cakes and Danielle would bring the first course, fish with rice, and a coconut cake for dessert. She could kill Joshua, just strangle him. The whole house had to be cleaned, but he didn't bother offering to help. No, he was over at Ilanit's. The nerve. Especially after he told Joseph to make sure he helped Lily in the kitchen when Ilanit's parents were here instead of sitting around expecting to be served. "They liked me well enough as a boyfriend," Joshua explained, "but they're not too sure Ilanit should marry me. They don't like the way Oriental men treat their wives. They think it's sort of like a harem affair, so if you'd just get up and do some work in the kitchen while they're here, it would help."

This time Lily put her foot down. "Your father works hard all day to support us. When he comes home, he deserves to be waited on, and I hope Ilanit will feel the same way toward you."

"Well, she won't, Mother. I don't see why Father can't pretend for one night that he helps around the house. And please, if you're going to turn on the radio, leave it on Gal Aleph so they can hear classical music. Whatever you do, don't turn it to any Arabic station. Ilanit's father thinks Arabic music is just a lot of noise. They're not well off, but they are cultured."

"Perhaps I should be reading a copy of Dostoevski when

they come in, your father meanwhile in the kitchen washing dishes."

Joshua clapped his hands and laughed. "That would be perfect, Mother."

"Joshua, you're a snob and you're ashamed of your own parents."

"I'm not ashamed of you. I'm just asking you to go through this once. Ilanit knows who I am. After we're married, we'll do things my way. And please, Mother, whatever you do, don't cry or shout or be emotional in any way. Her parents aren't like that. They're sort of—"

"Cold?"

"Well . . ." He shrugged his shoulders affirmatively.

Joshua remembered what he had forgotten to tell his father when he saw the Burgs coming out of their bedroom, ready to depart for his house. He had forgotten to tell his father to wear a tie. Oh, well, into the breach. Ilanit gave his hand a squeeze, even though it was sweating. He looked at her and she smiled her encouragement. They had already decided that no matter what happened tonight, they would still get married. It was just that it would be so much nicer if their parents got along. Hela, Ilanit's sixteen-year-old sister, found the whole thing amusing and was already giggling into her cupped hand. Giggling out loud was not permitted in the Burg household. It led to a lack of discipline.

They took the bus to his place. They could have walked it, but Mrs. Burg had trouble with her feet, especially if she had to put them into shoes instead of her house slippers. Joshua was pleased to see that his mother had a soft light on in the living room, candles on the table in the dining room, and was listening to Western music on the radio. So far so good. He watched his mother greet the Burgs. For the first time he realized how absolutely beautiful Lily was. Her hair, though streaked with gray, curled angelically around her face, her body was still sleek, and with her gold jewelry modestly displayed, she looked like a Persian princess. Impulsively he came up and gave her a kiss, which both surprised and pleased her. "Where's Father?" he asked.

"He called to say he was going directly from work to the synagogue."

"Your family's not religious, is it?" asked the secular Mr. Burg.

"Of course we're religious," Lily said, surprised that anyone would ask her that.

"We're not zealots," Joshua explained. "We celebrate the holidays and Shabbat. Please sit down. No, Mother, you sit too. I'll just go into the kitchen and bring out some nuts and crackers." It was definitely going to be a long night.

Lily sat with a smile and waited for what she knew she was going to hear next. "Mother, do you know where the hors d'oeuvres have gotten to?" Lily smiled graciously and excused herself. As if Joshua knew where they had been in the first place.

When Joseph got home from the synagogue, he said a quick hello to the Burgs, gave Ilanit a kiss on the cheek, then hurried to the bathroom to wash up. Joshua watched Mr. Burg. He was sure Ilanit's father expected Joseph to return in pajamas. That's how Europeans thought Iraqis dressed at home. His father might be just perverse enough to make an appearance in his striped flannels. But no, Joseph had put on his white shirt and brown pants. They were ready for the kiddush. Joseph offered the honor to Mr. Burg, but Ilanit's father refused. "What's wrong with the radio?" Joseph suddenly noticed.

"Shall I turn it off for you?" Ilanit suggested quickly.

"Couldn't you get the regular channel?" Joseph asked an embarrassed Lily.

"I'll turn it off for you," Ilanit insisted.

"No, I'll turn it off," Joshua said.

"Well, someone turn it off. It's getting on my nerves."

Joshua rushed to the radio and flicked it off. He gave his father a look that could kill, but his father was already reciting the kiddush. When it was over, he passed the wine cup to the Burgs, then to Lily who kissed his hand before she took a sip, then to his son who kissed his hand before he took a sip, even though he noticed the Burgs' stern disapproval, then to Ilanit who kissed his hand before she took a sip. *"Motec,"* Joseph said to her. Hela did not kiss his hand.

"Shabbat shalom lakhem," Lily said as they all sat down, even, Joshua noted with dismay, Joseph.

"Shall I help in the kitchen?" Ilanit asked Joseph.

He shook his head. "No. Lily's used to doing it all. Don't worry about it."

Joshua's hopes fell. It was definitely going to be an elopement. How could his father have forgotten the lecture he gave them just last night!

The meal went well, if one discounted the fact that Mr. and Mrs. Burg didn't eat much. Ilanit and Hela definitely dug in, and his father kept the conversation going by asking Mr. Burg about his work in the ministry of communications, asking Mrs. Burg about her work in social welfare. The only rough spot came when Mrs. Burg asked Lily what she did. "I look after my husband, my son, and this apartment," Lily answered very contentedly.

"But is it enough?"

Lily smiled broadly at her. "Well, now with Joshua getting married, there will be grandchildren to look after."

"Ilanit is planning to go to the university after the army," Mr. Burg said to Joseph so there would be no mistake about having children right away. "She's planning to study English literature. And Joshua?"

"Joshua will be joining the business," Joseph explained. "I need him with me. It's too big for me to handle alone anymore."

"But what about his university degree?" Mrs. Burg asked. "We had expected our daughter to marry an academic."

"If he wants to go to the university, I have no objection." There was a general sigh of relief. "As long as it's in the evening. Look, Ilanit and Joshua have known each other since high school. They know each other better than we know either of them. I'm quite content to let them lead their own lives. And my wife and I will be happy to have

Ilanit as a daughter. We're very fond of her." He smiled at his prospective daughter-in-law and raised his glass in a toast to her. After dinner they moved back into the living room where Lily served coffee. Then she disappeared into the kitchen while the Burgs discussed business with Joseph. Joseph promised Joshua and Ilanit a three-bedroom apartment of their choice free and clear. That would solve the biggest problem for the young married in Israel, a place to live. Mr. and Mrs. Burg countered by promising the happy couple a stereo system and a complete set of Beethoven's symphonies. "Plus," Mr. Burg added, "two subscriptions to the Israel Philharmonic."

Joshua didn't know how to express his gratitude. Luckily his father did it for him. "Great" Joseph said. "Now you two have everything."

The wedding took place on Ilanit's army base a day before she was to be demobilized. Lily thought it was a weird way to get married, but Joshua explained that a regular wedding would put the Burgs into debt, so they had decided to say this was what they wanted. The Burgs did have a reception in their apartment just for the families after the ceremony. Besides, having it on an army base meant that all their friends would be able to attend. Joshua even got a three-day pass to enjoy his honeymoon. Joseph had booked them a room in Nahariya so they could enjoy the beach. It was to Joshua a little slice of heaven being alone with Ilanit in a hotel room they barely left, and he intended to enjoy every second of it because while Ilanit could go home, get their apartment in order, and register for the spring semester at the university, he still had six months of service left in the army. So he took full and complete advantage of the occasion. Ilanit wondered fleetingly if it would have been better had they waited, but he assured her constantly that married or unmarried, she was the best, the only lay he would ever have.

42

Danielle absently swept the sponge across her kitchen table. She had not noticed the tears falling from her eyes until they splashed down onto the table while the inevitable swish of the sponge soaked them up again.

It had been four years. Time had stopped. For her. Why only for her? Ezra and Paula had returned to the Golan after the war, had another child. Albert and Segal were living happily on the moshav, producing flowers and a child they had named Hyacinth. Ovadia and Roberta had visited Israel last summer bringing Zachary, Deborah, and their new one, Gabriel born since the war. Shoshana had Ehud. New life. New loves. Time stopped only for her.

Danielle hated herself for what she was becoming. Mean, spiteful, vicious. Just like her mother. And why? Because she was alone. That was it. Because she was alone within herself and even herself wasn't answering.

She would never forgive herself for her attitude toward Roberta and her boy Gabriel when they came last summer. How hateful she had been. Ignoring the child, ignoring Roberta. She had gone to Shoshana's afterward and just cried and cried. "I can't help it," she told Shoshana. "I can't help it. I'm trying. Honestly." Shoshana had held her tight and rocked her the way she would Udie. "It's all right," Shoshana told her. "Really it is. We understand."

She didn't want their understanding. She wanted a husband and a son. Where the hell was Sami? God, how she hated him. It was so easy just to get up, go off to war, and die. That solved all his problems. But what about her? How much did any of his promises mean to her now?

Shoshana. Oh, Shoshana could forgive. Shoshana could be sweet and understanding. Why not. Shoshana had Danny's and her son.

It was Hanukah. Soon it would be Tu B'shvat, Purim, then Pesach and she would still be alone. She could not bear it any longer. She worked in the bank all day. She came home. She was alone all night. She didn't have to be. That's what that one businessman had said to her a few months ago. As if she wanted him in bed with her. He was fat and married. No, she would not do anything without marriage.

An arranged marriage? She had considered it. But she would not let those women put her on the block to be assessed by men she didn't care for. Valued not for love but for how much money she could put up and how much skill she had around the house. She was too good for that, or if not too good, then too private.

She laughed then when she considered what she held in her hands. It was her ad in this Friday's *Maariv*. She checked it carefully to make sure there weren't any misprints. No, it was all there, laid out. Now all she had to do was wait for her prince to come. She laughed and studied it again. "Iraqi woman, childless war widow, own apartment, seeks companionable male of similar background. Object matrimony. Box M29." Was this the call to a prince?

The week passed slowly for an anxious Danielle. She worked without thinking at the bank, then hurried to her box to collect any answers she might have received. For the most part she had a set of disappointments. Several real estate agents wrote her and asked if she wanted to sell her flat. A man wrote and left his number. She called. The first question he asked was the size of her apartment. She finished that conversation off quickly. Matrimonial agencies wrote, letting her know she would have a better chance if she listed with them. Several women wrote and said they too were widows and would she like to share her flat as they were living with their families. One man perked her interest, but he was a Russian and she could barely understand him so she gave up. The only nearly acceptable call back she made was on Wednesday and even then she wasn't too sure.

"Yes, I wrote you about your ad," the voice with a heavy Oriental accent said.

"Yes." She wondered how she sounded on the phone.

"It says here of similar background?"

"Yes."

"I'm not Iraqi. I'm from Yemen."

Danielle considered it. He was probably short, dark, and hairy. "Yes."

"I don't know if that is acceptable to you."

Well, she didn't know either. What could she say. "Well," she began just as he started to say something.

"I'm sorry," he said. "Did I interrupt you?"

"No."

"I just wanted to say, well, to tell you something about myself. If you're interested?"

"Yes."

"My name is Moshe Zichri. I'm thirty-four. I came with my family to Israel in 1948. We live in Ha-Tikva. For high school I went away to an agricultural school. I was going to join a moshav but my parents needed help. I work now in the custom house but I am saving my money to buy a flower shop. The reason I am not married so far is, well, there are nine children in our family and it has not been easy for my parents, but the youngest one is now just going into the army so perhaps there will be a period of rest. I am a hard worker," he finished off.

Well, she knew that. All Yemenites were. Oh, dear. He was waiting for her to say something.

"Miss. Are you still there?"

"Yes," Danielle said. There was a pause. "Do you want to hear something about me?"

"Well, perhaps your name, how old you are, and why you did not have any children."

"Yes. Well, I'm Danielle. I'm thirty-two but I will be thirty-three very soon. And we didn't have children because we waited and then I had a miscarriage. Then the war—"

"I understand," he cut in quickly. "Then you want children? Children are very important to me."

"Me too," she assured him.

"I wonder then," he said, "if you would like to go with me to the movies this Saturday night. There is a new American—"

"Yes."

"Yes?"

"Yes."

"That is good. If you will give me your address, I will pick you up at seven?"

She gave him her address. She put down the phone and was scared to death.

By the time Saturday night came, she was in a panic. At thirty-two she was a nervous wreck at meeting a man for a date. She could only thank God that she had not told anyone what she was doing but had begged off from the usual gathering at the Ewans with a headache.

Her bell rang at exactly seven o'clock. It was as if he had been waiting outside her door checking his watch. She straightened her dress for the last time and moved to open the door.

Why did she compare him to Sami? Sami was so big and blustering. The man who stood before her was dark and thin, but at least taller than she had expected, almost four inches taller than she was. "Moshe?" she asked.

"Yes," he said nervously and held out his hand. She grasped it and in that way guided him into her flat. She took it as a good sign that he stared at her rather than her apartment.

"You know I never asked your last name," he said.

He had a nice voice, rather soft with a pleasing Yemenite accent. "Danielle Nissan," she answered.

"Danielle Nissan," he repeated. "It's very musical."

"Do you like music?" she asked. What a stupid question. All Yemenites liked music, didn't they?

He smiled. "Shall we go?" he asked.

She got her coat and he helped her on with it. She was pleased to note that he did not let his hands rest on her shoulders.

The movie they saw was supposed to be a comedy about an American woman with a child who doesn't have a man until an actor moves in on her and they start sleeping with each other. It was an uncomfortable film to see with a stranger, and Danielle wondered if Moshe knew what it was about before he brought her here. She just wished Americans would make films without sex in them.

After the movie he took her out for cake and coffee. It was crowded with other moviegoers and a bit noisy, but she was able to hear him. He was telling her about his job in customs, which she assumed wasn't much as he was not even a clerk but was involved in hoisting crates and things.

"I've been saving," he told her. "Whatever I can. I know the flower business and there's this shop in Bnei Brak that the owner is trying to sell."

"Do you have the money for it?"

"No. It would have to be on loan."

"Banks don't give money out of the air."

"Maybe."

"I work in one. I know."

"It's what I want to do, you know. It's my future."

"If you invest everything in your future, you might not have anything for the present."

He smiled. "If I don't invest now, I won't have a future."

She considered it. "What about your family? Won't you still have to help out?"

"There were nine of us," he said. "Four sisters. Three are married, one is home with Mother. Five brothers. One killed in 'sixty-seven, one in the army now. My older

617

brother married and another one is hanging around like me."

Danielle nodded. "And what about your father?"

"He works as a shoemaker. He can support my mother. It was the nine children he had trouble with. And what about your family, your father?"

"I don't have one. I mean he's dead."

"And your mother?"

"She lives on welfare." Danielle felt she had to explain. "You see my father could not adjust to life here so he left for Iran and—"

"It's not necessary," Moshe said quickly.

"My two brothers are doing well. Both married. One on a kibbutz up north, one married into a moshav in the south. He raises flowers. You would probably like talking with him."

"If I may, your husband?"

"He died in 'seventy-three, in the Sinai. He was in the tank corp." She smiled, remembering.

"I'm sorry."

"Yes."

"And you stayed in the apartment alone?"

"Yes. My mother did not get along with my husband," she explained.

He nodded. "And you are—"

"I have my job, the apartment, and a considerable savings," she cleared it up for him. "In American dollars of course."

"Of course. As a banker you would."

She smiled. She stared at him now. He wasn't half bad. Dark of course, but his clothes were clean, probably due to his mother, he had good manners, he was soft-spoken. Of course he was from Yemen and that meant that his customs would be different from hers. Still, he had ambition and she liked that. Sami also had his dreams. But no, she mustn't think of him, not now. She wondered what this Moshe thought of her. She would probably never know. That was the thing in offering yourself and your apartment as part of a package deal.

When they had finished their dessert, he escorted her back to her apartment. "Would you like to come in and look around?" she asked.

"If you wish," he said.

She unlocked the door and walked in with Moshe behind her. She hoped that he wasn't thinking of what happened in that movie. She showed him through the apartment, lingering on the kitchen, the living room, and the balcony, but hurrying him past the bathroom and bedrooms.

"Very nice," he told her. "Very clean."

"Thank you."

"Well, for me it's all settled then," he told her. "We must of course meet each other's families before we set the date. And the marriage contract must be drawn. I promise you that for me your money is your money, the same with your apartment, and it stays that way in the contract. Of course if you want to help, I'd appreciate it, but as you said, the future is a risk. What I really want is a wife and a place to live and this is quite suitable."

"What?"

He looked at her as if wondering if she really wanted him to repeat it all.

"You don't even know me and I don't know you," she said.

He shrugged. "What should I know. You're nice, you're pretty." She flushed. "We have the rest of our lives to work out what we don't know about each other. Believe me, I can promise you that I myself will work hard for you and our children. I am not so old-fashioned that I won't help you, when you need it. And I would never think of raising my hand to a woman. My voice maybe," he conceded.

"I'm sorry, Moshe."

"I don't please you?"

"I don't know you," she tried to explain. "I think we should see each other more first."

"Fine," he said and tried to figure out his next move.

She helped him. "Maybe you would like to come over here Wednesday for supper. Then you can see if I'm a good cook," she teased and smiled at him.

"Wednesday," he agreed. "What time?"

"Six thirty. Is that too late?"

"Six thirty." He held out his hand. She took it. "I think you will be very happy with me," he said. "I know you will be. I know how to read. I read a lot of things about far-away places. And I tell jokes."

She laughed at him.

"That wasn't one of them."

"Sorry."

He smiled at her. "Good night, Danielle." He shook hands again.

"Good night, Moshe." She watched him from the door-way as he went down the stairs.

She could hardly wait until Sunday evening when after work she rushed over to see Shoshana. Shoshana was sur-prised but happy to see her and together they prepared supper for the two of them and Udie.

"He's very picky about what he eats lately," Shoshana was complaining. "Sometimes it drives me mad. I often think it's not worth the effort it takes to make him some-thing special."

Danielle wasn't listening. She was waiting for an appro-priate moment to tell Shoshana about Moshe.

"You're so excited tonight," Shoshana said when she fi-nally got the food on the table and Udie into his chair. "What's the secret?"

"I met a man," Danielle finally burst out.

"Danielle! You sneaky little devil."

"Oh, Shoshana, you have to promise not to tell anyone anything about this because if it doesn't work out, it will be terribly embarrassing and everyone will make fun of me."

"I promise. Now come on, out with it. How did you meet him?"

"This is the embarrassing part."

"I can't imagine you doing anything embarrassing."

"I put an ad in the paper."

"Oh oh."

"I can't tell you about all the weird replies I got. But then this Moshe writes."

"Who is he?"

"I'm telling you. He's from Yemen."

"Short, dark, and wiry."

"Well, a little bit taller than that. He's thirty-four and wants to get married. You see I advertised that I owned my own apartment. He's been helping to support his brothers and sisters, but now he wants to move out on his own. He wants to buy a flower shop in Bnei Brak and—"

"Does he have any money?"

"Not much I don't think. Well, he had enough to take me to the movies on Saturday."

"What did you see?"

"Shoshana!"

"Sorry."

"Anyway, we went out after the movies and talked, then he came back up to the apartment."

"Oh, my."

"Really," she said, disgusted. "You know me better than that. So I showed him around. And he says, well, he says that's settled. We have to meet each other's relatives and draw up a wedding contract. How do you like that?"

"He must have liked what he saw."

"He said I was pretty."

"Well, you are."

"Not that pretty."

"Don't be silly. You're very pretty. So what are you going to do?"

"I was shocked. I can't do things that quickly."

"Did you tell him?"

"I told him."

"So what did he say?"

"I invited him for dinner on Wednesday. He's coming."

"Good."

"If I like him, maybe I'll bring him to your father's on Friday, or Saturday if he has to go to his parents on Friday."

Shoshana laughed. "You don't want to do things too fast,

but in one week you're bringing him to our family, poor man."

"You think it's too fast," Danielle said, suddenly doubtful.

"No," Shoshana answered seriously. "Why wait? If he and you want each other, you're too old for a couple of years' courtship. But is he nice, is he decent?"

"I think he's both of those. I also think he's poor."

"So you must be very careful when the contract is drawn that you keep what's yours in your name."

"He already told me I can do that."

"That's encouraging. The contract must be ironclad so he can't get out of it and take your half with him."

"I don't want to talk business."

"Be sensible. Having money is half the battle," Shoshana told her. "You must promise me though, if you are going to bring him over to Father's on Friday, you must promise to call me. I wouldn't miss this for the world."

Danielle made fish with rice, bread, and a salad. She bought some beer because men usually like to drink beer and she wanted to make him happy.

This time he arrived three minutes early. "I'm early," he said as she opened the door.

"It's all right," she said. "Only three minutes." They laughed together.

He had brought her flowers. They were really lovely though he told her that the quality of the bloom was perhaps a shade off. It didn't matter to her. He asked her if he could wash up. He had come from work where he had gotten in an hour overtime and he felt dirty. She gave him a clean towel and showed him again where the bathroom was. When he came out, he looked a lot better, or at least less harassed.

She asked him if he wanted to eat. He came to the table and gratefully accepted the beer. He said the blessing over the bread and watched her while she served him. "The rice is Iraqi," she told him. "I hope you don't mind."

"It's good," he assured her.

"How do you know? You haven't tasted it."

"But I know it will be."

She shook her head and laughed at him. They ate in silence. She tried to remember what she had said to Sami over the dinner table but couldn't. Sami was always talking about the people he delivered to, the trouble they gave him, the logistics of delivering. Everything was a drama for him. But Moshe was very quiet.

"Did you have a good day?" she finally asked him.

He looked up. "I didn't drop anything on my toes today. That makes it a good day."

"Is it hard work?"

"No. It's boring. But there aren't many willing to do it, so the pay isn't bad. I am waiting though to be among my flowers, to buy that shop in Bnei Brak. I have ideas about displays and arrangements that I think are much more appealing than what's being presented now. And also this shop is in a good location. Friday, you should see it, everyone in and out all day. It's good. But the owners are getting old and sloppy. That's why I have to move quickly, before they lose the clientele for me."

"But isn't this rather too much to take on all at once? A family and a flower shop."

He thought it over. "If I take only the shop now, then I will never have a family because I will never be able to afford one. If I take only a family, then I'll never be able to afford a shop so I will never be happy. If I take them both, I won't know what hit me and I'll live like a blissful idiot."

"Are idiots happy?"

"Have you ever seen one frown?"

He helped her clean up. She didn't want him to but he insisted. "I want to show you that I can help in the kitchen," he said. She wondered if they were married, how long that would last.

She plugged in the heater. They sat down together on the couch in front of it. There was not much space between them, perhaps five inches. He took her hand in his and they talked some more. Then there was a silence between them that grew more awkward as he decided to turn and try to kiss her. She let him. It was soft and fearful. She had not been touched by a man since Sami and she had forgotten how good it could feel. She allowed him to draw her closer and kiss her again. She opened her mouth to him and felt his warmth within her. Cautiously, she raised her arms and embraced him. He was so thin and strong, so easy to hold.

He kissed her on her cheek and throat. She shifted beneath him. His hand reached up and encircled her breast. It slipped inside her bra and kneaded her. She could not stop him of her own free will. "Please, Moshe," she begged him, "it isn't right."

He knew what she said was true. He stopped himself and pulled away from her, his hand trailing over her stomach and across her thigh as he did so. They sat in silence, she burning with shame, he trying to recover. "We must get married soon," he said.

Neither of them moved. "I know," he said finally, "that for you this match will be much harder than for me. You have someone to compare me with. I have had no one. I know that the first love is the stronger. But I hope in time you will come to love me as I will love you."

43

Roberta came into the hospital emergency room and stared at the man sitting on the table with his foot propped up. She tried to guess by studying his leg whether this emergency was due to tennis or jogging. She wondered if these tennis buffs or jogging nuts ever guessed at how completely boring they were to other people, including her. They talked about concentrating on their orgasmic high, being in their own space, which would have been too good to be true. They were always in her space, her emergency room with either their elbows, knees, or feet out of whack. Two of her friends had made a huge profit opening their own therapy clinic for those "into their bodies." They had asked her to join. It would have been the wise thing to do, yet she could not commit herself to a life given over to self-indulgent hokum. She would have advised them all to take up swimming. She put on her professional smile. "Leg or elbow?" she asked this rather muscular good-looking man.

"Foot," the man said, indicating the obvious.

"Jogging?"

"Bicycle. I was pedaling along Springfield when some car came too close to me. I swerved and hit a light pole. My foot got caught between the pole and the bike." He watched while Roberta carefully angled his foot one way, then the other. "The doctor already did that. The technician already took X rays."

"Were you on your way to a tennis match?"

"For an hour in the pool at the Old Man's Gym."

She smiled at him. "I think I'm going to like you, Mr.—"

"Halaby. Judah Halaby. Say listen, why are you here? I thought all I'd have to do is soak it or something. I have to get out of the country. I just came to Urbana for a month to use some documents in your library. I have my sabbatical from Cornell coming up this year. My foot's going to be all right, isn't it?"

"Why? Are you climbing the Himalayas?"

"Very funny. I'm an archaeologist. I'm going to Israel for a series of digs and I can't afford any physical disabilities. I have to be able to pull my own weight."

"Stand up," she ordered. She moved to his right side and took a good deal of his weight. Someday she was sure she would need help with a wrenched back. She watched while he tried to put weight on his foot, then helped him sit back down. "I'm going to soak it and wrap it for you, give you a few exercises to do. The doctor says it's a bad twist. You'll have to be careful with it for a while." She moved around him professionally. "Where will you be staying in Israel? Jerusalem?"

"No. Tel Aviv. I'll be working in connection with the university there."

"Will your wife and children be accompanying you?"

"I have no children and I'm divorced. Is this interrogation part of the medical examination?" He watched while she wrote what looked like a rather long list of instructions down. But when she handed him the sheet on ankles, it had a name, an address, and several phone numbers. "What's this?"

Roberta smiled. "My sister-in-law. You'll love her. She works at the university as a translator, Arabic into Hebrew.

Before that she worked for intelligence. Very interesting woman. She lost her man in the Yom Kippur War and has a cute little boy. Believe me, I know Israeli women. You couldn't do better. Call her up." Roberta gave Judah Halaby a few more choice words on his recovery, then sent him on his way. She envied him. She thought about Israel often, about her friends, the family, Michael. They all seemed so far away. So much had happened since she left the country. Not only the war, but then Entebbe, and now this change in government. She wondered how Michael felt now, after the election in May, the first time in Israel's history that the Labor party was defeated. Menahem Begin's Likud party was in power, the hard-liners, the right-wingers, some would say the fanatics. No one claimed to have voted for Likud. They had voted against Labor, against corruption and stagnation. She wished she could be there, to see for herself what changes were taking place. But it was another year in Urbana. Another year of watching her life drift away from her.

It was October, 1977, four years since Danny's death. Shoshana studied her mirror. She definitely looked four years older. She put her hands on her cheeks and tried to smooth out the wrinkles around her eyes. It was no use. The minute she took her hands away, her skin crinkled up again. She admired Roberta's skin, so white and smooth. But then Roberta wasn't hit by the sun each day, or the sand. Ah well. October. The university was starting up again. That was what she hated about working in a school. The years were marked off so exactly. In intelligence the months had flown by. But at the university there was always a beginning and an end. Another year beginning. Another year shot to hell.

Udie was ever growing. Where were his diapers, where his baby talk? Now he was a little boy playing in the park, bringing his friends home. It was just too fast. Her life was disappearing.

David was coming over tonight. That was her fault. She shouldn't have encouraged him when he first called several years ago and said he desperately needed someone to do some extra work for him. "As a favor," he put it. She should have known better. Now every week he seemed to come at her with some new piece of work that absolutely had to be done immediately. Sure he paid well. But he wasn't like the professors for whom next week or month was "immediately" enough. It had to be right then for David. She thought she had left all that behind when she quit working for him. But now it seemed between the university and David she was back on full time. Still she couldn't resent him as much as she tried. He had been such a good friend to her, both he and Hava, and all she had were friends now. Stop it! she told herself. Stop this self-pity. You had Danny, you have his son. She turned from her mirror and studied the framed photo of Danny on her wall. It was an enlargement and his features were blurred. Already he looked old-fashioned, stopped in time. She fell back on her bed. A moan escaped her lips. It struck her again: He would never age, his face would never crease, his hair fall, his stomach sag. They would never grow old and laugh together remembering how they first met, first touched. Danny was dead. But then she smiled. Don't worry, Danny, she promised, I'll remember for the both of us.

The buzzer sounded. Udie rushed to the door while she quickly wiped her eyes and hurried from the bedroom. The door was already open, David was handing Udie a square box wrapped with a beautiful bow. He's going to demand something outrageous, Shoshana guessed. "Is this the Greek bearing gifts?" she asked.

David looked up at her innocently. She laughed, came forward, and kissed him on the cheek. He noticed the tears still trembling in her eyes and his face softened into concern. She turned away from it. He pulled her back into his arms and she couldn't help but let herself go. "Sometimes I'm so miserable," she admitted. He held her so briefly, then Udie called her, and she broke away to bend down and examine the new Leggo set "Uncle David" had brought him.

David sat on the couch waiting for her. She wasn't a girl anymore, he could see that when he studied her objectively. Her figure was fuller, her face lined around the mouth and eyes. Pretty would be too trite to describe her now. She was handsome, gorgeous, sublime. "Have you been dating like I told you?" he asked.

"Yes. When I'm asked."

"Is there anyone special?" he probed.

"No," she answered with finality.

"There won't be another Danny, you know," he said, annoyed with her obstinacy. Then to soften his words, he added, "Love comes in many forms."

"I don't need a lecture from you on love."

"Right, I forgot. You know it all. But as a friend let me warn you, what you had with Danny can't be repeated, so don't look for it. There are other ways of feeling. It doesn't have to explode through you all the time, but it's still love."

"Thank you, professor. Is this a social call or—" She laughed when he looked slightly guilty. "You know, David, I would be better off still working for you. At least then I could assign this urgent work of yours to someone else."

"Well, fine with me. The job is yours anytime you want it. You can't believe the inefficiency I have to put up with. And don't think I don't catch hell every time I submit your chit. But you know how I am, generous to a fault." Her laughter irritated him but he pushed on. "This time we're dealing with something you should enjoy doing. It's the diary of the chief of internal security in Baghdad."

"A diary? Why would he have one?"

"Who knows? Anyway his home was burgled and somehow the diary fell into our hands."

"Yossi's doing, no doubt."

"No doubt. Anyway, the word is that this Musa al Haykal is trying to move up the political ladder in Iraq, and there's not much higher to go from where he is now, so the more we know him the better."

"They're all a bunch of crazy men in Iraq."

"Crazy, yes. But crazy can be deadly if you have planes and artillery. Will you do it?"

"Fine. Send it over."

"I can't. It can't leave the cage."

"No, David, I'm not going to leave Udie and come into work again, especially not in the security area. It drives me nuts with someone looking over my shoulder all the time."

"Shoshana, to be honest with you, no one else has been able to make sense of it, so I'm upping the fee."

"I'd have to get a babysitter and—"

"Expenses included."

She considered it with a sigh. "When?" she asked.

"Starting tomorrow."

"I'll see what I can do. But believe me, you're going to pay."

"In blood, knowing you."

Really, she didn't need the money anymore. Why was she working herself down to the nub? It was not as if she wanted anything. She had a television. She had her driver's license, but didn't want to buy a car. Udie's education was guaranteed, so what was she pushing herself for? Still the next morning she called Moshe at the flower shop to see if she could borrow his younger sister Yael to baby-sit for her. She, like everyone else in the family, had held her breath after Danielle's marriage to see what the union would actually be like. It turned out to be much better than anyone could have expected. Danielle had simply blossomed under Moshe's care. It seemed he had a green thumb with women too. They were not well off of course. Danielle had given Moshe all her savings to invest in the flower shop, for which she claimed half ownership under pressure both from Shoshana and Joseph. But they were happy and the business was flourishing. Though it would be more difficult for them now that Danielle was pregnant and was under doctor's orders to take it easy. She had had to quit her job and was spending most of her time at home. Shoshana only wished she could spend her time at home, but the next day she faithfully reported to Ha-Kiriyah. She had known the reception guard for fifteen years now but it didn't matter. She had to be checked off a list, then escorted to have a card made up for her; her old card was considered worthless.

"How long will this job take you?" the clerk asked her.

"Forever if you don't hurry this up," Shoshana shot back.

She finally had her pass and hurried down the halls to the cage where original documents were kept. Here she had to wait while several phone calls verified her existence and the diary's existence before the diary was signed out to her and the security watchdog, who would remain in the room with her while she translated, appointed. The guard carried the diary and unlocked the room for her. She entered first and immediately went over to check the machinery. So often she was given the lousy equipment, but this looked relatively new and all the switches worked, so she hoped for the best.

Yossi Leskov, still heading intelligence, came just as she was getting down to work. "So you're doing this," he said. He felt immediately uneasy. He wouldn't admit to feeling guilty. He couldn't afford a conscience, he kept telling himself. But seeing Shoshana Ewan holding al Haykal's diary, he thought of Jacob Ewan.

It didn't matter that he hadn't seen her in years, Shoshana thought. With someone as important as Yossi, he couldn't waste his time on politeness. He flipped open the diary to a certain page. "I had someone look over this. Some of the names are indicated just by initials. People he saw frequently probably. Also the person who looked over this said it seems to be done in a sort of shorthand, so it won't be easy."

"Fine."

"Any questions?"

"Not yet. You'll have someone transcribe? Or am I supposed to do that too?"

"No. Hand in your tapes each day and we'll have someone type it up. You can check it over."

"Okay."

Yossi left and she got to work. Or tried to. If it was in some form of personal shorthand. This first day would be the hardest as she attempted to find out how this Musa al Haykal's mind worked. If it worked at all, she hoped it followed some normal pattern.

It was frustrating. She didn't think al Haykal could ever have meant to use the diary again, so why did he write it down? She needed a pad of paper, an unabridged dictionary, and a couple of aspirin. It took her an hour before she even started using the tapes. Then she got down the first day's entry, which started in 1973. Nothing important. Perhaps. Whom he saw, what he saw, how he felt about it. It seemed he was just beginning to keep his diary, had just been promoted to this new position as chief of internal security. The dates were clear always. Sometimes he would even jot down the time. Not every day, thank God, because as he wrote more, he began to abbreviate more. For his privacy? For his safety? Whatever. She called out for a magnifying glass. Some of the work was in pencil and it had smeared.

She worked eight hours, having the food sent in. At least she had something to do. Her watchdog was bored stiff. When she finally got home and into bed, it was almost twelve. Udie and Yael were sleeping. The phone rang. It was Yossi.

"How long will it take?"

"I don't know," she told him.

He hung up.

It took a while for it to happen. Sometimes it never did. But when it clicked, it made translating a relative joy. And with Musa al Haykal it happened. All of a sudden she was thinking his thoughts. She knew where he was going. The diary was precise and written for one purpose, to get what he could on his superiors, to be able to weasel his way onto their plateau, to join them if not through ability then through innuendo. No wonder Yossi wanted it fast. It would give him more information than he could probably ever use on the leaders of Iraq, at least from one man's perspective. What made this al Haykal easy was that his diary, because it was so businesslike, didn't have the swings in mood of most personal entries. She was moving right along when she was caught by her own name: "Had J. Ewan picked up. Surprised he was part of plot. Jew and Shi'ites? Jacob-Shi'ites? J-Kurds? Who else? That's it for him."

Shoshana was stunned. She read over what she saw before her, the letters remained the same. Jacob Ewan, her uncle. She flipped through the pages of the diary, scanning for a second mention of her uncle's name. Nothing. What was she to do? Once she put it on the tape and finished the diary, she would have no access to it. They would claim this section hadn't existed. No. She got up too abruptly. The guard asked her if anything was wrong. She nodded toward the bathroom. He looked at her desk. She walked slowly to the bathroom door, hoping he had not bothered to count the number of pencils lying on her desk. Once inside, she bolted the door, tore off a sheet of toilet paper, wrote down exactly what had been in the diary about her uncle, folded the paper neatly, and placed it inside the bottom rim of her bra. Then she used the facilities. The watchdog was yawning and stretching when she returned. She smiled at him, he smiled back. She got back to work, trying hard to concentrate.

She stayed late that night, hoping to find another mention of her uncle. But there was nothing. When she got home, it was near one o'clock. But that didn't stop her. She went to the phone and dialed. When a woman answered rather sleepily, Shoshana said, "Hava, this is Shoshana. Could I speak to David?"

She heard the phone being fumbled over. "What is it?" he asked ungraciously.

"David? My uncle is named in that diary."

"What?"

"My—"

"What time is it?"

"It doesn't matter."

"It's after one o'clock."

"My uncle is mentioned in that diary."

"Oh," he moaned.

"David?"

"I'm thinking. Shh. The Iraqi one?"

"Uncle?"

"Diary."

"Yes."

"Uh. What's—what was said?"

"Something about a plot."

"When was this?"

Shoshana checked her piece of toilet paper. "December 20, 1973."

"Shoshana, that's four years ago!"

"Something happened to him."

"Did you finish the diary?"

"Are you kidding?"

"Well, finish it and see what happens."

"David, it's my—"

"I know!" he exploded. "It's also the middle of the night!" She could hear Hava complaining to him. "I'm sorry," he apologized, whether to her or to Hava she didn't know. "I'll see you tomorrow." That must have been to her.

She hung up the phone, she got undressed and into bed but didn't sleep. She thought about her Uncle Jacob.

The next afternoon before she attacked the diary, she went to see David. He was busy of course, conference, but that didn't bother her. She opened his door and told him to hurry up, she was waiting. And while she waited, she walked down to her old department where Orit still held on to her job as head secretary. They kissed and hugged and Orit demanded to see pictures of Udie. Then Shoshana asked how it was going.

"Look at my desk. Look at the desks around you. It's terrible," Orit whispered.

"It does look rather hectic."

"He refuses to do any of the work himself because he's the boss. So he assigns it but doesn't like the way it comes back to him so he reassigns it. He's a classicist. He has a Ph.D. in Arabic language and literature from Hebrew University, but once he's past *marhaba* he can't speak it. He knows absolutely no colloquial Arabic. Everyone hates him and doesn't want to work for him. You should come back."

"Why did David hire him?"

"I gather it wasn't David's fault. Internal memo. This guy's father was a cabinet minister."

"But after the election?"

"After the election it was too late."

David was strolling down the hall toward them. She waited for him. "You see what you've done to me," he said to her as he looked around. "This used to be one of my most efficient departments. Are you sure you don't want to come back and restore this to its former glory?"

She took another look around. "Positive," she said. "I don't have the energy." She wished Orit good luck and then went back to the office with David.

"Have you been to work yet?" he asked her.

"No. Have you seen Yossi?"

"Yes."

"And?"

"After exploding, Yossi said, You are supposed to translate the material, not worry about what's in it."

Angered, she asked, "Did you tell him about my uncle?"

"Yes. He said, well, basically, that it was none of your business."

"David!" she protested.

"Look, I know. I'm just reporting to you what he said. He also said if you didn't concentrate on your work, you could be replaced."

Shoshana was upset and torn. She could easily walk away from the diary, but if she did, she might never find out what happened to her uncle. Still, Yossi's attitude demanded some action. "Tell Yossi I'm feeling suddenly quite ill. I can't make it today. Let him see how easy it will be to get someone else to decipher that shorthand." She stood and walked out. "Bravo," she heard David call softly.

Shoshana stayed away from the diary two days. David came by the second day to report Yossi had run through four translators so far with no success.

"You'll have to import more Jews, won't you," she said coldly. She knew as well as David did that her generation was the only one who could adequately translate the dialects into Hebrew. The younger ones might speak the language in their homes, but they could not read Arabic with anything like her fluency.

On the third day when she was in her office at the university, Yossi called her. "You win," he told her. "Finish translating the diary and we'll talk about your uncle."

She called Yael again and made the necessary arrangements. It took her well into October to finish the diary; it became more complicated again as al Haykal increased his connections and his power. It was blackmail, most of the material, information about prominent members of Baghdad society. Bribes, kickbacks, drugs, women, boys, the usual. Friendships built on intimate, dangerous knowledge that incriminated al Haykal along with those he served. What was dispiriting to Shoshana was that there was no second mention of her uncle's name. But when she was done with the diary, she set up an appointment with Yossi and he graciously consented to see her, only keeping her waiting for two hours and then acting as if she were the one taking up his time the minute she came into his office.

"My uncle," she reminded him coldly as he frantically searched through a stack of papers in an effort to avoid her.

He sat down finally and faced her. "When was the last time you saw your uncle?"

She shrugged. "When I left Baghdad. In 1950."

"That's twenty-seven years ago. When was the last time you heard from him?"

"I think my father heard from him in fifty-one."

"That's twenty-six years ago."

She waited. "Do you want a math award?" she finally asked.

He smiled unpleasantly. "Ah, Shoshana, there's something so appealing about you."

"We had a deal," she reminded him. "I finish the diary, you tell me about my uncle."

"Your uncle's been dead to you for over half your life. I think you should leave it that way."

"What do you mean?"

"I mean," he said carefully, "you wouldn't want to know."

She thought it over for a long time while Yossi tapped his pencil. Then she said, "If you had an uncle in Poland and you heard his name mentioned after all these years, wouldn't you want to know what happened to him?"

"Not if I suspected he ended up in a gas chamber."

"My uncle's dead."

"Yes."

"So what happened to him?"

Yossi wasn't saying. "Think it over," he told her. "If you really want to know, come back and we'll talk again. But, Shoshana, you don't really want to know."

Shoshana didn't know what she really wanted to know, but she knew one thing, that she was no longer going to carry this burden alone. That evening after seeing Yossi, she took Udie and went over to her sister's for dinner.

"We have to talk," she said to Joseph and Lily.

"It's money," Lily said.

"How much?" Joseph asked wearily but kindly. While Moishe Frayman was no longer under investigation, their contracts had not come rolling in with their former speed, and Joseph had to curtail his expenditures.

"No, I don't want money," Shoshana said. "I want you to listen carefully because I don't know how to put this."

"We'll listen anyway," Lily assured her.

"This past month I've been translating a diary of a top official in Iraq. In it he mentions our uncle, Jacob Ewan. I saw the head of intelligence today. He told me Jacob is dead. He wouldn't tell me how, he wouldn't tell me why. Just dead. He says if I want to know more, I should think it over and come back to see him. I gather it's rather unpleasant."

Joseph looked to Lily. It had been years since he had thought of Jacob Ewan, and even when he did, it was only in connection with the part Jacob had played in saving his life, by sending little Rahamin to warn Joseph that the police were coming for him. But it did not surprise him to hear that Jacob Ewan was dead. Life did not thrive in Iraq. Yet if Jacob were dead, what of his sons, Rahamin and Ephraim? He asked Shoshana. Where were his sons? Had they married, had children? And Jacob's wife, what of her?

"I know only that Jacob's dead," Shoshana protested. "Nothing more. Perhaps Yossi knows. Perhaps not. The point is, should we try to find out or would we really be better off not knowing, as Yossi says."

Her sister considered it. "Even if we were better off not knowing, what about Jacob's family?"

"We owe it to them to find out," Joseph agreed. "If we can no longer help them, we still must remember them."

"I'll call Yossi then. Would you come with me?" Shoshana asked Joseph. "If I can arrange it?"

"Of course."

"No."

"Yossi."

"I'm sorry, Shoshana. I said I'd tell you. I'm not going to have your whole family here. This isn't a Kupot Holim waiting room."

"My brother-in-law, that's all."

"No."

"All right," Shoshana relented. "When?"

"Friday afternoon. Three o'clock."

She agreed and hung up. On his end Yossi let the phone dangle. He beat an eraser softly on his desk. Three o'clock Friday. He had until then to come up with a story she would believe.

44

Shoshana was packing up her work at two on Friday, getting ready to leave for her meeting with Yossi, when a knock came at her door. "Come in," she called. The door opened and a striking, tall Oriental entered her office. "Yes," she said rather distractedly.

"Shoshana Ewan?"

"Yes. Did Yossi send you?"

"No. Roberta sent me."

She frowned at him. "Roberta?"

"If you're her sister-in-law."

"Roberta Ewan?"

"Yes. She thought we should meet so I came by to see if you'd like to go out next weekend."

She was annoyed by this interruption. "Look, I don't have the time now."

"Sorry," he said. But the way he said it meant that she was the one who should be sorry, he was doing her the favor.

Men, if you didn't treat them like babies, got hurt so quickly. "Listen, leave your name and your number and I'll get in touch with you when I can," Shoshana said.

"No, really, it's not necessary."

She sighed. "Do it for good old Roberta," she said with a slight smile.

He was reluctant but she held out a pad and pencil to him and he wrote down his phone number and name.

"Halaby," she said. "From Syria."

"Yes."

"Do you work at the university?"

"Teach and research, yes."

"So give me your university number," she ordered. "Maybe we can get together for coffee."

"I'll be waiting for your call," he said sarcastically, but she didn't have the time or the inclination to care.

Yossi kept her waiting, but only half an hour this time, and he had the decency to have his calls held once she came into his office. He had a file on his desk and she knew it was her uncle's. "I'm warning you one last time," he said to her. "You don't want to hear this." She waited. He began. "Your uncle Jacob did not leave Iraq with the rest of the Jews."

"I know that already."

"He was one of a thousand, two thousand who remained. Conditions are not good in Iraq for the Jews. They weren't good in the late forties, early fifties, and they got continuously worse. By then it was too late for most of the Jews who remained to leave. It was their own doing, you know. They had money and position and they didn't want to give it up." She sat and waited. "Jacob Ewan was targeted by British intelligence in, oh, 1964. He ran the Swallow's Nest. It was a nightclub with a brothel above it. All the top men in Baghdad frequented it. It was the perfect setup for an intelligence operation."

"It always was," Shoshana interrupted. "Why did they wait until 1964?"

"They tried before, I gather, without success. But with Kassem, your uncle was placed in jail for a time. When Kassem was murdered, he was freed. Any enemy of an old regime is a friend of the new one. I guess that term in jail was the writing on the wall for Ewan. When he was approached after he was set free, he made a deal with the British."

"Who was his contact?"

"He could have been called anything but he called himself Harris. Andrew Harris. He's gone now, on to another assignment, so I guess it doesn't matter my telling you. Anyway, Jacob was willing to work for Harris as long as Harris found a way to get Jacob's sons and their families out of Iraq."

"Jacob's sons have families?"

"I just said that."

"So where are they? If Andrew Harris promised Jacob he would get his sons out, why haven't we heard from them? No matter where they are, they knew we were in Israel. They would have contacted us somehow."

"Don't get carried away. They didn't get out. Jacob served Harris well. We—" He caught himself. "The British were generous enough to pass along a lot of the information they got from him to us. The problem was, as it turned out, that Mr. Harris wasn't the only one who could spot a good source of information."

"Musa al Haykal."

"Yes. He also latched onto Jacob and squeezed him. As a matter of fact, we speculate that that's how this al Haykal became chief of internal security, by using what he got from Jacob to promote himself. Of course Harris knew that Jacob was also dealing with al Haykal."

"Because Jacob kept begging him to get his sons out."

"Probably," Yossi conceded.

"So what happened?"

"Jacob Ewan got mixed up in a plot to take al Haykal's life. All the conspirators were caught and executed. Including your uncle."

"And his family?" Shoshana stressed.

Yossi was silent for a while, staring into space. "What is your impression of al Haykal from the diaries?" he asked.

She thought. "Despicable."

He was tapping his pencil again. "Jacob did try to make a deal. In prison. He told al Haykal that he would give him the top—a top agent in Baghdad if al Haykal would assure the safety of his sons and their free passage outside Iraq. Al Haykal agreed to his terms, we heard." Shoshana waited patiently. Yossi was slowing down. "He waited two hours, three hours, four hours, who knows. Time enough to make Jacob think his family was being put aboard a plane for Beirut. When Jacob was assured that his family was safe, he told al Haykal about Harris. But Harris had already fled the country. Ewan was questioned further, but his contact was with Harris, no one else.

"On Jacob's last night al Haykal visited him and told him he was going to die tomorrow. Jacob said it didn't matter. As long as his family was safe. The next morning when al Haykal brought him to the courtyard to be hanged, there were three nooses. Another door across the prison courtyard opened and Jacob's two sons were marched out. Al Haykal hanged the sons one at a time in front of their father. Jacob Ewan was the last to die."

Yossi sat silently as Shoshana cried noiselessly, the tears falling from her eyes while her heart was cold.

"You'll want a drink," Yossi said and poured her a brandy. She drank it. It turned her to anger.

"I can't understand it," she said. "Nine years and Harris couldn't get Uncle Jacob's family out of Iraq? Not one of them? Don't ask me to believe that, Yossi. Where is this Harris now? I'd like to pay my respects."

"I don't know."

"He had a diplomatic cover, didn't he?"

"He was passing as a British businessman. By now he's probably a Canadian artist in Poland."

Shoshana thought it over some more. "The family?" she asked.

"Jacob's wife died about a month after her husband and sons disappeared. I don't know what it was. High blood pressure. A stroke. Something like that."

"And her sons' families?"

"They're still there."

"What are they like?"

Yossi checked in the files. "The older son had a wife, two daughters, and a son. The younger son managed to produce a boy and a girl."

"What's happening to them?"

Yossi shook his head. "I don't know."

"Can they be gotten out?"

"Do you know the risk involved in moving women and small children?"

"So they will just disappear off the face of the earth too?"

"Maybe someday. Part of a settlement. The UN." Yossi shrugged.

Shoshana rose, then sat down again, her legs too weak. Yossi came around to help her. He called one of his men who drove Shoshana home. She spent the rest of the Sabbath evening holding on to Udie, who didn't understand it and squirmed to get back to his toys.

There was something worrying about Yossi's story though, something that didn't quite fit. Even as she told the details to Joseph, little things that Yossi said came back to her, things that did not make any sense. No, she was missing something. Or there was something he wasn't telling her. What she had to do was find Andrew Harris, or find someone else who could. She knew several people in British intelligence who worked in Israel, either at the embassy or for the UN. She could try to contact them about it. But their field of operations was Israel, perhaps Lebanon and Jordan also, certainly not Iraq. So they would have to refer the matter to London, and she was sure she would never hear of it again.

If Yossi was telling the truth. If Andrew Harris was British. She tried to visualize it in her mind. A British businessman walking up to her uncle and asking him how would he like to be a British spy. She couldn't see it. Her uncle was a businessman, not an adventurer. He knew what a risk he would be taking working for a foreign power. So would he work for the British, who had left the Jews to the mercy of the Iraqi mobs so often before? To her it would make more sense if British Andrew Harris approached Jacob Ewan as an Israeli, said we will free your children, bring them home to Israel. Yes, that made sense. Jacob would trust a fellow Jew. Now all she had to figure out was this: Was Harris deceiving Jacob Ewan or was Yossi deceiving her?

"We have to help the family," Joseph said after Shoshana related what Yossi had told her. "Could we bribe their way out? What can we do?"

But Shoshana wasn't really listening. She rose and left her family. There was something she could do. But it had to be done alone.

Sunday morning at the university she called the janitor into her office and asked him to ask for Oren Kohan after she dialed the number. The janitor thought she was crazy, but she was one of his favorites so he did as she asked. When Oren came on the line, Shoshana took it from the janitor and waved him out.

"Don't say my name," she said quickly. He didn't. Well trained, he waited for her to speak again. "Can you come over at nine tonight?"

"Yes."

She hung up.

Now she was filled with doubts about Oren. Would he know? And if he did, would he tell her? For old time's sake? For Danny?

Oren arrived ten after nine. "Sorry," he said absently. "Had to get the kids to bed." He flopped down in one of her chairs.

"Want a beer?" she asked.

"Fine. How's Udie?" he called.

"Growing," she answered, coming back in with the beer.

She sat down on the couch opposite him and tucked her legs under her. "I need your help, Oren," she said softly.

"So all you have to do is ask," he told her.

"I don't think it's going to be that simple."

He became serious. "Does this have anything to do with the visits you've been paying to Yossi?" She nodded. "Oh boy," he said and rose.

"Oren," she begged. "It's my family."

He sat down again. "You don't know what you're asking of me."

"One question only," she pleaded.

"Shoshana!"

"Someone working under the cover name of Andrew Harris? Was he ours?"

Oren got up and walked swiftly to the door. He turned to her before he opened it, gave her a single affirmative nod, and then he left.

Yossi? Yes, he could make time to see her. Anything for the bereaved.

"Shoshana," he said sympathetically. "What can I do for you?"

She sat down and fixed him with her stare. "Get the family out of Iraq and into Israel."

"Don't you think I want to do that?" he said sweetly. "Don't you think I want to do that for every Jew everywhere. I mean, that's our job, Shoshana, to protect the Jewish people. But I've already explained—"

"I know that Harris was your man."

The change was dramatic. "How did you find out?" He was back to the bastard everyone knew so well.

"You used my uncle for nine years. You used his love for his family and fed upon that love. And then when he was about to be destroyed, you didn't lift a finger to save any of them. You ran away. Nine years, Yossi. Don't tell me you couldn't have gotten them out if you had wanted to."

"You're wrong there. We tried. Your uncle and his family were being watched. We didn't keep them prisoners in Iraq, al Haykal did."

"He trusted you, as a Jew, and you failed him. Have you

ever thought what it would be like to see your sons hanged in front of your eyes?"

"Don't lay any guilt on me, Shoshana. Your uncle was no simple Simon. He was paid for what he did and paid well."

"And his sons, his grandchildren, his wife? What did you offer them?"

"It happens. It's over."

"So now your Mr. Harris is free to recruit some poor Jewish sucker elsewhere with pleas for Jewish unity in the face of adversity."

He sighed. "I'm sorry you're taking this so hard."

"I'm taking it more than hard, Yossi. I'm taking it to the press. And you'll get the credit you deserve for it because I'll make sure your name and Harris's are smeared all over the copy. And I'm sure a really diligent reporter could discover just exactly where this Harris is now. Oh, I know that look. Censorship? I won't go to our reporters. I'll go to the foreign ones. A quick trip to Cyprus. They file their stories, fly back. What can you do? It makes pretty good human-interest material, don't you think?"

"Shoshana, you're hysterical."

She smiled. "Not as hysterical as you're going to be."

"Let's talk this over."

"I've given my demand. Free his family."

"It can't be done that quickly."

"Should they wait another ten years?"

"Look, give me a week. A week is not long for these things, you should know that much."

"A week then," Shoshana said. "Oh, and, Yossi, I hear you're a real killer, besides being a bastard. Let me just say, it wouldn't help you if anything happened to me."

"Let's not be melodramatic."

"Do you know how many family members I have in Israel?"

"Too many?"

"And in the States? Blood is blood, Yossi. Remember that. A week."

* * *

The week did not lie empty before Shoshana. Yossi was busy acting, Shoshana reacting to the power he was exerting on those she loved. The first one to hear from him indirectly was Joseph. Joseph was informed by the prosecutor's office that he was under investigation. He asked for specifics. "You'll find out soon enough," he was told.

Yossi's doing, it had to be, Shoshana told her brother-in-law.

When Joseph didn't panic and Shoshana didn't relent, the next to hear from Yossi was Moshe Zichri, Danielle's husband. He found a box of candy that had been left on one of his shelves near the planters. It meant nothing to him. He assumed that someone had been looking around, put it down to lift a flowerpot, and simply forgot it. He put it aside in the hopes that the customer would come back for it.

That night as he and Danielle were eating dinner, he received a phone call. "Did you find a box of candy sitting on one of your back shelves?" the caller asked.

"Oh, yes," Moshe said. "I've saved it for you. You can pick it up—"

"It could just as easily have been a bomb." The caller hung up.

Moshe assumed it was an extortion attempt by a neighborhood gang, though he never expected that sort of thing in Bnei Brak. He told Danielle about it and then he called the police.

The police asked Moshe to meet them at his store. After he left, Danielle called Shoshana to tell her what had happened. She was surprised to hear Shoshana laugh.

"He called the police, did he?"

"Yes. I don't think it's so funny. Do you know what would happen to us financially if the store were bombed?"

"I don't think it's funny either. But don't worry. I think I know how to handle this."

Shoshana hung up and rushed over to Moshe's flower shop to find him consulting with the police. Moshe was surprised to see her but accepted her presence as a comfort. "The police were just asking if I knew anyone who has it in for me," Moshe said. "They say there's no extortion racket around here."

"As a matter of fact there is someone who has it in for us," Shoshana said, half to Moshe, half to the police. An officer got ready to write down her words. "It's a family matter," she said. "It has nothing to do with poor Moshe here. But this guy feels he was owed some money and he's trying to take it out on anyone he can."

"Who is it, miss?" the policeman asked.

"Yossi Leskov," Shoshana said. "He lives out in Zahala. Number twenty. He's the one."

"You're sure?"

"Quite sure."

"Okay," the policeman said. "We'll go check."

She wished she could have been there to see Yossi opening the door to the police.

The next morning she went to work as usual, not knowing what new catastrophe to expect. Yossi Leskov himself was waiting for her in her office. She was surprised; she looked around carefully to see what had been touched. "You're late," he snapped.

She smiled slightly. "Yossi, your week's not up. Are you giving in so quickly?"

"Shoshana, I'll stop playing games if you will. Let us both be reasonable for a change. I can't get your relatives out."

"You must. You're a very clever man, Yossi. I rely on you completely. You undertook to get them out when Mr. Harris was in Baghdad. You've just been a little slow in doing it. I will understand it that way if you move now."

"Shoshana, there's nothing I can do and there's nothing you can do. I'm sorry."

She sat down at her desk and looked through her phone book. Then she picked up the phone and dialed. "Who are you calling?" Yossi asked.

"The minister of defense."

"He's a good friend of mine."

"I wonder if your good friend will understand how you manipulated the prosecutor's office to open an investigation against Joseph, how you threatened to bomb Moshe's store."

Yossi put his hand down on the phone's button, cutting off the call. "Let's talk this over."

"We've talked, Yossi. And if the minister of defense doesn't understand things from my point of view, I'll go to the Knesset and have the question asked on the floor. Any way I move, Yossi, you at the very least have lost your job, no matter what you manage to do to me in the meantime."

"Look, listen to me, please. It is not a simple job to get someone in and out of a country, especially women and children. I can't just snap my fingers and have it done. But I've come up with an idea—after the police visited me last night, I will admit. If you listen and promise to keep quiet about it, I'll tell you what it is."

She nodded affirmatively.

"The diary, you remember that infamous piece of literature surely," he said, "gave us what we needed. You should feel proud. It is by your hand that we shall free them. The diary gave us hard evidence in his own hand that al Haykal is having intimate relations with several rather nasty Soviet intriguers. Worse than adultery. Political suicide. In the Iraqi eyes of the moment."

"So?"

"So we have it on good information that al Haykal is soon to be made minister of the interior. You realize what he'll control then. A step up for Russian influence surely. We're going to get him, Shoshana. Thanks to Andrew Harris and your uncle, we have pictures, we have tapes. And we have the fact that the Iraqi chief of staff, who was a cousin of the prime mover of the plot your uncle was involved in, hates al Haykal's guts and would like nothing better than to see him swinging from a gallows. Which could be arranged with our pictures and tapes. So you see, when al Haykal becomes minister of the interior, we're going to approach him and he's going to become our man in Baghdad."

"How do you know he won't refuse you?"

"After reading the diary, you can ask that? You know what kind of a man he is. He knows how the game is played. And I wouldn't hesitate to cut off his head if he got out of line."

"So how does this help my relatives?"

"Because, as an act of faith between friends, he's going to deliver your family safely across the border into Iran."

She thought it over and shook her head. "How can I trust you, Yossi? What you're talking about will take months, and how will I ever know you're keeping your word?"

"I keep my word. Once I've given it. And I have." He watched her. "They'll be free by Passover."

"That's almost five months. I can't—"

"And as an act of good will between us, I've put in a word for your brother-in-law. They've called off the investigation."

"Which makes me ask why they started it?"

"And to show you that I'm not a cruel man, we've arranged with the bank to pay off the loan on the flower shop. It's now completely owned by Moshe and Danielle."

She shook her head.

"Look, if I don't keep my word by Passover, you can still call the minister of defense."

She looked at him suspiciously. Five months. "I'm not the only one who knows about this. I've told selected members of the family in Israel and in the States."

"I get your point, Shoshana. Now is it a deal?" He held his hand out to her. With much trepidation she put her smaller one into it.

45

Shoshana was on edge. And when she retold the story of her run-in with Yossi; as she did to David Tal and Joseph, her condition became worse. The excitement had peaked, but the adrenaline was still flowing. But there was nothing for it. She would have to wait for Pesach. Until then she must force herself to sit at her desk in the university and translate water survey reports from Jordan. In desperation one morning she called David and asked him if he had something she could get her teeth into at the other end of the wire. "David?"

"I don't know how to tell you this, Shoshana, but Yossi's branded you a security risk. There's no way I can hand off any work to you. Shoshana!" he called when there was no forthcoming answer.

"That schmuck!"

"I know."

"That—"

"I know, I know, you don't have to tell me. I work with him every day. Look, if it's money you need."

"No. It's not money, David." She sighed as she hung up the phone. What did she need? She looked out her window

651

across the campus. It was one of those nice days before winter. The sun was shining. She would need only her sweater if she were going out. Going out where?

She opened her desk drawer for a mint. It was becoming an addiction and she had to see her dentist. She was puzzled for a minute when she saw the name and phone number there, but then she remembered the tall Syrian who had been in to see her a few weeks ago. Sent by Roberta of all people.

She didn't know if she dared. But then what the hell. She dialed his office number and asked for Mr. Halaby.

"Professor Halaby," the voice answered snottily. "Just a minute." Obviously his officemate. These professors were such pains on protocol.

"Yes." It was his voice.

"Judah?" she said. She sure as hell wasn't going to call him professor.

"Yes."

"This is Shoshana Ewan."

"Oh." Such excitement. Was he holding a dead fish?

"Shall we meet for coffee?"

"I don't think I—"

"Gilman, the faculty lounge. Twenty minutes? Fine then, I'll see you there." She didn't wait for his answer, she just hung up. She figured even if he wanted to call back, it would take him at least ten minutes to find her number. By then she would be out the door and for politeness's sake, he would have to meet her. Maybe she should leave now, just to be on the safe side. After all, her hair could use a little combing and her lips more coloring.

If she hadn't met a friend in the bathroom, she would have been right on time. But as it was, she was five minutes late to the faculty lounge. She opened the door and looked around. There he was sitting on a chair near the window. He rose when he saw her, but he did not smile. Well, okay, she had been abrupt with him when he first introduced himself, it was up to her to be pleasing now. She put on her brightest smile. "Hi."

He just nodded. "Hello. What can I get for you?"

"Coffee will be just fine." She sank into her seat and watched him as he went up to the window to order. She couldn't help but admire Roberta's taste. He was a good-looking man, tall, slightly arrogant, unattached, probably divorced. She could rely on Roberta to have ascertained that fact.

As he came back to her, he watched her staring at him. If he was flustered, he didn't show it. He helped her to the sugar and cream, then sat silent while she used them. It soon dawned on her that he wasn't going to say anything.

"I suppose you think I was rude the first time we met?" Shoshana suggested sweetly.

"I never call Israelis rude. It would be redundant."

"Ah." She decided not to be personally affronted by this insult. "I see we've made our usual first impression."

"I've been here before."

"Oh. Well. There are some nice things about us," she reminded him, only to become slightly unnerved as he waited for her to enumerate them. "So you know Roberta?" she shifted hurriedly.

He smiled. "Not really. I had injured my foot and along with the therapy she handed out your address."

"I see." This was becoming almost as bad as dealing with Yossi. She stood up and held out her hand. "Well, thank you for the coffee. I hope we meet again someday." But not too soon, she almost added. And yet when he stood and took her hand, his hand was soft and warm and strong. It affected her strangely. Startled by her own reaction, she turned and almost fled the lounge.

Judah Halaby's eyes followed Shoshana out of the lounge and caught sight of her again through the window as she made her way along the sidewalk. What a strange woman. It shamed him almost that he hadn't taken the trouble to be pleasant to her. Yet she had been so offhanded about it when he first met her, then she called up and practically demanded to meet him for coffee. Well, he had gotten his own back, but he felt there was an opportunity here he might be missing. He looked down the sidewalk again. She had disappeared.

Carolyn Haddad

* * *

Shoshana was trying desperately to concentrate on the 1966 Jordanian report on the use of well water in the West Bank. Besides being utterly boring, it was primary work, work she would have cast off on a newcomer in Translations as not fit for someone with her skill and years of experience. She was beginning to hate this job. And certainly coffee with a dark, handsome stranger hadn't helped. Maybe tea would have been better. Then she could have at least read the leaves. Her phone rang. It was a welcome interruption.

"Shoshana, this is Judah."

"Judah who? Hello?"

"Judah Halaby. You just had coffee—"

"Oh, yes. Professor Judah. How are you?"

"Fine. I—it's taken me this long to find your number. I wanted to know if you would like to go out with me, next Saturday night. Not this Saturday, but next?"

"Next. I got it." She checked her calendar. Stupid fool, she told herself, of course it's empty. You haven't been out with a man in two months. But if you can't even think of something to say to him over coffee, how are you going to spend a whole evening with him? Still, he was a man and here he was waiting patiently on the phone. "Yes. Why not."

"Great. I love positive women. Uh. Do you want to give me your address and phone number?"

"Sure." She gave it to him and then asked what time he would pick her up. "Okay," she said. "See you then on November nineteen."

And yet would she? For between the time of Judah Halaby's phone call and their date itself the most extraordinary thing happened. Anwar el-Sadat of Egypt had hinted that he would like an invitation to address Israel's Knesset, and Menahem Begin had formally invited the president of Egypt to Jerusalem. Sadat had accepted. His historic arrival was set for—November 19, 1977.

The country was in a joyous uproar. Peace was the only word thought of that week, hoped and prayed for, even by the most cynical. No more wars, no more deaths, please God, let it be so. The country was consumed by gossip, each citizen had some new tidbit that he had to pass on.

Shoshana met someone from the translation department on the street. She longed to work on this but knew she wouldn't be asked. Damn it! It made her mad to be an outsider at a time like this.

She had almost forgotten about her date when it suddenly struck her on Thursday that she was supposed to go out Saturday night while Sadat was landing at Ben-Gurion. Obviously something had to be sacrificed. She located Judah's number once again.

"Judah, it's Shoshana."

"Who?"

She laughed. "About this Saturday."

"Oh, that Shoshana. Yes, I've been meaning to call you but I didn't quite know how to put it."

She was struck by brilliance. "Listen, do you have a television?"

"No."

"Great. So come over to my apartment, bring a bottle of wine or some cake or something, and we can watch everything on my set."

"Are you sure your television works?"

"Of course it works."

"Because I have an offer from someone whose television I know works. He's an engineer."

"I've had my television for three years and it hasn't broken down yet."

"By the law of probability then this would be the time."

"Oh. I'm not going to beg."

"Okay, I'll come over. But I'm bringing my wrench and screwdriver."

"And a bottle of wine."

"Right."

* * *

She had made some salad. She had some sliced cold turkey and sausage. Then of course there were the nuts, the fruits, the candy, the coffee. It would have to do.

She didn't know when to expect him. Before the Sabbath ended. That was sure. He wouldn't want to miss a bit of Sadat's arrival. Neither would she.

He came around four thirty with the cake and wine. She grabbed them from him while he went over to the television to adjust it.

"We'll have to make do with stale bread," she called from the kitchen. "Perhaps I should go down and forage for something fresh."

"Nothing's going to be open," Judah told her.

"Nothing?"

"Nothing. Stores, kiosks, theaters. Closed. Everyone's home watching television. The picture looks okay."

Udie crept out of his bedroom to see who the stranger was. Judah, kneeling by the television, noticed him. "Hi," he said with a bright, friendly smile. Udie smiled in return.

Shoshana came from the kitchen. "Oh. You two have met." She went over to hug her son. "Udie, this is Judah. Judah, this is my son."

Judah's smile suddenly faded as he remembered something Roberta had said about Shoshana's husband being lost in the war. "This meeting between Sadat and Begin must be very important to you."

"Very," she agreed. She went back into the kitchen and came out with some nuts and fruits. They sat in front of the television talking sporadically in between the commentators. Udie sat unwillingly near them. Every time he tried to get up to play with his toys, his mother called him back. "This is historic," she kept telling him, but he didn't seem to care.

Finally the moment came. The plane landed, the carpet was rolled out, the door of the aircraft was opened, and there he was. Anwar el-Sadat, president of Egypt, on Israeli soil.

Shoshana held Udie tightly on her lap and did not hide the tears that flowed down her cheek. "If only there would be peace," she said. "I'd forgive those bastards for killing my Danny."

"Danny was my father before he died," Ehud explained to Judah. "But he's not here anymore."

Judah took the boy's little hand and gave it a kiss. He felt like such an outsider here.

"Do you think there will be peace now?" Shoshana asked.

"Why not?" Judah said. "If Sadat can come to Jerusalem, why not."

"Ah. There he is with Arik Sharon. They're actually smiling at each other. If they can smile at each other, there will be peace. And then you, Udie my darling, will never have to fight and I would thank God for that every hour of my life."

"I'm going to be a colonel like my daddy," Ehud said to Judah.

"The glamour you can have," Shoshana conceded. "Just not the risks."

The night wore on, every moment bringing a different joy. The food was hardly touched. Udie finally got fed up and put himself into bed. The statesmen were about to do the same.

"Why are they going to bed?" Shoshana asked. "I'm not tired."

Judah smiled at her. "I better go too," he said.

Shoshana glanced at her watch. "But where—will you have some place to go tomorrow for the speeches?"

"I'll find somewhere."

She was silent for a moment, considering things, weighing and balancing. "Look, do you want to spend the night here?" He glanced up at her, shocked. She blushed. "I didn't mean in my bed. I could move Udie in with me and then you could have his bed."

"I don't want to dislocate your son."

"Well, then the couch. It wouldn't bother me, honestly. And they're going to start the coverage first thing tomorrow morning."

Judah thought about it. She was right. They would start

early in the morning; he didn't want to miss any of it. And he was an adult, she was an adult. Two adult people could share the same apartment without sleeping together. His former wife had proved that point often enough. "Okay," he agreed, "the couch."

She smiled. "Fine. Come with me and I'll get you the sheets and towels."

Judah followed her into her bedroom. It was small but neat. Hanging on the wall was a picture of a man in uniform. "Is that your husband?" he asked.

"My husband? No." She looked up at him. "Danny and I were never married. We were going to be."

"Oh." She handed him his linens. They managed to maneuver around each other in the apartment until both were settled in separate rooms. Shoshana lay in bed but she couldn't sleep. Whether it was the Sadat-Begin meeting or Judah Halaby's presence in the apartment, she could not determine. All she knew was that things felt different. She rose and made her way to the bedroom door. She slipped into the hallway where she could overlook the couch. He was lying with one arm flung over his head and his legs outstretched. She stood there for the longest time studying him. Who was this man? What was he like? Whatever was he thinking? Why should she care? Suddenly like a ghost he rose to a sitting position and looked her way. She was startled. "Shoshana?"

"Yes?"

"Is everything all right?"

"I just wanted to know if you have everything you need." She fumbled. Even to her it sounded too lame to believe. "Good night," she said quickly. Then she vanished into her bedroom and left Judah sitting there.

What am I supposed to do now? Judah asked himself. Does she or doesn't she want me?

He rose and padded through the hallway toward her bedroom door. He stood in its frame. This woman was lying on her side, feigning sleep. He went over and sat down on the side of the bed next to her. "Shoshana," he whispered, brushing her long black hair away from her face. "What do you want?"

She turned over on her back. "I don't know," she answered.

He could barely see her face in the dim light filtering into the bedroom, but the white bow of her nightgown lay around her neck. He untied it and undid the top buttons while she stayed silent beneath him. He slipped his hand inside her gown and found her breasts. His fingers encircled and enticed them until Shoshana moaned softly, lifted up the covers, and invited him in.

"Disastrous," she was screaming. He thought he was at a soccer game, the way she was carrying on. "What a time lapse. I would have done it much better."

"I thought the translator was doing quite well," he protested.

"That's a Syrian for you," she said, disgusted.

"Thanks." He looked at her and laughed. He felt good, better than good, he felt terrific, he had to admit it. When he had woken this morning and found her cuddled next to him, he had wondered how it would be when she opened her eyes. She was still naked and when she woke, she did not try to hide herself. She was so small and defenseless, he felt so tender toward her that it hurt. And her childlike, trusting smile did nothing to dispel his caring. Of course it was embarrassing to both of them, Udie's asking at various times during the day if he had spent the night in his mommy's bed. But Judah did take it as a good sign that Shoshana had curled up with him on the couch, not minding Udie seeing it. But then this was during Begin's speech in which she had far less professional interest.

"They needed me," she told him.

"I know," he decided to agree.

She took him seriously. "Do you realize the whole world is watching and they used that idiot for Sadat's speech instead of me!"

* * *

Carolyn Haddad

Well, not quite the whole world. Roberta and Ovadia in Urbana, Illinois, were having a hell of a time locating the speechmakers Begin and Sadat. There were three channels serving Urbana besides public television, which was off the air. And since it was Sunday morning, the time slot was taken up with religious programming. The evangelicals were at it again, and the local stations weren't about to give up the attempt to convert another crazy for Christ just because an event of historic importance was taking place. So the Ewans of Urbana rushed to the radio, Ovadia swearing once more that he hated this place.

The winter was closing in. Last year 1976–77 had been the coldest winter on record so far. This year 1977–78 would break that record. Roberta only knew that in spite of her "liberation" it was Ovadia who flew off every other week to conferences, in California, in the South, away from the oppressive cold and the snow. Every time he left, the skies opened and the snow fell with a particular viciousness right on her walks and driveway. She longed for a southern climate where if she had to be responsible for the entire household, she at least could eliminate snowplowing from the list of her activities. Ovadia listened, as usual. He ignored. As usual. The bastard.

Later, a long time after she had seen her doctor for what she thought was a psychosomatic illness due to her own repressed rage and found instead that she had VD, later she thought if it had not been that, there would have come along some other reason for leaving Ovadia. She didn't think Ovadia realized how much she had come to hate him for what he had done to her. He had taken away her freedom, literally stolen her life from her. She had three children, she worked a forty-hour week, she took care of the house, and she took care of him. Whatever he had once been to her—her lover, her partner, her friend—he was no more. His deceit had finally killed any spark that might have remained between them and crippled her so that she could no longer visualize herself as a whole person. "You were the only one I had, Ovadia, the only one I loved. You knew that and you still did this to me."

He had always loved her, he loved her still, he protested over and over again to her as she packed her bag. "Do you think I want to lose you?"

She smiled at him even as the tears rolled down both their cheeks. "You wanted it all, Ovadia. The American Dream. The house, the car, the job, the kids, the wife. Well, you've got it all. Including infidelity and a divorce."

He held out his hands to block her way.

"Don't touch me," she told him. "Don't ever touch me again. You make me feel dirty."

He backed away from her and she walked out.

46

Shoshana lay back on the grass and watched through the sun's reflection on the water her son and Judah out rowing on the lake. Judah had Udie up on his lap, four hands gripping two oars, but they were making little progress. She hadn't wanted to go on the boat with them. "Why?" Judah had asked. How could she explain that she wanted to be apart so she could see them together? "I'll take your picture from the shore," she had said. But instead she lay in the grass and watched and wondered.

It was the beginning of April. The winter with its awful rain and cold was almost over. She wouldn't have to worry about buying more kerosene for her heater or the power outages that came from the downpours. Or how often and how bad Udie's colds would be. She felt at peace. It was silly, at peace. The Palestinians were raiding, taking their toll of children, the Israelis had marched into southern Lebanon. Begin refused to budge with his peace proposals, refused even to listen to his own people gathered as she and Judah had witnessed in Kikar Malkhai Yisrael to protest what they saw as his intransigence. Political peace she wanted desperately for the sake of Udie. Her personal peace she had found with Judah. Sometimes she thought so.

She remembered what David had said so long ago about love being different. Love was not the same with Judah as it had been with Danny. It was more mature, more accepting, certainly kinder. What surprised her was that neither one, neither Danny nor Judah weighed heavier on the scale of her affections. She supposed it was because they were both so different, and what they were prepared to offer, she was prepared to accept. So she watched Judah being a father to Danny's child and she was grateful.

Ovadia looked outside the window of his home in Urbana. It was April yet the snow still lay on the ground outside. He had not realized the totality of this prairie desolation until now. Somehow coming home to Roberta had always blocked from him the barrenness of Urbana, which she had seen so clearly all these years. But now Roberta was gone, and he was left in Urbana alone. He felt he was dying.

He had not heard from her for the entire month of January. During which time all the kids had been sick with the flu or colds, and he seemed to be spending half his time running them to the doctor's. And the clothes. Why was it that no one ever had clean clothes to wear? He did the wash once a week. Shouldn't that have been enough? The meals were dismal. The kids even liked the school food better. And they wondered where their mother was. They asked questions that he could not answer. Even the questions he asked himself seemed to have no response. Remorsefully, he set about examining his life. As far as he could see, he had done one thing wrong—he had lost Roberta.

The first week in February the children had received a letter from her. It was pages long, filled with details of how she spent her days and how much she missed them. The return address was a post office box in Kiryat Shmona. So that settled that. She had gone back to Israel. He should have guessed.

He wrote her immediately, trying to put into words what he was feeling about what he had done, how he wasn't living without her. Could he come to her? Would she come back to him? He never received an answer. If he had expected time or absence to heal, he was mistaken. The children now regularly received letters. He was mentioned in none of them. In desperation he called Shoshana.

Roberta got up at six, put on her pants, socks, and heavy work shoes, and headed over to the kitchen. She thought it ironic that in seeking liberation from the enslavement of her marriage and Ovadia's betrayal, she had ended up working on a kibbutz preparing the main meal for between two hundred and three hundred people. But there it was. She had come to Israel with a decision to make. She could go crying to Ovadia's family or she could strike out on her own. She chose striking out. It sounded more aggressive. With funds soon to be depleted, she applied to the Kibbutz Ha-Me'uhad movement in Tel Aviv. She was a little old, but they were used to dealing with crazies. They sent her as a volunteer to Kibbutz Dreyfus, the "American" kibbutz in the Galilee. "You'll love it," the clerk assured her.

She didn't. Why was it that all illusions seemed to shatter at the same time one needed something so desperately to hold on to. She had left Israel with two illusions still intact. The army—well, its lack of preparedness for the Yom Kippur War had taken care of that—and the kibbutz. Perhaps she had romanticized it too much from her days spent in several pleasant guest houses. But when she arrived at Kibbutz Dreyfus, she found it to be the coldest, most unpleasant spot in Israel, aside from Jerusalem. It didn't bother her that she lived in a shack. What bothered her was that the members of the kibbutz lived in baronial splendor while the volunteers and the hired outside labor served as serfs, doing all the work that the members deemed unpleasant or beneath their dignity.

Roberta took her turn of chores as they came. She didn't want to be socially discriminated against, so she planted trees in the rain; weeded the roses in the greenhouse, an activity that left her hands and arms scratched, as there were not enough protective gloves to go around; harvested with the hired help, either Arab or townspeople from Kiryat Shmona, while the kibbutz member directing the harvesting sat on his ass, shouting orders. She came back to her shack dirty and tired and sweating while the women of the kibbutz looked at her as if she was crazy. They were busy loafing, supposedly working in the children's houses, but actually gossiping took up a good part of their day. Many of the men too, those not involved with plowing the fields or light industry, rode around the kibbutz on their bicycles trying to look busy. She was so incensed—if she had to work, everyone should have to work—that she almost forgot about her marital troubles.

She found her real niche in the kibbutz when she was asked to work in the kitchen. At first she wasn't allowed to do anything important. Just wash up. Many were the times she almost fainted at the sink from the heat. Then her big break came when one of the women went on vacation and she was allowed to peel two crates of onions for the morning and evening meals. She did it so successfully that she was finally allowed to handle the food itself. She remembered her first big meal. Chopped liver for two hundred fifty. She ground up the meat, then asked how she was to mix it with the other ingredients. They looked at her as if she was an idiot. "With your hands!" the boss told her. She soon found herself up to her armpits in chopped liver and onions.

It didn't matter. She finally felt she belonged. Especially when they asked her if she would be willing to get up early to pressure-cook two hundred chickens for the sabbath meal. Of course she would. The pressure cooker was one step closer to the oven itself. And that was where the power of Kibbutz Dreyfus was located.

Still, as much satisfaction as Roberta found working in the kitchen, it ended as soon as she went down its greasy steps. After her work was finished, she was left alone to think her own miserable thoughts. The members of the kibbutz didn't even bother to be friendly to each other, they certainly weren't going to be pleasantly polite to the lowly volunteers. So she thought about what she was going to do with the rest of her life. She was staying here, that she knew. She would try to make a go of it in Israel, despite all its problems and her problems. She supposed it was back to Tel Hashomer. Michael had said there was always a place for her at the hospital. But she needed a place to live, that was the problem, with room enough for her and the three children. She could approach Joseph but would Joseph help her? Ovadia was Lily's brother after all. She should approach the Jewish Agency, but there she knew she would come away empty-handed and insulted to boot. So she continued in limbo, writing to her children, missing them, anxious, angry, lonely, mostly hurt.

After her first day of looking Shoshana had been tempted to ask Yossi for help. Where was Roberta! The post office didn't have an address, they didn't know what she looked like; the police in Kiryat Shmona had no idea whom Shoshana was talking about. This was agonizing. Was she supposed to comb the entire northern Galilee for her sister-in-law? Did she have any choice? Before night fell, she took a *sherut* to Danielle's brother Ezra. He was surprised but glad to see her. She handed him the obligatory box of candy and asked to stay the night. No problem, he assured her, as anxious to catch up on news from Tel Aviv as he was to show Shoshana around their new settlement. Over dinner in the common dining hall she explained the problem of Ovadia's missing wife to Ezra and Paula. "I've tried all the hospitals from Safed north," Shoshana protested wearily. "Nothing. God knows where she could be staying."

"Why not at a kibbutz?" Paula suggested. "It would be the easiest thing to do for someone coming into the country. Food and shelter provided."

"But Roberta is not the kibbutz type, believe me," Shoshana said kindly.

Ezra excused himself and let the women finish their

meal alone. When he came back, they were on their second cup of coffee. "Kibbutz Dreyfus," he told Shoshana. "I'll drive you there tomorrow."

Roberta was scrubbing the pots when she heard someone tapping on the screen across from her. She looked up and was surprised to see Shoshana Ewan. She motioned her sister-in-law to the side door, where they met on the steps amongst the cases of carrots, apples, and celery.

"Shoshana!" Roberta said excitedly. "What on earth are you doing here?"

"Ovadia sent me." Shoshana watched while Roberta's smile broke and the lines on her face hardened.

"That is none of your business, so butt out."

"Gracious as ever. Roberta, I've talked to Ovadia. You can't appreciate the depths of the agony he is going through without you. If what he says is true, I think you're making a big mistake. You should stay together, work it out, make amends."

"I've worked it out already. I'm here, he's there. It feels good."

"To be without the children?"

"I'm sending for the children as soon as I get settled. I'm leaving here soon. Besides, I can't send for them until their school year is over anyway."

Shoshana was trying to concentrate on what Roberta must be feeling, but the flies were swarming around her. She slapped at her arms and suggested they take a walk away from the kitchen. Roberta led her past the cow barns and the stable, across the road, onto the banks of the Jordan River, which this far north was just a stream leading into the Galilee. They sat down in the grass and watched the water pass them. "What are those rocks doing across the river?" Shoshana asked.

"All the kibbutzim along the Jordan try to dam the river for their fields," Roberta explained. "There have been several fistfights among the kibbutzniks when those dams are discovered. In most countries men fight over gold. In Israel it's water."

"I met that Judah Halaby you sent over by the way."

"Oh! And?"

"He's asked me to marry him."

"Oh, Shoshana, I'm so excited for you. I knew he was something special the minute I saw him." She reached out her hand. "I hope it works out for you. Maybe you can do the same for me one day."

"I think I can. I have this brother who's desperately in love with you."

"Oh, Shoshana, do you think he wants me back because he's in love with me? Don't be a fool. He wants someone to take care of the kids, do the laundry, cook his meals. He doesn't know what love is. I think he married me because I'm blond and Christian. I fit into his ideal of the American life-style. Like adultery."

"Maybe," Shoshana conceded. "Maybe that's why I chose Danny too. Because he was the epitome of the Israeli sabra and I was such an outsider here. But does that mean I wasn't in love because my need for him can be analyzed?"

"You and Danny wanted only one thing. To be together. Ovadia and I want different things. He wants the security, the serenity, the bourgeois comfort of dull, dead Urbana. The only excitement he seems to have needed all these years was another woman's body. I don't need security. I've had it all my life. It bores me. I'm staying here. You can call Ovadia and tell him that. You'll see how much his love for me means then."

Shoshana returned to Tel Aviv and called Ovadia. After she relayed Roberta's message, she expected Ovadia to promise to be on the next flight over. Instead he thanked her very distantly for her effort and hung up. So. Roberta was right. It made her review her marital inclination toward Judah Halaby more closely. Yet if Roberta's marriage had soured, look at Lily's and Joseph's. Were they not just as much in love today as they had been twenty-seven years ago? And Ilanit and Joshua were always bustling with adventure when they discussed their lives together. Even Danielle and Moshe lived comfortably, happily together,

expectantly full as she was with child. There was something to be said for marriage no matter how looming the
price of failure might be. She had been alone too long.
Udie needed a father; she needed a husband. And at thirty-
six it was not too late for a second child, a real family.

Roberta came south ten days after Shoshana had gone
north to find her. "I was coming down the kitchen steps,
dripping with sweat and chicken fat, when these American
tourists took a picture of me," she explained. "I figured
that was the time to get out." She was staying with Lily
and Joseph, working full time at the hospital. They had
told Meir that Roberta had received a grant to study in
Israel. He must never suspect the breakup of her marriage.
He wouldn't understand.

47

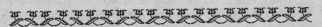

Judah Halaby was surprised one day to open the door of Shoshana's apartment and to find her sitting close on the couch, deep in conspiratorial conversation with an older man.

Shoshana sprang up when she saw him, while the older man just stared. "Judah! You're home early. Yossi, this is Judah Halaby, my fiancé," she said pointedly. "Judah, this is Yossi Leskov."

Yossi smiled, almost laughed as he rose to shake Judah's hand. Then he indicated to Shoshana that she should accompany him to the door. "You're sure Oren will be all right?" she asked him.

"Quite sure."

"Because he's a friend of mine," she reminded him. "You wouldn't—"

"Shoshana, you are more suspicious than I am and that's going some. Oren will just be sitting on the border between Iraq and Iran, waiting for your family. Actually this is working out better than even I expected." He nodded good-bye to Judah and left.

"What was that all about?" Judah asked as Shoshana came back to him. She sat down and told him briefly about her relatives in Baghdad, how she had found out about them through the diary, and how she had forced Yossi to free them. Judah looked at her in amazement. "Why do I constantly think of you as a fragile flower that needs protection? You're actually as tough as they come."

"When I have to be," she admitted. "If I weren't, I would have perished years ago. But I want to be that fragile flower, Judah; I want you to protect me and love me. Can you?"

He opened his arms to her. "Very easily," he assured her.

The first Shoshana knew that Oren and her cousins were safe with their family was when Rebecca, who had fled from Baghdad so long ago with Lily only to marry and remain in Tehran, called by phone to let them know of the miraculous arrival.

Shoshana wasn't there and could only hear secondhand from Lily what had happened. It seemed the crossing at the border had gone well, as expected. The family, with each woman carrying one suitcase, presented its papers to both crossing stations and was permitted entry into Iran, where Oren took over. Leila, Rahamin's wife, the one with three children, had collapsed as she stepped onto Iranian soil, the other, Tina, had merely cried hysterically. This reported by Rebecca via Oren, that "not very sympathetic Israeli" as Rebecca called him. "Oh, the stories," Lily said, "the stories they are telling about what the Arabs have done to our Baghdad. Thank God we left. Thank God. The camps, the tents, anything is better than what Jacob's family has been through. They're all dead or waiting to die over there."

"But our cousins are all right?" Shoshana asked.

"Yes," Lily answered. "And coming here. Joseph is seeing about apartments for them. After what they've been through, he doesn't want them to have to go to an absorption center. He wants the children in school immediately and the wives to have some comfort. Rebecca says the relatives there will give them what they can. But we must do so much for them, Shoshana. Towels, dishes, sheets, a washing machine. There's no time to waste. Beds, furniture, clothing for the children. Get your sweater on. Let's get going."

The sisters spent more money than they had. What they couldn't carry with them they had delivered to Lily's apartment, where they were finally forced to flee after the stores closed. Joseph was already there, telling Roberta all about the new set of relatives she would have to get used to.

"Did you get the apartments from the housing ministry?" Lily asked Joseph, out of breath as she was.

"I had to throw the official's chair through the window and threaten to castrate him, but I got the apartments."

"Oh, Joseph," Roberta said, "they're going to come and arrest you one of these days."

"Don't worry about it. Hurry up and eat. I've got the truck here and Joshua's coming over to help us move this stuff. And we have to see Meir."

"Tonight?" Lily asked.

"It's not something that we don't let him know about."

"Not about how they died though," Shoshana said.

"No. Not how. Just the deaths and the escape."

It was late but Meir was up reading the papers when they came to him. He opened the door and greeted them with a smile. "Where is your young man?" he asked Shoshana.

"At home working."

Meir shook his head. He was always afraid that now that she had someone decent the fellow would disappear on her. "So, what is this delegation about?"

"Sit down, Meir," Joseph said. Rahel was already in bed, so Lily went into the kitchen to prepare coffee. She felt for an instant the presence of her mother, Salemah, who had worked long and hard to keep the kitchen clean. It had sadly deteriorated under Rahel's care.

"Well, what is it?" Meir said when they were all settled.

Shoshana took her father's hand in hers. She kissed it. It was so old and gnarled now. She looked into his eyes, stared at him with fear and delight as she had as a child. Age had made him less imposing, yet there was power here still. "Father, you know that for us it is not how or where we die. What matters is whom we leave behind to remember us. A man's life passes, but his sons and his sons' sons live on to bless his name forever. Today the grandchildren of your brother Jacob were set free. Tonight they sleep in Tehran. Tomorrow, the next day, they will fly to Israel to live free with us."

Meir considered sadly what his daughter had to say. "And Jacob?"

"Jacob and his sons are dead."

In silence they watched Meir weep. For his brother, for his brother's sons, for the Jews of Iraq. He got up slowly, walked over to the cupboard, and took out his prayer book. "We will say kaddish," he said to Joseph. And the women listened in silence while the prayer for the dead was repeated and received.

All the relatives had come to the airport. Relatives they saw only at weddings and funerals, relatives they never saw. They came from all over the country to welcome Jacob's family home.

"I'm getting claustrophobic," Judah shouted to Shoshana.

She laughed. "Just watch Udie." She was having a good time trying to recognize everyone. When the plane finally arrived, as an exception the guards let the relatives onto the tarmac. And when the door opened and the women and children appeared, a high trilling of joy rose from among the women on the field.

"I thought I'd forgotten how to do that," Shoshana said to Judah.

The family rushed the plane in happiness, and soon Leila and Tina were surrounded and their frightened children were being raised and carried aloft by their male relatives.

Oren was standing on the sidelines watching it all. Shoshana rushed up to him and gave him a big hug. "God bless you, Oren."

"My good deed for a lifetime," he told her.

"Come, join us."

There was singing now and dancing. The other passengers were staring at these strange people as they tried to nudge through the crowd. The women had brought cakes, the men wine. Even the guards were given their fill. It would have gone on forever if they hadn't had to clear the area for a 747 from New York.

How Joseph ever got his hands on the women Shoshana would never know, but he finally loaded them onto his truck with their children and set off for Ramat Gan.

"It looks surprisingly like the truck we were taken to the barracks in," Meir said from the parking lot.

"Nothing like it, Father," Shoshana assured him. "Come on. Judah has his car."

"Ah, the earthworm."

Leila and Tina were settled but unsettled. They were in their flats on the same floor of a new apartment building in Ramat Gan. Lily had taken the children to school and registered them even though they wouldn't be starting immediately as the Passover vacation was almost upon them. Shoshana took her women cousins to the closest absorption center and registered them for the ulpan. It was all very confusing and hectic for the new families, but they were grateful for the help, if puzzled. The relatives from around the country had returned home, but the ones in Tel Aviv provided the newcomers with meals and company. They were all amazed to find the one thing that worried the women about Israel was the terrorist attacks. "After living in Baghdad," they were asked, "you worry about Arabs attacking you here?" But it seemed all the time in the papers the Iraqis had overplayed the Palestinian terrorist achievements.

* * *

It was Pesach. Roberta accompanied Lily and Joseph over to her father-in-law's for the seder. Lily had insisted on buying her a new dress for the occasion, even as she had done for Leila, Tina, and their children. "Ovadia will probably call. Then you'll have a chance to talk to him," Lily prodded her. Roberta did not take the bait.

"Are Joshua and Ilanit joining us?" she asked instead.

"After the seder at her parents' is over. It only takes them an hour and a half to finish."

"And Meir?"

"Four hours minimum," Lily warned her. It was a good thing they were already in the car, as Roberta looked as if she might want to back out.

When they disembarked at Katznelson Street, they found Judah Halaby parking behind them. His car disgorged a teetering eight months pregnant Danielle, her husband, Moshe, Shoshana, and Udie. There were cries of *hag sameah* and kisses all around before they started up the stairs. The two-room apartment of Meir Ewan, which he had bought all those years ago when he came from Iraq, was now one big table. There were places set for seventeen. Leila and Tina and their children were already there, having come by earlier to burn the bread. Roberta started at the children. Nadav, Rahamin's first born standing so tall by his mother, was seventeen. Next year he would go into the Israeli army. What must he think of that? And Rahamin's daughters, Ephraim's children about the ages Shoshana and Ovadia were when they first came to Israel in 1950. They looked puzzled, frightened, pleased. Roberta wondered how it had been for her husband when he had come, how it would be for her children.

Lily put her arm around her and said, "Too bad Ovadia and the children aren't here."

"If Ovadia and the children were here, we'd be out the window," Joseph noted.

The seder began. Ehud waited for his big moment and then on cue began the four questions: "*Ma nishtanah hallayla hazeh mikkol hallelot.*" He sang them with a clear, strong voice, and when he finished; he set down his Haggadah and waited for the applause. Instead there was an absolute silence, then peels of laughter. "Who taught him that?" Meir wanted to know. Judah confessed. Ehud knew the words perfectly, the only problem was that Judah had taught him the Syrian melody, at which point Moshe pointed out that the Yemenite was far different, so they were treated to yet another set of four questions.

The night passed. The adults' and children's voices mingled in the recitation of the ancient words. Meir did not falter until he recited, "This year we are here; next year we shall be in the land of Israel. This year we are slaves; next year we shall be free men." "Why is this night different from all other nights?" They answered their own question. The Ewans were free.

It was late, almost two in the morning when everyone got ready to leave. "That was the nicest seder ever," Shoshana went over to her father to say, before remembering her absent mother.

Meir took her hand and kissed her fingers. "I remember too," he said, as if guessing her thoughts. "We will remember them all tonight and they will rejoice with us."

Roberta lay in bed past sleeping. Contrary to Lily's predictions, Ovadia had not called. The switchboard must be jammed, Lily guessed. Roberta didn't know the reason, at this point would not even try to guess at it. The only thing she did know from this evening was she had not made a mistake. She belonged here. Even Meir agreed to that. When Leila told everyone she had never seen a Jew as blond as Roberta or even an American Jew before, no one bothered to correct her. They accepted Roberta now as Naomi had accepted Ruth. That was good.

Sometime in the middle of the night when sleep had taken her, the phone rang. She sprung up, slipped into her robe, and hurried to the bedroom door. Lily had taken the call. Roberta saw in clear slow motion Lily shriek, raise her hand to her mouth, and drop to the floor on her knees.

Joseph took the phone from her and listened. Without so much as a word, he put the phone back in its cradle and bent over to comfort his wife. When he noticed Roberta, he said simply, "Meir is dead. Heart attack. You must call Ovadia."

Roberta walked stiffly to the phone, put in the call, and waited. It gave her a moment to figure out the time difference. It would be only eleven in Urbana. Ovadia should still be up. The phone rang in the Benjamin apartment. Roberta picked it up and waited while the overseas operator put through her call. It was funny because as soon as she said hello, Ovadia recognized her voice. She thought that it had been too long, that they were too far from each other. He went on and on about how he had tried to call earlier, all the things he had planned for them. She finally had to break in to tell him his father was dead. Come home.

They had waited a day for Ovadia to arrive. There was time to contact everyone and all came. Meir was buried in Kiryat Shaul next to Salemah, the wife he had led forth from Baghdad twenty-eight years ago. "He lived a full life," everyone said over and over again. Good and bad, full. Roberta looked around at the gathering. Besides the family, Danielle, her brothers, and their wives had come, neighbors, fellow workers. If one were to walk through the crowd, one would hear any number of languages spoken. "It looks like a miniature UN," she whispered to Shoshana.

Shoshana wiped her tears away and smiled. "It's the family of Israel." She took Roberta's hand and squeezed it, held it tight.

During the shivah Roberta paid scant attention to the mourners who came and went. She had grieving of her own to do, as it seemed that her marriage was really over. She and Ovadia could not speak to each other. They tried, they stumbled. Their children were her only comfort now. On the sixth day after his arrival in Israel, Ovadia asked her if she would go with him, he wouldn't tell her where. He took her to Tel Aviv University, department of engineering.

There on the second floor he set her in front of an office and let her figure it out for herself. She fingered the Hebrew lettering on the cold metal: Professor Ovadia Ewan.

"That's what I was trying to tell you when you called," he explained. "It's taken me this long to make the arrangements. I've quit Illinois. The only place I want to be is where you are. And if you want to be here in Tel Aviv, that's where we'll be."

She turned and allowed him to take her in his arms. Now that the decision had been made, she felt an army of doubts assaulting her. "If we don't like it, if it doesn't go well," she promised him, "we'll fold our tent and steal away."

48

It was June. Shoshana and Judah and Udie had just been over to Danielle's to see the new baby boy. Barely over a month and growing rapidly. Danielle and Moshe had named the child Meir. Udie was fascinated and a little bit jealous. "What will you do if I have another child?" she had teased her son. He just made a face.

June. She and Roberta had just driven out to the airport to pick up Roberta's children. The three of them came off the boarding ramp weighed down with backpacks and shopping bags. "Now do they look like immigrants or do they look like immigrants?" Roberta asked happily before she rushed to embrace them. She had not trusted Ovadia completely to keep his word. So she had stayed in Israel as Ovadia returned to Urbana with the children to finish the school year. With Joseph's help she had bought a cottage in Ramat Aviv which they would remodel. She left it to Ovadia to sell the house, to pack, to tie up the loose ends of their life in America. Shoshana had to concede that perhaps Roberta knew her brother better than she did, for when Shoshana asked Ovadia if he really had resigned from the University of Illinois as Roberta had claimed, he told her confidentially it was only a leave of absence. "You never know with Roberta. She can change her mind so quickly."

As for Shoshana, she had her own decision to make, one that struck her without warning. She had casually mentioned to Judah how great it would be to have the family all together again now that Ovadia and Roberta were returning to Israel. Startled, he stared at her and asked her if she hadn't understood. After they got married, she and Udie would be returning to the States with him, to Cornell University in Ithaca, New York, where he taught, where his life was waiting to be resumed.

No, she hadn't understood. She hadn't understood at all. It never occurred to her that someday she might leave Israel. And despite Judah's assurances that they would keep the apartment and return each summer, she was uncertain. She sought advice from those she loved.

David said no. "Why should you leave? This is your home. He's a Jew. Let him come here to live." But was it really her home? Well, since she was nine, but sometimes she felt like such a stranger here, as if she didn't belong. And even David admitted she would probably not have another chance like this. "But look at it this way," he added, "you made out pretty well before you met him." But had she? Yes, she made out. With her job. With her child. But it wasn't like being married, being secure and committed. Judah would be good to her. She wouldn't have to wonder what she would be like or whom she would be with in ten years. She would have someone. And she liked the idea of living with Judah. She was interested in his work and liked to help him figure things out. They had fun together. He loved Udie. He was willing to see her pregnant again.

Oren said no. After he heard Judah was returning to the States. "I know what's best for you," he said. "Best for you is to marry him. But I'm thinking about Udie."

"Udie needs a father."

"That's just it. Udie has a father. Danny was his father. Can you see Danny in America? Or his child."

No. she couldn't. Danny would have wanted Udie to grow up as he had. Rude and overbearing, sure of himself, quick, ruthless, crazy, passionate, confused, Israeli. But Danny was in the ground. She was alive. And what would he say to her? She didn't know.

Roberta—Roberta even!—said go with him. "I came to this country because I love it, not because of ideals, and you know I have no illusions left. Go to America. See it for yourself. You can always come home again."

Come home.

It was unfair. Unfair to have everything and then to have only half of everything. Lily's advice: Take the man. "Enough already," she told her sister. "You're not some young pioneer. You've had your excesses and you've paid for them. Now settle down with someone who cares for you."

"I don't know."

"Look, Shoshana, you've given this country more than it ever gave you."

"It gave us a home."

"And you've served it. You went into the army. Against everyone's wishes, may I remind you. You worked for the government after that. We won't even go into raising the morale of a certain soldier. What more can they ask. That you live out your life here alone and raise Udie to die on some godforsaken sand dune."

"Oh, Lily."

"Save yourself, Shoshana. And your child."

"What will I do without all of you? Without my family?"

"We'll be happy for you. Joseph and I will be very happy for you. And you know in your heart that Father would have wanted you to marry Judah, even if it meant leaving Israel. Father was a pragmatist. Did he come here because he was a Zionist? No. He came because he wanted to survive. You must be pragmatic too. You can love a state or a man. Believe me, a man can do more for you."

683

Carolyn Haddad

* * *

Shoshana Ewan married Judah Halaby on June 14, 1978. The wedding had a strange dreamlike quality for her as people from her past floated in and out of her line of vision, wishing her love, luck, happiness. "You'll see," Judah promised her on their short honeymoon at Ha-Goshrim, "the United States has everything."

Well, almost everything. Not her family, not her country, not her loves.

It was funny that she was the one now being seen off at the airport, that she was the one who was waving good-bye frantically and kissing everyone in sight, only to get into the Departing Passengers Only section and have their flight delayed for an hour. No, that was wrong. They had planned it so they would go through passport control just as their flight was being called. She had planned it that way so she would have no time for second thoughts. No time to think about Lily and Joseph, or Danielle and Moshe with their baby. No time even to think about Roberta and Ovadia. But here she was waiting nervously with her coat folded over her arm and her travel bag clasped in the same hand as her purse. She wanted to call David or Oren and Nurit or somebody, but she had spoken to them all just last night, had said good-bye, and what more was there to say. She would see them soon, next summer, she promised. But they were already fading from her life.

Soon she would be in America, in Ithaca, New York, and when she heard Israel mentioned in the news, her heart would jump but she would no longer be there, be a part of it. She looked around at Judah, who was pacing the floor. Who was this stranger she was leaving her homeland for? She panicked, she wanted to get up and run, out of the waiting room, down the stairs, to her family, to the streets of Tel Aviv, to the people she knew and cared for, to the people she was sure of.

They called her flight but she still had time. Judah was looking at her, his lips were moving. She didn't hear him.

"Mommy, Mommy," Udie called to her. "Daddy says it's time to go."

She stood up. She walked over to Judah and let him put his arm around her. Then together as a family they walked to the boarding ramp.

Danielle Steel

AMERICA'S LEADING LADY OF ROMANCE REIGNS OVER ANOTHER BESTSELLER

A Perfect Stranger

A flawless mix of glamour and love by Danielle Steel, the bestselling author of *The Ring*, *Palomino* and *Loving*.

A DELL BOOK $3.50   #17221-7

**VOLUME I
IN THE EPIC
NEW SERIES**

*The Morland
Dynasty*

The
Founding

by Cynthia Harrod-Eagles

THE FOUNDING, a panoramic saga rich with passion and excitement, launches Dell's most ambitious series to date—THE MORLAND DYNASTY.

From the Wars of the Roses and Tudor England to World War II, THE MORLAND DYNASTY traces the lives, loves and fortunes of a great English family.

A DELL BOOK $3.50   #12677-0

A love forged by destiny—
A passion born of flame

FLAMES OF DESIRE

by Vanessa Royall

Selena MacPherson, a proud princess of ancient
Scotland, had never met a man who did not desire
her. From the moment she met Royce Campbell at
an Edinburgh ball, Selena knew the burning
ecstasy that was to seal her fate through all eternity.
She sought him on the high seas, in India, and
finally in a young America raging in the
birth-throes of freedom, where destiny was bound
to fulfill its promise. . . .

A DELL BOOK $2.95